YOU
SHALL
NOT KILL

Julia Navarro is a journalist, a political analyst, and the internationally bestselling author of seven novels, including *The Brotherhood of the Holy Shroud*, *Tell Me Who I Am* and *Story of a Sociopath*. Her fiction has been translated in more than thirty countries. She lives in Madrid.

www.julianavarro.es

[f] Julia.Navarro/Oficial

JULIA NAVARRO

YOU
SHALL
NOT KILL

GRUPOIII
IIIBOOKS

GRUPOⅢ
ⅢBOOKS

Grupo Books
An imprint of Penguin Random House Grupo Editorial, S. A. U.
Travessera de Gràcia, 47-49. 08021 Barcelona, Spain

ISBN: 9781644731246

Copyediting: Cillero & de Motta

Printed in USA

To my family, especially my grandparents Jerónimo and Teresa and my mother. In memoriam. And to all of my friends.

Acknowledgements

My thanks go to all those who help make it possible to transform stories into books.

To my editors, especially Virginia Fernández.

To all the booksellers and readers who have accompanied me on this journey so far.

To Lola Travesado, yet again, for helping me to understand the maze that is the mind.

And to Fermín and Álex, for always being by my side.

While writing this book, I had two inseparable companions: E. M. Forster's guidebook of Alexandria and my beloved Argos.

As you set out for Ithaka,
hope your road is a long one,
full of adventure, full of discovery.
Laistrygonians and Cyclops,
angry Poseidon — don't be afraid of them:
you'll never find things like that on your way
as long as you keep your thoughts raised high,
as long as a rare excitement
stirs your spirit and your body.
Laistrygonians, Cyclops,
wild Poseidon—you won't encounter them unless
you bring them along inside your soul,
unless your soul sets them up in front of you.

C. P. CAVAFY, *Ithaka*

BOOK I

1

Madrid, May 1941

The bells rang and dulled the voices that came from the grove. He recognized the man's voice. Yes, he was sure of it. It was the American. Who was he with? It must be some woman: out here in this secluded spot, at this time of the day, after such a long party ... He had tried that himself in the past, coming down into the trees to find a little intimacy, where he could run his hands over some girl's body. But not this time. He was trying to find a place to be alone so he could vomit. He had drunk too much. It was hard for him to walk, and the wine was forcing its way up from his stomach to his mouth, pushing to be let out.

He leaned back against a tree. He was too dizzy to keep on walking and slumped to the ground. He heard the American, talking more loudly than usual, and thought he saw someone hiding among the nearby trees.

His head was spinning. He threw up, and feeling marginally better, got to his feet again and went cautiously over to the trees. He didn't want to interrupt anything.

"Who's there?" he asked.

"Fernando" a voice replied.

Its urgent tone alarmed him. He stumbled towards it and lit a match, which chased away the shadows in the dark corner.

The American was holding Catalina's body in his arms. He was supporting her head with one hand, and with the other was pulling down her skirt, trying to cover her bare legs.

She was saying something, but he couldn't make out the words. He held onto the trunk of a nearby tree and stared at what was going on. Yes, the American was holding Catalina in his arms; and there, on the ground beside them, her stockings ...

"What have you done to her?" Fernando asked in alarm.

"Nothing ..."

Fernando bent down and lit another match, looking at the young woman's face. There was a bruise bulging on her left cheek, her blouse was torn, and her skirt was all covered in mud.

"Jesus! What have you done to her?"

"Nothing, I'm telling you. Don't worry; I think she's fine ..." the American said, as he stroked her face.

She opened her eyes, and then closed them again. He saw her lips bend into a smile, which was shortly followed by a grimace of pain. He didn't understand a thing about what was going on ... or maybe he did; his mind started to clear and he remembered that he had drunk so much because of her.

They had all gone to the Pradera de San Isidro to meet with some of their friends from the neighborhood. It was Antoñito's birthday and he had invited them all to celebrate it with him, making the most of the fact that, although it was only May, spring was already in the air. Antoñito's father, Don Antonio, sold goods on the black market. He had a general store, and throughout the war people had always been able to get food from him. Now he was proud of his close relationship with the victors, which meant that Antoñito had been able to promise that he would have a few bottles of wine for his twenty-fourth birthday party. Where had he gotten the links of chorizo from? And where, in fact, had the wine come from as well? It wasn't very good wine, but it had let them relax for a while, and forget about the war. There was no one in the whole neighborhood who would have dared miss the party. And no one's family, apart from Pablo Gómez's, was not in debt to Don Antonio. Pablo Gómez's father, Pedro, worked for the tax office. Antoñito and Pablo claimed to be friends, although in fact they fought over everything, especially Catalina.

He thought that he shouldn't have gone to the party, that he had no right to have fun while his father was in prison, but he hadn't been brave enough to tell Catalina that he wouldn't go with her. He wanted to be with her, and he was afraid that someone would take her from him. He knew that Pablo and Antoñito were on the prowl.

Someone had given her a glass of wine; she had held back to start with, but the afternoon was warm and encouraged her to throw caution to the winds. He saw her drink two or three glasses of wine, and turn into a different woman. She danced with him and he felt her body pressed close against his, but then she danced with other men in the same forward way.

Most of all, she danced with the American. Yes. In fact, Catalina had only asked him to accompany her to the Pradera because she liked the American. She had said as much a while back. And now she was there, stretched out on the grass, drunk, no stockings on, and her dress pulled up, leaving her thighs uncovered, while the American tried to get her to stand up.

"Help me," the American asked.

"Help you do what? Leave me alone …"

He heard Catalina speaking. It was hard for her to speak, or at least that's how it seemed to him.

"Marvin … don't leave me … it hurts …" she whispered.

"Don't worry, I'm not going to leave you … but you've got to try to sit up … I'll take you home … Fernando, why don't you want to help me?"

No, he didn't want to help him. It was hard for him to move, to tell the truth. He felt a wave of anger. How could they have done what they had just done? He had always thought that Catalina was such a good girl, and he knew that until that night she had not allowed anyone to do anything with her; she knew how to put the boys in their place, and even did as much to him, even though they'd known each other since they were children.

But here she was, half naked in the American's arms. It was obvious what had gone on between the two of them. He felt a shudder in his breast and felt like crying.

Marvin managed to get her to stand up. He put his arm around her waist and made her walk alongside him.

He looked at them without moving. He felt like being sick again. Let her go. There was nothing he could do.

"Fernando! Fernando! Can you hear me? Stop …"

A few days had passed since that afternoon at the Pradera. He hadn't seen her since, and had made no effort to do so. He hadn't seen Marvin either, but that was easier. The American lived in Eulogio's house, but never went out. The two of them—the American and Eulogio—were friends. A few months ago, the American had resurfaced, and Eulogio had opened his door to him. His friend had explained that he had met the American at the front, where the pair of them were wounded at the same time. Eulogio had come back from the front before the end of the war because he had been badly wounded while helping the American. It was at the battle of Jarama; he had almost lost his leg, and he was now crippled for life. When he came back home, he found out from his mother that his father had died fighting at the front in Aragon.

When the American showed up at his door, there was no need for him to remind Eulogio that they had met in the cold February of 1937, at the desperate battle that was Jarama; Eulogio had taken him in and waved away any attempt to pay for his lodging. Marvin said he was a poet. He had come to Madrid in the spring of 1936 to research Cervantes, but the war broke out and he decided to stay, thinking that the pain of war would be a good source of inspiration; he ended up working as a translator for American reporters who came to cover the conflict. He had become friends with Eulogio during those days at the front. Then everything that happened had happened, and Eulogio never thought that Marvin would be back. But there he was, ready to start working again on his *Spanish Civil War Notebook*.

"He's a writer, a poet," Eulogio explained to his friends. "He was at the front when the war started; he was a translator, not a soldier, but he was wounded at Jarama and he left," he said, importantly, but he never said that it had been he who had saved the American's life.

The thing that no one understood was why he had come back, and why Franco's forces had ignored the fact that he had been on the Republican side. But Franco couldn't have cared all that much about an American running around the streets of Madrid. Those streets belonged to the dictator now, and nothing could happen there without him hearing about it.

Fernando thought about all of this, and Catalina watched him. She didn't usually interrupt his musings. They had respected each other's silence ever since they were children, and she waited until she saw something in his face that gave a sign he was returning to the real world. Yes, he had been caught up in thoughts of Eulogio and the American, and had forgotten that she was there.

"They've told me that you've asked for a pardon for your father again. Do you think they'll give it to him this time?" she asked with interest.

Fernando shrugged. That very morning, he had paid Don Alberto García again, a lawyer who said he had an in with the government when it came to getting people pardoned. But so far, all he had done was leech money from them. His mother had sold everything they had of value, apart from the books. She couldn't do that. The books that filled the walls of the house were the things her husband loved most in the world, apart from his son and wife. Her husband, Lorenzo Garzo, was a scholar, as well as being a well-known editor and translator who worked as a director for the Editorial Clásica publishing house.

Fernando dreamed of following in his father's footsteps and working for the same publishing house. Ever since he was a child, he had paid close attention to everything his father did, and it didn't bother him in the least to come back from school, do his homework, and then spend two hours studying English with his father. "If you want to be a translator, then you need to know the language perfectly, and it's best to learn languages when you're still a child," his father had told him. And Fernando got down to work, thinking that one day he would walk in through the doors of the Editorial Clásica and that they would treat him with the same respect and care that they treated his father. He couldn't think of any better job than immersing himself in a sea of words.

Fernando was dreaming again. Catalina was patient, accustomed to her friend's vague moments.

"My mother says that she's just finished some crochet work that maybe you can sell. Tell your mother, but make sure my father doesn't find out. You know how he is."

Yes, he knew. Don Ernesto, Catalina's father, had family lands in Huesca, and the rumor was that until the war they had provided a steady income. It's not the case that the Vilamar family was very rich—at least, not as rich as some others—but they had been able to live well until 1936 came around. Don Ernesto was a shy man, Catholic and monarchist, and from the moment the war began, he had sympathized with the Nationalist side.

Don Ernesto had not gone to war because of his poor eyesight, and he had come down with a liver infection shortly after the war broke out and had had to stay in bed. And so he stayed in Madrid, waiting for fate to decide between the Republic and Franco, and hoping that the latter would win, as did eventually happen; no one in his district was surprised when he went out to cheer Franco's troops as they entered the city.

"I'll tell my mother," Fernando said, coming back to the real world with a start.

"Fernando ... about the other night ..."

"Don't say anything."

"I'm in love with Marvin. I'm going to get married to him."

"Has he asked you?"

"No, not yet ... but he'll marry me, don't you think?"

"I don't think any man will marry a girl who's easy."

Catalina slapped him in the face, looked at him angrily, and started to cry.

"How can you say that? I'm not easy, you know me."

"No? Well, I think it's only the easy girls that let the first man they meet do anything they want to them. I saw you, Catalina, you had your stockings off, your shirt was all in tatters, and your skirt ... You could see your thighs and Marvin had his hands on your legs ..."

"I ... Well, you might not believe me, but I don't remember it all that well ..."

"You don't say. Well, if you want me to help you bring it all back, let me remind you that you danced with everyone, especially Pablo and Antoñito. Pablo got a little insistent with you, and you asked me to get you out of there, and then, when I went to get a glass of wine, you disappeared with Marvin, who you'd been chasing all night."

She said nothing, trying to find an answer, seemingly more for herself than for Fernando.

"I've told you I don't remember much about what happened … But Antoñito and Pablo both insisted on dancing with me and taking me into dark corners. And I said no … but they got so pushy … It's better that if anything did happen, it happened with Marvin."

"So you don't care about what you did! You should be ashamed of yourself!"

"Don't talk to me like that! I won't let you!"

"And what are you going to do? Talk to your father? If he finds out, he'll slap you six ways from Sunday."

"He wants me to go with Antoñito; he says he's the only man in the district who has any future ahead of him," she replied gloomily.

"Well, I don't think Antoñito will be up for it, not if he's seen you with Marvin."

"I don't care whether he saw me or not: I hate Antoñito, he's a creep, he makes me feel sick. And I've told you, I want to marry Marvin. I hope he'll take me far away from here. I'd like to live in America. Have you ever read any of Marvin's poems?"

"No, I'm not interested."

She was upset by this answer. She knew that Fernando liked reading and that there were more books in his house than in anyone else's. Don Lorenzo was an editor and Catalina remembered what he used to say to all the neighborhood kids: "If you don't read, you won't understand life or even know who you are." She'd never understood what he was trying to say, but she didn't care. The war had interrupted her education, just as it had that of countless other children and young adults, even though her mother had tried to make sure that she kept on studying, "to finish herself," which was how she had ended up taking interminable piano lessons at her aunt Petra's house.

"Maybe what I teach you will come in use someday," her aunt said, although she knew full well that her niece wasn't all that talented when it came to music. But the classes were a form of entertainment for the pair of them. It was a way for Catalina to get out of the house without her father being worried, and for her aunt it was a way to gossip about the family. She had been widowed almost as soon as the war started, and although her husband, who had been a civil servant, had had some money saved somewhere, the war had eaten away at her capital. Doña Petra never stopped bemoaning the fact that her husband, without any need to do so, had joined the Nationalist troops and lost his life in the fighting in Aragon. But she was a resolute woman, and now that the war was over, she tried to earn a living in the hungry Madrid of those years by giving piano lessons and French classes at a convent school, the kind of place attended by the flighty daughters of black marketeers and all other kinds of crooks who thought that education could give their offspring at least a veneer of respectability, while their fellow citizens were barely able to feed themselves.

Catalina smiled to herself. She was losing herself in her own thoughts as well. This was the good thing about being with Fernando, that they didn't have to talk to each other if they didn't want to. They could sit in silence without the need to waste their words. Fernando was prone to introspection and even to forgetting that she was next to him, but she didn't mind, and didn't feel offended when he did so. There was no one more loyal to her than this clumsy young man.

They were silent for a while until Catalina grew tired of it, and coughed to bring him back to himself.

"When will you hear about the pardon?" she repeated.

Fernando shrugged again. He didn't have an answer. The lawyer had asked him to be patient.

"When you go to the prison to see your father, I'll come with you if you want. And don't forget to come by my house to get my mother's crochet work."

"I don't think that your father will let you come with me; he's annoyed enough already that your mother and you even talk to us."

"You know how he is … But he doesn't want you to have a tough time of it; he just thinks that your father chose the wrong side."

"And what about you? Do you think the same?" Fernando asked, his voice tense.

"I don't know what I think, Fernando. I was very scared during the war, and everyone in the whole neighborhood, apart from us and a few other families, was very scared that the Nationalists would come to the city … and I'm not a red, like you are, but I don't like Franco; I don't like Don Antonio Sánchez or Don Pedro Gómez, or their children. And Marvin was on the Republican side, and he's much more sensible than I am, so …"

"I thought you could think for yourself! Why do you care what Marvin thinks?" he broke in angrily.

"Of course I care what he thinks, he's more sensible than I am, and sees things more clearly than we do. You should be happy that Marvin was on the side of the Republicans. The other night he told me that it was a catastrophe for Spain that Franco had won the war."

"Leave me alone, Catalina, I don't want to put up with you right now."

Fernando turned his back on her and started to walk down to the Plaza de España, down to where the print shop was. He earned very little at this job, a few pesetas, nothing more; nowhere near enough to support himself and his mother. They had lost everything. His father's savings had disappeared with the Republic's now-worthless currency, and all they had left was the house. Don Antonio, the black marketeer, had said that he had a friend who was ready to buy it from them. But at the price he was offering, it would be better simply to make a gift of it.

And anyway, where could they go? He thought that his mother would die of the pain if she were ever forced to leave her house. She had inherited it from her parents and had lived in it her whole life. Fernando would have preferred to steal rather than force his mother out from those four walls that were her only point of support.

He worked as much as he could. In the morning, he did work for anybody who needed physical labor, hauling sacks and doing the most difficult jobs, and in the afternoon he worked at the print shop. In the evenings, he still found a couple of hours free to study. He wanted to be like his father, but he wasn't sure he'd be able to. He knew that the children of reds weren't given the same opportunities.

He ran into Eulogio, who was dragging his injured leg behind him.

"Where are you off to in such a hurry?" Eulogio asked.

"There's a lot of work in the print shop," Fernando said, not very eager to stop and chat.

"It looks like you're running away from someone. Your face …" Eulogio said, looking at his friend.

"Don't be silly! Who would I be running away from? You can't run away from Franco's supporters, anyway. They're everywhere."

"You're going to tell me that?"

Fernando didn't answer. Eulogio was right. When his friend came back from the war he had had to set aside his dream of being a great painter, and instead settle for a job that gave him enough to eat. And so by day, he painted, and by night, he worked as a night watchman at the warehouse of Don Antonio, the black marketeer. Don Antonio claimed to have hired him out of pity, because he had known him all his life, but he took advantage of the fact that he had fought on the Republican side to pay him only a few pennies, barely enough to live on. Eulogio gritted his teeth to suppress his anger, and told himself that any day now he'd go to the mountains to join the last few resistance fighters, for all that his mother had told him to accept the defeat: "We've lost the war, but because we're still alive, we need to keep going. And we can be happy that Don Antonio doesn't turn you in for being a red." He had accepted the job. He had done so because he did not want to add more pain to his mother's already great pain. And so they had sold the house that they lived in to Don Antonio, and they had moved into an attic. Eulogio consoled himself by thinking that the attic wasn't as bad as it could have been, that there were worse places to live. The ceilings weren't too low, they had three rooms as well as the kitchen, and they could see the walls of the Convent of La Encarnación from the windows. It was enough for him and for his mother.

"There are a lot of shameless people around … Don Antonio is getting his hands on the whole neighborhood: he buys houses for next to nothing and then sells them on for a tidy profit. Careful, because he's got his eye on your house. And you see what happened to me," Eulogio continued.

"I told you to hang in there," Fernando reminded him.

"And what, let my mother starve? I have to be grateful to him for giving me a job as a night watchman in his warehouse. If you saw what he keeps there ... I don't know where he gets it, but a truckload of scrap iron comes in every day. He's making a mint."

"His wife fooled us all. She said she didn't know where he was, and of course she did: he was a Falangist, so he could only be off at the front shooting people. I heard that when they took a town, he actually enjoyed executing the anti-fascists."

"Yes, she was clever. She managed to keep the shop open and give us all loans. And she swore she knew nothing at all about her husband when the workers' committee came to call. She tricked us all, pretending to be an abandoned wife, and turning her back on her husband. And then when he came back she met him with open arms."

"He taught her well. They set it all up beforehand, and he told her that the only way for her not to lose the shop was to swear that she had been abandoned. And the people around here all behaved well, because they could have told any one of the committees that her husband was with the Falange."

"But no one did, Fernando; I suppose it's because, in spite of everything, we've known them all our lives. Although I should say that my father could never get along with them."

"He could see through them ... Bunch of bastards."

"Well, and now Don Antonio is my boss and I'm the watchman at his warehouse."

"Yeah, you make a great watchman, I bet."

"How do you want me to earn a living?" Eulogio replied, upset by what Fernando had said.

Eulogio was twenty-eight years old, three years Fernando's senior, but they had always gotten along well. They had gone to the front together during the earliest days of the war, when the Nationalists fought to take Madrid. Fernando had enlisted without telling his father, causing the only argument the two ever had.

Lorenzo Garzo thought that it was his job as a Republican to fight to defend the values of the Republic. Fernando wanted to follow in his footsteps, and so he had joined a militia without telling him. He and Eulogio and a few other friends had spontaneously decided to join up and help the troops who were trying to stop the Nationalists from taking Madrid. All he remembered of this time was chaos and confusion. That was the first time he had held a gun in his hand. But the enemy was nowhere near him, so he didn't know if his shots had missed or hit the target.

When his father found out, he called his son to him and forbade him from returning to the front, saying: "Fernando, you shall not kill." But his son insisted, and his father grew very serious, pointed a finger at him, and said: "Son, you shall not kill. No one can be the same after taking another man's life." He agreed to his father's demand, and took part in the war as a member of the Popular Culture group. He risked his life taking newspapers and books to the trenches, as well as stocking libraries and hospitals and providing propaganda for the Frente Popular.

Don Lorenzo, Fernando's father, liked Eulogio's paintings and had spoken regularly about how good an artist he was. Fernando had adopted his father's opinions on art, and he had also found in the painter someone with whom he could talk and, above all, regret the past without fear of being turned in to the authorities. Where had Franco found so many supporters? He had always thought that Madrid was almost completely dominated by the Republican cause, and that was why the city had held out as long as it had. But now there were Franco supporters everywhere, and anything a person said that could be interpreted as a criticism of the regime brought with it immediate consequences. Everyone's biggest fear in those days was being reported to the authorities for having been on the Republican side. General Mola had told the truth when he threatened people with a "fifth column."

"Why don't you try to sell your paintings?" Fernando asked.

"These people don't understand art," his friend replied.

"Which people?"

"The ones who won the war. The ones who are now in charge. Marvin has promised to take a painting or two of mine to Paris with him when he goes. If it weren't for my mother, I'd go too … They understand people there, they understand Picasso, Braque, Miró … They appreciate them, and most importantly, they buy their paintings."

"Is Marvin going?"

"Well, not right away, but in about a month, I think. He says that since he's been here he's hardly been able to write. My mother has told me that she hears him writing all night long, and then cursing and throwing away everything he does write. The situation here doesn't inspire him."

"What kind of a poet is he?"

"I don't know ... But his work has been published in a couple of anthologies in Paris, and now he's writing a *Spanish Civil War Notebook*."

"I don't like your friend," Fernando admitted.

"What you don't like is the fact that Catalina has fallen for him. You're jealous, Fernando, you can see that from miles away. But it's not Marvin's fault that all the girls swoon over him, especially Catalina. Don't worry; as soon as he goes she'll come back to you, because there's no one else around who's worth the trouble. Pablo Gómez is sweet on her as well. Just look at the airs he puts on, just because his father works in a ministry. But Catalina doesn't give him the time of day. I wouldn't worry, because ..." Eulogio suddenly fell silent.

"What?"

"Nothing, nothing at all. Anyway, Marvin's an attractive man, and although he doesn't ever boast about it, you can see that he comes from a good family. Look at the clothes he wears ..."

Eulogio's brutal honesty hurt him, although Fernando knew that his friend wasn't trying to offend him. He was just incapable of anything less than complete honesty, and that stopped him from weighing his words with care.

"Do you think that all the girls like that American?" Fernando asked intently.

"Haven't you realized?" They think that he's ... I don't know ... different. He talks to them about abstract questions, about beauty, suffering, friendship, compromise ... all that kind of stuff! And he's not just doing it to string them along. He looks like he's in torment, as well, which helps: all the girls want to save him. You have to admit that he's handsome. How many Spaniards do you know who are blond with blue eyes? And he's tall. And as far as we're concerned, Fernando, all the girls from around here know us all too well. Your Catalina has fallen for him like all the others have."

"She's not 'my' Catalina. We're childhood friends, you know that."

"Yes, but you don't think of her as a sister. You've been in love with her ever since you were kids. I remember when you were a little kid, always hanging around her. If she fell over, you'd go to pick her up, and you'd always carry her books to school. You can't hide it, kiddo, you're head over heels in love with her. We've always thought that you and Catalina would end up getting married. And there's no one better than you, for all that her father wants her to marry Antoñito. I think she'd rather become a nun than marry the black marketeer's son. He's a wretched creature, isn't he, just like his dad, helping run the family business. I can't stand them, with their stupid mustaches. But you know, I'm supposed to be pleased, should thank them for not turning me in to the Falangists, for giving me a job."

"They take advantage of you," Fernando replied.

"Of course they do, but I try to take advantage of them as well. I grab something from them whenever I can. I lifted a bit of flour and some lentils today, as well as some cigarettes," Eulogio said, very pleased with himself, as he offered one of the cigarettes to Fernando.

They had chatted for too long, and Fernando was going to arrive late at the print shop. As they said goodbye, Fernando promised to come up to the attic that evening and smoke the promised cigarette.

He arrived late, but by barely a minute. He enjoyed his work in the print shop. It was as close as he could get to editing books, and much better work than what he did in the mornings, carrying bricks and running pulleys. His hands were callused and his back hurt. But he didn't complain. He didn't want his mother to suffer. She was already suffering enough over the idea of what might happen to his father.

When he got back home that evening, he found Marvin in the doorway. The American held out his hand, and Fernando didn't know how he could reject it.

"You left the other night, and it would have helped if you had given me a hand with Catalina."

"Hey, leave me out of this. You're not my problem," Fernando replied forcefully.

Marvin looked at him, ignoring his annoyance, and offered him a cigarette. Fernando hesitated before taking it, but it was an American brand. He lit up.

"How's your father?" Marvin asked.

"Same as always."

"They're executing a lot of people; I hope your father gets through all right."

Fernando threw the cigarette to the floor and crushed it under his shoe. He couldn't bear people talking about the fate that might befall his father.

"They won't shoot him," he replied angrily.

"It's tough to live here ... This country's not what it used to be. I remember the first few months of the war ... Everything was different."

"Why did you come to Spain?" Fernando asked, intrigued. It was the first time they had been alone together.

"Why? Spain is the country of Don Quixote and of Lope de Vega, Santa Teresa, Góngora, of Jorge Manrique ... Also, I didn't want to miss what was going on here. I think my best poems are from those first days ..."

"Did you send poems to any magazines?"

"No, I was a translator, but I also submitted a few articles, and whenever I had a moment free I wrote for myself. Then ..."

"Then what?"

"I went to the front a few times ... It was something I hadn't thought would happen. But a friend of mine asked me to translate for some American comrades of his. You can't imagine what it was like in Jarama ... The Nationalists attacked on all sides, and a guy shoved a rifle in my hands and said: 'Shoot, we don't need spectators here.' But I couldn't shoot. It would have been a contradiction; a poet doesn't shoot. Eulogio told me that you were at Jarama as well, that you took newspapers and books to the soldiers ... that you were with the Popular Culture group. I met other militiamen who were with the cultural front ..."

"But you didn't stay there for the whole war," Fernando said, reproachfully, shifting the focus of the conversation so that they would stop talking about him.

"No, I didn't. I was wounded that same day … Eulogio saved my life and … I had to make a decision: if I stayed there, it would be to kill, and forget about poetry forever. It would make me into another person; I was already turning into something I didn't want to be. I had the excuse of being wounded, and so I left."

"And why'd you come back?"

"Because I want to finish my *Spanish Civil War Notebook*. I couldn't stop thinking that if I came back then I'd be inspired, be able to forgive myself for having left."

"And did you?" Fernando asked with interest.

"Not completely. But I've decided to leave again."

"Forever?"

"Who knows? … I'm not sure. But I think I have to go back to France. That's the one thing I know."

"Where? The Nazis have taken over there. Why don't you go home?"

"To New York? No, there's nothing for me there. Everything important that's taking place in the world is taking place in Europe, at least now, and I don't want to miss it. Paris is the capital of the world, Fernando. You should go."

Fernando laughed bitterly. Go to Paris! He wanted to tell Marvin how stupid he was. He couldn't even let himself dream of making such a journey. His only wish was to get his father out of prison and earn enough money to support his mother. And when his father got out of prison, he wouldn't be able to work as an editor. The Nationalists wouldn't grant Republicans the power to edit and publish books.

"Yes, I guess I might go to Paris someday," he said, just to say something.

"In spite of the Nazis, I think I'm going to try to go to Paris," Marvin said, more to himself than to Fernando.

"Well, the Americans aren't at war with them."

"But we will be, I'm sure of that," Marvin replied.

They said goodbye. Fernando didn't want to speak to the American anymore, and anyway, his mother Isabel was waiting for him so they could eat. Soup made with a bone that gave it hardly any flavor at all, and a handful of rice.

"I've thought about working," his mother said.

"Going out to work?" You? We don't need it. We'll get along all right."

"I was talking to someone who owns a pharmacy, and they need someone to give them a hand with the house," his mother said, as though Fernando hadn't spoken.

"No! Get that idea out of your head, you're not going to do anyone's chores. And who is this pharmacist anyway, who can afford someone to clean his house?"

"He seems to be someone with very good connections. He has five kids and his wife is worn out. She needs someone to help her. I could do it, Fernando. I'll go for a couple of hours, and the money will come in very handy."

"No. I won't let you humiliate yourself in this way."

"Humiliate myself? You think that working is humiliating? There's nothing humiliating about washing, ironing, or cooking. It's all stuff I know how to do," his mother replied, twisting her expression into something that was almost a smile.

"No, of course there's nothing wrong with it, but you do it at home already, and when Father comes back he'll need you here. Do you think he'll put up with you working for a Franco supp-porter? He's suffering enough already, and this'll just make things worse. Who told you about this job anyway?"

"Don Bernardo."

"Of course, it would be the priest! Let him mind his own business and leave us in peace."

"He's a good man; he cares about his parishioners and ... well, he's been asking me for some time now why you don't go to church."

"Tell him the truth: I can't bear to see the flag draped over the altar, and I can't bear to see people bowing to it, and I can't bear to see them being asked to pray for Franco. And all priests are fascists."

"What are you saying? That's not true, there are all sorts, just like in the rest of the world."

"Oh, so how many priests do you know who supported the Republic?"

"Watch yourself, Fernando! Don't be a little boy; the Nationalists have won, and we have to accept it."

"I'm not going to accept it. I'll keep my mouth shut, but only until Father gets home."

"And then what do you think you're going to do? You'll put your life on the line by criticizing Franco? That's your goal? You think it's worthwhile? Your father won't allow it."

"My father risked his life for the Republic, and will never kneel to fascists."

"Your father has always been a dignified man, but he can't do anything now, nothing at all, not even if he wanted to."

They sat in silence. Fernando didn't want to argue with his mother, but he knew how stubborn she was, and it would be difficult for him to convince her not to take this job with the pharmacist.

"I'll try to find another job," he suggested.

"No. You have to be an editor and a translator, the same as your father and his father before him. Do you want to make your father even more unhappy? He wouldn't want you to stop trying to do that, not for anything in the world."

"Can't you see what's going on? Open your eyes, Mother: I was with Cultura Popular during the war, I was a militiaman at the front and no one is going to let me edit books, no one will let me be more than I am, carrying bricks in the mornings and setting type in the afternoons. I'll never be more than that."

"When your father comes back it'll all get sorted out and you'll see: they'll find a way to make you an editor. Maybe Don Bernardo will help us. He could be our backer, tell the authorities that we're decent people. You see how much he's helping us."

"To do what? To recommend you as a maid?"

"Fernando, all jobs have something worthy about them, and I won't have to be at that house all day, just until lunch time. I'll leave home at seven and I'll be back by three. You won't even know I'm gone. But don't ask me to sit around and twiddle my thumbs while you break your back, out every day at work … You're thinner every day … I can't see you do this to yourself …

and we've got nothing left to sell. Whatever I earn will help pay the lawyer as well … Come on, let's not argue."

He had to give in. He knew that his mother still thought of him as a little boy that she needed to protect. He felt angry and sad. Angry because he couldn't look after his household. He also felt hatred, a deep hatred for the Franco supporters who had put his father in prison and ruined their lives. His mother didn't complain, but he couldn't stop himself from being upset at the future that had been taken away from them.

"When do you have to go?" he asked, submissively.

"Tomorrow. I'll start work tomorrow. It'll be fine."

"They're Nationalists," Fernando said in disgust.

"Who isn't these days? You think anyone will dare say what they really think? This is over, Fernando, get used to it. The things your father taught you … you don't have to forget them, but you need to keep them to yourself."

"I'll come with you. They'll know that you're not alone."

His mother stretched out a hand and stroked her son's head.

"Run along. Go and smoke a cigarette with Eulogio before he has to leave for work."

"No, I won't go up today. Oh, Catalina told me that her mother has made some crochet cloths that she could give us to sell. Maybe Don Antonio will want to buy them."

"It would be good, but … don't call him Don Antonio, at least not when we're alone. He doesn't deserve our respect, doesn't deserve for us to call him 'Don' when we talk about him. And not just because he used to be a shopkeeper …"

"Why, then? Because he never went to school?"

"Well, there's that as well, but because he's a scoundrel, like all black marketeers. He's made himself rich by ruining other people. As soon as he can, he'll throw us out of this house."

"I won't let him, Mother, I swear I won't let him."

They declared a truce by settling down to read together. Fernando was reading Cervantes' *Viaje del Parnaso*, and Isabel was reading poetry.

"What are you reading, Mother?"

"'This burning ice, this frozen fire, this wound which hurts and yet one cannot feel: it is a wondered dream, a present evil, a tiring pause, a rest which tires one more …' You know who that is?" she asked with a smile.

"No …"

"Francisco de Quevedo. It's a poem I like a lot. It's called 'Definition of Love.'"

"You're a romantic, Mother."

The Madrid nights were growing cooler. His mother's persistent cough kept him awake and he was thinking that he should get a blanket from somewhere, just for her. It was an impossible dream. They didn't have any money. They didn't have anything left to sell, either, apart from their beds, a couple of armchairs and their dining table and chairs. His mother had said that she could sleep on the floor, but that they had to eat like civilized people. Also, when his father came back, he'd need somewhere to sit and write. And if he didn't get a job in a publishing house, then maybe he could earn some money by tutoring. Yes, they'd have to be allowed to do that; they couldn't be condemned to die of starvation, although they'd been hungry ever since the war started.

Fernando couldn't forget his father.

"What does it feel like to kill someone?" he had asked him, on one of his brief visits back from the front.

He saw how his father had stiffened, how his fists had clenched, and how he had closed his eyes and breathed in deeply as though he had to fill his lungs in order to reply.

"Nothing. That's the worst of it, you don't feel a thing. You shall not kill, Fernando, you shall not. You feel nothing when you kill, and the hell of it comes later."

"Lorenzo, what things you say!" his mother had exclaimed angrily, looking annoyed at both of them.

Then his father had gone back to the front and returned a defeated man.

When in November of 1936, the Republican government moved to Valencia, Fernando's father had convinced him that the cultural front had moved there as well. After a year, Fernando returned to Madrid because tuberculosis, rather than a bullet, had almost

34

put an end to his life. He only survived by a miracle. It was his mother's miracle, really: she had looked after him with no fear that she herself would fall sick.

The days went by in the capital; the bombs howled and the reports came in that the Nationalist forces had Madrid surrounded, but that the Republicans were resisting strongly. He followed the news from his bed, unable to leave the house. Then the news spread that Colonel Casado was negotiating a surrender, and then one day Franco's troops were in Madrid.

When the war ended, Lorenzo Garzo was imprisoned and sentenced to death. Fernando and his mother were sure that they would be able to get him pardoned and sent back home.

Fernando was barely able to sleep. He knew that his mother was also awake, but both of them lay silent. He got up before dawn. There was no better alarm clock than the bells of the Convent of La Encarnación. His mother usually went there on Sundays to hear Mass, or else to another nearby church, San Ginés. There, Quevedo had been baptized and Lope de Vega had gotten married. There were beautiful pictures there as well: one by El Greco, and others by Luca Gordano, Francisco Ricci, and Alonso Cano.

Taking care to make no noise, he went into the bathroom. The cold water of the shower cleared his head. He thought that it was almost a luxury to be living in this house, with a bathroom they didn't have to share with anyone. Ever since Eulogio had moved to his attic, he had had to wash in a bucket, or at the sink in his tiny kitchen. Yes, he felt very lucky to have this little bathroom that his father had installed before the war had touched their lives. He suddenly had an idea and almost burst out laughing. They might be able to rent the bathroom out. Eulogio had told him that the American, with great forbearance, had gotten used to the inconveniences of the attic, but that every now and then he complained about not being able to have a shower like God intended.

When Eulogio got back from guarding Don Antonio's warehouse, he'd go up and tell him that he could rent the shower to the American. If Eulogio wanted to take a shower, then Fernando wouldn't charge him anything, because they were friends, but the

American could pay, and would pay, because Americans have money, although he didn't understand why the American had decided to stay in the attic when he could very well have afforded a room in a better class of lodgings.

He didn't have any breakfast because there was nothing to have, apart from a bit of malt that he left for his mother.

"Fernando, don't go out without having breakfast," Isabel said.

"It's early, Mother, you can sleep a little bit more."

"It's half past five and I need to get ready. It wouldn't be good for me to be late my first day of work."

Fernando got dressed and waited for his mother to get ready so that he could go with her. When they went out into the street, he held her arm. They walked fast. They reached the pharmacist's house before seven o'clock.

The door was opened by a woman in a black dress and a white frilly maid's apron.

"Doña Hortensia is waiting for you: there's a lot to do. And who is this?" the maid asked.

"My son, Fernando."

"Well, he can go."

"All right ... Son, you can go, I'll see you later."

"I'd like to say hello to Doña Hortensia," Fernando replied, keen not to leave before he'd been able to judge the owners of the house for himself.

"The cheek of it! You really think that Doña Hortensia will waste her time on you? Go on, get out of here before she sends you and your mother away."

An elderly man came out into the hall. The maid coughed anxiously, but Fernando held the man's gaze.

"And you are ...?" he asked.

"Fernando Garzo, and this is my mother ..."

"Right, and what do you want?"

"She's here for the ironing, Don Luis," the maid interrupted.

"Ah, all right ... Yes, my wife told me that someone would come to do the ironing and help a bit around the house ... What's your name?"

"Isabel," she replied in embarrassment.

"Well, come on in, my wife's been having trouble with the house for a while. And you, young fellow, you'd best be off ..."

"I only came to see my mother safely to work and to see what kind of a place it was where she'd be working."

Don Luis looked Fernando up and down. For a moment Fernando thought he was going to be thrown off the property, but Don Luis gave him a slap on the back and showed him to the door.

"She'll be in good hands here. It's a good thing for you to take such care of your mother. Now get along with you, back to whatever it is you do."

Fernando left the house saying to himself that it might not be a bad place to work, but he hadn't even reached the street before he was bemoaning his bad luck. This was a man who had won the war, and he had to be a bigwig in the new regime to be able to permit himself a maid and hire another woman, Fernando's mother, to cook and iron. He felt a wave of hatred overcome him. His father was in prison, just because he was a Republican, and his mother, his dear mother, was forced to be a servant in that house. He spat on the ground. It was his way of getting the bitterness out.

When he got to the building site, his boss gave him a shove.

"You're late," he said.

"No, I'm not, Pascual. It's not even eight yet."

"And how are we going to put Spain back on her feet if we don't work? Don't be a slacker, and get those sacks of cement moving, over there where Pepe is ... I bet you spent all night with your books. Ooh, look at you, wanting to be an editor! All you can do is lift and carry things, kid. You should be glad they don't lock you up like your father."

Fernando said nothing. Why should he? Pascual was a brute, who barely knew how to read and who thought that sheer force was enough for a man to get by. He had fought on the Nationalist side and liked to boast of the number of reds that he had killed at the front. When they heard him speak, there were a number of men on the building site who had to bite their tongues. They couldn't permit themselves the luxury of talking back. It had been hard enough to get the job on the building site, as a way to make enough money to survive. It was better to keep quiet. Silence was a part of the punishment for the losing side.

"Don't get worked up about it, kid," one of the men said as Fernando brought him a sack of cement.

He went home at half past two. He was keen to see his mother and for her to tell him about how her first day at work had gone. He hurried back. He also wanted to speak to Eulogio about the shower.

He found his mother in the entrance to their house. She seemed happy, but tired.

"They seem like nice people. Doña Hortensia is very pleasant. She asks a lot of me, but there's nothing for you to worry about."

"And what about the husband?"

"You've seen him, he's a pharmacist. He seems to know lots of important people who seem to rate him highly."

"He's an old man."

"Well, he's older than his wife, a few years older. She can't be more than forty, and he ... well, he must be about seventy."

"And their children?"

"They've got five of them, all ages, but Doña Hortensia runs the house like a barracks."

"Did you get any food there?"

"No ... I made them lunch, lentils and an omelet."

"They could at least have given you something. Even just an egg."

"They didn't have to."

"Bastards," Fernando said.

"Please, don't be so bitter," his mother begged.

Fernando went up to see Eulogio and found him just out of bed. His friend had been napping, but now was up and ready to start painting. He heard Fernando's proposal of getting the American to pay for using the shower with interest.

"He's out at the moment, but I'll tell him as soon as I see him. I'm sure he'll say yes. Does your mother agree?"

"How could she not? Of course, we'll have to tell him not to waste water."

38

"Of course … And I'm going to take you up on it as well, your offer of showering for free. I'd like that, even if it's only once a week. How is it going with Pascual?"

"He works me hard. He doesn't like me much."

"You've got to put up with him. He's the site foreman and he takes advantage of lots of you, because he knows that you were Republicans. And you're lucky that he gives you work to do instead of reporting you to the authorities."

"I'm sick of him. He's always going on about the war and the reds, just so there's no doubt at all about what he thinks. And he takes advantage of the fact that my father's a Republican and in prison, and he pays me much less than another kid who does the same work as I do but whose father joined up with the Falangists as soon as the war broke out."

"I've told you, you've got to put up with it. Don't cause me any trouble. It was tough for me to speak to Don Antonio and get him to get you this job. You don't like Don Antonio, and neither do I. If he puts up with me it's because he knows that I know how much of a scoundrel he is, and that his friend, the foreman, steals building materials and sells them to Don Antonio at a cut rate. But there are so many people like us around at the moment, doing whatever we can do to get a job for a few pennies … Look around you, Fernando, even the Nationalists are hungry."

"Some people are hungrier than others."

"Of course they are. But don't fool, yourself, there are more people having a tough time than not. There are always sly people like Don Antonio around. But what can we do: they won the war."

"We're idiots to keep on calling him 'Don Antonio.' He used to be 'Antonio, the guy who runs the shop,' and now we're calling him 'Don' this, and 'Don' that …"

"We may not like it, but we've got to go along with it. And he's the one who puts food on our plates. And he might be a bastard, but he's given me work and you've got work through him, indirectly."

"But he threw you out of your house! Look at how you're living now!"

"We lost the war, Fernando, accept it. Your father will explain it all when he gets out of prison. Don Antonio used to have a shop and now he trades on a much larger scale. He's got the upper hand, and what can we do about it?"

"Well, I've got to go to the print shop now. Talk to the American and let me know what he decides about paying for the shower."

Although he was upset in general with his situation, Fernando liked working as a typesetter. He had only been there for three months, but he was such a quick learner that Don Vicente, the shop manager, who was both severe and gruff, sometimes gave Fernando a pat on the back. And as for Don Víctor, who was the actual owner of the place, Fernando couldn't deny that he had been good to him, which made the fact that he was right-wing all the more annoying.

"You're good at this job," his boss said to him one afternoon.

Yes, he was good at composing, and had even dared make suggestions a couple of times for how they could save paper.

They did everything at the print shop, from books to propaganda. Fernando sometimes asked himself if he was betraying his father when he set pamphlets glorifying Franco.

Marvin agreed to pay for the shower. Isabel gave in, resignedly. It would be useful for them to have a few pennies a day, and the American seemed a good enough fellow. They'd give him a key so that he could get into the house: not only because they thought he could be trusted, but also because there was nothing in the house worth stealing.

It was a large house, with three balconies facing onto the street. The living room, which was also the dining room, used to be very comfortable, but now was almost empty. There were two sliding doors, always left open, that led into a little room which they called the office, covered from floor to ceiling with Fernando's father's precious books. A couple of bedrooms, as well as the kitchen and the bathroom, made up the rest of the house.

Sometimes Isabel would imagine the moment when Lorenzo, her husband, would come home. He would come back exhausted, having spent so long locked away in prison without anything at all. She would explain to him that they'd had to sell their furniture, but at least they had kept the table and the office chair.

Everything else – the coat rack and dressing mirror in the foyer, the plate rack in the dining room, the headboards of the beds, and so on – all these no longer belonged to them. She knew that Lorenzo would hug her and would say that she didn't need to worry, that all those pieces of furniture were only objects, however much they had loved them. He would look over the shelves in the office and would sigh in silence to see that she had kept his books. For a man like Lorenzo, a lover of literature, books were part of his soul and he couldn't understand himself without them. Yes, he would stroke the spines of the novels of Cervantes, he would sink into the poems of Góngora, he would smile to see the old volumes of Calderón. And he would sigh with relief to see that *Romancero gitano* by Lorca and so many other books were still there, books that had formed his life and the way he moved through the world. And he would certainly hold back a tear when he saw that on the table in the office, the book of poems would still be open just as he had left it, on the same page with the same poem by Gómez Manrique:

> *I leave you now, my maiden,*
> *against my will;*
> *I leave your pure goodness*
> *with great anguish.*
>
> *I leave in great sorrow*
> *for this sad departure,*
> *and am weighed down by the thought*
> *that it will shorten my life.*

Isabel was desperate for him to come home. She struggled to escape from the nightmare that came to her every night. Always the same nightmare. She saw her husband saying goodbye to her, but she did not hear his final words. Then there would be a deafening noise and the slumped body of Lorenzo would fall to the ground. Dead. When she reached this point in the dream she would wake up screaming.

Fernando would come over to her and hold her tight without saying anything. He didn't need to. He also saw ghosts.

Isabel finished combing her hair. She looked into the mirror and smiled sadly. Her chestnut hair was already peppered with gray, and she was barely forty years old. She could not deny it. Her youth had disappeared in the war. Wrinkles across her face made her expression hard. The skin on her hands was rough and her skinny frame, the result of hunger, took all her beauty away from her. But she was sure that Lorenzo would still love her in the same way that she desperately loved the ruined and tortured body of her husband, paying no attention to his premature baldness, his sunken eyes, his arthritic fingers that had suffered in the cold during the years of the war.

She still saw her husband as the serious, dedicated youth who had lost track of time translating Shakespeare, Oscar Wilde, Daniel Defoe and Walter Scott, the boy who had seemed surprised that she would look twice at him, a girl who all the neighborhood boys chased after. Isabel had lived with her parents in a village in the sierra where her father worked as a vet, and where Lorenzo spent every summer with his parents.

Isabel was barely eighteen years old when they got married. She had been radiant that day, and that was how Lorenzo would always see her.

"Are you ready?" Fernando asked, bringing her back to reality.

"Yes, son, I'm ready. Let's go."

They walked quickly out of the house. It's not that the prison was a long way away, but they always got there early on visiting day. The guards liked making things difficult for the families of the losers.

Fernando had dressed up as well. He knew that his father was upset by how ugly things were in prison, and he suffered enough with the ticks and fleas there.

When they arrived at the prison, they had to stand around for a while, whispering with the families of the other prisoners. They all knew each other, after so many weeks meeting at the gates to this building, which had once been a convent, and which was now a prison for Republican prisoners.

Both mother and son looked for familiar faces, and if there were people whom they did not see, this was usually because the father, the brother, the uncle or the friend in prison had been shot.

Fernando felt his stomach turn to see his father so gaunt and somehow absent. Why wasn't he wearing his glasses? He didn't see well without them.

"Dad, where are your glasses?" he asked, as soon as they had greeted each other.

"Don't worry about that, son," his father answered.

"Did they take them away from you?" Isabel insisted.

"Well … they got broken. The guard at the door said I was holding up the line and pushed me and they fell off and … he stepped on them. I'm sorry."

Isabel held her husband's hand and tried to keep back the tears. Fernando clenched his fists to hold in his rage.

"Dad, you mean Roque, right? Roque … We've heard that he's a brute, and likes picking on people here," Fernando said angrily.

"Let's talk about other things. Are you getting any better food?" Isabel said, just to keep the conversation going.

"The same as usual. They call it 'soup' and it's always full of insects … We're so hungry that the men eat without looking … But tell me about yourselves …"

"Dad, the lawyer promised me that he'll give me some news in the next day or so. He says he's almost sure that you'll get the pardon. You'll see, you'll be home by Christmas."

"I'm sure of it … Lorenzo, I've started working. Don Bernardo, the local priest, has recommended me at the house of one of his parishioners. Don Luis is a pharmacist, and Doña Hortensia, his wife, is a good woman. They've got five children and need help with everything …"

"They're Falangists, Dad," Fernando added.

Lorenzo looked down in shame. He felt deeply upset to imagine Isabel forced by necessity into washing and cleaning in someone else's house. It's not that he didn't think that cleaning was a worthy job, but that she had to do it was just one more sign of the life that he had lost, perhaps forever.

"Do they treat you well?" he asked, stroking Isabel's cheek.

"Yes, of course they do. They're not bad people."

"Of course they are!" Fernando said.

"Come on, son, don't make your mother feel worse. Fernando, it's not the case that everyone who thinks differently from us has to be bad. There are good people and bad people every-where."

"Well, when you get out, see for yourself how they behave and then you can tell me what you think," Fernando said bitterly, and in a voice that was perhaps slightly louder than it needed to be.

"We've rented the shower to an American. I've spoken to you about him; he's a poet and lives upstairs in the attic with Eulogio. He was dying for a proper shower, and Fernando had the idea of letting him come and shower, and paying for it. The money helps," Isabel said, to shift the conversation onto a different topic.

"I see that you're figuring out how things work. Good. Renting the shower is a good idea, I think," Lorenzo said with a smile.

"We let Eulogio shower for free," Fernando said.

They got him up to date with all the news of their neighborhood, and Lorenzo listened to everything attentively, as if he could really be interested in how Don Antonio the black marketeer was doing, or what was happening with the Vilamar family.

"And what about you and Catalina, eh?" Lorenzo said with a glance at his son.

"She's not my girlfriend," Fernando protested.

"You know how the Vilamars are, Lorenzo: they aim high and want to secure their daughter's future. I think that Ernesto Vilamar wants to link his family to Antonio the black marketeer's. His son Antoñito is very keen on Catalina," Isabel explained to her husband.

"Well, if that's aiming high …" Lorenzo said with heavy irony.

"Antonio is dealing with a lot of money at the moment. He still has his shop, but if you could see the warehouse he's rented for the black market things … You won't recognize him when you see him, for all the airs he puts on."

"Well, but Catalina's always been very clear about doing what she wants; I don't think that she likes Antoñito," Lorenzo said.

"Maybe she doesn't like Antoñito, but …" Fernando fell silent.

"What are you saying?" his father insisted.

"She likes the American. Marvin is a poet, and was there when the war broke out, working as a translator for some American journalists, then he left. I don't know what it is about him, but all the girls seem to like him."

His father smiled and looked at him tenderly. He saw the pain and stunned sensation of one's first failure in love reflected on Fernando's face. He knew that his son had been in love with Catalina ever since they were both children.

"Don't worry about it, she'll grow out of him. I'm sure that you're very important to Catalina."

"Yes, as a friend," Fernando said, bitterly.

"You'll see … Don't get upset about it …" his father encouraged him.

The guards announced that it was time to go. Isabel gave her husband a loaf of bread and two hard-boiled eggs. She'd bought the eggs from Don Antonio the day before. She'd got the bread from the money she'd saved up from Marvin's showers.

"The eggs will be good for you," she said. "They'll give you energy."

"Of course they will. Look after yourselves. I love you."

"You'll be home soon, Dad."

It wasn't until they had left the prison that Isabel allowed herself to cry. Fernando put his arms around her shoulders, trying to console her.

"We'll get him pardoned, you'll see."

"But he's thinner every day, he's just skin and bones, and now with his glasses … Your father can't see anything without them. Lord, Fernando, we have to get him out of there."

"We will, Mother, you'll see. Dad hasn't done anything bad."

Isabel didn't reply. The victors were cruel to the vanquished. They didn't respect anyone, and most certainly didn't respect the Republican soldiers. There were firing squads every day, and she shuddered to think that one day someone would come to her door to tell her that Lorenzo had been shot.

2

"Did you tell Fernandito about the crochet work?" Doña Asunción asked her daughter.

"Yes, Mama," Catalina replied.

"It's been more than a month since I told you ..."

"That's true."

"Your father had better not find out about this ... You know he doesn't like it that we still talk to the Garzo family. I'm very sorry for Isabel. It must be very hard for her to work in that pharmacist's house. I don't know what I'd do in her place. The poor woman!"

"We have to help them, Mother," Catalina said.

"Of course, but we have to do it without your father finding out; you know what he's like."

Catalina gave her mother a hug. She felt very close to her. She knew that she would always protect her. Her mother was absorbed by her daughter, her only daughter, a gift from heaven after several failed pregnancies.

They were very similar, not just physically. Of medium height, with light chestnut hair and chestnut eyes with green sparks in their depths, and both of them fine-figured; they were very alike in character as well. Doña Asunción was very affected by the suffering of others, and tried to alleviate it if possible, which led to arguments with her husband. It was useless to look for empathy towards others in Don Ernesto. He was the youngest of six children, and had been brought up with harsh discipline. He had suffered in silence throughout the war, not just because of his liver complaint, but also because he had been unable to flee to the Nationalist-controlled areas. It upset and bothered him to think that most of his neighbors were Republicans, or, even worse, socialists. If he only knew for certain … For example, there was Lorenzo Garzo, the editor. He had never gotten along with him. It had always been hard for him to bring himself to greet him when they met in the street, and he had been upset that Asunción had gotten along so well with Isabel. Now Lorenzo was where he deserved to be, in prison. He was hoping that they would shoot him. Franco should not show any pity towards enemies; it was better to get rid of them, because they could be dangerous if they were left alive.

Doña Asunción said that now they had won, the best thing to do was forget about the war and try to get back to a normal life. She was so naive; well, she was just a woman, and women didn't know how to think. And she really didn't have anything to forget about: Petra, her only sister, was alive even if she had lost her husband during the fighting in Aragon. His brother-in-law had died for Spain like a patriot. He'd even been given a posthumous medal.

All he had was Catalina, and sometimes he thought that it was a blessing they had no other children, especially not any sons, as they would have been killed by the reds. Of course, he missed having another man in the house, missed having someone he could talk to, who would understand politics, given that his wife and his daughter were two saintly, ignorant souls.

Don Ernesto was glad that Andrés, his older brother, had gotten the family farm back. The militias had destroyed the house, confiscated the pigs and the sheep, but the land was still there and would come back into the family's possession. The bad part of it was that the man who until the start of the war had been the estate manager turned out to have been an anarchist, and had actively encouraged the reds to ruin it. He gave thanks to Franco and to God that justice had been done. The estate manager had been shot. But that was not enough to wipe out the pain that had been inflicted on them. They had killed his father, although he was an old man, and his nephew Andresito, who was little more than a child. Amparo, his sister-in-law, had gone mad. And now

Andrés ran the farm with the help of a trustworthy man, a Falangist from a nearby village. Don Ernesto didn't like Falangists all that much: he thought they were a little blunt and he could do without their baggage, but it was better a patriot than a red.

He had lost two other brothers at the front, and a third hadn't made it out alive from the secret police headquarters on Fomento Street. He didn't want to think about what had happened to his sister the nun when another group of militants had broken into her order's cloister.

But at that moment his biggest problem was Catalina. His wife was too soft on her. Asunción was too tolerant of her daughter's behavior, just as his sister-in-law Petra was. The two sisters came from a good family; their father had been a tobacco wholesaler, bringing in goods from the Canary Islands. They had studied at a convent school, and had learned everything that two good young women should learn. His father-in-law had gotten him a job at the family firm, but the whole thing had gone to pieces during the war and the poor man had died without having the satisfaction of seeing the right side win.

And now Don Ernesto was trying to make his father-in-law's firm a going concern once more. After all, who didn't smoke in this day and age? Although he had hope for the future, he was also worried, because they had run up a vast number of debts during the war.

He had to arrange a good marriage for Catalina. His daughter was no longer a child and he didn't like to see her not keeping herself busy. As soon as the summer was over, he would have to find her something to do, because the classes she took with her aunt Petra weren't enough to keep her occupied. His wife kept on saying that they had to make Catalina into an educated woman, but that seemed a little eccentric to him. Why would a man want to marry a bluestocking? It was a Republican idea, giving women an education. Thank the Lord, things were now back to the normal way. The important thing was for Catalina to get married to someone with enough money to keep her well.

Antoñito was a good choice. The shopkeeper's son was a good match. Don Antonio was rich. He had gone into the black market after the war and earned money; now, he earned even more. He traded in everything, but the most important thing was that he had good connections with some of the current ministers, thanks to his brother Prudencio, who had been assistant to a colonel. Antonio, the shopkeeper, had been a Falangist who had fought against the reds and had come back to Madrid with the Nationalist troops, to become Don Antonio, and his oldest son, Antoñito, was a good match. He wasn't all that handsome, but he wasn't ugly either: the really ugly ones were his two sisters, Paquita and Mariví, who were two little girls who had nothing good going for them at all. He could also marry Catalina to Pablo Gómez, he supposed, the son of Don Pedro who worked in the tax office and lived on the fifth floor.

Don Ernesto looked up from the papers on the desk in front of him. The bank had just refused him a loan.

He heard his daughter laughing, and imagined her chattering away to his wife. Bless them, for they had nothing to worry their heads about.

He rang the bell and the maid came in.

"Tell my wife and daughter to come to the office," he ordered without looking up.

Two minutes later Doña Asunción and Catalina stuck their heads around the door to the office.

"What do you want, Ernesto?" his wife asked.

"I wanted to tell you that Don Antonio wants to organize a picnic in the countryside in a couple of days. I just wanted to give you a bit of warning, Asunción."

"Don't worry about me, although I must say that I do find those people a little difficult to get along with, they're so … well, it's not quite the done thing to say as much, but you can tell what their upbringing has been, what kind of family they come from."

"Wasn't it you who told me that the important thing was whether people were good or not? There you go. Don Antonio may not come from a good family, but he's shown a great aptitude for business. He got rich during the war, and is getting richer with every day that passes. He deals with important people, so why we shouldn't deal with him, I don't know."

"Ernesto, before the war you didn't even give him the time of day. I think that back then you wouldn't go into his shop."

"Why should I go in? Isn't the house your job? Look, Asunción, don't try to complicate matters; things have changed and a new order is in place; people with talent are being allowed to get ahead."

"But Don Antonio is so ordinary," the woman insisted.

"Well, of course he hasn't had much education, but he's an upright man, and he was on the right side, not like the Republicans, or the bloody communists and anarchists. We will always have to thank Franco for cleaning up that trash."

"But, darling, you were a monarchist," Doña Asunción reminded him.

"That's why I'm on Franco's side: he's brought back order and he'll bring back the monarchy soon enough."

"I don't know. Men don't like giving up their power, and I can't imagine Franco, after winning the war, handing the country over to a king," Asunción said.

"What would you know about it? All I wanted to say was that we're going to this picnic out in the countryside on Sunday. It'll be a good chance for Antoñito and Catalina to talk."

"What would we have to talk about, Papa?" Catalina said in annoyance.

"Well, the two of you are young and have a great future ahead of you, and it would be good for you to get to know one another," Don Ernesto replied.

"But we already know each other, Papa, and you didn't let me play with Antoñito or his sisters when we were younger. You said that I couldn't be friends with a shopkeeper's children because they weren't the right kind of people." Catalina knew how to irritate her father.

"You say the most stupid things! And anyhow, things have changed. Don Antonio is a businessman and his older brother Prudencio is a brave soldier who knows a number of generals. Catalina, you must be aware that nobility is acquired through brave actions on behalf of the king and of the country."

"But Papa, everyone knows that Don Antonio's brother was nothing more than a quartermaster, and that he stole whatever he could get his hands on."

"Catalina!" Don Ernesto looked furiously at his daughter.

"And what has Don Antonio done for the king or for the country? I'm sorry, Papa, I didn't know, I thought that he was nothing more than a black marketeer who cared nothing about anything apart from getting rich. And as for Antoñito, I know that you want him and me to … but that's not going to happen, he's disgusting. I'd sooner be a nun than marry him …" Catalina continued, almost unaware of her father's rage.

"So this is the kind of education you want to give your daughter? I'd never have dared to speak to my father like that! Children don't have the right to their own opinions; all they can do is obey their parents, who know what's good for them. Don't you dare say again that you'd prefer to be a nun, because I will take you personally to my sister's convent in Aragon. And then you'll see how Aunt Adoración will whip you into shape."

"Why are you fighting? Of course we're going to go to this picnic in the countryside, and of course Catalina will talk to Antoñito, and … well, the Lord knows if they are meant to be together," Doña Asunción interrupted him, afraid of the direction the conversation was taking.

"Oh, and I don't want you to see Fernando ever again! The only thing that kid can bring us is more problems. His father's in prison for being a red. I don't want to have anything more to do with those people," Don Ernesto said angrily.

"But Ernesto, the Garzos aren't bad people; Isabel's father was a vet up in the mountains. And as for Don Lorenzo, the poor fellow, he was the director of the Editorial Clásica publishing house, and he was a good editor and I'm sure he's done nothing wrong. You've got a lot of the books that he published. I'm sure he'll get out of prison," Doña Asunción said, afraid that all she could do now would be to make her husband even angrier.

"Oh, so he hasn't done anything! That's rich! So, fighting alongside the reds isn't anything important?"

"Well, he is a Republican, or he was a Republican, just like so many people, and I don't think we need to shoot all the Republicans, because that would mean shooting half the country. And, until the war broke out, there was no shame in being a Republican," his wife insisted.

"Have you ever heard anything like it! That I should have to hear something like this in my own house! What are you teaching our daughter? If you carry on talking like that, she'll believe that there's nothing wrong with being a Republican! They almost destroyed Spain, almost handed it over to the Bolsheviks!"

"Ernesto, calm down; I'll get you a coffee and a bite to eat. The doctor says you need to eat well. Catalina, go and set the tray and bring a cup of coffee to your father."

Catalina left her father's office muttering to herself. She had always been an obedient daughter, but she was certainly not going to get anywhere near Antoñito. She felt disgusted simply thinking about him. She still remembered his birthday in the Pradera de San Isidro. Well, she didn't remember it all that well, only that Antoñito had pressed against her during their dances, and Pablo Gómez had done the same. They were so disgusting, both of them. She didn't remember any more, but just thinking about it made her stomach turn over. At least Marvin had been there. Every time she thought about the American, she felt a shiver run all over her body. She was in love with him and her father would have to accept that. Marvin was a polite man, and his family had to be at the same level as the Vilamars, although she didn't care at all if they were not. He was her boyfriend, her fiancé, almost, or at least that's what she felt. And as for Fernando, she was not willing to break their friendship, whatever her father might say. Catalina stopped dead at the door to the kitchen. She realized that this was the first time in her life that she was ready to disobey her father, consequences be damned.

Meanwhile, Doña Asunción tried to calm her husband's rage. Don Ernesto was not well, and his doctors insisted that he should try to avoid stress.

Doña Asunción's marriage was not happy, but she didn't even say that to herself, and she crossed herself just for thinking it. It had not been easy to live with a man in poor health, a melancholy, tyrannical man. She had had to tone down her joy in life and her happiness in order not to upset her husband, who was unnaturally upset just to see her smile. But he had been a good husband; she had never wanted for anything, and he had never been upset or angry that they had not had any more children. He had been satisfied with Catalina, whom he undoubtedly loved.

Don Ernesto coughed to attract his wife's attention.

"Asunción, if Antoñito does marry our daughter it will be very good for us."

She looked at him expectantly, without daring to say anything else. She knew her husband was irritated by questions.

"We have to be realists, and not think too much about the new regime. Or would you prefer us to be governed by socialists? Franco is a fine man and he knows that the Spaniards need someone to take the helm. You'll see how Spain will start to prosper now."

"But I don't understand why you think that it's so important for Catalina and Antoñito …"

"Because Don Antonio is a member of the new social class that will govern us. We could marry our daughter off to someone who is one of our people, but you must know that many of our friends have been left with nothing and are doing all they can merely to keep up appearances. If she's with Antoñito she won't want for anything. And she will know how to make him a better person."

"If you say so, Ernesto …"

"Yes, Asunción, I do say so, and I won't let Catalina have her flighty little ideas about anything. Our little girl is becoming a woman now, and her duty is to accept whatever it is that we decide. There's no arguing with that."

"Of course, of course, Ernesto," Doña Asunción said, not entirely convinced.

"Ah, and one more thing. Even though the war is over, we need to be prudent when it comes to our expenses. I'm going to see my brother in Huesca next week. I want him to give us a loan."

"A loan? But why …"

"Good Lord, Asunción, don't be so silly! We have expenses and obligations."

"Yes, Ernesto, you're right."

Catalina pushed open the door with her foot and came in carrying a tray with a coffee pot on it, and a little plate with some tea cakes. Her father's face lit up and he waved her and his wife out of the room. He preferred to eat cake when he was by himself.

What Don Ernesto had not told his wife was that they were short on ready money, so short that they barely had any at all, and that Don Antonio, as well as being in the black market, was a loan shark, and as the bank had refused Don Ernesto his loan, he had had to go to the shopkeeper and borrow a fair amount of cash. If his brother did not come through and give them an even larger loan, Don Ernesto would find himself in a very sticky situation indeed.

At that very moment, Marvin was musing to himself as he looked at the wall of the tiny room he rented in Eulogio's attic.

He shouldn't really have rented that apartment. He didn't need to suffer the same poverty that Eulogio and his mother did. He had enough money to rent a room somewhere else, or even stay in a hotel. But he had been scared of coming back. He had not fought with the Lincoln brigade, but he had been in Spain and seen his comrades fighting, and his way of participating in the war had been to work as a translator. Maybe Franco and his deputies were aware of which foreigners had been on his side and which had not. What if they arrested him? He had no illusions about his bravery: he knew that he was really a coward.

Of course, his parents were too important for the Spanish to dare to arrest him. He had several letters of recommendation, as well as the protection of his embassy. Franco wasn't going to go head-to-head with the Americans.

Even so, it had been stupid of him to stay with Eulogio. But he wanted to be close to the man whom he had liked and respected during the war, and who had saved his life. They had gotten along well when they met each other at the front; he had been surprised by the joy and comradeship that the amateur painter had shown. Marvin thought that he was a mediocre artist, but he never said so out loud.

Why had he come back? Perhaps he hadn't forgiven himself for not fighting. During the war, but especially when he left Spain, he would always say that a poem could do as much for a good cause as throwing a grenade, shooting a rifle, or storming the enemy lines. But he hadn't been able to convince himself of this fact, and this had led him into a crisis of confidence. Ever since he had left Spain, he had written no poetry worthy of the name.

His family had insisted, from New York, that he come home. His father was a steel tycoon, and it was a disappointment for him that his son had turned out a poet. Luckily enough, Marvin's younger brother, Tommy, was willing to keep his father's dreams alive, and the family business would stay in family hands. They sent Marvin an allowance every month that allowed him to live without worry. His mother, who had an artist's soul, would not have let it be any other way; and, in the end, it was her steel mill that the family had inherited, and which her husband now ran.

"Would you like a coffee?" Piedad, Eulogio's mother, asked, sticking her head around the door into Marvin's room. He seemed caught up in the book he was reading.

"Real coffee?" he asked in surprise.

"Yes, Eulogio took a handful from Don Antonio's warehouse. A few kilos came in yesterday, and you know what my son's like … Well, and Don Antonio doesn't pay him all that much …" Piedad tried to justify Eulogio's petty theft.

"I'd love a cup of coffee," Marvin said with a smile.

"What are you reading?" she asked.

"It's a book that Eulogio lent me, and that I think Fernando's father published. Lope de Vega's *Rimas sacras* … 'If dryness and cold are the first signs of rigorous and wild death, then my hard heart and its ice are signs that I should fear …'" Marvin read out.

Piedad smiled. And Marvin thought how much he liked this woman. She was very attractive, but she seemed not to realize it. She had lost her husband at the front, and had almost lost her son, who she saw coming back one day, barely able to walk. Marvin owed his life to Eulogio, because it was Eulogio who had picked him up when he had been wounded, and who had run with him as bullets whizzed all around them, and who had forced the doctors to leave their patients and come to help the American as a matter of urgency. But Eulogio had paid a price for his assistance, as he was left crippled, and it was these wounds that had kept him away from the front for the last two years of the war.

Piedad never complained. She accepted her fate without blaming anyone. Things were as they had to be, she said, when

Eulogio and Marvin sat around discussing how upset they were about Franco's triumph.

Jesús Jiménez, Eulogio's father, had been a minor editor at a Madrid newspaper, and had translated from French as well. He put in his extra hours as a translator at the same publishing house where Lorenzo Garzo, Fernando's father, worked.

He was a good man: shy and spiritless was how Piedad always used to describe him, but she would always add that although her husband had been a lover of peace, he had not tried to avoid the debt he owed the Republic, and had gone to fight at the front, where he lost his life.

Before the war, the family had been reasonably well off. As far as Eulogio's vocation as a painter was concerned, he'd had it since childhood. He could sit for hours drawing on a piece of paper. His dream was to become a great painter, and his mother and father had encouraged him by paying for him to study at the San Fernando School of Fine Arts.

Marvin was a keen and curious observer of the families that had come together in this building in the Calle de la Encarnación. They were all petty-bourgeois families. Well, most of them had been petty-bourgeois, but they were all now struggling to survive.

He went over the list of neighbors in his head: there were the Garzos, on the first floor; the Jiménezes, on the second floor to the left, until they went to live in one of the attics; the Garcías, on the fifth (the head of the household was a lawyer) ... There were also the Gómezes, whose only son Pablo was Antoñito's constant competitor. Next door, a slightly grander establishment, was where the Vilamars lived. Don Ernesto did not approve, but his daughter Catalina was on friendly terms with all her neighbors. Doña Asunción, her mother, was a good woman, always ready to lend a hand if need be.

Piedad came in with a cup of coffee and put it on the table, where a few blank pieces of paper lay.

"Inspiration hasn't struck, dear?" she said.

He was slightly taken aback by such a direct question, and frowned, although he knew that Piedad hadn't meant anything in particular.

"Maybe a coffee will help me," he said.

"This country is dead, Marvin, don't you see? You can't get inspiration from the dead. You're not going to write anything here. You need distance and … well, I don't want to poke my nose in where it's not needed, but you need to forgive yourself as well. You have nothing to feel bad about. I heard you speaking with Eulogio and I know that you can't sleep at night because you left before the end of the war. Why should you have stayed? You were wounded, and it wasn't your fight anyway, Marvin, it wasn't a fight for most of us here."

He was surprised by how profound Piedad's comments were. He thought that she was little more than a simple housewife, with more concern for survival than for the good of people's souls.

"I'm full of ideas, but when I try to write them down I find I can't; they sometimes just vanish."

"And what are these ideas that you want to turn into poems?"

"The struggle for liberty, because it is the greatest gift that any human being can have; failure; fear; despair …"

Eulogio's mother listened with interest. She had sat down in front of him and was looking at him with such intensity that Marvin thought she was reading his thoughts.

"Those are good ideas, Marvin, wonderful ones; you'll think of something. But you haven't come back to Spain to find inspiration, but rather to sort out a problem you have with yourself. You are looking for a reason why you left and, I think, you are really looking for forgiveness."

"No, that's not quite it," Marvin said, but he was astounded by the woman's sensitivity.

"I think it is. As far as I know you were here for a couple of months, working as a translator for some American journalists, and then you got wounded and you left. It's not that different from what other people did."

"I settled for being a translator. I didn't want to fight," he admitted, looking down to the ground.

"And why should you have fought? You didn't come here to kill anyone. And even so, you went to the front, and met Eulogio …"

"Well, we didn't really get to know each other there. He was a friend of Pepe's, an anarchist, who also did translations for various newspapermen. Eulogio and I met on the front line and that was where I was wounded ... But he had the worst of it, after risking his life to save me ..."

"Yes, he's lame, but he's alive, like you are. The wound in his leg stopped him from having to go back to fight. I won't say that I'm not sorry he's lame, but I'd prefer to have him like that than to be mourning his death."

"I understand," Marvin said, although he truly didn't understand the woman.

"I don't know if you do, but it doesn't matter. I understand you. Go home, Marvin. You won't find the answer here, the way to scare away the ghosts that hunt you at night and make you scream in your sleep."

"Scream? I'm sorry, I didn't want to bother anyone ..." he replied uncomfortably.

"It's no bother. I just feel sorry for you," the woman said, heedless of how humiliating that sounded.

"I'll be gone soon."

"As far as I'm concerned you can stay as long as you like; we need someone to rent the room. It's just that I don't think you'll find the answer to your problems here. I've told you as much already."

"Thank you so much for taking me in ... I wanted to be with people I trusted."

"Trusted? Yes, you were lucky. My son's a wonderful man. But you have to be careful nowadays; everyone is being reported, and people have been rounded up and carted away just because they're accused of being reds."

"But you ..."

"Yes, my husband was one and my son is one, and that's why I've had to ... Well, we all have our secrets."

Marvin looked down at the ground. He didn't know for sure, but he had heard wicked rumors that the woman had slept with Don Antonio so that the black marketeer would give Eulogio a job and keep the Falangists away from him and his mother.

He looked up, straight at her. She seemed lost in thought. He could see why Don Antonio might have fallen for her. She was of medium height, thin, with curly chestnut hair and a skin that was so fine it seemed to be made of porcelain. Her eyes were stubborn, but also tired. Perhaps her hands had been smooth, but they were callused now, the nails broken. But even so, she still gave off an almost unconscious air of sensuality. And as for Don Antonio, Marvin thought that he wanted to enjoy the favors of another woman, a woman not his wife, simply because he could.

He didn't judge her. She was a survivor, a woman who grasped life and took from it what she could, not for her own sake, but for her son's. She had not been defeated, but she knew that she had no more fight left in her.

The woman looked at him and smiled, which made him even more confused.

"My husband was a section editor ... he worked for a newspaper and did the French classics for Editorial Clásica. But don't think that he was just any old editor. We lived well, nothing to boast about, but well just the same. I loved him, yes. I loved him. He only had eyes for me, and wasn't one of those men who's always looking for the next thing." She said this with disgust, and must have been thinking about Don Antonio, who had kept one wandering eye on her.

"Why did he go to the war?" Marvin asked, made uncomfortable by the personal turn in the conversation.

"He said that he couldn't look himself in the mirror if he didn't do anything. He was a socialist and was appalled by the fascists. That's why he went to the front, and why, in spite of all my protests, he did nothing to stop Eulogio doing the same."

"Could he have stopped him?"

"I don't know, but he didn't even try. And then he lost his life and my son nearly lost his leg. And the only thing I want now is for him to work and do well. I don't know if he's any good as a painter, but that's not important. No one needs artists here, and so he'll have to work something out if he's going to earn a living. I don't mind if he paints in his free time, but only when he doesn't have to work."

"He's a good painter," Marvin said, unconvincingly.

"I don't like his paintings all that much, but I don't understand them. The only thing I want is for him to do his job well and make Don Antonio trust him. If he can do that, he'll never starve."

"But Don Antonio is …"

"A scoundrel, a man who can't be trusted. You think I don't know that? But he needs people who can keep their mouths shut. Eulogio won't say anything about Don Antonio's business, and he'll be paid well for his silence. I know that what I say isn't all that nice, but what can you do? The only choice left to us at the moment is to survive."

"But you can survive without … well, there are other ways to …"

"Really? Name one. Name it." She spoke harshly.

Marvin said nothing. Who was he to say that dignity was more important than hunger? He knew people who had barely enough to eat, but even so did not sell their soul or their body to the victors.

"Don't judge me. What do you know about it?"

The woman had read his mind. He felt a wave of heat rising to his face. He didn't want to upset her. Not just because she was his friend's mother, but also because he looked at himself with contempt and had no right to feel contempt for anyone else.

"I'm not judging anyone. I'm very grateful that you let me live here."

"My son thinks that you're his friend," she replied with a shrug. "I hope you don't judge him as well, just because he works for Don Antonio."

"No, I don't," he managed to say.

"Don't say anything about this to Eulogio. Well, I'll let you get back to work. Ah, I forgot to say. This morning, when you were downstairs in Fernando's apartment, Catalina came to see you. She said she needed to talk."

"Catalina?"

"Yes, Catalina Vilamar. The prettiest girl in the neighborhood. Everyone's head over heels for her, but she must like you in particular, because she wouldn't have dared come and find you otherwise."

"No … I don't know her. I've seen her a few times around the neighborhood, but nothing more."

"Nothing more? Well, I think she must have her eye on you, if only because you're a handsome American. Fernando Garzo has been in love with her since they were kids together. Antoñito, Don Antonio's son, wants to marry her; Pablo wants to marry her as well; everyone else can't take their eyes off her, so don't tell me that you're the only one who doesn't notice her at all. You have to admit she's pretty; a little thin, perhaps, but who isn't thin after a war? Even the Vilamars ... Her father had a good job, but they've had problems."

"Catalina is very pretty, yes, but I'm sure that ... she's not my type. I don't know why she came here or what she might want from me."

"Well, if you don't know that you're not as clever as you like to think. She has a thing for you, which makes me feel sorry for Fernando, who loves her so much ... But that's how it is with young people. Good for you. But be careful: Don Ernesto, Catalina's father, will fly off the handle if he finds out that his daughter and you ..."

Marvin sighed with relief when Piedad left him alone at last. The conversation had upset him. The woman had stirred him up inside so much that the anguish he tried to hide now flared up once more.

She was right. He wasn't doing anything here, and he didn't want to get mixed up in people's little squabbles. He didn't care about anything. He was interested in the overarching drama that had been the war, and the triumph of Franco, and the consequences that this would have for the future of the country. Why should he care that Fernando was in love with Catalina? Or why should he care that Eulogio's mother went to bed with Don Antonio, and that her son pretended not to know about it? It was stupid, all this local drama when there were really important things going on. The desolation felt by the losing side, the arrogance of the Falangists, poverty, hunger, hate, despair ... All of this inspired bitter poetry in him. Everything he wrote was the result of his own personal pain, because he hadn't managed to make peace with himself for having left when he was wounded just after the start of the war.

Only he knew that he was a coward who hated the fact that it was pain that was the source of his inspiration, being surrounded by the living dead who wanted nothing from life, because they knew they had lost at it. Of course, the winners were far away, as though they were no longer a part of his world.

3

Don Antonio Sánchez was smoking a cigar. It tasted wonderful. Of course, with his money he'd been able to get his hands on some real cigars.

He had just closed a deal with a man who had a textile factory in Catalonia. He was going to sell shirts to the army.

Prudencio, Don Antonio's brother who worked in logistics, had alerted Don Antonio to the opportunity: the soldiers needed winter shirts. He had heard his colonel say as much. And the army was likely to buy shirts from people who either already had shirts available, or who could offer them wholesale.

Mr. Soler, the owner of the textile factory, had told Don Antonio that he could have several thousand shirts ready in only a few weeks. And as soon as he made them, he would send them to Madrid, to Don Antonio's warehouse, where they would be bought by the army in a deal Prudencio was to organize.

Soler could be trusted. Maybe he was exaggerating a little when he said that he owned a textile factory: Don Antonio had seen it and it was nothing more than a few machines in the basement of the house where the man lived. Several women worked there, paid a pittance. But to have a job, even if it paid very little, was to be better off than those who had nothing.

"And now that we've signed the contract we should go and have something to eat, eh, Soler? My treat," Don Antonio said.

They left the warehouse and walked to a pub close to Plaza Opera. The innkeeper knew Don Antonio, because he sold him his wine.

"What's on the menu today, Perico?" Don Antonio asked.

"Lentil stew. And for you, a couple of fried eggs as well. Shall I make you up a plate, Don Antonio?"

"As long as there actually are lentils in the stew."

"You'll have lentils. You can trust me."

They washed down the lentils with a couple of glasses of cheap wine, of a kind that Don Antonio provided, and which Perico made stretch with a little water.

Prudencio came to join them.

"I went to your house. Your wife told me that you were in the warehouse, and there they told me that you were here," he said to his brother by way of explanation.

"Mari would be annoyed to see you at my house at this hour," Don Antonio said.

"But your wife is a saint, and she told me that you wouldn't be eating today, because you had a meeting with Soler."

"Well, what did your colonel tell you about the shirts?" Don Antonio asked.

"It's all fixed. He'll order them if you give him a good price. I've told him that no one will sell them cheaper or better, because you are a patriot, and there is nothing too good for this wonderful country. As soon as the order comes through to buy them, just put in your quote and we're off to the races. I've got you the papers where it says how many you need to supply and how much they'll cost."

Don Antonio ripped the paper out of his brother's hands and read it carefully.

"But they want us to give them the bloody shirts! No way, at this price there's no deal."

"Let me see the paper," Soler said anxiously.

"How greedy you are, Antonio. Do you think the army's made out of money?" Prudencio said, looking at Soler out of the corner of his eye.

"Greedy? If they want their soldiers to have shirts, they'll have to pay for them!" Don Antonio was angry.

"Come on, come on, don't be like that ... We'll earn less than we predicted; we won't become millionaires, but we'll still make a decent profit: it's a lot of shirts," Soler said, giving him back the paper.

64

"If they want our shirts, they'll have to pay for them," Don Antonio repeated.

"What are you saying? Don't you think there are more people bidding for this contract? I know that there are more offers coming to HQ, and they'll have a lot to choose from. If it's not us it'll be someone else … You can say what you like Antonio, but don't ask me to speak to the colonel again, because he won't buy anything. You know he doesn't like scams of any kind, but he trusts me and is sure that I won't do him wrong, and that all he's doing is a little favor, because you're my brother."

"Prudencio is right. We'll earn a bit less, but we'll earn something at least, and the important thing is that the shirts lead to other commissions," Soler said.

"You think that we're going to earn money with this, these, these pennies they're paying us?" Don Antonio asked his Catalan partner.

"You know we will, and I'm ready to sell the shirts at this price. And when I get back to Tarrasa I'll send you a package with all the different sizes of shirt in it, so that Prudencio can show it to the colonel. I'll make them the best so that the colonel won't have any concerns. Then the others we make won't be as good, of course, but they won't be terrible."

"I don't know, Soler … If they get used to us selling to them cheaply, they won't be keen for us to raise the prices in the future," Don Antonio complained.

"We've got to understand that the war has just finished, and that there's no money, and they're not going to spend too much on shirts," Soler insisted, trying to convince his partner. "By the way, Prudencio, how much is the colonel going to take as his cut?"

"Nothing, Soler, nothing at all. He's not a crook. If he tells me that the army's going to buy something or other, it's because he knows me to be loyal and he trusts me. As he says, it's better to deal with patriots, and as Antonio's my brother …"

"And how much is your cut?"

"Same as usual. Antonio knows …"

"All right. Anyway, if we come to a deal then we'll all be better off," Soler said.

When the lunch was over, Antonio and Prudencio said good-bye to the Catalan and walked back towards the Puerta de Tole-do, where the warehouse was. They walked in silence to begin with, but it was Prudencio who spoke first.

"I don't think there's anything to be done about Don Loren-zo Garzo. I've been asking around, and he's not in a good spot. He's redder than a tomato, and he went to the front of his own accord ..."

"Are they going to shoot him?"

"They haven't said anything to me about it, but I guess so. The ones they've got in Porlier prison have it bad, although it's no bed of roses for the ones in Comendadoras either. But why do you care about him? Don Lorenzo was never a friend of ours: he never came into the shop, never said hello to us in the street."

"He's an intellectual, and intellectuals always have their heads in the air; they never notice anything," Antonio replied.

"Well, let them shoot him for being an intellectual. Who needs intellectuals? They've done enough harm to Spain, lining up alongside the communists. And all intellectuals are Freema-sons, anyway," Prudencio said.

"Piedad asked me to fix it. Piedad, Eulogio's mother," Anto-nio said quietly.

"That woman's no good for you, brother. She'll ruin you. She made you get her son a job at the warehouse, and now she's try-ing to fix things for Garzo. You can't let yourself be pushed around like this."

"Eulogio does a good job. And he keeps his mouth shut."

"But he was with the Republicans. If it weren't for us ... Well, he'd have been shot already."

"But he was only there for a couple of months before getting blown up," Antonio said.

"Yes, but how many of us did he take with him? Don't try to wriggle out of it, Antonio. I know that you get what you want from Eulogio's mother, but don't let her get in your head. Any-way, I don't know why you go for someone like that; your wife's much better-looking."

"Hey, don't talk about my wife like that, okay? I won't have you making comments. She's the mother of my children, and that's it. I respect her and I have a very special place for her in my heart."

"Yeah, and the other one's got you on a leash."

"Shut up. What do you know about women anyway?"

"I don't know, but I know about this one that her husband and her son were both Republicans and that if you play with them you are playing with fire. If you weren't such a big man in the Falange … At least they think it's funny that you're going after these women, because if they didn't …" Prudencio was unstoppable.

"You're right, brother, I guess you could say she's got me by the short ones. I started to use her when I came back from the front. She was afraid that her son would be taken away, just like so many others, for having fought with the reds. She was very grateful that I could help her."

"And she paid you well in her 'gratitude.' Well, and you got her house as well. You bought it for nothing, and sent her up to the attic, so you're not as far gone as it might appear." Prudencio laughed to himself; he thought he was being witty.

"Business is business. What use did they have for such a large place, anyway? They're okay in the attic. She and Eulogio don't need anything better than that. And she knows that it's thanks to me that she still has her son. What more could a good mother want? She owes me."

"Well, if you want to keep on sleeping with her, make her go to church; they've told me that Don Bernardo is getting annoyed with her because she doesn't go very often, and when she does she doesn't take communion, doesn't even confess."

"You want her to confess to the priest that she's sleeping with me? She's a sensible woman," Don Antonio said, defending his lover.

"But it attracts attention. Don Bernardo's got a bee in his bonnet about it."

"And how do you manage to find out about everything, Prudencio?" Don Antonio asked suspiciously.

"I keep my ear to the ground," Prudencio replied, with a giggle.

"You've got it nailed to the ground."

"What about Antoñito and Catalina, then? Are they formally engaged yet?"

"My son's pushing for it, but she's resisting him. You know that the Vilamars always pretend to be better than everyone else in the neighborhood. But Don Ernesto hasn't got a cent; he's ruined and I'm lending him money, so the girl will end up making the right decision."

"How much have you lent to Don Ernesto?" Prudencio asked with interest.

"A few thousand pesetas, and he's still asking for more."

"And you keep on giving it to him, like a fool."

"We're going to be fathers-in-law together."

"We'll see, Antonio. The girl's a flighty one, and I don't know that she'll obey her father."

"What do you mean? Of course she'll obey him, or her father will give her one she won't forget. And anyhow, when did children start disobeying their parents? Catalina is very young and she's a dreamer, but she'll do what her father tells her and get married to my little Antoñito. You'll see, Prudencio, you'll see."

"If you say so," Prudencio said, unconvinced.

"Fine, let's talk about other things. I'm meeting up with some friends this evening to drink and then go to the brothel at Corredera. You coming?"

"I can't, Antonio, I need to get back to the barracks, my colonel's driver is sick and he needs someone he can trust to take him to a meeting. He asked me to do it, and I can't say no to my colonel."

"Of course, you mustn't say no. It's good for us that he trusts you so much. Well, you can come out with us some other time."

"I wonder what the whores in Madrid are like," Prudencio said.

"There are lots of them, brother, much more supply than there is demand. Lots of the women on the street were decent women until recently. But we don't care: the only thing that matters is to relax a bit. Kick back."

"And doesn't Mari get upset?"

"My wife? How'll she ever find out about it? You say some odd things, Prudencio."

"And what about Piedad?"

"I don't need to explain anything to her. When I need something from her, I call her to the shop and we go into the storeroom and that's that. What did you think?"

Prudencio didn't think anything. He admired his brother Antonio, and had always admired him. Prudencio knew he was weak, and Antonio was a man in the prime of his life, full of vigor. He wasn't surprised that his wife didn't complain about him, and he was also sure that Piedad didn't have too bad a time of it in the storeroom, either.

More than a month had gone by since Antoñito had last seen Catalina on the night of his birthday party out at the Pradera de San Isidro. They had met in the neighborhood since then, but they had barely greeted one another. He remembered that night very well, and smiled to himself when he thought about it, even though he was annoyed now, standing at the door to the Vilamars' house.

He straightened his jacket and stroked his mustache. He rang the bell and waited impatiently for someone to open the door. No, he wouldn't have been there if his father hadn't told him to go. He'd said that he had to deliver a dozen eggs and a chicken to the Vilamar house.

Doña Asunción opened the door and looked at him in surprise. She wasn't expecting visitors, much less Antoñito.

"Good afternoon, Doña Asunción; this is from my father," he said, holding out a basket with goods inside wrapped in brown paper.

"Ah … How strange, we haven't ordered anything; it must be a mistake of some kind …"

"No, no, not at all. It's no mistake: my father wanted to give this to you. It's a dozen eggs and a chicken. They came in fresh today, and because Don Ernesto isn't in the best of health, my father thought he might like some chicken and some eggs."

Doña Asunción looked at him in surprise, still undecided as to whether or not to take the basket.

"It's very kind of your father, but … I don't know … it's a surprise and … I don't know if I can accept it," she replied, obviously taken aback.

"But I can't tell my father that you didn't want to take the basket. He'll get annoyed." Antoñito didn't want his father to give him a telling-off and call him useless.

Catalina stuck her head out of the door that led onto the entrance hallway.

"Who is it, Mama?" she asked.

"Antoñito. He's brought us … he's brought us a present from his father."

The door opened all the way and Catalina came out into the hallway and stood in front of Antoñito, looking at him in disgust.

"What a surprise to see you here. Don't you know it's rude to come to someone's house without giving them any warning?"

"It was nothing to do with me. My father sent me. If you don't want his present, I'll just tell him and that'll be the end of it," he replied, somewhat defiantly.

"No, it's not about not wanting his present; we're very grateful for his generosity, but … well, we're not accustomed to these things," Doña Asunción managed to say, looking angrily at her daughter.

"We're not good enough friends to accept presents." Catalina spoke to Antoñito without bothering to hide her annoyance.

"Well, as far as I know, you live here thanks to the loans you get from my father, so there's no need to be so picky," he replied, viciously.

"What are you saying? I don't have to stand for this. Get out of here, and take your basket with you. And don't you dare come back without telling us in advance." Catalina held the door open and shooed Antoñito out.

He hesitated. He thought for a second about leaving with the bag and telling his father that the Vilamars, once again, had treated him like an inferior. But he knew that his father, as well as getting angry with the Vilamars, would get angry with him, and accuse him of doing things badly.

He left the basket on the ground, turned, and left the house without looking at either mother or daughter. "Let them do what they want," he thought. If they dare go back to the shop and return the basket, then let his father deal with those two harpies, putting on airs when they were nothing more than two starving women. He wanted his father to arrange the wedding already, give him the chance to knock some sense into Catalina: she'd have no choice but to put her head down and accept that her family were in a bad way, and that if it weren't for him, then the Vilamars would be begging in the streets.

"I can't stand him," Catalina said as soon as the door closed.

"He's not a bad boy, but maybe a little slow. Let's ask your father what to do with the basket; if he says we have to keep it, then we'll have to."

"But we can't do that, Mama! It's a humiliation. I'd rather starve than have those hicks offer us charity."

"Your father … Well, I think he's got some business dealings with Don Antonio, so I don't think we can treat him like this."

Don Ernesto clenched his jaw and frowned while his wife and daughter explained to him what had just happened. How dare the storekeeper send him a basket of eggs! And a chicken! Who did he think he was, a charity case? He was about to send Catalina over to Don Antonio's shop to give the basket back, but he stopped himself. He owed him a great deal of money, and the last thing he could afford to do now was upset him. So Don Ernesto took a deep breath, sighed, and put his thoughts in order. The black marketeer was a brute, a Falangist in all respects, even if he didn't wear the uniform, who walked around with his chest puffed out; he was also a patriot, and it was thanks to people like him that the country hadn't fallen into the hands of the reds. Don Antonio was uneducated and knew nothing about how to behave. They had to excuse the lack of tact he had shown in sending them a basket of food: it was just a friendly gesture, another way of getting Antoñito and Catalina together. It wasn't the best way, but he hadn't intended to offend them: quite the opposite. Also, although Asunción didn't know this, ever since the war had ended and Don Antonio had come into Madrid alongside Franco's troops, taking back control of his shop, the Vilamars had only been able to afford to eat thanks to the credit the store extended to them. More importantly, Don Ernesto was trying to get back on his feet thanks to a loan Don Antonio had made him to help refloat the tobacco business his father-in-law had left him.

Asunción thought that her husband paid the bills every month at the grocery shop, but the truth was that the bill rose and kept on rising. It would only be paid off on the day when Catalina walked out of the church on Antoñito's arm.

"Of course we have to accept the present. We are good clients, and it is only natural that Don Antonio would want to give us a little gift," Don Ernesto said.

"But, Papa …!" Catalina protested.

"If you say so, Ernesto … I'll make a potato omelet this evening, and we can roast the chicken tomorrow," Doña Asunción said, as it would never have occurred to her to contradict her husband.

That afternoon, Catalina wrapped up the two packages of crochet work that her mother had made and decided to take them over to the Garzos' house. Nearly two months had gone by, and Fernando hadn't come to pick them up. He was still angry with her. He had no reason to be, Catalina said to herself. They weren't boyfriend and girlfriend, and they had never been, and she had never even suggested that they might be. She was fond of him, as they had known each other since they were children, and Fernando was very clever and helped her with her schoolwork. He had also helped her when any other boys were annoying her. Every boy in the neighborhood knew that pulling Catalina's ponytail would mean getting a punch from her friend.

She went into their building and smiled at the doorwoman, who was sweeping the entryway.

"I'm coming to see the Garzos," she said.

"I don't know if Fernando is there, but his mother certainly is."

She ran up the stairs to the first floor and pressed the bell hard. Isabel opened the door and invited her in.

"Catalina, it's so long since I saw you last. Fernando is just about to come back. Come in, and sit down. Would you like a glass of water?"

"Thank you, Doña Isabel; I only came to bring you these cloths that my mother made, and also a couple of eggs."

"Oh, yes! Fernando did say something about it … Thank you

so much: your mother is very good at crochet work. Thank her, and for the eggs as well."

"How is Don Lorenzo?" she asked kindly.

"You can guess … The prisoners in Comendadoras are in a bad way; they scarcely get anything to eat. He's so thin … I hope we manage to get him a pardon, because he won't last for much longer," Isabel said.

"Of course he'll be pardoned! Don Lorenzo is a good man; we all know that. Don't be sad; he'll be home soon, you'll see. I pray for him every day. And ask the Virgin for help."

"Well, I hope the Virgin listens to you, because no one up there has been paying me any attention for a good while now …"

Fernando came into the kitchen and saw his mother and Catalina taking to each other. He liked to see them together; they were the two women he loved most in the world, the only two women he loved. Who else could he love?

"I didn't know you were going to come," he said to Catalina as he came over to give his mother a kiss.

"I brought the crochet work, because you didn't come by to pick it up …"

"I have a full-time job, Catalina; I'm not free to do whatever I want, not like you are."

Isabel looked at her son in confusion: he had spoken so harshly. She thought that he must be angry, and this upset her, because she didn't even know that the two of them had argued.

"I know you work, Fernando, and … well, I don't want to bother you. I'll be off. I'll go up to Eulogio's house now: I've got a couple of eggs to give to his mother, and I wanted to have a word with Marvin."

Catalina's openness made Fernando feel physically sick. Hadn't she realized how much she had upset him? Isabel realized at once what the problem was.

"Marvin's a very nice young man; he fits in well here. He'll leave good friends behind him when he goes," Isabel said, trying to smooth things over.

"I don't think he'll go; I think he likes Spain too much," Catalina replied.

"You're wrong there. Marvin is planning to leave very soon,

perhaps in a couple of days; there's nothing more for him to do here," Fernando replied, without trying to hide his antagonism.

Catalina looked at him in confusion. Why was Fernando speaking so angrily?

"Well, it's normally hard for good poets to find inspiration, but I don't think that's Marvin's problem. And I know that he likes Spain and has no intention of leaving. Perhaps he used to, but now … No, now he's not going anywhere," she insisted.

"That's what you'd like, but the American is going to leave, Catalina. You'll see."

"He'll do what he has to do, won't he? Catalina, say thank you to your mother from us; she's always so generous and kind," Isabel said, to try to stop the argument.

"My mother has said that whenever you can, she'd like to invite you by for coffee. Perhaps you could come and visit us one of these days."

"Of course. Tell your mother that if it's all right with her, I'll come by for a bit on Thursday."

"Of course, and that'll work well, because she won't have to worry about my father so much on Thursday: he's going to Huesca to see his older brother, and will be away for a few days. Thursday is perfect. You could come as well, Fernando. I'll bake a cake, how about it?"

"I have a full-time job, Catalina; I don't have time to come and eat cake," he replied grumpily.

"All right. Well, I'll make the cake anyway, and give your mother a big slice to bring back with her," Catalina said, determined to ignore Fernando's sour mood.

Once Catalina left, Fernando's mother berated him. She understood her son's frustration at Catalina's indifference, but she didn't want him to become bitter.

"You weren't very nice to her."

"If you say so …"

"Yes, I do say so. Come on, Fernando, you'll never get anywhere like that. I know that you're in love with her, but it's only natural for her to like the American, and it will pass, and if it doesn't pass then there's nothing you can do. No one can control other people's feelings. I would love it for Catalina to be your fiancée, but if that's not how she feels about you then you can't force things; you'll find a woman who does appreciate you and who values you. And you'll laugh when you remember your schoolboy crush."

"Leave me alone, Mother. I don't care about Catalina, but I hate that she's crazy about the American and doesn't see that he couldn't care less about her. She's making a fool of herself."

"You can't fool me, Fernando. You've been in love with her ever since you were a child. And you're making that all too clear by treating her like you do. If you want her to pay any attention to you, you have to pretend not to care."

"I'm not going to play games, Mother; if she doesn't love me, then she doesn't love me. And I don't care anyway."

But he did care, so much that his chest hurt, thinking that Catalina could even now be knocking on Eulogio's door and asking to see Marvin. "She's so insensitive; she can't control herself," Fernando thought to himself, even as he was fighting not to run upstairs and interrupt the conversation between the two of them.

It was Piedad, Eulogio's mother, who opened the door. She looked at the young woman in surprise before inviting her in.

"Come in ... come in ... What can I do for you? My son's just gone over to the warehouse; you know he starts work at seven ..."

"I'm sorry for bothering you, Doña Piedad, but I wanted to see Marvin," she said, resolute.

"Marvin? Of course, I'll tell him to come through. Come through into the kitchen: it's a little room, but at least we've got chairs where we can sit."

Catalina didn't sit. She stayed standing and tried to control the anxiety that she felt.

Marvin came into the kitchen followed by Piedad. He was confused by Catalina's visit.

"What are you doing here?" he asked abruptly.

"I came to see you; we haven't seen each other since that day in the Pradera to celebrate Antoñito's birthday. I didn't want to interrupt you; I know you're working a lot." She looked at him with a smile.

Catalina's gaze was enough for Piedad to realize that the girl was in love, and that the American seemed either not to notice or else not to want to show anything in front of her.

"I've got things to do. If there's anything you need … Catalina, would you like a glass of water?"

"No, thank you. I don't want anything."

Well, I'll leave you to speak …" And Piedad left the tiny room and went into her even tinier bedroom, sitting on the bed to wait for Catalina to leave.

"You know, Marvin, everyone's saying that you're planning on leaving soon. I know it's not true, but it upsets me to hear it."

"Well, it's not like I'm going tomorrow, but I was thinking of heading back to France; I don't know when, given that the Germans are there. Europe is at war. I can't stay in Madrid forever, and I'll have to go someday," he replied, unaware of why Catalina was here and why she was so bothered about what he might do.

"I'd love to go to Paris: life there must be so different from life here …"

"Well, if you want to go to Paris then I'll be your guide, although it's not the best moment to go," he said, just to say something.

"Would you really show me Paris?"

"Of course … it would be a real pleasure to see you there. Do you like the theater? We could go to the theater; I could show you the cafes … there are no cafes more beautiful than the ones in Paris."

"And the Eiffel Tower? I'd love so much to climb all the way to the top," Catalina exclaimed.

"I don't know if you can climb all the way to the top, but I'd be happy to show it to you."

"Do you have a house in Paris?" she asked.

"I have an apartment, close to Notre Dame."

"And is it nice?"

"I think so. You'd like it; it's very comfortable," Marvin said, unaware of the effect his words were having on Catalina.

"That would be marvelous! I would love to go. My parents won't want me to go, but they'll have to get used to the idea. Are you sure you don't mind my coming to Paris with you? Have you really thought this through?" she asked, looking at him very seriously.

Marvin did not understand the meaning of this conversation. For him Catalina was no more than one of the neighborhood girls, flighty, but a good person in general, if a little flirtatious, and that was that. It wasn't that he wanted Catalina to come and visit him in Paris, but he was too well-mannered to refuse her a visit.

"What's there to think about? If you come, then you will be looked after. You'll like Paris, you'll see."

Catalina jumped from the seat she sat in and threw her arms around Marvin's neck, giving him a loud kiss on one cheek. He didn't know how to react and stood frozen for a few seconds. It was Piedad who saved him. She hadn't been able to avoid hearing the conversation because the walls in the attic were so thin that it was impossible not to know what was going on in the kitchen.

"Are you sure I can't get you a glass of water?" Piedad asked, walking into the kitchen.

Catalina lowered her arms and stepped back a little from Marvin before answering.

"No, really, Doña Piedad, thank you so much … We're just talking, but maybe it would be better to go for a walk and finish this conversation. What do you think, Marvin?"

"It's very late … and I was writing … but … all right, I'll take you home," he said, unenthusiastically.

Catalina kept on asking him about Paris, about the places he'd take her, the names of his favorite cafes, the friends he had … Marvin replied reluctantly, but she didn't notice. She was happy. The words of the American had led her to believe that not only was he in love with her, but also that he was eager to take her away with him.

Later, in the solitude of her room, Catalina realized that they hadn't spoken about the wedding, but she put that thought to one side. They would get married, of course they would. How else could she go to Paris if not as his wife? Her father would oppose the match, but with her mother's help she'd end up convincing him. She wasn't going to give in: she was going to marry Marvin and live in Paris. She felt a stab of preemptive nostalgia thinking of her mother, but pushed it aside at once. Her mother would come to see her a lot, and she would go back to Madrid as well. Traveling back and forth might even be fun. Also, Marvin was rich, she knew that for a fact, because his parents had a steel mill in the States, and so when they were married, she'd have enough money to go shopping in all the fashionable shops of Paris when her mother came to see her. They'd have such a good time together that she was already starting to enjoy the life that awaited her in the French capital.

She couldn't help but feel a bittersweet sensation when she thought back to that night in the Pradera. She remembered that she had been in pain, and slightly confused, although she had heard women gossiping about how physical love, especially the first time, was not particularly agreeable.

She had been in pain for a few days, but she had felt better knowing that she had been in Marvin's arms and that it was his hands that had stroked her face and had pulled her skirt down to cover her legs. He had been so attentive, so delicate …

Neither of them had spoken of that afternoon. He was too much of a gentleman to do so, and she was grateful to him for that. It hadn't been right of her to let things go so far. She was pleased to find out not only that Marvin didn't think less of her, but also that he was in love with her, and eager to start a life together.

She had decided to tell her mother that she was going to get married, but that night, at dinner, her father seemed thoughtful and her mother worried, and Catalina had learned that when she had important announcements to make, it was best to pick the right moment.

Piedad was making an omelet when Marvin came back and went into the kitchen.

The American sat down at the table, prepared for a good meal. There wasn't much to eat in the house, as in most of the houses in Spain, but Eulogio always managed to get something from the warehouse, and they seemed to trust Piedad in Don Antonio's shop, so there was always something to eat.

Everyone in the neighborhood gossiped about Don Antonio's relationship with Piedad, but Eulogio seemed to be unaware.

Some mornings, when Eulogio came back from the warehouse and went to bed, Piedad got dressed and went out without making any noise. When she came back, she would always be missing a hairpin, or her clothes would seem disheveled; her face would be blushing, and weary.

They tended to eat alone, given that Eulogio was out at the warehouse most of the evening and all night. After supper, Marvin would lock himself away in his room and try to write, or else go out to spend time with some of the friends he had made in Madrid. But that evening he felt upset because of Catalina. The girl unsettled him, overwhelmed him; he saw in her a strength and a determination that seemed unstoppable.

Eulogio made fun of him, saying that he had made the most beautiful girl in the neighborhood fall in love with him, but Marvin thought that Catalina loved life more than anything else, and that Spain was too narrow and prudish for someone like her. And as for him, he felt a great admiration for her, precisely because Catalina had what he did not: an undeniable desire to enjoy life.

Piedad and Marvin ate dinner together in silence, each one sunk in their own thoughts. When they finished, Marvin offered, as he always did, to do the dishes, but Piedad couldn't imagine having nothing to do, so she washed the plates while he went back to his room to face the blank page that waited for him until he could find out a way to fill it with words.

He tried for a while, but, once again, needed to accept that inspiration had abandoned him for the day; disappointed, he headed off to find a cafe.

On the way out, he ran into Fernando.

"Where are you off to?" he said.

"I'm taking the trash out; what about you?"

"I'm going for a stroll; it's too hot here."

"If you want to, I'll come with you," Fernando offered. "But not for very long; I've got to get up early tomorrow morning."

"I'm so old," Piedad thought to herself. She looked at her face in the mirror and could only see wrinkles, and a grimace setting in around her mouth. A few gray hairs fought to be noticed in her chestnut bob. "My husband thought I was beautiful, and maybe I was, years ago, but now …" She wondered why Antonio the black marketeer would feel so much for her. She still couldn't see why he had worked so hard to get her to become his lover.

She remembered like it was yesterday how Franco's troops had taken over the city and how the people who had left to fight with the Nationalists had gradually made their way back to their homes. Antonio came back in his Falangist uniform, preening himself and boasting of his war record.

While he had been away, his wife, Mari, had taken charge of the shop. Although she had made it look like her husband had abandoned her and she had no interest in politics, she was still very quick to welcome him back into her arms and hand the shop back over to him.

The neighbors hadn't thought that she opposed the Nationalists; some of them had even reported her, but no one could ever prove that she was anything more than a simple woman who wanted her daughters to be safe, given that her son, Antoñito, had gone off to join his father and fight with Franco's troops.

Piedad could remember the afternoon when she had gone over to the shop to ask Antonio to let her have some potatoes, and maybe some eggs, on credit, and he had looked her up and down and invited her into the storeroom. She had followed him, thinking that maybe he didn't want to extend her any credit in front of the other customers.

The shop boy stayed behind, helping a couple of other clients.

"Your husband was killed at the front, right?" Antonio had asked.

"Yes," Piedad had said, bluntly.

"He was a red, and wanted Spain to fail."

"My husband was an honorable man, an upright man, who did what he had to do," she said.

"And your son also fought against us; he deserved to get his leg blown off."

She stepped forward and slapped his face. Antonio accepted the blow with a grotesque giggle.

"Oh, so you still think you're somebody … Well, let me tell you what we're going to do now. You can take your clothes off, and then you know what will happen. Yes, if you don't do what I want from now on, I'll hand you over to the authorities. I'll get my friends to arrest your son for being a communist. He's a parasite as well, a cripple with no job. A feeble imitator of the man who painted *Guernica*, what was his name? Picasso? There is no place in our Spain for reds like you. Your Eulogio will go to prison. A few months of sitting around and then the garrote or else the firing squad at dawn. That's all he'll have to look forward to. If you don't want him to be picked up you'd better get your clothes off now …"

Piedad looked at him with all the hatred she could muster. Then she walked over to him, and stood close enough to smell his bitter sweat and sour breath.

"Yes, I'll take my clothes off. But not only will you protect my son; you'll give him a job. Eulogio can do anything."

Antonio hadn't expected this reaction. He looked her up and down, wondering what to do.

"You can't give me conditions. You'll have to go through with this if you want to keep your son; I don't care about anything else."

"You'll pay him a decent salary that will let us both live," she insisted, as though she hadn't heard what he had just said.

"You're crazy! Who do you think you are?" he said, loudly.

"You've been wanting to see me naked for years. You think I don't see your disgusting glances at me whenever I come to your shop? If I have to become a whore, then I will be paid and I won't do it out of fear. Franco supporters like you have taken everything from us; if you want anything else, Antonio, then you'll have to pay for it. And pay upfront."

"Take your clothes off," he repeated, and came over to her, ready to tear her blouse open by force.

But Piedad walked away and, heading to the door, smiled back at him.

"You know what? I think Eulogio could do a good job of looking after your accounts and managing the warehouse you've just bought."

"But he's a cripple!" Antonio cried out.

"He's a brave man, far braver than lots of people with two working legs. He'll be able to help you."

"I don't need anyone sticking his nose into my business."

"All right, Antonio. It's your call."

"Send him to me and I'll see what I can do for him. Now take your clothes off."

"Not today, Antonio; I'll do it when you sign a contract with him, that says how much you'll pay. The sooner you do so, the sooner I'll take my clothes off. Would you like me to send him along straight away?"

"Crazy woman!"

"I'll send him along to see you. Oh, and one more thing. If you tell my son, or anyone else, that this is our agreement, then I'll kill you, I swear that I'll kill you. And don't waste your breath with threats. You're going to get me sent to prison? So what! This whole country is a prison: I'll only be a little bit more confined. And if they shoot me, so what? You think I'm so desperate to live? I hate living, knowing that your kind are in charge. I don't have anything to lose, Antonio."

Piedad went back into the shop and, in front of the astonished shop boy, reached into the sack of potatoes, placing several in her bag. Then she went over to the counter and took a couple of peppers and some tomatoes. She left without looking at anyone.

Her next battle was with her son, Eulogio, who refused to go to the black marketeer's shop to get his job.

"How am I going to work for a Falangist? It would be a lie, Mother!"

"Look around you, accept the state of things. They've won the war, and they are the ones who can give you work, so there's nothing we can do but accept it. I don't want you to become a beggar, like so many other people wounded in the war. We don't have anything left to sell, Eulogio, so we need jobs. Antonio is prepared to give you one, and it's no worse than other jobs."

"We could go to France. I'll find something to do there; I don't mind working at whatever I can get. We can start again," Eulogio suggested.

"How on earth are we going to go to France? The Germans are there. But if it's what you want to do, then go. I'll stay here. I'll understand if that's what you want to do, but I'll be happy just knowing that you're alive. I don't want anything else and I'm not strong enough to go into exile. I'm sorry, son."

She kept her eyes on him, forcing herself not to cry. She could read the confusion and even shame in her son's eyes. Eulogio couldn't understand how his mother could hand herself so easily over to the victors; he thought it was better to go into exile, or even die of hunger, rather than work for the fascists.

They barely spoke for several days. They avoided each other, sunk in their own pain.

Piedad didn't go back to Antonio's shop and even avoided going near it so that she wouldn't be seen. Then one day the police came to her house asking for Eulogio. They took him away. Someone had turned him in. She didn't think twice. She went to the shop. They told her that Antonio was in the warehouse. She ran to it. She was not frightened, not scared off: she asked a lad carrying a couple of sacks where she could find the black marketeer. When Antonio appeared, he made a show of being surprised to see her. In fact, he had been expecting her.

"They've taken Eulogio to the station. Someone has accused him of being a communist."

Antonio shrugged indifferently and looked her up and down. Lust burst from his sweaty pores.

"You'll get him out of there," she said, with a conviction that she didn't quite feel.

"Who, me? What do I care about your son? Let him rot, the traitor."

Piedad walked over to the door and closed it. Then she undid her blouse and took off her skirt. Antonio looked at her in satisfaction. He had been waiting for this.

When he had had his way with her, he burst out laughing. Piedad had to put up with that, while she tried to hold back the vomit that rose in her gorge.

"Let's go to the station," she said without looking at him.

"No need. I just need to make one phone call and they'll let him go."

They did. Piedad heard the conversation and it made her eyes widen in surprise. Antonio had asked a friend, who in turn had a friend at the police station, to arrest Eulogio, but to press no charges until he himself should ring. He told them to let him go, said that the boy and his family had had enough of a scare, and were now well aware of who was in charge.

"No, don't worry, I promise you he's harmless. Yes, he's the son of a red, and he was on the wrong side, but he's an unimportant cripple; I've got it under control. I just wanted to give him a fright, just in case he thought of doing something he shouldn't. You let him go: I'll take care of him from now on."

Piedad thought that if she had had a knife in her hand at that moment, she would have plunged it into his guts. Her son's arrest had been nothing more than a ploy, the black marketeer's vile way of getting control over her and turning her into his slave. She had learned her lesson, and found out how Antonio worked. She only had two choices open to her now: either she could flee to France, or she could put up with the weight of Antonio's body on her own.

"Come by the shop on Friday morning. My wife won't be there. And you know what will happen if you don't come: I won't be able to save your son a second time. Oh, and I've got a friend who's keen on buying a cheap apartment in the neighborhood. I mentioned that yours was for sale."

"Mine is not for sale," she replied.

"Yes, it is. I'll give you some money for it, and your son and you can live in the attic; I think there's some space up there."

"I don't want to leave my home," Piedad insisted.

"You have no right to a home. Why do we have to be generous to the reds? If I were Franco, you'd all be shot. But the Caudillo is merciful; he has a good heart."

"His heart's black, like yours," she shot back.

"Calm down, dear. Look, until I get tired of you, enjoy what you have. Come by this afternoon with your son and the documents for your house. We'll close the sale then. My friend will give you a few days to move out. And now go away: I've got work to do."

She could remember every detail of the first time that she had allowed Antonio to manhandle her body. She still blamed herself for this, although for her son she was ready to do this and more. She felt ashamed when she thought of her dead husband. Would he forgive her? Can a man ever forgive his wife when she gives herself to another?

Her husband would definitely have said that exile was better. But she had not felt that she was strong enough to leave and go to another country, one where she knew they would not be welcome. Many of the Spaniards who had fled had been confined to camps in the south of France, and she did not want that for her son.

Leaving Spain, she thought, could be even worse than staying, for all that it was harder by the day to get used to the arrogance of the victors.

The worst part of it had been telling her son that they needed to sell the house. They had released Eulogio after lunch; when he came back home, they hugged one another, and stood like that for a long while.

She didn't tell him that Antonio insisted that she sell their apartment, but rather that she needed some money.

"But we can't do that, Mother! I don't even want to have to think about you living in an attic. I'll work for the black marketeer, but let's not leave this apartment."

"No, it's not enough. We have to be realistic about it: what do we want with such a big place? We can't keep it up, Eulogio, and you know that. It costs a lot. And we'll still be in the building, just in the attic. The doorwoman showed me the attic where Fidel, the musician, used to live. Do you remember him?"

"Of course I remember him. Poor man, his wife and daughters killed by the bomb that fell near the Gran Vía. And then, to get so sick ..."

"It's the largest living space in the attic; it's got three rooms, all very small, but a kitchen and a little dining room as well. And it has its own bathroom. We'll get by."

"And what about father's books? They won't fit in the attic."

"Eulogio, please! We'll fit what we can, and the rest will have to be packed away."

"But ..."

"Oh, and you will work for the black marketeer. He'll give you a salary. You have to stop dreaming, boy. You won't be allowed to carry on with your studies, and as for being a painter ... I know that you've got a lot of talent, but your pictures don't fit in here. They don't understand you, Eulogio, and what can we do about that? Come on, we have to accept things as they are; we need to survive, no more than that."

In the end, her son accepted the deal. He had been very frightened when they took him to the police station. No one had said anything to him in all the hours he had been there, apart from the fact that he was a red and that he'd get what was coming to him. When they let him go, they offered no explanation, and he did not ask for one either; all he wanted to do was go home. But the fright had been enough for him to realize that he now had only two choices: to go to France or else to try to conform to his mother's wishes. Eulogio promised himself that he would convince his mother, but while he was working on her he'd bend like a reed, keep his mouth shut and silently curse the fascists who had taken away his leg and his future.

They said nothing to each other, but Eulogio and Piedad's hearts both sunk when they closed the door to what had once been their home for the last time, climbing up the stairs to move into the attic, three flights up.

The money that the black marketeer had given them was barely enough for them to pay for the attic. Her husband's desk didn't fit there, nor did his bookcases. There wasn't even space for the sofa. Piedad sold what she could, in spite of Eulogio's reproaches. The day they took the desk, her son cried.

Piedad told herself that she had no other choice than to accept the situation. Antonio had won the war and she had lost. She was a part of the victors' spoils, and so she had to hold back her nausea and grow used to the garlic on Antonio's breath, the bitter sweat that covered his body, his rudeness and, above all, the feeling of being treated like someone who had no right to do anything other than give him pleasure.

She learned to use her body and allow her mind to float free. She thought about absurd things, like Eulogio's trousers that needed to be hemmed, or whether or not she had the supplies to make mashed potatoes; even while Antonio was grunting like a pig above her, she managed to disappear and let her mind take her to places she liked to visit: the Retiro gardens, the blossoming almond trees in the Tiétar Valley … Places she had visited with her husband and her son, and where she had felt happy.

When the black marketeer finished with her, she would get up and clean herself as best she could before returning to the attic. They met wherever he wanted. Sometimes in the storeroom, sometimes in the warehouse, sometimes even in the car that Antonio had just bought and which he flaunted around the neighborhood.

She didn't care. The only thing she wanted was for him to finish quickly once he was on top of her.

Piedad knew that there were rumors in the neighborhood, and prayed that they would never reach Eulogio's ears. Her son would never forgive her for having surrendered to this humiliation, even if she had done it to save him. But what did he know about how much a mother is prepared to do to save her children? While Antonio was still using her they could rest easy; no one would bother them.

Sometimes she felt a deep sadness when she came up the stairs and walked past the door of what had once been her apartment, where a regime-supporting friend of Antonio's now lived.

They were a family who drew people's attention in the neighborhood, because they seemed not to need anything when everyone else lived in hunger. Of course, the new owners of the apartment liked to show off and pretend that they had things they did not, but even so, Piedad couldn't help but hate them deeply, hate them for having become the owners of her house, the place where she had been happy with her husband, the house where she had brought Eulogio into the world.

She took a long time to get to sleep that night. She couldn't help thinking that she had fallen into a hole from which she would never escape.

Catalina refused to go to the picnic that Don Antonio organized. She had woken up feeling nauseous and had been retching since early morning. Also, she didn't want to go back to the Pradera de San Isidro.

"Sick or not, you've still got to come," her father warned her.

"Ernesto, if the child's not well … Don Antonio will understand; he won't be angry."

"What do you know about it, Asunción! We can't disappoint him. You know that it's an important day today: Don Antonio wants to announce the engagement."

"What engagement? For God's sake, Ernesto, you're really jumping the gun here! They need to get to know one another first, and then decide. I think it's a good idea for the two families to work together, and see if Antoñito and Catalina like one another, but you have to give them time. It's like you don't know your daughter: she'll try to please you within reason, but she won't let you inflict a fiancé on her."

"This is your fault, Asunción, for the way you brought her up. My mother had six children and none of us would have dared go against what my father wanted. I married you because my father told me to, or don't you remember?"

Asunción nodded. How could she not remember? She had accepted the marriage that her parents had worked out, but although she didn't dare say as much to her husband, she wanted Catalina to marry a man of her choosing; her daughter would be sensible enough to choose a good man, she had no doubt of that.

"Let her rest for a bit, and then we'll see how she feels …" she suggested.

"Not a chance! Let her get dressed and ready to go to the country, and if she's sick, then let her be sick under a tree."

There was no way to change Don Ernesto's mind, for all that his wife pleaded and begged: Catalina had to get up and get dressed and go with her parents.

Don Ernesto didn't like to drive—in fact he practically never did so—but there was no way to get to the Pradera de San Isidro without driving or walking, and his health was too poor for him to allow himself such a long walk.

Asunción had managed to buy a box of candies to take for their hosts.

"We're making fools of ourselves, Mama," Catalina said.

"What do you mean?" her mother replied in surprise.

"It's ridiculous to take sweets to a picnic in the Pradera. We wouldn't do it even if we were going for tea at a decent house … And I really can't come, whether or not Papa gets annoyed. All I want to do is throw up."

"You had too much to eat last night," her mother said.

"You think soup with noodles is too much? And a little bit of odd-tasting chicken?"

Asunción didn't answer. Catalina was right, the chicken didn't taste of chicken. They had bought it in the street from a woman. It hadn't looked like chicken when they bought it, but the woman had explained that she cut the birds up in order to make more money from them, and promised that they were chickens from her own village. It was odd that she sold them in pieces rather than whole. She had had very little to eat, but she had also slept badly, and vomited, but she felt better now. As for her husband, he had not wanted to eat anything besides soup, so he had escaped the effects of the chicken.

"Catalina, you can't go against your father. I don't know what business it is that he has with Don Antonio, but it has to be important."

"So, Papa has business with a black marketeer? That's a good one! Think how low we've fallen!"

"How can you say things like that? If your father has to do business with Don Antonio, it's because he has to and that's how things need to be. It's not for us to question his decisions. Oh, Catalina, how badly I've brought you up! Children don't have the right to criticize their parents."

"I'm not going to the Pradera, and that's that!" Catalina said angrily.

But she did go. Her father came into the room and ordered her to get up, indifferent to her tears.

When they reached the Pradera, even Don Ernesto found it hard to hide his discomfort at being in a group with Don Antonio and his family. Mari, Don Antonio's wife, was there with her two daughters, Paquita and Mariví. So too were Don Antonio's brother, Prudencio, with his wife and children, and a few Falangist friends, and some soldiers with their families.

Don Antonio greeted the Vilamars by slapping Don Ernesto on the back so hard he knocked the wind out of him. He put a wineskin into his hand.

"Have a good swig to perk yourself up, and let the women go over there together. Mari has brought too much food, so take advantage of it. Catalina, Antoñito and Pablo are over there playing football, so stop wasting your time and get busy," Don Antonio said, with a guffaw that was so loud it attracted everyone's attention.

Asunción went over to Mari timidly and gave her the box of candies. The black marketeer's wife didn't open the box and didn't even say thank you. Mariví and Paquita looked enviously at Catalina who, even though she was feeling ill, looked beautiful.

"Antoñito, Catalina's here!" Mari called to attract her son's attention. "Come on, she's waiting for you to pay her some attention."

Catalina was about to say that as far as she was concerned, Antoñito could carry on doing whatever the hell he wanted, but her mother pinched her arm.

Don Ernesto, Don Antonio, and Prudencio had walked a few steps away from the rest of the group and were talking seriously.

Doña Asunción's pleasant face reflected how desolate she felt at that moment. Mari and the other women talked at the tops of their voices, and it was clear how common they were. It took her a while to get into conversation with them, as they looked at her with mistrust: aware, just as she was aware, that they were from very different worlds.

Mariví, Don Antonio and Mari's youngest child, sidled over to Catalina.

"My brother felt you up that last time," she said, making Catalina turn red as a tomato.

"Don't be ridiculous! No one has ever laid a hand on me," she protested.

"I saw how you were dancing; how close he got to you; there wasn't room for a cigarette paper between the two of you ... But

I don't think my brother likes you. He doesn't like easy girls."

Catalina lifted her hand and was about to give the girl a slap, but at that moment Antoñito came over towards them.

"Oh, so you came. I suppose you were hungry," he said, looking at her disdainfully.

"Hungry? You think we came here just to get a meal? That's all I need!" Catalina said, growing tense.

"Well, just look at it, all the food that my mother's brought, more than there'd be in your house in a year," Mariví said in a disgustingly sweet voice.

"I think that ... well, I don't know what it is you're thinking, but you're very wrong if you think we're here to eat. We're lucky and we can eat well in my house, every day."

"Sure, because my father gives you credit," Mariví said.

"Gives us credit? What are you talking about? All right, I know that you don't like me, and if it were up to me then I wouldn't be here, so just leave me alone and get on with your lives," Catalina said, barely able to hold back her rage.

"Let's go and take a walk, because if we don't then my father's going to be annoyed," Antoñito said, grabbing Catalina by the elbow.

She jumped back, wrenching herself from his grip. She felt queasy at the man's very touch. She walked a few steps away and started to be sick in earnest.

"Ew, how disgusting! She's throwing up!" Mariví shouted, drawing everyone's attention to Catalina.

Asunción ran over to her daughter and put one hand on her back and the other on her forehead. When Catalina had finished purging the bile from her stomach, her mother took a handkerchief out of her bag and wiped her daughter's forehead.

The women came over, curious, and Asunción explained that they had eaten chicken last night and that they'd both felt bad afterwards. "Chicken? Well, they've got to be well-off if they can afford chicken. We haven't eaten chicken since before the war, and then it was only at Christmas," one of the women said. They all started to speak at the same time and Asunción took this opportunity to walk a little further away with Catalina.

"Are you very ill?" she asked worriedly.

"I told you before we left the house, but father insisted, and now look at what a spectacle I've made of myself," Catalina complained.

"Make an effort, come on, for your father … Try to rest a little, talk to Antoñito and then we'll tell your father that we need to leave because you're not feeling very well, but at least he'll see that you're obeying him."

"So now I have to show him that I'm a good daughter? When have I done anything different from what he told me? I want to go now, please, Mama, I can't deal with these people, they're all so …"

"I know, but we need to listen to your father. Please, dear, talk to Antoñito," her mother begged.

A little way away, Antoñito looked at them in disgust while Pablo Gómez laughed. The women had gathered around the cloths that were spread on the floor laden with food. After the men had finished their game, they came over, hungry. Don Antonio and Prudencio, flanking Don Ernesto, came over as well. Only Mari didn't settle down to eat, upset that the poor little rich girl had vomited.

"Well, if she's not well, it's better for her not to eat," Mari said.

"Yes, better for her not to eat anything. I think it would be good for her to have a walk and breathe the air … It'll help settle her stomach," Asunción said, just to say something.

"Well, Antoñito should go with her. Come over here, son, and take her for a stroll; she'll get a bit of fresh air and it'll make your father happy to see you together," Mari said.

Her son went over to Catalina again and took her by the elbow once more, pulling her along.

Catalina struggled as much as she could, in spite of the effort she had to put in to contain her nausea. Antoñito walked quickly, as though he wanted to get this over with and get Catalina back to the others. He spoke first.

"You're going to ruin the party," he said.

"Me? You've never been ill, then? I should have stayed at home, but my father insisted; he didn't want to upset your father."

92

"He owes him too much to even dream of it," Antoñito said with a touch of arrogance in his voice.

"What are you saying? My father owing your father money … Don't say such stupid things!" Catalina herself was deploying the arrogance of the upper classes.

"If it weren't for my father, then you wouldn't be able to eat. What with that and the loans, stop giving yourself airs. You would be starving. And you know that when we get married you'll know what's what. You've never picked up a broom in your life, and I want my wife to know how to run a home, not just be some lady who looks at herself in the mirror all day. Look at my mother: we've got money, but she cleans the house, makes the food and looks after me and my sisters and my father. That's what a woman should be like."

"Marry you? I'm not going to marry a yokel like you. I'd sooner join a convent," Catalina said, witheringly.

"You'll do what they tell you, and if my father has decided that we're going to get married, then that's what's going to happen."

"But who does your father think he is?"

"It's you who has to stop thinking you're better than the rest of us. You don't have any money; you owe my father a lot, and you are a part of the payment."

They stood still without speaking. Catalina felt like her head was about to burst as she tried to force Antoñito's words into her mind so that she could understand what was going on. It couldn't be true.

She turned around, ready to go and get her father to clear all this up, but Antoñito took her arm again and held her still.

"We're going to get married. It's a done deal, and you can start getting ready to be a proper woman or else you'll feel the back of my hand."

Catalina shook herself free of Antoñito's grip and started to run. Her mother, who had kept her eye on them all this time, went over to her. Catalina had no time to say anything, because she was once again overcome by a fit of vomiting.

Don Ernesto looked at them in annoyance and got up and went over to where they stood.

"Will someone tell me what's going on?"

"She's sick, Ernesto, and we're going home," Asunción said firmly.

"We can't leave!"

"Yes, we can. We've shown our faces and now we can go, no one needs to feel offended; it's enough that we came ... I ... I want to go as well," Asunción said, and her voice was a plea.

Don Antonio came over to them, looking grumpy. Catalina was ruining the day, he thought to himself.

"Are you still throwing up?" he asked, with a look of anger.

"I'm sorry, Don Antonio, but we need to leave; my daughter's not feeling well ... I think it must be food poisoning ... Maybe the piece of chicken I bought wasn't chicken after all," Doña Asunción explained.

"Of course it wasn't chicken! It must have been lizard, or something like that. There are lots of people who go out hunting lizards and then sell it as chicken: don't tell me you didn't know that? What planet are you on?" He raised his voice so much that the rest of the guests turned to look at them.

"Lizard! No ... It's not possible ... the woman told me it was chicken ..." Asunción mumbled.

"Right ... chicken! ... And you think that they sell chicken already diced into unidentifiable little chunks? What were you thinking, woman?"

"She told me that she cut it up like that to make it go further ... I only bought some little bits ..." Asunción felt embarrassed as she carried on explaining herself to the black marketeer.

"And what shall we do now? I was thinking about making the announcement that Catalina and Antoñito were engaged," Don Antonio complained.

Don Ernesto took charge of the situation and, much to his own regret, backed up his wife's opinion.

"I'm sorry, Don Antonio, but you can see that my daughter isn't feeling well. There'll be another chance in the future. Catalina has made the effort to come, out of her respect for you and your family, but we're going home now. We'll talk again tomorrow, or whenever is good for you."

The black marketeer looked them up and down and turned

his back on them, muttering "We'll see." Don Ernesto was left feeling very worried. Even so, he gave one arm to his wife and the other to Catalina and walked over to the car that was parked a few yards away. None of the three said anything until they were back home. Asunción took her daughter to bed, and when she returned to her husband, she found him in a furious mood.

"That girl will be the death of us!" he said when his wife appeared.

"Good Lord, Ernesto, don't blame her for getting sick! You've seen how she is: we need to call a doctor."

"And what are you going to tell him: that you tried to be too clever and bought lizard instead of chicken? Until she's thrown all of that rubbish up she won't feel better at all. Give her some Carabaña mineral water; that'll help her get it all out."

"Yes ... you're right ... But. If she doesn't get better I'll call the doctor; we can't leave her like this ... and ... well, I wanted to say something ..." Asunción wrung her hands nervously.

"What do you want to say?" her husband asked, not really wanting to hear her.

"I don't like those people, they're just so ... so coarse ... and those women ... they didn't stop making personal remarks about me ... they didn't feel comfortable with me, and I wasn't comfortable with them. And Mari, Don Antonio's wife, is ... Well, no, I refuse to let her become Catalina's mother-in-law. She hates our daughter: if you could only have heard her talking about her behind her back, saying she was stuck up and so on ... I had to make an effort not to talk back, because I knew you'd be angry, but I'm not going to see her or speak to her again."

"Well, she'll be Catalina's mother-in-law whether you like it or not!" Don Ernesto said, getting angrier by the minute.

"I'm not going to allow you to marry our only daughter to that lout ... Antoñito is ... is ... he's a lout."

"Lout or not, Don Antonio wants Catalina for his son and I will give her to him. It's finished, Asunción, signed and sealed."

Doña Asunción didn't dare say more. She was not ready to stand up to her husband, but even so, she was sure that she would have to do so in the future to stop her daughter being married off to the black marketeer's son. She thought that they couldn't marry into such a low-class family, however much they might need their money.

She'd go and see her sister. Petra always had answers for everything, and loved Catalina very much.

Piedad handed Marvin a letter that had come that morning. It was from his father, telling him that he would visit Europe in September.

> We haven't seen you for a long time, son. Your mother would never forgive me if we came to Europe and didn't spend a few days together at least. I'm telling you in advance so that you can organize a trip to London, even if only for a few days. I think that there's not much point to you being in Madrid: the past is in the past. You have to look to the future, and I would like to talk to you about it. I've never understood why you went in for poetry so much, though your mother has convinced me that we shouldn't stand in the way of your vocation. But you should agree along with me that you can be a poet in New York just as well as in Europe, and your family is here, not there. Your mother misses you a lot, and so does your brother Tommy.
>
> I've sent a letter to our ambassador in Madrid so that he can put your papers in order and allow you to cross over to London without any trouble. I've reserved rooms at the Mayfair Hotel. I'll see you there on September 20th.
>
> Your father,
>
> PAUL J. BRIAN

It occurred to Marvin that he had stumbled upon an excuse for leaving. He was fooling no one; he'd been trying to find a pretext to leave for weeks. He needed one to leave Madrid.

He had come back to Spain to try to finish his *Spanish Civil War Notebook*, yes, but more than that, he had wanted to find a way to forgive himself and assure himself that the people he had served with at the front still thought of him as their equal and didn't blame him for having left. And so the minute the Spanish

Civil War in Spain was over, he had asked his father to pull some strings and send him back under the auspices of the Madrid Embassy. His father had not been enthusiastic about the idea, but his mother had sided with him once again. If Marvin wanted to go back, then he must have his reasons for doing so; they only had to make sure that nothing would happen to him, and so they pulled all the strings they could, even going as far as the White House. The owner of one of the greatest steelworks in the United States had certain privileges.

Slumped on his bed, Marvin felt a jolt of nostalgia. He wasn't going to miss the cramped attic, but it would be hard to say goodbye to Eulogio. He was the best friend he had ever had, the best and most unexpected.

Eulogio had seen him cry at the front, trembling in fear, and had saved his life, had run out under a hail of bullets and never spoken of it again. He had been generous, had shared everything he had, especially his affection and understanding. They had spent so many nights talking over all that had happened, and partially exorcising the ghosts that haunted him day and night.

Their friendship had been most firmly cemented by the fact that neither of them was the same again after the war. Part of their souls and bodies had stayed behind, on the field of battle.

He regretted spending his days wandering around in a stupor, seeing how the new regime had changed the city. It wasn't that the buildings had changed, but the people were not the same as they had been when he came to Madrid for the first time shortly before the war. Where had the people gone, his people? The Republicans, the communists, the socialists, the anarchists? And all of Azaña's supporters, those well-intentioned bourgeois people.

Madrid was scared, or at least that's what he thought. The people turned the other way if you made even the slightest mention of politics. He saw the terror in people's eyes, the defeat, everyone knew that the best thing for them to do was not to give an opinion, not say a word that could compromise them in the eyes of the victors.

Not a day passed without arrests, without someone reporting their neighbor as a communist; some of these reports were simply the result of personal vendettas.

Marvin could only talk freely with Eulogio, and with some of his friend's friends. But even so, they lowered their voices as they spoke, and looked around cautiously, even if they were safely at home.

There were two kinds of people in the streets: the victors and the survivors.

The winners of the war had their victory written all over their faces. The men walked upright, even defiantly.

And as for the losers like Eulogio, they preferred to sink into the crowd, not to attract attention. The new regime was looking for people who had fought in the war on the losing side. There was no compassion for them.

He had heard Piedad say that Eulogio had joined the militia almost as soon as the war started, but that he came back soon, and wounded, and so the neighbors stopped paying him any attention. Or at least, that's what she thought.

He lit a cigarette and took a deep drag. He didn't like the harsh tobacco, it wasn't even tobacco, really, but he put up with it, even though he thought that he would enjoy contraband American cigarettes more. He thought that when he left, in spite of everything, he would miss Madrid. He didn't know why; perhaps it was because he could sense the undertow of resistance that still flowed here, and this had a positive effect on his depressed mind.

There were a couple of soft knocks at the door.

"I forgot to give you this. Another letter. Catalina Vilamar brought it by this afternoon."

Piedad looked at him with interest, trying to read in his face the effect that a letter from Catalina might have. But Marvin did not react, merely held out his hand indifferently; he felt nothing but indifference, and maybe a little overwhelmed by her. She seemed to be immune to the general desolation of the country, as though she refused to take part in it. She wasn't insensitive, Marvin thought, but she had a survival instinct that was stronger than that of others. Catalina was not prepared to submit to Spain in its defeat, and in spite of everything, she chose life. She was not one to regret the past.

He opened the envelope and read the letter, a typical young woman's letter.

My dear Marvin:

I haven't heard from you for a week and it seems like forever. We need to meet and talk about our journey to Paris. I still haven't told my parents of our plans. I know that my mother will understand and will give us her blessing, but my father … the poor man; it will be hard on him. He still wants me to marry Antoñito. But I've already told him I'd rather become a nun.

I know you're very busy, but please try to find a moment when we can talk. We could arrange a chance meeting, if you'd like: I go to Mass at San Ginés every morning at nine. Please, don't make me wait any longer!

Yours,

CATALINA VILAMAR

He would have to see her. He'd have to tell her that he was going to London and that this was not the moment to go to Paris, much less for a young woman to go to France. She seemed to be unaware of the fact that Europe was at war. Maybe he could show her the city one day, but little more than that; he wouldn't look after her, and of course Catalina's parents wouldn't approve. Even though she clearly showed that she liked him, they were still virtual strangers. A few months ago, neither had known the other existed; they had not spent enough time in each other's company for them to travel together, for all that she dreamed of seeing Paris. No, he couldn't take on that responsibility at all. He would talk to her, peel the scales from her eyes. If she calmed down one day and traveled to Paris with her parents, he would of course show her around, but it was not likely to happen, so he had to let her down.

When Eulogio came back in the morning, Marvin was still asleep. His friend's shift ended at eight, and that was when he came home, always walking, in spite of the fact that it was hot.

Eulogio's habit was to wake him up and share a cigarette and a cup of the coffee-like drink that Piedad made for them. If Eulogio had managed to get a handful of beans, they would even have real coffee.

After breakfast, Marvin would usually go down to Fernando's house and have a cold shower. But that morning, in spite of the fact that his friend seemed to be more tired than usual, he had a lot to talk about.

"My father's coming to London in September, and so I'm going to leave. He wants us to see each other, and you know how badly the war is going, how the Germans are winning ... I don't know, I think it's better for me to go sooner rather than later," he said.

"Good for you; not everyone can leave here."

"I'd love to be able to invite you to Paris, but the Germans are there ... There's more than enough space for two in my apartment ... Maybe after seeing my parents I'll go back to France ..."

"You know I can't leave, Marvin, that I can't abandon my mother. What would she do without me? She's suffered enough, losing my father."

Marvin was surprised by how much the Spanish valued their family ties. He had left home when he was seventeen, without thinking about the effect it would have on his parents; if it had affected them, then they never said anything. This was the American way of life: children had to find their own path, with no interference. He could have decided to stay and run his parents' steelworks, and they would surely have liked him to do that, especially his mother, but she was also the one who had encouraged him to become a poet. She had told him, ever since he was small, that what he wrote was really good.

Now his mother's main worry was not seeing, him but the uncertainty that filled Europe ever since Hitler had come into power. 'This man will cause a massive disaster' was a common refrain of her letters.

He pushed his mother out of his thoughts and carried on talking to Eulogio.

"Well, if you do decide to come, then my house is your house, remember that."

"I know, I know. You know what? I'm pleased that you're going. Don't look at me like that, it's not that I want you to go, but I think it's the best thing for you. You have to do what I've done, even though it hurts: accept that there's no fixing the past and that there's no other choice for us than to carry on moving forwards. You think I like working for the black marketeer? If you knew how much I hate him ... But what can I do? I went to the war, I lost my leg, my father was killed ... I've only got my mother left, and it's only for her that I don't pack up my things and head into the mountains to try to find the people who still have the strength to fight. We've lost, Marvin, yes, but at least they haven't taken away what little life we have left. It's hard, but we have to stop asking ourselves what we did wrong and why what happened has happened."

"It's not that easy, Eulogio, at least not for me."

"And you say that to me! Look, if it weren't for my mother ... Tell me, have you found any answers these last few months? Are you feeling better, looking at the misery and poverty that surround us? Don't you see that these people are filled with the despair of losing, and cast down by the constant struggle just to survive? I'm not talking about hunger, that's not the most important thing, the worst of it is knowing that Spain is in the hands of the fascists and that we can't do anything to stop them even if we lay down our lives to oppose them."

"You're telling me that the only thing we can do is let life carry us where it wishes ..." Marvin said sadly.

"Yes, you poet, it is. There's no other choice for now. You have to go, Madrid is a cemetery. You can leave, so leave. The answers to the questions that are hurting you so badly are not here."

"And where are they?"

"In your head. But maybe there are no answers."

Piedad made them some more would-be coffee and took the mugs away; they barely noticed her, sunk in conversation as they were. They both knew that they were saying goodbye, perhaps forever.

They went out at noon for a walk. Eulogio had stopped feeling tired; he had talked too much. They walked down as far as Gran Vía, apparently now called the Gran Vía of the General Supreme, and from there to the Puerta de Alcalá. On their way back, they bumped into Fernando.

Eulogio said that Marvin was leaving.

"When?" Fernando asked, keen that he leave as soon as possible.

"I'm going to go to the embassy this afternoon, and if there's not too much paperwork, then it'll be in three or four days," Marvin said, paying no attention to Fernando's surprising eagerness.

"If they let you come in, there's no reason for them not to let you go out," Eulogio said.

"And you came to Spain before the war broke out, so they might not know that you were with the Republicans," Fernando said naively.

"Pah, they know everything! They just don't want to be on bad terms with the Americans. Especially not with someone who's got the protection of the ambassador. You know that Marvin's family is very important," Eulogio added.

"Yes, I have had the embassy supporting me. If not …" Marvin fell silent.

"If not, then you wouldn't have dared come back," Fernando said, ignoring the fact that his words cut Marvin to his core.

"I would have come back," the American said.

"More fool you if you had! You know how Franco's supporters treat people who aren't on their side," Fernando insisted.

"Will you say goodbye to your friends?" Eulogio asked.

"Yes, some of them at least. I'll go to Juan's house and try to see Pedro and his wife as well; Chelo has always been very kind to me."

"We could all meet up and have a drink," Eulogio said.

"If he's going in three days then there's no time," Fernando said, who couldn't wait for Marvin to leave Madrid and go as far away from Catalina as possible.

"I should say goodbye to Catalina as well. She'll be upset if I leave without saying anything."

"You're going to break her heart." Eulogio immediately regretted what he had said when he saw the expression on Fernando's face.

"No … I don't know … I know she wants to see Paris, but it's just a girlish dream. She's so full of life …"

"All right … Well, we'll see if you have time to say goodbye to everyone," Eulogio said, trying to steer the conversation in a different direction.

Fernando said nothing. He hadn't known that Catalina wanted to travel to Paris. She had never said anything, but if Marvin knew it, then it was because they had discussed it. He couldn't carry on fooling himself. Catalina was in love with Marvin; she had said as much herself. And he knew what had happened that night at the Pradera de San Isidro. Marvin had gone too far, and Catalina had given herself to him. He didn't know how much of herself she had given, and really didn't want to, either. He felt a sharp pain in the pit of his stomach. This always happened when he thought that she didn't love him.

"Okay, I'm going home, it's too hot to stand around in the street," Fernando said, bluntly, and sped up, reaching the door to their building and vanishing inside before they could catch up with him.

"What's the matter with him?" Marvin said in surprise.

Eulogio didn't know if he should tell the truth. He knew that Fernando was in despair to see Catalina so obviously in love with the American. After a moment's hesitation, he decided to tell the truth.

"It's not your fault, but until Catalina met you, it was assumed that she and Fernando were going to get married. They've been inseparable since they were children, and the whole neighborhood even made jokes about it."

"But what's that got to do with me?" the American said, not understanding what Eulogio was trying to say.

"You haven't done anything bad at all, quite the opposite in fact; I think you haven't even noticed her, but she's had you in her thoughts this whole time … She's in love with you, or at least she thinks she is, and Fernando's suffering because of it. I don't even know how he's let you use the shower in his apartment. If it weren't for his mother, and how much they need the money …"

Marvin looked at Eulogio in astonishment, as though he didn't really understand what had just been said. Catalina was just one of the many people he had met in Madrid, and he hadn't been attracted to her, or ever thought that she might be attracted to him. As Eulogio spoke, Marvin felt extremely uncomfortable. The last thing he wanted was for some woman to set her sights on him. He was preoccupied enough trying to escape from his ghosts without needing to deal with a silly little girl, which is all Catalina was.

"I'm sorry," he managed to say.

"Why are you sorry? These things happen. I don't think that Fernando has anything against you in particular; he knows that you didn't make the first move, that it was Catalina."

"Move? What move? No ... no ... you're wrong ... there's nothing between Catalina and me, I give you my word."

"I believe you, my friend, of course, but we've all seen how she looks at you and how she searches you out all the time. That night at the Pradera, all she did was sniff around you, and everyone thought that you did more than just talk to her. Look, don't worry about it, Fernando will get over it ... And if you leave, then I'm sure she'll forget about you and go back to thinking about Fernando. Well, actually, I don't know ... she's very headstrong and she's spoiled as well ... an only child ... All that nonsense about wanting to go to Paris ..."

"She said that she'd like to get to know the city, that she's always dreamed of traveling, but she doesn't seem to realize that France has been overrun by the Germans." Marvin seemed to be speaking to himself more than to Eulogio.

"Yes, of course she'd like to get to know Paris, who wouldn't? But she wants to go because you have an apartment there; if you told her you were going to Sebastopol, you'd see how quickly her love for Paris would pass."

"I'll talk to Fernando ... I want him to know that I don't care about Catalina ... I think he's a wonderful person, like his mother ... and he must be suffering so much, with his father in prison ..."

"Leave it, Marvin. You'll be gone in a few days and things will get back to normal between them, I guess."

Isabel, Fernando's mother, got back a few minutes after her son. She went over to him and kissed his cheek, a gesture which he accepted indifferently. He wasn't in the mood for maternal affection. The conversation he had had with Marvin and Eulogio had upset him, but also annoyed him.

"Was work bad this morning?" his mother asked, when she

saw that he did not react to the kiss or her hug, not like he normally did.

"Is it ever good? There's nothing good here, Mother, nothing. Don't you get it?"

"You can't fool me, you're angry, and both of us know why ..."

Fernando didn't reply, and went instead to the bathroom to cool down. The heat made him angrier still.

His mother called to him that food was ready. Potatoes with paprika. They had it very often, and they were lucky to even have this. If his father hadn't been in prison, they would have been able to say that they were lucky, to have survived the war and have something to put on their plates.

They sat in silence. When he was in a bad mood, his mother normally let him be. When they had finished, she started to wash the dishes and he got ready to head over to Don Vicente's print shop, where he was still being shown the ropes.

Sometimes Fernando thought that he would be very upset if September rolled around and the new rulers of Spain wouldn't let him go to college since his father had been arrested for being a Republican and was still in prison. But he had learned to enjoy his job at the print shop, and every now and then let himself dream that one day he might run one himself.

"Don't be late," his mother said as he left.

"I won't be," he replied.

He met Marvin on the stairs. The American said he was walking the same way and offered to accompany him, but Fernando said no.

"Marvin, I'm in a hurry, I'll be late."

"Right ... well ... it's just that ... I want to say something to you."

Marvin took him by the arm and made him stop.

"I want to say something, and I hope you'll believe me. I know that you and Catalina ... Well, that you've always been close and that she's very important to you."

"Why do you care about Catalina and me? Don't stick your nose in other people's business," Fernando replied angrily.

But Marvin didn't back down, and even held him tighter, to make him listen.

"I don't get involved in other people's business, Fernando, but I think Catalina has got involved in yours. I just want you to know that I'm not interested in her, and that even if I had been, I would never have come between the two of you."

"Leave me alone, Marvin! I don't want to talk about Catalina with you or anyone else. And anyway, you've got something going with her and I haven't."

"You have to hear me out: I'm not involved with anyone. I'm not interested in Catalina, and I don't think she's really interested in me either. I think she's flighty, a dreamer. She's caught on me because I'm new, but I'm sure that when I'm gone, things will get back to normal. In any case, I promise that never, ever will I get between the two of you. Please remember that, Fernando."

Marvin let go of Fernando's arm. Fernando pulled himself free, then went down the stairs three at a time without giving the American any answer.

4

"He's gone? It can't be! No, he can't have gone, you can't do this to me."

"Come in and calm down," Eulogio said to Catalina, who was about to burst into tears.

Eulogio had arrived home at nine in the morning after his night shift in the warehouse. He was tired and had gone to bed as soon as he could, but before he could fall asleep, he heard the doorbell and his mother talking to someone who turned out to be Catalina. He got up and pulled on his pants, then went to see what was happening.

Piedad had just told her that Marvin had left four days ago and she, incredulous, was starting to raise her voice and deny that such a thing was possible.

Catalina was frozen in the doorway, and Piedad held out her hand to invite her in. If she stayed there, then the whole building would hear what was going on.

"Sit down, I'll get you a glass of water. And put your shirt on, son," Piedad ordered.

"There must have been a mistake," Catalina said as she sat down.

"He had to go sooner than he expected. Apparently, one of the diplomats from the British Embassy had to travel now, and invited him to go with him. Marvin accepted because it was the safest way to travel. He would have liked to say goodbye to everyone he knew in Madrid, but he wasn't able to," explained Piedad.

"But he should have told me. He can't have gone without me!" Catalina replied, unable to hold back her tears.

"He'll write to you, don't you worry," Eulogio said, coming into the room fully dressed.

"I have to go to Paris … You have to give me his address … I have to go." Catalina wasn't listening.

"What are you saying? Paris is controlled by the German army. It's not easy to travel, with things as they are, and who would go with you on such a trip? Your father's not in the best of health, and your mother … well, I don't think she'll leave your father alone to come with you on a trip like that. And there's one more thing: Marvin hasn't gone to Paris, he's gone to London to see his parents," Eulogio said.

"Didn't he leave a letter for me?" Catalina asked hopefully.

"No … No, he didn't leave anything. He had to go so quickly …" Piedad said, moved by Catalina's tears.

"And now what am I going to do …?" she said.

"Wait, and stop behaving like a little girl," Eulogio said severely.

"It's just that … well, you don't know, but Marvin and I … he promised that he'd take me to Paris, that he'd look after me, that he and I. …"

"You know what? I don't think Marvin promised anything at all, apart from to behave like a good host if you happened to come to Paris one day. And to do that, the war needs to come to an end. The Germans are in control of half of France, and they are in Paris. But you know that already. I think you've gone off on a flight of fancy, not that Marvin has encouraged you." Eulogio was not looking at her as he spoke.

"But you can't say things like that," Piedad protested.

"Mother, you know how close Marvin and I were; I know that the only feeling he has for Catalina is friendship, and there's no doubt about it," Eulogio replied angrily.

"You don't know anything! Nothing at all! Marvin and I are going to get married, I tell you! And if he has gone, then it's because of something that has come up and forced him to go. His father might have made him go to London because he has something important to tell him. Yes, that must be what's happened," Catalina replied, convincing herself with her own words.

"Believe what you want, it's your funeral," Eulogio replied, shrugging.

Catalina stood up and went to the door, followed by Piedad.

"Thank you for being so kind ..."

"Don't mention it, and try to stay calm: you'll see how everything will sort itself out," Piedad replied.

When mother and son were alone together, Piedad reproached Eulogio for having spoken so harshly.

"You didn't need to be so tough on her. She's a good girl."

"A good girl, but a very flighty one. To hear her speak, you'd think that Marvin had agreed to marry her, and I know better than anyone that he's done no such thing."

"She must have been confused by Marvin's friendliness ..." Piedad admitted.

"I know I wasn't kind, but I wanted her to snap out of it."

"Poor Fernando," Piedad said.

"Yes, he's still in love with Catalina. I hope she comes to her senses: she deserves someone who really loves her," Eulogio said, still a little angry.

Catalina walked quickly and did nothing to hold back her tears. She refused to accept that Marvin could have left without saying anything to her. Not only did he love her, he was also a gentleman, and after all that had happened between them at the Pradera de San Isidro, he couldn't just abandon her. Another man could, perhaps, but not him.

She blamed herself for not having stopped his departure. Now she thought that she should have realized that Marvin's silence had a cause. But they had met a couple of times in the street, and once he had walked with her for a good long time without telling her that he was leaving soon. She remembered that Marvin had mentioned his father's letter, but that he hadn't once said that he was going to travel alone, without her.

She stopped for a moment to fight back nausea. She had been feeling sick for two weeks and had often been forced to stay in bed in the mornings for longer than usual.

That very afternoon she was due to go to the doctor with her mother. She didn't care what he told her; she even fantasized about being diagnosed with a serious illness, for then Marvin would have to come back for her. Then she abandoned the thought. No. That wasn't good. It wasn't worthy of her, even though she said to herself that she would be willing to do anything to make him come back.

She passed the black marketeer's wife in the street and didn't say a word to her. She disliked her as much as her son. Antoñito came to their house every evening and stayed for at least an hour. Her mother kept an eye on him as she came in and out of the salon.

She and Antoñito barely spoke. She would have a cup of coffee, the same coffee that he brought as a gift every week, and they would trade a couple of banal observations. Neither of them felt happy in the company of the other, but she could see in Antoñito's eyes that he wanted her to belong to him. She shuddered to think what he might be capable of. He spoke to her with a powerful sense of resentment, as though it was her fault for having been born into a family that had a place in the world, while he was simply the son of a shopkeeper.

"You have to get ready for when we're married; you'll cook and clean like my mother does," he warned her constantly. "I don't like layabouts; if you think you're going to get up any later than eight o'clock, then you're sorely mistaken." "Don't look at me so openly; well-brought-up women don't look men in the face; they look down to the ground." "You won't have any opinions; you'll think what I tell you to think about everything. That's the least of it." His words painted a picture for her of how her life would be once they were married.

Catalina didn't care, because she knew it would never happen, for all that her father was insisting that she marry Antoñito. She had allowed him to come and visit so as not to upset her father, but she was tired of it now, and would inform him of his mistake very shortly. She was not going to marry the black marketeer's son.

When she got home, she went to her room and slumped on the bed. She was tired and her nausea exhausted her.

Her mother and father came into the room, surprised that she hadn't come to greet them when she got back.

"What's wrong?" her mother asked, putting her palm on her daughter's forehead.

"She's got a stomach upset. Let's see if the doctor can give us some medicine his afternoon. Don Antonio wants the wedding to take place at the end of the year, and I've told him that this is a little hasty, but if that's how it has to be, then that's how it has to be," Don Ernesto said.

"That's not important now; we need to find out what's happening to the child. She hasn't been right for a couple of months now. Look how pale she is," Doña Asunción replied.

Catalina didn't say anything to either of them. They always just said the same things anyway.

"She looks all right; she's even put on weight," Don Ernesto said.

"You go back to your office, Ernesto, and I'll stay with her. I'll boil up some herbs that Petra gave me."

When they were alone, Doña Asunción looked at her daughter more worriedly than even she would have liked to admit to herself.

They went to Don Juan Segovia's office that afternoon. Asunción and he had known one another since they were children, because their parents had been friends. If her husband had had any say in the matter, she would have changed her doctor, because Don Juan had always been on the side of the Azañistas, and even though he didn't get involved in politics, he had been unable to escape the effects of the war.

The doctor examined Catalina, asked her a few questions, and when he was finished told her to sit down.

"Well, if I'm not mistaken, and I don't think I'm mistaken, your problem is that you are pregnant. Am I right?"

Doña Asunción cried out and protested, looking fearfully at the doctor.

"What are you saying? Good Lord, Juan, how can you think that the girl might be pregnant? It's just that everything she eats makes her feel bad … And she's getting married, I don't know if you knew: at the end of the year Catalina's going to get married to Antoñito Sánchez."

"Right, the black marketeer's son … I heard something about it, but didn't want to believe it. Catalina and that boy … I don't know … Well, it looks like they've been a little hasty in doing things that they should have left until after the wedding, and that's had consequences."

"No, no, no! That's impossible! How can you suggest that my daughter …?"

"Come on, tell me, girl: am I right or am I wrong?" Don Juan asked Catalina.

She was stunned. When Don Juan and her mother spoke, it was as though their words came from far away, as though they weren't right next to her, looking at her.

"Catalina, say something, for God's sake!" Asunción demanded.

"Give her a chance to rest for a second. I'll get her a glass of water; it's only natural for her to be in shock."

Don Juan left the room and Doña Asunción stood in front of her daughter.

"It's not possible … tell me that … you …"

Catalina said nothing, and her mother grabbed her by the shoulders and shook her, trying to get her to come around.

Don Juan came back with a glass of water which he gave Catalina and made her drink.

"Right, the best thing is for you to tell your parents what happened. You must have been pregnant for a couple of months at least. When did your periods stop?"

Both women blushed at the direct question, but Don Juan was a doctor, and had been through a war, and had no scruples at all when it came to speaking to a young girl who had behaved in an unbecoming manner.

Catalina swallowed while she thought. She could not accept what Don Juan had said, but the doctor was right: it was a couple of months since she had last bled.

"Catalina, listen to me: if you want me to help you then you have to tell me the truth. I understand that you weren't expecting it, but when you do things like that, then … well … these things happen. You and Antoñito should have waited until the wedding; it was only a couple of months, but what's done is done. If you don't want to be showing too much when you get married, you have to bring the wedding forward to September or October at the latest; you're thin and don't eat much, which is very easy these days, and then no one will notice it at the wedding."

"Juan, don't say such things! Catalina isn't ... Catalina wouldn't ... she's not ... she's not ..."

"She's pregnant, Asunción. I know that it's a big shock for you, and I don't want to think what you'll say to your husband, but these things happen: they've happened before, they happen now, and they'll carry on happening in the future. All you have to do is get them married as soon as possible: problem solved. I'll make sure that Catalina stays healthy."

"Please, tell him he's mistaken!" Doña Asunción begged Catalina.

The doctor looked at her with sympathy and Catalina started to cry in despair. He made a gesture to Doña Asunción indicating that she should say nothing and to let the girl unleash her feelings. After a while, when it seemed as though the girl had no tears left to cry, the doctor spoke again:

"The best thing is for you to tell your parents everything. They're going to be surprised and upset, but you're their daughter, the apple of their eye, and they'll sort things out for you in the best possible way. As for Antoñito ... he'll have to be a man and step up to sort out the situation."

"It wasn't him," Catalina murmured.

"What did you say?" Don Juan said, unsure that he'd heard correctly.

"It wasn't Antoñito." And Catalina burst out crying again.

Doña Asunción fainted, and the doctor and Catalina had to help her. Her daughter held her up and fanned her, and Don Juan went to get another glass of water.

The tables had been turned, and it was now Doña Asunción who cried in despair, upset by what she was going through.

Don Juan had to wait quite a while for mother and daughter to be calm enough for him to start the conversation again.

"It's not my business to ask who it was that you did things with that you shouldn't have done, but the sooner you tell your parents, the better. I suppose it must have been some young man you know, and that he'll take care of things, eh?" the doctor asked.

"Fernando! It was Fernando!" Doña Asunción shouted, apparently in the grip of a revelation.

"Fernando Garzo? The editor's son?" Don Juan asked.

"No, it wasn't him … It was … Marvin. It was with Marvin."

Her voice breaking, Catalina explained to Don Juan who Marvin was, and how they had become boyfriend and girlfriend without telling anyone, and how one night at the Pradera de San Isidro what had happened had happened, but that now he had gone to London without telling her, but that she was sure that as soon as he found out he would come back to marry her.

"But you have to get married to Antoñito! What will your father say?" Doña Asunción groaned.

"The important thing is for her to marry the father of her child, don't you think, Asunción? And anyway, I don't think that Antoñito is going to want to take charge of a child that isn't his …"

They left Don Juan's office supporting each other as they went: both of them seemed to lack the strength to walk unaided. Mother and daughter were both in a state of shock, incredulous at what the doctor had told them.

"But how could you have done such a thing?" Doña Asunción asked, in tears.

"Mama, I don't know … It was Antoñito's birthday, when we all were invited to the Pradera … I drank wine and it went to my head … I didn't realize what was happening; I don't even remember it all that well … But let me say, I am happy that it was with Marvin. I love him. I hate Antoñito. I won't marry him, whatever Father says."

Doña Asunción squeezed her daughter's arm, unable to say that it was Antoñito now who wouldn't want to marry her.

She shuddered when she thought about what would happen if the American didn't come back, or if he refused to take responsibility for Catalina and the child they were to have together. He was a foreigner, and there was no way to pressure him into fulfilling his obligations. She trembled when she thought about what her husband's reaction would be: she knew he was a good man, but he was overwhelmed at the moment by his debts. For him, the wedding had become a solution for the difficult situation they found themselves in.

"I don't know how we're going to tell your father. The shock could kill him," Doña Asunción said.

"I'm sorry, Mama, I'd never forgive myself if anything were to happen to Papa because of me: what can I do?" Catalina asked worriedly.

"I don't know. I just don't know."

Mother and daughter both walked slowly, knowing that from this moment on, their lives would never be the same again.

It was hard for Catalina to cope with the idea that she was to be a mother. She said that maybe Don Juan had made a mistake, and she plucked up the courage to ask her mother if a woman could ever get pregnant if she had only done "it" once.

"Yes, my dear, yes, that's our lot in life," Doña Asunción said, almost overcome with worry.

Don Ernesto was in his office, talking to Don Antonio. Catalina and her mother came in and greeted the two men, who looked at them in surprise, as they could see that the women had been crying. Their eyes were red, their faces were puffy, and they couldn't hide the fact that something had happened.

"You look tired. Go and rest while I finish talking to Don Antonio," Don Ernesto said.

"Yes … it's hot … you know that the heat in Madrid is difficult to bear," Doña Asunción replied.

"It must be really something today," Don Antonio murmured, surprised by how bad the two women looked.

As soon as the black marketeer had gone, Don Ernesto called for his wife to come and tell him how the trip to the doctor's had gone. Doña Asunción burst into tears, unable to tell her husband the truth.

"What is it? Asunción, if the girl's sick, tell me …" Don Ernesto said in great distress.

But his wife was unable to reply and started crying even harder, so Don Ernesto called for his daughter. Given how much his wife was crying, he was starting to worry that Catalina was suffering from some fatal disease.

When they had managed to calm Doña Asunción, Don Ernesto, unusually for him, sat down next to his daughter and took her hand, as though he were trying to encourage her, and insisted to his wife that she tell them what had happened.

Doña Asunción looked at her daughter, not knowing what to say, and Catalina, shocked by her mother's tears, decided that she should tell the truth herself. She didn't know where she managed to get the strength, but she managed to tell her father directly.

"I'm pregnant. Don Juan says I'm two months gone. It's not Antoñito's child; the father is Marvin, the American." She said all this while looking her father in the eye, watching as his expression changed. He moved from incredulity to anguish to anger.

Don Ernesto stood in front of his daughter and gave her a slap that knocked her to her heels. Catalina took a step back, trying to keep her balance, and cowered against the wall with her hands in front of her face as her father raised his hand again.

"Ernesto, for God's sake! Leave her be! I'm begging you, Ernesto!" Doña Asunción cried out, trying to get between her husband and her daughter.

But Don Ernesto's anger was such that he pushed his wife out of the way and slapped Catalina's face again and again.

"You slut! You whore! How could you have done something like this! You bitch! Harlot!"

Catalina listened to him in terror. She had never seen her father like this before. He was always so upright, such a gentleman, incapable of raising his voice, and now he was unrecognizable: red in the face, his eyes bulging, spit flying from his lips with each new insult.

She withstood her father's blows as best she could, but finally she doubled over and fell to the floor as her mother begged her father not to hit her any more.

Doña Asunción bent down, trying to protect her daughter with her own body as her husband started to kick his daughter.

"I'll pull that bastard out of you with my own hands! You won't have this child, I swear to God you won't have it!" Don Ernesto shouted.

Both mother and daughter were beaten again and again until Don Ernesto felt faint and had to grab the back of a chair to steady himself.

Crying, Doña Asunción tried to pick Catalina up off the floor.

"My girl, please get up … please … my girl …"

One of Catalina's eyes was so swollen she could barely see out of it, but she could sense that her father was recovering from his moment of weakness, so she made an effort and stood up. Then, held in her mother's arms, she let herself be led to her room. Once she was inside, Doña Asunción pulled the bolt across and helped her to lie down on her bed.

"Don't worry, Mama," Catalina said, more upset by her mother's distress than by the pain of her father's blows.

"We'll go to the doctor: he can't have ... My poor daughter! Forgive your father ... forgive him ..."

"Forgive him? Never! Never!" Catalina said, unable to hide her anger.

"You have to forgive him ... forgive him ... men are like that; honor is the most important thing for them," Doña Asunción begged, wiping her daughter's forehead with a perfumed handkerchief.

Catalina's nose was bleeding and, besides her eye, she had other bruises all over her body. Doña Asunción was in no better shape, but she didn't complain: her only concern was for her daughter.

"Stay here. I'll go get some water and something to eat. When I leave, lock the door and don't open it to anyone until I come back."

"Mother, stay here ... Papa is capable of anything ..." Catalina said, terrified.

"No, he won't do anything to me ... he's a good man ... Forgive him, please, it was just the shock of the news. We have to let him get used to it ... It'll all get sorted out, you see; your father loves you; you're the apple of his eye ..."

Catalina didn't reply. She hadn't recognized that raging animal as her father. She had expected to be scolded and punished, but not subjected to the violence that he had used against the pair of them.

When her mother left the room, she pushed the bolt across. Suddenly she felt deeply afraid of her father, and put her ear to the door to listen in case her mother should start screaming, ready to run and help her.

But she heard nothing and threw herself down on the bed in

despair. She closed her eyes and tried not to think, but it was impossible. She said to herself that maybe she had been a little blunt in how she had informed her father; perhaps she should have broken it some other way, or have let her mother explain things that night, when she and Don Ernesto were alone in their room together. But there was no going back. The worst of it was that she would have to face her father again.

Suddenly she sat up with a start. What if she were unable to get in touch with Marvin? She didn't know where to write to him. Only Eulogio had his address, and he wouldn't give it to her unless she explained why it was so urgent that she speak to him. But if she told Eulogio that she was expecting Marvin's child, then he wouldn't be able to keep his mouth shut, and sooner or later the whole neighborhood would know it, which would be terrible. They would gossip about her behind her back; she could just imagine the things they would say. It was only then that she realized the gravity of the situation.

She lay back to wait for her mother to return, running her hand over her belly. She felt nothing. Was it really possible that she had Marvin's child inside her? "A child," she thought for the first time. She was going to have a child that she didn't want. She immediately regretted the thought. Of course she wanted to have children with Marvin, but only when they were married, not just whenever. But what about him? Would he be angry when he found out that he was going to become a father? Would he think that it had been her fault? No, he couldn't think that: what had happened in the Pradera had been pure chance, and he knew that. And it had been Marvin who had been unable to hold himself back, anyway, because she had drunk so much that she didn't know what she was doing; the wine had gone to her head and removed all her willpower.

Her back hurt where her father had kicked her, and her vision was still blurry from the blow to her eye; she could feel one of her teeth wiggle loosely as well. She didn't want to look at herself in the mirror, as she was afraid of what she might see.

She lay drowsily on her bed until a couple of soft knocks at the door brought her back to herself. She heard her mother whisper her name.

She opened the door and Doña Asunción came in quickly. She had a tray in her hands with a glass of milk and a piece of bread.

"I'm not hungry," Catalina said.

"You have to eat: if not for you then for the child," Doña Asunción said, looking at her daughter's belly.

"Did Papa … did he say anything?" Catalina said.

"I had to make him an herbal tea. He's very upset; it was a big shock for him."

"It wasn't my fault," Catalina said.

"It doesn't matter … What's done is done. Now we all have to face up to it."

"But you're not so angry with me." Catalina looked almost pleadingly at her mother.

"Angry? I don't know what I feel … I still can't get my head around the idea that you're … well, that you're pregnant. I haven't had a chance to think about it and I'm … well, I'm surprised. I'd never have thought that you … I showed you how to behave around boys and then this foreigner turns up and you let him seduce you …"

"Mother, please help me!"

"Of course I'll help you, but I don't know what we need to do. As soon as your father has calmed down we'll talk to him and make some decisions. The only thing I'm sure of is that the American will have to come and take responsibility. If it's necessary, I myself will go and tell him as much. Isn't he in Eulogio's house? Piedad is a good woman and I don't think that she'll tell everyone you're pregnant. But the sooner you get married, the better. It's a shame we won't be able to organize a proper wedding."

"Mama … Marvin left. Eulogio told me that he's gone to London, and I don't have his address. If Eulogio doesn't give it to me, I won't know how to find him …"

"What do you mean? How can he have left without telling you where he was going?"

"He left without saying goodbye." Catalina started to cry again.

"What a disaster!"

Doña Asunción sat on the edge of the bed and wrung her hands. Her lower lip was trembling. Catalina folded herself into her mother's arms and stayed there for long time.

"Wherever he is, we need to find him and make sure he comes back as soon as possible," Doña Asunción said.

"Eulogio knows his address, but he won't tell us how to find Marvin in London if we don't tell him why we want to find him," Catalina said.

"Why should he care? We shouldn't have to give explanations. Maybe Fernando could give you a hand: isn't he Eulogio's friend?"

"And what? Should I tell Fernando that I'm … that I'm expecting Marvin's child? I can't do that, Mama, I just can't."

"You don't need to explain everything," Doña Asunción said doubtfully.

Catalina burst into inconsolable tears once again. The realization had dawned that her life was no longer just her own.

Her mother made her drink the milk and eat the bread, and then left her alone. She needed to put her thoughts in order as well, and struggled to hold back her tears as she walked to her room.

Her husband was sitting in an armchair by the balcony, the window wide open. It was very hot. The mug of herbal tea was on a table near where he sat, and Doña Asunción saw with relief that it was empty. She sat in a chair.

"She has to have an abortion," her husband whispered.

Doña Asunción gave a jolt, shocked by what she heard. She didn't dare say anything, but looked worriedly at her husband.

"I'm not going to let her marry that American. She's engaged to Antoñito, and she will marry him. But she needs to get rid of what she's carrying in her belly first. Let's find someone who can sort out the problem for us. There has to be someone in Madrid who can deal with such things. No one must find out, not that she's pregnant, nor that she's gotten rid of it." These last words came as a warning to his wife.

"But we can't … it's not possible … we're Catholics … Catalina won't allow it: she's in love with the American and wants to marry him … Good Lord, Ernesto, how can you even contemplate something so monstrous!"

Don Ernesto slammed his fist down onto the table and the cup fell to the floor and broke.

"Are you as mad as your daughter? We are ruined, hadn't you noticed? I owe a lot of money to Don Antonio, and without his help we won't even be able to eat. Don Antonio wants his son to marry a real lady, and Catalina is the woman closest to hand."

"And you don't care about handing your daughter over to that yokel?" his wife said.

"What kind of a world do you think we're living in, Asunción? The war destroyed your father's business; all we have are debts. My brother isn't doing that much better; he's trying to get the farm working, but for the time being, they're only making enough to live on. There's no other way out; Catalina isn't used to going without, and Antoñito will give her all she needs."

"But she doesn't love him. She hates him ..."

"Did we love each other when we got married? Our parents arranged our marriage because it was the best thing for both of us, and here we are now, and has anything bad happened? You've been an exemplary wife and I've been a faithful husband, and what more could you ask for?"

"But we can't force her ... The American could come and ask for his child back ..."

"What child? There won't be any child: I'll make sure of it. She'll have an abortion."

"I will not allow my daughter to commit a mortal sin!" Doña Asunción got to her feet and stared defiantly at her husband.

"And what, isn't it a mortal sin to commit impure acts? She'll go to Hell just the same."

"What are you saying? Ernesto, you need to rest, and we'll talk about this tomorrow. We're on edge and saying things we don't mean ... God forgive us!"

"Yes, God forgive us, but the girl will have an abortion."

Catalina rose just after dawn. She washed herself quickly and went out of the house without making any noise, keen to see Eulogio on his way back from the warehouse. She met Fernando instead: he was on his way to work.

"What are you doing out at this hour of the morning?" he asked in surprise.

"I have to see Eulogio," Catalina said without thinking.

"So early? He's just about to come back, but why do you need to see him so urgently? What's going on? You've got a black eye and your arm is bruised ... Did you fall down?"

Catalina said nothing, but bit her lower lip until it bled.

"Hey, if you don't want to tell me, don't tell me, I don't care. Goodbye." And Fernando turned away moodily.

"Don't go ... It's not that I don't want to tell you ... it's just that ..." And she burst out crying.

Fernando stopped dead in surprise. He had never seen her cry, not even when she was a little girl and fell over and scraped her knees.

"What happened?" he said, putting an arm around her shoulder.

Catalina cried all the harder; Fernando was scared.

"I'll take you home now; I don't think you should be wandering around the streets like this. And tell me what's happened; you know you can trust me."

"Whatever it is?" she moaned.

"Yes, anything," he said.

She still didn't know whether to speak. She needed to confide in someone, and there was no one better than her beloved childhood friend, but she was too ashamed to tell him that she was pregnant.

Fernando grew impatient, but he didn't want to leave her alone in the street in such a state. He'd get to work late, and the site manager was likely to fire him. But even so, he knew that she was the most important thing to him in the entire world, and that if he lost his job because of her it wouldn't matter. He loved her so much that he was willing to give his life for her.

Catalina burrowed into his arms looking for comfort, and he couldn't help feeling deeply uneasy.

"Come on, let's sit down on a bench and you can tell me everything."

They walked the short distance to the Plaza de la Encarnación and sat very close to each other on a bench. He took her by the hands and smiled.

"Whatever's happened, I'll help you sort it out."

"You promise?" she said, pleading.

"I swear."

"You're so good to me!"

"All right, tell me what's happened."

"Well ..."

"Come on, Catalina, if there's someone you can trust, then it's me," he insisted.

"I'm pregnant." She spoke in a whisper, and wiped away the tears that ran down her cheeks.

Fernando let go of her hands. His eyes must have revealed a great deal of pain and despair, along with indignation, because at that moment, Catalina regretted having confided in him. They sat still for a few seconds, looking at one another without truly seeing each other, despairing, unable to give each other support.

Finally Fernando recovered a bit of control over himself and, fighting against the rage that he felt, said:

"Who was it?"

"You know who it was ... You remember that day in the Pradera?"

"Marvin."

"Yes."

Fernando clenched his fist and hit the bench. He didn't feel any pain, even though he had taken the skin off his knuckles. He was so angry that if Marvin had been in front of him at that moment, he would have crushed him like an egg.

"How could you ..." he said.

"I ... I don't know what happened ... I don't even remember it ... I'm sorry, Fernando, I'm so sorry ..."

And her sorrow was sincere. She looked worriedly at Fernando: she couldn't bear from him to think less of her, much less for him to decide to turn his back on her forever. In that instant, she realized the depth of the bond they shared, and how deep it would always be. She knew that he loved her and that she had ignored his love, but whatever she did, he would love her completely and generously, as he always had.

She sat very quietly, while Fernando, his eyes staring into the distance, tried to control his emotions.

"What are you going to do?" he asked in a tired voice, as though he were an old man.

"I'm going to ask Eulogio to give me Marvin's address. I'll write to him in London and in Paris, and tell him what has happened and ... well, I hope he'll take care of things, and come back to marry me."

Catalina's words were agony, like salt on an open wound.

"Are you sure he'll come back?"

"Yes, he can't leave me like this ..."

"Right ... So you're going to tell Eulogio that you're pregnant ..."

"I don't have a choice; he's the only one who knows where Marvin is. I'm ashamed of telling him, and worried that he'll tell everybody else, but what else can I do?"

"I could ask him."

"You? You think he'd give you the address?"

"Eulogio is my friend, the best friend I have, and I'm sure that he can keep a secret, but it would be best if, until Marvin comes back, you didn't tell anyone that ... that you're ..."

Catalina lowered her head in shame. She knew that Fernando was trying to protect her, and that made her feel even more guilty.

He passed his hand over his face, and then looked at her so intently that she looked down at the ground.

"My father hit me," she confessed.

"Those bruises, was that him?"

"Yes, he got furious; I thought he was going to have a heart attack or something; I've never seen him like that, screaming ... I'm scared of him now."

"I won't let him hit you. I'll speak to him," Fernando said, certain that he would.

"No, no ... it's better that you don't come to the house; I don't know what he might do."

"And he doesn't know what I might do if anyone hurts you," Fernando replied, very seriously.

"Will you help me?"

"I have no choice. Now go home, and I'll talk with Eulogio today."

Fernando spent the rest of the morning thinking about Catalina, his concentration fractured. Pascual, the foreman, shouted at him a couple of times for being distracted; his big mistake was to give Fernando a shove to make him concentrate, to which Fernando replied with a haymaker that left the man sprawled on the ground.

The rest of the workers looked at Fernando in shock. How had he dared to hit an older man, the foreman of the whole project? He'd be fired for sure; and anyway, the shove hadn't been strong enough to merit a punch in return.

The foreman got up, wiped the blood from his lip, and turned to Fernando.

"You're fired, and I will turn you in to the authorities. The children of reds deserve no compassion. You'll end up in prison like your father, and then they'll shoot the pair of you."

One of the workers held Fernando back as he tried to punch the foreman again.

"Come on, kid, don't make it worse. Get your stuff and get out of here and don't do anything stupid."

That's what he did. He left the building site with no remorse in his heart. The foreman was a nasty piece of work, and would have gotten the punch he deserved sooner or later.

He wandered around the city with no clear goal in mind. His part-time at the print shop didn't earn them enough to live on. For the first time in his life he was not sorry that his mother had gone to work at Don Luis' house. At noon, before he went home, he went up to Eulogio's attic. Piedad opened the door.

"He's still asleep; he got back very tired today. I'll tell him that you stopped by."

When he got home, his mother realized that something had happened, but she didn't ask what.

They ate potatoes with a little bit of paprika, and then shared an apple that Doña Hortensia, the pharmacist's wife, had given Isabel.

His mother waited for the frugal meal to be over before she asked what had happened.

"I punched Pascual and he fired me."

"Why on earth would you punch the foreman? There could be consequences ... What did he do?"

"He pushed me."

"Right, and was that a good reason to punch him?"

"Everyone has his own idea of his dignity, and I'm not going to let people raise their hands to me, foreman or no."

Isabel looked at her son and knew that the fight with the foreman had been the result of something else. Fernando wasn't violent – quite the opposite in fact – so it must have been something more than a push that had provoked such an excessive reaction.

"What else?" his mother asked.

"What else? What do you mean?"

"What else happened?" his mother insisted, a serious expression on her face.

"Nothing."

"You can't fool me, Fernando. I'm upset if you don't trust me, but don't lie to me."

His mother's worried face touched his heart. He didn't have the right to put any more weight on her shoulders.

"I don't want to lie to you, Mother, you're right: today wasn't a good day."

Isabel sat in silence waiting for him to speak.

"Mother, I'm going to say something that has to stay between you and me."

"You think I'm a gossip?"

"No, of course you're not, but it's not about me; it's about someone else."

Fernando swallowed. He trusted his mother, but it was hard for him to tell her about Catalina. Isabel had always been kind to her, but he had the feeling that they weren't really on good terms, probably because it was no secret that Catalina was not in love with him.

"Catalina is pregnant," he said bluntly and looked at his mother, waiting for her reaction.

"Who's the father?" she asked, emotionlessly.

"Do you think it's me?"

"No, I know it isn't you."

His mother's reply upset him. It made him sad that it was so clear to everyone that for Catalina, he had never been more than her childhood playmate.

126

"Marvin," he replied. "The American."

"The American … Yes, it must have been him," she said, without a single sign of surprise.

"You seem so certain: why did it have to be him? It could just as well have been me."

"You? Of course not. She doesn't love you like you want to be loved. Catalina is a good girl, but you know she's got her head in the clouds, and so it's only natural that the American entranced her. She has to be smarter now, and not do things she shouldn't."

"Her father gave her quite the beating."

"Lord preserve us from the fury of peaceful men. And her mother?"

"Her mother is trying to protect her, but she wants her to write to Marvin and tell him what's happened so that he can come back right away from London."

"He won't come back," Isabel said.

"How do you know? I'm sure that he left without knowing that Catalina is pregnant; he's not my friend, but I think he's a good man and he'll do his duty."

"I'm not saying that the American is a bad person, but he's got his own problems. From what you told me, and the very little I've spoken with him, he came back to Spain looking for a way to forgive himself, and I think he left the same way he came. I don't think he can deal with anything that isn't his own pain. But I may be wrong. I hope I am, for Catalina's sake."

"I can't bear seeing her so defenseless."

"You'll have to accept that Catalina isn't for you. She'll never love you like you deserve, like you need. She's fond of you, I'm sure of it, but she doesn't see you as the man you are. Did she ask for your help?"

"I offered to get Marvin's address for her from Eulogio. If she went to ask for it, then she'd have to tell him what she needed it for."

"And what excuse are you going to use with Eulogio?"

"I don't know, maybe that he left some books and papers and if he wants me to send them on to him? I don't know."

"It's a good excuse. Credible."

"Mother, why are you being so harsh?"

"Harsh? No, I'm not being harsh; it's just that Catalina's problem is the consequence of her own stupidity and confusion. I still cry, my son, I still cry for your father in prison, for the uncertainty of not knowing if he'll ever come back to us ... I cry for all those women and children and brothers who wait for the door to be opened, for such a short length of time, so that they can see their families. I cry for what Franco and his crowd are doing to our country. But don't ask me to cry for a girl who has been stupid enough as to let herself be seduced."

"What have you got against her?"

"She's a good girl, but she's selfish and flirtatious. She knows that you love her, and how you love her, and she leads you on just to keep you tied to her; it's very useful for her to know that you are always there for her, unquestioningly, and she doesn't care how much you will suffer just because you love her," Isabel said.

Fernando said nothing. He knew that his mother was right, but even so he was still prepared, with no prospect of any reward, to be Catalina's knight in shining armor.

Eulogio scribbled down the address of Marvin's apartment in Paris.

"But he's not there; I told you that he's gone to London to see his parents who have come to Europe to try to convince him to come back to New York. I don't know where he's staying in London. But if you want to send the books to Paris ... Of course, the most likely thing is that they'll never arrive. And if you leave some books behind when you leave the country, they're not likely to be all that important to you. Although one never knows with Marvin ... He's not all there; he's a poet, unstable."

With the address in his pocket. Fernando sighed with relief that he had managed to complete the mission that he had set himself for Catalina. He had to help her, he said, even if this meant losing her forever. He could not bear to see her suffer, pregnant and cast out by society for her condition.

That afternoon, in the print shop, Don Vicente asked him what was worrying him.

"You look preoccupied; have you had any news about your father?"

"We've got a meeting with the lawyer tomorrow. I hope he gives us some good news."

Then he told Don Vicente that he had been fired from the building site, and why.

"Oh, you're a little firebrand, you are ... hitting the boss ... Well, I'd better be careful not to upset you, or I'll get my block knocked off," Don Vicente said with a smile.

"You're not like Pascual: he's a fascist and a bad man. I'm not going to let anyone get away with insulting my father," Fernando replied.

"But you have to hold yourself back. The right way to solve a problem isn't with your fists. Your father would have said the same thing. And be careful what you say, the walls have ears, even though Don Víctor is a good person; he was on the side that won the war, for all that he respects your father. We published and keep on producing some of the Editorial Clásica books that Don Lorenzo was working on before the war."

"I know that, Don Vicente. My father spoke very highly of you as well, and I'm very glad that Don Víctor gave me a job."

"I've told you before, Don Víctor is a good man, one of those who helps everyone without wondering if they were reds or blues. And stop calling me "Don Vicente": I may be in charge of the print shop, but I'm only a typesetter, and proud of it."

"It's just out of respect ..."

"I know that you respect me; I wouldn't have it any other way. But just call me by my name."

"Yes, Don Vicente."

"What did I just say?" The typesetter chuckled at Fernando's face.

"Yes ... yes ..."

"Look, let's work something out. Why don't you come in the mornings as well and I'll ask Don Víctor to pay you a bit more ..."

"Do you think he'll want to?"

"There's no harm in asking. You know what? Maybe it's good that you left the building site. It wasn't for you, even though nowadays we always have to work at what we can get, not what we want, and we have to be happy about it, because there's no choice."

"Thank you, Don Vicente."

"Really? Really? Vicente, just call me plain Vicente, it's not that hard."

The next day, when Fernando got into the print shop, Vicente told him that he should go to Don Víctor's office.

Fernando felt suddenly nervous. Don Víctor had always been friendly towards him, but he was a man who compelled respect. He knocked at the door and waited to be invited in.

"Come in, son ... Sit down."

"Thank you, Don Víctor."

"So, Vicente has told me that you'd like to work a few more hours at the print shop."

"Yes ... Yes, it would be very useful."

"And what about the building site?"

"Well ... I had a problem with the foreman."

"What kind of problem?" Don Víctor looked closely at him and seemed almost able to read his thoughts.

"I'm not going to lie to you. We had an argument and ... well, I punched him ... I know it's not right, but he was rude about my father."

"Right ... I understand you. I wouldn't have let anyone insult mine either. But don't get into the habit of swinging your fists all over the place. Your father, Fernando, is a true gentleman, an upright and educated man. I've always liked him, in spite of our political differences. A good editor, one of the best. I can still remember our conversations. He liked very much to bring in the texts personally. He would say: 'Víctor, treat this one with kid gloves; it's very special.' He liked poetry and history best."

"Thank you, Don Víctor." Fernando was surprised and relieved at Don Víctor's reaction.

"Don't thank me. This war ... we should have found a way to avoid it."

"You won," Fernando plucked up the courage to say.

"Won? Well, one side beat the other, but what of it? Will we ever learn to look at one another without hatred or anger? Will we be able to grow past the things we've done? I ... Well, I don't like revolutionary leftists, and don't think that they had the solution to Spain's problems in their hands; I think they were making them worse, to be honest. I argued about this with your father. I'm a Catholic and I like order, that's it. But I don't need to give you explanations, do I? Tell me how your father is ..."

"He's suffering, Don Víctor. He's not complaining, but he gets thinner every day. He's in a tiny cell with thirty other men. They're packed in like sardines. The food is nothing more than garbage. But he doesn't give up hope."

"I'll go and see him this week. Is he still at Las Comendadoras?"

"Yes, that's where they're keeping him."

"Well, I'll go and take him a book; I hope they let him read. And ... well, I'm not promising anything, but I'll talk to some friends of mine, to see if there's anything that can be done."

"If you could, I'd be eternally grateful. I still don't understand why they've sentenced him to death. Our only hope is for them to commute the sentence."

"I'll see what I can do. And now go and speak to Vicente: he'll tell you what your new hours should be and what you have to do."

"Thank you, Don Víctor."

"Don't mention it. Really."

When he left the print shop it was after nine o'clock, but it was still light in the streets. He went home, hoping to find Catalina there: she only lived two doors down from him, so there was every chance they might meet each other. But instead he saw Antoñito and Mari, who had just closed up the store for the night. They said hello to one another but did not stop to talk. He also saw Piedad and two local boys he had been in the same class with at school.

He walked up and down the street, and eventually attracting the attention of the doorwoman, who knew him and started chatting with him.

"What's up? You're not going upstairs? Prefer to stay out in the cool?" This was Pepita, the doorwoman for his building, a fat woman in spite of the fact that everyone in the neighborhood was hungry.

"It's too darn hot, and I want to stretch my legs …" he apologized.

"Your mother's home. She got back a while ago."

"All right … Fine … I'll go up now …"

He didn't like having to explain himself to the doorwoman. She wasn't a bad person – he'd known Pepita since he was a child – but she kept a sharp eye on the comings and goings at the building. While Madrid was Republican she had seemed to support the Republic, but when Franco's troops came into the city, she had no trouble adapting to the new situation. If anything, she seemed even more conformist than before.

He decided to go upstairs. Isabel was darning her best blouse, the white one, the one she wore to go to see the lawyer, as they planned to do the next day.

"Hello, Mother."

"Are you feeling better?" she asked worriedly.

"Yes … And I spoke to Don Víctor. Don Vicente recommended that they give me more work to do in the mornings: the salary isn't much better, but it will give me something to do until I find something else."

He also said that Don Víctor had offered to try to do something for their father. Isabel's heart swelled with hope.

"I wish he could do something. I know that his brother-in-law is with the Falange. Your father and he always got on well together in spite of their political differences."

"He doesn't seem to be a bad egg. He gave me work because Don Vicente explained our situation to him."

"Yes, he gave you work because of your father. We have to go to the lawyer tomorrow afternoon," she reminded him.

"I know. I hope he gives us some good news and that we can have father home soon."

The doorbell rang and Fernando went to open the door. It was Eulogio, who wanted to have a smoke with him before going to the warehouse.

Eulogio knew that Fernando couldn't afford to spend a penny on cigarettes, and neither could he, but Don Antonio gave him some on occasion, and when he didn't, then Eulogio helped himself to them as required.

"Smoke?"

"Of course, come in."

They chatted for a while about nothing much. Then Eulogio said goodbye and went off to work.

Meanwhile, the pre-dinner hour at the Vilamar house was far less harmonious.

Don Ernesto had just come home after spending a large part of the day out, and neither Doña Asunción nor his daughter knew where he had been. When they heard his key turn in the lock, Catalina ran to hide in her room, and her mother prepared to face the wrath of her husband.

"Tell the girl to come to my office," he said, without even saying hello to her.

Doña Asunción didn't dare ask her husband anything, and went to find her daughter.

"I'm not going to see him. What if he hits me again?" she asked fearfully.

"You've got to go, or I'll be worse," her mother begged.

The two women went into the office together. He was sitting behind the oak desk that he had inherited from his father, and which his father had inherited from his father, and so on down the generations.

Don Ernesto waved them to the monastic-style chairs in front of the desk. They sat down without protest.

"A friend has told me about a woman who helps get rid of bastard children. She lives in the center of town, in La Corredera. You'll go to see her tomorrow morning. She costs one hundred pesetas. Here they are."

"But Ernesto, it's a mortal sin; you're condemning our daughter to the flames," Doña Asunción moaned.

"I don't care about her soul. She is the one who has endangered it, not me. We have a problem now, and as for the Hereafter, we'll have to face it when it comes. We can't face the shame or the consequences of this pregnancy. Antoñito won't want to marry her, and as for Don Antonio … No, we can't let it happen."

"But Ernesto, you're a Catholic: are you going to confess to Don Bernardo that you made your daughter get an abortion? I would die of shame, and I'd have to confess it too. And as for Catalina, when she dies she'll go straight to Hell."

"Then let her, let her, let her!" Don Ernesto shouted, slamming his fist onto the table. His face reddened and a vein in his forehead started to pulse so alarmingly that he put his hands to his temples.

Doña Asunción fell silent in shock, and Catalina, pale, was hardly able to breathe. When Don Ernesto recovered from the intense burst of pain in his forehead, he looked at them with such hatred that he scared them all the more.

"If you are ashamed to confess to Don Bernardo, then find yourself another priest, and if Catalina goes to Hell, as she very well might, then that's where she has to be to atone for all that she has done. I will not allow her to ruin this family. We survived the war in this city surrounded by Reds, terrified that every day those scum from the Popular Front would come and dig us out of our house to shoot us. We can't let this slut destroy us now."

"But, Ernesto ..."

"Silence! You have to obey me. You will go with her to this woman's house tomorrow, and when you return, we'll be able to put all this behind us."

"But what about the danger? There are lots of girls who die when they do this ..."

"I'd rather she was dead than dishonored," Don Ernesto spat.

"Good God, the things you say!"

"Don't argue with me anymore, Asunción, or it'll end badly."

His wife lowered her head, and the tears that she had held back until that moment started to flow. Catalina squeezed her hand to thank her for her defense. She swallowed, then spoke.

"I'm not going to go to Hell, not for you and not for anyone. I have committed a mortal sin, that's true, but the Lord can forgive me; what no one can forgive is murder. You can hit me as much as you want, Father, but I will not go to that woman's house, and I will have this child, and if the Lord wills it I will marry Marvin. By tomorrow at the latest I will have his address and I will write to him; I am sure that he will write back, because he loves me as much as I love him. This is what I will do, and if you prefer me not to be seen while all this is happening, then I will leave the house." She said all this in a single breath, with no pauses, controlling the fear that fluttered in her stomach.

Her father stood up, and before she could realize what was happening, he slapped her so hard that she fell to the ground. Doña Asunción bent over to protect her daughter with her own body, and so she was given another blow intended for Catalina.

"Whore! You're a whore! And still you dare tell me that you're going to disobey me! If I need to I will beat you to death, but this bastard will never be born! I swear it on my life!"

Catalina did not cry this time. She swallowed her tears and stood, with her mother's help. Once upright, she went over to her father and stared at him with the same hate that she saw in his eyes. She held back her own desires, to slap him, kick him, spit in his face. She stood very still, ready to take as many blows as he was going to give her.

But her mother stood between the two of them, and pulled her to the door before Don Ernesto could do anything else.

"Go to your room, and I'll be along in a moment. I have to speak to your father."

When they were alone in the room, Don Ernesto sat back down behind his desk, and she sat down in one of the chairs.

"Ernesto, you can't carry on hitting her. She's our daughter, our only daughter, blood of our blood, for all that she has made a mistake now. She's not the first woman to make a mistake, and she won't be the last," she said, as she felt the burning pain of the blow that her husband had given her as she protected her daughter with her own body.

"Mistake?" her husband shouted. "You call getting knocked up a mistake?"

"I know that Catalina has done a bad thing, but we can't add sin onto sin. I will not let you condemn her to Hell."

"What? You won't let me? How dare you!" Don Ernesto stood up, his eyes bloodshot.

Doña Asunción looked at her husband, worried that he was going to hit her. This man, so taciturn and frail, so modest, had turned into a different person, one it was hard for her to recognize.

"We went to see my sister Petra this afternoon. We told her what's happened, and she's given us a solution," she replied to her husband in a trembling voice.

"How dare you air our dirty laundry with your sister? Now the whole world will hear about it!" he shouted.

"You know that Petra is discreet, but she's also my sister and she loves Catalina like a daughter, her only niece. From the outside she saw things much more clearly," Doña Asunción said apologetically.

"And what has your clever sister told you?" Don Ernesto asked scornfully.

"When Catalina starts to show, she should go to Petra's house, if the American hasn't shown up by then. If Marvin turns up in time, then they can get married, quietly, and that's that; she won't be the first or last woman to get married when she's pregnant. But if he doesn't come, then … well, Catalina will spend her pregnancy there, and when she's had the child, then … well, it will be hard, but Petra will take it to the orphanage. And so Catalina will be able to come back to her life as though nothing has happened. All you have to do is delay the wedding to Antoñito. Tell Don Antonio that we're taking her out of town for a while because she's sick, or because my sister is sick and she needs to be looked after. Whatever seems best to you. If Marvin comes, we end the engagement, and if he does not, then all we need to do is wait."

"And … Well, who'll help deliver the child? I don't think that you or Petra are likely to be good midwives."

"I'll go to see Don Juan: he may know someone who can help us when the time comes; he's our doctor and has known Catalina since she was a child. It was he who realized she was pregnant."

Don Ernesto thought for a while. He had never paid his wife too much attention; he didn't think she was all that bright, but she and her sister Petra might have hit on something this time. He definitely felt uneasy committing a crime against this infant who was yet to be born. He was a good Catholic and knew that God would keep score. But they needed to make time somehow. The problem was convincing Don Antonio. He was a brute, accustomed to everyone doing what he wanted, especially when people owed him money: Don Ernesto owed him more than he could ever pay back.

His wife waited, expectantly, praying silently that her husband would agree to the plan.

"How many months along is she?" he asked, quietly.

"Almost three …"

"So she'll start to show pretty soon."

"Yes, one more month."

"It's now August, so the bastard will be along around February."

"Yes."

"Don Antonio won't want to wait so long …"

"We'll make excuses. Catalina can write to Antoñito while she waits, string him along."

"All right. Let's do it. But while she's with us, I don't want her leaving the house except to go to Mass. And the same when she's with your sister Petra."

"Don't worry; we want to leave some gifts with the baby at the orphanage, so we'll have a lot of sewing to do."

"Has Catalina agreed?"

"To begin with, no, she cried and resisted, but my sister convinced her that it was the best thing to do. And it's a solution in case the American doesn't turn up, even though we hope he will."

Her husband sat in silence for a while, tapping his fingers rhythmically on the surface of the table. Doña Asunción prayed once again, this time for her husband not to change his mind.

Don Ernesto, although he was a stubborn man, was also a good Catholic, and Petra's solution was starting to seem better than his own.

"How could she have done this to us?" he asked his wife, calm now.

"She's a silly girl. She doesn't remember what happened. It was Antoñito's birthday. And you agreed that she could go with him and the other kids from the neighborhood to La Pradera. I remember that I thought it was a bad idea." Doña Asunción justified her own position.

"And how was I going to refuse? Don Antonio insisted that Catalina go to his son's party."

"Some party! People celebrate their birthdays at home, not out in a park with a few bottles of wine. But of course, you can't expect anything from those people," Doña Asunción said cuttingly.

"People go to the Pradera de San Isidro to spend Sunday afternoons with their families. I don't think there was anything wrong with letting the girl go."

"Ernesto, you know that Catalina is very innocent and isn't used to drinking. Apparently Antoñito insisted that she drink straight out of the wineskin. Just think! I mean, children from other neighborhoods might do that, but she …"

"Don Antonio gave me his word that Antoñito would look after her," Don Ernesto said.

"Well, he didn't."

"At the very least, if she was going to sin, she could have sinned with Antoñito," Don Ernesto muttered.

"God forgive you! How can you say such a thing?"

"I don't know if the Lord will forgive me, but I do know that Don Antonio won't forgive me a single peseta of what I've borrowed from him."

"Oh, we have sunk so low," Doña Asunción said, and couldn't help giving him a disappointed glance.

The next day, Fernando and his mother arrived at the office of Alberto García, the lawyer, half an hour before their appointment. He was not a bad man, although they suspected that he took advantage of the desperation of the people whose family members were in prison. There were so many prisoners that he could make a good living from it. More often than not he didn't manage to achieve anything, but the families paid, pawning and selling everything they owned.

This time he gave them the same excuses as always. Lorenzo Garzo's case was being processed; they had to wait and be patient. Oh, but they did need to bring in a letter from the local priest to say that Don Lorenzo had always been a good Catholic.

Fernando lowered his head and his mother spoke.

"My husband has always been a good man, beloved and respected by the people who knew him. An upright man. Nothing more than an editor. Is that a crime?" Isabel insisted.

"I'm sure it's not, madam, but you don't need to convince me. You still need to include a letter from the priest in your husband's file."

Isabel knew that the battle was as good as lost. Don Bernardo would refuse to give them a letter guaranteeing that Don Lorenzo was a good Catholic. He only knew Lorenzo from walking past him in the street, and Fernando's father had never set foot in a church. The priest suspected that Lorenzo was a Freemason, and had said as much more than once to Isabel, who herself was definitely a good Catholic.

"If Don Bernardo doesn't give us the letter, what will happen?" Fernando asked.

"Well, things might get difficult. We need someone from the Falange, as well as a priest, to write in support of your father."

"And what do the Falange and the Church know about my father? Who are they to certify anyone's goodness?"

"Jesus, Fernando, don't get your back up; Don Alberto's only trying to help us." Isabel held her son's hand worriedly, fearing the consequences of his outburst.

"Look, kid, there are a lot of traitors in Spain, and it's only logical that Franco doesn't trust them, and so we have to prove that your father isn't one of the people who are poisoning the country. It's a question of sorting the wheat from the chaff."

"So anyone who's not a Falangist, or who doesn't go to church, is worthless?" Fernando said aggressively.

The lawyer looked him up and down, bored, before replying:

"Well, if you ask me straight out, then the answer, these days at least, is yes."

"You're wrong," Fernando said, looking him straight in the eyes.

"Look at the big man! I'd be careful what you say, there are people out there who might get the wrong idea. Look, I'm an honest man and I'm just stating the facts: if you get these two letters than you'll probably save your father, and if you don't, then ... Lord only knows."

They paid him the twenty-five pesetas that each visit cost them. It wasn't right, and it made them save their last pennies and end up hungrier than they needed to be.

They left, almost despairing. Isabel had tears in her eyes, and Fernando's face was clenched in anger.

"What are we going to do?" Isabel asked her son.

"I'll go and see Don Bernardo, given that he doesn't pay you any attention. What a terrible priest; it's a shame that no one got rid of him in the war."

"What are you saying? Don Bernardo has helped us; it's thanks to him that I've got a job in Don Luis and Doña Hortensia's house. He recommended me and we need the few pesetas I earn."

"Yes, he helps you, but you're nearly a saint. He wants my father to be shot simply because he didn't go to church and everyone knew he was a Republican. Say what you want, but he's a scoundrel."

"Fernando, I forbid you from going to see Don Bernardo. I'll go, I'll get down on my knees, I'll beg. He'll listen to me this time. I'll do all the penance he tells me to."

"Like you always do, though I don't know why. You spend days praying the rosary: I suppose it's the penance the priest gives you for having married someone who was a Republican."

"Oh, be quiet, son, you say such silly things ... We'd better hurry to be at the prison in time to see your father. Where's the package?"

Isabel had wrapped a few crackers, a couple of apples and a piece of potato omelet in a napkin. She hoped that they wouldn't confiscate it at the prison gates. She was particularly worried about the potato omelet: she had tried to make it since she knew her husband liked it.

Lorenzo Garzo walked with short steps, as though in spite of his extreme thinness his feet were still too heavy for him. Fernando saw that without his glasses his father looked vague, almost absent.

The three of them started to speak all at once, wanting to know how things were going.

"Okay, let's take turns, or else we'll never understand each other," Don Lorenzo said, raising his hand to silence his family.

"We've just come from the lawyer: he doesn't promise anything, but he's not saying it's impossible either."

"That's a good sign, Fernando," Don Lorenzo replied, trying to cheer up his son.

"You'll see, they'll let you out soon ... You didn't do anything," Isabel said, with more conviction than she actually felt.

"Of course, of course ... Don't worry, it'll all turn out fine in the end. And now tell me what you're doing and what's going on in the world."

They said nothing of how hungry they were; it would have been cruel, when he was all skin and bones himself. Fernando told him how he had been fired from the building site, and how with Don Vicente's help, Don Víctor had taken him on to work in the mornings as well.

"Don Víctor is an upright man, one of the good ones, and as for Vicente ... Learn from him, Fernando, he can teach you a lot. Typesetting is an honorable trade, better than many. And I'm afraid that our dream of your becoming an editor like me ..."

"Don't say that, Lorenzo, Fernando will be an editor: why on earth wouldn't they let him study?" Isabel said, although she knew that they didn't have enough money even to try such a thing.

"Well, we shall see. The important thing is that Fernando is a good person. Things should have worked out differently, but there's not much we can do about it at the moment, so we should be realists. That doesn't mean give up, my son, but think about things realistically."

"I'm not going to give up, and we still have your books. I'll be able to prepare myself for anything and everything."

"Look after my books, Fernando, they are my greatest treasure, apart from you two."

"You can trust me."

"Of course I trust you. Of course."

Isabel insisted that he try to eat a bit of the potato omelet; she wanted to see her husband enjoying the food himself. Lorenzo obeyed his wife, but even though he was starving, he couldn't eat it.

"You don't like it?" his wife asked, disappointed.

"Of course I like it! But my stomach is somehow blocked … It's been hurting a lot recently."

"You have to see a doctor," his wife said, as though this were even a possibility.

"When I get out of here, don't you worry."

But they were worried. Don Lorenzo seemed to be getting worse by the day.

"I have to do something," Fernando murmured.

"What are you going to do? The only thing left for us is to get Don Bernardo to give us the letter the lawyer's asking for. I'll go to his house right away. And as for a certificate of good conduct from the Falange … I don't know, maybe Don Antonio …"

"The black marketeer? We've never dealt with him. He won't give it to us."

"Well, but you know Antoñito, you went to school with him, you could talk to him. And he seems like a good kid: he invited you to the Pradera de San Isidro for his birthday, remember?"

"And I went because you made me."

"We can't do anything to upset them, Fernando, we owe them so much at the moment …"

"And we're paying them well."

"Look, now's not the time to be proud; we need to do whatever it takes to get your father out of prison. If you don't want to talk to Antoñito, then I'll talk to Don Antonio."

"Don't even think about it! I don't want you on your knees to that fascist."

"Fascist or not, he can give us the letter that the lawyer's asking for. And if I have to go down on my knees to him, then I will. Don't you think that your father's life is worth more than that?"

"Your dignity is worth more," Fernando replied.

"I'm not going to abandon your father. Maybe you could speak to Eulogio: he might be able to help us."

"How?"

"Doesn't he work for Don Antonio? He could be the go-between … Don't be so proud, child, we can't afford it."

His mother was right: he'd talk to Eulogio. His friend always gave him good advice, and he knew the score with Don Antonio. He was also very aware of the contempt in which Eulogio held his boss, from whom he openly stole goods, without any remorse.

He went up to his friend's attic, but Eulogio had already left to go to the warehouse, so he decided to go and see him there after dinner.

When he arrived, he had to wait for Eulogio to finish stacking some sacks of potatoes that had come in that afternoon, as well as a few boxes of cheap wine and more sacks of rice and lentils.

Eulogio paid Fernando no attention until he had finished stacking the sacks. When the last box of wine was in place, he waved him to sit down on a sack of lentils.

"Shall I roll a cigarette? I haven't stopped working since I got here. You see these boxes? Don Antonio told me to stack them so that tomorrow he can fill them with something, I don't know what, that he's going to take over to the barracks where his brother Prudencio works. It's got to be a bribe. We sent a box with a few bottles of wine across there a few days ago."

"He's a generous man, your boss," Fernando replied.

"Generous? Don't think so. Whenever he gives something, it's because he hopes to get much more in return."

"I need you to do me a favor," Fernando said impatiently.

"Of course, what do you need?"

"I need your boss to sign a letter stating that my father is a good man. The lawyer's told us that there's nothing to be done without a letter from the Falange and one from a priest."

Eulogio sat in silence for a moment. Fernando wasn't asking him for a favor; he was asking him for a miracle. Don Antonio hated the reds, and he thought that Fernando's father was one of them. And Don Lorenzo had never spoken to the black marketeer; he was one of the people in the neighborhood who even he found it difficult to greet when they met in the street.

"Impossible," he said to his friend.

"Will you ask him?" Fernando's voice was shaking.

"Yes, I'll ask him, but I don't think he'll want to write the letter. You must know that Don Antonio never liked your father. I've heard him speak out against him lots of times. He said that they'll knock some of the namby-pamby intellectualism out of him in prison. He's a brute, Fernando, and you know that very well."

"Yes, I know," Fernando agreed heavily.

"And Don Bernardo, will he write the letter?"

"I don't know: my mother's going to talk to him. We got home late, so she'll have to go tomorrow. I hope that he'll feel a little bit of compassion, being a priest and all."

"Don Bernardo? I don't want to upset you, but I have my doubts. He lost two brothers in the war, and the militia came to his village and shot all the fascists … It's difficult for him to forgive," Eulogio said.

"But he's a priest," Fernando insisted.

"I'll never forgive the people who killed my father, even if it was in the war. All Fascists are the same to me, so I can understand the Fascists when they say that all reds are the same. We never forgive blood crimes; even a priest wouldn't." Eulogio knew that his words would hurt Fernando, but he didn't want to give him false hope.

"I have to try," Fernando said in despair.

"I'll help you as much as I can. I'll ask him tomorrow. Now take a sack and put some potatoes in it. There are tomatoes as well, and a couple of onions, and put some lentils and chickpeas in too."

"Don Antonio will know they're gone."

Eulogio shrugged. He was prepared to get a dressing-down from the black marketeer if it meant helping his friend. He put a bit of bacon in the sack as well.

"But he'll know it's missing!" Fernando protested.

"No, not him. This isn't very much, after all; I pocket something myself every day."

"Your mother doesn't care?" Fernando asked, intrigued as to how Piedad might react.

"I don't think so. She wouldn't be able to steal herself, but she doesn't say anything to me and I don't think we should feel guilty about stealing from people who have ruined our lives. I lost my father and yours is in prison. We don't owe them anything, Fernando."

"We owe them our shame, Eulogio. We owe them that."

As he walked home, Fernando was thinking about how to get Marvin's address to Catalina. He hadn't been able to see her that day or the day before, but he couldn't wait any longer, given the seriousness of the situation. He had no choice than to ask his mother for help. He couldn't go to the Vilamars' house because Don Ernesto would throw him out on his ear, but his mother could go over with some excuse quite easily.

When he asked her, Isabel looked worriedly at her son.

"So you want me to go to the Vilamars' house and slip this paper to Catalina, and if she's not there, then to her mother."

"Yes, that's what I'm asking."

"And what's written on this paper?" Isabel asked severely.

"An address, the American's address."

"Right. And what is my excuse for going to their house?"

"Say you need to speak to Doña Asunción … something like that …"

"I'll go tomorrow when I get off work; I could do it first thing, but Don Ernesto would be surprised if I turned up at his house at eight in the morning asking for his wife."

"Thank you, Mother."

"You're a good boy."

"Me? Why?"

"Because you're helping the girl you're in love with marry someone else."

"Mother!"

"Fernando, you've never managed to fool me. You're head over heels for Catalina, and have been since you were both children. I know that you've been very upset, deeply hurt to know that she's in love with another man."

Fernando lowered his head in shame. His mother was right. His soul hurt him, at least the part of his soul that lay closest to his heart, pressing down on him so hard that the pain was almost unbearable. This was his soul, the part of him that roamed his dreams at night and made sleep unbearable, impossible.

"Everyone falls in love with the one they want, and there has never been anything between me and Catalina, nor any hint that anything might happen," he said, his heart breaking.

"She's a flirt, and you've been too silly to see it, but she's always leading you on. I'm not saying that she does it maliciously, but she's like all flirts, and likes to have a group of admirers around her to pay court."

"Don't talk about her like that," he said, upset by his mother's accuracy.

"I'll do what you ask of me, Fernando, but not for her. I'll do it for you."

"Doesn't the situation affect you?" he asked, surprised by her harsh words.

"I don't wish her any harm," she replied.

"Catalina is a good person and deserves the best," he said.

Isabel shrugged and paused for a few seconds before answering her son. She didn't want to make him any sadder than he was already.

"I've known her since she was a child and have nothing against her. I just don't like to see you suffering for her. You think she's worth more than she's actually worth, that's all."

Fernando preferred not to say anything. The important thing was that the note with Marvin's address would get to the Vilamars' house and into the hands of Catalina or her mother.

"And where did you get all this from?" Isabel asked nervously, pointing at the sack with the tomatoes peeping from its top.

"Eulogio gave it to me. Six potatoes, three tomatoes, two onions and a head of garlic, a fistful of lentils, a fistful of chickpeas and, best of all, a piece of bacon." Fernando smiled slightly.

"Good heavens! If Don Antonio finds out … I don't know if we should accept them …" Isabel wondered.

"Of course we should. Eulogio says that the fascists have ruined our life and he's right. Don Antonio is a fascist, and one of the worst of them, a black marketeer."

"Yes, but we're not like him, and I don't think it's right for Eulogio to take things that don't belong to him, even if it is food …"

"Mother, Don Antonio isn't going to notice that he's missing a few potatoes, and we are very hungry."

"But it's not ours," Isabel insisted.

"It is now. Don Antonio takes advantage of everyone and sells his products at prices we can't afford, even though he knows that here in the neighborhood, like in the rest of Spain, everyone's very hungry. Look, think of it as a present from Eulogio, and there's an end to it. You make very good potatoes fried in bacon fat. Come on …"

146

Fernando took the sack into the little kitchen and emptied it. Isabel seemed to hesitate, and then accepted.

"He's given you a good load of bacon, we'll have food for two or three days. But the best thing now is to make a salad: the tomatoes are very ripe and won't last another day."

Isabel would have liked to be firm in her refusal of Eulogio's gift, but she felt hungry from dusk till dawn with no respite, while that fascist Don Antonio got rich at the expense of other people's hunger. She still didn't like it that poverty and hunger could steal even a grain of her dignity. She knew that her husband would not have accepted those tomatoes or those potatoes, or even the garlic. She hesitated again, but Fernando brought her back to reality:

"Come on, Mother, stop thinking so much: we're both hungry."

Isabel started to wash and cut the tomatoes. At least they would not go to bed hungry that night.

The next day, when she got out of work, Isabel went to the Vilamars' house to carry out her son's request. She felt uncomfortable going at this time, around two in the afternoon, when she might very well barge in on the family sitting down to eat.

Catalina herself opened the door to her and asked her in.

"No ... I'm not going to stay; I just wanted to find out how your mother is ... I haven't seen her at church for days now ... but it might be because we go to different services," she said, excusing her visit as she secretly slid the piece of paper that Fernando had given her into Catalina's hand.

Catalina clenched her fist tight and smiled, sure that the paper contained Marvin's address, the address she had begged Fernando to find for her.

"Doña Isabel, please come in ... I'll tell my mother ..."

"No, I don't have time ... Tell her that I stopped by ..."

"My father isn't home, although we're expecting him for lunch," Catalina said, encouraging Isabel to step in.

Doña Asunción came out into the hall to see who was talking to her daughter, and she too insisted that Isabel come in.

"Just for a second … How's your husband's case coming along?"

"The lawyer is noncommittal; he says we need to get some letters of recommendation. But it's not easy to get them, although Don Bernardo might be able to give us some help."

"Is there anything we can do?" Catalina asked, anxious to help.

"I don't know," Isabel replied uneasily.

Doña Asunción looked worriedly at her daughter. She didn't think that her husband was in the best of moods for someone to come and ask him to intercede in the Lorenzo Garzo case. Even so, as she was a kind woman, she offered to try.

"Look, Isabel, Ernesto is about to get back; if you'd like, why not stay and explain the situation to him and see if he'll help?"

But Isabel decided not to try her luck, and to avoid a face-to-face meeting with Ernesto Vilamar. She wasn't afraid of him, but she'd never felt all that comfortable around him. She was sure that he'd find her presence in his house, at this hour, confusing.

As soon as Isabel left, Catalina ran to her room and unrolled the paper. Fernando had carefully written down the address she longed for: Marvin Brian; Apt. 3; 25, rue de la Boucherie; Paris (V).

And a note: "Marvin is in London and I'm not sure he'll go to Paris."

Catalina went to find her mother, who was mashing potatoes.

"I've got it! Fernando got it for me!" she said enthusiastically.

"What are you talking about, dear?" her mother said distractedly.

"Marvin's address. I'll write to him at once to tell him that … well, I'm sure it'll be a surprise for him, but he's a gentleman and I don't think he'll let me go through this alone. And he's in love with me, of course."

Doña Asunción looked at her daughter with a degree of anxiety. The number of alleged gentlemen who had abandoned girls after having their way with them was not a small one. She didn't know Marvin, and didn't know if he was in love with her daughter, for all her daughter's own insistence.

"Yes, write to him, but don't get your hopes up too much …

He might not want to hear about the whole thing, or the letter might not even get to him. The Germans are in Paris, and he might want to steer clear of France, because of those liberal ideas of his you were telling me about ..."

Catalina didn't want to imagine that this might happen. She had become convinced that after Marvin met with his parents in London, he would return to Paris. It was the city he loved and he had promised her that he would show it to her, all of it.

When Don Ernesto got home, he found his daughter in a good mood, less listless than on previous days, although she still avoided him. He greeted her with a nod and did not try to kiss her, although he usually would have. She had not forgiven him for beating her, but he was sure that the anger would pass with time. Which father would not have done the same, if his daughter had told him that she had dishonored herself?

He told them over lunch that he would take the train that afternoon. He needed to talk with his brother.

When he came back two days later, Doña Asunción found her husband in a very grim mood. He had been depressed every time he came back from Huesca recently. She tried to cheer him up.

"How was Andrés?" she asked worriedly.

"You know how things are ... My brother's life has been destroyed."

"And Amparo?" she asked, although she already knew the answer.

"She's still not all there."

"Maybe with time ..." she said, unconvinced.

"You know that's not going to happen. She's completely crazy and has good reason to be. Imagine if such a thing had happened to us ... Those bastards turned up at the farm and weren't happy with just burning everything, they ordered everyone to come out into the courtyard. My brother asked them at least to treat the three farmhands well, but those bastards just laughed at him and said that they worked for landowners, so they were as guilty as the rest. And then, as well as insulting them and beating up my brother ... they took ..."

"No! I know what happened. Don't tell me again! Don't keep on reminding me of it! What's done is done, and we can't change it."

"How can you say that?" her husband said.

"The war brought out the worst in people and they committed many atrocities," she said.

"They killed my father and Andresito! My brother's only son. When a militia man pushed his mother and he tried to help her the bastard shot him right between the eyes. He didn't even have a chance to defend himself," Don Ernesto continued, bringing to mind memories that broke his heart.

"Good God, Ernesto, don't talk about it anymore!" Doña Asunción took her husband's hands and held them between her own.

"They laughed about it … then they pretended they were going to shoot them all … and that's when Amparo lost her mind. And you want me to forget it all? Never! I'll never forgive them. I hope that one of our side sent them to Hell."

It wasn't the first time that Don Ernesto had recalled what had happened on his family farm. But he seemed very affected, and told the story as though for the first time.

"We have to forgive them, Ernesto … It isn't Christian to feel hate."

"Let the priests say what they like! I'm not going to forgive the people who killed my father and my only nephew, and who ruined my brother's life!"

"But Ernesto, we were at war … there were bad people on both sides … We have to forget about it."

"You can forget if you want. All I want is for them to shoot all the reds they've got locked up in their prisons."

"But they weren't all murderers … there are people who were on the other side but who didn't hurt anyone. What about Lorenzo Garzo? He was a good man," she said, plucking up her courage.

"A Freemason! That's what he was. You're silly, Asunción, and think that everything can be fixed by praying. Don't you care that they killed my father and my nephew, that they killed your sister's husband? I don't think Petra would like to hear you talking like this."

"Petra's husband was killed at the front and ... well, I'm sure he killed other people as well. Let God forgive them all."

"Right, let God forgive them, because I'm not going to forgive anyone. Have you forgotten how frightened we were all through the war? I was scared every day that they were going to take us to one of their police headquarters. Or is it that you don't want to remember how one of my brothers never came out of the police station on Calle Fomento?"

"But God protected us," Doña Asunción said stubbornly.

"And why did he protect us? Look, let's not keep on talking, or it'll only be worse."

"But we have to forgive each other, because the anger will poison our blood otherwise."

"Asunción, I don't know if you're stupid or what, but I won't let you say that we all need to forgive one another. I am not going to forgive the murderers of my father or of Andresito, or the people who assaulted my brother and his wife."

"You know that I am very fond of your brother and his wife and that I am always praying for the souls of your father and of Andresito ... and of your other brothers who died at the front."

"Well, keep on praying," he said, grumpily.

"Isabel came by earlier. She's worried about her husband ... You know that Lorenzo Garzo is a good man and a good editor ... You praised his editions of the classics."

"People seem to be one thing and then are something else. Lorenzo Garzo is a Republican, a Socialist and a Freemason."

"Well, a Republican and a Socialist, perhaps, but a Freemason ... we don't know that ... Let's not let ourselves be swayed by rumor. Isabel told us that they're working on getting her husband a pardon and that the lawyer said that it would help to have some letters of recommendation to say that he is a good man. I thought you could write one ..."

"Don't be ridiculous! What are you saying! I'm not going to ask for clemency for a red. How can you ask me that, knowing what they did to my family?"

Doña Asunción was scared to see her husband so agitated. She was worried that he might have a fit, and she blamed herself for pressing him to intercede for Isabel's husband when he had just got back from visiting his brother Andrés. She tried to calm him down by changing the subject:

"I was speaking to Catalina ..."

"Don't talk to me now about that hussy: her job now is to have the brat as soon as possible and then marry Antoñito. Don Antonio sent me a note to tell me that he wants to make the engagement official this Christmas. His wife wants them to get married in the spring."

"They can't have an engagement party this Christmas! Catalina will be seven months gone by then."

"She'll have to have it earlier. I've told you, the engagement will be announced at Christmas."

That afternoon, while Don Ernesto was locked up in his office going over papers covered with sums, and Catalina was sitting by the balcony letting out one of her dresses, Doña Asunción went to visit Don Juan.

This was not just because he was the family doctor, but because she trusted his good judgment.

Don Juan had spent the morning in the hospital dealing with all kinds of patients; in the afternoons, he opened his house to friends and acquaintances who were looking for medical help.

He was not expecting Doña Asunción, and was surprised when his elderly housekeeper announced her arrival.

"Well, well, well, Asunción ... What a surprise! I didn't expect to see you again so soon. Is Catalina well? And Ernesto? Don't tell me it's you who's feeling under the weather ..."

"I'm as healthy as I can be, given the circumstances. I've come to ask for your help and advice."

"Well, sit down and I'll get the maid to bring in some coffee."

She looked at him in thanks and couldn't help letting out a light sigh of relief. Given that they had known each other since childhood, it wasn't strange that the two families saw each other every now and then. She had even been a little sweet on him, but had never dared to confess it, not even to her mother. And so when her parents had told her that they were arranging a marriage between Ernesto, the Vilamars' boy, and herself, she had not been brave enough to refuse.

Ernesto had started to visit the house on a daily basis while members of the two families sewed the wedding gown.

She could still remember the day when her parents and the Vilamars had organized a meal to announce to their closest friends that their children were going to get married. Juan congratulated her, without even suspecting that she was secretly in love with him.

Juan Segovia had married a very beautiful woman, Pilar, who he had always loved very much.

"You look thoughtful," he said when he came back into the little room that served as his doctor's office. "And, now that I get a good look at you, what's that bruise on your left cheek? Let me take a look ..."

"No, it's nothing, Juan ... he hit me ... it's been a difficult few days ... Ernesto ... well, you can imagine that it's been hard for him to find out that Catalina was pregnant."

"And he ... Good Lord! He hit you?"

"No, of course not ... but he tried to slap Catalina and I got between them ..."

"Ernesto is my patient and your husband, but even so ... Oh, I won't say anything I might regret."

"My sister Petra has had an idea about how she can help Catalina."

"What is it?"

"She should have the child and then hand it over to an orphanage. It's for the best. Ernesto wanted ... he wanted her to have an abortion."

"But he's crazy! How could he think of anything like that? Catalina hasn't behaved perfectly, but sending her to get an abortion ... it's not just that it violates God's law, but where would she even get one? From some woman in an attic? Do you know how many women die trying to get an abortion?"

"That's why Petra thinks the best solution is to take the child to an orphanage."

"But what about the young man who put Catalina in this way?"

"Well, he's an American who has left Spain. He used to live in Paris and now ... well, we don't really know where he is: he went to meet his parents in London, and then ... I don't know, Juan,

I don't know if he's going to go back to the States with his parents, or if he'll go back to Paris or somewhere else. But Catalina has written him a letter and when I leave here I'll take it to the post office. I'll send it to the Paris address, but heaven knows if it will get to him."

"And what do you want me to do?"

The maid came in with a tray and two cups of coffee, and the two of them sat in silence until she left.

"To get back to what I was saying, I want you to look after Catalina until the day of the birth. I want you to visit her at my sister's house, for her to be your patient as she has been all this time, and for you to recommend us a midwife or some woman who knows how to bring a child into the world. And ... well, you know a lot of people: maybe there's a couple that can't have children who would like to adopt the baby ... That would be the best. I think it would be better for Catalina to know that the child is in good hands."

The doctor said nothing for a few seconds. He couldn't refuse Asunción anything. He would help her, of course he would help her.

"I'm your family doctor, and so Catalina will carry on as my patient. I'll go to visit her at Petra's house. I'll look after her pregnancy and bring in a good midwife for when the moment comes. But tell me, does Catalina want to hand her child over to an orphanage?"

"No, Catalina doesn't, but Ernesto is inflexible. The war ... We've lost a lot, Juan, and things aren't like they were before. I know that Ernesto would be angry if he found out I'd told you, but ... we've got problems ..."

"And who doesn't have problems, after going through a war? We've all got problems, Asunción."

"Things aren't going well for Ernesto ... Money troubles ... He had promises to keep. The shopkeeper, Don Antonio Sánchez, who's making a mint on the black market ... he loaned us some cash ..."

"Since when have shopkeepers done that?"

"Well, Don Antonio is an important man now. He was in the war and he's got some friends in very high places, and Ernesto had to go to him to sort out some problems, and the solution ended up being worse than the problem. But he has a son, Antoñito, and Ernesto and Don Antonio want the boy to marry Catalina. But of course, he won't marry her if he finds out that she's expecting another man's child."

"And does she want to marry him?"

"She doesn't like it, but she'll have to go along with it. It's a law of this life that one has to obey one's parents. You know that."

"Did you obey yours, or did you marry Ernesto because you were in love?"

Asunción blushed. The question caught her off guard, with no time for her to prepare to defend herself as she should.

"You're blushing." Don Juan's eyes twinkled.

"Well … I did what my parents thought was best for me."

"And what would you have liked to do?"

"Juan, don't ask me such things! I've been married for a long time now. I was seventeen when I got engaged, and eighteen when I was married off …"

The doctor came over to her and took her by the hand, bringing the blush back to Asunción's cheeks.

"I remember, I remember … I came to your wedding with my parents. You were very beautiful. But you could have waited," he insisted.

"Why do you say that? I … I didn't make any decisions … Waiting … What was there to wait for?"

"To find a man you fell in love with. I married Pilar because I loved her and she loved me, but I have to admit that my parents weren't very happy with the match. They had another girl in mind for me. But I couldn't have been happy with anyone but Pilar."

"But you were able to influence your parents, which I never could. And so you had an advantage that I didn't," Asunción dared to say.

"Haven't you been happy?"

"I'm probably too romantic, that's what Ernesto always says. I have been a good wife, and I am a good wife, and I have grown used to the marriage, to not wanting anything apart from what I've got."

"That's not quite the same as being happy," he said.

"It was enough for me, and it is still enough. My father was sick and was worried about what might become of me when he wasn't there. He wanted to see me married and looked after."

"Well, you are lucky to still have Ernesto. I've had two years, two interminable years, where I've not been able to think of anything other than the loss of Pilar and my daughter. I lost them both. The hardest part was not being able to do anything to prevent it. You can't imagine how frustrating it is for a doctor not to be able to do anything to save the lives of the people he loves. Oh, the damn war!"

"Damn tuberculosis."

"The war, Asunción, the war: I was at the front and they were here, suffering all kinds of deprivations, just like everyone else. They got sick, and when I came back on leave the disease had advanced so far that it was impossible to do anything. Little Pilarín died first, and you can't imagine what it was like for Pilar and me to have to bury our daughter. Pilar gave up, and followed after her."

"Well, let's be thankful that it is all over. Things aren't easy, but Ernesto says that Franco will know what to do."

"But what does that fool know about anything?"

"Juan, how dare you! You fought with the Nationalists," Asunción said.

"Shush, Isabel! Your husband is how he is … I'm not surprised that he would have started supporting Franco after being a monarchist, but you …"

"I'm pleased that Franco won the war. What did you want, a revolution? No, Juan, I was scared of the idea of people rioting in the streets … communists, anarchists, the followers of Largo Caballero … all of them full of hate and ready to fight against anyone who didn't think like them."

"Things aren't that simple, Asunción. People were sick, sick of corruption, sick of politicians who couldn't deal with the country's problems, sick that a few people had everything while the rest of us had barely enough to eat."

"But you're not a revolutionary … You fought against them …"

"No, Asunción, I'm not a revolutionary, and I don't like revolutionaries, much less the chaos that they spread throughout any country they touch. I'm speaking about the people, the good people who scrape by day after day just as they always do."

"You sound like you support the reds!" Asunción was scandalized.

"What I'm saying is that things don't just happen. If Spain had been a prosperous country with politicians who were capable of giving the people enough to eat, then no one would have even wanted a revolution."

"If you didn't agree with the Nationalists, then why did you fight with them?"

"I've told you that I didn't like the Popular Front, but the war caught me in the middle of a Nationalist zone. I was serving as a military doctor when it all started, don't you remember? And my regiment was one of the ones that joined the coup. And I thought, just like you, that the revolutionaries didn't look like they had the solution for Spain. But I would have wanted to remain loyal to the Republic. You know how much I supported Azaña."

"Ernesto says that Azaña has to take a lot of the blame for what happened."

"Your husband's a ... well, no, it's his opinion. I'm not going to argue with Ernesto via you; we argue enough whenever he comes in to see me himself."

"And so you don't like Franco?"

"I don't like anyone, Asunción, I don't like anyone, and Franco least of all. But I also know that the solution for Spain isn't to have a revolution or turn ourselves into Russia. If they'd just let Azaña do his job ... The only thing that's left to us now is to wait and see what happens, but I don't like that there are so many people still in prison, or being shot, and that people are worried about being turned in if they speak a word against Franco. I'm a man of order, an upper-class man, and if the revolutionaries had won they might have killed me, just for that, for being one of the bourgeoisie, as they used to say before the war. Do you know what I was most scared of during my years at the front?"

"No."

"I was scared that I might come face-to-face with my brother. He was with the Republicans, and I was with the Nationalists, and I didn't know where he was. I asked myself what would happen if we met on the field of battle. Would we have killed each other? Would I have fired first or would he? That's the nightmare I had throughout the whole war."

"I'm sorry they killed José Mari."

"Yes, they got him at the Battle of the Ebro, and I grieved for him as my parents grieved for him, and as other brothers and other parents grieved for the men who killed my brother. There is nothing to be proud of in a war, nothing. Nothing at all."

"The reds killed Ernesto's brothers and attacked the convent of his sister the nun ..." Asunción said.

"Yes, and what do you think the Nationalists did when they got to a village? They rounded up the reds and killed them and threw them into a ditch. War is an atrocity that brings out the worst in all men, for all that it hides behind the idea that it is justice to kill one's enemies, which is only a smokescreen to keep you from despair when you see your hands covered with blood, the blood of other men."

"But now it's all over; we've won the war. You too, Juan."

"Me? No, I haven't won any war; no one's won the war; we all lost. How much time will have to pass before we forgive one another? It won't be easy, Asunción. Don't be naive and think that we're at peace now. No one gets out of a civil war unscathed. No one trusts anyone anymore: the man you meet in the street, red or nationalist, might be the person who shot your son, or your brother, or your father. I'm a doctor, but I've fired a gun as well. I've killed. Maybe I killed the husband of one of the women who comes into the surgery to see me. It's only wicked people who can feel happy after a war is over. There's nothing to be proud of, nothing."

"Would you rather the other side had won?" Asunción asked the question, but was afraid of what the answer might be.

"I would rather no one lit the fuse that led us to kill each other. That's what I would have wanted. But I'm a contradictory man, a selfish man, and I also want to be sure that Spain won't become the next Russia. I don't believe in revolution, if that's what's worrying you. Let's stop talking about this. You've got enough problems without me worrying you with politics."

"You know you can talk to me."

"I've been a widower for two years, I feel lonely and don't have anyone. My parents are dead, my brother is dead, my wife is dead and my daughter too. I've got nothing to be happy about. But let's get back to Catalina's problem: you don't need to worry; although there are too many orphans here at the moment, I'll ask around and find out if there is a good family that can take care of her child."

"Thank you, Juan."

Asunción was flustered when she left Juan Segovia's office. The conversation had upset her.

She wander aimlessly for a while; she had no desire to go home, even though she knew that Ernesto might get annoyed if she were late. But she needed to be alone for a while, to put herself back together inside, and return to her role as the subservient wife when she crossed over the threshold of her home.

When she at last came home, her husband was still in his office doing the accounts and Catalina was in her room letting out another dress for later on in the pregnancy.

"Will I get very fat? I don't have a dress with enough spare fabric to let out."

"That's not your problem now; also, when you're in Petra's house you should try to avoid going out so that no one can see you, so it doesn't really matter what your clothes are like. I went to see Don Juan and he's promised that he's going to find a family to take care of the child you're going to bring into the world."

"But I don't want to give my baby away!"

"I know, and it will be hard for you, but there's no other way out of it. You can't bring up a child by yourself. It'll be a scarlet letter, and no one will want to marry you."

"But Marvin will come. Did you take the letter to the post office?"

"Of course I did, but we need to think about what will happen if he doesn't get it, or even if he doesn't want to have anything more to do with you."

"Don't say that! I told you, Marvin loves me."

"Child, men are men, and they run away from women who cause them problems. There are a lot of men who will seduce a woman and then leave her without thinking about the consequences."

"Mother!"

"My child, pray that Marvin will come back, but if he doesn't, then you'll have to give the child away and marry Antoñito."

"I'll never marry him! I hate him; he always smells of sweat, and his breath … No, no, I'll never marry him."

"You'll have to do it, Catalina. You're not a child anymore and … well, there are things you need to know even though your father and I don't want to trouble you with our problems."

"What problems, Mother?" Catalina asked worriedly.

"The war's over and we've been left with almost nothing; we're ruined, and it's only thanks to Don Antonio that we're surviving … He loaned money to your father, but things aren't going well and there's no way to pay him back."

"And that means I've got to marry his son? My father's put me up for sale?"

"What are you saying?" You father thinks that Antoñito is a good match, and that he's got enough money to give you a good life and make sure you never want for anything."

"I'd sooner starve than marry him."

"Catalina, children have to obey their parents, who always know what's best for them."

"And isn't this what's best for my father? That Don Antonio forgives his debts?"

"How dare you say such impertinent things! We owe Don Antonio a great deal, and if it weren't for him then we wouldn't even be able to put food on the table, so it is only right to be grateful. Let's not talk about this anymore. I'm going to make supper, and so you should come to the kitchen and help me. You see what it means to be ruined: we've had to get rid of the maid."

5

Isabel rang the bell at the sacristy door. The evening Mass had just finished, so she was sure that she'd find Don Bernardo.

There had not been that many people in the church, but the priest made sure to carry on the custom of giving seven o'clock Mass every day. He asked her to come in.

"Come in!"

"Good afternoon, Don Bernardo ..."

"Come in, Isabel. What are you doing here at this hour?"

"I'd like to talk to you."

"You could have come at five, to pray the rosary."

"I couldn't make it then, although I wanted to, Father. Doña Hortensia and Don Luis sometimes have guests over on Saturdays and she asked me to stay behind and give her a hand."

"The Ramírezes are good people, the best," Don Bernardo said.

"Yes, of course. I'm very grateful to you."

"I know it can't be easy for you ... Not all that long ago you had servants of your own, and now ..."

"I don't mind working, I promise," Isabel said sincerely.

"Well, what's troubling you?" he asked her kindly.

"It's like this. The lawyer who's dealing with my husband's case insists that we need as many recommendations as possible to make sure that the pardon comes through. And ... well, I was hoping you could give me a letter to say that Lorenzo has always been a good person, trustworthy ..."

"Right ... but I know him so little, he never came through here," the priest said regretfully.

"Well, he had his own ideas; he wasn't very religious ..." Isabel said.

"No, he wouldn't be, as a Freemason," Don Bernardo said, looking her straight in the eyes.

"Goodness, Don Bernardo, don't pay any attention to rumors!"

"I don't, my dear, I don't, but there are times when the rumble is such ..."

"I ... I'd like you to give me a letter of recommendation, and if you could, ask other people to do the same thing."

"Which other people, Isabel? You must have a list already."

"If it's not too much trouble, could you ask Don Antonio for one? He and his brother are influential people in the new regime ... And the Gómezes as well: Don Pedro works for Revenue and is well connected."

"And why can't you ask them?" Don Bernardo asked.

"Well ... the truth is we never got on all that well with the Gómezes or Don Antonio. I don't know if they'd give me the letter if I asked for it ... But you ... they won't say no to you."

"What you're asking me for won't be easy," the priest said.

"I know, Don Bernardo, but if you could ..."

"I won't promise anything, but I'll see what I can do."

Isabel left the sacristy with a bittersweet feeling in her heart. She could certainly hope that Don Bernardo would ask Don Antonio to write the letter, but she had no guarantee that the black marketeer would say yes. And she didn't really think that Don Pedro Gómez would want to help either. Whenever they met in the entrance to their building, he would turn his head without even looking at her.

When Isabel left, Don Bernardo walked out of the sacristy and took a stroll while he smoked a cigarette. He couldn't refuse to help Isabel: she was a good woman who had never failed in her duties to the church, despite the fact that her husband was a Freemason. He had no doubt that Lorenzo Garzo, as well as being a Socialist, was a Freemason. And it turned his stomach to think of doing something for a Freemason, but he couldn't not help Isabel: it would be a betrayal of his conscience.

He decided not to think any more on the subject, and went to the warehouse where he hoped that Antonio Sánchez would not have yet gone home.

He was lucky. He found him in his tiny office going through some account books.

"Don Bernardo, upon my word! Good to see you here. What is it that you want?" the shopkeeper said, pulling his mouth into a smile and looking suspiciously at the priest.

"Who says I want anything?" the priest said grumpily.

"Because you wouldn't be here at this time of the day otherwise: it's nearly nine o'clock and that's no time for a priest to be out in the streets." The shopkeeper liked to tease the priest.

"Well, you're so sharp that there's no point wasting any time. I've come to get you to write a letter on behalf of Lorenzo Garzo. A letter that will help him get a pardon."

"That's a good one! Why should I write a letter for Garzo? He's never been my friend. And from what I hear, he's an inveterate Freemason. I'm not going to put myself at risk by sticking my neck out for a Freemason, and you shouldn't do so either," he said, and looked expectantly at Don Bernardo.

"Antonio, before you judge anyone, take a look at yourself, because you're not exactly a saint yourself. When was the last time you went to confession? Or Mass? I haven't seen hide nor hair of you for months. So don't judge others, because, as the Gospel has it, let he who is without sin cast the first stone," the priest said, annoyed at the shopkeeper's attitude.

"All right, all right, I give in. So I don't go to Mass? Right, but I'm a good man, a man who fought on God's side in the war, the winning side."

"Don't bring God into this," Don Bernardo said uncomfortably.

"What, now you're telling me that God wasn't on Franco's side? What kind of a priest are you?"

"The kind of priest who looks after his parishioners. Let's leave God in peace, because this is something that has nothing to do with Him. It's about lending a hand to a neighbor, writing a letter that says nothing more than that Lorenzo Garzo is a good man."

"You're asking me to lie? I can't say something I don't know to be true. Garzo raised his hat to me when we passed in the street. We aren't friends, and have never been friends."

Don Bernardo was in despair: the shopkeeper was digging in his heels.

"I'm only asking for a letter that won't commit you to anything. Antonio, think about your attitude: I don't like it. The war's over, and it's tough enough for these poor people who lost."

"Poor people? I can see you weren't at the front. Sons of bitches!"

"Antonio, watch your tongue!"

"I'm sorry, Don Bernardo, but I get so angry when I think about the damage those scum did to Spain. Can you really forget about all those priests who were taken out and shot? And the convents they burned?"

"I'm not saying it's easy to forget," Don Bernardo admitted, "but Isabel is a good woman and she's afraid of losing her husband. My duty is to offer comfort to those who suffer." As he spoke, he grew ever less confident about his mission to the shopkeeper's office.

"Well, Father, I can't refuse you anything. I'll talk to my brother and see what can be done," Don Antonio said, his mind made up not to do anything.

It was enough for Don Bernardo to leave his house with a clear conscience. He wasn't convinced that Don Antonio would do anything for Lorenzo Garzo, but at least he had done all that he could.

And as for Don Pedro Gómez, he'd speak to him when he next came to confession.

6

The London hotels were completely full.
There was not a single free table in the
hotel restaurant. In spite of the fact that the room was crammed
to bursting, conversation was barely audible. People spoke in
scarcely more than a whisper. Even so, they had asked the *maître
d'* to sit them at a corner table so that they could speak freely.
Marvin looked around nervously. His mother wouldn't stop
talking; she talked so much that he had stopped listening a while
back. He had no interest in the things she said. News from her
friends in New York; the holiday they had spent at one of the
beaches near Boston; the invitations they had to accept when
they got back to America; the investments that the steelworks
was making.

His father was silent, bored at his wife's constant chatter.
Marvin waited for him to cut the monologue short.

"Honey, don't you think that Marvin should tell us what he's
been doing all this time? We haven't seen each other for ages."

"You're right ... not since he was wounded in Spain. How
awful! I still remember how upsetting it was ... at least we could
bring you to New York ... But then, as soon as you were better,
off you went to Paris again. Son ... I. ... I don't want to think
about what happened to you in Spain. You could have been
killed, and in the end, what does this war matter to you? Although your best poems are the ones you wrote about the war,
I have to give you that."

"Yes, Monsieur Rosent says that my best work comes from
those days."

"Yes, yes … your editor … It was lucky that this French editor included you in the anthology of young poets that, as you know, I gave to all our friends. We're very proud of you, Marvin, you know that. But tell me, why haven't you published any more poems?"

"I've lost my inspiration, Mom. That's why I went back to Spain."

"Just for that, son?"

Rose Brian looked at her son and he was unable to hold her gaze. She knew him too well for him to be able to deceive her. His mother was intelligent, very intelligent, and although he tried not to speak about what had happened in the Spanish war, she knew that even if the wounds of his body had been healed, the wounds of his soul were still open.

"And so, you've not written any more poems?" his father asked, more out of affection than interest.

"Barely a few lines worthy of the name, Dad."

"That tends to happen when a person has been traumatized. You shouldn't worry about it. One day you'll see the poems begin to flow again. Don't chase after it, let it come to you," his mother said firmly.

"We'd like you to come back to New York. I need you there, son. I've got new projects on the table," his father interrupted, in an attempt to bring the conversation around to more practical matters.

"You know I'm no fan of business; that's what Tommy's for."

"Your brother is very young; he's still in college."

"But he's working with you already."

"I wouldn't go that far: let's say he's feeling out how the company works."

"Dad, I'm not planning on going back to New York, at least not now."

"But, son …"

"Leave him, Paul. Marvin has the right to choose his own path. He's not like you or Tommy."

"And what are we like?" Paul Brian said, looking angrily at his wife.

"Magnificent, simply magnificent … but you're made from

different stuff than Marvin. You have to get it into your head that Marvin isn't interested in either steel or business."

"And what's he going to live on?" Paul asked angrily.

"As long as I've got what I've got, a good chunk of shares in the steelworks, and a satisfactory investment portfolio, he doesn't have to worry about anything besides writing. We're very lucky to have a poet for a son," Rose replied.

"Don't you think he should earn a living for himself?"

"You don't understand anything, Paul, because you don't read anything, much less poetry. Each one of us is born with different talents, and we should thank God that we have two children with such different skills. Tommy's going to be a good businessman, and Marvin will be a great poet. We should accept them as they are."

"I can't stand these arguments," Marvin said. "If we're going to carry on like this, then I'm leaving."

"Wow. As soon as we speak about something that you don't like or that isn't quite right for you, you run off," his father said scornfully.

"No, I just don't want you and Mom fighting over me. You're right, of course, I should earn a living without expecting you to maintain me. It's not fair that Tommy should be studying and working and that I …"

"… and that you should be an extraordinary poet," Rose said.

"I've only published a couple of poems …"

"But the critics loved them, in the States and in France. Look, son, God's given you a gift, the gift of making words into poetry and touching people's hearts. Don't waste it. It'd be a sin."

Marvin took his mother's hand and held it between his own. He knew that her love was unconditional, the solid and unmovable rock on which he could always rest for a while and feel safe.

"Thank you, Mom."

"Don't thank me, son. But I'd like you to come to New York for a while, or at least not let so much time pass between visits. I miss you, and it's not easy to come over to Europe, what with all that's happening."

"Yes, no one knows what's going to happen with this war in Europe," Paul Brian said, trying to lessen the tension between him and his son, and keen to take the conversation in a new direction.

"There's only one decent choice, to fight against Hitler. I can only hope that our country will join in as well," Marvin interrupted.

"You a communist?" his father asked in alarm.

Marvin shrugged. He knew what he was not, but not so much what he was.

"Oh Paul! You do say such silly things! Of course Marvin's not a communist, but no man in his right mind would support that man Adolf Hitler. Churchill's done what he had to do. The first thing to do is to defeat Germany, and for that you need the help of the Soviets. Then, when Germany's no longer a danger, Churchill and Stalin can go back to being enemies."

"That's one heck of a lesson in political strategy," Paul said admiringly, enjoying his wife's perspicacity.

"I'm only saying what's plain to see, darling."

"Marvin still hasn't answered my question," Paul Brian insisted.

"I don't know what to say … If you ask me what I think of the working conditions for men in Europe and in the States, then I'll tell you something you know very well, that things aren't easy for people, that most of them are exploited, that they pay for every cent they earn by working ever harder, that a few people get rich thanks to their poorly-paid workers, and I don't think it's fair that they have no rights and live in poverty and filth. Communists claim back dignity for workers, and if you ask me if I'm on board with that, then I'll tell you openly that I am. But I also know what they're like; I met a few of them in Spain and I've not seen this 'new man' they keep on talking about. But that's just because human nature is what it is: I've seen some of these 'new men' behaving just as horribly as the people they were fighting against. You know what, Dad? I think the important thing isn't what you say, but how you behave. And so I don't care what label you want to stick on me, but I do care a great deal how my friends see me."

They were quiet for a while after this, and it was Rose who then took her son's hand again and squeezed it while she looked at him proudly.

"We do the best for all our workers," his father said.

"It's not just about you being a good boss; it's about them having rights that go beyond their relationship to their boss, good or bad. That's the issue," Marvin replied.

"Well, their unions keep an eye on what happens in the factories."

"I know, Dad, I know, but sometimes it's not enough."

"Our son's not a communist, Paul, it's just that he can't bear to see injustice in the world."

That night Marvin turned all of this over in his mind. He knew that he was a privileged man. Someone who could fantasize about the future without worrying about how much money he had in his wallet. His mother looked after him. But what would he really be like if he had to work in a factory from morning to night? Would he sympathize with his comrades, or would he struggle against them in order to earn an extra penny? Would he stand up to his superiors, or would he keep his head down, not rock the boat, try to gain their trust? Would he curse his situation or put up with it? What would he be capable of doing in order to keep his head above water? No, he didn't know what kind of a man he was. The only thing he knew with certainty was that he could not bear the wounds, both physical and mental, that he had received in the Spanish war.

He had decided not to go back to New York with his parents. He knew that this would upset his mother, who wanted to have him close for a while, but he felt unable to even imagine sinking himself into the kind of life that being in New York would bring to him. He did not know what kind of a man he was, but if there were any way of finding it out, then it would be here, in this Europe that was now bleeding from the effects of a war that, if Germany won, would change the face of the world.

When he told them he was intending to return to France, his father frowned and tears came to his mother's eyes, but neither of them tried to dissuade him. It wouldn't have been worth their time.

"But the Germans are in Paris," his mother reminded him.

"I'm from the US; the Germans haven't got anything against us," he said in order to dispel the anxiety that he saw in his mother's face.

"Roosevelt's not going to be able to keep looking the other way; this isn't simply a war between Europeans, it's a question of values. You yourself said that you hoped America would go to war against Germany," his father said.

"There was more at stake in the Spanish war than the problems of Spaniards," Marvin replied.

"My boy, you've got to forget about Spain, about everything that happened to you there," his mother begged.

"You know that's impossible. I can't, Mom, you know I can't."

"So when are you planning on leaving?" his father asked.

"I'll stay with you here for a few days in London, then I'll go to Switzerland and from there to Paris."

"We could come with you," Rose suggested.

"I don't mind. You can stay in my house: I've got a spare room. It's not that big, but you'll be comfortable enough."

"Good idea," Paul said.

Paris seemed to pay no attention to the Germans who were there pretending to be its masters. The city had decided to carry on living.

Paul and Rose Brian moved into Marvin's apartment on the rue de la Boucherie. It wasn't very large, with only three bedrooms, a kitchen, a salon and a bathroom, but it was bright and seemed very bohemian in a way that struck them as being peculiar to Paris, and just as Rose had expected.

The doorman had kept all of Marvin's correspondence, and when he handed it over Marvin was surprised to see a letter with Spanish stamps on it.

He had left Madrid more than a month ago, and in all that time he hadn't stopped thinking about how absurd his last period in Spain had been. Eulogio had been very generous, offering him a place to sleep, and Piedad had done all she could to make him comfortable in the musty attic, with no space at all for anyone to have even a moment of privacy.

Once he had gotten his parents settled into their room, he shut himself away in another one to read the letter. He hadn't seen whose address was on it, and was surprised to see Catalina Vilamar's name on the envelope.

My dear Marvin:

I know that it is very daring of me to address you in this way, but as you will see, I think the circumstances allow it.

I hope that the news I have to give you will, after the initial surprise, make you happy.

I'm pregnant. I'm three months gone. I got pregnant in May, on Antoñito's birthday, at the Pradera de San Isidro. Do you remember what happened? I am sure that it was then, because I haven't been with anyone on any other occasions, and so it can only have been at that time. I know that you remember and that's why I'm writing to you, because I think you ought to know. You behaved so kindly to me that night! I lost my head because I'm not used to drinking, but I think you know that I'm not "easy."

You can imagine how my parents reacted. I can't blame them.

You say that you would be happy for me to come to Paris: I don't want to force you into anything, but can I come? Maybe you could send a letter to my parents to tell them that you're expecting me, or else you could come and find me if that were easier. My situation is very difficult: I can't have a child as a single woman. My parents have decided that when the child is born they'll hand it over to another family, or to an orphanage. If I had to do that my heart would break. But I trust you; I know I can trust you; I know you wouldn't abandon me to my fate, because you are good and honorable.

I'm sorry to be a burden, but if I can't turn to you, then who can I turn to?

I await your reply: please, don't take too long!

Yours, with all my love,

CATALINA VILAMAR

He read the letter twice. He felt sympathy towards Catalina Vilamar, but not so much that he felt any responsibility towards her. The last thing he needed was to take someone else's problems on his shoulders; he had enough with his own. He knew that this might look like selfishness, but he was in no position to face up to Catalina's problem: she had behaved in a very foolish way that evening at the Pradera de San Isidro. Let her suffer the consequences of her actions.

Eulogio had warned him that Catalina had fallen in love with him, which meant that Fernando had stopped coming by. According to Eulogio, Fernando was in love with Catalina.

He thought that all of this was unimportant and didn't concern him. He'd write to her to tell her that for the time being he couldn't have her in Paris, but maybe later on. Or, even better, he'd just ignore the letter, as though he'd never received it. When all was said and done, he had no special bond with Catalina, and felt no obligations towards her.

He ripped up the letter. That was that.

He did, however, think of writing to Eulogio. He felt that he was the most loyal of his friends. He had been loyal to him on that fateful day when they were surrounded by the Nationalists. Perhaps he would never return to Spain, but even so, he wanted to keep his friendship with Eulogio alive. He thought of buying something to send to him, maybe some proper cigars. He'd buy something for Piedad as well. Eulogio's mother had looked after him as though he were her own son. Stockings, yes, he'd buy her some stockings and maybe a scarf or a blouse. He was sure she'd like them.

That afternoon, while his parents were out visiting some friends, he went to see his editor on the rue des Rosiers, in the fourth *arrondissement*, in Le Marais.

Monsieur Rosent had the blinds down in his little bookshop, at the back of which was his office. He published only books of poems that moved him, and his younger authors came to him because they had not been able to find any other editor willing to pay the costs of editing their work. His altruistic attitude had led him to publish a few books that had been successful, and these poets had remained loyal to him, even rejecting the invitations of other, more prestigious publishing houses. This loyalty made it possible for Rosent's list to include some of the best poets of the period.

Marvin knocked at the door and waited impatiently until he heard Monsieur Rosent's unsteady footsteps.

"*Entrez, entrez.* I'm happy to see you again."

"Are you well, Monsieur Rosent? I'm surprised to see your blinds down at this hour …"

"I'm trying not to attract anyone's attention, but it's useless really: the Germans have this part of the city, where there are so many of us Jews, under special observation. Captain Dannecker has become our worst enemy."

"Dannecker? Who's that?"

"He's an SS captain, and his job is to deal with the 'Jewish problem' that some newspapers are talking about. You've come here at a bad moment, Marvin: lots of Jews are being deported. Who knows when it will be my turn?"

"But that's absurd, you're French!"

"Yes, I'm French, a French Jew, which is all that matters to them. Some Jews left Paris when the Germans invaded, but after the armistice a lot of them were too trusting and returned to their old homes. It was a bad decision, given what's happening now. They've taken a lot of Jews to the camps in Pithiviers and Beaune-la-Rolande."

"And you, why haven't you left? You should get out of here as soon as possible; if you need help, you know you can count on me."

"*Merci, mon vieux.* I hadn't planned on going until now; I thought I was too old to run away, but now I know that Theodor Dannecker's troops could turn up any day and then …"

"They'll take you God knows where."

"Yes, that's right. But sit down. I've got some tea you're sure to like. I'll just put the kettle on."

They spoke all afternoon. First about what was happening in Paris, and then about poetry. Marvin handed him an envelope with a few poems in it, which Monsieur Rosent read attentively.

"Is that all you've written since going back to Spain?" he said when he had finished, looking him right in the eyes.

"I can't write, I don't know how to write, the words have stopped coming and I don't know how to find them."

"These poems … they're not as good as the ones you wrote before. You know that, *n'est-ce pas?*"

"Yes … I know … I told you already, I don't know how to write."

"You have to take hold of your pain, all your feelings, your ideas, and put them into words without allowing the pain to destroy your capacity to express yourself."

"Maybe I'll never again write poems like the ones you put in your two anthologies of young poets."

"Oh, so there's that as well! It happens. Lots of authors are afraid that they'll never again match the level of what they wrote before, the work that was praised by critics and readers. I didn't think it would happen to you. If you start to worry about what other people think you'll always end up failing. You have to be true to yourself, to what you feel and what you want to say. If other people like it, then good, but if they don't, then you don't need to worry. Don't let the vanity of success gnaw away at you, because then you'll fail at the most important thing: letting your words flow and finding their true meaning in relation to each other."

"You know what happened to me in Spain …"

"Yes, and don't think I don't understand your suffering, but this pain should make you a better poet rather than paralyzing you out of fear of failure."

"I'm not the same as I was."

"You can't be, but you have to live with the wounds you brought home from the war, wounds on your body and your soul. We don't have power over the past, Marvin, and there's no way back after things have happened."

"Do you know how many of my dreams I've had to set aside? I'll never be able to have a life like other people."

"And why does your life have to be like that of other people? Stop feeling sorry for yourself, stop regretting things that aren't in your power to change. You love poetry and it can be the best companion to you in your life, and it can give back to the rest of us these words that fly over your soul, leaving their warm breath behind."

"And so …"

"Keep on writing, and keep these poems."

"I will."

"All I hope is that you come back here with some poems before they come for me. I'd be very happy to publish a collection of your work, although I don't know if I'll have time, at least not in Paris. I have a daughter, Sara, you know her. She got married a little while before the war began and then left with her husband to Alexandria, in Egypt. He's an editor as well. They have a bookshop and a publishing house in the center of London, and a branch in Alexandria. He is Jewish: his father's British and his mother's a Jew, born in Alexandria to a Greek family. Sara wants me to go and live with them and carry on publishing books."

"And will you?" Marvin asked, worried about what might happen to his editor.

"I don't know. I have friends who say I should leave right away. They've even arranged tickets for me, but I'm still refusing to go. What can I do in Alexandria?"

"They say it's a beautiful city," Marvin said.

"Yes, Sara tells me that the light there is unique."

"If you go … maybe I could come with you."

"Why?" Rosent asked, intrigued by the suggestion.

"I may need to get out of Europe, get away from what's happening here. The war is spreading like an oil spill."

"Egypt is under British control, but they say that King Farouk sympathizes with Hitler," Rosent whispered.

"Even so, I think I'll go. I've never been to the Orient."

"Marvin, the world is at war, and war's going to come to Egypt as well."

"I can come with you. If you decide to go then I shall."

When the meeting with his editor was over, Marvin went out to eat with his parents; he couldn't refuse to go, and he didn't want to disappoint them, especially so as not to add to his mother's anxiety. And so they had dinner at Maxim's, despite the disgust they felt at sitting surrounded by German officers, with women who they flaunted as though they were trophies.

"Look at them … So arrogant," his father whispered.

"They're the masters of Paris, and they're not leaving any room for doubt," his mother replied.

"But those girls …" Marvin's father seemed upset.

"Come on, Paul, don't be such a prude. You'd need to be really brave to stand up to the invading army," his wife replied.

When they got back to the apartment, Marvin went to his room, keen to sit down and write. The conversation he'd had with Monsieur Rosent made him to want to lose himself once again in the magic of words transforming into poetry.

He wrote all night. He tore up a lot of pages, and others he put into a folder, keen to go back to Rosent's bookshop and get the approval of his editor.

In spite of the Germans, in the late summer of 1941, Paris was still the most beautiful city in the world.

His parents' presence didn't upset him, but he felt a certain degree of relief when they left. His mother kept complaining about the ominous presence of the Nazis. As for his father, he grew ever more certain that it would be impossible for the United States to remain neutral, especially given the fact that the Germans had invaded the Soviet Union on June 22.

Marvin wrapped himself up in his new poems. He wrote, tore up what he had written, started again, and again, and when he was finally happy with what he had written he read it out loud to convince himself of its quality.

He forgot about Monsieur Rosent, and even forgot that Paris was an occupied city. But reality caught up with him abruptly the night that his editor turned up at his apartment without warning.

"I'm sorry to come like this, but I couldn't wait."

Marvin asked him to come in, worried by how pale and nervous the old man looked.

"Sit down, I'll get you something to drink …"

"We don't have much time. I need you to do me a favor. Buy my bookshop, and become the owner of my publishing house. No, I'm not asking you to do this because I need money, but to save the building, this house that has always stood for poetry."

"I … Well, I don't know … I don't understand."

"You know that they're confiscating the property of Jews. I received a notice. I won't let my books end up in the hands of the Nazis. My lawyer Monsieur Dufort prepared this document for you to take to the notary: the bookshop will be yours, as well as all the books and manuscripts in it. You are an American; they can't take it from you. It's symbolic, the amount of money; you don't even need to pay me. All I ask is that you keep hold of my little world in case one day … Maybe one day this war will end and Sara and her husband will come back. She's my only daughter and she loves poetry as much as I do … You are an honorable man and I know that I can put everything I own into your hands. Save the shop, please, Marvin, I beg you."

He didn't even read the document; he signed it straight away. Monsieur Rosent gave a sigh of relief.

"Now all you need to do is make your ownership of the business worthwhile," he said, and held out a hand.

"What about you?"

"Some friends are going to hide me. They're going to take me to Vichy and then to Nice, if that's still possible. But you have to go to the shop and collect all the manuscripts that are ready to be published. Publish them, and if you can't, then take them to Sara, and she and her husband will do it. They're poems that deserve to see the light of day."

"I'll go to Nice with you … You can carry on editing books there," Marvin replied, overwhelmed by the situation.

"I'm not the best traveling companion … a Jew … no, save the poems, save the books, save the shop … That's all I ask. I've put Sara's address on this paper. I'll never publish another book. How much time do you think it'll take the Nazis to deal with the rest of France? The free zone isn't really free. Pétain is Hitler's puppet, for all that so many Frenchmen would pretend not to know it. And as for this city, my dear city … you can see for yourself, there are so many Parisians who prefer to pretend that they are still free, and who drink and laugh as though the Nazis were nothing more than props in the background. It's very depressing."

"Let me help you …"

"You're already helping me."

"I need to pay you for the bookshop. I'll go to the bank to-morrow."

"I've put a sum in the contract, but I don't want you to give me even a single franc. I'm not selling it to you: I'm leaving it to you in trust until Sara can come home."

"But …"

"I know you're doing me a great favor, and I don't have the right to ask it of you, but I trust you: you're my last hope."

Monsieur Rosent gave him a hug and then left. It took Marvin some time to react. He didn't know what to feel or to think or to do, and so all that was left was for him to cry.

When he had stopped crying, he sat down to write a letter. He needed to share with someone his anguish and his possible fate, and so he wrote to Eulogio. Destiny had bound him together forever with his Spanish friend. They had been together on the same front, and each of them knew the scars carved in the other's soul.

7

Madrid

Fernando waited impatiently until the eight o'clock Mass was over. It was Sunday, and Catalina had gone out early in the morning to go to Mass at San Ginés. There wasn't a large congregation at this hour. Her pregnancy wasn't visible – she was still thin – but her parents wanted to avoid the possibility that any particularly attentive eyes might spy out the truth.

He hadn't seen her for days. They didn't let her leave the house, and even though waiting for her as she came out of church brought with it the risk of meeting Don Ernesto, as it was Sunday, he knew that he wouldn't have many other chances.

She trusted him, and in spite of how much it hurt him to know that she was pregnant by another man, he loved her too much to leave her to her fate.

When he saw mother and daughter come out of church, he went straight over to them. "How are you? Have you had any news from Marvin?" he asked, without giving Doña Asunción time to react to the sight of his unexpected presence.

"It's only been a week since I wrote to him. But I know that as soon as he reads the letter he'll come for me," Catalina said with a smile, not seeing how deeply her words wounded Fernando.

"When are you going to your aunt's house?"

"I can still stay here for a few more days, but when I go remember that you've promised to come and see me …"

"I will."

"What are you saying?" Catalina's mother protested.

"Fernando is like a brother to me, and if it weren't for him then I could never have got Marvin's address. I've already told you that I tell Fernando everything and he knows what the situation is."

"Lord, if your father ever finds out …" Doña Asunción said in a fright.

"Mama, Fernando knows that I'm pregnant with Marvin's child: how could I hide it from him? I trust him, and know he'd never do anything to hurt me."

"Please don't worry, Doña Asunción: you know how fond I am of Catalina, and I wouldn't do anything at all that might hurt her. If I'm here, it's because I haven't seen her in days and I'm worried about her."

"They don't let me leave the house. My father's worried that someone will find out that I'm … well, that I'm pregnant."

"Could I speak to Catalina alone for a moment?" Fernando asked Doña Asunción.

"No, of course not. She has to come back home with me; if she doesn't, then her father will be angry with both of us, as we won't be able to tell him where we've been."

"Of course. In that case, let's do this: go back into the church and sit down and I'll come in behind you and sit in the pew behind you, and then Catalina and I will be able to talk quietly."

"I don't know … there are people who might see you in the church …"

"What are they going to see?"

"Yes, it's the best solution: we'll talk in the church," Catalina said, and walked back inside without waiting for her mother.

Doña Asunción followed her, protesting, and Fernando brought up the rear.

Sitting on a pew in the last rows of the church, far from the altar, leaving Doña Asunción praying with her rosary, Catalina and Fernando looked at one another and tried to hold back their laughter.

"How are you feeling?" he asked.

"Terrible: I spend all day throwing up and my face is green."

"You're as beautiful as you always are," he flattered her.

"Right. What can I do about it? I've told you that I'll still be at home for a few days unless my father decides to send me away sooner. But you know the address: come and see me as soon as you can."

"Do you think Petra will allow it?"

"What choice does she have? Fernando, I don't want anyone to find out the state I'm in, and I'm going to go to my aunt's house because of that, but I don't have any secrets from you and I told my aunt as much when I went to see her a few days ago."

"And what did she say?"

"She said I shouldn't have told you, that the fewer people that know about this the better, that you shouldn't come to see me because if my father found out it would be the worse for me, and he might put me in a convent … In short, everything I expected her to say."

"And so? How am I going to come to see you? They won't let me in."

"You just come."

"Don't be a child, Catalina, things don't work like that."

"You're going to leave me by myself? I can't bear it. I think I'll run away."

"Don't say that!"

"In that case, promise you'll come to see me."

"I promise."

"Thank you, Fernando, and now tell me about your father."

"We've got another meeting set up with the lawyer. I don't know what to think; I don't want to lose hope, especially because of my mother. You don't know how much she's suffering. They're shooting so many people …"

"They can't shoot your father! He hasn't done anything!"

"And you think that'll stop them? No, Catalina, Franco and his kind shoot people for revenge. It's not enough that they won the war: they want us all to know that they're made of iron, that there'll be no mercy for the people who stood up to them. This is how they can make sure that the people won't stand up to him, won't do anything against him."

"You have to wait for the pardon; I'm sure it'll be granted."

"I don't know … I'm not sure."

"Come to see me, Fernando: I won't be able to bear being alone."

"I promised, and I'll come."

Catalina took his hand and squeezed it, and he trembled.

After speaking to Fernando, Catalina was worried. It hurt her to see her friend suffer because of his father's fate. If there was only something she could do …

Fernando left the church before the two women. Catalina and her mother stayed a little longer.

Doña Asunción was worried by her daughter's silence and asked her what Fernando had said to leave her so upset.

"He's afraid for his father: he's spent too much time waiting for the pardon to come through … If it doesn't come through, I don't know what will become of Fernando," Catalina said.

"We'll pray for them," Doña Asunción said, sweetly convinced that prayer could bring about miracles.

"Mother, isn't there something we can do? Do you think that Father …? Well, he knows lots of people … Maybe he can do something for Fernando's father."

"I don't want to think how your father would react if you dared ask him … He's so angry with you …" her mother said.

"But what if you asked? You haven't done anything to upset him."

"I already asked him, and he didn't want to hear it. I don't know, it's hard: he's been so angry about everything lately and it's not easy to speak to him …"

"Maybe Papa could speak to Don Antonio. He's such a supporter of Franco that he must have some kind of sway with them, and can make them give Fernando's father a pardon," Catalina said, sure that the shopkeeper could do something for the Garzos.

"I don't know …"

"Please! Ask Father again," Catalina begged.

"The things you ask me!" Doña Asunción said, scared at the prospect of insisting that her husband try to get a letter of recommendation for Lorenzo Garzo.

"Promise me!" Catalina insisted.

"Well … I'll see if I can find the right moment."

When Fernando got back home, his mother saw how upset he was. Isabel was cleaning the study.

"You've got up early for a Sunday," Isabel said.

"I went to San Ginés to see Catalina; her father won't let her out of the house."

"I'm not surprised."

"Mother! Can't you feel the least bit of sympathy for her situation?"

"I don't want to argue with you; Fernando, but we've got problems enough of our own without adding Catalina's as well. We have to go to the lawyer tomorrow: you think there'll be good news? I'm so scared …"

Fernando hugged his mother and held her for a long time.

A little while later he went up to Eulogio's apartment to talk to him for a while. It helped him calm his nerves and he was always an optimist in any situation.

Piedad opened the door and Fernando saw that her eyes were red, as though she'd just been crying.

"Is Eulogio there? I can always come back later …"

She didn't reply, but left the door open for him to come in, and went back to the kitchen.

Fernando stood still for a few seconds, upset, not knowing whether to stay or leave; then Eulogio came out to see him. His friend looked suddenly aged, as though a fifty-year-old had suddenly taken up residence in his twentysomething body. His face was clenched, he looked distant, he smelled of sweat and tiredness was written all over him. He'd been up all night, just like so many others, looking after Don Antonio's warehouse.

"I don't want to bother you, I was just coming to smoke a cigarette, but …"

"Wait, I'll put on a shirt and come with you."

"No … you don't need … later, perhaps …"

Eulogio left him standing there and went into his room; he came out a moment later, buttoning up his shirt. They went out of the attic without saying goodbye to Piedad.

"Let's go."

When they got downstairs, Eulogio took out his tobacco and rolled a couple of cigarettes. They walked for a while in silence, smoking. Eulogio seemed to be lost in thought and Fernando didn't dare break his friend's silence.

When they got to the Plaza de Santo Domingo, Eulogio cleared his throat and started to speak.

"I'm screwed. I punched Prudencio, Don Antonio's brother."

"Prudencio? Why?" Fernando asked in surprise.

"He's a son of a bitch."

"We know that already, him and Don Antonio."

"Two assholes."

"Yes," said Fernando, without daring to ask Eulogio why he had hit Prudencio.

"Has anyone said to you that my mother … that my mother's got an arrangement with Don Antonio?"

Fernando said nothing, shocked at the question.

"So they have told you," Eulogio said.

"No … no … what are you saying? You've just put me on the spot. How could you say something like that?"

"Tell me the truth, Fernando … I can't bear the thought of making a fool of myself working for that fascist, who took our house from us … How could my mother have gone with such a bastard?"

"You're going to pay attention to rumors? Look, I don't know what Prudencio said to you, but he's the kind of guy who doesn't deserve the time of day."

"He came to the warehouse last night with a woman. You can guess what type of woman. He had been drinking, but wasn't completely drunk. He said that he had some friends over and wanted to keep drinking, but that he hadn't got anything in the house, so he'd just take it from the warehouse. I said that he couldn't take anything without Don Antonio's permission. He said that everything in the warehouse was his, that his brother wouldn't have anything without him, wouldn't be anything. He was right, I guess, but I said that I was in charge of the warehouse and that nothing could leave it, not a crate of wine or of spirits, without Don Antonio's permission. He got in my face then, I suppose he wanted to impress the whore he was with, and said that he was going to take whatever he wanted, because it was all his. She started to goad him on, saying that he wasn't going to let himself be stopped by a loser like me. And then I turned to her and told her to shut her trap. And she got angry and told Prudencio to put me in my place or that she would go. Prudencio ordered me to apologize and I laughed. "Apologize? To that? Come on!" She started to moan and say that I wasn't treating her like a lady, and that if Prudencio let that happen then she had nothing more to do here. I got really angry then and said that there was no lady here, as far as I could see. And then Prudencio got up in my face and said, "Hey, kid, you should know a lot about whores because your mother's the biggest whore in the neighborhood, so treat this woman like a lady and take the wine out to my car." I punched him and he fell over onto a sack of potatoes. He got up and wanted to hit me. The whore stood between us crying. Prudencio was red with anger and he said ... he said that I was a piece of shit and a loser, who couldn't do anything, and that if his brother hadn't been screwing my mother we'd both be dead of hunger. He said I was a useless loser and swore that since my father fought for the Republic and I was another shitty little red, he was going to make sure I went to prison, where all the reds go before being put up against the wall. And so I got past the whore, gave him another punch, and left. I've been here all night, in the street, not knowing what to do. I was scared of speaking to my mother, scared that she ... that she would tell me the truth."

Eulogio got out another cigarette and lit it while Fernando tried to find the right words to say. Of course, he had heard rumors about Piedad and Don Antonio. There were always people ready to stir the pot by complaining about other people's behavior.

"Did you know, Fernando? Tell me the truth ... I can't bear to think that everyone knew about my mother and Don Antonio ... Everyone apart from me ... I bet you all had a good laugh!"

"How can you think of saying such a thing? Laugh at you? Who's going to laugh at you? I didn't know anything about it, Eulogio, because I don't listen to stupid people. I only know that your mother is a good woman who has suffered from losing her husband, your father, in this damn war, and who has made sacrifices to move on. Your father was an intellectual, like mine, and your house was always comfortable, just like mine. And your mother and mine now take any work they can to make ends meet, and there you have it: my mother cleaning other people's shit in a house of fascists, and yours sewing and cleaning in a sweatshop. And Don Antonio? The bastard made you sell your apartment, and now he's sniffing after ours as well, desperate to get us to sell it for a pittance so he can pass it on to his friends."

"But did you know, Fernando?"

"Know what? I'm telling you, I don't care to listen to what other people are saying, and especially if they're talking nonsense about people I care for and respect."

"Fernando, you knew and didn't tell me anything! You let them make a fool of me."

"Please, Eulogio, stop thinking about what other people say or don't say!"

"I asked my mother, and she couldn't lie to me, but she didn't want to deny it either. How could she have done something like that? Is her dignity worth so little?"

"Don't judge your mother! You have no right. Come on, let's go home. You look terrible. Take a shower, rest a bit, and don't upset your mother."

"I'm not going back to the warehouse."

"You know what you need to do … But it wasn't a good idea to punch Prudencio."

"Wouldn't you have done the same?"

"Yes, if someone had insulted my mother I'd have done just what you did," Fernando admitted.

They walked back in silence. Fernando was asking himself how he could soothe the pain and anger his friend felt, and Eulogio was lost, seething with uncertainty.

They went upstairs, and when they got to Fernando's apartment, Isabel opened the door before they had a chance to say goodbye to one another.

"I saw you coming from the balcony. Come in, the pair of you," she ordered, looking serious.

Eulogio wanted to make his excuses and leave; he didn't want to speak with anyone, and certainly not Isabel. But Fernando's mother didn't give him the chance to protest.

"Eulogio, I've just seen your mother and we spoke for a long time."

He didn't know what to say.

"I went up to the attic to ask to borrow some salt, and I found her crying. She told me what happened, and I have to admit that you did well to give Prudencio that punch. He deserved it."

Fernando was surprised at this: he knew that his mother was a pacifist.

"But you shouldn't have judged your mother. You don't have the right. Everything she has done, all the good and the bad, she has done with one single aim in mind, always: to protect you."

"I'm sorry, Doña Isabel, but I'd rather not talk about my mother ... It's between us, and it's no one else's business but ours."

"You're right, I'm getting involved in your business, but it's because I care for you both. You're still young, Eulogio, for all that you've been to war. Your mother has suffered because your father was killed at the front. She's been left alone, widowed with a son who's marked as a red. A wounded son. This damn war took our lives away from us, all that we had. You wanted to be an painter, remember? Your father was very proud of you, convinced that you'd manage to achieve your dream. But that dream's been taken from you. Your mother doesn't want your life to be taken from you as well. You know that lots of the people in the neighborhood are Republican like us, but now they're quiet, not because they're afraid of losing anything material, but because they're afraid of being killed. It's the only thing some of them have left to lose."

"Mother, I think Eulogio's right and you shouldn't stick your nose in his business," Fernando interrupted.

"I can't stand injustice," Isabel said angrily.

"Right ... But if it's all the same to you I'll go up to my apartment now," Eulogio said.

"It's not all the same to me. You will stay here and listen to what I have to tell you. Lots of the winners in this war spend all their time trying to report their neighbors as reds. Your mother was forced to sell your apartment and accept the attic where you now live. That wasn't the worst of it. She had to bow to that bastard Antonio Sánchez's blackmail: he hasn't stopped telling her that unless she lets him have his way, then you'll go to prison, and she fought back as much as she could. But she didn't have the power to stop the shopkeeper calling in some favors: don't you remember the day you were arrested? There isn't a mother in the world who wouldn't do anything to save her son. And there's more: listen to what I've got to tell you, Eulogio. If it were a question of saving my son's life, I'd even sleep with Franco himself."

"Mother!" Fernando cried out, scandalized.

"You're saying some very strange things," Eulogio said, uncomfortable.

"Well, that's the way it is," Isabel said bluntly.

"Dignity is worth more than life, and I'm not going to live a life without dignity," Eulogio said, angrily.

"You know what, Eulogio? Your mother, the same as me, the same as so many other women, are nothing more than women, normal human beings, and our heroism in times like this consists in keeping you alive, even if we have to pay a heavy price to do so, even if we have to pay with what you call 'our dignity.' Yes, it's more heroic to do what Guzmán el Bueno did, to throw down your own knife so they can slit the throats of your own children before your eyes, but no mother would throw down a knife for them to kill her own child. I wouldn't do it, Eulogio. I'd rather burn in hell than have anything happen to Fernando. I've never been in a situation like that, but your mother has, and she did what she had to do. You care too much about things, you men do, because you think that women's bodies are your property."

"Mother, please, stop talking!" Fernando said, shocked by what he was hearing.

But Isabel didn't listen. She looked fixedly at Eulogio, forcing him to lower his eyes.

"Your mother's dignity is not to be found between her thighs, but rather in her honorable behavior throughout her life; it's in the love she bore and still bears for your father; it's in the sacrifices she's made to save you. That's where her dignity is. A man like Antonio Sánchez can't take a scrap of dignity from your mother. The one who's lost his dignity is him, taking advantage of a mother's love. That's all I wanted to say, Eulogio. And now, if what I've said has made you think even a little, go upstairs and hug your mother."

Eulogio nodded and left without saying goodbye.

Fernando was angry with his mother, but he didn't say anything until Eulogio had left.

"How dare you, Mother! You don't have any right to say what you said to Eulogio. You made him upset. It's enough for him to be feeling what he's feeling without you trying to make him feel guilty. You can say what you want, but you have to understand that any son would be upset to find out that his mother … well … that his mother's with a man who isn't his father."

"Eulogio's father is dead, and so even if she hadn't been blackmailed, Piedad didn't owe anyone anything, and can do whatever she wants with her life, even have a relationship with someone as disgusting as Antonio Sánchez."

"There are other ways of surviving in this world," Fernando protested.

"Yes, and she was working, destroying her eyesight sewing in a workshop. If it was only a matter of getting enough to eat, Piedad would never have slept with Don Antonio, but he threatened her son."

"He's a fascist!"

"Yes, Fernando, we know that already, and it's precisely because of that that he's all too capable of carrying out his threat. Piedad lost her husband in the war, and her only son's been wounded, so don't expect her to stand by twiddling her thumbs while they cart him off to prison. Your father is in prison, Fernando, and I hope he'll get out … We've been left with nothing, and have even had to sell the beds in order to pay the lawyer, but I promise you, son, that if someone guaranteed me that my husband would be released from jail in return for my body, then that's a price I would pay without complaint."

"Mother, I don't know you … you say such things …"

"You know nothing, Fernando."

When Eulogio went into the attic, he found his mother sitting down, staring off into space. He stood in front of her, fighting with himself. He loved her, but at the same time he hated her. He was moved by her pain, but he detested her behavior. He would have preferred for his mother not to have given in to Don Antonio, even if it meant that he went to prison. He felt that his mother was now a different person for him, no longer the perfect woman he had so loved and admired. The woman before him was one who had surrendered.

"I'll go out to look for work tomorrow," he said, in a bitter voice, "so don't even think about going back to that bastard Don Antonio. If he wants me to go to prison, let him send me. He's right, of course: I'm a red and I hate the fascists just as much as they hate us."

"I'll do whatever you say, Eulogio, I … I'm sorry … forgive me … I thought that it was the only thing I could do to protect you … I swear I held him off as much as I could, but he … you know how he is …"

"Yes, I know how he is. I suppose that as well as sending me to prison he'll do what he has to do to get us thrown out of this hole."

"No …he can't do that … the attic is ours …"

"Right. The apartment was ours as well, and he took it so that we could pay the debt we owed him. He made us sell it to cover the debt and the tiny amount he gave us in exchange we used to buy the attic."

"He's a bastard."

"Swear to me that whatever happens, you're not going to humiliate yourself again, not in front of him or anyone. Swear it, or else I'll leave and you'll never see me again."

"Don't say that, son! You're my whole life … I … I couldn't live without you …"

"Swear it, Mother."

"I swear it, I swear … Whatever you want, Eulogio."

"You've behaved as though I was a child … you protected me without telling me what I needed protecting from … you stopped me from deciding about something that affected me as well as you."

"I'm sorry, I'm so sorry … please forgive me!"

Piedad got up from her chair and went over to her son and took him by the hand. Eulogio didn't draw back, but neither did he hold her close as she had hoped he would. His mother choked back a sob. They stood very still for a few moments.

"I'm going to paint for a while," he said, moving deftly aside. She nodded.

Catalina closed her suitcase. It was already noon, and her father had said that was when he would take her to her aunt's house. She was already four months along, and keen to be out of her house. She couldn't bear her father's resentful glances. They had barely spoken to one another since the day he had hit her.

Her mother suffered to see it, and asked her to understand her father, but Catalina refused. It was enough for her to try to stop the waves of hate she sometimes felt towards him. She thought that she would miss her house, especially her mother: she needed her so much!

Her aunt Petra had put a room together and was happy to have her niece visiting, even in such circumstances. She would stay with her until after the birth, until she had handed the child over. It wouldn't be easy for Catalina, but it was the best solution. Her niece wasn't the first or the last flighty young thing to have made this kind of mistake; the important thing was to avoid the consequences. That's what orphanages were for; better still her sister Asunción had explained that Juan Segovia, their doctor, was looking for a good family to take the child, so they wouldn't have to go through the shame of handing it officially over to the foundling hospital. Even so, she would have been ready to do it out of the huge love she felt for her sister Asunción and her niece.

"Have you got everything you need?" Doña Asunción asked her daughter.

"Yes, Mama, I've got it all."

"Think carefully, you always forget something when you go on a trip," her mother insisted.

"I'm not going on a trip, and if I forget something you can bring it; you've promised to come and see me every day at Aunt Petra's house."

"Yes, I will. I'm so sorry you have to go ..."

"Don't worry," Catalina said, giving her mother a hug.

"I'll tell your father you're ready, although I think he's already waiting in the street with the car ..."

"Mama?"

"Yes, my love?"

"Promise me that if Marvin writes then you'll bring me the letter at once."

"Of course! There's nothing I'd like better than for that boy to come back here and marry you. It would be the best for all of us."

"Well, not for Papa," she said sourly.

"Your father loves you; you have to see that. It's been very difficult for him to deal with this … You're our only daughter and we want the best for you."

"Sure. Come on, Mother, he wants me to marry Antoñito just so he can get out of what he owes his father."

"Don't say that! Your father only wants you to be happy."

"You know I'm right."

"Don't judge your father, Catalina; parents shouldn't be judged."

"I'm not going to give up my child, Mama."

"Oh, don't start that again! It's the only way."

"I'm not going to do it, Mama. Would you have abandoned me?"

"That's not the same. You're our legitimate daughter."

"And my poor child, who hasn't done anything wrong, has to suffer because of what I've done? It's not fair, Mama. It's me who should be punished, and suffer the consequences of my actions, and if that means that people point at me in the street and I can never get married, then that's how it has to be."

Doña Asunción hugged her daughter. She didn't want to argue with her. She knew that Catalina would fight against it with all her strength, but that as soon as the child was born, they would take it away without even letting her hold it. That's what Juan Segovia had recommended, and he was a doctor, so he ought to know.

Fernando walked quickly. He was worried about his friend. He couldn't stop asking himself what he would have felt if he had been in Eulogio's shoes, and if what his mother had said had been true, that she was ready to do anything to keep him from prison.

What about him? What was he prepared to do to keep his father out of prison? "I'd kill for my father," he said to himself, and then blushed, thinking that a woman could give her body for the same thing, to save someone she loved.

He was going to see Don Víctor and ask him to give Eulogio some work in the print shop. His boss was a good man, but the print business wasn't the same as what it had been before the war, and maybe he couldn't pay to take on another apprentice.

He walked along Gran Vía, thinking about the havoc wreaked by the war. The signs of it were written on everyone's faces. He could tell the winners from the losers. The winners weren't noticeably richer or better-off; they were as hungry as the rest, but there was a glint of hope in their eyes that wasn't there in the eyes of the losers. He was a loser. He couldn't help returning to the moment when his father told him to look after his mother while he was at the front. The other thing his father had said that day also played over and over in his head: "You shall not kill, Fernando, you shall not kill."

He couldn't help but think about what the lawyer would say when they went to see him. They had done everything Don Alberto had asked of them; his mother had managed to get a letter from Don Bernardo interceding for his father. It hadn't been easy, because the priest, as he had done on many other occasions, had blamed his mother a little: "A shame, Isabel, that you married a Republican." Isabel had replied as she always did: "My Lorenzo is a good man, an exemplary father and husband who has never hurt anybody."

Fernando had promised that if the priest's letter did the job and his father was pardoned, then he would show his thanks by going to Mass every Sunday and every holiday.

He walked around with no clear plan of where he was going, eventually relaxing a little. He could have gone out to look for some of his friends, but he didn't want to talk to anyone. Anyway, he liked being alone. His mother had gone to the church to pray. There were a lot of widows in the parish, and prayer was a way of getting some kind of consolation, or at least, for those who know they have nothing to hope for, of finding a way to get the interminable hours to pass more quickly. Going to church was a way for women to have some time to themselves, even if it was to repeat the *Kyrie Eleison* mechanically as they thought of other things.

He, too, needed time to pass more quickly.

Piedad left her house early. She walked quickly because she liked to be on time. The owner of the workshop was a good woman, a little simple, who made all her employees say the Angelus every day at noon.

Piedad had been religious before the war began. Not a saint, but a believer at least, although the war had taken her away from the church. It wasn't that she no longer believed in God, but he clearly was indifferent to her problems, and so she treated him with the same indifference.

Suddenly a hand grabbed her by the shoulder.

"Stop there, you ungrateful bitch!"

Don Antonio's voice shocked her, but she turned, ready to confront him.

"I'm late, let me go," she said, as she tried to wriggle away from the hand on her shoulder.

"Your pig of a son hit my brother Prudencio and broke his nose. I'm going to end him, the bastard, son of a bitch, red. How dare he disrespect my family! You're a bunch of starving rats who owe me everything! You'll see just how powerful Antonio Sánchez is!"

"Let me go! And leave me alone: I've got to go to work! Do what you want: you're the real bastard, so do what you want."

"Bitch! How dare you talk back to me? You're a slut! A fucking slut who's no use to anyone!"

"Do what you want, Antonio. It's over. You're not getting anything more from me. I've humiliated myself, and accepted that you ... but not anymore. I don't want to see you again."

"You'll pay what you owe me!"

"Owe you? I don't owe you a thing!"

"Of course you do? You think that you paid your debt with your nasty little apartment? Not at all. We fed you throughout the war. You owe me everything!"

Piedad gave him a shove and started running. People looked at her without daring to get involved. He followed after her, screaming: "Bitch! Slut! Whore!"

Don Antonio wanted to get his revenge on her and on Eulogio. He was going to turn him in, pull whatever strings needed to be pulled to get him taken away. He'd accuse him of whatever it took. Hadn't Eulogio fought on the side of the reds? He didn't need anything else: a red was always a red; those bastards never repented. He'd make sure they took him for real this time, but not just to give him a scare: he'd teach him that you had to respect Antonio Sánchez and his family.

He didn't like the idea of giving up that little slut Piedad, but he had no choice. Prudencio had demanded that he do something about Eulogio, and this was what he was going to do.

When Piedad got to the workshop she drank a glass of water. She was out of breath and her heart was pounding so fast that she could count each and every one of its beats.

She sewed with much more effort than she normally did. She needed to get rid of all the tension she had built up. How long would it be before they took Eulogio away? She was sure it would happen. Don Antonio was going to have her son arrested again, and this time there was nothing she could do.

When she went home that afternoon, she went to Isabel's house first. She needed to let off some steam with her friend.

Isabel listened to her patiently, moved by what she heard.

"What can I do?" Piedad asked after she had explained everything about her meeting with Antonio Sánchez.

"He's a bastard, and you can't expect anything but the worst from him. I'm so sorry, Piedad! I don't know what to say ... Would you like me to talk to him? Maybe he'll listen to me ..."

"No, don't even think about it! Your husband's in prison and he might think about hurting you as well. No, no, no: you can't talk to him. It wouldn't do any good."

"But someone has to stop that man. We have to think of something ... what if we tell Don Bernardo?"

"It'll be worse: Don Bernardo will just say I'm a sinner."

"Don Bernardo is a good man, Piedad, a priest who's a little uptight, but I don't think he'd ever hurt anyone."

"I'm not saying he's a bad man, but I don't think he'll help me. Antonio's very powerful in the neighborhood; everyone owes him something. He tries to smooth over the fact that he's never in Mass on Sundays by giving Don Bernardo lots of little presents: eggs, flour, tomatoes ... and Mari makes sure that everyone knows she puts ten pesetas in the collection plate every Sunday ... you know how it is."

"But that doesn't stop Don Bernardo from scolding him."

"That's true too. But I don't think he'll get involved ... It won't do any good."

"He helped us. He wrote a letter on Lorenzo's behalf," Isabel replied.

"That's different ... You're a Catholic; you didn't stop going to church even during the war, and it's the least that Don Bernardo can do for you."

"Yes, but Lorenzo ... you know that Lorenzo never set foot in a church."

"Neither do I, Isabel. And Don Bernardo doesn't owe me anything. My husband, may he rest in peace, and my son never set foot in church. You know that my husband Jesús was an atheist; he never hid it, and he stopped going to Mass. And so the priest has no reason to help us, and I understand him."

"Let me try," Isabel insisted.

"No, I'm telling you: you're not going to get anything out of him, and you may have to ask him for another favor in the future, for Lorenzo. I'm sorry, I'm so caught up in my own problems that I didn't ask how he is."

"We're going to see the lawyer tomorrow to see how things are going with the pardon. As for Lorenzo, you know how he is; he doesn't complain about anything, but he's thinner every day and his glasses are broken. It's so hard not to cry when I see him."

"I'm so sorry," Piedad said.

"Well, let's get back to your problem, where at least we can do something. Fernando has told me he's going to talk to Don Víctor, the owner of the print shop. He's a good man, and if he can then I'm sure he'll find a place for Eulogio."

"I didn't sleep all night, thinking that maybe we should leave,"

Piedad said, without paying any attention to Isabel's flustered statements.

"Leave? But where would you go? Half of France is in the hands of the Germans, and as for the rest, Pétain's government doesn't treat the Spaniards who flee there all that well. You don't want to end up in a labor camp."

"My son's in danger, Isabel. I'm afraid that Antonio will get him arrested."

"Pray it doesn't happen! We have to do something …"

That very afternoon Fernando spoke with Don Vicente in the print shop.

"Eulogio can be trusted, absolutely. Do you think that Don Víctor will take him on? I promise you that if he gives him a job he won't regret it."

"I don't know what to tell you, because even if Don Víctor does want to give him a job, he won't be able to. You know that the print shop isn't working like it did before. The war is over but the country is destroyed; no one has any money, and we survive rather than live like real people. I can't ask Don Víctor to take anyone else on. You know there's no work for more people. I can't do it, Fernando, I'm sorry not to be able to help your friend, but you have to understand."

Fernando bowed his head so that Don Vicente wouldn't see his anger and frustration. He knew that the print shop didn't make much money, but he had been sure that Don Vicente would take pity on Eulogio.

"Will you excuse me? I'll go and work on the machine: there's a lot to do," Fernando said.

The printer let him go without saying a word. He knew that he had disappointed his apprentice.

After work, Fernando walked rapidly back home. He wanted to see Eulogio and tell him that he had failed in his effort to find him a job, but he went to his house first so that his mother wouldn't be worried. He found Isabel sewing up one of his shirts, taking advantage of the last rays of the afternoon sun.

"Hello, Mother, I'm going up to the attic to speak with Eulogio, and then I'll be straight down."

"Wait a moment, son … I spoke to Piedad this afternoon. Don Antonio came out to find her this morning when she went to the workshop to clean it. He caused a real scandal in the street and he threatened her. Piedad thinks that he'll get Eulogio arrested. I don't know what we can do to help them. I said that maybe Don Bernardo could help them, but she refused, and says that the priest won't help them because Eulogio is an atheist."

"I'm an atheist as well!" Fernando replied, an angry expression on his face.

"Lord almighty, the things you say! You're not an atheist: you're baptized, you had your first communion and you're confirmed. So don't tell fibs."

"Mother, the fact that you believe doesn't mean that I believe. I'm sorry, but I've never seen God anywhere. What is God doing for my father? If he's omnipotent and perfectly good, then why does he let a good man like my father end up in prison?"

"You can't ask God to give you explanations. And anyway, it wasn't God who put your father in prison."

"But he let it happen. Let's leave God out of this, Mother."

Isabel nodded in resignation. She was a fervent Catholic, and nothing that could happen would alter her faith, even though she too begged God for help though so far his only response had been silence.

"Someone has to stop Don Antonio," Fernando muttered.

"We don't have any power over him. It has to be someone he respects … But that man doesn't respect anyone," Isabel said.

In the end, Fernando decided not to go up to Eulogio's apartment: he didn't want to add a further piece of bad news to the events of the day.

"I'm not hungry; I'll go for a walk."

"But where are you going to go at this time of night?" Come on, stay with me …"

"I won't be long, but I need to be alone for a bit so I can think."

Without knowing why, he set off towards Doña Petra's house, which looked onto the Retiro. It was only a few days since Catalina had moved to her aunt's house and he missed her a lot. He knew that he couldn't turn up there, much less at this hour of the night, but at least he would feel close to Catalina.

What he didn't expect at all was to run slap-bang into the three of them.

"Fernando! Fernando, what a nice surprise! But what are you doing here?"

The young woman had thrown off her mother's arm, and ran to see him under the shocked gaze of her aunt.

"Well … I wasn't expecting to see you," Fernando said sincerely.

"Well, if you came over here it wasn't impossible that we would meet each other. I had to give it my all to get us to leave the house, but as it's night it's not likely that we'll meet anyone we know, but here you are, I suppose. I gave you my aunt's address. You see, Auntie, that Fernando's come to see me?"

"No … well … I mean, it's not that I didn't want to see you … but I swear I wasn't expecting to today."

"Good evening, young man," Petra said, looking him up and down.

"Doña Petra, Doña Asunción … I do hope I'm not bothering you, that really wasn't my intention … I swear I wasn't expecting to meet you."

"We just came out for a moment to take the air," Catalina's aunt replied, "and it's clearly something we shouldn't do again. You see, Catalina, how you always run the risk of running into someone? Luckily it was only Fernando."

"I understand … It was just so stifling today, and Madrid at this time of year is always so hot," Fernando said, still in shock.

"Why don't you come up for a bit with us? You won't mind, will you, Auntie? Then you can walk my mother back home so she's not alone in the streets, all right?" Catalina proposed.

"No … I don't need to … I'll be off now … Your father will be expecting me, and it's already a little late …" Doña Asunción apologized, uncomfortably.

"But it's still daytime, Mother! You said that Father had an important meeting and that he'd be back late. Come on, stay a little while longer." Catalina held onto her mother, kissing her to try to make her change her mind.

"Well …" Doña Asunción didn't know what to do.

"The best thing is for us to go back home, because you need

to rest. And it's almost nine o'clock, it's really no time for your mother to be in the street," Doña Petra argued.

"But Fernando can go with her now. He should at least come upstairs and drink a glass of water," Catalina insisted.

The two sisters gave way in the face of the young woman's insistence. It was better for them to give the young man a glass of water and send him off than for them to stay in the street in full view of the world, and of people who might know them.

Catalina made Fernando go through into the sitting room, and brought in a tray with a bottle of water and four glasses.

"You look bad, has something happened to you?" she asked worriedly.

"No ... nothing ..."

"Do you have news from the lawyer?"

"Don't worry ..."

"Of course I'm worried! Tell me what's happening, Fernando, for God's sake, you look like someone's died."

"Don't be silly," her aunt Petra scolded her.

"Why don't you leave us alone for a bit so we can talk?" said Catalina, ignoring her aunt and her mother's expressions of reproach.

"Catalina, will you learn to behave!" her mother snapped.

"What's wrong with having a chat with Fernando?" Catalina insisted.

"I don't think it's a very good idea, given the situation," her aunt interrupted.

"The situation? Fernando is my best friend, and he knows that I'm pregnant and he's helping me find Marvin. I don't have any secrets from him."

Asunción and Petra looked at one another without knowing what to do or what to say, knowing that Catalina would get her own way.

"All right, but only five minutes. I'll be leaving in five minutes, and Fernando will come with me," Doña Asunción said, looking severely at her daughter.

When they were left alone, Catalina took Fernando's hand and squeezed it in a gesture filled with affection and understanding.

"What's going on? Don't tell me that it's nothing: I know you and I know that there's something troubling you," she said, and put her hand on Fernando's chest, making him shiver.

He didn't hold anything back, and told her what had happened with Eulogio, the punch thrown at Prudencio, the threats Don Antonio had made against Piedad, the fear that they might be arrested at any moment.

"My mother says that someone should speak with Don Antonio, someone with authority who he respects. But who?" Fernando said.

Catalina sat silently, her gaze lost in the distance. Fernando looked at her, thinking that every day he loved her more.

"I'll ask my mother," Catalina suddenly said.

"What? What? I don't understand," Fernando said, shaking himself out of his reverie.

"He respects my mother. My mother is a woman, a proper God-fearing woman. If my mother tells Don Antonio that she's found out about his dealings with Piedad and that if he does anything to hurt her or Eulogio there'll be consequences …"

"That's crazy. Anyway, what consequences could there be if people find out? He likes to think of himself as a stud."

"But I don't think his wife will think it's funny, or his children. The only person Antoñito feels any respect for at all is his mother: he'd never forgive his father for embarrassing her in front of everyone. It's one thing for there to be rumors, and quite another for the dirty laundry to be out there, in public."

"You're such a dreamer. Your mother can't just stand up in front of Don Antonio and throw this business with Piedad in his face. I don't think it will help at all, and also I don't think your mother would do anything like that. She doesn't know Piedad at all."

"I'll convince her," Catalina said, very sure of herself.

"Come on, Catalina, don't talk nonsense!"

"You'll see. Mama, Mama!"

Asunción and Petra came running when Catalina called them. They both looked worried.

"Mother, is it true that you think the same about Don Antonio that I do?" Catalina blurted out.

"Where's all this coming from?"

"I'm not going to marry Antoñito unless you do something for me."

"Catalina, for heaven's sake!" her mother said in despair.

"What now ..." her aunt protested.

"Don Antonio is a pig and the two of you know it. He's blackmailing a woman. He's been doing it for a long time. He abuses her. You know what I mean."

"What are you saying!" Doña Petra protested.

"Don Antonio has been abusing Piedad for a long time now. He got Eulogio arrested and now he's blackmailing her. Either she does what he wants, or he'll send her son to prison. Piedad had to give in to save her son and Don Antonio now takes advantage of her whenever he wants. And now Eulogio has got into a fight with Prudencio, Don Antonio's brother, who is the aide to a colonel, and the shopkeeper is getting his own back by threatening Piedad."

"That's enough, Catalina! I don't want to hear you say such things, this is nothing to do with us," Doña Asunción said sharply, giving her daughter a scandalized look.

"Yes, it is to do with me, Mother. I can't bear injustice, and I couldn't sit by if they arrested Eulogio. We all know what they're like, the people on the winning side."

"Catalina!" her aunt shrieked. "How dare you criticize Franco? Your uncle died defending peace and order. We're a decent family."

"And why is it only us who are decent? Why? Because we won the war? And everyone on the losing side is wicked? Marvin doesn't like Franco!"

Asunción and Petra looked at Catalina, fear in their eyes. More than anything else, they didn't understand her. They knew that she was a rebel, and that she'd always been one, but for Petra, the suggestion that Franco winning the war wasn't the best thing that could have happened to Spain was going too far.

"Fernando, what ideas are you putting in her head? You come here to tell a story that ... well ... a story that has nothing to do with us and which we shouldn't even listen to," Doña Petra said to Fernando.

"I'm sorry, Doña Petra, it certainly wasn't my intention to upset you … I'm sorry I went into something that was worrying me; Eulogio is my friend: we live in the same building and have known each other since we were just boys," Fernando apologized.

"But that doesn't justify your coming here and talking about your neighbor's personal affairs, especially with Catalina … with Catalina being as she is," Petra insisted.

"I am pregnant, yes, but that doesn't mean that I have to stop caring about the people who are important to me. And I am worried about what happens to Eulogio: you'll remember that he is very good friends with Marvin. Eulogio is the best friend that Marvin has in Spain. They met at the front, they were both wounded there, and when Marvin came back to Madrid after the war, he lived with Eulogio and his mother."

"Catalina, you are behaving very badly," Doña Asunción interrupted, feeling ever more annoyed at her daughter.

"Mother, I want you to do something. You spend so much time asking God for handouts, why don't you get him to do something for Eulogio as well?"

"Blasphemy! How dare you?" Doña Petra said, upset at her niece's forwardness.

"Blasphemy? God forgive me: I'm a good Christian and I'd never blaspheme, not for anything. But you have to accept what I'm saying: it's not enough for us to ask the Lord to take care of all our problems when we can solve them ourselves or solve the problems of others."

Catalina's mother and aunt were lost for words, and looked at her in shock. Fernando, for his part, felt that he loved her even more for her bravery.

"I'm sorry to be the cause of this argument. It's best if I go. I'll come back some other time."

Petra was about to tell him that he would not be welcome, but her niece got in first.

"Don't go, Fernando: if my mother refuses to speak to Don Antonio I'll speak to him myself."

"You are not going to leave this house!" her aunt shouted.

"Are you going to tie me down? I'm not looking for trouble, but I'm really not going to let you lock me away here," she said bluntly.

"Oh, Lord, what a scandal!" Doña Asunción said. "And all

for that woman, who would have done better to have resisted Don Antonio than to have lost her honor."

"You think less of Piedad because she chose to save her son's life by … well, by doing that? So, I suppose you have a worse opinion of me, for having allowed Marvin to … well, for ending up pregnant?"

"Oh Lord, what an impossible child! I'm not sure I'll be able to be responsible for her," her aunt said.

Asunción looked anxiously at her sister. If Petra didn't look after her daughter, then her husband might very well return to insisting that they find a woman to "take care of" the child.

"What do you want, Catalina?" she asked her daughter, her lower lip trembling.

"I want you to go to Don Antonio and tell him that you know he wants to hurt Piedad and Eulogio, and that if he dares to do anything against them, then you'll make sure that his wife hears all about it, and that you'll also tell Don Bernardo, and not in the confessional."

"How am I going to do that? Absolutely not!"

"All right, then I'll do it myself. I don't care about standing up to the shopkeeper. I don't have any respect for him. I find him as disgusting as I find his son."

"You see the problems you're causing, Fernando?" Doña Asunción said.

"You don't know how sorry I am, I swear it wasn't my intention …"

"Maybe not, but you've really put your foot in it," declared Doña Petra.

"Mother, tell me that you'll do it. I will do it myself, and I'll tell you something else: even if Father hits me again, I'm going to tell Antoñito that I'll never marry him because I'm going to have Marvin's child."

Doña Asunción blanched, then flushed, about to burst into tears. Ever since Catalina had gotten pregnant she had become impossible. She was no longer the child she had been, a child who had talked back, but that always let herself be persuaded; it was as if the fact that she was going to be a mother had made her feel even more secure in herself.

For her part, Doña Petra was confused, without knowing what she could say, much less what she could do.

"Catalina, you can't ask your mother to speak to Don Antonio. It won't be any help and you'll put your family in a difficult situation. I told you about Eulogio because I needed to speak to somebody, but your mother and your aunt are right, it's not your business. We'll think of something," Fernando said, with as much conviction as he could muster.

"Don Antonio is a bad person, and there's no other way to deal with him besides giving him a taste of his own medicine. Either we threaten him, or he'll do anything," Catalina said, unwilling to back down even an inch.

Doña Asunción took a sip of water, and pulled her skirt down as if she wanted to cover her knees even more, although they were already fairly invisible.

"I will speak with Don Antonio. I will. And you know why? Because I never thought that my own daughter would blackmail me. You know very well how your father would react if you dare to stand up to Don Antonio, and all the more if you say to Antoñito that ... that you were pregnant. We would be ruined, my daughter, and you will have no future at all."

"I'm not blackmailing you, Mother," Catalina replied, feeling scared herself now.

"Yes, yes, you have blackmailed me. You're forcing me to get involved in a situation that does not concern us, for me to help Piedad and her son, who are people we know, but with whom we don't have any relation. You want me to stand up to a man like Don Antonio, who is no gentleman, and who is very rude, and who knows how he could react? If he goes and complains to your father, I don't even want to think about what might happen. But I would prefer to take on this responsibility rather than have you do something stupid, because then ... I don't know what your father might do."

Catalina hugged her mother, but Doña Asunción did not respond. She felt exhausted and disappointed with her daughter. She had enough to do making sure that nobody found out about her daughter's state, as well as making sure that the pregnancy went well, and then finding a family to take care of the child.

"Asunción, you shouldn't do it," Doña Petra dared to say.

"I know my daughter, and I know that she is quite capable of confronting Don Antonio. And now I'm going to leave. Ernesto will already be at home, and he will start to be worried about where I am. And you, Fernando, come with me."

Fernando walked alongside Asunción in silence. She did not scold him, and he did not dare apologize any more. When they reached the Vilamars' door, he nodded goodbye, and ran to his house.

Isabel was angry. She had been waiting for him for hours. She did not understand why her son wouldn't share all his troubles with her, and preferred to go and speak to his friends, or else just go out walking by himself, lost in his own thoughts.

Asunción knew from her husband that Don Antonio went to the warehouse very early. She calculated that she could run into him when he left his house at around seven o'clock. Her stomach hurt, as did her head, from the fear that she felt about having to confront the shopkeeper. He was a disgusting man, and perfectly capable of shouting at her or of saying unpleasant things. The worst would be if he went to complain to her husband. Ernesto would never forgive her. And he was right, what she was going to do was ill-advised. But she was ready to do anything for her daughter. Catalina was the most precious thing she had in the world.

"Where are you going so early?" Ernesto asked when he saw her dressed up to leave.

"To the seven o'clock Mass. I've got lots of things to do today, so I decided to go to church early."

"What are these things that mean you've got to go to Mass at such an early hour?"

"I need to get the house in order and organize lunch, but today I also need to help out at the parish clothes bank. Lots of people here are in need, and Don Bernardo has asked anybody who has any clothes that they don't use anymore to give them to the church. I have to see what we can contribute. This afternoon I want to go back to Petra's house to help Catalina adjust the clothes that she took with her; they're too tight now."

"All right, you do what you have to do. I'll stay here at home."

"Don't worry, as soon as I get out of Mass I'll come straight back."

"Try not to be late."

She left her house walking uncertainly, afraid that somebody might see her hanging around in front of Don Antonio's house, but either fortune or the Lord was on her side, and she had barely reached the corner when she met him.

"Good morning, Doña Asunción. You're out early."

"I'm going to seven o'clock Mass," she replied, trying to find strength to say to him everything that she had practiced in her mind all night long.

"God be with you, then."

"Don Antonio, now that I've bumped into you, I've got something to say …"

"Yes? Tell me."

"For Christian people, fidelity and the vows that we make in the marriage ceremony … they're sacred. People who don't obey them are a bad example to their children."

Don Antonio looked at her in annoyance. What was it that this holy old bat wanted to say to him? He'd thought she was a prude, but why on Earth was she addressing him in the street?

"I don't understand you, madam …"

"It's very simple. To my great distress, I've heard the rumors that were going around the neighborhood about you and Doña Piedad … Well … You know what I'm talking about … I don't want to pay attention to them, but you have to understand that I'm worried … You know, my daughter and your son … I still haven't spoken to my husband: I wanted to ask Don Bernardo's advice first."

"You shouldn't pay attention to what people in the neighborhood say. There are a lot of jealous people around," the shopkeeper replied bitterly.

"They even say that you blackmailed Doña Piedad and threatened to report her son Eulogio, and that one of these days they are going to take him away to prison. God, say it isn't so! We all suffered enough in the war. Tell me it's not true … I haven't slept since I heard."

"Madam! Keep your nose in your own business, and don't spread gossip about things that have nothing to do with you or anybody. Goodness gracious!" the shopkeeper replied, raising his voice.

"I'm worried about the kind of family that my daughter is going to marry into. I need to know that it's a Christian family where everybody obeys the laws of our Lord. That's why I'm going to tell Don Bernardo everything that I am telling you, so that he can advise me what to do, because when someone is quiet in the face of other people's sins, then they're an accomplice, don't you think? And I don't want to be an accomplice to your sin, Don Antonio. You should respect your lady wife and your children. Imagine how upset they would be if they found out that you don't honor their mother as you should. Should I tell your wife, María, what everybody is saying? Should I just keep silent? I don't know what to do … As for this boy, Eulogio, is it Christian to do wrong to a poor cripple who's no danger to anyone? Don Antonio, you must understand how confused I am …"

"What are you saying? Are you threatening me?" the shopkeeper shouted.

"Me? Heaven forbid, nothing could be further from my intention! I just thought I should be honest with you before I spoke with Don Bernardo. It's just that they've told me that you were going to report poor Eulogio, and you had threatened Doña Piedad … You must understand that I need to get advice from a priest, and that he in his turn will give you good advice, so that you don't do anything that's impossible to fix."

"That's a good one! I have to put up with you blackmailing me! You're penniless, and it's only thanks to me that you have anything to eat at all!"

"And we are very grateful for your generosity, Don Antonio. Well, it was good to see you, and if I've made a mistake, then please forgive me. I'd like nothing more than to know that neither Eulogio nor Piedad are going to be in any trouble."

"Of course not, what do you take me for? You must understand, madam, that I am a good Christian, and that the only thing I've done is to help this poor family, whom you mustn't forget are not really an example to anyone, given that Piedad's husband died at the Battle of the Ebro fighting against Franco. And his son barely had time to fight because he was wounded in the first month of the war. I've helped them to survive, I helped them sell their apartment and to move to the attic, and I gave Eulogio a job: you must know that he is very ungrateful."

"You're taking a real weight off my shoulders, Don Antonio! So, Eulogio and Doña Piedad don't have anything to fear from you?"

The shopkeeper coughed uncomfortably. He had at that moment been going to see some friends to get them to arrest Eulogio that very morning. "Curse that woman!" he said to himself.

"I don't persecute women or cripples. I've got enough with my Mari. God be with you, Doña Asunción, and try not to get involved in things that don't concern you. I hope that you don't let your tongue wag and tell Don Bernardo any gossip."

"Now that I know that neither Doña Piedad nor Eulogio has anything to fear from you, and that you are a loving husband and father, what would I have to tell him? And now you must forgive me, or I'll be late for Mass."

Don Antonio was silent as he watched her leave. "She's a real shrew," he thought, fearing that Catalina too might turn out like her mother and make life impossible for his Antoñito.

For a moment, he thought about doing what he had planned, of taking revenge on Eulogio and on Piedad, because he knew that if he didn't, his brother Prudencio would be angry. But if he did, then he was sure that Doña Asunción would talk to Don Bernardo, and that he would unleash a scandal that the whole neighborhood would talk about. The priest was a strange man; he didn't seem to care that Don Antonio was a black marketeer, but he was very strict as far as morals were concerned. He was a priest, and not a man, and didn't know anything of what men needed, and so he would condemn him for having "used" Piedad. She would also be scolded. But she wouldn't care, because he knew that for Piedad, God was nothing important.

As for his Mari, she would never forgive him, and was even capable of leaving him and going to her mother's house. His son Antoñito loved him, but he was a mama's boy, and would take his mother's side.

He cursed Doña Asunción in several imaginative ways as he walked to the army headquarters, which was where Prudencio was.

His brother was surprised to see him. He didn't like Antonio to come there. His colonel was very suspicious.

"But what are you doing here? You know you shouldn't come," Prudencio chastised him.

"I can't report Eulogio."

"Why not? Of course you can. Hey, don't tell me you had a roll in the hay with Piedad and she made you change your mind? That woman is a bitch who's got you by the balls, but you should be strong, not give in, and you'll be finished with them."

"I'm telling you, I can't, damn it! Dona Asunción has threatened to tell Don Bernardo and Mari everything."

"Doña Asunción? But what does she know!"

"Well, I met her on the way to Mass and she told me that she had heard rumors in the neighborhood that I was going to report Eulogio, and that I was giving it to Piedad, and that it was her Christian duty to tell Don Bernardo, because she was worried that her Catalina was going to enter a family where the laws of the Church and God are not strictly obeyed. The old bag's a witch."

"Well, talk to her little peacock of a husband and get him to put her straight and stop her from meddling in men's affairs."

"I wish! He's another holy roller, and wouldn't stop his wife from telling Don Bernardo everything. You know that for that sanctimonious crowd, their first duty is to the priests, and they tell them everything. No, Prudencio, neither you nor I can let Eulogio get arrested, or else Dona Asunción is going to ruin me with Mari and my children. You know how my wife is, and if she finds out about Piedad, she'll have my balls."

"Well, it's weird that if the whole neighborhood knows then she hasn't heard anything. Mari maybe pretends to play dumb, like all women do, but only because it suits her."

"Look, I don't know if she's playing dumb or if she really doesn't know anything, but if she finds out, then it'll be worse than the war. And if Doña Asunción decides that she won't let her daughter marry into a family where we're not all a bunch of bedwetters, then Mari will never forgive me either. She wants Antoñito to marry that wet blanket Catalina."

"It's a mess, and no mistake. Damn … Well, you've got to do something to Eulogio, because I won't let him get away with giving me a black eye."

"We're not going to do anything, at least not until Antoñito and Catalina are married. The only satisfaction I can give you is that Eulogio's not going to come back to the warehouse and they can die of hunger … unless Piedad starts working the street corners."

"The day that Antoñito and Catalina get married, you report Eulogio and I'll make sure he's shot."

"Well, that's something to look forward to, but better keep schtum about it."

"And when's the wedding going to be?"

"Well, we haven't got a date yet; apparently, Doña Petra, Doña Asunción's sister, isn't very well, and because she's a widow and doesn't have any children, Catalina has gone to look after her; I think she's going to be in the country for a season or so. And then there's the engagement; Doña Asunción is a real stickler, and thinks they need to have at least two years of being engaged. Her husband thinks she might let them get away with just one year, but you know what the Vilamars are like: it's all about appearances."

"Antonio, two years is a long time, and one year's not short either. We have to deal with Eulogio before then." Prudencio protested.

"Look, I'm not going to screw with the wedding, so you need to wait. The day they get married we'll deal with Eulogio; until then, you're going to have to live with it."

The shopkeeper went away, leaving his brother upset. But no matter how much Prudencio complained, he wasn't going to bring his own house down around his ears. Mari wanted Antoñito to have a wedding with all the trimmings, and Don Ernesto Vilamar's mother was the daughter of a marquis, so Catalina was aristocracy of a kind. Mari already saw herself dolled up in a mantilla, walking with her son to the altar. Fucking women! He was sick of trusting the Vilamars. And Catalina was such a weak little thing, too thin, and always giving herself airs … and she was a little scrounger, for all that her father was gentry.

Isabel darned Fernando's only shirt. As soon as her son got back from work, they would go to see the lawyer. She had been saving up money in an envelope from what Doña Hortensia paid her.

She had to admit that they were good people. They were Franco supporters, of course, but they treated her well and Doña Hortensia always treated her with respect, saying "please" and "thank you" even as she ordered her around.

They knew from Don Bernardo that her husband was in prison, but they never mentioned his situation. Isabel thought to herself that she couldn't have borne it if they had. She didn't want to speak about Lorenzo with anyone who couldn't feel what she was feeling, and that meant that she could only confide in other losers like herself.

She fixed herself up as best she could, tying back her hair and pinning it in place. She took out the only stockings she had left and put them on carefully, worried about getting a run. Then she put on the black skirt, blue blouse, and a light sweater. She couldn't stop worrying about Piedad. She was afraid that Don Antonio would carry out his threats against Eulogio at any moment, and she knew that poor Piedad would be unable to hold herself back. "If they take my son, then I'll kill Antonio, I swear it," she had said. Isabel shuddered, because she knew that Piedad was desperate enough to do what she promised.

She started to feel a sharp pain in her stomach. The same pain she felt before every visit to the lawyer.

Finally, Fernando came in and washed himself quickly. He was worried as well.

"Be patient, that's the most important thing; don't get cross with Don Alberto, keep your temper: he's doing all he can," Isabel advised her son as they walked along at a fairly brisk pace.

"The thing he's best at is taking money we don't have away from us," Fernando protested.

"The money's not important, son: the important thing is that they let your father go."

"That's what I'm complaining about: he's been in prison for two years already, and the lawyer tells us lots of stories but hasn't managed to get a pardon sorted out. I don't care about the money, Mother, I'd pay with my own life if we could get Father out of prison, but I think they're just taking advantage of people like us."

"Don't say that! Don Bernardo says that the lawyer is a good man and that we can trust him."

"And you believe whatever the priest tells you?" Fernando exclaimed in anger.

"And why shouldn't I believe him? Has Don Bernardo ever hurt us? He's doing everything he can for us."

"Father never went to Mass."

"But I always did. Your father never stopped me from going to church. He's always respected my faith. Faith is something that I didn't lose even with the war, and if I didn't believe in God, then I don't know how I'd put up with everything we've been through," Isabel said gently, trying to avoid confrontation with her son.

Don Alberto made them wait for quite some time. When he opened the door to his office, they saw a very upset couple. The woman in particular could barely hold back her tears. Isabel grasped her son's hand and couldn't suppress a shudder.

"Come in, come in, Mrs. Garzo," the lawyer said.

The man seemed uncomfortable. Fernando didn't know if it was because of the couple who had been there previously, but he felt uneasy.

"Today's not a good day ... Well, I should tell you as soon as possible ..."

"Tell us what?" Isabel asked, afraid of what might be coming.

"They've started to refuse pardons ... Don't ask me why, but they're making their policy a great deal harsher ... No one knew this was happening ... they only said we'd have to wait a little bit longer ... That's how things are ... I really wish I could have given you better news," he said.

"You're telling me that my father has to stay in prison?" Fernando asked in an icy voice.

"Yes ... for the time being, yes ... it's just a matter of waiting ... I'll carry on trying."

"Tell me exactly what the situation is, and what we can hope for, if indeed we can hope for anything. But we want to hear the truth: don't string us along any more." Fernando raised his voice.

"Look, son, I know how you feel, but ..."

"I'm not your son. I'm the son of a good man, who is now in prison."

"Look, Fernando, you have to trust me when I say that I'm doing everything I can. If it were up to me, your father would already be out of prison. I know that he's a good man and no danger to anyone, but it's not up to me. If your mother and you aren't happy with my work, then … well, there are other lawyers."

Isabel was shocked. Don Alberto's voice made clear how upset he was at Fernando's attitude. They couldn't afford to look for another lawyer, one who might charge more. She looked at her son and knew that he was thinking the same thing, but that his pride wouldn't allow him to take a step backwards.

"Don Alberto, we're very grateful for everything that you're doing, and we know that my husband's case is in good hands, but you have to understand our impatience … It's been two years now since the war ended … My son misses his father and I … well, you can imagine. We live thinking that something might go wrong … They shoot prisoners every day; you can imagine how upset we are," Isabel said, a plea in her voice.

The lawyer adjusted his cuffs and straightened his tie. He did so mechanically as he thought about the answer he could give Isabel.

"Well … I'll carry on trying to do the impossible, which is what I need to do in order to get a pardon for your husband, believe me."

"You don't know how grateful we are; you're our only hope," Isabel said, avoiding her son's gaze.

"When will you have some news?" Fernando asked, trying to hold back the anger that he felt.

"I don't know … a couple of weeks … maybe more … They've stopped giving out pardons, but that doesn't mean they won't start again. It may just be that so many people are asking for them that the bureaucrats are overwhelmed," Don Alberto suggested.

"Let's hope it's that," Fernando muttered.

"You've got to have faith," the lawyer said.

"Faith is what keeps us going, Don Alberto," Isabel replied, something like a smile flitting over her face.

"Make an appointment with my secretary in a month, and let's see if I can tell you something then. Of course, if there's any news before then I'll tell you at once."

They left the office and met the secretary in the waiting room. She had the bill already drawn up.

"It's the same as always," the woman said.

Fernando took out the money and paid without saying a word. They didn't speak until they were down in the street and Isabel started to sob. Her legs were trembling, and she held tight to his arm.

"Son, you nearly pushed Don Alberto too far back there," she said.

"I'm sorry, Mother, but he's a hypocrite through and through. He's taking our money and giving us nothing but pretty words in return. He's got connections: he could do something more for Father," Fernando replied.

"Don Bernardo recommended him, and he always says that we're in good hands."

"I don't know, Mother. I'm not sure that's true, and just thinking about Father makes me desperate. He looks so lost since he broke his glasses. We'll go and see him on Sunday."

Isabel accepted this idea, still crying. They were each sunk in their own grief, and didn't speak until they were back home.

Pepita told Fernando that Eulogio had come and asked for him a couple of times.

"I told him that you went out looking very dressed-up," the doorwoman said, keen for them to tell her where they had been.

It wasn't until after supper that Fernando gathered the strength to go up to Eulogio's attic. He didn't want to speak, but he didn't want to ignore his friend's troubles either.

"Come in, come in," Piedad said as she opened the door. "He's in his room."

Eulogio was stretched out on his bed, looking at the ceiling. A cigarette butt hung from his lips.

"Did you see the lawyer?" he asked Fernando.

"Yes, and he told us that they're not giving out any more pardons at the moment, so my father will stay in prison for a while longer. You can guess how we're feeling."

"Screwed, just like everyone. Bastards!" Eulogio shouted.

"Don't swear; you've always been able to control yourself," Fernando said.

"You're right ... Hey, I got a letter from Marvin."

"Oh ... is he all right?" Fernando asked unwillingly.

"Yes, but he says that the situation in Paris is pretty impossible, what with the Germans everywhere, and that he's bought a bookshop, and that he's thinking about going to Alexandria."

"To Egypt? What's he going to do there?"

"He thinks it will be good for his inspiration and for his writing. He's sent me the address in Alexandria."

"Right ... Okay ..." Fernando didn't know what to say about Marvin: he didn't care what he did.

"I'm thinking about leaving," Eulogio said suddenly.

"Leaving? And where are you going to go? Not Alexandria too?"

"I don't know, maybe America. Things aren't good in France for us Spaniards. They'll arrest us in the free zone and send us to labor camps."

"But if you go to France, then Marvin will give you a hand. It's the least he can do for you, after you put him up for a few months."

"Yes, but the Nazis are in Paris, and so it's not really the best place to go, which is why Marvin is going to leave. As for the free zone, it's not free at all. Pétain is a lackey of the Nazis. I think the best idea is to head West, maybe go to Argentina. They speak Spanish there and it won't be hard for me to find a job."

"But America's a long way away ... it's easier to go to France."

"All I know is that I should go. Don Antonio's not going to be satisfied with firing me. He's a bastard and I'm sure he'll try to do something more to us."

"And what about your mother? Are you going to leave her here?" Fernando's question was a reproach.

"I'll be honest with you: I prefer to go by myself. And she always says that she's too old to start all over again, and that she'll stay here and see what God has in store for her."

"Right, but God hasn't really been on our side recently, if he ever was, and so you'd better convince her to come too, because Don Antonio is capable of anything."

"My mother doesn't want to leave Fernando."

"Really? She's not an old woman. Have you thought about what might happen to her if she stays here? If Don Antonio can't get his revenge on you, then your mother's the next obvious choice. He's got no shame."

"I don't know how my mother could have … I think I'll never be able to forgive her …" Eulogio said, closing his eyes and trying to block out the shame he felt when he thought about his mother's relations with Don Antonio.

"Look, I didn't want to say anything to you, but there might still be a solution … Catalina has asked her mother to speak to Don Antonio. Well, she's actually asked her to threaten him that she'll tell Don Bernardo about what he's been doing to your mother …" Fernando blushed.

"What! No, no way … Who does Catalina think she is to stick her nose into our business! If you did this I'm not going to forgive you. How dare you tell everyone what's happened?"

"Catalina only wanted to help you. If Doña Asunción talks to Don Antonio, it might slow him down."

"No! I don't want anyone getting involved in our lives! You like Catalina, and she's not a bad girl, but she's got her head in the clouds, and she's flighty and badly brought-up: a little rich girl who doesn't know anything at all about life. And her mother is a sanctimonious old biddy. The Vilamars have always looked down on us. Who does she think she is to talk to Don Antonio! How dare you, Fernando!" Eulogio raised his voice angrily.

"I'm sorry to have upset you. I was worried for you and told Catalina. I thought you had a better opinion of her, Eulogio."

"She's a spoiled brat, that's what she is! She's got her hooks into you and that's it."

"You're not being fair to her or to me. It's true that Catalina is very important to me, and although you don't acknowledge it, she's kind and generous and always ready to help other people. And she is very fond of you. You're right that I shouldn't have said anything to her, but she would have found out anyway. No one's talking about anything else in the entire neighborhood. Everyone knows that Don Antonio fired you … Well, I'm off." Fernando was upset at his friend's reaction.

Eulogio let him leave without saying anything. He was in despair, and felt that his life had taken another unexpected and unpleasant twist. He had lost his father in the war, and then had gone to fight himself and come back crippled. Now, at the age of twenty-eight, he thought of himself as an old man, as though he had already lived several lifetimes. Had he been unfair to Fernando? No, he thought, probably not. He knew that Fernando was well-intentioned, but he felt humiliated that he had spoken to Catalina about him and his mother. The whole neighborhood was gossiping about them. He knew it. But the fact that he knew it didn't make it hurt any the less whenever he remembered it.

His mother barely went out anymore. She tried to leave the house as soon as the sun came up so that she didn't run into any neighbors. She was a proud woman, and felt ashamed. At least in the workshop, where she went to sew during the week and to clean on the weekend, they didn't know anything about what had happened.

He felt angry again as he remembered his life before the war. His father, a newspaper editor, had also translated books for the Editorial Clásica run by Fernando's father. And he had still found time to teach people how to read and write at one of the Casas del Pueblo, the local trade union offices. His mother, well, she had supported Azaña and was sincere in her admiration of his time as president of the Republic. He looked up to his father. What he had done seemed important. They had lived without any luxuries, but comfortably, and his father's dream had been that his son would become a great painter. But the damned war had taken away both their lives.

He thought about how stupid he had been to think that he was cleverer than Don Antonio, stealing a few things from the warehouse. Don Antonio gave away nothing for free, and had used his mother's body in exchange for every crumb that Eulogio took away with him.

Piedad had told him why she had given herself to the shopkeeper. To get her son out of prison, to stop him being judged for some imaginary crimes. Don Antonio had blackmailed his mother using the only thing he could: Eulogio himself.

He left his room and found his mother sewing elbow patches

onto a shirt. She looked older. It was the first time that he felt she was defeated. He would have liked to have given her a hug, but he couldn't. He was overcome with resentment. Maybe it would have been better for them to take him away to prison, for at least there he would have had nothing to be ashamed of.

"I've decided. I'm leaving," he said.

"You're going out, now?" she asked.

"No, I'm leaving Spain. I'm telling you. There's nothing for me to do here apart from see other people laugh at me. And Don Antonio isn't the forgetting kind. Sooner or later he'll accuse me of something and they'll arrest me."

"Where are you going to go?"

"I thought I'd go to America."

"But … America is a long way away …"

"It's better that way. I'm not coming back. There's no life for me here."

"Eulogio … I … I thought you'd stay closer to home …"

"No. If I go, I'm going for good, so I can forget all of this."

"Forget me as well?" Piedad said, hoping her son wouldn't notice her grief.

Eulogio was silent and didn't dare say anything. He would have liked to have said that she was the first person he was going to forget about, but he knew that this would cause her a great deal of pain and that then he'd feel bad. No, he couldn't forgive her, but he couldn't hurt her either.

"I told you days ago that I was going to leave, and you said that I shouldn't count on you coming with me," he reminded her.

"Because I'd be no use to you. That's why I'll stay here. I just hope that Franco doesn't last that long, and that you'll be able to come back, you and all the people who have already left."

"Don Antonio hasn't got anything against you, so I guess he won't do anything to you," he said, knowing that his words would ring in his mother's ears like a reproach.

"If I've lost your father and now I lose you, then there's nothing else that can happen to me; no one can hurt me at all. But … you know what? I won't ask that you understand me, but I will ask you not to hate me. I did what I thought I had to do and I would do it again, a thousand times, before seeing you locked away in prison and losing the best years of your life. A mother would pay any price for her son."

"I would have preferred to go to prison rather than feel this shame, but what's done is done. There's no turning back now. As soon as I can, I'll be off."

Piedad looked down at her needle. There was a lump in her throat. Her son had seen her and judged her, and his verdict was implacable. They were lost to one another forever. And she felt, more than ever, that she hated everyone who had helped ruin their lives.

Back in his room, Eulogio reread Marvin's letter. He missed his friend. Their conversations, and their companionable silences. They could be together without any need to say anything. What they had gone through at the front had brought them together forever.

> My dear friend,
>
> I'm sorry I haven't written before now, but my parents were here until a few days ago, though that's not really an excuse for not sending you my news. I've also been writing a lot. I'm not happy with what I'm writing, but maybe one line in ten, or twenty, is worth preserving.
>
> I've bought a bookshop, for reasons which I will tell you. Monsieur Rosent, my editor, has sold me his business. The Jews are suffering terribly here, persecuted by the authorities, and Monsieur Rosent is getting it bad as well. This wasn't what I planned, but the circumstances have changed and the war makes us do strange things.
>
> I'm more and more pessimistic about how the war's going to end. If Germany has dared to invade the Soviet Union, it's a sign either of their madness or their strength. Maybe both. I don't want to imagine a world with Hitler at its helm, and so I wonder if I shouldn't do something, but just thinking about fighting … No, you know I can't do it. Because I'm a poet? No, because I'm a coward. That's the only truth.
>
> But I don't want to carry on burdening you with things that are hurting me.
>
> My friend. I may go to Alexandria for a while. It's a trip to do

with the sale of the publishing house. Sara Rosent lives there. She's my editor's daughter, and she'll be in charge of her father's property one day; I'm just a temporary guardian of her inheritance. I'm also drawn to the idea of spending some time in a place like Egypt, where the war isn't making such big waves as it is here.

I'm sending you Sara Rosent's address in case you need anything from me.

Until next time, with a brotherly embrace,

MARVIN BRIAN

Two days later, Doña Asunción arranged to bump into Fernando. It was harder and harder for her to escape from her husband, who asked her constantly about her comings and goings. But Catalina had insisted that she go and find Fernando and tell him about her conversation with Don Antonio, as well as to ask him to come and see her. She was bored in her aunt's house.

Fernando was coming back from the print shop when he ran into her.

"Good afternoon, Doña Asunción. How is Catalina?" he said with a slight bow.

"She's well ... very well. She wants you to go and see her, although my sister Petra's not very keen on the idea of your coming over ... We're very worried ... If my husband found out that you saw Catalina, I don't know what he'd do ..."

"No one, least of all Don Ernesto, is going to find out from me."

"My daughter's very fond of you, Fernando, and she says that she trusts you more than anyone else in the whole world ..." Doña Asunción confessed.

"And I feel the same about her: we've known each other since we were children."

"Yes ... Well, I want you to know that I've spoken to Don Antonio, and I think he won't be causing Eulogio any more trouble."

"Wow! That's excellent news. Are you sure? He's not really a very trustworthy man ..."

"I know ... Well, I don't really know ... It's all so difficult! He's promised to do nothing to hurt Piedad or Eulogio, and I think that he'll keep his word ... I ... I told him that I was thinking about talking to Don Bernardo because I was worried about the rumors there were about him and Piedad. I think he got scared. He knows that Don Bernardo would be very angry."

"You've been very brave," Fernando dared to say.

"It wasn't easy, and if my husband finds out ... I don't want to even imagine what might happen! We shouldn't carry on talking; people make up rumors about the silliest things."

"I'll go see Catalina whenever I can. Tell her."

"Is there any news about your father?"

"They say that they've put pardons on hold ... We're desperate."

"I'm so sorry. If you think we can do anything ..."

"No, I don't think you can. Thank you anyway."

"Say hello to your mother from me."

"I will, Doña Asunción."

He would have liked to go and tell Eulogio what Catalina's mother had just told him, but they had spent a couple of days avoiding one another. They were hurt by each other's attitude.

When he got home, he described his conversation with Doña Asunción to his mother.

"She's a good woman, and I guess it must have been hard for her to face up to that brute of a shopkeeper, who's only scared of his wife and of Don Bernardo. They're the only ones who can slow him down. And so Doña Asunción did well to tell him that she was going to see Don Bernardo."

"The poor woman is worried that her husband will find out about all this chicanery," Fernando said.

"Yes, I don't want to think about how Ernesto would react. He's a difficult man. And the Vilamars aren't in such a good situation as they have been in the past, and I think that Don Antonio is giving them a hand," Isabel explained to her son.

"Goodness, Mother, I didn't know you were so up-to-date with what's happening in the neighborhood!"

"People gossip a lot, Fernando, and sometimes you hear things you'd rather not."

"You know what? I'm worried about Eulogio. I don't want him to go without us saying goodbye."

"Well, you know what you have to do. Go upstairs and talk to him."

"But he's angry at me, I told you already."

"So what? You're friends. You've always been friends, even though he's a bit older than you. I remember when he decided to go to the war you cried because you wanted to go with him. There's no sense losing a friendship over a silly question of pride, Fernando. I'm sure he's as upset as you are that you've stopped talking to one another."

"Maybe I'll go up and he'll throw me out."

"I don't think so, but if he does, then too bad. And he'll get over it."

"Mother ..."

"Don't be so proud! Go on, go up and talk to him. He needs you. I'll meet up with Piedad to go for a walk one Sunday: she's almost too scared to go out in the street. It's one thing to have people spreading rumors about you, and quite another to have everyone take it for granted that you and the shopkeeper are having an affair."

"The odd thing is that Don Antonio's wife doesn't know anything," Fernando said.

"No one dares tell her. You know that the last person to find out about these things is always the one who's closest to them. Eulogio never suspected anything about his mother, and the whole neighborhood was murmuring about it."

"You're right ... Well, I'll go up to the attic and see what happens."

"You're good friends, Fernando, you'll sort it out."

He found Eulogio painting on a piece of cardboard. He barely paid him any attention, so engrossed was he in drawing things that looked like silhouettes.

They stayed where they were for a few minutes without saying anything, until Fernando felt uncomfortable and began to speak.

"I met Doña Asunción, and she promised me that Don Antonio won't bother you. She threatened him with going to speak to Don Bernardo."

"And what would she have said to Don Bernardo: that my mother was getting it on with Don Antonio?" Eulogio said bitterly.

"I think you're exaggerating a bit. Wasn't it you who spoke about a free society in which men and women were equal, and no one could blame a woman for doing as she pleased?"

"Don't test me, Fernando! Leave me alone!"

"All right, I'll leave you alone. You're bitter about this. The war didn't do it to you, but you let Don Antonio do it to you, and he's not worth one tenth of what you're worth, much less what your mother's worth. Do what you want, Eulogio, but know that Don Antonio won't lift a finger against you. It's not that I trust him, but I think he's not stupid enough to allow Don Bernardo to get involved and for his wife to find out."

Fernando turned away and was about to go downstairs, when he felt Eulogio's hand on his shoulder.

"You're right: that man has ruined my life, and the worst of it is that I can't forgive my mother."

"She doesn't deserve that. I'm sure that mine would have done the same for me, and the last thing on my mind would be to blame her for it. Your mother has shown that she's willing to pay any price for you."

"I would have preferred it if they'd taken me to prison."

"And what good would that have done? Your mother's suffered enough, losing your father, without having to lose you as well."

"Don't get preachy."

"No, I just came here to tell you that you could be at ease. No sermons."

"I'm going to America: there's nothing for me here. Franco's not going to give up on his power, for all that my mother thinks he won't last long."

"I don't know what's going to happen … I hope your mother is right! But things as they are … they still put people in prison, and still shoot them, and make us too scared to even blink," Fernando said.

"You see, they won the war, but it still wasn't enough for them," Eulogio muttered angrily.

"Well, I'm off. I've got to get up early tomorrow. Tell your mother what Doña Asunción told me and maybe that'll calm her down."

When Fernando was gone, Eulogio went into the kitchen, where Piedad was mashing a boiled potato with a little parsley to give it some flavor. That was the evening's meal.

Piedad listened to her son with a serious expression on her face, although she was greatly relieved that Don Antonio was not going to be able to harm them.

"Doña Asunción is a good woman," she said.

"You're too kind. The Vilamars are right-wingers and they always have been. And now they love Franco more than Franco loves himself. I hate them," Eulogio replied.

"The Vilamars were monarchists, and we've never seen them hurting anyone. And before the war, when they had some money, Doña Asunción helped us as much as she could, and Don Ernesto has always been very polite to everyone," Piedad said.

"What are you saying? That's all I need to hear! I never thought that you'd defend people like that. Weren't you a supporter of Azaña?"

"I'm not defending anyone, I'm just saying that they're not bad people."

"Don Ernesto a monarchist, and Doña Asunción a God-botherer ... What can you expect?"

"And does that make them bad people? Look, I think you need to judge people by their actions."

"Well, because of their actions, they need to be condemned: they support Franco! Franco! And now look who's defending Franco supporters?"

"I'm not defending Franco supporters: I'm saying that the Vilamars are good people."

"I don't understand you! I find out something disgusting about you every day," Eulogio said. He left the kitchen, slamming the door shut behind him.

Piedad burst into tears. She blamed herself for arguing with her son about the Vilamars. Eulogio was right, what did they care about her? She should have held her tongue and not gotten into an argument, because her son was very sensitive and it was all her fault.

Eulogio had always been an optimist, even managing to hold it together when he had been wounded at the front, but he had changed since he found out about her and the shopkeeper. He was bitter about everything, and worst of all, she couldn't do anything to make him forgive her.

She stayed in the kitchen, sobbing quietly. She wasn't brave enough to go into the room and give her son a hug. She knew that he would reject her, push her away as he had done over the past few days. Every time he refused to kiss her, she felt a sharp pain in her chest. Although doctors say that the heart doesn't hurt, her own heart was about to explode with pain.

Piedad didn't sleep at all that night, and neither did Eulogio. Three floors further down, Isabel was also awake. She couldn't stop thinking about her husband's fate. She tried to be brave for Fernando's sake; she didn't want to make him feel worse, but she had a bad feeling about the situation. Fernando, lying in his bed, had his eyes shut, but he wasn't asleep either.

On Sunday, Isabel and Fernando got up as soon as the sun had risen. They wanted to get to the prison first so they could be a part of the line of prison families.

The guards carefully checked everyone who had a family member or a friend in the prison. It was hard for Fernando to keep quiet in the face of the humiliation. He suffered. His mother told him every time that they should be quiet: any word out of place might mean that they wouldn't let them see his father, or else retaliate against him.

Their clothing was shabby and showed its age, but they tried to dress well, because his father had always been an elegant man. "You respect others by dressing well," he used to say to Fernando when he was a child.

Isabel had washed her hair and put it up in a bun held in place by pins. She was wearing a worn-out white blouse and a dark blue skirt. Her shoes were clean in spite of the fact that they were old. Fernando was wearing one of his father's old jackets.

The families of the prisoners waited impatiently. Fernando and his mother were early and stood around with the other early risers. They usually spoke to an old man who cheered them up. Don Arturo, for that was his name, had his eldest son taken prisoner in the Comendadoras, and had lost two other sons in the fighting. "The tragedy is that my middle boy fought on Franco's side, and my youngest, the apple of my eye, turned out to be an anarchist. And now I've lost them both," Arturo would say as he tried to hold back tears. "I just want the oldest one to be all right; he was a supporter of Azaña, and a teacher ... But Franco seems to hate teachers as well, and I'm afraid for him."

That day the guards seemed to be in a worse mood than usual, and they coldly told several families who were waiting at the door to leave. When this happened, it was because the prisoner had been transferred to another prison, or worse, because he had been shot after being denied a pardon.

When Isabel showed her documents to the guard, he looked through a list in his right hand.

"Lorenzo Garzo ... he's not here. Next!"

"What do you mean, he's not here? You must be mistaken: my husband is here. You know that perfectly well, we come here every week to see him. There must be some mistake," Isabel said nervously.

"I've told you, he's not on the list! Get out of the way. Don't cause any trouble!" the guard shouted.

"Listen, my father's in here. Lorenzo Garzo, have another look," Fernando said, feeling a wave of icy sweat rush over his whole body.

"I've told you, get the hell out! He's not here." The guard gave Fernando a push.

Isabel, terrified, grasped her son by the arm, worried that he'd be unable to control himself.

"Tell me who we can talk to," she said, trying to keep calm.

"How should I know? He's not here, and that's it. It's not my job to know what happens to the criminals we keep here. Get out!"

For a few seconds, Fernando and Isabel thought they were living in a nightmare. It can't be, they said to one another, there must be some mistake, but the guard wasn't going to check his list again.

A young woman who was waiting in the line came over to them and said in a low voice:

"They must have shot your husband. A month ago, they told me the same thing when I came to see my brother. Now I hope they're not going to say the same thing again about my other brother."

"What are you saying?" Isabel asked in terror.

"I know it's hard for you to believe it ... The same thing happened to me. But when they're not on the list it means they've been shot," the woman insisted.

"Not my father ... not my father ..." Fernando mumbled.

"They'll write to you and tell you everything ..." the woman said, just as her turn to enter the prison came.

Fernando held his mother tight. Both of them were trembling. They didn't know what to do or what to say, or where to go, or who to speak to.

"Don't worry, Mother, we'll get back in the line. Look, let's get into another line and maybe he'll be on the other guards' list."

"Yes, yes, that's what we need to do. There must be some mistake. If anything had happened to him, then the lawyer would have told us ... He'd know ..."

"Of course, Mother, you'll see. Everything will get cleared up."

They got back into the line. They waited impatiently for another hour, trapped in the same nightmare.

"Lorenzo Garzo isn't here," the guard said without even looking at them.

"He has to be here. We're working on his pardon, we saw the lawyer just this week," Isabel said with a note of hysteria in her voice.

"Look, if I say he's not here, then he's not here. Get out."

"But he has to be here!" Isabel said, about to break down.

"If you carry on like this we'll have to arrest you. You're blocking the line." The guard's manners were no better than those of his colleague.

"It can't be true." Isabel was starting to cry.

"What can't be true? There's nobody innocent here, so ... Get the hell out!"

Isabel collapsed and Fernando was barely fast enough to catch her. He took her over to the corner and made her lean against the wall.

"Mother, for God's sake, calm down! Nothing's happened to Father. We'll go to the lawyer tomorrow and he'll tell us what's happened and sort this out, you'll see ..."

"Don't you realize, son? Haven't you heard what that woman said? Your father ... they ... they've ..." Isabel couldn't carry on speaking, because her sobs caught the words in her throat.

"Don't say that! Father's alive! I know it! I know that nothing's happened!" Fernando shouted.

They walked away, hugging each other close and supporting one another. Tears ran down Isabel's face, and bitterness was etched on Fernando's.

When they got home, they were unable to eat a single bite. They wouldn't have been able to force down a mouthful even if they had been invited to a banquet. They spent the rest of the day talking about what might have happened. Fernando insisted that it was all a big mistake, and Isabel wanted to believe him, but at the bottom of her heart she knew that her husband had been killed.

On Monday morning, Isabel got up without any strength in her limbs. She was exhausted. She hadn't slept all night, and her eyes were red from crying. But she had to go to the Ramírezes' house. Don Luis and Doña Hortensia got up early, and they were not fond of tardiness.

When she got there, Doña Hortensia was drinking a cup of malt.

"Look at your face, Isabel. Are you ill?" she asked, worried.

Isabel couldn't contain herself and burst into tears as she told the whole story.

Doña Hortensia was silent and looked straight at her. On the one hand, she was sorry that Isabel's husband had been shot; on the other, it was clear that this was because he had been a red.

The woman asked herself how it was possible that upstanding people like the Garzos could have fought on the wrong side.

"Come, now, don't cry. I'll ask my husband, and maybe he'll be able find something out. He's got good friends. He'll find something out. I'll talk to him, and you get started on the ironing ..."

Isabel wiped away her tears with the back of her hand and went through to the kitchen. Doña Hortensia went into her bedroom, where her husband was just finishing getting dressed.

"Luis, I know you're in a hurry, but Isabel has just arrived and she can't stop crying ... They went to the prison yesterday to see her husband, and they told her that he wasn't there ... She fears the worst ... Can you find something out about it?"

"Everyone will know we've got a red in our kitchen ..." he protested.

"She's a good woman, and Don Bernardo recommended her, and I've never had any complaints about her. She's a worker, a good worker, and she's clean and quiet. She's not to blame for what her husband did. So please, see what you can do," Doña Hortensia said, pushing her husband slightly.

"I'll ask, but I can't promise anything. I don't like it when we get into trouble for other people."

"Is it a sin to ask a question? For God's sake, Luis! I don't think that it could harm us to try to help the poor woman. And whether you like it or not, there are lots of reds left in Madrid, and what would you have us do with them? We all have to live here. The important thing is that we won the war. We have to be merciful."

"The things you say ... Well, I'll ask, but nothing more than that."

"Well, if there's anything else we can do ..."

"Hortensia, don't get started, it's one thing to ask a question, and quite another to get caught up in the affairs of that family."

"Luis, we have obligations to our neighbors. And I'm not going to spend my life checking who's a red and who isn't. I don't care: the only thing that matters is that they're good people."

"How can you not care? That's all I need! Look, Hortensia, don't say such things, because we really will end up getting into trouble. The enemies of the Fatherland ..."

"Shush! Don't start with your speeches. Look, I don't think that Isabel is anyone's enemy, and as far as I've been able to find out, everyone loved her husband as well. Even Don Bernardo wrote a letter in his favor asking for him to be pardoned. Lorenzo Garzo was the editor of Editorial Clásica, and we've got several of his books in the house; I don't think an editor can hurt anyone."

"An editor who fought for the reds in the war," Don Luis replied grumpily.

"How boring you get with all these colors. They were wrong and they lost. What more do you want?"

"I'm going to be late. I'll tell you something about this Lorenzo Garzo this afternoon."

"If you could ask and also get him let out of prison ..."

But Don Luis had already left the house and didn't hear what his wife said. She had given him a headache. Even so, he knew he would have to ask about this Garzo. Hortensia wouldn't leave him alone until he gave her a proper answer.

That Monday, Fernando thought that the hours went by unforgivably slowly. He was keen for the afternoon to come so he could go to Don Alberto García's office and ask for explanations. He couldn't believe that the lawyer wouldn't know what his father's fate might have been. The only possibility that he could think of was that his father had been sent to another prison; he couldn't bear to imagine anything else.

Don Vicente had to call him out a couple of times, seeing him sunk in his own thoughts in front of the printing machine.

"What's the matter with you today? You look struck dumb or something ... Come on, pay attention."

"I ... I'm sorry ... I was distracted."

"I can see that. Did you sleep badly?"

"It's not that ... It's just that ... Well, that too: I didn't sleep a wink all night. It's just that ... I went with my mother to see my father yesterday, and they said that he wasn't there. The guard wouldn't tell us anything else."

"Ah ... Well, it could be a mistake. Come on, leave the printing to me and go find out. It's not a visiting day today, so it should be easier for you to speak to someone."

"I thought that when I got out of here I'd go and speak to Don Alberto, the lawyer who was working on the pardon."

"Do both. Go to the prison and then go and see this Don Alberto. These are tough times, Fernando. People want to get rid of everyone who isn't on their side. Whatever's happened, you're a man and you need to think about your mother. You're all she has. You know how much I respected your father, an upright man and a good person. Just thinking about the afternoons we spent together at the Athenaeum …" the printer remembered.

Fernando nodded gratefully. Don Vicente had always been a good friend of the family.

As soon as he left the print shop, he went to the building that had once been the Convent of the Comendadoras, but which was now a prison.

It was not the only religious institution which the victors used to lock up their enemies. Francisco Tonel, a lieutenant colonel in the cavalry, was in charge of public order in Madrid, and had twenty-one prisons spread out throughout the city. Sixteen were for men and five were for women. But what scared the losers the most was not the fact that their family members were in one of those prisons, but that every day many prisoners passed in front of one of the five military tribunals who decided whether the people who had been loyal to the Republic were to be allowed to live or else condemned to die.

Isabel used to say to Fernando that he was lucky to have his father in the Convent of the Comendadoras, which was only a few blocks from their house. At least he would feel close to them.

Fernando came to where the guards were, and stood in front of them, asking what had happened to his father.

"You told us yesterday that he wasn't on the list. Does that mean he's been transferred?"

The man looked him up and down with a mixture of condescension and commiseration.

"If he wasn't on the list, it means that he's been sentenced. Last week a lot of people were taken to the military tribunals."

"Did they take my father?" Fernando asked, terrified about what the reply might be.

"Go in and ask. It's not my job to hand out information. Anyway, I don't know who your father is. There are three thousand men here, and it's not like I have to know them all."

A prison official listened unwillingly to his story.

"I don't have to give you explanations. You'll get a letter telling you where your father is."

"But you must understand that we're worried. My mother is in despair … If you would only be so kind as to tell me where they've taken him …"

Fernando left the Comendadoras with a bitter taste in his mouth. He hadn't been able to find anything out, only that his father was no longer there. He walked quickly to Don Alberto García's office.

The lawyer was annoyed that Fernando had come to see him without an appointment. He had one client with him already, and another one in the waiting room, and so he told Fernando he had to wait. For two long hours, Fernando waited. When the door to the office finally opened, the lawyer looked sorrowfully at Fernando.

"I was going to tell you … but I've been very busy …"

"Tell us?" Fernando said, feeling fear hit him right in the gut.

"Well … It's a terrible thing … all our efforts have been for nothing. I'm sorry."

"I don't understand …" Fernando whispered.

"The court-martial rejected the appeal and … well … your father was shot," Don Alberto said, knowing that he would have to deal with Fernando's reaction.

"Bastards! Sons of bitches!" Fernando said, muttering the words that flew from his throat.

"Calm down! Calm down, son! Don't say anything: it won't help your father, and it might hurt you in the future as well."

"They killed him!" And the tears began to flow down Fernando's cheeks, eventually turning into inconsolable sobs.

Don Alberto García didn't like these scenes of sorrow, though he was required to be present at so many. He didn't like trying to get prisoners pardoned, but he kept on doing it because it was a good source of money. He didn't try to cheat people. He told them the truth: he would do whatever he could do, which wasn't much, and he couldn't guarantee a happy ending to their quest.

"Fernando, look, you knew that this might happen. I know how you're feeling … It's not easy to lose a father. I remember when I lost mine."

"You father died in his bed, and mine was shot," Fernando said, looking at him with hatred.

"The result's the same: you lose a father. And at your age you need a father very much … I know …"

"What would you know about it?" Fernando shouted.

"I promise you, I did everything I could."

"Why didn't you tell us?"

"I was going to tell you today … I didn't hear about the decision of the court-martial until Saturday evening … and I couldn't just go to your house and tell your mother …"

The lawyer looked worriedly at Fernando, who didn't stop crying, with an expression of hatred on his face. He knew that Fernando wasn't a bad kid, but he was worried that the boy might turn violent. One time a woman had slapped him when he told her they had shot her fiancé. He stood there silently, waiting for Fernando to win the battle against his tears. It was better this way: words would only make him angrier.

"How can I tell my mother?" Fernando said to himself. "She won't be able to deal with this. Oh God, what have we done!"

Don Alberto poured him a glass of water from a jug covered with a white cloth that he had on his desk. Fernando took it.

"Look, you still owe me a few pesetas, but given the circumstances, I could let it slide. Is that all right?"

"No, no, no. You'll be paid. The Garzos don't accept charity from anyone." And Fernando took the money he already had prepared out of his pocket.

"Don't be proud … I'm just trying to be kind …" Don Alberto said, very pleased with himself for his generosity.

"We don't owe anyone anything. We don't accept charity," Fernando replied angrily.

"All right … I won't insist …" The lawyer put the money away in the top drawer of his desk. "Now that you're here, I'll give you the papers … this is the court-martial's ruling against the commutation of sentence … You need to go to the address I'll write here and get your father's death certificate."

"You mean my father's murder certificate."

"Come on, Fernando, please be careful what you say! I know that you're a good boy and I understand your pain, but I don't want to hear this. You can't disrespect an official tribunal. You have to respect the law."

"What law, Don Alberto? Wasn't it enough to win the war without shooting all the losers?

"No one's going to shoot you, so stop talking nonsense. Come on, drink some water and calm down. Tell your mother that I'm here in case she needs anything ..."

"I need my father," Fernando said angrily.

"I'm sorry, kid, you know I'm sorry, I'm not happy about this either. I was certain that they'd commute the sentence ... but it wasn't to be."

The lawyer stood up to indicate that the meeting was over. He had nothing more to say. It wouldn't help either of them to carry on talking. He held his hand out to Fernando, who seemed to hesitate before shaking it.

When he was in the street, Fernando wiped his tears with the spotless white handkerchief that his mother laid out next to his clothes every morning. It was his father's. They still had six of his handkerchiefs that Fernando now used.

He couldn't wrap his head around the idea that his father was no longer in this world, that he had ceased to be. Just thinking about it left a pain in his chest that was so sharp he thought his heart was about to stop beating. The hatred he felt was so great that it scared him. He was terrified of telling his mother. Would she be able to handle it? His parents had been very close. He had never heard them argue. He had been lucky enough to grow up in a family where harmony had reigned supreme precisely because of the deep love that suffused his parents' relationship.

He walked for a long time. He needed to calm down before speaking to his mother. He didn't want to break down in front of her.

And suddenly a terrible idea unfurled in his mind: he would kill his father's killers. He knew that he wouldn't be able to get all of them, but maybe one at least. He had to choose who. Maybe one of the members of the court-martial. Yes, that would be a good revenge, to let those bastards know that they couldn't get away with their own crimes.

Or he could get one of the guards at the prison. Those bastards had made his father's life a misery by denying him any solace. Or maybe … yes, maybe it would be better to kill one of the soldiers who had been in the firing squad. He had to think, had to find the right way to take revenge. But he would have his revenge, even if it cost him his life, even though he knew that if that happened, his mother would never recover.

When he got home, night was already falling. He was surprised to find that there was no light on: maybe his mother had gone out. Sometimes she went to pray the rosary at seven o'clock, and would spend a few minutes talking to Don Bernardo or the other women who found their consolation in saying prayers.

When he turned the light on he nearly jumped out of his skin. His mother was sitting in a chair by the wall. She was pale and still, as though she were dead.

"Jesus, Mother! You scared me! What happened?"

She barely moved her face to look at him, and he jumped back again.

"What is it?"

Suddenly he understood. He didn't have to give her the news about his father's death. She knew. That was it.

"Mother … you know … Who told you?" he asked timorously.

Isabel took some time to be able to get the words into her mouth, to articulate them and to let them flow from her lips.

"Doña Hortensia," she managed to murmur.

"Doña Hortensia?"

"She asked Don Luis to find out about your father. They told him today."

Fernando went over to his mother and fell to his knees, burying his head in her lap. She started to gently stroke his hair. Then they held each other and let themselves give in to their tears. They cried, with no wailing and with no words, silently, sitting so close to one another that their tears mixed together as they fell.

Reality came slowly back into focus, and Isabel and Fernando slipped back into their working routines. Neither mother nor son hid their despair.

Isabel had grown old overnight. Wrinkles had attached themselves into the corners of her mouth, making it into a rictus of bitterness. Her eyes looked smaller, and her skin, which had always been very white, looked pallid.

She cried silently. She cried on her way to work, she cried at night when she lay in bed, she cried when she did chores at home. Her tears became as natural as breathing.

Fernando cried as well, but he made sure his mother didn't see him. He didn't want to add to her suffering.

"If I'm still alive it's because of you," his mother confessed one night.

"Don't say that … we have to live, Mother, we have to do it for Father. He wouldn't have wanted us to have given in. We have to stay standing and fight for his memory. We have to live, Mother, we have to live and … take our revenge."

"No, son, vengeance ruins the one who uses it, and anyway, we couldn't even if we wanted to."

Isabel stopped going to church. She had lost her faith.

Don Bernardo came over to their house one Sunday after the noontime Mass.

Fernando opened the door and stood in the doorway without asking him in.

"Well, what, you're not going to let me in? I've come to see your mother; I know you're a lost cause …" the priest said, trying to contain his rage at Fernando's defiant gaze.

Isabel heard the voices and came out at once. She looked at the priest with no emotion on her face, not even curiosity.

"What do you want?" she asked without making the slightest gesture to welcome him in.

"I want to talk to you, my daughter. You haven't been seen for two weeks. I know about your husband, and I am very sorry for you. I pray that God has taken him into his bosom."

"Don't bother. My husband doesn't need your prayers," Isabel said defiantly.

"What are you saying? Come now, I understand how you are

feeling, but don't turn your back on our Lord," Don Bernardo protested, uncomfortably talking past Fernando, who still blocked the doorway.

"God has turned his back on us, so we're through." Isabel's voice betrayed her anger.

"You're not going to let me in? I have brought you comfort," the priest insisted.

"Comfort? No one can comfort us. No one. Do you think there are any words that can lift the suffering I feel at having lost my husband? Do you think there's anything that can lift the pain my son feels at the loss of his father? Words can't do anything. Leave us with our pain," Isabel said.

"My duty is to stop you from losing your soul."

"You should worry about the souls of the people who murdered my father," Fernando interrupted. "They're the ones who need your prayers. But even if God did exist, I don't think there are prayers that would save them from hell."

"God Almighty! How dare you say such things? Careful what you say, Fernando. Thou shalt not tempt the Lord thy God." Don Bernardo was losing his patience.

"Why not leave us alone?" Fernando's reply was defiant.

"Isabel …" the priest insisted.

"You've heard my son. We don't need your consolation." And she turned and walked away, leaving Fernando facing Don Bernardo.

"If that's the way you want it … I hope your mother comes to her senses," the priest murmured.

Don Bernardo turned his back on the young man, who shut the door brusquely.

Fernando went to the kitchen, where his mother was peeling a potato. Isabel looked intently at the potato, as though it required all her attention.

"I didn't know you'd stopped going to church," Fernando said.

"Why would I go? Do you know how much time I spent praying for God to save your father's life? How foolish I was! If God didn't stop other people from being shot, why would he take any notice of me? We're through. To each his own."

"So you're done with God …"

"Don't think it was easy, Fernando." Isabel spoke without looking at her son.

"No, I suppose it can't have been for you. Ever since I was little, I never saw you miss a chance to go to church; and Father never went at all."

"Your father had his reasons, which I always respected, just as he respected my beliefs."

"That's how Father was, always respectful with everyone. But are you sure you don't want to go to church?" Fernando asked, as he knew that prayer had always been a consolation for his mother.

"Yes, I'm sure. And now let me get on with the potatoes. Doña Hortensia has given me a couple of eggs and I'm going to make a potato omelet. Have you seen Eulogio?"

"Yes, I told him about Father …"

"I know, Piedad came down to speak to me. They're good people, son. I'm going out this afternoon. To go for a walk with Piedad. She's suffering a lot. Eulogio doesn't realize how much he's making his mother suffer. She might not have done things in quite the right way, but you can't forget that everything she did was to help him."

"I know, Mother, I know, but … would you have allowed Don Antonio to have his way with you to save me?"

Isabel sat in silence for a few moments while she thought of her reply. She had asked herself the same thing more than once and still had not come to any satisfactory answer. Sometimes she thought that loss of honor was a small price to pay for her son; at others, she thought that there must always be other choices. But one thing she was sure of: that she must not judge Piedad. She had always liked the Jiménezes. Eulogio was the spitting image of his father, Jesús. And on many occasions, Lorenzo had struck up a conversation with him on the stairs and the two ended up chatting in one another's houses over a cup of coffee. They were both keen on politics, and Jesús Jiménez liked to discuss the newspaper with Lorenzo.

She and Piedad had tended to speak whenever they met in the entryway or in the neighborhood, but this Sunday would be the first time they went out together. Piedad had suggested that they go for a walk, and Fernando had insisted that his mother accept.

"You can't stop leaving the house. You need to get some fresh air," he said, but Isabel stubbornly refused to leave the house apart from to go to work. "Father wouldn't want you to lock yourself away," Fernando had insisted. "It's not good to leave the home when you're in mourning," Isabel had said. But her son had convinced her that grief was not incompatible with going out for walks. And that if she didn't leave the house she'd end up driving herself crazy. "I don't know what's wrong with going out for some air. And if the stuck-up old women criticize you, then let them. Nothing's going to bring my father back."

For Piedad it was a relief that a woman who commanded respect should go out with her to take a walk. For Isabel, it was a way of defying the neighborhood hypocrites: leaving the house with a woman who was the focus of rumors about her relationship with the shopkeeper.

"Mother, you haven't said anything," Fernando insisted, bringing her out of her reverie.

"Right ... Who knows ... It depends on the circumstances ..."

"Well, I don't think you'd ever do it," Fernando said.

"Who knows, son, who knows ... Well, what are you going to do today?"

"I'm going to go and see Catalina."

"Right ... How's the pregnancy going?"

"I haven't seen her for nearly three weeks ... ever since we heard about Father ... I suppose she'll be all right. Doña Petra doesn't like me coming by, but Catalina insists that I don't pay her aunt any attention."

"She's such a flighty child. You can't go to a house where you're not welcome," Isabel said severely.

"Doña Petra is afraid that Don Ernesto will find out. And you know how strict he is."

"It doesn't matter if it's Ernesto or Petra who doesn't want you to visit. You should respect their wishes," Isabel said.

"I'm not going to, Mother."

"When are you going to accept that Catalina isn't for you?"

"Never."

"What?"

"Never, Mother, never. I love her and I will always love her, whatever happens, whatever she does."

"This is going to stop you from being happy."

"Maybe you're right, but things are as they are. A life without Catalina wouldn't be worth living."

"You are very young, Fernando, and if I were still able to believe in God I'd ask him to help you find a woman who deserves you. But I'm not going to, because I know it would be useless."

Autumn had come to Madrid, and it was cold, but at four o'clock on the dot Piedad rang the Garzos' doorbell. She wanted to go out, and she couldn't think of anyone better than Isabel. They both suffered so much that they had no need to engage in pointless small talk, and were happy just being silent together.

Fernando opened the door to Piedad and invited her in.

"What about going down the Gran Vía? We could walk as far as the Retiro …" Isabel suggested.

"That's an excellent idea. I need to get out," Piedad said with a smile.

"Mother, I've saved up a couple of pesetas … Maybe you could have a coffee," Fernando said as he handed his mother two coins.

"I don't know … two women out by themselves …" Isabel said.

"What's wrong with that? I don't think it's a sin to drink coffee," Fernando said.

"You keep the money, son. Times being what they are and all."

"Mother, I saved them up for you. Please do it for me. You go out so rarely …"

"And I don't know if I should do it while I'm in mourning. I don't know if it's a good thing to leave the house."

"Mourning is something we have within ourselves. Dressing up in black means nothing at all," Fernando said.

"Of course it means something. It's a way of expressing the pain that we feel. I couldn't wear anything else," Isabel said.

Piedad listened to them without saying anything. She was envious of the obvious affection that Fernando and Isabel shared. She would have liked her son Eulogio to show her the same degree of affection. But as soon as she had this thought, she pushed it to one side. Eulogio had been a dedicated and loving son until he had heard about Don Antonio. No, she couldn't blame him for anything. She deserved his contempt.

Fernando left at the same time as his mother and Piedad. He thought that he'd stroll over to Doña Petra's house with the hope that Catalina hadn't gone out for a walk.

His grim state of mind was not matched by the warm rays of sun that lit up the Sunday afternoon. He remembered that his father had often said that Madrid had the most beautiful light in the world, and today he saw that this was true.

He did not just want to see Catalina that evening. He also wanted to ask her something. It wasn't going to be easy for him, and maybe she would say no, but he had to try.

He hadn't stopped talking about how he would get his revenge. He had spent the last two weeks going to Comendadoras to see when they took the prisoners out to face the firing squad. They took them out first thing in the morning, before the city woke up. They took them over to the wall by the Cementerio del Este graveyard, and lined up the firing squad there. He had seen that afterwards the soldiers stood back a little and that some of them smoked cigarettes. He thought that he could go up to them then and shoot one of them at point-blank range before running away. He knew that he wouldn't have any chance at all of survival, but he didn't care. But chance came to his aid. On one day when he was wandering around Comendadoras, he bumped into Don Arturo, the old man they used to see when they went to the prison on Sundays.

He was surprised to see Fernando.

"Goodness, I didn't think I'd see you here … I heard about your father. I'm sorry," he said sincerely.

Fernando asked after his son, and the old man was barely able to hold back his tears.

"They shot my son this morning," the old man said in what was barely more than a whisper.

"I'm sorry ... I feel your pain." Fernando was filled by an anger that was so strong that he himself was scared.

At this moment, two men who were walking past them looked them up and down with contempt. Fernando was about to get angry, but the old man took his arm and forced him to stay still and say nothing. When the men had left and were a good distance away, Don Arturo explained who they were.

"Didn't you recognize them? The taller one is one of the prison guards, Roque, a real son of a bitch, and the other one is his son, a soldier, one of the ones who shoots the prisoners. I think he's called Saturnino. He usually comes with his platoon to Comendadoras to take the prisoners away. So, the father's a jailer and the son's a soldier. It's not the first time I've seen them. The son comes to find his father so they can go home together."

"Right ... the old man's a real bastard. He threw my father's glasses on the floor and stamped on them," Fernando replied.

"There's no prisoner who has a good word to say about him. He likes to humiliate people: he deserves to get a bullet in the head," Don Arturo muttered.

Fernando shuddered and knew at this moment that he had found the man who would be the object of his revenge. He also knew how he would do it. He felt a wave of satisfaction to imagine the moment at which he would shoot the pair of them. The father a jailer, the son a murderer. It was only a question of waiting for a moment like this afternoon to repeat itself. He'd follow them, and when they were distracted, he would shoot them. Yes, that's what he'd do. It would be easier. An eye for an eye. He only had one problem: he needed a weapon. He didn't know anyone whom he could ask for one, but he knew that there was a pistol at Doña Petra's house. Catalina had told him as much: she had helped her aunt clean out some drawers one day and had found a lumpy package wrapped in several bundles of cloth. She was just unwrapping it when her aunt shouted at her to stop. "That's your uncle's pistol. I keep it there. I don't like weapons, but I'm not going to get rid of anything that belonged to my husband," she explained. Catalina thought that this was a sufficiently interesting discovery to tell Fernando about it. She had told him as though it were a great secret, and he had forgotten all about it until he started to plan how he was going to get his revenge on his father's killers.

He wondered how Catalina would react when he asked her to give him the pistol that her aunt kept so carefully.

When he got to the door of Petra's building, he was pleased to see that the doorwoman wasn't there. He didn't like that nosy woman; she always asked him where he was going even though she knew already.

He went up the stairs two by two. He wanted to see Catalina and share the pain that he had felt in his soul ever since his father's death. He rang the bell a few times and the door opened, revealing Catalina's silhouette.

"Finally! I thought you were never going to come," she scolded him as she stood to one side to allow him to come in.

Doña Petra came into the hall and looked at him with compassion before giving him a hug.

"Fernando, please accept my commiserations. My sister Asunción told me what happened."

"Thank you, Doña Petra," he managed to say, moved by the woman's embrace.

"It's not difficult to accept a loved one's death. I know that very well: I'm still grieving my husband's death at the Battle of the Ebro."

"Aunt, please! That's not the same thing at all," Catalina said, seeing how Fernando's face had crumpled at her words. "It's one thing to die in a battle and quite another to be executed."

Fernando didn't know what to say, and for a moment thought about leaving. Doña Petra's husband had died in the war, fighting on the side of Franco. His father had been executed in Franco's name. The difference was so great that it was hard for Fernando not to say something cutting to Catalina's aunt.

"Anyway, come in, I'll make some hot chocolate. Asunción brought it yesterday. It's a present from Don Antonio," Doña Petra said as she led them through to the sitting room.

"I don't want any," Catalina said.

"Why do you care where it comes from? You have to eat; you have to think of the child," Doña Petra said.

When the two of them were alone in the sitting room,

Catalina hugged Fernando. She threw her arms around his neck and pulled him close to her, trying to express just how much affection she felt for him. Fernando trembled to feel himself so close to Catalina's body. He felt her warmth, and her rounded belly, stretched by the child she carried within.

"You should have come sooner! You must have been suffering a lot. And what about your mother? I haven't stopped thinking about you ever since Mama told us the news. I'm so sorry … Your father was such a good man … I imagine you've written to Marvin to tell him. I've done so as well. He hates the fascists … He'll be very upset to hear it."

The very mention of Marvin made Fernando's heart sink. He was sad to find out that for Catalina, Marvin was still very much present.

"I don't have anything to say to Marvin," he said angrily.

Catalina said nothing in the face of Fernando's upset. She refused to accept that her friend was in love with her, although her mother and her aunt never stopped telling her this. She loved him a great deal, but had never stopped thinking of him as the brother she'd never had. She took his hand and invited him to sit down.

"I'm so sorry, believe me. I wish there was some way I could help you. Any way at all."

He would have left if he had not needed the pistol. But it was the only chance he had to take his revenge.

Although Doña Petra was still in the kitchen preparing the hot chocolate, Fernando lowered his voice.

"That's why I'm here, to ask you for something."

"Whatever you want … whatever I can do …" Catalina said expectantly.

"I need you to give me your uncle's pistol," Fernando said, lowering his voice even further.

Catalina looked at him in surprise, almost as though she hadn't understood.

"I know that it might cause you problems, but if you don't help me …" Fernando whispered.

"But what do you want a pistol for?" she said in a changed voice.

"Shush, shush, don't let your aunt hear."

"Fernando, you're scaring me ... I don't understand what you want ..."

"I'm going to kill the people who murdered my father. I need a pistol for that. I need you to give me your uncle's pistol. If you don't help me ... I don't know what I'll do, but I swear I won't stop until I have my revenge."

Catalina sat still, staring straight at him. She didn't know what to think, what to say, or even what to feel. At that, moment her aunt came into the room and put a tray on a low table. Three cups for the hot chocolate and some tea cakes.

"It'll be a minute until the hot chocolate's ready," she said and left the room again.

"If I give you the pistol my aunt will find out," Catalina said in a whisper.

"She doesn't have to ... I'll try to give it back to you, although I don't know if I can promise that ... I'm going to leave the country. There's no place for me here."

"You can't leave! What about your mother? I think that this desire for revenge is driving you mad. You have to calm down, Fernando, or you'll be making a big mistake."

"Will you give me the pistol?"

"No ... I can't ... don't ask me that ... They'll find you, and they'll know who the pistol belongs to, and they'll come for my aunt ... who knows what they could do to us ... for God's sake, Fernando, think!"

"If you don't help me, I'll kill him with my own hands," he replied calmly.

"But who are you going to kill? You don't know who shot your father ... No one knows the names of the men in the firing squad," Catalina said, growing ever more agitated.

"I know one of them ... his father is one of the guards at Comendadoras. He goes to see his father and help him round up the accused. He goes to pick his father up in the afternoons and walk him home. I'll kill the pair of them." And Fernando told her just how and when he was planning to do it. It would be the next Saturday. The guard's son always went to find his father then.

"Here it is ... you're going to love it, a real hot chocolate with milk ... I'll give you some to take some to your mother. She'll really enjoy a good cup of hot chocolate. She's so thin ..." Doña Petra said.

Fernando tasted the hot chocolate. He couldn't remember the last time he'd had a cup. It must have been before the war. He didn't refuse one of the tea cakes that Doña Petra had brought along either. Catalina finally gave in and had two cups and some tea cakes. She could never resist chocolate.

"Don't drink it so fast: you've barely eaten anything today ..." her aunt said. "You know what, Fernando? Catalina is impossible to deal with, and we're in such a state at the moment ..."

When they had finished the hot chocolate, Doña Petra put the cups on a tray and took them through to the kitchen. They made small talk about unimportant topics, mostly the people in Catalina's old neighborhood. When the two of them were left alone, they felt uncomfortable. And they were surprised at the feeling, because it was the first time they had felt such a thing.

"I'm leaving. I hope that everything goes well for you. I wish you all the best," Fernando said, getting up.

"You're not coming back?"

"No. I've told you what I'm going to do. They'll hunt me down and shoot me, although I'll try to avoid it, if only for my mother's sake."

"You're going to ruin her life if you do this!" Catalina said.

"I hope that you'll keep my secret," Fernando said.

"Of course. You know that I'm not someone who runs her mouth, and I'll never say anything that might get you into trouble. If ... well, if you manage to do this, where will you go?"

"I'd like to go to France ... There are lots of Spaniards there, but the French apparently treat us fairly badly. But when the war started, one of my father's friends went to Paris. He said he was going because he refused to participate in a fratricidal war."

"And what does your father's friend do?" Catalina asked.

"He's an accountant ... But I don't know what he does now."

"So you'll go to Paris ..."

"Maybe, we'll see."

They said goodbye in a worried fashion. Fernando had to hold back his tears, thinking that this might be the last time they saw one another. He asked himself if he could cope with Catalina's absence. He couldn't imagine himself without her: it hurt him as much as the thought of leaving his mother.

He walked slowly back home. He knew that his mother would suffer untold torments when he disappeared, and much more if she found out that he had killed two people. Fernando was certain that he would kill them, even if he lost his own life in the attempt.

When he got home, his mother was there, sitting by the balcony and looking into the abyss.

"What are you doing, Mother?" he asked as he gave her a kiss.

"Thinking … I can't stop thinking about your father. Not a minute goes by that I don't think about him. I'll never be able to forgive his murderers, never." Isabel took her son by the hand and squeezed it tight.

"Neither will I," Fernando said.

"I hate them, I hate them so much that I want to kill them all. And that scares me, knowing that I would be able to do this, that if I could I wouldn't hesitate to visit on them all the wickedness that they have done to us. I'll never forgive them, Fernando, never. The worst of it is that they'll be here for a while … Piedad thinks that when the war in Europe is over the foreign powers will help free us from Franco, but I don't think that if England wins the war they'll come and free us. When have the English ever done anything for us? And France? Impossible! The leftists under Léon Blum turned their backs on us … We're alone … no one will come to rescue us, and these bastards will do what they want with the country. We're the losers. If they'd released your father, I might have just put my head down and carried on, but without him … What more can we do?"

They held each other tight for a long time. Fernando was surprised at how intense his mother's hatred was. He'd always thought of her as someone who was almost preternaturally calm and thoughtful, and suddenly he found out that she was just as angry as he was. He remembered how his father had been impatient with him, and had told him that before speaking or acting he should reflect for a while and not let himself be carried away by his emotions.

He had never seen his father lose his temper, or raise his voice, even when someone was arguing with him.

He wondered if the war had changed his mother. He realized he didn't care about the answer. He was relieved to find that his mother felt the same raging hatred as he did; maybe this would make it easier for her to forgive him when she found out that he had killed two men.

On Monday morning, just as he was leaving his building, he ran into Eulogio.

"I haven't seen you for days," Fernando said.

"You know where to find me," his friend said grumpily.

"Have you found anything?" he asked, even though he knew that the question would make Eulogio's mood worse.

"No one wants to give a cripple like me any work. I don't have any training, I don't have any skills, and my father was a red." His answer was filled with bitterness.

"So what are you going to do?"

"I've told you, leave. The worst thing is that I'm going to have to ask my mother for money for the train."

"And where are you going?"

"To America. I'm going to try to get to Lisbon and put myself onboard one of the boats going to America. I don't care if it's the States or South America. I'll work to pay my passage. They always need help on a boat, and though I may be a cripple, I'm not an invalid."

"I may come with you," he said, and immediately regretted it.

"What do you mean? Are you thinking of leaving? Why would you leave? If you go I don't know what your mother will do ..."

"The same as your mother, weep and lament. But I have a reason to leave."

"Really? Well, tell me what it is, because you have a job and you've been cleverer than us: you've still got the house."

"I'll come up and see you this evening, and if you've got a moment we can go out for a bit and I'll tell you. But don't say a word, my mother doesn't know anything about this."

"Don't worry. I won't say anything."

All the way to the print shop, he couldn't stop blaming himself for having opened up to Eulogio. For his plan to work out, it was essential that no one know the least thing about it. He had told Catalina, of course, but he was sure that she would keep his secret.

Two days later, Catalina woke up sweating and vomiting. She had had a nightmare about Fernando dying. Also, with every day that went by, she was more and more weighed down by the pregnancy. Fernando's visit had upset her. She was scared. She thought that he was all too likely to kill the jailer and his son, especially if the latter had participated in the arrests.

Her aunt had been shocked to see her like this, and although she had tried to joke about it, and said that Catalina's face was as green as a lettuce, she was scared, and she had called her sister Asunción, who was just about to arrive.

Catalina had argued with her aunt because she hadn't wanted to upset her mother, but she hadn't managed to make her back down. Doña Petra said that it was a lot of responsibility for her to have her niece there in her "state," and that it was her duty to make sure that nothing happened to her. She was worried to see her niece with such dark circles under her eyes: they surely couldn't be a sign of anything good. She was her aunt, not her mother, and the best thing would be for her to allow her sister to take charge of the situation.

Doña Asunción had been worried by her sister's phone call. Petra was not one to exaggerate, and if she said that Catalina was looking bad, then surely something was up with the girl.

She had just set the table with coffee and plates. Her husband was putting on his tie.

When Ernesto Vilamar came into the dining room, he did not notice how nervous his wife was, although she slipped a little as she served him his coffee.

"Careful, Asunción …"

"Yes … Sorry, Ernesto, I don't know where my head is this morning … It's about the girl … Petra called to say that Catalina looks terrible and is feeling worse. As soon as we've had breakfast,

I'll go to see them. I'll call Juan Segovia as well, I think she probably needs to have a doctor take a look at her."

"What she needs to do is have that bloody baby already. Don Antonio has asked me about her again. I think that he doesn't believe that Catalina is out of Madrid looking after some relative. He told me that his wife is insistent that they need to get to know one another before they get married, and that even though they are officially engaged, she's never seen a couple that didn't even write to one another. This has to come to an end, Asunción. It would have been better for her to have gotten rid of the child."

"God forgive you, Ernesto! How can you say that you would have preferred for Catalina to have an … Well, I'm weighed down enough by the responsibility of thinking that we'll have to give the child away, without you saying things like that as well."

"You're too soppy. Don Bernardo has all of you churchgoers under his thumb. What does a priest know about real life? The girl should give birth and we can forget about all this nonsense."

"Well, Don Antonio and his son will just have to wait."

"Asunción, you'll have to do something, because Don Antonio isn't going to wait forever. His witch of a wife keeps on putting the screws on him …"

"Well, tell them the truth, that Catalina slipped up and is expecting a child. If Antoñito loves her, then he'll forgive her."

"You're insane! What sort of a man would marry a woman who had gotten pregnant without being married? You don't know what you're saying. You should have taught your daughter better. You go to church every day, but she …"

"You have no compassion, Ernesto," Doña Asunción plucked up the courage to say.

"What we have, Asunción, are debts. Either Catalina marries Antoñito, or we're going to lose the house and live under a bridge. Is that what you want? We're ruined. The bloody war has ruined us. I am tired of telling you that your father's business went under during the war. And the farm in Huesca … My brother Andrés is working his fingers to the bone, but still can barely scrape a living."

"And is there no way forward?" she said, afraid of the answer her husband would give.

"None."

"What about my inheritance?"

"Your inheritance? How do you think we've managed to survive? There's nothing left of your inheritance."

"But to hand our daughter over to these people ..."

"And what are children for if not to obey their parents? The child has grown up thinking that she's a princess. It's time for her to face the facts."

"We could try to find her a husband who wouldn't be so unpleasant as Antoñito."

"And where are we going to find such a gem? Antoñito is the choice we have at the moment, and it is Antoñito she will marry."

"But ..."

"No buts. Asunción, we need to face up to reality."

When Doña Asunción reached her sister's house, she was frightened to see the state Catalina was in. She put her hand on her forehead and knew that she was running a fever. Thank goodness, she thought, that Juan Segovia had agreed to come and see the girl before lunch.

They spent the rest of the morning feeling very nervous. Catalina was dizzy and unable to control her vomiting, and her mother and her aunt were terrified. Doña Asunción didn't remember feeling so bad when she had been pregnant with Catalina. And as for Doña Petra, she had never had children and knew nothing about pregnancies, but even so, she realized that her niece must have something badly wrong with her.

The doctor came to the house at two o'clock on the dot, and Doña Petra almost embraced him, so grateful she was to see him.

"Come in, come in, Juan ... Catalina's very sick ... We made her lie down, but she won't stop throwing up, and says that her stomach hurts ..."

"All right, all right, I'm sure it's not that bad ..."

Once he had had a look at her, the doctor's diagnosis was that the chocolate hadn't agreed with her and that it was nothing more than indigestion, but he also said that the child seemed to have turned in the womb.

"I don't know ... it could mean that the child might be getting ready to be born. I hope not, because at six months ..."

"Almost seven," Catalina said.

"Six and a half," Doña Asunción agreed.

"It's dangerous, very dangerous. I'll call the midwife and get her to come over from the hospital this afternoon. And you shouldn't move at all. Don't even step out of the bed. You could lose the baby."

"Lord! Marvin will be so upset," Catalina said.

"Stop talking about Marvin!" her aunt said with a tinge of hysteria in her voice.

"He's the father of my child! Whether you like it or not, this child has a father, and that father is Marvin."

"Please … don't make this any harder than it needs to be." Doña Asunción was about to burst into tears.

"Catalina, you have to accept that you can't keep the child. Do you really want to shame your parents and your family? And as for you, do you think that any man will want to marry you?" the doctor scolded her.

"Marvin will. I know he'll be proud when he finds out we've had a son."

"Don't be a child … you've caused your parents enough harm. As soon as the baby is born, we'll hand it over to a good family. They're waiting for it already. They'll look after it as though it were their own flesh and blood. It won't want for anything. And you can get married to Antoñito, have more children … you'll see."

"No! I'm not going to marry Antoñito, I'd sooner die. I hate him. And I'm not going to give my child away. You go and find another child for that family. They won't have mine."

Don Juan made a sign to the two women not to get into an argument with Catalina. She was a child, with no judgment of her own, and there was nothing she could do in the end other than obey. Let her play at being a rebel as much as she wanted. He would take the baby away as soon as it was born. But why argue with a little girl? Of course he was worried to see the baby so low in her belly … He was almost afraid they might lose it.

They left her alone in the room in almost complete darkness, for all that she begged them to open the windows and let her see the light that came through the branches. But her aunt Petra refused. She wasn't going to allow her niece to disobey a single one of the doctor's recommendations.

"I'll be back this afternoon with the midwife. Meanwhile, she should be calm and drink nothing apart from chamomile tea to settle her stomach. And don't let her get out of bed: things could get really bad."

Catalina had made a decision. She realized that no one, not even her mother, would support her in keeping the child. She was not prepared to hand it over to anyone. It was her child, hers and Marvin's, and she was sure that he would never forgive her if he found out that she had given their child away. If she did it, she'd lose him forever. She only had one choice, and that was to leave. She couldn't even wait for the child to be born. She had to go as soon as possible. She'd leave, go to France, find refuge with Marvin. He'd look after everything. Just thinking about it made her feel relieved.

The afternoon was already well under way when the doctor came back with the midwife. The woman examined her brusquely.

"If she doesn't stay on complete bed rest, then I don't know what's going to happen to the child ..." the midwife said, supporting Don Juan's diagnosis. She even said that the baby might be born prematurely.

"Maybe we should take her to the hospital," Doña Asunción suggested, worried for her daughter's life.

"We'll wait a few days; if she stays absolutely still and doesn't leave her bed at all ... Don't worry, Asunción, Catalina is strong and it will all turn out well," the doctor tried to comfort her.

"The worst isn't the thought of her losing the child, but of something happening to her. And may the Lord forgive me for saying what I've just said," Asunción said, crossing herself.

"There's still a high chance that the birth will be premature," the midwife said.

"Let's all keep calm. The girl has to keep calm, and I'll come by tomorrow and see if I should take her to the hospital," the doctor said.

They left Catalina alone in her room and went to the living room, where Petra insisted that they have a cup of coffee.

It was drizzling, and Don Juan didn't need much encouragement to decide to stay, but the midwife excused herself, saying that she needed to attend to at least a couple more births that evening, and so had to get back to the hospital as soon as possible.

As soon as the midwife had left, Doña Asunción once again expressed her fears for her daughter.

"I don't want to imagine that anything might happen to her ... For the love of God, promise me that she'll be all right!"

"Come, now, Asunción ... You're too worried about this. I won't lie to you: there is a degree of risk, but there's nothing we can do at the moment. Let's wait, for a day at least. Trust me."

"She's my daughter, my only daughter ... I can't live without her." And as she spoke, she started to cry.

"Don't be so dramatic, Asunción." Her sister tried to console her. "If Juan says that Catalina will be all right, then you have to trust him."

"Her face is all wrong, don't you see?" Doña Asunción said.

"She's been throwing up a lot ... Who would think of drinking hot chocolate while pregnant?" the doctor said.

"It's my fault. She hasn't been eating at all, and I thought that I could tempt her with a little bit of chocolate," Doña Petra apologized.

"All right, but in her state ..." the doctor said.

"But she's not going to have a premature baby because of a cup of hot chocolate ..." Now it was Doña Petra who looked like she was about to cry.

"Let's stop talking about it. We're not getting anywhere. She should stay in bed and relax, and that's all we can do for the time being. Please don't get nervous, because nerves can be contagious. Catalina has to be calm, with nothing to worry her. By the way, you said that the father hasn't been to see her ... Is that right, Asunción?"

"Yes, that's right .... Ernesto is so angry ... He's so upset ... Who would have thought that our daughter would ... would do something like that ..."

"And what about the engagement to Antoñito Sánchez?" Don Juan wanted to know.

"Well, it's still on, but I don't know what's going to happen ...

Ernesto says that Don Antonio is growing impatient, and that his wife won't stop asking about Catalina, and is very suspicious that she's been out of the house for so long," Doña Asunción explained.

"Yes, it's a real problem ... Well, let's hope that everything turns out well and that as soon as Catalina's had the baby she can get married to Antoñito. Your daughter needs a husband," the doctor said.

"She's an only child ..." Doña Petra said.

"Right, but she's spoiled and that's why she's so rebellious," Juan Segovia said, not letting himself be convinced by Petra's argument.

At that very moment, Fernando was coming home from work, and after he had greeted his mother he went up to the attic where Eulogio lived.

He had barely knocked on the door when he heard his friend's agitated voice. He turned around, prepared to walk away because he thought that Eulogio and his mother were arguing, but he had only got to the top of the stairs when the door opened. Piedad stood in the doorway, drying her eyes with the hem of her apron. There were tears on her cheeks.

Fernando felt uncomfortable, and saw the same discomfort on Piedad's face.

"I ... Well, I'm sorry ... I was coming to see Eulogio ... I'll come by some other time ..."

He could hear Eulogio's voice, and soon he hobbled into view.

"Let's go and smoke somewhere I don't feel disgusted," he said, slamming the door.

"We could talk tomorrow ..." Fernando said, trying to escape from this embarrassing moment.

"I need some air. I can't cope with her anymore. I think I'm going to leave tonight."

"Your mother ... Well, I don't think she deserves this treatment," Fernando said as they walked down to the door to the street.

"She's a whore. And she deserves what whores get."

256

"What the hell are you saying? I don't want to hear you speak like that about your mother. It's not fair and you have no right to insult her like that. Your mother is a good woman."

"A good woman who goes to bed with the first man to come along?"

"You know that's not what happened ... everything she did, she did for you ... It's like you don't realize that we lost the war. Your mother lost her husband, your father, and didn't want to lose you. How many times do we have to have this conversation?"

"You're right: we've done this before, so don't come here and try to preach to me anymore."

"I don't want to preach to you, but I just can't bear to see how you treat her. It's not worthy of you."

"Right ... so the worthy thing to do is sleep with the shop-keeper. Drop it, Fernando!"

They walked along for a while without speaking to one another. Fernando felt very distant from his friend. He didn't like what he was seeing in him. He loved him, and he had known him all his life, but Eulogio's bitterness was hard for him to see.

"You said you had something to tell me," Eulogio said, interrupting Fernando's thoughts.

"It doesn't matter."

"Don't you trust me?" Eulogio said.

"I don't feel comfortable ... I like your mother, I respect her, and I think she's been very brave to do what she did. There are certain things that it is hard to do ... especially if by doing them, you become someone you don't want to be. Your mother has done what she did and that has marked her for good, but those are the consequences of the damn war and the arrogance of the victors."

"You're good at giving speeches. What a shame there are no parties anymore, or else you could have gone in for politics," Eulogio said scornfully.

"I'm not here to talk nonsense. We've all got problems, so the best thing for me to do is to go home. My mother's waiting to give me supper and I'm exhausted."

"Come on, Fernando, don't annoy me. Tell me what you've had to keep so secret."

"I don't think I can trust you, with your morality such as it is; if you treat your mother like that, then I can't imagine what you'd think of me …"

"Right, now you're really annoying me! So, you don't trust me? You're such a little boy …"

"Goodbye, Eulogio, I'm going home."

Fernando walked away as fast as he could, but his friend caught him up in spite of his limp.

"Yes, I'm bitter … I hate how I treat my mother, but I can't help it … It's shameful … But I'm going to leave. I can't carry on like this … I can't keep on tormenting her and hating myself as much as I do." And as he spoke, he burst into tears.

Fernando was upset by Eulogio's tears. He didn't know what to do, but eventually hugged his friend to calm him down. When Eulogio had finished crying, they carried on walking in silence.

"I'm going to kill two of the men responsible for my father's death," Fernando said, and immediately regretted his words.

Eulogio stopped in his tracks, frozen by his friend's announcement.

"What did you say?" he asked in a low voice.

"I'm going to kill one of my father's jailers and his son, who was in the firing squad. I'll do it in a day or so if I manage to get hold of a pistol, but if I can't get one, then I'll use a knife or my bare hands," Fernando said in a monotone.

"You're crazy!" Eulogio said, still astounded.

"Yes, I'm crazy. Crazy with pain that my father was murdered. Your father died fighting at the front, and mine was killed with a single bullet. I won't stop until I have my revenge."

"But it's impossible … They'll catch you, and they'll shoot you too …"

"Yes, that's what will most likely happen. I know," Fernando said calmly, accepting his fate as he spoke.

"Come on, don't say stupid things … I know that you want to do something like that, but it won't get you anywhere except in front of the firing squad. You blame me for how I behave in front of my mother, but can you imagine what it would mean for yours if they shot you? Your mother would go mad. And she's very Catholic …"

"I know that my mother would suffer a great deal. When we found out that my father had been shot she stopped going to Mass, but now she's started to go again," Fernando admitted.

"You can't do it ... And anyway, where are you going to get a pistol from?"

"I'll kill them with or without a pistol," Fernando said.

"But who are these men? Why them?" Eulogio was terrified.

"I told you already. The older one is one of the jailers at Comendadoras, and his son is a soldier and one of the members of the firing squad. If I could kill the whole squad I would, but I'll settle for just one of them."

Eulogio was so taken aback by Fernando's words and attitude that he didn't really know what more to say.

"You can't do it," he murmured.

"I'm going to do it," Fernando said firmly.

"You can't! Don't be stupid! They'll have weapons: do you think they'll let themselves be slaughtered like lambs?"

"I've been watching them for weeks. I know how and where I'm going to do it. I want to ask you one thing: forget what I've just told you."

"Right ... yes, forgetting it now ... What's wrong with you? I know you want to have your revenge, that you hate those sons of bitches, but the person who has to forget about this madness is you."

"Let's talk about something else, or rather, maybe I should just go home. I'm tired. I've told you already that we've got a lot of work to do at the print shop."

"I'm your friend, Fernando, we may have our differences of opinion, but you know you can trust me," Eulogio said, surrendering in the face of the fact that he would be unable to change his friend's mind.

"It's enough for you to keep silent," Fernando said.

"I don't know anyone who has a pistol ... Well, that's not quite true: Don Antonio has one. It's in his desk drawer in his office ..."

"Do you think I could steal it?"

"That you could? No ... Neither you nor me. It was in a locked box. You'd have to force the drawer ... And anyway, now they've got a real brute in to guard the warehouse. He's not all that bright, but he's got a pair of fists on him that'd break your head wide open."

"If you tell me where Don Antonio's office is in the warehouse and which drawer the pistol's in …"

"No … It's not a good idea … I don't know why I even told you …"

"You offered to help me," Fernando reminded him.

"Yes, but not to kill someone."

"You're not going to kill anyone. I'm going to take care of those two guys."

"Yes, but if I help you with the pistol … I shouldn't have said anything …"

"But you have told me. There are only two people who know where I can find a pistol. Catalina and you."

"Catalina? She's full of surprises. Is she still in her family's house in some village somewhere? There are lots of rumors all over the neighborhood … Mari is pretty angry."

"I don't care what the shopkeeper's wife thinks."

"Right … But how does she know where to get a pistol?" Eulogio insisted.

"Because she has a family member who has one. That's all. I asked her to get it for me, but she doesn't want to."

"Of course. I wouldn't want to help you with this either. Look, Catalina and I are on the same side for once."

"Yes, both of you just pretend to be friends with me." Fernando knew that he'd provoke Eulogio.

"Hey, I'm your friend for whatever you need, but I'm not going to let you risk your life. That's what you'll do if you insist on going through with this. And it won't help you at all. You won't be able to kill them and all they'll do is shoot you too."

"That's my problem, not yours or Catalina's."

"I'm fond of you, and we've known each other since we were children … I'm not going to let them kill you just like that."

"I shouldn't have told you, and I shouldn't have told Catalina either."

"Does she also know that you want to kill these two men?"

"Of course, I explained it to her the same as to you."

"That's all you need! She's not going to keep your secret," Eulogio said.

Fernando stopped still in front of his friend, so suddenly that Eulogio took a step backwards.

"Stop judging her! I won't let you! Catalina is fond of me and I trust her like I trust myself. I've never been anything but certain that I could put my life in her hands. She would never betray me. You got that?"

Eulogio was taken aback by Fernando's reaction. He knew Fernando was in love with Catalina, but not so much that he had lost his head over her. Even so, he didn't oppose his friend's statement. He thought that if he did, then he would lose him forever.

"All right, all right ... don't get like that ... I know she's not a bad girl ... Well, if you trust her then that's that and I've got nothing to say."

"That's right, there's nothing you can say. Now forget what I told you and I'll sort it all out myself."

"No, I won't let you do that. I'll come with you. If you manage to get a pistol ... well, I'll be near you and we'll get away together. You'll have to escape. Come to Lisbon with me, and we'll find a boat that'll take us to America. No one will find us there."

"We'll see, Eulogio, we'll see."

Fernando hadn't gone back to see Catalina and she insisted to her mother and her aunt that they should tell him to come and see her because she wanted to talk to him. But neither Doña Asunción nor Doña Petra had allowed themselves to be convinced. The doctor had warned them that Catalina could lose her child. They had to be ready. Doña Petra was scared that this could happen while she was alone with her niece, even though Juan Segovia had said that he would make sure Catalina went straight to the hospital.

For all that the doctor, her mother, and her aunt spoke about her behind her back and in whispers, Catalina had realized what might happen, and much against her will, stayed in bed and obeyed all the doctor's advice. But she had also made a decision. She was not going to let them take her child away, and so she would have to escape. If Fernando had not had this crazy idea of killing two men, then she would have asked him to help her escape as soon as she gave birth, but as she was sure he would go through with his plan, she had no choice but to ask him to take her with him when he fled, even if that meant putting the lives of herself and her unborn child in danger.

For the first time in her life, she was confronted by a dilemma in which all possible outcomes were bad. If she had the child, it would be taken away from her at once, and she wouldn't even be able to hold it in her arms. If she fled, then she would put its life in danger: most likely she would lose it then as well.

She wept inconsolably as she tried to find a solution, but her tears did not help her see more clearly, and in fact only added to her despair.

One morning, she woke up and found she had made her decision. She would flee with Fernando, even if it meant putting her life and her child's life at risk. Marvin would never forgive her if she gave birth only to have the child taken from her and given to some strangers.

Fernando wouldn't accept her on his flight. She only had one way of convincing him: to steal the pistol that her aunt kept so jealously hidden. That was the price she would have to pay. And she would tell him straight out. He could have his revenge and she could avoid losing her child. That would be the deal. She had to tell him, but she didn't know how. Fernando had said goodbye to her forever, as he would have to flee if he carried out his plan for revenge. She was nervous because she knew she had very little time, but Catalina decided to wait until her aunt went out to give her music lessons at the school, and then leave the house and go to find Fernando at the print shop where he worked.

That morning Doña Petra came into her room to bring her breakfast.

"Wake up, Catalina, I've got to go. I've made you some coffee from the beans that your mother brought me, and a nice piece of bread. You'll be able to eat it with no problems."

"All right, Auntie … But I'm not very hungry."

"But you have to eat, for you and for the child. You know what might happen if you don't look after yourself, so eat, please.

I'll be home a bit late today because I get out of the school at noon and then I need to do some shopping. But I won't be too long."

"Don't worry, Auntie, I won't leave my bed."

"That's right, don't move, and when I get back I'll help you wash yourself."

Doña Petra kissed her niece on the forehead and went out, worried that while she was away, something might happen to her niece.

She had scarcely left the room when Catalina jumped out of bed. She went to the bathroom carefully, making sure not to slip. The mirror showed her face to be blotchy and far too pale. She took a little time to make herself look presentable. She was cold and put on two jerseys and some thick stockings. Her dress would barely fasten, even though she wasn't that fat.

Then, without hesitating, she went to her aunt's room and looked in the chest of drawers for the bundle that she knew held the pistol. She didn't forget to take the bullets out of the little box where they were kept. She took them out carefully and wrapped them in a handkerchief that she put into her bag. She left the box where it had been. She unwrapped the pistol and wrapped it again in one of her petticoats. She crumpled several sheets of paper and made a bundle which she wrapped up again with the fabric that had been used to cover the pistol. She slid it to the back of the drawer, praying that her aunt wouldn't realize. Then she went back to her room and took out her purse with a few pesetas that her mother had given her.

She took an old hat of her aunt's and pulled it low on her head, not just to protect herself from the cold, but also to hide her face in case she bumped into anyone she knew.

She stumbled out of the house. She was a little dizzy, but she knew that she wouldn't necessarily have more opportunities to escape in the future.

The cold air woke her up, but even so, she walked along clinging to the wall, afraid of losing her balance.

It took her a while to make it to the Plaza de España, and from there about fifteen or twenty minutes more to reach the building where Don Víctor's business was based. It was a little after ten-thirty, so Fernando would be at work.

The large wood-and-metal door was closed, but even so, she could hear the clicking of the Linotype machine through it. She tried to open it, but wasn't strong enough, so she looked for a bell. She waited impatiently, feeling her legs tremble under her.

A child of no more than twelve years old opened the door. He was wearing blue overalls and his hands were stained with ink.

"What do you want?" he asked in surprise.

"I'm looking for Fernando Garzo."

"Fernando? He's working, and I don't know if he can come out." Now the gaze of surprise had turned into one of open curiosity.

"Tell him that it's Catalina Vilamar, and that it's urgent."

"Are you his girlfriend?" The boy now looked amused.

"No ... no ... Please, tell him to come out ..."

The boy closed the door and Catalina waited, worried that he wouldn't tell Fernando anything. But two minutes had scarcely passed before the door opened again and Fernando was standing in front of her.

"What are you doing here? Are you crazy? You shouldn't leave your bed. Do you want something to happen to you?"

"I had to talk to you, and as you won't come to see me ..."

"I'm working, and ... well, you know, I've got other things on my mind."

"Yes, that's why I wanted to speak to you."

"Now's not the time."

Don Vicente's voice interrupted them.

"Who are you talking to, Fernando?" he asked, angrily.

"I'm sorry, Don Vicente, but one of my neighbors has come to see me ..."

"We don't allow visitors during office hours," he said, looking at them both in annoyance.

"I am sorry ... If it weren't an emergency then I wouldn't have come ... It's a family matter ..." she apologized.

Don Vicente looked at her closely and took a while to recognize her.

"You are ... I think I've seen you on a few occasions ..."

"Yes, I'm Catalina Vilamar, and I live next door to Fernando ..."

Catalina remembered seeing this man with Don Lorenzo Garzo.

"Yes ... Right, I know you ... Well, you have to understand that you can't just turn up here because you feel like it." Don Vicente seemed to realize that the young woman wasn't feeling well.

"I just wanted to have a minute to talk to Fernando; it won't be long. I promise you that if it weren't important then I wouldn't have dared come here like this."

"Two minutes. No more. If Don Víctor finds out he'll be annoyed. We don't bring problems from outside to our work," he said severely.

"Two minutes. I promise," Catalina replied.

As soon as Don Vicente had left, she gave the bundle to Fernando.

"What's this?"

"The pistol," She replied in a low voice. "I'm giving it to you in exchange for you taking me with you."

"What?"

"I don't want them to take my baby away, and they will, as soon as it is born. I thought that if I insisted then they'd let me keep it. But Mama says that Father won't change his mind. As soon as I've had the baby they'll make me go home and marry Antoñito. Help me, Fernando. You have to help me to keep my baby and get away from Antoñito." Catalina was crying as she spoke.

"Catalina ... What I'm going to do means ... no ... no, you can't come with me ... I don't even know where I'm going. It would be very dangerous for you ... If they catch me, they'll think you were my accomplice, and you know what will happen ... I wouldn't be able to forgive myself if anything happened to you because of me ... Go on, go home, and I'll come and find you later."

"No, Fernando, I won't go until you promise you'll take me with you. I only brought the pistol to make a deal with you. You need the pistol, and I need to escape. Tit for tat. I trust you and I know that if we make a deal you'll hold up your side of the bargain," she said, with more certainty than she actually felt.

"I can't! Please, Catalina, go home!"

"If you won't help me, then … well, I'll sort something out myself. I don't want to stay and wait to have my baby and then have it taken away from me. I'll go today. I hope that if they ask you then you'll say nothing."

Catalina turned away and tried to hold back her tears. She wasn't angry with Fernando. She understood him. If he took her with him then he would have to take more risks, and so Catalina had no other choice than to run away by herself. Perhaps the best thing would be not to go back to her aunt's house. Fernando's voice brought her back to herself. She felt his hand on her shoulder stopping her from leaving.

"I'm not going to abandon you; I don't want anything to happen to you … I hope it will all turn out all right …" And he held her tight.

"Thank you … Thank you … for not abandoning me. I only have you left."

"Now go home and. …. Take that thing you brought with you. I'll come and see you this afternoon when I get out of work."

"Yes … yes, please … come …"

Don Vicente, watching them from a window, hadn't missed a single detail of the scene. He thought that Catalina had put on weight, and suddenly he had a thought which he immediately wanted to push aside: that the girl might be pregnant. But was it possible that she and Fernando …? He had thought he was such a fine young man …

He went to meet him and made a sign for him to come into his office, which was a cubicle from which he could see the whole shop floor.

"Fernando, I don't know what problem you have with that girl, but you must understand that there can't be any more scenes like this." And he waited for Fernando to give him an explanation.

"I'm sorry, Don Vicente, it won't happen again. Catalina is a good friend and she's in a bit of trouble: she wouldn't have come here otherwise."

"Can you tell me what it's about?"

"I'm sorry, but it's a matter of confidence, and I can't speak about other people's problems."

"Good for you," the man said, a little annoyed because he

wanted to know what was going on. "Well, get back to work, and don't let this happen again."

"I promise you it won't."

For Fernando, it seemed that the hours passed more slowly than usual in the print shop, and he even plucked up the courage to ask Don Vicente to let him leave at seven instead of eight.

"May I ask where you're going to go?" he asked suspiciously.

Fernando gritted his teeth. He didn't want to lie to this man who had always treated him well.

"Don Vicente … I …. Well … I need to do something for Catalina …" he stammered.

"All for that girl … Hey, I hope you're not going to start doing stupid things, because some men lose their minds over women. You're lucky, because Don Víctor has just left. He's got a cold and went home early."

"Thank you, Don Vicente. I'm in your debt, as always."

"Your father was a good friend, Fernando, and it's my job to help you, but you need to learn to help yourself as well."

Catalina had to hurry to be back home before her aunt returned. The effort not only tired her out, but gave her a sharp pain in her belly. She had barely had time to put on her nightdress when she heard the street door open. She put the pistol under the mattress, because she didn't have time to put it back in its rightful place.

Doña Petra thought that her niece was paler than usual, and for all that she tried to hide her pain, it was clear that something was wrong. She was frightened and called Don Juan, and then her sister Asunción. An hour later, the midwife was examining the young woman. Don Juan had thought that this was necessary. He thought that her belly was too low.

Doña Asunción and Doña Petra waited nervously, seated in the living room. When the doctor and the midwife came in they both stood up so suddenly that they bumped into one another.

"Calm down, ladies, I don't like seeing you so nervous. Catalina is all right," the doctor said, but not with any great degree of conviction.

"I think that she's going to go into labor any time now," the midwife corrected him.

"Then we have to take her to the hospital," Doña Asunción exclaimed at once.

"All in good time …" And there was reproach in the doctor's eye, aimed at the midwife for having upset the two women.

"Juan, I don't think we should take any risks … if the girl goes into labor here …" Doña Petra couldn't hide the fear she felt at such a possibility.

"Do you think that if she were going to go into labor I'd stand here twiddling my thumbs? Maybe she is going to give birth prematurely, but it's not going to happen right now, and she's better here than in the hospital. Petra, you have to trust me," the doctor said.

"And we trust you, we do trust you, and we'll do whatever you say," Doña Asunción said, not wishing to contradict the doctor.

Doña Petra pursed her lips. She loved her sister and her niece, but she felt that she had taken on a responsibility that was not hers. She said nothing.

"Let Catalina rest. I'll be back later this evening when I get out of the hospital, and I'll make a decision depending on how I see things then."

For all that her mother and her aunt insisted, Catalina refused to eat. She was so tired and in so much pain that the only thing she wanted to do was close her eyes and sleep.

"Asunción, I'm so worried …" Doña Petra confessed when they had left Catalina in her room.

"I'm scared too, Petra … But we have to trust Juan, he knows more than us."

"Yes, yes … but I'm worried that something might happen to her when I'm here by myself."

"Thank you so much for all you are doing for us. I know it's a lot to ask, but we wouldn't be able to do anything without you. Ernesto is so worried about our situation … The only way to get out of this hole we're in is for Catalina to marry Antoñito."

"But she doesn't love him," Doña Petra said, in support of her niece.

"You think it doesn't break my heart to imagine my daughter married off to that …. that yokel?"

"Doesn't Ernesto own some of the land out in Huesca?"

"I've told you, it's not worth anything at the moment. We're ruined, Petra, the war has left us with nothing."

"But Father got him a job, and your husband still has it, a good job," Doña Petra insisted.

"I thought the same, but Ernesto tells me that no one knows where the money is now, or if we ever even had it."

"And what about your dowry? Father gave you a very generous dowry."

"I don't know, but he told me there's nothing left," Doña Asunción admitted, lowering her eyes in shame.

"What will we do if Catalina refuses to hand over her child?" Doña Petra wanted to know, worried because she knew her niece's stubbornness.

"I don't even want to think about it … The poor girl, to force her into something like that … The only comfort I can get from the situation is that Don Juan has told me that the family he has found to take the child is well-off, and they're good Christians. At least the poor child's clothes are nearly finished. I'd hate to hand it over with nothing."

"Yes, we've made about half a dozen sweaters. And I'll show you the scarf I've nearly finished."

"I've brought some diapers as well. You'll say I'm over the top, but I've made twenty. And I'm finishing the cross-stitch shirts. It'll be the most beautiful baby in the world."

"You know what, Asunción? I'd like you to stay, what with Catalina like she is …"

"I've told Ernesto not to expect me back until suppertime, and I've brought a couple of shirts to finish them off here."

The two women spent the rest of the afternoon engaged in sewing. Every now and then they went into Catalina's room and were pleased to see her sleeping peacefully.

At eight on the dot, the doorbell rang and surprised them.

"It must be Juan," Doña Asunción said.

But she was wrong. Doña Petra was surprised when she opened the door and saw Fernando.

"You? Here? ... Catalina isn't very well, and she's not up to seeing visitors." She didn't invite him in, expecting that Fernando would turn and go.

"I only want to see her for a moment," he said firmly.

"Right, but it's not possible today. She's not well. We called the doctor."

Fernando and Petra's voices made their way through to Catalina's room, and a minute later she appeared at the door with no shoes on and wearing a camisole, while her mother tried to get her to go back to bed.

"Fernando! Come in, come in. Aunt, let him in."

"But he can't ... You're not well ..." Doña Petra complained.

"I've had a nap and I feel much better. Don't argue, and let me speak to Fernando. Come on." And she took his hand to lead him to her room.

Doña Asunción and Doña Petra followed them, shocked at Catalina's behavior.

"I need to speak to Fernando by himself," she said, looking at them defiantly.

"You can't go to your room alone with a man!" her aunt said, scandalized.

"What do you think's going to happen to me? Fernando's like a brother to me, and anyway, I'm already pregnant ..."

"Good Lord, the things that girl says!" Doña Petra crossed herself, shocked at her niece's words.

"Come on, dear, we've had enough headaches already, you don't need make things even more difficult. It's not right for you to have a man in your room, and for all that you like Fernando and consider him your brother, he isn't, he really isn't."

"All right, we'll talk in the kitchen." And Catalina, without letting go of Fernando's hand, pulled him after her towards the kitchen.

"You'll make yourself even more ill! Go back to bed at once," her aunt begged, seeing that her niece was beginning to shiver with cold.

"Only if you let me speak to Fernando."

"You can't, dear, you have to understand." But Doña Asunción knew that this was a losing battle.

270

"Well, we'll go to the kitchen, then." Catalina said.

The two women gave in in the end. The most that Catalina agreed to was allowing Fernando to be sat on a chair at the foot of the bed, to preserve a certain distance. But she was inflexible in her demand that they be allowed to speak alone.

Fernando sat on the edge of his seat and looked fixedly at Catalina. He admired her determination. He knew her very well, and was aware that when she set her mind to something it was impossible to stand in her way.

"I'm not feeling very well ... I shouldn't have gotten out of bed. Don Juan says I may lose the child."

"Then don't get up again," Fernando said with a degree of severity.

"I told you this morning, I'm not going to give up my child. What would Marvin think of me if I gave up our child? I am certain he'd hurt me. I'll find the strength somewhere, Fernando ... The Lord will help me. And you. I need you as well. I know that we're in danger, and that maybe we won't succeed, but we have to try at least. I've thought a lot about what you want to do ... I don't agree, but I'm not going to judge you."

"So, you've decided ..."

"Yes, I have no other choice. Either I escape, or they take my child and force me to marry Antoñito. Come over here."

Catalina got out of bed and started to lift up the mattress.

"What are you doing?"

"Shush, don't raise your voice or else my aunt and mother will come to see what's going on. I've hidden the pistol under the mattress. It's best if you take it."

Catalina gave him the bundle and got back into bed while Fernando tried to find a place to hide the pistol. He ended up putting it in his overcoat pocket.

"I'll kill them on Saturday at eight o'clock in the evening. Then I'll meet up with you and Eulogio at the station. We'll try to catch a train there."

"Eulogio? You've told him about this as well? Fernando, there are things that the fewer people who know, the better ..."

"Eulogio is my friend. He won't betray me. He wants to go to America and is trying to convince me to go with him."

"America … But Marvin is in Paris … I have to go to Paris …" Catalina was about to burst into tears.

"Look, the first thing to do is for us to escape. They'll chase after me because of the two men I'm going to kill, and they'll chase after you for running away from your aunt's house. We'll see where we can go: I'm not sure we'll even be successful."

"We could get on a train that's going to France," she almost begged him.

"I don't want to promise you anything that I won't be able to deliver," he said.

"Then …"

"If you want I'll give you back the pistol," he said sincerely.

"No, it's not that … It's that I don't want to go to America. I want to find Marvin."

"From what Eulogio tells me, Marvin's thinking of leaving France as well."

"That's not possible! He likes living in Paris."

"Come on, don't be a child, don't you see that most of Europe is caught up in a war that's almost as bad as ours was?"

"But the Americans aren't involved in the war."

Fernando shrugged. He was tired. He loved Catalina, but his decision to kill two of the men who were responsible for his father's murder was stronger than any sense of affection.

"I can't decide where you should go. All I can do is promise to take you wherever I go. To try to get you out of Spain. Afterwards … Well, you'll have to decide if you are going to come with me or go looking for him."

They sat in silence for a few minutes without even looking at one another. Fernando was waiting for Catalina to make a decision, although he was sure what it would be.

"Yes, the first thing to do is to get out of here, and then look for Marvin. Eulogio can help me. They're friends and he'll know where he is."

"You're right, they're friends and maybe that's why he hasn't wanted to tell you anything about Marvin."

"I'll tell him that I'm pregnant and then he'll help me. He'll understand that Marvin has a right to know that he's going to be a father, and that he should come to find us as soon as possible. Yes, Eulogio won't be able to refuse me his help."

"His first loyalty is to Marvin," Fernando said, trying to stop Catalina from giving herself over to vain hopes.

"If he's loyal to Marvin, then he won't have any choice other than to help me, because the child is his."

"I'll talk to Eulogio and come back on Wednesday or Thursday to give you some more details."

"I think we need to go with you to Comendadoras," Catalina suggested.

"No. I don't want you and Eulogio involved in what I'm going to do. You have to stay out of this, at least until we escape. If they catch me, there's no need for you to suffer my fate. They'll shoot me."

"But we need to be with you and help you," she insisted.

"If you want to come with me, you'll have to do what I say. I'm going to go now, and you need to rest, because what we're going to do won't be easy."

Don Juan came just as Fernando was saying goodbye to Doña Asunción and Doña Petra. The two women were a little upset at having to justify Fernando's presence in the house, but the doctor didn't seem to pay it much attention.

"Fernando Garzo seems like a good kid. A shame he's not the father of the baby," he said, making the two women smile.

After examining Catalina, he said that she was much better, but that she still shouldn't move. Catalina promised that she'd stay in her bed until she gave birth, and Doña Petra huffed suspiciously. She knew that her niece wouldn't keep her promise.

Fernando was distracted over supper with his mother. Isabel was tired, although she tried to hide it from her son.

"Mother, don't force yourself to talk: I know you don't want to."

"Of course I want to speak to you, and listen to you, and find out how your day went. I don't know, I think there's something up. You look worried."

"No, there's nothing wrong with me," Fernando said, trying to sound convincing.

"You can't fool me. There's something wrong, something weighing on your mind. Whatever it is, you know you can always count on me."

"I know, and … oh, Mother, if you only knew how much I love you!"

"I love you too, Fernando, and now we've only got each other left. But tell me what's worrying you."

"Nothing, Mother … it's just that … I would have liked to have gone to the war and fought alongside Father, to have killed a few fascists."

"Don't say that! Fernando, I'll never forgive them for killing your father, but you must remember what he said, and never, ever forget it. Do you remember? 'You shall not kill.' Never forget what he said."

They hugged and Fernando felt how thin his mother was. And he cursed the people who had condemned them to this situation.

Eulogio came by their house after a while. Isabel was reading out loud. Fernando was listening to her, absorbed as he dusted his father's books.

"The eye that you see is not an eye because you see it: it is an eye because it sees you. To speak to someone, first you must ask and then listen … Never set your boundaries, or trace your profile: all of that is external …"

"If I'm bothering you …" Eulogio said when Fernando opened the door to him.

"What are you talking about? Come in."

Isabel looked up from her book and smiled.

"My husband liked reading out loud. We used to sit in this room after supper, the three of us, and each of us would choose what we were going to read. I've chosen Machado this evening, from his 'Proverbs and Songs.' What would you like to read?" she asked Eulogio.

"I don't know … I've always preferred prose, but my father liked Sor Juana Inés de la Cruz … He knew a few of her poems by heart; I think the one he liked the most was 'Lyrics for the Feeling of Absence'" Eulogio replied.

"I know the one … Wait …" Isabel got up and went to the bookshelves, where she found an anthology with some of Sor

Juana's poems. She flicked rapidly through the pages and gave a satisfied smile. "Here you are. Take a look."

Eulogio obeyed his friend's mother and started to read:

"My beloved lord / listen to my tired complaints / as I trust the wind / will soon bring them to your ears / if their sad noise does not vanish / like my hopes, into the wind. / Hear me with your eyes / as your ears are so far away, / without anger / my sighs are echoed in my pen; / and since my coarse voice does not reach you / hear me, deaf man, as I complain in silence."

His gaze grew misty and he looked over at Fernando, who understood that his friend wanted to see him and talk to him alone.

"I'd like to go out and have a cigarette," Fernando said.

"It's very late," Isabel put in.

"Mother, after spending the whole day working it'll do me good to get out a little. Get some fresh air."

"No point in getting some fresh air: the night's cold and it's about to rain," Isabel said, trying to convince her son to stay.

But Eulogio seemed keen to speak to him and to say something that he couldn't in front of his friend's mother. He didn't want her to know about their plans. She'd get upset and tell them not to do it, and he'd be unable to refuse because he loved her more than his own life.

"I'm sorry to have turned up without telling you," Eulogio said once they were in the street.

"Tell me what you want, because it's awfully cold," Fernando complained.

"I've been down to the station to see which trains leave on Saturday evenings. We don't have many choices. The longest-distance train is the one to Lisbon, so we'll take that one. We'll have to buy tickets and I don't know about you, but I'm flat broke."

"I don't have a penny to my name either. Whatever I earn I give to my mother, and I'm not going to ask her for it. It's enough that she's going to have the shock of her life."

"Well, we're screwed, then. We'll have to get on the train once it's moving and hope that the conductor doesn't catch us."

"We could do that, but Catalina couldn't. It's not possible for her to get on while the train's moving. It would be too much for her."

"Catalina? You want her to come with us? No ... Don't count on me if you're thinking of taking her."

"Well, that's how things are. She's coming with me." And Fernando looked so intently at Eulogio that his friend couldn't hold his gaze.

"The girl will be the death of you," Eulogio said angrily.

"She gave me her uncle's pistol on one condition, that I take her with me. And that's what I'll do."

"Why does she want to go with you? She's not used to hardships of any kind. We'll go to Lisbon and then we'll have to find a boat that we can get passage on to America. They could take us on board as able seamen, but as for her ..."

"Eulogio, you have to swear to me on your father's memory that you won't say a word of what I'm about to tell you. If you do ..."

"Don't you threaten me ..."

"I'm not threatening you. I'm asking you to swear on your father's memory."

"What's so important that I need to do that for?" he asked, intrigued.

"Just swear it, Eulogio."

"How am I supposed to swear on my father's memory if I don't know if it's worth it?"

"Well, we're done here then. To each of us his own way," Fernando said.

"What? Hey, you're just making things more difficult. To swear on my father's memory ... There's nothing sacred in the world for me except his memory. It's all I have left."

"That's why I'm asking you to swear on it. If it weren't important, I wouldn't ask you."

"It's not easy to have you as a friend," Eulogio said, protesting.

Fernando didn't reply. He understood why Eulogio was so unwilling. He wouldn't swear in vain on his father's memory either. But he couldn't tell him about Catalina without a prior promise. He knew that Eulogio didn't like Catalina much, and if his tongue got the better of him and he went around saying that Catalina was expecting Marvin's son ... He didn't want to think what people would say about her. He had to protect her.

Eulogio's promise shook him back to himself.

"I swear on the memory of my father that I will repeat nothing of what you say to me. I will keep the secret you ask me to keep until the end of my days. I swear it." Eulogio swore with as much solemnity as he was capable of, as the first few drops of rain began to fall on his head.

The two friends looked seriously at one another and Fernando, lowering his voice in fear that someone might hear what he said, told his friend that Catalina was almost seven months pregnant and that the father was Marvin. He explained in detail that her family wanted her to marry Antoñito Sánchez, that they had arranged the marriage already, and that when the child was born they would hand it over to a family that had no children. He described Catalina's anguish, her refusal to abandon her son, her self-respect and her commitment to Marvin, and her quest to find him wherever he might be. He spoke of her with pain and admiration, without hiding from his friend the fact that he was in love with her, and that it broke his heart to know that she was expecting another man's child. Catalina had played her cards, had offered the pistol in exchange for help with her escape. And he would hold up his end of the bargain.

Eulogio listened to his friend without interrupting him. And his face changed as the story progressed. When Fernando had finished the story, he paused for a few seconds before replying.

"It's not possible ..."

"I saw them, Eulogio, I saw them ... They were on the ground and ... Well, she was half naked."

Eulogio seemed confused. But even so, he gave his friend a hug.

"You can trust me." It was all he felt capable of saying.

The drizzle had turned into a full-blown rainstorm, and they were soaked.

They agreed that Eulogio would go to pick up Catalina and take her to the station. They'd wait for him there. If he didn't turn up, it would be because he'd been caught, or arrested, or even worse. In any case, they shouldn't wait for him. They'd take the train to Lisbon. Catalina would decide what to do when they got there, because Eulogio wasn't going to change his plans and was clear that he was going to board the first ship that would take him.

As he had some free time, Eulogio promised Fernando that he would spend the next few days plotting out the movements of the jailer and his son the soldier. Fernando had checked that every day at eight on the dot the son went to find his father and then they walked together back to their house in the Corredera Baja. They would walk along, chatting without a care in the world, and they hadn't noticed that every now and then they bumped into the same young man.

It was Wednesday, and there were only three days to go until their flight. Fernando was nervous, and it was hard for him to contain his anxiety in front of his mother. He was worried above all things by the idea that he might not see her again. Things would have to go very well indeed for him to be able to have her at his side once again, one day. On the other hand, he was worried that if they found out who had killed the two men, and could not find him, then they would carry out reprisals against his mother. Whenever that thought came to his mind, he thought to himself that what he was doing was madness, and that maybe he shouldn't even consider it, as nothing was going to bring his father back. But his desire for vengeance was stronger even than his good sense.

Eulogio was also making him nervous. He came by their house at dinnertime. Isabel said nothing, but it was clear to Fernando that his mother was confused by Eulogio's constant presence. He insisted that they needed to think about all the details. But everything was in place and all they needed to do was act.

One day he found Eulogio waiting for him at the print shop.

"What are you doing here?" he asked grumpily.

"I'm here to go over Saturday again with you."

"But it's all sorted out already. I think you're nervous, and that makes me worried. And now I need to go to find Catalina. She has to know everything we've agreed, and she needs to know she can trust you, because you're the one who's going to pick her up."

"I'll go with you," Eulogio suggested.

"No, that's not possible. It's hard enough for her aunt to let me come in without you being there as well. It would be a perfect excuse for her not to allow me to see Catalina. Go home."

"I could wait for you at the door," Eulogio insisted.

"I said no already, and it's a waste of time."

"I don't have anything to do ..."

"Well, why not just relax. Or else go to the station and see how we're going to get on the train, the three of us, without breaking our necks."

Doña Petra opened the door to him and couldn't disguise the fact that she wasn't pleased to see him.

"Fernando, you know that this isn't the time ... You know that Catalina needs to rest."

"I know, Doña Petra, but I couldn't come and see her at any other time. You know how worried I am ..."

"Yes, I know you've known each other since you were children, but in the circumstances I want to be clear with you: I don't think it's a good idea."

"You don't know how grateful I am that you let me see Catalina, in spite of the fact that you've got reservations."

"All right, go in, but only for a minute. It's late, and we need to have dinner and then pray the rosary."

He found Catalina on her bed with her eyes closed, and so pale that he grew scared.

"Come in, Fernando, come in," she said in bare whisper, making a very great effort.

"I've told Fernando that he can only stay for a couple of minutes, so no getting into conversations," her aunt warned her.

"We won't talk much, I promise, but let us be alone for a bit," Catalina asked.

Doña Petra clenched her jaw and left the room, very much against her better judgment. She knew that if she didn't, her niece would get out of bed, and she was afraid that just moving would cause problems.

"Tell me what's going on, Fernando," Catalina said, holding out her hand.

"You look bad ... I ... I think you ought to reconsider coming with us. Anything could happen to you ... Think of your child ..."

"I'm doing this for him. So don't worry, I'll find the strength somewhere, and won't get in your way."

"For God's sake, Catalina! It's not about getting in our way, but the question of your child's health and your own. You could go into labor at any moment, and what will we do then? We don't have any money and we don't know how to help you. And how are you going to get on the train? We'll have to do it while the train's moving and hide ourselves. Don't you see the risks?"

"Enough! We had an agreement, and you have to hold up your end of the bargain," she said angrily.

"I don't want anything to happen to you," he admitted.

"That's up to God," she said resignedly.

"Catalina …"

"Don't cause me any more problems, please," she said, closing her eyes once more.

All right, then … Eulogio will be by the door at about six o'clock. You'll go to the station with him. I'll come and find you as soon as I've done what I'm planning to do. Can you get out?"

"I will."

"Yes, but your mother always comes to see you in the afternoons, and your aunt doesn't normally go anywhere," Fernando reminded her.

"I'll think of something. I'll be at the door to the building at six. And now open the first drawer of the chest of drawers."

"Why?"

"Take my jewel box and empty it. It's not a lot, but if you sell them, then you'll have enough for three train tickets and some food."

"No, I won't do it," Fernando protested.

"You said as much, I can't get onto a moving train. The jewels I brought here are the ones I like the best. My first communion medal, my grandmother's wedding ring, the pearl earrings that my mother gave me when I turned sixteen and which she had been given by her mother … there are three or four gold rings, and my bracelet with little gold coins hanging from it, and some silver bracelets … Oh yes! And a cross."

Fernando was upset, looking at Catalina. He knew that these jewels had a sentimental value for her, and that her heart would break to lose them. But he obeyed her, knowing he had no other choice.

"There's a wallet underneath my handkerchiefs. It's got a bit of money in it, not much, but it'll come in handy. And now get out of here before my aunt gets worried. Tell Eulogio that I'll be by the door on Saturday at six o'clock."

On his way back home, Fernando swore to himself that, whatever happened, he would protect her to the end. No, he would never abandon her.

When he got home, his mother was waiting impatiently for him.

"You're very late," she said worriedly.

"I went to see Catalina. She's not looking good."

"Poor girl ..."

"I told you that the doctor won't let her leave her bed because he thinks that it'll bring the birth on, and she's not yet seven months pregnant. Tell me, Mother, what do you think might happen to her?"

Isabel was worried at her son's preoccupation. He was so loyal and loving towards that girl ... No, Catalina didn't deserve Fernando's love.

She tried to find words that wouldn't add to her son's anguish.

"There are lots of women who give birth in the seventh month, and they get along fine. Catalina will be in the best hands. You shouldn't worry."

"What about if she suddenly goes into labor? Could she die? And the child, what about the child?"

"Fernando, don't think about such things ... I'm not going to say that things would be easy if she went into labor this very moment, but the doctor will know what to do. And as for the child, well, poor little thing! It would be in the hands of God."

Eulogio was sitting on his bed reading a letter from Marvin. He had found it on the table when he came in. His mother was washing clothes and barely greeted him. The silence between them hurt Piedad, and it made him uncomfortable. So he shut the door to his room, desperate to know his American friend's news.

My Dear Eulogio,

I'm leaving for Alexandria tomorrow and didn't want to go
without telling you. I told you I was planning to go to Egypt,
but not as soon as all that, and so you'd be right to ask me
why I was leaving so quickly; but you will understand if I tell
you that a few days ago my former editor Monsieur Rosent suddenly disappeared. You can guess how upset and worried I am.
The only consolation I have is knowing that Monsieur Rosent
was able to save his business by selling it to me.

I feel overwhelmed by the responsibility I've taken on. I've
asked my literature teacher at the Sorbonne to look after the
bookshop until I return. I think I spoke to you about him before: his name is Alain Fortier and he was the one who encouraged me to take my poems to Monsieur Rosent.

Fortier can't look after the bookshop full time, but he'll do
whatever he can; that is to say that he'll publish what he can, but
not too much. I found a lot of folders in the bookshop with
manuscripts prepared and ready to be published, and so he'll get
in touch with the authors and tell them that Monsieur Rosent
isn't around anymore and that they'll have to decide what to do
with their manuscripts.

Alain Fortier is very fond of Monsieur Rosent. One of his
students, Jean, will help him out as well. I think they'll deal with
everything okay.

But because I'm overwhelmed with the thought of so much
responsibility, I'm going to go to Alexandria to tell Sara Rosent
about the situation.

No one knows how long this war will last or how it will turn
out. France may end up being a vassal state of Germany forever.
England is holding up by herself, but with the entry of Russia
into the war maybe things will change. Not even Napoleon was
able to beat the Russians.

Like I told you in my last letter, Sara Rosent lives with her
husband in Alexandria, which is where he comes from original-
ly and where his family has a flourishing publishing business.
I won't hide from you the fact that in spite of the war I am quite
tempted to spend a while in Alexandria, and go across to Cairo

to see the wonder of the world that is the Pyramids. Can you imagine! I don't know if I'll be able to, but I'll try. I think that Alexandria will be a balm to me after this depression that has been eating me up and which is becoming chronic.

And now, my dear friend, I'd like to make you an offer which you will no doubt think is a little crazy, but even so I'd like to try it out on you. I'd like to invite you to join me on my Egyptian journey and come with me to see the Pyramids. I know that it's difficult, and that the Germans and the English are waging war on the Egyptian border and that it won't be easy to get to Alexandria, and I don't even know how I'm going to manage. As for the price of the voyage, don't worry: I'll cover it; it's the least I can do as a thank you for having me in your house for so long and so generously. Let me treat you at least. I hope it will be possible to get this crazy little plan on the road.

Sara Rosent's address is at the bottom of this letter. Write to me there or – even better – I hope to see you there one day.

Your friend forever,

Marvin Brian

Eulogio was both surprised and flattered by Marvin's proposal. Suddenly Alexandria seemed to him like an unexpected gift that he could not refuse, even though he was eventually aiming to move to America. Marvin could help him. Once they met up in Alexandria, he could get him to help with his journey to the much-desired New World. Yes, that's what he'd do. As for Fernando and Catalina, they would have to decide what to do once they got to Lisbon.

A gray mist had spread over the city, stopping even a single ray of light from getting through.

Isabel was worried by her son's evident depression. She knew that there was something wrong with him, but ask as she would, he always claimed to be fine. It hurt her that he was so guarded. Ever since he was a child, Fernando had always brought her his worries and preoccupations.

Leaning on the balcony, Fernando looked out vaguely into the world. He could sense how worried his mother was. He had been tempted to tell her what he was going to do, but he knew she would try to stop him. The worst part of it was having to leave without saying goodbye. That night he had written a letter that he would leave on her pillow for her to find the next day. He imagined her reading it and weeping. He wondered if perhaps he had made a mistake, if it were really fair to inflict so much suffering on his mother. He was going to leave her forever, because it would be difficult for him to go back to Spain or for her to meet up with him, although the latter was not impossible.

The one thing he was sure that he would not regret was killing the two men who, to him, represented his father's killers. Their family would suffer just as his family had suffered. Didn't the Bible say something about an eye for an eye? Well, that's what he was going to do. Even so, he couldn't stop himself from thinking about the words his father had said when he refused to let him travel to the front: "You shall not kill, no, you shall not kill." Yes, he could still hear his father's deep voice. But he wasn't going to obey him, not this time.

He wondered what Catalina would do to get past her aunt. Doña Petra barely left her alone, and as it was Saturday, it would be even less likely for her to do so, as the good woman was ever more worried for the health of her niece, who was getting weaker and weaker. It was obvious that she would pose difficulties for their escape plan. But there was no turning back now.

"I'm ready …" Isabel said, bringing him back to himself.

"Well, let's go, I'm going to be late," he replied.

"Doña Hortensia has told me that she doesn't need me this afternoon, so I won't be too late coming home."

"Well, when I get back from the print shop I'll go for a walk with Eulogio."

"In this weather? They say it's going to rain all day …" she said worriedly.

"Mother, you know that after working all week I like to take a bit of time to relax. All we do is go for a walk and maybe meet up with some friends. I don't know if I'll be a little late; in any case, don't wait for me to have supper."

Isabel was surprised at her son's statements. It wasn't normal for Fernando to go out, far less for him to come home late. All he usually did was go for a walk with Eulogio and smoke a cigarette, but not much more. She pursed her lips but said nothing else. She couldn't blame him for wanting to go out with his friends; he was right, he was a young man and had the right to relax a little.

They walked together a little while as they did every morning. Fernando liked to walk with her until he headed off to the print shop.

Isabel didn't know why she felt an immense depression, as though a hand were wringing her insides. She saw that her son was upset, lost in his thoughts, with an angry expression on his face and his gaze lost in the middle distance.

When they got to the corner where they usually separated, Fernando hugged his mother so tight that she got scared.

"I love you, Mother, so much. You do know that, don't you?"

"Of course, my son ... how could I not? But ... Fernando ... I don't know ... I feel there's something worrying you. You've been very quiet for a few days, but today there's also ... something like anguish."

"What are you saying? No, there's nothing, I'm a little tired, but that's because I don't get a break in the print shop, but I'm glad they give me so much work. I love you, Mother. I love you."

"But, Fernando ..."

"Go on, run along or we'll both be late."

He hugged her again and the pair of them walked their separate ways, both of them equally upset. Isabel felt terrible. Fernando was secretly bidding her farewell.

The hours passed more slowly than they usually did. He hoped that with Catalina's money, Eulogio would have got them three third-class train tickets: he had also asked him to sell the communion medal, a couple of rings, and the golden bracelet with hanging pendants. Eulogio knew a lot of people and he had been able to find a buyer who didn't cheat them too much.

Fernando had kept the rest of the jewelry, hoping that they would not need to sell it, although he wondered what they were going to do and what they were going to eat when they reached

Lisbon. At least Catalina would be able to sit down on their journey. The two men would try to get into one of the goods wagons. They didn't have a penny to spare. Also, it didn't seem right to him that they should spend her money.

Don Vicente had to call him back to himself a couple of times. "You're very distracted, Fernando. Your head's elsewhere and you're here to work. And stop looking at the clock: you've been staring at it since you got here this morning."

Fernando swallowed, worried that his unease should be so evident. Don Vicente noticed everything, and when they came looking for him, he was bound to say that he had been behaving strangely that Saturday at work.

Catalina was in a bad mood. She hadn't slept well because of her nerves. Also, her aunt Petra had been especially annoying that morning, insisting that she eat when she couldn't do anything, not even drink a glass of water.

As if that weren't enough, they'd told her that Don Juan was coming by to see her, and she was sure that her mother would be there as well, like she was every afternoon. In spite of having told Fernando not to worry, she realized that she didn't know how she was going to escape. She had spent several hours already praying to God and the Virgin Mary to help her.

At nine o'clock on the dot Don Juan arrived. He seemed to be happy that morning, in spite of the fact that the rain had dyed the whole day gray.

"How are you today?" he asked.

"The same as always," she replied.

"Let's hope that the child hangs on in there until it gets to seven months …" the doctor said as he examined her.

"Well, there's not long to go. The seventh month will start on December the fifteenth," Catalina said.

"I never trust the accounts that pregnant women keep. You have to carry on lying down, and we'll see what happens."

She accepted all the doctor's recommendations without complaint. On other occasions, she might have rebelled against his insistence that she was not to move from the bed, but today she couldn't care less about anything that Don Juan might say.

"Your aunt says that you have no appetite. That's not good. Don't you know that you're hurting the baby?"

"You can't even see that she's pregnant: she hasn't got fatter at all; I think she's even losing weight," Doña Petra complained.

"Well, we need to sort that out. Times are hard, but a pregnant woman has to eat."

Catalina heard her aunt and the doctor speak but she paid them no attention. The only thing that she wanted was to be left alone. She had to pack clothes for her child and for herself. She couldn't take much, just what fitted in her bag.

Shortly after Don Juan left, her mother arrived. She was surprised, because she hadn't expected her to come until the afternoon.

"Ah, Petra, I need your help," Doña Asunción said as she came into her daughter's room. "Don Bernardo has decided that this afternoon, right after the six o'clock rosary, that we need to have a raffle. Everyone has to bring something to raffle, and with the money that they earn from the tickets he's hoping to have something to give to the poor of the parish. He says that there's a lot of poverty out here. As if we didn't know that already! And everyone has to bring something."

"And what do you want me to do?" Petra asked in alarm.

"Look, I thought that maybe we could give them some of your husband's old suits that you're still keeping."

"Asunción … I don't know … How am I going to give my husband's suits away? I gave all his clothes to the parish already, and there's only the suit that he got married in left."

"Well, give them that … What do you want it for?"

"Well … I don't know …"

"I'm going to take them one of Ernesto's jackets that's still in good condition, and a couple of his ties."

"Right … but your husband is still alive, and mine isn't," Doña Petra said.

"For God's sake, Petra, with all the poverty there's around here, and you don't want to give up something that's no use to you anymore …"

"All right, let me think …"

"I've promised it to Don Bernardo already."

"Really? Why did you do that?" Doña Petra was getting angry.

"Because he asked for a suit for the raffle and said that there are a lot of men who don't have any decent clothes to wear to work."

"Give them one of Ernesto's," Doña Petra replied angrily.

"Ernesto's a petty man, and you know that it's hard for him to carry out acts of charity, especially with his own belongings. And he doesn't have all that much anyway. We're giving away the jacket and two ties."

"Mama!" Catalina shouted, impatient because her mother had not yet come through into her room.

The rest of the morning Catalina had to sit nervously through a long discussion between her aunt and her mother about clothes.

Doña Asunción apologized to her daughter and said that because of the raffle she wouldn't come to see her that evening, but promised that on Sunday she wouldn't let her out of her sight. And Doña Petra muttered between her teeth that it didn't seem right to her to leave her alone to look after Catalina that afternoon, because, like every Saturday, she had been invited to have tea by her friend Doña Josefa, the widow who lived on the first floor. Doña Josefa organized innocent little card games with two or three other widows, and Doña Petra was one of the fixtures at them. Ever since Catalina had been at her house, she hadn't been able to go to these parties as regularly as usual. She had organized the tea parties herself for a while, but hadn't dared to do so since Catalina's pregnancy became more noticeable.

Catalina started to pray in silence and give thanks to God and to the Virgin. They had heard her prayers. That afternoon her mother wouldn't come to see her, and with a little bit of luck, she'd be able to convince her aunt to go down and play cards with the widow on the first floor.

This shook her out of her bad mood and she even agreed to drink a cup of soup with her mother and eat a bit of a potato omelet that her aunt had made. She kept her eyes on the clock, willing time to pass faster than it did. Her mother went at two o'clock, and her aunt sat down at her side, hoping she'd sleep for a while. Catalina was tired from so much nervous exertion, too tired to sleep, but she closed her eyes so that her aunt would leave her alone.

As soon as Doña Petra was convinced that her niece was asleep, she left her bedroom on tiptoes.

Around five o'clock, the doorbell rang. Doña Josefa, the widow from the first floor, had come to ask Doña Petra to go and play cards. She asked about Catalina, whom she didn't see anywhere.

"She's in bed with the flu," Doña Petra explained.

"She's had the flu for an awfully long time," her neighbor said.

"She gets over it, then gets it again … She's very weak … Catalina doesn't eat anything, and that's what lets all the germs get to her," her aunt said.

"Odd, she's been looking a little fatter recently …" Doña Josefa said, not without a degree of malice.

"I wish that were true! She's thin as a noodle."

"Well, there's no harm in leaving her alone for a while, is there? I mean, if it's just a touch of the flu?" the widow said.

"She's pretty demanding … Maybe she'll want something," Doña Petra said.

"When you've got the flu, all you want is to be left in peace."

And without hesitation the widow walked over to Catalina's room and knocked lightly at the door, then walked straight in. Doña Petra followed her, afraid that she might realize her niece's true condition.

"My dear, how long since I saw you last! You really do look bad, are you sure it's just a touch of the flu?"

"Yes, yes … of course, Doña Josefa … But it's very contagious, don't come too close," Catalina said.

"Right, I won't come over … But in spite of how you look, I don't think there's so much wrong with you that your aunt can't come down to play cards for a bit."

"Of course she can! Nothing's going to happen if I just stay here for a moment. The only thing I want to do is lay quietly in my bed," Catalina said as sweetly as she could.

"No, I don't like it, you could need something at any moment," Doña Petra said, looking for her niece's support.

"I'd feel worse if you didn't go down; it's three weeks that you haven't been thanks to me."

"I don't know what's wrong with your aunt, she barely leaves the house now … Stuck here all day, I'm surprised you don't get bored …" Doña Josefa guessed there was something they weren't telling her.

"Well, I came here to keep my aunt company, she was so alone all the time … but that doesn't mean that she should stop doing the things she's always done. Please, Auntie, don't let it be for my sake that you don't go down to Doña Josefa's house. If you don't I'll feel terrible."

"But, Catalina …" Doña Petra muttered.

"You've heard what your niece said, so come downstairs with me and help me get the tea things ready. It's five-thirty already and the other ladies must be about to arrive."

Doña Petra could struggle no longer and begged Catalina not to get out of bed.

"I won't be long," she said.

"Please, Auntie, have fun with your friends, and I hope you win your game; you always say you're very good at it," Catalina said, desperate now for the women to leave.

When she heard the door shutting, she got carefully out of bed and knelt down in front of the little table where the painting of the Virgin was kept, and prayed to her to be allowed to get out of the house quickly, without any further upset.

At six o'clock on the dot, she left the house with a little bag in her hand. She was wearing her overcoat and had her head wrapped in a scarf to protect herself from the rain and the cold. She felt weak, and shivered as she walked, but she was sure that God and the Virgin were on her side and that nothing could happen to her. The proof of this was in the fact that she had started the morning with no idea about how she would get away from the house, and now here she was.

Eulogio was waiting for her at the corner. He was soaked. He came over to her and took the bag she was carrying.

"Can you walk?" he asked.

"Yes, yes, if we go slowly …"

"Fernando told me to take a tram; it's not that expensive."

"That would be better," she agreed.

There weren't many people on the tram. Few people ventured

out on an afternoon that was so cold and so wet. Even so, they sat in silence, worried that they might say something that would sound strange to anyone who might overhear them.

The tram left them close to the station, and then they walked a while.

"The train doesn't go until nine o'clock," Eulogio said. "We'll wait on a bench until Fernando comes. Here's your ticket."

"What about you?"

"We're going to hitch a ride. Fernando didn't want to spend a penny of your money. I agree with him."

"But the money's for the three of us. We're in this together. Please, don't let me travel alone," she almost begged.

"Catalina, we don't know what's going to happen to us when we get to Lisbon. You and Fernando will have to decide where to go … You'll need all the money you can get. There's no point spending it on two more tickets."

"But I don't want to travel alone," she protested, with a touch of anguish in her voice.

"We'll try to come through and see you in the carriage. It will be safer for you: you know what Fernando's planning on doing. If they arrest him, at least you'll be free. Just imagine what might happen to you, and your child."

"And what are you going to do when we reach Lisbon?" she asked, as though the question could lift her out of the apprehension that she felt.

"I'm going to find a boat to take me to Alexandria."

"Alexandria? Why there? Didn't you want to go to America? What are you going to do in Egypt?"

Eulogio regretted having spoken. He hadn't even had a chance to speak to Fernando about Marvin's latest letter.

"Marvin's in Alexandria. I'll meet up with him and from there I'll go to America."

"Marvin's in Alexandria? How can he be in Alexandria?"

"Well, it's a long story …"

Catalina listened to him with great attention, drinking in every one of his words and trying to control the beating of her heart, as she was now certain where Marvin was and what she had to do.

"I'll go to Alexandria as well. I have to see him, he has to know that we're going to have a child. You don't know how happy I am!" And she took his hand and squeezed it tight.

She wasn't surprised by Eulogio's silence, as he sat there, cursing himself for having spoken too much. Fernando and Marvin wouldn't forgive him. No, he couldn't let her come to Alexandria. He blamed her for putting him in such a difficult situation. And as for Fernando … he couldn't be happy to see Catalina running into the arms of another man, even if he would reject her. But there was no turning back now. He had to face up to the consequences of his indiscretion. The die was cast, and he would soon find out whether for good or for ill.

It was not yet eight o'clock. Fernando watched the facade of the convent-prison without seeing any kind of movement. The doors were firmly closed.

He held the butt of the pistol in his overcoat pocket. He felt the coldness of the iron in his hand.

He looked at the clock again, but time was passing with excessive slowness, almost as though it were laughing at him. The noise of the rain stopped him from hearing footsteps coming up behind him. It wasn't until a young man walked past him that he realized it was the soldier, the jailer's son, one of the men who had shot his father and torn his life away from him. He felt hatred run through his guts, but he didn't have a chance to do more than that, because at that moment the door to the prison started to open, letting a group of men out who said goodbye to one another before splitting up and heading off into the rain. The soldier walked over to where his father was standing, and after greeting him, set off with him quickly to get out of the rain.

Fernando cocked the pistol and followed them closely. As the rain picked up, he took the pistol out of his pocket and whistled. The two men turned, but the rain was so heavy it stopped them from seeing the face of the man who had whistled, or from realizing what was happening. Fernando shot the father first and, as his son tried to react, turned the pistol on him.

He had killed them face-to-face. He would never have shot someone in the back; that's why he had whistled, to attract their attention. He went over to them and saw the open, blank eyes of the two men; they were lost, looking into the darkness of the night.

He heard voices and quick footsteps, and started to run, to get away from that place as quickly as possible. The night and the rain were his allies. He had to get to the station. He couldn't abandon Catalina. He thought about what he had done and felt nothing. He might have been too scared, or else his mind might simply have seized up. The only thing that concerned him now was to escape, to flee, to flee, to flee …

Catalina and Eulogio were waiting impatiently for him. It was seven minutes to nine. Eulogio was waiting for Fernando by Catalina's carriage.

He guessed it was Fernando when he saw the sodden figure running towards him. Catalina gave him a hug when he arrived and Fernando told her to get on the train, and that he would come and see her as soon as he could.

"I was so afraid something would go wrong …" she said, without letting go of his neck.

"Well, here I am, so don't worry. Now get into the carriage, because you're soaked."

He helped her to get in and find her seat. There was an elderly couple in the carriage, and a young mother who was carrying a small baby wrapped in a shawl. They looked at the pair curiously, although they said nothing.

"Well, you'll be fine here; I'll come to see you in a minute."

The seat was nothing more than an uncomfortable wooden bench. Catalina sat next to the woman and the child. Then Fernando and Eulogio ran back to the goods wagons, hoping to jump onto one once the train started moving. This they did. They fell down next to one another among some huge packages, and waited for their breathing to calm down. Eulogio spoke in a low voice:

"Did you do it?"

"Yes …" Fernando said nothing more, and looked up at the ceiling of the wagon.

Each of them lay in his own silence as he set his emotions in order. They took a long while to start speaking again. Eulogio told Fernando about his indiscretion in telling Catalina that Marvin was in Alexandria, and that she was now desperate to go there no matter what.

"But how could you! You've gone crazy!" Fernando said.

"Marvin will be angry, I know. And he won't want to see her, I'm sure of that," Eulogio said, "so you'll have to convince her to go somewhere else. It won't be hard. She's pregnant and the sea is very dangerous. There are German ships everywhere, and they don't care about sinking passenger vessels or cargo ships."

"You don't know her," Fernando said angrily.

"I know I've messed things up, and I'm sorry. I don't even know why I told her."

Eulogio explained the details of Marvin's stay in Alexandria, and his decision to go meet him there and then find another boat to take him to America. He thought that Marvin might be able to help him get there, and that he might give him a letter of recommendation.

"Don't we have enough problems without Catalina being desperate to go to Alexandria as well? What are we going to do there? I thought I was going to convince her to come with me to America, and now you tell me that we're going to have to spend some time in Alexandria," Fernando complained bitterly.

"I've said I'm sorry. Look, I'm worried. I've been through hell today thinking about what you were going to do and worrying that it might go wrong. I didn't even say goodbye to my mother."

"Now you care about her?" Fernando said, refusing to show any sympathy for his friend's plight.

"She's my mother," Eulogio said very seriously.

"You've been giving her hell without caring about her, and now your excuse for screwing things up is to say that you were worried about not saying goodbye to her ... You're just a blabbermouth, that's it."

Eulogio stood up quickly in spite of his bad leg. Fernando did the same. They stood in front of one another, measuring each other up. Their fists were clenched, and every muscle in their bodies was tense.

"The best thing will be for each of us to go his own way when we reach Lisbon. It wasn't a good idea to leave together," Eulogio said angrily.

"All right. We'll do it like that."

"And Catalina?"

"None of your business," Fernando said, turning away and going to a corner where he sat down a long way from his friend.

Eulogio lay down and closed his eyes. The argument with Fernando hurt him, but there was no way back. They had different aims. He had done enough just waiting for him at the station, knowing what he had just been doing. Had he really killed those two men? It was hard for him to imagine his friend killing people in cold blood. But you never really knew people, that was the truth of it. His own mother had surprised him by sleeping with the shopkeeper, even though she said her aim was to save him. His mother had always seemed to him to be a worthy woman, upright and principled, incapable of doing anything that might shame her son, and even so she had given herself to Don Antonio. It made him sick just to think about it.

The rumble of the train lulled him into sleep. He had spent days without sleeping well because of his nerves.

Fernando lay with his eyes open. Every time he closed them, he saw the faces of the two men he had killed. They were surprised and then frightened, and then they fell to the ground. He relived the moment in which the younger man took a step forward and held out a useless hand, perhaps trying to stop him. He also heard what the older man had muttered, his last words: "Son of a bitch," as he collapsed, dying.

No, he couldn't close his eyes because then their faces came to him and he felt a rough pain in his guts.

He had killed. He had killed in cold blood. When he pulled the trigger he felt no fear, no pity; then, when he ran towards the station, he felt no remorse either. But now guilt wrapped itself around him so tightly that he wondered whether to get off the train and give himself up. Should he do it? Yes, he decided. But if he did it, then he would be condemning his mother to absolute, unending pain. He knew that they would pass sentence on him and shoot him and that she would have to live with her husband's death and her son's, and her own death as well, because she would have been left without anything to live for.

He also looked into his soul wondering if there was any speck of fear there. Yes, he was afraid, afraid they would arrest him, and torture him, and kill him. But even so, and even with guilt pouring down on him and starting to steal his breath, he told himself he would do the same again.

He thought of his father, of the days he had spent in prison, of how he had been thin and clumsy without his glasses, how he had scratched himself openly because of the fleas and bedbugs, how he had coughed up blood, but how he had always maintained his dignity and always sadly asked his wife and his son to maintain it as well.

He knew that his father would not have agreed with his revenge, but even this knowledge had not been strong enough to overcome his desire to give pain for pain, anger for anger, life for life.

No, he would not close his eyes, maybe he would never sleep again, if the two men he had killed were now permanent residents of his brain, begging eternally for their lives.

As for Eulogio, he knew that he hadn't spoken to Catalina about his plans for any other reason than his spontaneity and his inability to keep his mouth shut. But it was true, his carelessness had created a problem for the three of them. There would be no way to convince Catalina to get on a boat with him to go to America. He knew her well, and knew that she would insist on traveling to Egypt, and that's what she would do even if she had to swim.

He was upset by the idea of having to try to go to Alexandria. For a moment he envied Eulogio his carelessness. It was a part of his character.

After a while he got up and wondered how he might get through to the carriage where Catalina was. He had promised to go to see her, and he would, even if he had to risk his life by jumping from carriage to carriage.

Meanwhile, Catalina was uncomfortable in the face of her traveling companions' interrogation. The elderly couple wrapped up their curiosity in a false concern at seeing a young woman traveling by herself. As for the woman and her child, she divided her attention almost equally between the baby and Catalina, asking her without pretenses why she was traveling alone and pregnant, and if her husband was one of the two men who had taken her to her seat.

Uncomfortable, she avoided the questions as best she could, but her interlocutors didn't give up, and their curiosity made them ask the same things again and again.

"It's not good to travel alone," the elderly woman said.

"I suppose your husband must have been that upright-looking fellow. He shouldn't leave you here at the mercy of anyone who might come along, especially not in your state," the elderly man added.

And so it went on, questions being asked again and again until Catalina wanted to scream, but she decided instead to say that she was very tired and that she was going to sleep for a while. But she couldn't manage to do so, and as soon as the carriage door opened, she opened her eyes.

"Fernando! How good of you to come. Look, I'd love to walk with you for a while, my legs are swelling up. This bench is so uncomfortable ..."

They left the compartment and walked down to the end of the carriage. Fernando was frightened that the conductor might appear: he had already had to avoid him on two occasions as he made his way to Catalina's carriage.

"I can't stay long, the conductor's wandering around everywhere, and the last thing I want is to be caught without a ticket."

"You should have bought tickets for the three of us. It was silly not to," she scolded him.

"We're going to need all the money we can get our hands on. Don't you realize that you might give birth at any moment?" he said.

"You're right ... But third-class tickets aren't that expensive."

"Don't worry about us, we're fine."

"These people are unbearable: they don't stop asking me questions, they want to find out who my husband is."

"And what have you told them?"

"Nothing ... Well, almost nothing."

"What have you said?"

"That you're a family member traveling with me to meet up with my husband."

"All right …"

"It wasn't that much of a lie: you're almost like my brother."

Fernando's mouth suddenly felt bitter. His heart broke every time she insisted that she loved him like a brother. But he couldn't blame her at all. Nobody has power over another person's emotions. The only thing he could do was wait, to always be with her until she looked at him one day with other eyes and loved him as much as he loved her.

"The less you say, the better."

"They asked me about Eulogio as well. I said the same about him, that he was family. But they're surprised that we're not traveling in the same carriage. I hope they don't say anything difficult in front of the conductor."

"Try to sleep and then you won't have to talk to them. It's better. Are you hungry?"

"Not really … Hey, Fernando, did … did you manage to do what you had to do?"

"Yes."

"And are you all right?"

"Yes."

"All right … I want you to know that I was praying for everything to turn out well. And whenever I've asked Jesus or the Virgin for something they've listened to me. And … what did you do with the pistol?"

Fernando gave a start. It was in his overcoat pocket; he'd forgotten about it. He put a hand in his pocket and felt the cool metal of the butt.

"Don't worry, it's here."

"And wouldn't it be better for you to throw it away? If they arrest us and they don't find the pistol, they won't be able to accuse you of … of what happened to those two men."

"You're right. I'll try to wipe my fingerprints off it and then I'll throw it onto the tracks. Don't worry. Go back to your carriage and go to sleep."

"And if they ask me where you are?"

"Tell them I'm in another carriage."

He went back to Eulogio. He couldn't hear his breathing, so he guessed he might be awake. Perhaps they should talk. If they had argued it was because they were nervous and overcome with anxiety. But who should take the first step? Eulogio had been wrong to tell Catalina where Marvin was. They might get to Alexandria, but the American might refuse to acknowledge the child that Catalina was going to have, and that would drive her into despair. But the worst of it all was that they knew nobody in the city.

"Was she all right?" Eulogio asked in a hoarse voice.

"Yes, I've just been to see her, she's fine. The people in the compartment are a bunch of gossips and won't stop asking questions, but I'm sure she'll be able to hold her own."

"I'm sorry we fought. You're right, I'm a blabbermouth. And I more than anyone shouldn't have told her where Marvin is. I've failed you and I've failed him."

"It'll be hard for him …"

"Marvin will never forgive me if Catalina turns up on his doorstep to tell him she's pregnant."

"Don't talk about it anymore. He's got his problems and we've got ours. We'll get out of this. I'm going to throw the pistol away."

"Don't do it … If they find it, they'll find us."

"And if they find it on us, what then? I'm going to clean the prints off it and throw it into the train tracks."

"And if anyone sees you?"

"It's the middle of the night, it's raining, I don't think anyone's looking out of the windows, and even if they were then they wouldn't see anything."

"Your mother will be worried." And as soon as he had spoken, he regretted speaking.

Fernando felt as though a hand were clamped around his neck when he heard Eulogio mention his mother. She must by now have found the letter that he left on her pillow. He knew that she would be weeping inconsolably, and he felt extremely wretched.

My dear mother,

By the time you read this letter I will be a long way away, but I will always, always, hold you in my heart.

I can't say why I have gone or where I am going; all I can do is promise that I will do whatever I can to make sure that one day we are together again. I can't bear the idea of not being with you, but believe me when I say that there is no other choice. I will work hard and try to find a way back to you, and I won't forget what you have taught me, or what Father has taught me. I will try to be the man you wanted me to be and come back one day for you to feel proud of me and forgive me the pain that I am causing you.

It is only you, Mother, who can understand me and forgive me, and I beg you, never forget me, and don't ever stop loving me, no matter what happens, and forgive me.

Your loving son,

FERNANDO

Isabel couldn't stop crying. She had read the letter several times, trying to understand why her son had left. Fernando was gone, and he gave no reason, but he begged her to forgive him. What had he done, or what was he thinking of doing? She shuddered when she thought about why he might have left. No, she didn't want to think of anything apart from maybe his desire to find a better life outside of Spain, in some country where he could breathe the air of liberty, and wouldn't be afraid of speaking out, or of having people point their fingers at him and calling him a red, a Republican, a Freemason.

Yes, Fernando had gone to another country to look for work; she could understand that, but she felt a clear certainty in her heart that there must be some other reason. She wondered if he had traveled alone, if he had told anyone about his flight; she wondered where he was headed; she asked herself so many questions that she was afraid that the veins that ran across her forehead would explode: she felt them growing tighter with every tear she shed.

How could she live without her son? Where would she find the courage to do so?

She didn't sleep that night, and fell into bed holding Fernando's letter to her chest, thinking about the last few days, their last few conversations, his farewell to her in the morning. She tried to analyze every gesture, every word, every gaze.

She didn't know what time it was, only that the morning was shifting into the afternoon, when someone rang the doorbell. And then rang again.

Piedad apologized to Isabel when she opened the door. She looked gaunt and worried.

"I'm sorry to bother you, but I just wanted to ask Fernando if he knew where Eulogio was. He didn't come home to sleep … I don't think anything's happened to him, but … well, some of his clothes are missing and … What's the matter?"

Piedad gave a start to see Isabel's face covered in tears.

Isabel ushered Piedad into her house, and when the door was closed, she hugged her.

"Good Lord, Isabel, what's going on! You're frightening me … If anything's happened to Eulogio, tell me …"

Isabel couldn't hold back her tears, and she couldn't speak, and so she held Piedad tightly until she impatiently begged her to answer her questions.

"Fernando has gone … I don't know where," she said as she cried.

"He's gone, and Eulogio?" Piedad felt a sudden pain in her chest.

"I don't know …"

It took both of them a long time to feel calm enough to sit and talk about what had happened. They guessed that Fernando and Eulogio had run away together and this frightened them, but at the same time they found it vaguely comforting, to know that their sons were not alone.

"Did he leave you a letter?" Isabel said, without showing Piedad Fernando's.

"No … You know that Eulogio is furious with me … He can't forgive me for Antonio … If he's gone, it must be because of that, because he won't forgive me. He's been saying he'll leave for quite some time, but I didn't imagine he'd do it without saying goodbye. It's odd, though: how could Fernando leave without saying goodbye?"

"Yesterday, when we were going out to work, he held me very tight and said he loved me more than anyone else in the whole world … I should have realized he was saying goodbye to me," Isabel said, trying to explain to herself Fernando's behavior.

"Yes, but you're so close to one another … To go like that, without saying anything … Fernando's got no reason to do a thing like that," Piedad insisted.

"Don't torment me! I can't stop asking myself why …" And she started to cry again, with such intensity that Piedad was afraid she would faint.

At that very moment, Ernesto Vilamar was cursing his daughter in silence while his wife cried. Petra had called them to say that Catalina had disappeared. She was so frightened and upset that she had called Juan Segovia as well, sure that he would know what to do. The doctor had come, worried by Doña Petra's urgent request, and had been surprised when he heard what she had to say:

"Catalina convinced me to go downstairs to play my usual Saturday hand of cards, and she said she was fine. I didn't want to, but she insisted so much … She said she wanted to stay in bed and there was nothing wrong with me going down to relax for a couple of hours. I was a little later than I thought, but I was back at nine. The house was silent and I thought that she must be asleep. I went into her room. She'd made a bundle with her pillow and covered it so that I'd think it was her. The room was dark and so I didn't look closely, but went back out. And then I came back a bit later to see if she was awake and wanted something, but the room was still silent and so I thought that she must be deeply asleep and it was better to let her carry on. You can't imagine how shocked I was when I went in a few minutes ago with the breakfast tray and found that what I'd thought was Catalina was actually a pillow. Where can she be?" And Doña Petra and her sister cried together.

"So Catalina probably left yesterday evening before you got back … The question is, where did she go, and who could have helped her escape? She's really in a very delicate condition … it's a complicated pregnancy … she could lose the child at any moment. And that's not the worst of it; one has to think about what might happen to her as well," Don Juan said, without hiding the worry he felt.

"What are we going to do?" Doña Asunción said, almost shouting, looking at her husband.

"We're going to give her a damn good thrashing when we find her. She's shameless ..." Don Ernesto said.

"Come on ... come on, don't say such things, Ernesto. I understand your reaction, but she's your daughter and she's always been a good child. A little flighty, yes, but a good kid," the doctor said, trying to inject a little calm into the proceedings.

"She wanted to have this child ... she kept on saying that she wouldn't give it away ... that she wanted to find the child's father," Doña Petra said through tears.

"That's it: Catalina was not prepared to give away her child and that's why she's left," Don Juan said.

"We only wanted to do what was best for her," Doña Asunción said, still crying.

"Right, well, it's understandable that she didn't want to give up her child. There are a lot of women who change their minds at the last minute," the doctor replied, "but let's just think for a moment ... Someone must have helped her ... she could barely walk ..."

"Yes, she didn't leave here alone," Doña Petra admitted.

"Who could it be? No one knows about her condition," Don Ernesto said, but the frightened gazes of his wife and his sister-in-law alerted him to the truth.

"Well, these things can't be hidden completely," Don Juan said, trying to help the women out.

"You're hiding something. Tell me, Asunción, who else knew about this? Don't lie to me. Who was it?" Don Ernesto was tense.

Doña Petra started to sob inconsolably, which made her brother-in-law all the more suspicious.

"You owe me an explanation," Don Ernesto insisted.

"Oh! Ernesto, I ... I didn't want to tell you so as not to upset you, but Catalina told Fernando Garzo because she wanted him to help her get in touch with the American. And ... well, Fernando has been coming to see her ..." Doña Asunción closed her eyes, scared at the expression on her husband's face.

"Can it be? You've tricked me! Of course! A chip off the old block! Your daughter's just like you ...! The same shamelessness as you! You let Fernando Garzo, the Freemason's son, come and visit her! How dare you behave like that behind my back?" Don Ernesto shouted.

"That's enough, Ernesto! Stop talking such nonsense and behave like what you are, a gentleman. You will not talk to Asunción like this, at least not in my presence, because I won't allow it."

Don Ernesto looked in astonishment at the doctor, who had got to his feet and was standing in front of him.

"What do you mean, you're not going to allow it? Asunción is my wife and Catalina is my daughter, and so I'll speak to them however I please, do you understand?" he shouted, beside himself with rage.

"I'm not surprised that Catalina decided to run away, with a lunatic like you breathing down her neck," Juan Segovia replied.

"This is the last straw! How dare you!"

"Of course I dare speak like this! You're in the wrong at the moment and you're saying things that are unworthy of a father and a husband," the doctor replied.

"Please, please!" Doña Petra begged, upset by the way the situation was developing.

"Yes, let's all calm down. It's clear: Catalina has run away and she must have had the help of Fernando Garzo, which is a relief because he's a good young man, serious, responsible and in love with her, so she couldn't be in better hands," the doctor said.

"That's all I need!" Don Ernesto was finding it difficult to hide his rage.

"Fernando will look after her and, of course, he will send us news of how she is," Don Juan continued.

"But we don't know if he's with her ..." Doña Asunción murmured.

"Well, we need to find out. I think, Asunción, that you should go to the Garzos' house, and then Fernando's mother will have news for you," the doctor advised.

"But what if she hasn't gone with him?" Doña Petra said.

"Of course she's with him. Fernando is like a brother for Catalina, she told me so herself," the doctor said, "and the boy's head over heels for her, and will do whatever he can to help her. If Catalina wanted, he'd even marry her," he added.

Don Ernesto, a little calmer now, nodded. And so he decided to allow his wife to go to the Garzos' house while he stayed at his, with Doña Petra and the doctor. Doña Petra would have liked to have stayed in her own house, or else gone with her sister, but she didn't dare stand up to Don Ernesto, who blamed her for Catalina's flight.

Isabel and Piedad both jumped when they heard the doorbell ring. For a moment they thought it might be their sons, but that dream was shattered when Isabel opened the door and found Doña Asunción weeping openly.

"I'm sorry to bother you, but I need to ask you a question," Doña Asunción said, pushing into Isabel's house.

"What's going on? Isabel said, trying to stem her own tears and confused at Asunción's appearance.

Piedad came to the door, also surprised by the arrival of this visitor. The three women looked at one another for a few seconds without knowing what to say. Doña Asunción swallowed, not knowing if she could speak with Piedad there as well.

"My daughter has disappeared. She left yesterday afternoon and we think that Fernando helped her run away," she said out loud, all in a rush, without addressing anyone in particular.

"Catalina's gone?" Isabel said in amazement.

"Yes … she …" Doña Asunción couldn't say anything more.

"Our sons have gone as well," Piedad said, astonished with how the situation was developing.

"They've gone? Where?" Doña Asunción wanted to know. Isabel invited her to sit down. The three women sat in silence, wondering how much they could say and how much they had to keep hidden. The girl's mother decided in the end that it wasn't worthwhile trying to play down the gravity of the situation.

"Catalina is pregnant. I don't know if Fernando told you." Isabel said nothing, and it was Piedad who spoke.

"Who's the father? Is that why she left? Eulogio said that she went to look after her aunt who wasn't well …"

"That's the excuse we gave. We didn't want people to see her putting on weight. We took her to my sister Petra's house. We wanted her to have the child and then give it up for adoption."

"Poor little thing!" Piedad said.

"Poor little thing? Worse for her to be a single mother and unable to get married. We decided to do what was best for her," Doña Asunción defended herself.

"But what about the child's father? Doesn't he want to take any responsibility for her?" Piedad insisted.

"The father is that American friend of Eulogio's, and as you know all too well he's gone away, and Catalina has written to him and he hasn't written back," Doña Asunción replied.

"Marvin! Good Lord!" Piedad said, unable to believe what she was hearing.

"Yes, Marvin …" Doña Asunción said.

"But Marvin's a good boy, I'm sure that if the child is his then he'll take care of it," Piedad said.

"Well, for the time being we don't know anything about him at all. Catalina's almost seven months gone and is threatening to refuse to hand over the child. Fernando is the only one who knows about the situation; he's been visiting her these last few months. But you have to know that, given how close you are to your son." Doña Asunción looked expectantly at Isabel.

"Now I understand," Isabel said, and her face seemed to relax.

"What do you understand?" the other two women asked in unison.

"Fernando helped Catalina, and Eulogio helped Fernando. My son is in love with your daughter, and has been ever since they were children, and he'd do anything for her, even help her to find Marvin."

"Why would Eulogio have to help them?" Doña Asunción asked.

"Because he wanted to leave … there's no future for him here. Catalina and Fernando running away will have helped him make up his mind to take the last step," Piedad said, the pieces falling into place for her as well.

Suddenly Isabel started to laugh as well as cry. She felt relieved to have worked out why her son had left. Fernando was a romantic, and here he was with the chance to be Catalina's knight in shining armor. Perhaps he had gone away with her in the hope that the girl would appreciate the gesture and accept his proposal of marriage – that is, if Marvin didn't want to take her. Yes, that was very like her son.

Knowing that he had left with Catalina and Eulogio took a great weight off her shoulders. Now she knew that she hadn't lost him for good.

Piedad understood immediately why Isabel was smiling, and she herself calmed down as well. Doña Asunción alone didn't understand why hope had replaced despair on the faces of the two women.

"Look, Asunción, your daughter is in good hands. Fernando and Eulogio will take care of her. When Catalina has had her child, she'll need to make a decision. The important thing is that none of the three is lost and that they're together and can help one another," Isabel said, seemingly having overcome her grief.

"Another thing to think about is how they will deal with her giving birth. But they're smart and I'm sure that they'll know how to deal with the situation," Piedad added.

"But where are they?" Doña Asunción shouted in desperation.

"We don't know … I suppose they've gone as far away as possible so that we can't find them," Isabel said, feeling a sudden shudder of pain.

"Nothing'll happen to them," Piedad said.

"But my daughter … she's not well … the doctor told her to keep to her bed because she was in danger of losing the baby … anything might happen." Doña Asunción was almost begging in front of these women who had suddenly seen their hope revived.

"Nothing will happen to them. You'll see. Calm down," Piedad recommended.

"Catalina was going to get married …" Doña Asunción said, and she started to cry again.

"Who to? You said that Marvin didn't reply to her letters," Piedad interrupted.

"To Antoñito. My husband arranged the wedding. Antoñito, of course, knows nothing about Catalina's state, or else he'd have broken it off … and now … What are we going to tell them?"

"Catalina's broken the engagement … that she wants to stay with her aunt … Anything," Isabel advised.

"He won't accept it! The shopkeeper is a horrible man and we ..."

"You're in debt to him like everyone else," Piedad said.

"How did you know?" Doña Asunción asked in fright.

"Because Antonio and Mari make sure that everyone in the neighborhood knows who owes them money, and they are much more boastful when it comes to you, because they never would have dreamed that they could be in a position of power over the Vilamars," Piedad explained.

"So everyone knows ..."

"That you've got money troubles? Who doesn't have them? There's no shame in it," Isabel interrupted.

"I'm not surprised that Catalina would have run away ... marrying Antoñito is a fate most people would want to escape from," Piedad said.

"And what are we going to do now? Please, don't say a word to anyone about Catalina!"

"Of course not!" Isabel replied, offended. "Do you think that all we do is gossip? We won't tell anyone: you're the ones who have to think of an explanation for why Catalina disappeared."

"And what are you going to say about your sons?" Doña Asunción asked.

"That they've decided to emigrate and look for a better future," Piedad replied.

"Yes, that's what we'll say," Isabel agreed.

"And me? What will I say to Ernesto?" Doña Asunción asked, terrified about what her husband would say.

"The truth. Tell him that Catalina is well, and that nothing's going to happen to her because Fernando and Eulogio will look after her, and that they are childhood friends of hers and care for her a great deal," Isabel recommended.

Doña Asunción left the house feeling devastated. Maybe a little calmer, though, after Isabel's final words: she was right, Fernando and Eulogio would look after her daughter. But how would Ernesto take the news? She was frightened of what his reaction might be. His main concern was not his daughter's well-being, but the planned wedding to Antoñito, which was the only thing that could get them out of their economic bind. And now that Catalina was gone, what would they do? And how could they justify her absence? And they didn't know if their daughter would return. She burst into tears again, worried by the problems that now faced her.

Don Ernesto hadn't stopped complaining all the time his wife was at the Garzos' house. Juan Segovia had to hold back his anger in the face of Ernesto's resentful quibbles. As for Petra, she cried and blew her nose every now and then. She was too scared to think, and every time her brother-in-law looked at her, implying that it was her fault that they were in this situation, she burst out crying with even greater intensity.

When Asunción came back home, the three of them surrounded her at once to find out the news. She told them that Catalina had fled with Fernando and Eulogio, and that neither Isabel nor Piedad knew where they could have gone, but that the two women felt happy to think that the three of them were together, and they should be happy too, to know that Catalina was in good hands.

"But you are just astonishingly stupid!" Don Ernesto shouted.

"Watch your language, at least while I'm here," Don Juan said angrily.

"Can't you see how disastrous the situation is? What are we going to say to Don Antonio? God Almighty, why are you doing this to me!" Don Ernesto shouted out, paying the doctor no attention.

"Calm down, Ernesto, you'll do yourself in," his wife asked.

"Of course I will! And it'll be your fault, yours and your useless sister's. We put Catalina in her hands and she goes off to play cards ... Who would do such a thing?"

"Catalina would have run away one way or another," Juan Segovia interrupted, "so don't you go blaming anyone for what happened. Maybe you're the guilty one, for wanting to push her into a marriage that she didn't want," he said, wanting to defend Doña Petra.

"Right, now I'm the guilty party! The only thing I've been focused on is my daughter's well-being, on making sure that she's not treated like a slut just because she's a single mother. And as for Antoñito, there's no better match possible. She won't want for anything when she's married to him."

"I'm not going to say more than I should, but I'll speak my mind because of the friendship we bear each other. Who was going to get the most out of this marriage? Come now, Ernesto, as well as Catalina's future financial well-being, the wedding to the shopkeeper's son was designed to get you out of a hole," the doctor said, looking at Ernesto mistrustfully.

"How dare you! Insulting me in my own home!"

"No, I'm not insulting you, Heaven forbid, but I can't cope with the injustice of putting your own responsibilities and problems on other people's shoulders. You need to find an excuse and stop the wedding, because I don't think we'll be able to find Catalina."

"I'll take this to the police! I'll make her come back if I have to drag her back myself!" Don Ernesto said defiantly.

"And then the whole world will know that she's pregnant and that she has run away because she didn't want to give her child up and marry Antoñito. Is that what you want? That's what will happen if you go to the police."

"You want me to sit back and not go looking for my daughter? What sort of a father do you think I am?" Don Ernesto was shouting again.

"Do what you think you need to, but use your head, and make sure that the cure isn't worse than the disease," the doctor recommended.

"Juan's right … if we go to the police we'll have to say that she ran away because she was pregnant, and Don Antonio will find out eventually. Antoñito won't want to marry her, and she'll be marked out in public as well," Doña Asunción said, daring to stand up to her husband.

Ernesto Vilamar put his head in his hands and said nothing, apart from:

"My God, what a tragedy! My God, what a tragedy!"

BOOK II

1

Marvin opened the doors to the balcony and let the light flood into his room. At this hour of the morning, it was still cool and the sun didn't heat things up too much; for the first days of December, this was a blessing.

He closed his eyes and breathed in the pure air of the morning. He didn't open them until a hand lightly touched his shoulder.

He turned and smiled. He had thought that he would never feel something this close to happiness.

He felt Farida's body next to his and it did not bother him at all; instead, it made him feel calm. This was how it had been ever since they had met.

He owed Monsieur Rosent so much! Not just for believing in him as a poet, but also because it was through his daughter Sara that he had met Farida. If Monsieur Rosent hadn't made him the temporary owner of his property so that he could hand it over to Sara, then he would never have come to Alexandria and they would never have met.

Wilson & Wilson was in the center of the city. It was a small bookshop. Wall to wall and floor to ceiling, its shelves held authentic treasures.

The owner, Benjamin Wilson, was Sara's husband.

Wilson traveled all over the world looking for rare books, especially rare collections of poetry. Unique editions. He bought them and sold them, and published his own material as well.

When he had gone to Paris, it was always to see Monsieur Rosent, who would often have something he might be interested in. Neither Wilson nor Sara had shown any obvious interest in one another, but on his last trip to France he had asked her to marry him and she had accepted. This was before the Germans had occupied Paris.

Sara was no longer a child: she was nearly forty and had never shown any desire to marry. It was enough for her to read poetry and help her father to run the handcrafted publishing house where budding poets came looking for advice and to get help publishing their first volumes. The Rosents also sold books by the great poets of the world.

Benjamin Wilson was from an English family, but had been born in Alexandria. His grandfather had inherited a business buying and selling antiquarian books in London, but before he had taken it on, he had traveled to Africa and the Orient writing long travel articles for the London newspapers and working every now and then with the Foreign Office.

He married a rural aristocrat and they had one child, Robert, who had not followed in his father's footsteps, but who had preferred to try his luck in the Army. He came to Alexandria in 1895 as an officer in the permanent garrison that Great Britain kept there, as well as in other cities of Egypt, as a result of the peace agreement between the two countries. Robert had married an Egyptian woman, the daughter of a Greek family that had moved to Alexandria from Thessaloniki. She gave him a son, Benjamin. Marvin had heard people say that Benjamin Wilson's mother was Jewish, but this might be no more than rumor, and he hadn't dared ask Sara about it.

Everyone called Benjamin "Mr. Wilson." His father, Robert Wilson, thought that he should study at an English school, and so in spite of his wife's protests, he had sent him to study in London under the guardianship of his grandfather, who took the chance to instill in him a love for reading in general and poetry in particular. The young man learned whatever his grandfather could teach him and never thought about doing anything besides publishing, buying and selling books. Grandfather Wilson was a strange man, who would travel vast distances to find rare books, an activity which gave him immense satisfaction and joy. Grandfather and grandson were inseparable. On his grandfather's advice, Benjamin had decided to serve his country by going into the Foreign Service, but the old man got sick and all his plans fell through. When his grandfather died, Benjamin Wilson decided to return to Alexandria as his father asked him: his father was also afraid for his wife's health.

When he got back to Alexandria, Benjamin Wilson made two decisions: to keep the London bookshop open, and to open a branch in Alexandria.

When he came back to the city, he realized just how much he missed its light; above all, he missed the mixture of people from all over the world that gave Alexandria its unique personality.

Sara Rosent had told Marvin all this, and it was all he needed to know. He had hit it off with Mr. Wilson from the start, and ever since he had come to Alexandria to find Sara, not a day had passed when he had not gone to the bookshop. It was also a place where writers met up, and where he had met Farida for the first time.

"What are you thinking about?"

Farida's crystal-clear voice brought him back to himself. He turned to her and smiled.

"I'm thinking about the day that Sara introduced us, and how odd she and Mr. Wilson are together."

"Odd? I think they go well together, and they are happy, which is the most important thing. I have known Benjamin Wilson for many years, and I promise you I had never seen him smile."

"I owe them a debt I can never repay."

Farida looked at him expectantly while he took her hand.

"What debt is that?" she asked.

"Having brought us together."

"It was lucky for us both. I've told you, though, that we were bound to meet. It was fated."

Marvin was sometimes surprised by the things that Farida said. He didn't reply, but he embraced her and she embraced him back. Marvin thought that if happiness existed, then it could be found in this moment.

He had been saved from himself by meeting Farida. She was older than him, more than forty. She was tall and dark, with olive skin, and slender: she seemed so sure of herself that it was formidable.

Shortly after his arrival in Alexandria, Sara had invited him to a poetry reading. It was a meeting of a few poets who did nothing more than try to dazzle one another. Writers in other genres also attended, which was why Farida was there.

Once the poets had finished reading their most recent writings, Sara led the conversation onto other, thornier topics such as Good and Evil, conscience and duty ...

Everyone spoke, but when Farida spoke, silence fell and everyone listened with respect and fascination.

Sara whispered in his ear: "Farida is a philosopher." Later on, he found out that she had written five books, including a veritable encyclopedia on Alexandrian philosophy and its doctrines.

"There's a long tradition of arguing about everything here, and of asking questions with no answers. After Greece, I'd say that Alexandria is the second most important place in the world for philosophy," Sara explained.

Marvin asked her to introduce him to Farida, and was a little taken aback when Farida asked him to go for a walk with her.

They left Wilson & Wilson and wandered through the city. Marvin didn't know Alexandria very well, but she guided him: the rue Rosette, the church of Saint Athanasius, the Convent of Saint Catherine, the Moon Gate ...

Farida asked where he was staying. Marvin replied that he had been lucky enough to be invited by Sara to stay in her own house. The Wilsons lived in Bolkly, a residential neighborhood where the majority of the inhabitants were foreigners, most of them British.

Sara and Benjamin Wilson's house was as large as it was beautiful, and from the terrace there was a beautiful view over the sea.

She listened as he spoke, until he realized that he was sharing with this unknown woman the ghosts that had taken up residence within him ever since the war in Spain. He told her everything: his fear in the battle; his wounds, both to his body and his soul; the way that poetry seemed to have frozen within him; his conviction that the future would bring him nothing.

"Come with me," she had said. And he let himself be led away to her house in an old building in the Corniche District, whose balconies leaned out over the sea. The morning greeted them as they were speaking, and he didn't know when he fell asleep, but when he woke up, Farida stroked his forehead and her smile brought him back to life. From that day on, they had not been apart.

Sara hadn't asked him any questions when he came to her house for his luggage, as though it were the most natural thing in the world for him to go and live with a woman he had met the day before. She only told him one thing about Farida: that she was a wealthy woman. She had been married to a man who, when he died five years previously, had left her a fortune. She wrote, thought, and traveled to wherever she could be assured of a good discussion about human nature.

Marvin was surprised to realize that he really knew very little about Farida. He had bared his soul in front of her, but she had not shown him her own.

When he got to her house he asked Farida to tell him who she was, what she desired, what she felt, and the night caught up with them and then the morning again, and they woke up wrapped in one another's arms.

And that morning was as happy as all the other mornings when they had woken up together.

Marvin sighed and looked Farida deep in the eyes.

"What shall we do today?" he asked expectantly.

"Write. Benjamin Wilson wants to publish a book of mine. And you should do the same. Look at the sun on the waves, let the air come into your lungs and caress your heart. Smile or cry, but write."

And he did. He obeyed her as though he were a child. Farida had shaken the shadows from his soul, and had returned to him the pleasure of feeling alive.

2

The morning fog had dissipated when the train drew into Lisbon station. Fernando and Eulogio had jumped out of the train a few miles back, and had told Catalina that this was what they were doing, and that she should wait for them without moving.

Eulogio had hit his arm, and it was swelling minute by minute as they walked. He had also hurt his ankle and was finding it difficult to walk. As for Fernando, he was bruised from head to foot. They took longer than they had thought to walk to the station. Catalina was waiting for them, as worried as she was scared, and above all upset to be the object of so many curious eyes. A ticket collector had come and asked her if she was lost, to which she replied that she was just waiting for someone to come and pick her up.

And she waited until she saw her two friends come hobbling along.

"What's happened to you? Have you hurt yourselves? We need to go to a doctor!"

"And how are we going to pay him?" Eulogio said grumpily.

"I've still got some money, and the jewels … We could sell them."

"No, don't worry, it's nothing," Fernando said as his face twisted with pain.

"Don't treat me like an idiot! We're going to a doctor right now." And without giving them any chance to reply, she went over to the ticket office and asked with her best smile where she could find a doctor. The similarities between Spanish and Portuguese helped her to be understood with no trouble. Once she had gotten an address, she made the two men follow her, barely speaking to them.

The doctor was an old man who was deaf, and he didn't have anyone waiting to consult him, so he could see them at once. He diagnosed Eulogio with a sprained ankle and a serious contusion on his wrist; and as for Fernando, he seemed to be sound, although very bruised by his fall.

Catalina paid the old man without haggling, and asked him where the nearest pawn shop was. He gave them an address not very distant from where they were, and warned them not to get cheated.

"But you, young woman, are the one who really worries me ... Your belly ... I'd say that you're about to give birth. You're very pale, are you well? You don't need to answer that, I can see that you're not well."

But she wouldn't allow him to examine her. With Catalina leaning on Fernando's arm, the three of them left the surgery to go to the pawnbroker's. Once there, they handed over all the jewels. The money they got would barely be enough to let them survive.

They sat on a bench on an avenue that led down to the sea. They talked about what they were going to do. Catalina laid down her demands.

"We need to find a boat that will take us to Alexandria. We'll be able to pay for our journey with the money from the pawn shop. Marvin will help us once we get to Alexandria, for sure."

"And where are we going to find a boat going to Alexandria? Haven't you noticed that there's a war on, and that the Germans sink every boat they come across?" Fernando replied in a slightly surly voice.

"Look at the port, out there ... it's full of boats. Let's go and ask someone," Catalina said stubbornly.

"And what if none of them is going to Alexandria?" Fernando insisted.

"Well, there has to be at least one making the trip, or that will drop us off somewhere close," she said, more certainly than she felt, making an effort for them not to see how tired she was, or how weak she felt.

They walked slowly. Neither Eulogio nor Catalina could walk at any speed at all. They found themselves under the curious gaze of several people once they arrived at the port. Fernando wondered if they would be looking for them yet, and if someone had pointed the finger at him for the murder of those two men. He wouldn't be safe until there was a sea between him and justice.

They didn't want to leave Catalina exposed to the gazes of the sailors, so they went with her as she asked all the people she met about a boat leaving for Alexandria. But they couldn't give her a positive answer. They were just about to give up and admit that they were unlikely to travel to Alexandria when they saw a sailor walking briskly towards a midsize cargo ship that looked like it was getting ready to depart. They asked him.

"That boat is the *Esperanza del Mar*, and it runs on the Egypt and America routes. A few months ago, a couple of Germans nearly sunk it, but the captain got lucky."

"And does he take passengers?" Catalina asked impatiently.

"He doesn't like to take them, much less women, but he has taken passengers every now and then," the sailor admitted.

"What's the captain called and how can we find him?" Fernando asked.

"He's called Captain Pereira, but they call him the Portuguese. He's always in a bad mood, but he's a great sailor, and his men will follow him into the very jaws of Hell itself. They put their trust in him. They say he has the devil's own luck, and the sea holds no secrets from him."

"Right ... And where can we find the Portuguese?" Fernando insisted.

"If he's not in his boat, I'd try that cafe ... but the lady shouldn't go in there, especially not in her condition," the sailor said.

They went into the cafe and the men's rough gazes focused on Catalina right away. She didn't look down or let anyone think that she might be intimidated. Fernando took her by the hand and squeezed it tight to encourage her.

Eulogio asked for the Portuguese, and the man behind the bar asked why they were looking for him.

"We'll tell him when we see him," Eulogio replied.

"Well … go ahead … look for him," the man replied grumpily.

Catalina lent on the bar to gather strength so as not to fall over. She was tired and sick, and her belly had been hurting for some time now.

"We need to speak to the captain of the *Esperanza del Mar*; maybe you would be kind enough to tell us where we can find him …" she insisted.

The man looked her up and down and thought for a while before speaking.

"The Portuguese don't like strangers, miss."

"I understand, neither do I," she said.

Fernando saw Catalina's legs trembling and put an arm round her shoulders to keep her standing.

The sailors began to murmur among themselves, annoyed at the presence of the three strangers. One of them came over to where they were standing.

"Get out of here, kids. Right now!"

"Could you not shout please? There's no need. You want us to leave, and we will leave as soon as we know where we can find the Portuguese or his boat." Catalina looked the man in the eye, taking in his weathered face, rough after a lifetime of fighting the sea.

"Greenhorn!" The man looked at her disrespectfully.

"Please respect the young lady," Fernando said.

"Or else …?" The sailor was getting ready for the fight he was going to have with this young firebrand.

"Or else I'll punch you in the face," Fernando said without blinking.

The sailor laughed and launched himself towards Fernando, but he was quicker and tripped the man and made him fall, which made all the other men laugh. Even so, Fernando knew that the man would be a better fighter than him, as he'd never been involved in anything more serious than a scrap with the boys in his neighborhood. He wasn't afraid for himself, but for Catalina.

"What sort of men are you, that you can't respect a pregnant woman? Bunch of cowards!" Catalina shouted.

Several sailors got up from where they were sitting and came over towards them, ready to dole out a beating. Catalina stood in front of Fernando, but he moved her to one side so she wouldn't get in the way of the fight. Eulogio came and stood next to his friend, knowing that the battle was lost before it even started.

"All right!" came a voice from the back of the cafe. "Sit down! Or are you going to fight with a woman?"

The sailors went back to their seats and sat down expectantly.

"I'm the Portuguese. Who in Davy Jones' name are you?"

Catalina was almost ready to hug the man; he stood upright and proud, in spite of the scars on his face and the fact that he was old enough to be her grandfather. His gray, almost white hair and his wrinkles bore witness to that fact.

"Thank you, sir, I'm very pleased to meet you." She held out her hand with a smile.

"Captain, we're looking for you because we want to go to Alexandria," Fernando explained.

The Portuguese let out a guffaw that was echoed by the other sailors.

"You're surprised? Well, it's very important for us, so don't laugh," Catalina said.

The old captain looked at her in surprise. She couldn't be any older than his granddaughters, but even so, she was very much in control of herself. It didn't seem like it would be easy to scare her.

"So, it's important for you to go to Alexandria ... Well, go on."

"We want to travel on the *Esperanza del Mar*," she said, looking him in the eyes without blinking.

"All right ... So you've decided which ship you want to travel on as well."

"Sir, could I have a word with you alone?" Catalina said, surprising not only the captain but also Fernando.

"Impossible," Fernando said.

"We won't let you go alone," Eulogio added.

"I want to speak to the captain by myself. I'm sure there won't be any danger," she insisted.

The Portuguese was disconcerted, but at the same time he couldn't help but feel curiosity about what this young woman would say, so fragile-looking, but sure of herself in a way he had seen in very few people before her.

"I don't mind," he said, looking at Fernando and waiting for his acceptance.

"Let's go outside," Catalina suggested.

"But it's raining buckets!" Eulogio protested.

"Don't go outside. If you want to speak to the captain alone, do it where we can see you," Fernando said angrily.

"Let's go into this little corner," the captain said, pointing to an empty table.

Catalina walked boldly after him, aware that all the sailors were looking at her and making jokes which she would prefer not to hear.

The captain pointed to a chair and invited her to sit, which she did, relieved. With every minute that passed her belly hurt more, and she was worried just how much longer she might be able to last.

"What do you want to ask me?" he said bluntly.

"You can see that I'm pregnant. The father of my child is in Alexandria, and I need to get to him."

"Right ... I thought that young Galahad over there was your husband."

"Fernando? No, he's like a brother to me."

"So, your husband is in Alexandria ..." The captain guessed that the young woman was in some kind of trouble.

"I'm not married. Not yet. But I'll get married as soon as I set foot in Alexandria. That's why I have to get there as soon as possible. I'm in a very precarious situation," she said, lowering her voice.

The Portuguese sat in silence, unsettled by the confession. Catalina, undaunted, carried on speaking.

"Fernando and Eulogio are childhood friends of mine. They want to go to America, because you know how Spain is now, after the war. But they're very generous and are going to help me meet up with the father of my child. I ... Well, my family wants to make me give the child up as soon as I have it, hand it over to be adopted, but I won't do that: I'd sooner die."

Fernando and Eulogio were looking nervously at Catalina and

wondering what she might be saying to the captain of the *Esperanza del Mar*. Whatever it was, the old man coughed uncomfortably.

"Will you help me?" she asked the captain, looking him straight in the eyes.

The Portuguese hesitated. In spite of himself, the young woman's confession had moved him. He had spent years on the high seas, ever since he had signed on as a cabin boy to earn some money for his poor widowed mother. He had never known his father, and he had suffered this absence without complaint. The sea, the wind, all the countries he had seen and, above all, all the men he had encountered, sailors such as himself, they had given him no room to show weakness. But this girl had not just brought him back to his childhood, his absent father, she had also reminded him of his two granddaughters, who must be more or less her age. They were the people he most loved in the whole world, even more than he had loved his wife, who had died, or his only daughter, who had given him the gift of the two girls.

Catalina didn't interrupt his thoughts. She knew that she couldn't pressure this man, who was at this very moment deciding her fate. Finally, she saw his head move as he looked at her gravely.

"We are at war, you know? The sea is filled with German submarines that have no respect for cargo ships. I've had more than one run-in with them in which I've almost lost the ship. It's not safe to travel by boat, especially not with all the miles between us and Alexandria."

"I know, but do you think I care about the risk? I have to find my son's father. And it wasn't easy to leave my home without knowing what awaited me."

"You ran away?" he asked in alarm.

"Yes," she said sincerely. "I told you that they wanted me to give my child up for adoption."

He hesitated again, but couldn't help admiring the girl's determination.

"My boat is leaving at seven. Everyone has to be on board by four o'clock."

"How much will it cost?" she asked, worried that they wouldn't have enough for the journey.

He named a sum that stopped Catalina dead, but she didn't give in.

"We don't have that much money. We'll give you what we have and we can work on board doing whatever you need. I can clean and cook and sew ... and Fernando and Eulogio are strong."

The captain laughed so loudly that it frightened her, and Eulogio and Fernando came to her side in alarm.

"What's happening?" Fernando wanted to know.

"Your young friend here wants to pay for your travel by cooking or sewing ... I don't think she can do anything, but maybe you'll be able to lend a hand. We pay for our tickets in advance."

Catalina opened her bag and took out her purse, handing the captain all the money she had. He took it without counting it.

"We'll take the gangplank away at six o'clock," he said, getting up and leaving without giving them time to say anything else.

They saw him look grumpy as he left the cafe. Fernando and Eulogio didn't know what to say or to think.

"What did you say to him?" Eulogio asked.

"The truth. I told him the truth. He'll take us to Alexandria."

"You've given him all our money, we haven't got a penny," Fernando said worriedly.

"Well, we still have things we can pawn," Catalina said, holding out a couple of rings.

"They won't give us much for them," Eulogio said.

"I've got a cross ... I'm wearing it. I didn't think I'd ever get rid of it, because my grandmother Agustina, my father's mother, gave it to me. She asked me never to part with it, and said that the cross had protected her ... I suppose if we pawn it it's a very concrete way of getting protection."

"What are you saying? The rings, okay, but I won't let you pawn the cross," Fernando seemed almost angry.

"It's mine, and I'll pawn it if I want to. We can't be left without money, even if it's not very much."

"We haven't eaten all day," Eulogio said, who seemed to think that Catalina's plan was not a bad idea.

"We'll go back to the pawnbroker's and see what they give us," she insisted.

The afternoon was wearing on, but there was still some time before they had to board the ship. Fernando was worried about Catalina. He saw that she was exhausted, and her face showed the marks of pain.

"Are you all right?" he insisted.

She said she was all right. She knew that if she told him the truth, that her contractions had started, then he'd never let her get on board.

They didn't know what to do until the time came to board the ship, or where to go to shield themselves from the wind and the rain. Once they had pawned the rings and the cross, they decided to keep the money until they got to Alexandria, where only God knew how long it would take them to find Marvin. The few people who walked the streets in this weather looked at them mistrustfully.

And so, when they got back to the port, they showed their documents to a customs official who barely paid them any attention. It was raining so hard that all he wanted to do was to stay in his warm shed.

They found a more or less sheltered spot where they could wait and, shivering, let the time pass until they could board the boat.

Catalina started to cough. She was soaked to the skin, and she couldn't stop shivering, for all that Fernando tried to warm her by holding her in his arms.

The time passed so slowly that they started to feel desperate. After a while, Catalina insisted on heading to the boat.

"Let's ask them to let us on board. We are passengers after all."

"But the money we've given the captain isn't even enough for one ticket!" Eulogio said, worried that they'd be thrown off the boat if they tried to get on before the stated hour.

"Well, we could at least try," Fernando said, worried by Catalina's shivering.

The gangplank was in position on the *Esperanza del Mar*, and they walked up it very slowly. A sailor came out to meet them.

"We've bought tickets to Alexandria, and the captain told us to be punctual, because as soon as dawn broke he was going to pull up the gangplank," Catalina said, with a certainty she didn't feel.

"Stay there, no one can board the ship without the captain's permission, and he's given the order not to let anyone on board until four o'clock. I'll talk to the bosun."

Two sailors stood in front of them, making it clear that they would not be allowed to board the ship without the proper permission.

"It's three thirty ... there's only half an hour to go ..." Catalina said.

But it was useless. At four o'clock, the sailor who had gone to ask about allowing them on board came to let them on.

"Come with me, I'll take you to your cabin. You'll have to share. This isn't a passenger ship, although the captain allows passengers from time to time. We weren't going to take anyone on this trip. No one is mad enough to risk his life dodging German submarines."

They didn't complain about the fact that they'd have to share a cabin. They felt pleased to be finally under a roof.

The cabin was small. There were two beds screwed to the wall, a table, a couple of chairs and a tiny wardrobe.

"This door here leads to the head," the sailor said, pointing.

"And the captain?" said Catalina.

"He's preparing for departure. And he's in a foul mood. I wouldn't go to see him until we're out at sea. I heard him telling the bosun that he was stupid to allow himself to be talked into letting you on board, and the best thing would be to send you all home. I'll bring you some coffee."

They agreed that one of the beds would be for Catalina, and that the two men would take turns in the other.

Catalina went into the tiny bathroom to change her clothes because she was exhausted.

"Get to bed and try to sleep," Fernando ordered her.

"I don't know if I'll be able to sleep, but I'll get some rest. I hurt all over and I think I've caught a cold."

"My arm and my ankle are hurting. With all the walking we've done, I think the sprain's gotten worse," said Eulogio.

"Well, let's not complain. We've been very lucky. The best thing is for us to stay here and not get in anyone's way, or else the captain will change his mind and throw us off the ship. We should try to rest," Fernando said.

"The important thing is that we're together and headed to Alexandria." And for the first time that day, Catalina smiled.

Eulogio fell asleep almost as soon as his head hit the pillow. Catalina closed her eyes, but she couldn't sleep. Her contractions were growing sharper. She started to tremble with fear. She knew that at any moment she might go into labor.

Fernando was sitting on one of the chairs, and he had fallen asleep as well. Catalina watched him, pleased to have him by her side. She felt safe with him.

Light started to filter through the porthole. The cold gray morning greeted them, while the ship started to cast off.

It took them a while to leave the port, and then they were out on the dark Atlantic, which seemed to churn up especially fiercely as they came.

The boat was pushed around by the waves, which came over the deck and left it soaked in water.

A noise woke Eulogio at the same time as Catalina screamed. Fernando had fallen off the chair where he was sleeping.

"Have you hurt yourself?" Eulogio asked, sitting up in bed.

"No ... no ... I fell asleep without noticing, and I fell over ..."

"I think I'm going to be sick ... the boat never stops moving ..." Eulogio said, trying to contain his nausea.

"I'm not that well myself ... I've never been on a boat, and I didn't think it would move so much," Catalina admitted.

"The best thing is for you to close your eyes and try to sleep. I'll go and ask what's going on," Fernando said.

But when he went out on deck the wind knocked him over, and a sailor picked him up and shouted at him to go back to his cabin and stay indoors. Fernando tried to find the Portuguese, but another sailor told him that the captain was at the tiller and couldn't be disturbed, especially not when the ship was dealing with waves twenty feet high. He was going back to the cabin when he ran into the sailor who had shown them to their cabin earlier. He felt a little relieved to see him.

"My friends are feeling very seasick," he said.

"It's normal, but the only thing to do is eat something. Go to the canteen, which is at the end of the hallway, and ask them to give you something to take to your friends."

"I don't think they'll be able to eat anything ... They're pretty sick."

"But that's why you need to settle your stomach. Anyway, I can't hang around, we've got an emergency on our hands." He lowered his voice. "As well as the storm, they say there may be a German submarine around here."

"Might it attack us?" Fernando asked in alarm.

"Of course! Their main aim is to sink as many enemy ships as possible."

"But the captain will know what to do ..."

"Captain Pereira is one of the best ... but it's not easy to avoid torpedoes ... So, if you can pray, give it a shot, and pray that the submarine has something better to do than to send us down to Davy Jones' locker. And, seriously, go to the canteen."

Fernando walked along the narrow passageway, trying to keep his balance. The blows of the waves tossed the ship from side to side, and he fell a couple of times. He got to the canteen feeling very clumsy and it was hard for him to push the door open: it seemed much too heavy.

Two sailors were sitting in the canteen drinking coffee. He saw that there was a tray with a few slices of bread on it on the table. He said hello, and went over to the men.

"Sit down and have a cup of coffee. It'll do you good," the older of the two men said. He had a strong accent that Fernando couldn't identify.

"My friends aren't feeling very well," he explained again.

"Don't worry, they'll get over it," the sailor replied, ignoring the young passenger's worry.

Fernando was upset by this man's lack of consideration and looked him up and down slowly, surprised to see the wrinkles that lined his face, but also the scar that ran from his forehead to his chin. He thought he must be about sixty years old, and was surprised to see such an old man on a boat like this. Of course, the captain must be about the same age.

"You're traveling with a pregnant woman. Your wife?"

"They said there were three passengers," the other sailor said.

"Yes, there are three of us ... and ... she ... she's not my wife. She's ... a family member. She's pregnant and not feeling too good."

"How far along is she?" the older sailor asked. He seemed to have a degree of authority.

"Let's see. We're in December, so … seven months."

"She shouldn't be traveling. It's very risky," the man said severely.

"But the captain does what he wants and never talks to you, Doc," the younger sailor said.

"Are you a doctor?" Fernando asked hopefully.

The sailor laughed, looking scornfully at the man whom he himself had called "Doc."

"Just to be safe, make sure you don't get ill. If you break your left leg, he might put a cast on your right," he said, heavy-handedly.

Doc opened his arms in a gesture of resignation, smiling as he did so. He was used to this kind of humor.

"But are you a doctor?" Fernando insisted.

"It's a secret that's been revealed to no one. So I suppose you have to think that Doc is more or less a doctor," the sailor replied.

Fernando drank a cup of coffee and ate some bread he had dipped into it. He immediately felt his stomach settle.

"Your friends should eat something," Doc advised.

"I'll take them a bit of bread," Fernando agreed.

"They could use some tea as well," Doc said.

"And water, get them to drink water," the younger sailor rec-ommended. His name was João. He helped Fernando prepare a tray with bread, two cups, a teapot and a bottle of water.

"Let me help you," he offered. "You're not used to the way the ship rolls, and the tray will end up on the floor."

On the way to the cabin, the sailor explained that the war looked to be getting more complicated.

"I've heard some of the officers say that Japan has attacked the United States."

"That can't be true!" Fernando said.

"Yes, apparently they bombed one of their Pacific ports. The captain is worried."

Fernando didn't know what else to say. The war, which he had thought of as something distant, was now ever more present in their lives. He thought that the Spanish had had enough with their own war, and that if he was there now, in this boat, it was because of their own damn civil war.

Eulogio was in the bathroom fighting against his nausea. He cursed the day that he had gotten on board this ship. Catalina stifled her cries of pain by biting the sheet that covered her. The contractions were continuous, but the worst of it was that she was soaked in a liquid that flowed from between her legs. She didn't know if she had gone into labor or if she was losing the child.

When they came into the cabin the smell of blood and vomit surrounded them all, so the sailor tried to find a place where he could put the tray and then leave as soon as possible.

"What's going on?"

"I'm dying ... I think I'm bleeding ... It hurts so much. Please help me!" she begged.

As he sat down beside her to try to help her sit up, Fernando felt the wet sheets.

"You're bleeding!" he said in alarm.

"Yes ... it started all of a sudden, but I can't move ... I'm not strong enough ..." Catalina was trying to hold back her tears.

"Go and get Doc!" Fernando begged the sailor, who was looking curiously at the scene.

"I don't think he knows about midwifery," João replied.

"Please, go and look for him!" Fernando shouted, giving him a push.

Eulogio came out of the bathroom holding himself up against the wall. He couldn't stand up. The cabin was spinning around him.

"Help me," he begged his friend.

For a moment Fernando didn't know what to do. Eulogio needed help to get into bed, but he couldn't leave Catalina.

He decided to prioritize the most urgent case: Eulogio could be dealt with and then he could go back to Catalina. He helped her to sit up and made her drink a glass of water.

"I can't ... Please, don't make me drink anything," she said.

"It'll do you good. Don't worry, Doc's on the way."

"Who's Doc?"

"Well, I think he's the doctor, or something like that at least. He'll know what to do, you'll see."

"I'm dying," she said, lowering her voice.

"No, don't say that! Don't even think about it. It's just that … Well, maybe the baby's coming a little early, or else you're suffering from the movement of the ship. You can't imagine how much wind there is or what the rain's like. It's a miracle we're still afloat."

He didn't want to say that there was a German submarine lurking. It would just have made them more worried. He looked at Eulogio out of the corner of his eye, worried about his friend, although he knew that he was only seasick.

Fernando helped Catalina put a towel between her legs, but it was very soon covered in blood, and so he got another, and then Eulogio's sheet. There was no way to stop the hemorrhage, which flowed without ceasing. Suddenly Catalina gave a terrifying shriek. This was at the exact same moment that a couple of knocks on the door announced Doc's arrival.

He pulled back the sheet that barely covered Catalina's body, and an expression of concern appeared on his face.

"I can't do anything," he said, turning away.

Fernando jumped to his feet and grabbed him by the arm, holding him back with all the strength that he could muster.

"I don't know if you're a doctor or not, but if you know anything about medicine, then please help me, or else she'll die."

"I don't know anything about giving birth. I've never even seen a birth before. I don't know what to do. The girl is bleeding out, that's what I do know."

"Do something!" Fernando shouted, holding Doc's arm so tight that his face twisted in pain.

"I can't do something I don't know how to do."

There were a couple of hollow knocks at the door. Doc broke free of Fernando and opened it. Pereira came in unannounced, followed by the young sailor.

"They told me that the young woman was dying."

The sailor had told the captain what he had seen in the cabin. He knew that if something happened and he hadn't told the captain, then he wouldn't be hired back onto the ship ever again.

"I can't do anything," Doc said.

The captain looked at the situation for a couple of seconds

and didn't say anything, even as he watched Catalina bleed unstoppably.

"You'll have to do something. Improvise," he ordered.

"You know I can't!"

Pereira looked at him so furiously that Doc lowered his gaze in submission. Fernando didn't dare say a word.

The captain turned to the sailor.

"Go and find sheets, towels, and hot water. And someone has to come and clean up this pigsty, the smell is unbearable. And you, Doc, go to your medicine chest and bring scissors, a scalpel, iodine or whatever you think you'll need. I'll help you."

Doc left at once, relieved to be able to leave the cabin, and the young sailor went to carry out his orders.

"Take her nightdress off," the captain ordered Fernando.

"But ..."

"She's soaked in blood. We're going to clean her."

"She doesn't have another one," Fernando said worriedly.

"Well, give her one of your shirts, or whatever you have, and see if there's a bowl in the bathroom. Bring it here, even if it's filled with cold water."

They cleaned off the blood that covered part of Catalina's body and she came back to her senses, weeping bitterly. When Doc came back, along with the young sailor, the captain stood aside.

"You have to get the child out. Now. It may be dead."

There was terror in Doc's face, and he took a step backwards. But the captain pushed him until he stood in front of Catalina.

"We'll hold her while you try to get the child out."

"No, I swear I don't know how to!"

"You'll do it, Doc, or I'll throw you overboard. Damn it! I should be on deck trying to stop this boat from getting shot to hell. We've got a bloody storm and German submarines all around us, and I don't know which of the two is worse. So don't make me waste my time."

"You shouldn't have taken these three onboard!" Doc said, panicked.

"Of course I shouldn't! You think I don't know that? But they're here, so we have to stop this problem from getting even worse."

At that moment, Eulogio threw up again, but no one paid him any attention. Fernando held Catalina by her arms while the captain tried to clean the blood that flowed from between her legs. The bed was as soaked as the shirt, which barely covered her body.

Doc came resignedly over to her and opened her legs without looking very closely. His hands were trembling and he looked up at the captain as though he were hoping that he would change his mind and order him out of the cabin. But all he did was recoil at the sight of the captain's stern face.

Catalina was still screaming. She felt as though Doc's hand was stirring up her very guts. And each scream ran into the next, so that eventually the captain shouted in turn:

"Shut the hell up!"

Fernando turned to the captain, furious:

"Don't shout at her! She's suffering!"

Doc was getting ever more scared. His hands were inside Catalina's body. Sweat ran down his face. He stayed like this for a good while, as the silence in the cabin grew ever more ominous. The young woman kept crying out, but in a muffled voice.

Time passed. For Catalina, these minutes were a nightmare, and seemed interminable.

Doc finally pulled out a tiny body covered in blood. It slipped from his hands and lay between the young woman's legs. She carried on screaming while Fernando tried to calm her.

"I don't know if it's dead," Doc whispered to the captain, as he rummaged inside Catalina again to try to find the placenta.

The infant was still connected to its mother by an umbilical cord, and as Doc pulled out the placenta, Pereira let go of Catalina's legs and went towards the bloody bundle on the bed. He took a knife out of his jacket pocket and cut the cord, separating the infant from its mother; then he took it in one of his enormous hands and with the other gave it a couple of slaps. But the lump of bloody flesh gave no signs of life. Doc didn't move, and looked at the captain, who tried again and again.

Fernando gave a sudden start. Catalina had stopped screaming.

"She's dead!" he cried in fright.

"She's just fainted," Doc replied.

336

Eulogio managed to get back on his feet, and although he was stumbling, he came over to Fernando. He thought he would die, he felt so sick, but he knew that his friend needed him.

The captain gave the newborn infant another slap on its buttocks, and to everyone's surprise, it gave a weak little whimper. It was such a feeble sound that at first they thought that they'd heard wrong, and so he slapped it again, and this time they heard it mewl quite clearly.

"I think it's a girl," the captain said, looking at the tiny body he held in his hand.

"Yes, it looks like it," Doc agreed.

The girl whined again, and seemed to wriggle in the captain's hand.

"We'll have to clean her," Pereira said.

Doc took the child apprehensively. He seemed not to know what to do, and Fernando brought a towel over.

"Yes, the most important thing is to clean it well," Doc said.

The two of them tried to clean the blood from the tiny body. Doc focused on the nose and eyes. The girl seemed to have difficulty breathing.

"I don't think she'll survive," Doc said.

"She'll survive," Pereira maintained.

"How do you know?" Eulogio asked very quietly as he tried to stay on his feet.

"She'll survive, although what happens to the girl and to all of you isn't my problem. Try not to get in the way until we reach Alexandria."

His rough words, though, were contradicted by his imperceptible gesture of tenderness: he came over to the girl, who was still in Fernando's arms while Doc cleaned her, touching her forehead with a finger before leaving the cabin without saying another word.

They put the baby on the bed and Fernando looked through Catalina's bag until he found a shawl and a diaper. The tiny child seemed to have little strength even to breathe.

"What can we do?" he asked Doc.

"Not much. In any case, I'm not the person to tell you. I suppose the best thing is to give her to her mother. They say that a mother's warmth is important for newborn children."

The infant was whimpering without pause. Fernando looked at her in fear; he didn't know how to put on her diaper, and so he just wrapped her in the shawl.

"We could at least try to wake Catalina up," he said to Doc.

"She's better off unconscious. It was a difficult birth. She's lost a lot of blood. She's in bad shape," he diagnosed expressionlessly.

"Are you going to let her die?" Fernando raised his voice and was about to put the baby down so he could force Doc to look at Catalina.

Doc gave a start. The shine in the young man's eyes was the sign of a storm that he didn't know he'd be able to deal with. He went over to Catalina, asking Eulogio to fill the bowl with fresh water and bring some towels. It was all Eulogio could do to fulfill that request. The sailor had left a few towels on the chair, so he took one and gave it to Doc, then went into the bathroom for more water.

Doc did nothing except wipe away the blood that covered half of Catalina's body. Then he asked Eulogio to look for sheets and another towel.

Working together, the two of them managed to get rid of the dirty sheets and fit fresh ones to the bed. Then they covered Catalina and Doc slapped her gently, trying to rouse her from her faint. He soaked a piece of cotton wadding in a liquid that he had with him in a little flask and passed it under Catalina's nose. It seemed to make her rise up from the shadows in which she had sought refuge. Meanwhile, Fernando rocked the child in his arms, shocked at how fragile she seemed, and that every now and then she stopped whimpering and he thought that she had given up the ghost.

"Put the child with her mother," Doc ordered Fernando.

Catalina gave a start when she felt the little body by her side. Then she smiled and moved her lips a little as she said:

"My son, here you are." Then she closed her eyes again.

"It's a daughter, a little girl," Fernando whispered into her ear.

Catalina seemed not to have heard him. Then she opened her eyes and looked around, startled.

"A daughter? No, it can't be … It's a boy, I was going to have a boy …"

"Yes, you thought that was the case, but it's a girl," Fernando said.

"She's very small and weak. She's not in good shape," Eulogio said, holding back another attack of nausea.

"The child needs to eat," Doc said.

But neither Catalina nor Eulogio nor Fernando seemed to know what to do.

"What shall we give her?" Fernando asked.

"Well, her mother can feed her." Doc started to walk towards the door. He felt disgusted by the smell of blood and vomit, and the only thing he wanted to do was to leave that cabin at once.

"But she's very weak," Fernando protested.

"That's not my problem," he said, feeling relieved to be getting out of there.

Fernando helped Eulogio back into his bunk. In spite of his efforts, given the state he was in, there was no way he could be of any use. As for Catalina, she seemed to have fainted again and for a moment he thought she had died, as he didn't see any signs of her breathing. The child whimpered again and shivered with cold.

Fernando put the little child into the bed and covered her up. He hoped that Catalina's body would give off enough warmth to help the little creature live. But he was frightened to see that her body was cold and getting paler all the time.

"Eulogio, I'm going to get help. I'm afraid that the two of them are dying. At least make sure that the child doesn't fall out of the bed."

"You can count on me," Eulogio managed to say.

Fernando left the cabin, prepared to go all the way to the bridge. The captain had to do something. He could at least make sure that Doc didn't ignore Catalina and her daughter.

The wind was still knocking the *Esperanza del Mar* around, pushing it ceaselessly back and forth. The deck was awash with water and the rain fell without slackening.

The sailors bustled here and there, carrying out the officers' orders. No one seemed the least bit interested in him.

He got to the bridge and argued with a sailor who was guarding the door. It wasn't until the captain realized that he was standing there that he was beckoned in.

"How are they?" Pereira asked.

"Catalina has passed out again, and the girl … she's breathing very badly …"

"She's premature and doesn't look all that healthy. The most likely thing in such cases is for the child to die," the captain admitted.

"We have to do something," Fernando begged.

"Look, don't ask me for more help. I shouldn't have let a pregnant woman on board my ship. Now go away, this damn German submarine has decided to sink the lot of us. So maybe none of us will survive. And we've just found out that the United States has declared war on Japan, which means they're all in with this whole war."

"Why?" Fernando asked.

"Don't you know that the Japanese and the Germans are allies? The war's going to burst its banks …" the captain said, as he looked out over the sea with his binoculars.

"We are eternally in your debt, and that's why I'm asking you to do one more thing for us: please order Doc to come and help us." Fernando was at that moment more worried about Catalina than about the Americans entering the war.

"Doc? Help you? He's done enough for one day."

"If he doesn't help they will die," Fernando said in anguish.

"Don't blame me for something that hasn't happened yet! I don't know who let that girl go on a journey, but whoever did is as crazy as she is. And I'm crazy as well, for giving in to her demand to take her to Alexandria."

"You're experienced, at least … you helped Doc during the birth."

"I have a daughter and two granddaughters," the captain murmured.

"Right, then tell me what we should do now … I'm desperate," Fernando admitted.

The captain cursed, and ordered the ship to make a turn. Then he told a sailor to go and find Doc, wherever he was.

"Tell him to go to the passengers' cabin. And you, don't bother me any more!"

"Thank you."

Fernando left the bridge and went back to his friends. Catalina seemed to be coming back to her senses. They gave her a glass of water. The child kept on making little crying noises.

"She has to eat something," Eulogio murmured.

"What?" Fernando asked.

"Well, Catalina could give it … you know, women have milk when they give birth …"

"You're right."

Catalina was conscious again and seemed to be listening to them. Fernando helped her put the child to her breast. But the little creature didn't seem to find anything there.

Fernando left the cabin and found Doc, who was accompanied by João.

"The captain has ordered us to take the mother and the child to the infirmary," Doc said grumpily.

"The child … needs to eat, and her mother … can't provide any food …" Fernando explained.

"Let her try again," Doc ordered.

"It's just …" Catalina said, "I think I don't have any milk."

"Sometimes it takes a day or so to come in … the child should carry on trying," Doc recommended.

"And if it doesn't …?" Catalina said, worriedly.

Doc was silent as he tried to think of an answer. He didn't know what to do in such circumstances.

"We'll give her sugar water," he said uncertainly, "but not very much and very carefully."

He sent João to fetch some, and soon he was back with a glass of water to which he had added several spoonfuls of sugar.

Fernando sat next to Catalina, who held the baby while he used a spoon to try to get the child to swallow a couple of drops of the liquid.

"My little girl … Give her to me, Fernando … I'll feed her," Catalina said.

"She's cold," João said, who spoke as though he was an expert in such matters.

It was only to be expected. All she had on was a badly fastened diaper and a shawl. Fernando went back to the wardrobe and looked around until he found a shirt and a jumper, and a little blue-edged baby's smock. Catalina had always wanted a boy. All the clothes they had made were for a boy, which suddenly seemed to him to be absurd.

They dressed the girl quickly, frightened by how much she was shivering.

Doc watched without saying anything until the child coughed and started to spit out the sugar water.

"If you've finished, we should take them to the infirmary," he said, looking at Catalina with no sympathy at all.

Fernando and Doc lifted her up, wrapping her in the sheet. She barely had the strength to keep her eyes open.

"Hold onto my neck," Fernando said.

Catalina couldn't even raise her arms, and so Doc had to lift her into Fernando's hold. João picked up the child.

When they went out into the hallway, they found themselves the object of the sailors' stares.

The infirmary wasn't very large. They put Catalina on a cot and laid the child next to her. Doc set up a screen so they would have a little privacy.

"This is where men come when something happens to them," he said, referring to the need to have a screen.

Fernando smiled. Catarina was much better here: at least the infirmary wasn't full of vomit and blood. Everything was clean.

"I can't look after her all day," Doc warned.

"I'll look after her," Fernando assured him.

"If you need me, I can lend a hand, if the captain allows me to," João offered.

Fernando's smile turned into a worried grimace when he looked at Catalina and saw that she was as pale as the dead.

"She's lost a lot of blood, but I can't do anything for her. She's in danger and so is the baby, the baby especially if she can't be made to eat," Doc warned them.

"But there must be something we can do," Fernando said desperately.

"I promise you, I don't have the knowledge or the training to save her."

Even so, he took her pulse and asked João to bring some soup from the kitchen. Fernando didn't dare ask anything more: he clung to the faith that the ignorance which the man claimed was not as absolute as he wanted it to appear.

The girl's little body was wracked by shivers; now, as if that were not enough, she started to vomit the sugar water she had just been given.

Fernando thought about his mother. She would have known what to do, and for a few seconds he regretted having left Spain. He felt alone, helpless, and he could not hide the fear that consumed his soul when he saw Catalina and her daughter both closer to death than to life.

The captain came in at that moment and stood in front of the cot where mother and daughter lay together.

"She looks bad," he said.

"Their lives are in the hands of God," João said, and then immediately regretted having spoken when he saw the captain's face.

"Shut up. And get back to work," Pereira grunted.

"Captain, this sailor ... Maybe you could let him help me ... at least until my friend Eulogio gets better. I don't know what to do, and João is more on top of things ..." Fernando asked.

The captain muttered something that they couldn't make out. Then he went over to Catalina and took her hand. He looked at the little girl, who wouldn't stop shivering.

"She's freezing cold. She shouldn't have been born yet, and she's traumatized. Put a blanket on her, and put her next to her mother's body. She needs her warmth. What can you do for them?" he asked Doc.

"Nothing."

The blunt response seemed to stagger the captain, who let out a curse.

"Don't tell me you can't do anything!" he shouted.

"I don't know what to do! I've never been present at a birth, I've never dealt with a newborn child. I can fix broken legs, deal with fevers and pain ... But don't ask me to do things I don't know how to do."

"Doc, you have to save their lives," the captain ordered.

Pereira left the infirmary without saying anything else. He was expected on the bridge. The sea was even wilder, and the rain meant that visibility was down to almost nothing. This crossing was turning into a nightmare.

João followed the captain, although he was back very soon with a mug of soup, saying that the captain had given him permission to help Fernando as much as he could.

"We have to keep them warm: we could put more blankets on them and feed the mother some soup," the sailor said.

Doc waved Fernando over to one side of the room, so that he could speak to him without João or Catalina hearing.

"They are both in danger. It might be that neither the mother nor the child survives," he said.

"They have to survive," Fernando said, although he was worried by the thought that Doc might not be exaggerating.

"They are both very weak. It's not likely that a baby born at seven months survives under any conditions, let alone these ones."

"But there must be something we can do," Fernando insisted.

"The captain threatened to throw me overboard if they die ... and he's capable of fulfilling his threats," Doc said.

Meanwhile, Captain Pereira was giving constant orders to the officers of the *Esperanza del Mar*. His face showed just how tense the situation was. Doc came onto the bridge and tried not to bother him. He asked himself why Pereira was so upset about a woman and a child he had only just met. Maybe he was getting old and sentimental. But he abandoned that idea. The Portuguese wasn't easily swayed. He had seen him ride through storms where it seemed at any moment that the *Esperanza del Mar* would sink down to the bottom of the sea, and he had seen him engaged in life-or-death struggles with men who were stronger than he was, and he had seen him impose discipline on a crowd of unruly sailors with a single glance.

In spite of the fact that Pereira was of an age where captains normally decide to return to dry land, he wasn't planning anything of the kind. He said that he would die on his boat and that his tomb would be the sea. And so Doc still asked himself why Pereira was so obsessed with this young woman and her child.

"Captain, it looks like the submarine's moving away," the radio operator said.

"They'll be back," Pereira declared.

When he saw Doc, he waved him over.

"How are they?" he asked.

"Bad. I've told you already: they're likely to die."

"And I've told you that if they do then I'll throw you overboard."

"Well, you'll have to do that, then, because they are going to die! There's not the right equipment in the infirmary to deal with a woman who's just given birth to a premature child, but even if there were, then they'd still die."

"You're wrong: they'll live because they want to live."

Doc shrugged his shoulders. He knew that when the Portuguese got an idea into his head, it was difficult to reason with him. He still remembered the day they had met, thirty years before. Some men were about to kill him in a drunken brawl in Hong Kong. Pereira came past and stopped to observe them. When he saw three Chinese sailors ganging up on Doc as he fell to the ground, he came over and kicked and punched until the three men retreated. He fought with them and gave Doc time to get back to his feet. They were lucky, because two sailors from the *Esperanza del Mar* joined the fight and the attackers realized they were outnumbered.

Pereira didn't ask Doc why they were fighting, but even so, he felt obliged to tell him. Gambling. Damn it. He had a debt he couldn't pay, and they wanted to settle it with his life. They said goodbye without thinking that they would see each other again. But two days later they met at the port. A sailor from the *Esperanza del Mar* had fainted and was laid out on the dock. Doc came over and treated him. He said they shouldn't move him until they found out what was wrong with him, and then he examined him carefully and found a wound on his forehead, the result of a fall. The man was unconscious, and Doc recommended that they take him to his ship to clean the wound. He went with them. Pereira told him to get on board and help with the patient, if he knew how to. He did so. Later, when he was about to disembark, Pereira asked him if he was a doctor or a nurse. He didn't answer. He never answered that question. Every man has a secret. The Portuguese looked him up and down and didn't insist. All he said was that the ship's doctor of the *Esperanza del*

Mar had needed to disembark in Mogadishu because he had caught malaria. They needed someone who could look after the men aboard ship, and he asked Doc if he could. Doc shrugged without promising anything, and from that day forward, the *Esperanza del Mar* had been his home.

"You should have a coffee, you're exhausted," he said to the captain to change the subject.

Pereira did nothing apart from ordering him to return to the infirmary.

"I can't be there all the time. I've done all I can for them," Doc said.

"I'm not asking you, Doc, I'm ordering you."

Catalina had her child in her arms, and although she had barely enough strength to hold her, she had put her once again to her breast.

"I don't know if I'll have enough milk for her." Catalina whispered, so weak she felt.

"There's powdered milk onboard … We can give her milk," Fernando said.

"Newborn babies can't have the same milk that we can," João said, to Fernando's surprise.

"You know a lot about children," he said.

"Of course, I've got eight brothers. I've seen how my mother deals with the little ones. She always wanted a girl, but she had to settle for nine boys. I used to help her with the little ones."

The night came upon them without them noticing. Fernando started to feel a little calmer to see that Catalina, although she was weak and pale, had taken charge of her daughter, and was hugging her close to keep her warm. João had brought another mug of soup and a piece of smoked meat which, although Catalina initially refused it, he forced her to eat.

"If you don't eat you won't have milk," João said.

Catalina, in the face of this threat, made an effort to keep the meat down.

Fernando realized that he hadn't eaten since the previous day. He hadn't even had time to feel hungry, and he had completely forgotten about Eulogio.

"João, could you bring me something? A bit of bread would be enough."

The sailor winked at him, and when he came back it was with something more than a piece of bread. Another mug of soup and a piece of cheese, which settled Fernando's stomach.

"The weather will calm down tomorrow, that's what I heard," the young sailor said.

"I hope God hears you."

Then he asked João to stay with Catalina for a moment while he went to the cabin to see how Eulogio was doing.

He was lying in the bed with his eyes closed.

"Are you asleep?" he asked in a low voice.

"I wish I could sleep. I'd throw myself overboard if I could. I never thought I could feel like this. I think I'll stay in Alexandria forever. I can't imagine what it must be like to sail to America," Eulogio said, trying to hold back his nausea.

"You'll get over it," Fernando said, just to say something.

"I felt like I was dying, my friend; if you hadn't needed to help Catalina, I think I'd have asked you to help me die."

"Don't be silly. Do you want me to bring you anything? Maybe if you ate something you'd feel a bit better."

"Even thinking about food makes me want to throw up."

"But Doc says that if you're seasick then you need to eat something."

"Well, I won't."

"At least drink some water … Look, here's the sugar water that João brought for the baby."

In the face of his friend's insistence, Eulogio took a few sips of water.

"I'll be with Catalina all night," Fernando said.

"Don't worry about me. The poor girl, I thought she'd die. And the baby … poor thing … I wonder what will become of her."

"They've got me."

"Well, but you're not the father of the baby, and you know that Catalina won't stop until she finds Marvin. And you still have to decide what you're going to do with your life. I keep on wondering if it wasn't stupid of us to set off for Alexandria."

"Now's not the moment to be questioning things. There's no way back now. We'll see what happens when we reach Alexandria."

"Yes, but you have to admit that it was stupid of us to set off for a place where we've got no future."

"We'll see. Look, let's take each day as it comes. And now the important thing is that Catalina and the baby stay alive, and that you get better as soon as you can."

"Yes, but …"

"Come on; Eulogio, don't be down about this. What's done is done."

"I'm thinking about my mother … I think that … Maybe I wasn't fair to her …"

"No, you weren't. But that can be fixed. As soon as we get to Alexandria, write to her and tell her. That'll make her feel better, and you as well."

"We'll see," Eulogio said.

"I'm going back to see Catalina now. Do you need anything?"

"I need to get off this boat," Eulogio joked.

"Try and get some rest. They say the weather will be better tomorrow."

"Let's pray they're right."

"Well, I don't know if prayers will help, so let's just trust in Captain Pereira," Fernando replied.

João was sitting by Catalina. He was still alert, even now that both mother and daughter seemed to have sunk into a deep sleep. He made a sign to Fernando not to speak in case he woke them up.

Fernando took over from him in the infirmary, and sat down next to the bed for the rest of the night. He must have fallen asleep at some point because Catalina's feeble voice woke him. She asked for a glass of water and he brought it to her solicitously, then she fell back asleep, hugging her daughter's little body close.

It was the baby's cries that woke him later. Catalina put the child to her breast, and she calmed down. And so the night passed.

Dawn came, and the rain declared a truce. The sky was gray, but at least there was no rain falling, which was a relief for everyone. As for the wind and the waves, they still bore down with force on the boat, but less strongly than the night before. Pereira's prediction was coming true. The captain came down to the infirmary, followed by João.

Fernando raised himself and let them stand by Catalina's bed. Captain Pereira looked at the pair of them for quite some time, and his face relaxed.

"They'll be all right, I know it," he muttered to himself.

Then he stood in front of Fernando and asked him to follow him, leaving Catalina and the baby in João's care.

"Look, I need to record the birth of the child. When we get to Alexandria, they'll need a document which records the birth and its circumstances, and so I'll need the full names of the father and the mother, as well as the name of the baby."

Fernando hesitated. He didn't know what to say about the baby's father. He didn't know what Catalina would say. And that's what he said to the captain. Pereira frowned, but agreed to wait until Catalina woke up.

"I've already made a note in my log about what happened, so we'll have to obey the normal rules, especially so that the young woman can have proof that the child is hers."

"I'll talk to her as soon as she wakes up … I … Well, I want to thank you. We owe you so much. I don't know what would have become of us without your help …"

The captain cut him short with a brusque gesture, and spoke angrily:

"I should never have let you come aboard. I want to get rid of you as soon as possible." And he left.

Fernando was undaunted by the Portuguese's words. He guessed that deep down, the salty old sea dog was a good man.

When he later explained to Catalina what Pereira needed, she didn't seem concerned, and said in her thin little voice:

"Let him produce a document that says she's my daughter. We can't do anything else until we find Marvin. Everything will get sorted out in Alexandria, but until then she should be registered as only my daughter. As for her name … You know, it's odd: I thought she would be a boy and that I'd call him Marvin after his father, but now … I don't know, maybe I could name her after my grandmother, or Marvin's mother, who's called Rose, isn't she? You could ask Eulogio. What do you think?"

"Well, you're the one who has to give her a name."

"You remember my grandmother Adela? My mother's mother?"

"Yes. She lived with you during the war," Fernando remembered.

"Adela's a nice name. She loved me so much. I miss her a great deal, and the house was so empty when she died. Of course, I love my grandmother Agustina, my father's mother, very much as well. Both of those are good names."

"Which one do you like more?"

"I don't know … I can't decide. I'm so tired …"

"I think you look much better now. Yesterday … I thought something was going to happen to you."

"I'm worried for my daughter, she's so little and so weak."

"Doc has said that you need to keep her warm. Don't let her go. Your skin is the best thing for her."

"She's not eating much …."

"She seemed hungry yesterday," Fernando said.

"Well, today she's barely … Look, she opens her eyes and closes them again at once."

The door to the infirmary opened and Doc came in, followed by Eulogio. Catalina smiled to see him.

"I'm so glad to see you up and about! Poor boy! You had a rough time of it yesterday," she said, grateful that he had come to see her.

"You had it worse. How are you? How's the baby?"

"I'm better and the baby's very well. She doesn't even cry, she only grizzles a little."

Eulogio came over and looked at the child in surprise.

"Is she sleeping?"

"Yes, she sleeps nearly all the time. She doesn't eat much and she's very cold."

"She'll be all right, you'll see. One day she'll be proud of having been born in a storm in the middle of the Atlantic Ocean."

They spoke about unimportant things for a long time while Doc, on the other side of the screen, attended to a sailor who had fallen over and broken his arm. Another sailor waited impatiently to get some kind of medicine that would help him with a persistent cold, and two more turned up with bruises and scrapes that they had gotten from slipping on the deck in the middle of the storm.

They heard Doc talking bluntly to these men. He didn't seem to care about their complaints. He didn't give them much time, either.

It was late in the morning. When Captain Pereira came back, he found Eulogio and Fernando with Catalina, who had dozed off again. She was very weak and still bleeding a little. And although she didn't complain, she felt her insides burning.

The Portuguese looked at her out of the corner of his eye and then spoke to Eulogio.

"So, you're better, then?"

"Not completely, but I'm much better than yesterday. João came by this morning to ask me if I needed anything, and although I said no, he brought me a cup of tea and a piece of bread which helped settle my stomach."

Pereira didn't respond, and looked at Catalina again. He couldn't help asking himself what it was about this girl that moved him so much. Perhaps her innocence. Yes, that must be it. He had not met innocence very often over the course of his life. Catalina's innocence must be the same that he had sensed in his wife when he first met her, forty years earlier. The same innocence that his daughter had inherited, and the same innocence that flourished in his granddaughters' eyes.

He coughed as he sensed Catalina looking back at him. She had opened her eyes and was smiling.

"Well, miss, I need to write a document that will inform the authorities of the birth of this child, so that it matches the captain's log. I need your full name, the name of the father, and the name that the child will be baptized under."

Catalina grew serious and cleared her throat as she looked the captain straight in the eye.

"My name is Catalina Vilamar Fernández. My daughter is Adela Vilamar. I can't tell you the father's name, because he doesn't even know that he has a daughter. I am going to meet him in Alexandria, and that will be the moment when he acknowledges us and looks after the child. Until then, the girl will have my name."

"And what if you don't find him? What will you do? I suggest you give your daughter some name, at least, and I'll put it on the document so that your daughter has a father even if it's a made-up one. It would be better for you."

"I'm not ashamed of my daughter. And although I haven't done things quite properly ... and ask myself how it's possible that ... well, I don't regret it. And so I'm not going to live as though I were ashamed. Adela will be Adela Vilamar until we find her father."

The captain accepted this in silence. He was surprised by how stubborn the girl was, and put it down to her lack of life experience. However much he felt responsible for her, almost against his will, he didn't want to get more involved in the issue than he had up to this point.

"All right, I'll write up the document. Two witnesses need to sign it, as well as Doc. Maybe your friends should sign."

"Yes, I want Fernando and Eulogio to be the witnesses."

That afternoon, the sea started to calm down, although the wind still stirred up the waves.

The next few days, Eulogio and Fernando started to have a bit more time to breathe the clear sea air up on deck while João looked after Catalina. The captain had relieved him of his duties and sent him to help Doc in the infirmary. The two friends were worried by Catalina's state. They had seen her come very close to death, and she was still so weak that she could barely move. As for little Adela, they didn't think she'd survive, because she scarcely moved or even cried. Catalina kept her close to her breast, both of them covered by four blankets that helped them to keep warm. The baby started to suckle a little better as well.

The days went by peacefully. The German submarine seemed to have stopped trying to send them to the bottom of the sea.

The captain kept coming to see Catalina and the baby, much to the disgust of Doc, who had found out that Pereira wasn't as hard as he appeared to be.

3

Madrid

Don Antonio was pacing impatiently around the warehouse. He had fought with his wife that morning because she was spending more than she should on the preparations for Antoñito's wedding. As far as her son was concerned, Mari thought that no expense should be spared. She was insistent that her husband acquire an apartment on Calle Arenal from a family that was in financial trouble, though this was nothing that Don Antonio didn't do as a matter of course. She was ordering all the furniture that Antoñito wanted, and had ordered herself some brocade to make a dress for the wedding. She was going to be the maid of honor and therefore had to shine. And she had bought some velvet for her two daughters, Paquita and Mariví, in dark blue and bottle green.

Not content with that, she had bought solid gold rings for Catalina and Antoñito as well as a necklace of real pearls for the official engagement announcement. The Vilamars were going to find out just what it meant to marry into the Sánchez family.

That morning, she had insisted that her husband buy a tailcoat. He had refused, that's where the argument had started and, as Don Antonio knew all too well, it wouldn't end until she got what she wanted. As if that weren't enough, Don Ernesto had called first thing in the morning to say that he needed to talk to him urgently. And, of course, this all had to happen on the day when a large consignment of goods for Christmas – when they hiked all the prices – was due to arrive.

Don Ernesto arrived at eleven on the dot. His serious face and exhausted appearance alerted the shopkeeper.

"What's so urgent that we need to talk about it?" he asked rudely, as a greeting.

"Can we talk in private?" Don Ernesto asked, looking at the young men working in the warehouse.

"Well … it must really be important … Come on, there's not much room in the warehouse, but there's a room at the back with a table and a couple of chairs. We can sit there."

Once they were sitting and facing one another, Don Ernesto looked down at the table, trying to find the words that he had spent so much time rehearsing in his head.

"I don't have much time at the moment, so spit it out. If it's money, don't bother asking for it, because I'm sick of looking after the whole family. And the marriage is costing me an arm and a leg. When's Catalina going to be back, by the way? My wife says it's not normal for someone to spend such a long time away from home."

"That's what I came to talk to you about," Don Ernesto said in an apprehensive voice.

Don Antonio looked at him suspiciously. It suddenly occurred to him that he was going to hear some bad news, a thought that annoyed him even more.

"Come on, then."

"The wedding's cancelled. Catalina doesn't want to get married. She says she doesn't love Antoñito, and that if there's no love, then she's not going to get married."

"What? No, no, no, no, no. There'll be a wedding, of course there'll be a wedding, even if you have to drag your daughter to the altar. What a bitch!"

"How dare you insult my daughter?" Don Ernesto got to his feet indignantly.

"I'll insult her, and I'll insult you and I'll insult the whole fucking family! You're a bunch of scavengers who wouldn't even have a place to call your own if it weren't for me! You know how much you owe me? Yes, of course you do. And so your daughter's going to walk to the altar without complaining, otherwise I'll call in the whole of your debt on the spot, and if you can't pay then you'll go to prison."

Don Ernesto was still standing up, and Don Antonio saw that his jaw was trembling.

"There won't be a wedding. Catalina has decided and that's that. I'm sorry about causing you such inconvenience, but I think your son won't really care either way, he's never shown the slightest sign of love for Catalina. It's best for the both of them."

Don Antonio hit the table with such force that all the papers on it flew into the air, and Don Ernesto started to worry that things would get even worse. The shopkeeper stood up, took him by the lapels of his jacket and started to shake him.

"Scavenger! Bastard! Fucker! Tell your daughter that either she gets married or else I won't stop at putting you in prison, but I'll finish her as well! That bitch won't marry anyone if it's not Antoñito! Or my name's not Antonio Sánchez!"

"I'm not going to accept your insults. You are offending me and my daughter. Behave like a gentleman, please."

"A gentleman? If your daughter isn't here tomorrow, then you'll face the consequences. I'll call in all your debts. You know what that means. You'll have to leave your house, and your brother will have to leave his farm. You'll lose your land … I'll put you in prison. I swear that if there's no wedding than you and your brother will go to prison. And your wife and your sister-in-law will starve in the streets. Or my name's not Antonio Sánchez!"

The indignation he felt at these insults was making its impression on Don Ernesto, who felt sweat forming on his brow despite the chill present in the warehouse.

"I'm not going to stoop to your level. Think again, and you'll see that you can't force my daughter to get married if she doesn't love Antoñito. I guess you want the best for your son, and won't want him to marry someone who doesn't love him."

"If she doesn't love him she'll put up with it! You and your family have cost me too much money to come to me with such nonsense!"

"Money's not everything in this world, Don Antonio. Do what you think is right. I just came to tell you that the wedding is off. Good day."

Making an effort to keep his dignity, Don Ernesto walked steadily to the warehouse door, trying to ignore the shopkeeper's insults.

When he reached the street he let out a sigh, and in spite of the rain, which meant he could barely see his hand in front of his face, he felt relieved to be back in the fresh air. He would be soaked when he got home, but it didn't matter. He needed to think. He knew that Don Antonio's threats were more than just hot air. He was most worried that they'd take his brother's farm. He would ask Don Bernardo to intervene. He knew that the priest would not allow the shopkeeper to go through with his threats. As for Asunción, he knew that she'd start to pray straight away: that was how she dealt with everything.

Don Antonio went home at noon. He had to tell his wife and his children about Don Antonio's visit and the fact that the wedding was off.

Mari was testing the noodles in the chicken soup.

"You're just in time," she said grumpily.

He sat down at the table next to Antoñito and his daughters and waited for his wife to serve the soup.

"It's too hot," the youngest complained.

"Deal with it. Blow on it and eat it," her mother replied.

"I need to tell you something," he said, and looked at his wife, afraid of what her reaction might be.

"Right? What is it?" she asked with only mild curiosity.

"Catalina Vilamar doesn't want to get married. Don Ernesto came to tell me." He looked at Antoñito to see what his reaction would be.

"I don't care," Antoñito said indifferently.

"You don't care!" his mother shouted. "How dare that starving little hussy reject you! No, that's not going to happen! Have you ever seen such a bitch!"

"I don't like Catalina, she's stupid and wet. If I married her I'd have to hit her every day. I'd rather not," Antoñito said.

"You're an idiot! A cretin!" his mother shouted.

"Shut up!" Don Antonio shouted.

"What are we going to do with the velvet for the wedding dresses?" Mariví asked.

Her mother gave her a loud slap, which served to release some of the rage she was feeling.

Mariví shrieked as the blow landed.

"Don't be a brute! Don't hit the girl!" Don Antonio shouted.

"What we have to do is say that I don't want to marry her because she's a bit too easy, and that she flirts with everyone and that I don't want to marry just anyone. And anyway, I want you to know that the girl I really like is Lolita." Antoñito said all this at a rush without caring what his parents thought.

"Who is Lolita?" his father asked.

"Haven't you seen the tailor's shop they've just opened on the Gran Vía? It's where they make the uniforms for the Generalísimo," Antoñito explained. "Lolita's the daughter of the owner."

"And how do you know her?" his mother asked, astounded at the sudden appearance of this Lolita.

"Pepe Ramírez introduced us. She's his cousin."

"Your friend from school?" Paquita asked.

"Yes, Pepe, my friend Pepe. He took me to see his uncle's shop just in case Dad or I might need a tailored suit one day. Lolita works there as a cashier. She's a decent, pretty girl, and I've seen her a few times, always with a chaperone. Her parents are very strict."

"A tailor's daughter!" Mari was about to burst into tears.

"The daughter of the owner of a tailor's shop, which is something very different," Antoñito said grumpily.

"But she's a nobody," his mother insisted.

"She is all she has to be, a girl from a good family. Her father is a patriot who thinks that Franco is the best thing that could have happened to us. He was in the war. Lolita is prudent, obedient and submissive, unlike Catalina. I want to marry her, and I hope you won't make too much trouble. I suggest we tell everyone that it was me who didn't want to marry Catalina." Antoñito looked at his father and waited for his response.

Don Antonio was thinking about what his son had said. It wasn't the same to marry a tailor as a Vilamar, but if the tailor's shop was the one he thought it was – a very new one that had opened in the center – then it was clear that Lolita's father wasn't a good-for-nothing. And Pepe Ramírez came from a wealthy family: they had three dairies in Madrid alone.

"You'll marry Catalina! With all that we've done for the

Vilamars, they've got no choice other than to marry their daughter to you, or else we'll have them all in prison. Antonio, tell your son," Mari said.

But the shopkeeper kept on thinking about the situation. Of course he'd ruin the Vilamars and he would enjoy seeing Don Ernesto in prison for reneging on his debts, but at least if they said that it was Antoñito who broke off the engagement to marry this Lolita, then there wouldn't be any humiliation involved. It wasn't what he'd imagined for his son, but given the circumstances, it might be a solution.

"Ernesto Vilamar will pay for this. And as for this Lolita ... we'll see ... I'll go to the tailor's to meet her father. But for now, let's not talk about weddings."

4

Alexandria

The Egyptian coast sketched itself into view as dawn began to break.

Captain Pereira was on the bridge with a cup of coffee in his hand. The presence of seagulls, skimming across the waves in search of scraps, showed how close they were to land.

It wasn't very far to Alexandria. It had been a difficult crossing, not just due to the waves and the storms, but because of the submarine that had tracked them for several hours: they knew all too well that the Germans had no scruples about attacking merchant ships.

The sailors were waiting for the captain's orders. They were keen to reach port: there were few places in the whole Mediterranean that offered as many pleasures and delights as Alexandria.

It was early, but Catalina was trying to feed Adela. Doc had told her that she did not have enough milk, that she should feed the child with powdered milk. She used a spoon to pour the liquid into her daughter's tiny mouth. She felt a little better, in spite of the rough crossing that had made her feel nauseous the whole time, but she had no illusions when it came to her daughter, who barely had the strength to struggle for life.

Catalina prayed day and night to the Lord, asking Him not to punish this little creature, who had done nothing wrong. Whether it was because of her prayers, or whether it was because Adela's hour had not yet come, the little girl kept on living. But Catalina had not recovered from the premature birth either. She had lost a lot of blood, and it was hard for her to stand up. Her head wouldn't stop aching, and her stomach was always in pain.

Doc looked after the pair of them because he didn't dare go against the captain's orders. Doc didn't have anything in particular against this mother and child, but he thought that they shouldn't be here: not on this boat, not at this time.

Eulogio hadn't dealt well with the sea either and spent more time collapsed on his bed than on deck, but he still went down to the infirmary every day to see Catalina.

As for Fernando, he had managed to get his way into the captain's good books, either because they both liked playing chess, or else because the captain didn't like talking and Fernando didn't mind keeping quiet for the long mealtimes they shared with the other officers of the ship.

If ever he asked a question, it was always something to do with the sea. Also, when he was not with Catalina, he tried to help the sailors as much as he could. The captain knew about this, but didn't say anything.

That morning, when the sun rose, Fernando was walking across the deck and saw the captain.

"We'll reach Alexandria today," Pereira declared.

"I thought we'd never get here," Fernando admitted, looking out over the land on the horizon.

"Where will you go?"

"Where? I wish I knew. You know our situation. Catalina wants to find the father of her child, and we don't know if he's still in Alexandria. If we find him, we'll see what happens next."

"Do you think he'll want to take responsibility?"

Fernando weighed his reply. He didn't want to betray anyone's trust, but he also wanted to give an honest answer.

"It's most likely that he's not in the city. He goes from place to place. We know he came to Alexandria to hand over a document, the title deeds to some property, that his editor gave him to pass on to his daughter, who is married and lives in the city. Marvin's editor is a Jew, and things have gotten pretty bad for Jews in France. I think that he sold Marvin the bookshop and the publishing house as a way of saving them, but on the condition that he come out here and find the daughter and give her the deeds. Once he's met with Sara Rosent and done his duty, the most likely thing is that he's headed off somewhere else."

"Sara Rosent? So she's the daughter of the editor of this friend of yours?"

"Well, Marvin's not really my friend, he's Eulogio's: they met on the front in the war in Spain. I don't know anything about Rosent apart from what Eulogio has told me, and all that he got from Marvin."

"I know Sara Rosent," Pereira declared.

"You know her? Really?" Fernando didn't know what to say, he was so surprised.

"Everyone in Alexandria knows about Mr. Wilson and his wife Sara Rosent. They own one of the most important book-shops in the city, and publish collections of poetry, and hold events at the shop every week. Poets and all kinds of other writers meet up there to talk about books and all kinds of other things. The bookshop's called Wilson & Wilson, and it's by the rue Cherif Pasha, near the rue Rosette. It shouldn't be difficult to find. But where will Catalina stay if she can't find Marvin? She and her daughter need a place where they can rest and get better, and if Marvin's already left the city …"

"I can't stop thinking about what we're going to do once we land. Catalina and Eulogio are such optimists … But I'm not so sure that things are going to work out how they hope."

"Do they have any money left?" Pereira asked, avoiding Fernando's gaze.

"We gave everything we had to pay for the tickets … I know that you have been very generous, because we didn't have enough for even one passage … I don't know how we can ever thank you, we owe you so much."

Pereira looked forward, again avoiding Fernando's gaze. He didn't want anyone to thank him, or praise him for his actions.

"They can't live without money," the captain said.

"I'll do whatever it takes to earn some. I know English; my father taught me," Fernando said.

"Right …" Pereira seemed to be thinking about something.

"I'm not a fool. I know it will be difficult. We're coming to a city that none of us knows anything about. The most important thing will be to protect Catalina and Adela. The little thing's so small and weak … She doesn't even cry."

They sat together in silence. The captain took out a pack of cigarettes and offered one to Fernando. They smoked in silence as they put their thoughts in order.

"Your friend Eulogio should be the one to look after you; he's older, and he's been in the war, which will have made a man of him. No one who's served on the front can ever be a child again."

"He was wounded."

"That's what I mean. He might be able to help you."

"He's done a lot for us already."

"Yes, but even so … Dammit, I can't leave you alone once you get off the ship! Lord knows what will happen to you."

"You shouldn't worry," Fernando said, with a firmness of tone that he did not feel.

"I have a good friend. Madame Kokkalis, Ylena Kokkalis. She's Greek. She's got a big house, with three rooms that she rents out. I'll give you a letter for her, and you'll at least have a roof over your heads until you find this Marvin, or get a job that'll pay for a room and a ticket back to Spain."

"No, we're not going back to Spain. Maybe Catalina wants to, but Eulogio and I will never go back."

"Why? Don't you see you haven't got anything, anything at all? Alexandria isn't a city for kids. Haven't you realized there's a war on? The Germans are getting closer, and the Alexandrians are on their side, just like the rest of the Egyptians. They can't stand the English. The quicker you get out of here, the better."

"Eulogio wants to go to America, and I may go with him: it all depends on Catalina. I'll never leave her, unless she decides to go back to Spain. I'm not going back there."

The captain looked at him with interest. He could guess that Fernando's determination never to go back to Spain must be motivated by something important. But he wasn't surprised by his loyalty towards Catalina, because it was clear that he was in love with her.

"Why don't you marry her?"

"I want to, but she doesn't love me. Well, she loves me like a brother. We've known each other since we were children."

"And you have always been in love with her, unless I'm mistaken?"

"Yes. Maybe she'll change her mind one day."

:a didn't say just how difficult it was for fraternal feel-
hange into ones of romantic love. Better to let the kid
for himself.

right. We'll be in Alexandria soon; you'll be able to disembark in the late afternoon. I recommend that you go straight
to Madame Kokkalis' place and get some rest. You can start looking for your friend tomorrow."

Fernando stayed up on deck while the captain went back to
the bridge. It was morning now, and the air had grown warmer;
the sky was blue, with only an occasional cloud to darken it.

His mother's face came to his mind, and he felt a sharp pain
in his chest. He told himself that he did not regret having killed
the men who killed his father, but his conscience stung with having abandoned his mother. He hadn't slept well since they fled
Madrid: his nights were filled with the image of his mother crying, and the faces of those other men. Roque and Saturnino Pérez
came to visit him, night after night.

If he did finally make it to America, he would get Eulogio to
write to Isabel and tell her that he was all right. He didn't want
to do it before then: they might still be looking for him. And if
they were, he didn't know if they could send an order from Spain
that would make him come back, accusing him of being nothing
more than a criminal. There was no other choice than to wait, let
some time pass before getting in touch with his mother again.

He was so caught up in his own thoughts that he didn't hear
Catalina's approach: she was walking slowly, leaning on Eulogio's
arm.

"Penny for your thoughts?" she said, holding Adela tight to
her chest.

"You shouldn't take the baby outdoors: it's cold," he said.

"Doc told me that we have to get up, that we're coming into
Alexandria and will be disembarking this afternoon. Eulogio's
helping me," Catalina said with a grimace.

"It won't hurt Adela to get a bit of air. Doc didn't think it was
a bad idea to come out on deck," Eulogio added.

Fernando didn't agree, but he didn't want to get into an argument. And they were out already, so if Adela was going to get a
chill, there was nothing he could do to stop it.

"Are you worried?" Catalina asked, sensing that there was something the matter with her friend.

"Yes, of course I'm worried. So many things have happened since we left Madrid that I haven't had a chance to think," Fernando replied.

"Well, the important thing is to get off this boat. I think I'd probably prefer to swim to America." Eulogio seemed to be in a good mood.

"We don't have any money," Fernando reminded them.

"But Marvin will help us." Catalina sounded convinced.

"Perhaps, but we've got to find him first. We don't know if he's in Alexandria or if he's already moved on. And if he's not there …"

"But he has to be there! Tell him, Eulogio, tell him that Marvin will be there." Catalina sounded like she was begging.

Eulogio didn't know what to say. Fernando was right: perhaps Marvin was no longer in Alexandria, and then what would they do? They didn't have any money; they didn't know anybody. He knew that they had been hasty and careless. Catalina and Fernando were inexperienced, naive, but he was an adult and should have thought more about what they were doing.

"Fernando is right. We were too hasty getting on the boat to Alexandria. But, well … we'll see what happens," Eulogio said, feeling uncomfortable with the situation.

"Captain Pereira is going to give me a letter of introduction to a friend of his who rents out rooms. We'll go to the woman's house this evening, and start looking for Marvin tomorrow, but even if we do find him, I'll still have to get a job to pay for the room and for our tickets out of here. I don't think that we'll be as lucky as we were in Lisbon, and find a captain who's willing to take us almost for free," Fernando explained.

"It'll be difficult to find a job; we don't speak Arabic," Eulogio said worriedly.

"It's the English who are in charge here, even though they've officially got a king. The Egyptians have been under British protection since 1882, so I suppose that, as well as speaking Arabic, they won't find it too difficult to hear us speak English," Fernando said.

"Well, you might know English because your father was a translator and an editor, and put the works of important English authors into Spanish, but I'm better at French, and as for Catalina …" Eulogio was growing more worried by the minute.

"I speak French well enough," Catalina admitted, "although I'll make the effort to learn English."

"Alexandria is an international city, filled with people from all over the world; it won't be hard for us to make ourselves understood." Fernando didn't wish to scare them.

"And what about this woman? How's she going to rent us a room even though she knows that we don't have enough money to pay her?" Catalina asked.

"She's a friend of the captain," Fernando said, taking Adela in his arms and walking with her below deck. She had started to cough, and he was scared that she'd caught a cold.

Catalina let her go. She knew her daughter was safe in her friend's arms.

Time passed, but too slowly. When they reached the port, they had to wait for the authorities to get on board the ship and examine its cargo, as well as speak to the captain.

Pereira told the port authorities about his passengers and the unexpected birth of a child.

The customs officials asked a few questions of Catalina, Fernando and Eulogio, and checked their papers. Catalina told them that she was going to look for the father of her child, and the two men said that they belonged to the losing side in the Spanish war and were fleeing from Franco's fascist regime.

If it had not been for the captain, the English customs officials might not have let them disembark. But Pereira spent a long time with them in his cabin, and when they came out, they limited themselves to telling the three adults not to get into trouble. Fernando didn't dare ask the captain how he had managed to convince the Englishmen to leave them alone. It was Eulogio who whispered a brief explanation into his ear: "The captain does favors for the British. I heard him talking to one of the sailors. Sometimes he allows men to travel; no one knows who they are. Other times he transports packages that are taken away to the garrison at Alexandria. Pereira is against the Nazis." Whether it was for this or for some other reason, it was clear that the Portuguese had a certain reputation among the British.

They bade farewell to the sailors who had been their companions on the journey, and also to Doc, who seemed relieved to see the back of them.

Catalina went to see the captain and, without thinking twice about it, gave him a resounding kiss on the cheek.

"Thank you, captain; I'll never be able to pay you back for what you've done for me, for my daughter, for all of us. You are one of the best men I have ever met and you will always, always have a loyal friend in me. I hope I can pay you back for your generosity one day. And ... well, when I meet Marvin and we baptize Adela, I would love for you to be the godfather. Would you? Please?"

Pereira didn't know what to say. Catalina reminded him so strongly of his granddaughters that he found it difficult to refuse her anything, and so he accepted, although slightly reluctantly. She gave him another kiss, overjoyed that the captain was to be the godfather to her child.

The *Esperanza del Mar* was to spend at least a week in Alexandria, and Catalina was sure that in this time they would find Marvin, and that she could get married and have their child baptized.

They left the port and walked quite some distance, asking people on the street how to get to the church of Saint Sabbas, in the Greek Quarter, because the captain had told them that it was near this church that his friend lived.

Adela was carried by Catalina, and then by Eulogio, and finally ended up being held by Fernando. The three friends took turns holding the baby, who spent most of the journey asleep.

Ylena Kokkalis lived in a beautiful building. A young woman opened the door to them and looked at them with frank curiosity while Fernando explained in his perfect English that Captain Pereira had sent them, and that they had a letter for Madame Kokkalis.

The young woman invited them in, and then asked them to wait in the large hall.

Ylena Kokkalis was a woman of medium height, with dark chestnut hair and olive-brown skin. Fernando and Eulogio would both refer to her later on as "very pretty," in spite of the fact that she must have been more than fifty.

She read the captain's letter carefully, and when she had finished, she put the envelope away and looked at them with a smile.

"Well … Captain Pereira has asked me to put you up in my house even though you have no money to pay me, but he has assured me that he will cover your bills until you can find a way to earn your rent, so that's settled. However, I only have one room free at the moment: all the others are occupied. There are two beds in it, and it is large, so I can get a sofa moved in as well. That's the best I can offer, I'm afraid."

They accepted immediately, glad to have found a place to shelter them. They thanked her in English and in French and she laughed at the jumble of languages.

"You sound like you're real Alexandrians already … We all speak so many languages here."

"But no one speaks Spanish, I'd guess," Eulogio replied.

"Ah, you'd be surprised. There are people here from all over the world, and more of them than ever, now that the war's started. You might meet someone from Spain."

They went with her to the room, which was large. They could tell that it would be bright in the morning. A few minutes later, the woman who had opened the door to them, along with another, older woman, came in, pushing the sofa that Ylena had offered them.

Fernando decided that he would sleep on the sofa and that Catalina and Eulogio could have the beds. Eulogio tried to argue, saying that he was oldest and he should sleep on the sofa, but Fernando stuck to his guns.

Adela started to whine, as she always did when she was hungry, and at that moment Ylena knocked on the door.

"I forgot to tell you that there's a bathroom. But you have to help keep it clean, because it's shared with the other two lodgers. Mr. Sanders has been here for five years now, and he's very demanding about cleanliness, as is Monsieur Baudin."

Ylena Kokkalis told them that if they had any problems, they should take them up with Dimitra and Ilora, the two maids.

Catalina decided that she needed a bath, and Dimitra found a towel for her, as well as giving her information about the other two lodgers. And so she found out that Mr. Sanders was a retired colonel in the British army, as well as an archeologist. He had served with the Alexandria Regiment and, as he was a bachelor and had no one waiting for him back in England apart from a happily married sister and a few nieces and nephews, he had decided to extend his stay in Egypt; until the war had broken out, he had indulged his passion for archeology. And as for Monsieur Baudin, he was a cotton merchant and a widower who had decided that it would be more trouble than it was worth to carry on living in the house he had shared with his wife, and so had moved into Madame Kokkalis' house, where he was well looked after. Monsieur Baudin had a married son who also lived in Alexandria, but who could not persuade his father to come and live with him and his wife. Baudin visited them often now that they had a child: his grandson, the main source of happiness in his life.

Dimitra also told Catalina that Madame Kokkalis was very strict about punctuality. She was very annoyed whenever her guests came down late for breakfast, which was served at seven on the dot, and was equally upset if they didn't tell her whether or not they would be staying for lunch or dinner.

But, even given all this, Dimitra praised Madame Kokkalis to the heavens for her kindness. The only thing she knew about her was that she had been born in Alexandria, although her parents were Greeks. She had never married, because when she was younger and had been about to do so, her fiancé, a sailor, had drowned. He was Captain Pereira's nephew; they had met one another for the first time during one of the *Esperanza del Mar*'s stops in Alexandria. But what looked like it was going to be a happy story ended in tragedy, because a storm blew up in the Atlantic just as the vessel was headed for Egypt. They did not sink, but the boat was in very bad shape; worst of all, several sailors were washed overboard. Pereira's nephew was one of them. The captain saw him fall and did not hesitate: he threw himself into the water to save him. Both of them nearly died. Pereira had to fight his way through the waves to rescue him; he reached the body, but his nephew was dead by the time they brought him back to the ship.

Pereira insisted that they keep the body in storage to bring it back to his fiancée. She was grateful to him for this. At least there would be a tomb for her to visit and mourn her love. In spite of the fact that she had other suitors, she never married. There were rumors later on that she had a relationship with a very rich Alexandrian, an influential figure in the court of King Farouk. But nobody knew this for sure.

Pereira visited her every time his ship landed in Alexandria. He was always well-received and over the years he had developed a deep friendship with her.

Dimitra said that Ylena's eyes lit up every time she saw Captain Pereira.

Catalina told Fernando and Eulogio all these details, and had to wait for her two friends to have a bath as well before they went down to the dining room.

They were hungry, and interested to see what food would be on offer.

Ylena introduced them to the other two lodgers without giving any explanations about who they were. Then they all sat down at the table, with the Greek at the head.

It was a number of vegetable dishes, a purée made of chickpeas that she said was called "hummus," and a fish whose name they didn't even catch. It seemed to them the most exquisite meal they had ever eaten.

Monsieur Baudin was very pleasant and praised Adela, who spent the meal asleep in Catalina's arms. Mr. Sanders was polite, but he showed no interest at all in the new guests, and even less in the child: he looked at her askance, worried that this little creature could perhaps ruin the peace and quiet of his home.

Monsieur Baudin discussed the latest news of the war with Mr. Sanders. He was worried that Germany had declared war on the United States.

"But what did you expect? From the moment that the Japanese bombed Pearl Harbor, it was clear that America couldn't sit back and do nothing. And once they had declared war on Japan, it was only a matter of time before Germany declared that it was going to support its allies."

"Maybe things will go better now that America is going to fight," Monsieur Baudin pondered.

Mr. Sanders looked at him with a certain arrogance, as though he were offended that the Frenchman was suggesting the British might need help.

After the meal, they all went back to their rooms. With Catalina and Eulogio sitting on their beds and Fernando on his sofa, they spoke about the meal, and above all about how happy they were to be back on dry land. Then, before they went to sleep, each one of them spent some time alone with their own thoughts.

Adela was the first of them to wake up. Catalina fed her, and after changing her, left her on the bed so that she could go and have another bath.

It was five thirty in the morning, and there was not a sound in the house. She knew that she couldn't be long, because Dimitra had told her that Mr. Sanders used the bathroom at six on the dot, followed by Monsieur Baudin at six fifteen.

As soon as she was ready, she woke Fernando.

"Hurry up; it's nearly six: you've got time to wash before Mr. Sanders."

Fernando jumped out of bed and, although he was as fast as he could be, he was still surprised by the two blunt knocks at the bathroom door that announced the arrival of the Englishman.

Eulogio had to wait for Mr. Sanders and Monsieur Baudin to use the bathroom, and they ended up hurrying, with only a few minutes before they had to be downstairs to breakfast with Ylena.

After breakfast, everyone went to do their own business. Catalina was keen to start searching for Marvin. The night before she had arranged with Eulogio and Fernando that they would go to Wilson's bookshop to ask Sara Rosent about Marvin, and that she would stay at home until they came back. Catalina had wanted to come, but she had not been able to convince her friends to let her go with them. They said that they had no idea where the bookshop was, and that they didn't want to run the risk of Adela getting involved in any trouble, given that they knew nothing at all about the city.

The truth was that Eulogio didn't want Marvin to see Catalina before they could explain to him what had happened. He felt that bringing Catalina to Alexandria was a betrayal of the American's trust. They had to talk to him and give him the opportunity to decide what to do about Catalina. Fernando assented.

Following the directions that Ylena Kokkalis had given them, it was not hard for them to find Wilson's bookshop, which was relatively nearby. A huge sign reading WILSON & WILSON hung over a door made of wood and glass. A well-organized window display showed off a few books of poetry.

They pushed open the door and found themselves in a room that was bigger than they had expected, filled with shelves that reached from the floor to the ceiling; there was a counter, better described as a table, where a person could look at the books at their leisure, and even some comfortable chairs at the back of the room. Behind them, a door led to a back room. The door was ajar, and through it they saw three men deep in concentration, reading. The room smelled of wax and books. Fernando found it comforting.

A woman came out to greet them. She was tall, thin, about forty years old, with her hair tied back in a bun from which a few rebellious curls escaped. She looked at them with piercing green eyes.

"Can I help you?" she asked with a slight smile.

They introduced themselves and tried to explain, nervously, that they were looking for Sara Rosent, but that they really were trying to find Marvin Brian. Eulogio spoke in French, Fernando in English, and each of them constantly interrupted the other, making it impossible for the woman to understand them.

"I think I can tell by your accents that you are Spanish, no?" she said in very good Spanish.

"You speak Spanish?" Eulogio asked in surprise.

"Indeed. So, if you want, we can speak your language and it will be easier for everyone. I think I understood that you are looking for Marvin Brian ..."

"Yes, we're friends of his. He wrote to me to tell me that he was coming to Alexandria, and encouraged me to come and find him," Eulogio said.

The woman looked at them curiously, then asked them to sit down in the green leather armchairs at the far end of the room.

She offered them coffee, which she brought on a silver tray. Once they were settled in, she asked them to start from the beginning.

Eulogio, as he was Marvin's friend, took the lead, and Fernando nodded along.

"Well, you've found me. I am Sara Rosent. As for Marvin … he never mentioned any of you, much less that he was expecting you to come to Alexandria."

"But he is here, isn't he?" Eulogio asked impatiently.

Sara Rosent didn't reply, but simply smiled. They didn't want to insist that she give them an answer, and so they waited until they had finished their coffee at their leisure: strong, aromatic coffee that jolted all their senses into wakefulness.

To their surprise, Sara didn't mention Marvin, but instead asked them where they were staying. They told her, and she said that she knew Ylena Kokkalis and would send them news at her house very soon. Eulogio insisted again on knowing where Marvin was, but Sara repeated firmly that she would tell them that afternoon.

Catalina grew angry when they came back without any news of Marvin, and said that she would go herself to speak with Sara Rosent. She wouldn't be able to refuse to tell her anything when she saw Adela. Eulogio advised her to be patient.

Barely two hours had passed when a young man came to the house and gave Dimitra an envelope for Eulogio. Sara Rosent invited him to come back to the bookshop, alone. There was not a word about Marvin.

Eulogio showed the letter to Fernando, who read it and shrugged. Sara's behavior seemed strange, but they decided not to mention it to Catalina, who was still angry and still insisting that she would go personally to Wilson & Wilson. They finally calmed her down, and Fernando suggested going for a walk with Adela.

When Eulogio pushed open the door to Wilson & Wilson, he saw Marvin at the back of the room sitting next to Sara on one of the green leather chairs. The American jumped up when he saw Eulogio come in. The two friends embraced.

Sara discreetly left them alone. She knew that the two friends needed to talk in private. She went over to the counter where one of her employees was organizing the books.

Eulogio and Marvin both started to speak at once, each trying to tell the other the news from their lives over the past few months, before breaking out laughing at the chaos of their conversation. Marvin, aware that the presence of his friend in Alexandria was something extraordinary, invited him to be the first to tell his story.

Eulogio did not leave out a single detail: he told Marvin everything about the discovery of his mother's relationship with Don Antonio, and how his pride had kept him from forgiving her, even though he knew that she was only doing it to save him. What he did not say was that Fernando was in Alexandria because he had killed two men. The explanation he gave was that Fernando had not wanted to abandon Catalina, who was desperate to come and find Marvin, to make him aware of the fact that she was pregnant and to ask him to take charge of the situation. And so the three of them had fled Spain. Eulogio apologized to the American for having told Catalina where she could find him.

He didn't hold back on the details about the journey either, about Captain Pereira's kindness, Adela's premature birth and the fact that they had no money to live on while in Alexandria.

Marvin's face showed a range of emotions, from stunned shock to worry.

"I live with a woman; her name is Farida Rahman. She's a philosopher. I love her more than life itself, precisely because she once saved my life. Farida is everything to me: my present and my future. You'll meet her soon. She knows everything that happened to me during the war in Spain, and how I've been running from myself ever since, unable to find a moment's peace. She's teaching me how to beat back my ghosts; she has given me back my hope."

"But she … she …" Eulogio stammered.

"She's a woman who doesn't care about the same things as other women," Marvin continued. "Her only desire is to understand the essence of what it means to be human, to plumb the depths of the souls who cross her path on her journey through life, to draw conclusions that she can test in the fires of argument. I love her with all my heart."

"Will you speak with Catalina? Will you tell her … ?"

"Never! Catalina means nothing to me … I barely know her, and no way am I going to take responsibility for her problems. I know that she's a good girl, a little scatterbrained, and I don't want anything bad to happen to her, but I can't do anything for her. What made you think bringing her with you would be a good idea?" Marvin couldn't hide the tone of reproach in his voice.

"It was foolish of me to tell her you were here. I'm sorry. Maybe if you spoke to her …"

"I don't have to, and I don't want to account for myself to Catalina. I'd like to help her solve her problem, but I don't know how."

"But we have to do something with her …"

"The best thing is for us not to see each other. It'd be worse for her; she'd just feel humiliated if I told her I don't care for her. It's better if this 'love' she says she feels for me can just trickle away. And as for the child … I don't know what to say … I've already told you what happened that night at the Pradera de San Isidro. I'm sorry for the poor girl, but I'm not in a good place to take on a daughter."

"I'll have to ask Fernando for help, because I don't know how I'm going to deal with Catalina."

Marvin promised to help them. He'd give them some money and look for a job for them if they decided to stay in Egypt, given that Europe was racked by war and there was no safe place for them to go.

"I wanted to go to America, but now that it's entered the war …" Eulogio stammered.

"You want to go to America? Well, that can be sorted out. Don't worry about the war: America's a long way from Europe. The hard part will be getting there … I'm going to New York in a couple of months. Of course, Farida's coming with me. I want her to meet my parents and my brother. Well, she's the one who really wants to meet them, to find the missing pieces she still needs to sort out the puzzle of my life. You can come with us. You don't need to worry about anything. I'll ask my father to give you a job in New York. You'll have to work on your English, which is pretty bad. So work on that until we go. Fernando's isn't bad: get him to give you lessons."

"It'll be a dangerous journey," Eulogio said.

"Yes, it won't be easy to find a ship that'll take us. It's harder to get across the Atlantic nowadays. But we'll manage."

"And what will we do with Fernando and Catalina?" Eulogio asked, worriedly.

"I'm sorry, my friend, but what might happen to them isn't my problem. I can help them without them finding out about it, but nothing more. And of course, they won't come with us to New York."

At that moment, a woman stepped decisively into the shop. Eulogio guessed that this must be Farida. Sara, who was dealing with some customers, smiled at her and pointed to the green arm-chairs where he and Marvin were sitting.

She came over and stood expectantly in front of them. They were both quiet, like children waiting for their teacher's approval. Marvin stood up and ushered her to a seat.

"Farida, this is my friend Eulogio. I've told you about him ..."

"At last we meet! I'm Farida Rahman," she said with a broad smile.

Eulogio stood up and held out a hand, unable to tear his eyes off her, not so much because of her beauty, but rather because of the strength of personality that showed in her face. He tried to hide his surprise at seeing how old Farida was. She was much older than Marvin. He guessed that she must already be forty.

Sara came over with a tray and put another pot of coffee on the table. Then she left them to themselves.

Marvin explained to Farida why Eulogio had come, as well as the situation with Catalina. Marvin was firm in his insistence that he was not going to see her, much less explain himself to her, not only because he felt no connection to her, but also because he thought it would be better for her; she wouldn't understand his flat refusal and would feel far worse if they did meet.

Farida listened in silence, nodding every now and then as she served the coffee.

"A woman who has come all the way to Alexandria for you will not stop until she finds you, no matter where you are. She will get to you, eventually."

"So what should I do?" Marvin asked worriedly.

"Don't do anything you don't want to do. She means nothing to you, so you don't need to hurt yourself by baring your soul to her. You don't owe her anything, and she doesn't owe anything to you. But you must be aware that she'll become obsessed with you."

Eulogio listened with fascination to Farida's melodious French accent.

They talked for a while, trying to decide the best way to keep Catalina away from Marvin.

How many hours did they spend talking? They didn't realize that the afternoon had slipped away until Sara returned to their corner.

"It is late, but if you want to stay here, you can. Benjamin is waiting for me and I have to go, but Akim will be here for a while," she said, looking over at the young assistant who seemed very busy reorganizing books on the shelves.

"It would be better for me to go back to Madame Kokkalis' house. Fernando and Catalina will be worried," Eulogio said.

"Ah, what an extraordinary woman Ylena Kokkalis is. She's a good friend and a keen reader. She can recite the *Iliad* from memory. And she always has clear and original opinions about poetry," Sara said.

"Goodness! She's so serious that I'd never have guessed that she likes poetry," Eulogio said in surprise.

"She's an educated woman, almost as smart as Farida. Don't ever forget, my friend, that a single woman needs to win people's respect," Sara said.

In the street, Marvin slipped a few bills into Eulogio's hand. They agreed that the next day he and Fernando would come to the reading that the bookshop held every Thursday.

The first shadows of night were creeping through the city when Eulogio reached Madame Kokkalis' house. He found Catalina feeding Adela while Fernando lay sprawled on the bed.

"What happened?" Catalina asked impatiently.

"Nothing important. I came as soon as I could, but I ran out of cigarettes and I need to smoke," Eulogio said, making a signal to Fernando that he immediately understood.

"Let's go out and smoke while Catalina finishes feeding Adela," he suggested, even though he knew that Catalina's suspicions would immediately be raised.

"Now you're going? That's it! Stop keeping secrets: I want to know what's going on," she said.

"But I need to smoke a cigarette now. I'll talk about everything with you later." Eulogio left the room before Catalina had a chance to protest, waiting for Fernando to follow him.

Rain suddenly began to fall in a thin drizzle, and Eulogio walked so fast that Fernando had to hurry to catch up.

"I don't know if it's a good idea to talk in the street."

"Yes, but I can't say anything in front of Catalina."

He gave a quick, staccato explanation of the situation. Fernando listened with an expression of concern on his face, which changed to one of surprise when he heard about Farida. But the most troublesome part wasn't that Marvin had chosen to wash his hands of Catalina, but rather how they were going to tell her without hurting her. They decided that they couldn't lie to her outright. Catalina was clever, and she had left everything to come and find Marvin. It wouldn't be easy to pull the wool over her eyes. So they decided to tell her that Marvin was in love with another woman.

Eulogio's main concern was how to remain loyal to his friend, while Fernando was preoccupied with hurting Catalina as little as possible.

When they came back into the room, Adela was asleep in her mother's arms. Catalina looked at them with a worried expression.

"It's like she finds it hard to breathe," she said, without addressing either of them directly.

"Oh ... But it looked like she was getting better ..." Eulogio replied.

"She's been fussy all afternoon," Fernando explained.

Adela opened her eyes, and started to breathe faster. It looked as though she were choking.

"We have to call a doctor." Catalina, anguished, held her child tight.

Eulogio went out to find Dimitra, who was in the dining

room clearing the supper dishes. He explained what was happening to Adela, and Dimitra nervously told him to stay put while she fetched her mistress.

Ylena came down with Dimitra to the room where her new lodgers were staying. She took in the situation at a glance.

"We'll take them to Dr. Naseef's house straight away. Come on, we need to hurry. We'll ask Monsieur Baudin to take us in his car," Ylena said.

Monsieur Baudin opened the door in his dressing gown and immediately agreed to do as Ylena asked.

Dr. Naseef's house was near Saint Mark's Church.

Adela was shivering. It almost looked like she was drowning. Catalina muttered prayers while she held her daughter tight.

"Hurry up," Ylena ordered Monsieur Baudin as he drove along.

Baudin drove at speed down the Boulevard Ramleh, turning onto rue Debbane and then continuing on to the rue de L'Église Copte, where the cathedral of the Coptic Orthodox Patriarch could be found. A little further along, he parked his car, and everyone got out and followed Ylena, who hurried to the doctor's house.

An elderly woman with brown skin and an expression of curious interest on her face opened the door. She smiled when she saw Ylena and showed them in while Ylena explained what was going on.

Dr. Naseef came in at once and examined the child with a serious expression on his face. Adela shivered and whimpers escaped from her little mouth.

"She has pneumonia," the doctor said.

"Pneumonia? But how?" Fernando said, shocked at the diagnosis.

"We have to take her to the hospital. Right away," Dr. Naseef replied.

It didn't take long to get there: the Egyptian Government Hospital was virtually next door, just past the British Consulate.

They followed Dr. Naseef down a hallway until they came to a room where he asked everyone but Catalina and Ylena to wait.

Fernando and Eulogio didn't even bother to sit down. They

paced up and down the room, worried about what might happen. Monsieur Baudin took out a pack of cigarettes and offered them around to help calm their nerves.

It wasn't until an hour or so later that Ylena came into the room, looking anxious.

"The baby's very sick … the doctors don't know if she'll make it … she's so small … and it doesn't help that she was born prematurely."

Ylena opened her bag and took out her own packet of cigarettes.

"And Catalina?" Fernando asked.

"She'll stay with the baby, but we can't do anything here," Ylena said.

"I'll stay; I can't leave her alone," Fernando replied.

"I don't think they'll let us be with her. Dr. Naseef has said that only Catalina can stay. It's understandable; there are other sick children in there, and they are with their mothers. Monsieur Baudin will take us back, right? The most sensible thing to do is to wait until tomorrow."

"But … what if something happens to Adela? No, we can't leave Catalina alone."

"Do whatever you want, I don't care if you sit in this room all night," Ylena replied testily.

"I will, then."

"Well, I'll go and tell Catalina that you're here, and then the rest of us will go home."

"I'll stay too," Eulogio said.

Ylena shrugged. She understood why the two Spaniards wanted to stay, but there was nothing else she or Monsieur Baudin could do.

Fernando and Eulogio sat on the bench in the waiting room in silence, each of them lost in his own thoughts. They didn't have anything to say. All they could do was wait. As dawn was breaking, they both fell asleep.

They woke up with a start when a woman and a child came into the room. They greeted them with a nod. Barely a minute later, two women and three children walked in. More and more people came until the waiting room was crammed to the gills.

"We should go and ask what's happening," Eulogio suggested.

They found a nurse, explained why they were there, and asked for Dr. Naseef. The nurse told them where they could find him.

It was clear that Dr. Naseef hadn't slept all night. He didn't beat around the bush; he explained to them that, although Adela had made it through the night, her chances of surviving the attack of pneumonia were slim. He summed up the little girl's situation, reproaching the two men for having allowed Catalina to make an ocean crossing in the depths of winter while pregnant, which had caused her to give birth prematurely. Adela was not strong enough to survive. Dr. Naseef added that although Catalina had refused to let them examine her, they'd had to do so during the night because she had lost consciousness.

Both men asked to be allowed to see Catalina and the child, and although the doctor initially refused, he ended up granting them permission.

They were shocked to see Adela with a needle sticking into her arm, connecting her to the medicine that they hoped would save her. Catalina was stroking her daughter's arm and running her fingers through her hair while she softly spoke to her. It took her several seconds to notice the presence of the others.

"Dr. Naseef thinks that Adela is going to die," she said, her face contorted by distress.

They didn't know what to say, and looked at her in silence.

"He's wrong. Adela wants to live, and she will live. We will both live," she said.

Fernando and Eulogio looked at each other worriedly, noticing a spark of madness in Catalina's eyes.

"You have to tell Marvin to come. He has to know what his daughter's going through. She needs him. I'm sure that Adela will get well as soon as her father is by her side too. Go find him." Her tone brooked no argument.

They left the hospital without knowing what to do. They didn't know if Marvin would be willing to come. And if he didn't come, they didn't know how Catalina would react.

They wandered uncertainly in a random direction, looking for Ylena's house. Fernando asked a man for directions, and he told them to take the tram. They did so using the money that Marvin had given Eulogio.

They were in such a state of shock that it didn't even occur to them to tell Ylena how Adela and Catalina were. It was Dimitra who came to tell them that Madame Kokkalis was waiting for them in the dining room.

Ylena was talking to the other two lodgers, who immediately asked for an update on the situation.

After drinking a cup of tea with them, Ylena recommended that they sleep for a while. She would go to the hospital to be with Catalina. Monsieur Baudin offered to take her, as he said it was more or less on the way to his office.

Eulogio and Fernando decided to take Ylena's advice. They felt exhausted, in a mental stupor, unable to make a decision.

Dimitra woke them up after a few hours with a pair of sharp raps at the door, ordering them to get up so she could clean the room. They obeyed. Also, they were hungry.

Ylena had come back from the hospital and could only tell them that Adela was still in critical condition. They had examined Catalina and come to the conclusion that she was anemic. She tried to cheer them up by telling them that Dr. Naseef was a good doctor and that if anyone could save Adela, it would be him.

Fernando insisted on going back to the hospital. Catalina, in turn, insisted that they go and find Marvin. The two men gave in.

Late in the afternoon, Eulogio reminded Fernando that they had arranged to go to the bookshop and meet Marvin. They would tell him what had happened, and maybe he would have some ideas of his own about what to do.

When they arrived, Sara was serving some customers. Marvin and the other guests at the reading had not yet arrived. Feeling nervous, Eulogio decided to go out for a walk and to smoke a cigarette, and Fernando stayed looking at the books.

He enjoyed picking up the old editions, handling them carefully; it was though he was afraid of hurting the pages so filled with poetry and history.

He didn't realize that a man had been watching him for a while, and gave a start when he came and stood next to him.

"Do you like poetry?" the man asked.

"Yes … I like books in general, all books, not just poetry. The ones here are extraordinary. My father would have loved to have seen them …"

"Your father?"

"My father was an editor … He translated English and published editions of the best English authors."

"And you have inherited his love for literature," the man said.

"Yes. I grew up surrounded by books."

"Do you write?" the man asked.

"Oh, no! I don't have a talent for writing, but I am good at telling if other people's writing is any good. My father taught me how."

"And what do you do?"

"Before the war I studied literature; I wanted to be an editor."

"Do you mean the current war, or …?"

"I mean the Spanish war. I'm Spanish."

"Right … Your English is excellent."

"My father taught me. He said that I had an ear for languages, just like he did."

"Do you speak other languages besides English?"

"A little French … and when I was a schoolboy I was very good at Latin and Ancient Greek."

"And what do you do now?"

Fernando shrugged, and stared at the person with whom he had been speaking; though they had been talking for a while, he had no idea who the man was. He was tall, with dark salt-and-pepper hair and deep gray eyes; he was well-dressed and radiated self-confidence.

"The war ruined everything. Since then I haven't done anything, really. I couldn't keep studying."

"Right … I'm very sorry to hear that … Well, I don't think I introduced myself. I'm Benjamin Wilson." He held out his hand, shaking Fernando's proffered hand firmly.

Sara came over to them, smiling at her husband as she did so.

"I see you've met … Fernando Garzo is a friend of dear Marvin, and Eulogio Jiménez is too. He's just gone out for a walk before the others arrive."

Sara offered them a drink while she greeted the guests, who

were starting to trickle in, leaving them alone while she went off to welcome the new arrivals.

"What brings you to Alexandria?" Mr. Wilson asked.

"I left Spain because … well, because I had no choice. I was on the losing side in the war. My father was shot. It's hard for the son of a Republican to make his way in Spain today. As for why I'm in Alexandria in particular … well, it's as good or bad a place as anywhere else. There's nowhere safe in Europe now that the Germans have started this war. My friend Eulogio wants to go to America, and maybe Marvin will help us get there. Of course, America's joined the war now, so I don't know what will become of us. We're traveling with a childhood friend of ours and her daughter as well …"

Fernando ran his hand over his face as though trying to stop his tongue from moving, giving him time to order to his thoughts. Why was he talking so openly to this unknown man? He barely knew anything at all about Mr. Wilson, and yet here he was, telling him everything.

The door to the bookshop opened and Marvin and Farida came in. Benjamin Wilson walked over to them, greeting them with obvious affection.

Fernando was shocked by the ease with which Mr. Wilson moved between languages. He had spoken to Fernando in English, and with Sara in French, and now he was speaking Arabic to the woman who had come in with Marvin, who – judging from Eulogio's description of Farida – must have been Farida herself.

Marvin shook his hand and introduced his companion. At that moment, Eulogio came back and joined the conversation. More and more guests started to arrive. Akim, the Wilsons' assistant, went around setting up low tables and chairs.

Fernando and Eulogio explained to Marvin and Farida what had happened the night before, and how Catalina was insistent that they take him to the hospital, convinced that it would help save her daughter's life.

"Jesus, this nightmare has to stop! I thought I'd stay another month, but if Farida's all right with it, we'll leave as soon as there's a ship to take us to America," Marvin said, annoyed at what he had just heard.

"I told you that this girl will follow you wherever you go," Farida reminded him.

"And what if you talk to her? What if you say ..." Eulogio fell silent at the expression on Marvin's face.

"Now even you're telling me I have to speak to Catalina! I don't understand you, Eulogio. How can you even suggest that?" the American said reproachfully.

"I'm sorry; you're right. It's just that ... Catalina's driving us crazy and ... well, we have to tell her something."

"Truth is always the shortest path," Farida said, looking Marvin straight in the eye.

He couldn't bear her scrutiny; his face crumpled into a mask of pain.

They stood there in silence, waiting. Fernando was the first to speak.

"You have to understand that what Catalina is going through isn't easy. Her daughter is dying."

"You're making me feel like a heel," Marvin said.

Farida took his hand and held it between her own. The American felt a comforting wave of warmth. She made him feel like he was not alone, and that whatever he did, he could count on her support. This calmed him down.

"I don't want to talk to Catalina. I don't have to. I'm not going to be a father to her daughter. She made her own decisions and I made mine. So sort out the problem however you can." Marvin's voice was steady again.

"He's blind, but one day he'll see the light," Farida said.

Sara gestured to them that they should sit down. Fernando was dazzled by the conversations that took place among the guests; they talked about poetry, about history, about the war that was breaking out between Germany and Britain, not just in Europe, but in neighboring Libya as well.

A young man read some poems that were applauded by some and greeted with ironic criticism by others. And, to Fernando's surprise, Farida spent a large part of the evening arguing with a man who claimed that Gnosticism had been very important in ancient Alexandria.

"I don't agree; it was too complex an idea to be adopted by

the common people. Also, no one likes to admit that Humanity might be a big mistake, much less that the breath of life was the result of a decision made by the demiurge. Could a minor god really have created humankind?"

From the Gnostics, they moved on to discussing primitive orthodoxy, Philo, Clement of Alexandria, Origen Adamantius …

Sara whispered in Fernando's ear: "We're debating the nature of God just as we did a thousand years ago. Farida is unique. She can take any philosophy apart, and show the ones that aren't based on strictly rational premises."

Night had long since fallen, and the group of friends would have carried on talking until dawn if a few blunt knocks on the door hadn't broken the mood. It was Akim who answered, and a man bustled into the room, looking for someone. That someone was Mr. Wilson.

Wilson got up and gestured to Sara, then walked to a door at the back of the room, followed by the new arrival.

Sara kept the conversation going for a few minutes more until Farida suggested that it was too late for them all to carry on talking.

Marvin insisted that Fernando and Eulogio have dinner with him so that they could talk more in a relaxed setting.

"But it's too late. I want to go to the hospital to see Catalina, we don't know what might have happened to her," Fernando said, trying to leave, ashamed to have enjoyed the evening so much.

Eulogio, in turn, accepted the invitation, hoping that Marvin could help him solve his problems. He couldn't stop asking himself what might happen to the three of them if they were left alone in this city, abandoned to fate.

Alexandria was full of surprises, a melting pot of all kinds of people, a modern Babel, which marched to the beat of a drum he couldn't hear. So Eulogio convinced Fernando to come with him to eat with Marvin and Farida; later, he would take him to the hospital himself.

Farida drove them carefully through the streets, which were empty because of the rain. They went to a restaurant by the sea. They relaxed as they ordered some food.

Marvin asked them what they wanted to do, if they were going to stay in Alexandria or go to America.

Eulogio knew without hesitation that he was going to go to America. They had only come to Alexandria to find Marvin. The city was a great mystery to him.

As for Fernando, he explained that his fate was bound to Catalina's, and that he would not abandon her, especially not with Adela in her current state. And so it would be Catalina who would decide if she wanted to stay or go somewhere else. He would go with her anywhere, other than back to Spain.

Farida and Marvin listened to them in silence, weighing up every last word and gesture the two friends made.

"We'll go to America, although we'll stay in Alexandria for a while. I'm finishing a book that Benjamin Wilson is going to publish. I've been working on it for two years," Farida said.

"I'm writing again. I thought I was done with poetry, but thanks to Farida I can get down to it once again. Sara has read my manuscript and wants to publish it as soon as possible. It was a relief for me to get past her strict critical assessment," Marvin added.

"When will you go, then?" Eulogio asked.

"If Catalina weren't here, then we'd stay for a little while until we knew what America joining the war means. But Catalina is starting to become a problem." Marvin looked annoyed.

"A problem you can solve if you just go see her. Whether you like it or not, you have a responsibility towards the child," Fernando said cuttingly.

Marvin looked at him in confusion and Farida stroked his arm.

"Fernando, I'm not questioning your decisions, I'm not asking you why you're here, so I'm begging you, please respect mine. I don't have to see her: I don't owe her anything and she doesn't owe me anything either," the American said.

"But what happened at the Pradera de San Isidro ..." Fernando couldn't continue because Marvin interrupted him in a rage.

"It's none of my business if she's brought a child into this world! It was her decision! I'm not going to deal with the consequences! I barely know her ... Catalina is your friend, not mine;

she's just a flighty little girl who doesn't know what she wants. You should be careful and not get caught up in the web of her fantasies."

"Don't speak about her like that!" Fernando stood up, facing off with Marvin.

Farida brought them back to their senses and asked them to think for a moment instead of getting caught up in a fight that wouldn't help anyone.

"It's very much a credit to you, the love that you bear for Catalina. That's what life is … You, Fernando, have decided to bind your fate to a woman who can never love you because she is chasing a dream. Dreams are the fruit of our imagination, and we can toy with them as much as we want; we can stretch them out forever and pursue them for a lifetime. And as for Marvin, he has the right not to take part in Catalina's dreams. It's his decision."

"Well, what are we going to do?" Eulogio asked, worried about the turn the conversation was taking.

"I've told you, you can come to New York with us, and I'm sure that my father will give you a job. But in spite of Catalina, we're not going to go just yet; I know it will be difficult to avoid her, but I hope you'll help us with that. I'll help you, and won't let you suffer. Farida has spoken to Ylena Kokkalis, so you don't need to worry about the bills during your stay at her house. It's the least we can do given the situation," Marvin said.

"You don't have to do that," Fernando said uncomfortably.

"No, no, of course we have to do that. No one has been more generous to me than Eulogio. I survived in Spain thanks to him. He dragged me away from the firing line with his own body; he was wounded, but even so, pulling himself along, he was able to get me out of danger. And then he and his mother took me into their home and shared everything they had."

"You don't owe me anything, my friend," Eulogio whispered.

"I owe you my life. And I'll never be able to do enough to make that up to you."

They sat in silence as though there was no more for them to say, but then Marvin spoke:

"I had lunch today with the Wilsons. Sara is very generous,

like her father, Monsieur Rosent. As for Benjamin, he always wants to please Sara. I explained your situation, and asked them for advice and help."

"And how can they help us?" Eulogio asked impatiently.

"I don't know yet ... I suggested to Benjamin that Fernando could help him editing his books, as he has a degree of experience and knows English as well ... As for you; Eulogio, Farida knows a man who is an architect and who has a business building houses and public buildings. Farida's friend can give you work for a while," Marvin continued.

"As what? I don't know a word of Arabic." Eulogio's voice was bitter.

"My friend is old and had an accident at work, and he needs someone to take him around, a kind of assistant. His current assistant is sick and he needs someone to help him out," Farida said.

"I won't be any use to him: we'll have to mime at each other to communicate," Eulogio insisted.

"This is Alexandria, don't forget; everyone here has the gift of tongues," Farida replied with a smile. "But let me just say that Sudi is half French on his mother's side. He traveled through Spain looking for traces of Islamic architecture. He lived for a long time in Granada. So you'll be able to get by with Spanish and French. You won't have any problems. And as for Arabic ... you can decide to study it or not as you need while you are here." Farida looked at him, waiting for a reply.

"I'd like to go to America," Eulogio said firmly.

"Then we'll find a boat to take you," Marvin replied.

"But I don't want to go yet ... Not while Catalina's daughter is so sick, or before Fernando's decided what to do. So I'll take this job and we'll see if I can do it."

"And what about you, Fernando? Do you think working for the Wilsons is a good idea?" Marvin asked.

"I hope I'll be able to be of some use to them ... Now I understand why Mr. Wilson was asking so many questions," Fernando said.

"Well, Benjamin always asks questions. That shouldn't surprise you. He's the best-informed man in Alexandria. Nothing happens here that he doesn't know about immediately," Farida said.

It was about ten o'clock when they finished eating. Farida tried to insist on taking them to the hospital, but they turned down her offer. Fernando needed to walk and to think. Eulogio agreed with him.

They walked for some time without speaking.

It was Eulogio who broke the silence.

"What do you think about these jobs, then?"

"We should be grateful to them; it's not easy for two Spaniards without a degree between them to find work. And we need money, we can't rely on their kindness forever. It's true that Marvin owes you a great deal, but he doesn't owe Catalina and me a thing, and even so, he's being very generous to us. I just can't understand why Marvin won't acknowledge what he did ..."

"Catalina will insist on seeing him," Eulogio said, worriedly.

"Yes, I know her, she won't take no for an answer. And Adela's part of the equation as well. She wants a father for her daughter."

"Yes, but ... Well, Marvin's not going to be that father, you heard him. He refuses even to speak to her."

"I don't judge him, Eulogio. He'll have his reasons, Catalina doesn't mean anything to him, but the poor baby ... Catalina won't give in and she'll insist on seeing him," Fernando said.

They had to ask a couple of times where to find the hospital before they reached it.

They went up the stairs, anxious to see Catalina and fearing the worst. When they got to the baby's room, they were surprised to hear a loud, commanding voice that they recognized immediately. It was Captain Pereira.

Catalina was sitting up in a chair with her child in her arms. She was holding the baby to her breast, although the little thing seemed to be asleep. Pereira was looking worriedly at the pair of them. The two men shook hands with him in a friendly greeting.

Catalina brought them up to date with the situation. Adela was still fighting, although she was growing weaker and weaker. Even so, she was convinced that her daughter would survive. Pereira agreed, as though he were sure that this was the only possible outcome.

"And Marvin? When's he going to come?" There was a spark of hysteria in Catalina's voice.

"He's not coming." Eulogio spoke so bluntly that Catalina jumped.

"What do you mean, he's not coming? That's impossible! You told him that his daughter had been born?"

"He's with another woman, and he doesn't want anything to do with you."

Catalina stared at Eulogio, incredulous. It seemed that she couldn't comprehend what her friend had just said. Captain Pereira coughed uncomfortably.

"I don't believe you," Catalina said.

"That's how it is," Eulogio insisted.

"Say it's not true, Fernando," she begged.

"Marvin's not coming. Eulogio's telling the truth. He's with another woman."

"He's living with another woman? Where? I'll go and talk to him. She can't stop him from meeting Adela, and then he'll decide what to do."

"That's not possible. He doesn't want to see you, and they're not going to stay in Alexandria. They're going to leave in the next few days," Fernando said, speaking softly, as though the words that he knew would hurt her didn't want to leave his lips.

They sat in silence. Catalina's face was pure bitterness. She looked almost like she had been beaten.

Adela started to whimper, and Catalina stroked her little face.

"You know that Ylena has managed to get us a room just for ourselves in the hospital? Adela can rest here, and doesn't have to hear the other children crying or their parents talking." Suddenly she started to rock the baby and sing to her, too forcefully, as though she had lost her wits.

The three men looked at her worriedly. Pereira left the room to find a nurse.

Catalina looked upset when the nurse came into the room, and she held her baby close to her.

"I'm just going to examine the child," the nurse said as she reached for the baby in Catalina's arms, looking to put her in the crib.

"She's better off with me." Catalina tried to keep hold of her.

"As soon as I've had a look at her … I need to check that her temperature hasn't gone up … She's still finding it hard to breathe. I'll tell Dr. Naseef, who's on duty today."

The nurse took Adela's temperature and checked the pulse on her tiny arm. Then she left the room.

Catalina carried on rocking her child, worried about the intense heat that radiated from her sick little body.

"I'll look for Marvin, and I swear I'll find him. I know that he'll look after me and Adela. He can't refuse when he sees me," she insisted.

They didn't contradict her. Neither did Captain Pereira. They just looked at one another.

Dr. Naseef came into the room without trying to hide his anger.

"Visiting hours are over. You have to respect the rules, just like everyone else here. So get out."

Then he started to examine the child, worry etching itself onto his face.

Captain Pereira, Eulogio and Fernando waited until the doctor came out of the room. They wouldn't leave without knowing how Adela was.

The doctor came out and stopped dead when he saw them.

"It's a miracle that she's lasted as long as she has, but I don't think she'll make it through the night. Her temperature's gone up and she's finding it hard to breathe. The nurse will give her a shot. She's in God's hands now …"

"You're a doctor, not a priest, and so don't leave things that are your job up to the Lord to handle." Fernando spoke angrily.

Captain Pereira held his arm hard to stop him from getting carried away. He understood his desperation, but he wouldn't achieve anything forcing a confrontation with the doctor like this.

"I've spent years fighting against disease, and yes, sadly I have lost many battles. But yes, in some of these battles that seemed impossible, there have been miracles. You don't have to believe me, but I hope God will grant us a miracle this time."

He turned and left, leaving the three men mulling over his words.

"Ylena says that Dr. Naseef is a very religious Copt," Eulogio said.

"God is everyone's personal business," Pereira replied. "You have to be aware of His presence ... But I've only seen His absence ... We can't blame Dr. Naseef for anything, anyway. I know him, he's a good doctor and a good man. Adela is in the best possible hands. If he can't save her, then no one can."

They left the hospital. Fernando and Eulogio were exhausted by what had been a very intense day; Pereira was haunted by the pall of death that was hovering around Adela.

None of the three slept well that night. The captain couldn't stop thinking about that day, not so long ago, that he had assisted Doc at Adela's birth, and the feeling of holding her in his arms, as if she was already dead.

The next day, Fernando got up early and went back to the hospital. Catalina was asleep next to her daughter's crib. He walked up to her slowly and looked at her, aware of how much she had changed. Catalina's face was tense, with fine lines of suffering etched around her mouth. She must have sensed his presence, because she opened her eyes and leaned, worried, over her child to see if she was still breathing. She gave a sigh of relief.

"I must have fallen asleep," she apologized.

"I'm not surprised, you must be exhausted. If you think it's a good idea, let me stay with you tonight and look after Adela, so that you can get some sleep."

"You think I can sleep while my daughter is fighting for her life?"

"She won't be alone, I'll be with her."

"But you're not her father, and a sick little girl should be with her parents, who are the people who know better than anyone what she needs. If Marvin came ... but I wouldn't even leave her alone with him."

Fernando felt a sharp pain in his stomach to hear Catalina speak. But he said nothing.

The nurse came in, treading softly, and was surprised to see Fernando there at such an early hour. She went over to the child and took her temperature. Then she wiped Adela's body with a warm washcloth.

"Her temperature's down … that's a good sign."

"But she's still throwing up, and can't keep the milk down."

"The doctor says not to force her. It's better to give her a bit of whey and some sugar water."

"She's so weak …"

"Don't despair … Adela really wants to live … I've never seen a two-month premature baby survive pneumonia, and look at her, she's fighting so ferociously," the nurse said.

"Will the doctor come?"

"He's not in yet, but he'll come to see you when he is. The duty doctor will stop by first."

When they were alone, Catalina smiled at Fernando and squeezed his hand affectionately, then moved over to him and gave him a hug. She let him put her arms around her and felt how strong he was.

"I don't know what I'd do without you," she said as she kissed him on the cheek.

"You don't need me, Catalina. You're strong, stronger than you think."

"I'm not, if you only knew … But I can't let myself give in, there's Adela to think of. Tell me, is there any news? Is it true that Marvin's going to leave, like you said yesterday?"

"Marvin is going to leave, along with the woman he's living with. We told you."

"Will he come back?"

"I don't know."

"Where are they going?"

"I don't know that either … Maybe back to his country. You know that America's joined the war."

"Damn wars! I hope he won't be stupid enough to join the war and fight."

"Who knows …"

"And this woman, who is she?"

"Farida? She's a philosopher, very prestigious in Alexandria. She writes books."

"Right … a philosopher … Does he love her?"

"Yes … But I can't answer that question."

"Who can I ask, if not you? Fernando, are you sure they're going to leave?"

"That's what they said."

"So what are we going to do?"

"For the time being, work. We need money. When I have enough, if you'd like me to, I'll buy you a ticket back to Spain. Maybe your father will calm down a bit when he sees Adela."

"And you? Are you going to go back?"

"I can't, Catalina, you know I can't. I killed those men. I don't know if they're looking for me … I'll never go back."

"Are you going to stay in Alexandria?"

"I don't know. Well, I know that I'll be with you and go with you wherever you want besides Spain. We don't have any choice at the moment other than to stay in Alexandria. It was foolish to come, but it would be worse to leave now that Adela is sick. And the war is spreading everywhere."

"You said you were going to find some work …"

"Yes, Mr. Wilson has got me working for his publishing house … That'll help us to keep a roof over our heads. Ylena is very generous, but we can't live in her house forever without paying. Eulogio's found a job as well. He's going to help a builder, a man who is sick and needs someone to take him around."

"So Eulogio's going to stay as well."

"It's a temporary job so he doesn't have to sit around while he waits to finally leave. You know that he came on this journey so he could get to America, and Marvin is going to help him."

"Life is so odd, Fernando … Here we are, the three of us, in a foreign city, where nothing holds us together. We're going to have to learn to survive."

"And we will survive."

"I'm not going back to Spain either. When Adela is better, I'll go find Marvin, and if he has left Alexandria by then, I'll go find him wherever he is. I'll get to him. I'll go all the way to America if I have to."

"Don't think about that now."

Sara was dusting the books when Fernando came in. She told him to go to her husband's office, which was on the first floor. Akim went with him. There was a door in the bookshop that opened onto a hallway where, to Fernando's surprise, the little publishing house could be found. Two men were working at a single table, another one a little further away was absorbed in his work with a manuscript, and at the end of the hallway, a small room with a half-glass wall housed the printing press. It was a modern machine, not a large one, but the best that money could buy.

Three men were walking around it. A staircase in the far corner led up to the second floor, where Benjamin Wilson had his office.

It was more than just an office: there was a waiting room and a meeting room, as well as a little kitchen and a reception desk where a middle-aged woman, her chestnut hair twisted up in a bun, was typing.

The woman smiled at him and stood up. Fernando was surprised by how firm her handshake was. "I'm Leyda Zabat, Mr. Wilson's secretary. He's waiting for you. Thank you for bringing him up, Akim," she said, dismissing the young man.

The office smelled of pipe smoke and beeswax. The mahogany furniture was all British, obviously, as were the hunting scenes that hung on the walls. One picture, behind the desk, stood out from the others. It was a portrait of a middle-aged man who looked astonishingly like Mr. Wilson. Fernando couldn't take his eyes off it as the pair of them shook hands.

"My grandfather," Benjamin said, looking at the painting.

"You look very like him ..."

"Yes ... I'm proud of the resemblance."

Wilson invited him to sit while he looked at him, taking the measure of the young man. He thought that Fernando had some of the qualities he needed, but was also deeply inexperienced.

"Did your friend Marvin explain what the work would be, if we manage to come to an agreement?"

"He said that I would be an editorial assistant."

"Do you think that you're ready for this kind of work?"

Fernando paused before replying.

"I can try, at the very least. Like I said yesterday, my father was an editor, and I watched him do his job. But I'd be lying if I said that I'd worked at all as an editor before today. When the war ended, I found a job in a print shop. The owner knew my father. They published books that he had translated. I know what printing and editing involve, but I don't think I'd dare claim to be an editor."

Wilson liked Fernando's sincerity, although he thought that the boy was almost too honest, bordering on ingenuous. But the boy's father had obviously instilled values that would remain with him forever.

"Our editorial assistant has just gotten married and is going to move to Cairo, where his wife's father has a good business. So the job is available. Let's try it for a month, and we can see if you'll stay on after that. I do recommend that if you are going to stay in this city for any length of time, you should start to study Arabic. Alexandria may be a Babel, but Arabic is essential."

"I'll do it, Mr. Wilson."

The salary was better than he had thought, so Fernando accepted the job without hesitation.

Benjamin Wilson invited him to get to work at once. He was to follow the orders of the editor, a man called Athanasius Vryzas. The man was very old, or so it seemed to Fernando. He had been a literature teacher, and he loved poetry above all things. He had been the editor for Wilson & Wilson in Alexandria for many years, and he had a good eye for discovering new talent. Benjamin Wilson trusted him, and occasionally brought him on business trips to London.

Vryzas greeted Fernando pleasantly and set him to read through some manuscripts that were waiting in the pile. There were four poetry collections.

"Read them carefully, and write a report on each of them. Don't be afraid to say what you think. We're very strict here when it comes to quality."

By evening, he had read the four poetry books and written the reports, which he left on Vryzas' desk; the editor had left a little while earlier. He was surprised by the number of people who visited the publishing house; they came to browse through the books, or to try to convince the editor to publish one of their manuscripts, or to see Mr. Wilson, who had spent the whole day in his office.

When he left Wilson & Wilson, he was in a better mood than before, and if he had not missed his mother so much, then he might almost have felt at ease in this surprising city.

Eulogio was waiting impatiently for him at Madame Kokkalis' house. Dimitra reminded them that punctuality was extremely important to her mistress, and that she was waiting for them in the dining room along with Colonel Sanders and Monsieur Baudin.

They spoke to their fellow lodgers and found out that Ylena and Monsieur Baudin had both been to the hospital, and that Adela had shown slight but noticeable signs of improvement. Dr. Naseef wouldn't say that she was out of the woods yet, as he didn't want to give them any false hope, but the girl was still alive, in spite of his proclamation that she wouldn't last the night.

Fernando and Eulogio ate well. The two friends wanted to be alone so they could talk about their day, and as soon as they had finished eating, they went off with Monsieur Baudin and Mr. Sanders to the library. Every night they would go there to smoke a cigar, drink a glass of port and, if they felt like it, play a game of chess. Ylena would usually come and talk with them for a while as well. She liked to smoke too.

Sanders was explaining the powerful enemy that the Allies had in Erwin Rommel.

"He's not just clever, he's talented, you have to admit it. And I've spent my life in the army," the colonel said as he took a drag on his cigar.

"Do you think Churchill was right to swap General Archibald Wavell for General Claude Auchinleck?" Monsieur Baudin asked.

"Of course, my friend. Who stopped them in Tobruk? It wasn't easy to stop Rommel."

"Rommel's coming for Egypt," Ylena said.

"Don't worry, we won't let him get here, Auchinleck knows what to do," Colonel Sanders replied.

"The Germans have a great many friends in the court; even, they say, King Farouk," Monsieur Baudin said.

"No country wants to answer to another country, and the British have spent too long doing whatever they want in Egypt," Ylena said again.

"Would you prefer them to be under the Germans' heel?" Colonel Sanders asked.

"I'm an Alexandrian, but I'm also a Greek, and my ancestors came here with Alexander, when he founded the city ... So many armies have passed through here wanting to take control ... But to answer your question: of course I wouldn't like Germany to take control of Egypt. I shudder when I turn the radio on and hear Hitler's voice ... that man is taking war to every corner of the world, and I hate his ideas about the superiority of the Aryan race. But you know that, Colonel, or else you wouldn't be living in my house."

They laughed and Ylena filled their glasses again.

"Of course, we have to be more afraid of the Germans than the Italians ..." Monsieur Baudin said.

"There's no such thing as a small enemy, my friend," Colonel Sanders said. "You know we lost the *Neptune* in the Gulf of Sirte yesterday. It's not official yet, so not a word to anyone."

For Eulogio, things were working out better than he had thought they would. Sudi Kamel, the builder Farida knew, was an older man: too old, Eulogio thought, to go running around from place to place without stopping.

He had lost his only son, who was going to inherit his business. He had two married daughters with well-positioned husbands: both were officials in the court of King Farouk and lived in Cairo. They showed no interest in moving away from the center of power to manage a business they knew nothing about. And so Sudi Kamel felt he had to keep working until the end of his days; as he explained to Eulogio, lots of his family members depended on the continued success of his business. He also hoped that one of his grandchildren – presently all teenagers – might, when they reached adulthood, start to take an interest in the family business.

Eulogio's job was simply to travel with him and help him do whatever he needed. It was a job that he could easily do, given that his new boss – just as Farida had said – spoke Spanish as well as French.

It was cold that night. December made its presence known in Alexandria. Fernando thought that it would soon be Christmas, and he was overcome by a flood of nostalgia. He'd had very little time to think since they had fled Spain. Survival was their principal aim, and to survive, he'd had to put all memories of why they were there to one side.

"I'll get up early tomorrow to go to see Catalina before work," he said.

"I'll go with you. Mr. Sudi asked me to go and pick him up at ten o'clock, so there's time to visit the hospital before then."

"Catalina will be pleased to see you."

"I think the only person she wants to see is Marvin."

"He has to be honest with her," Fernando said.

"We can't blame him. Catalina means nothing to him now."

"But he's the father of her child and she deserves an explanation even if it's just to say that he doesn't love her and that he won't look after her and her child."

"Fernando, don't be unfair to Marvin. He's got his reasons and he's been through a lot. At least he has Farida now. I think that she's the only person who can save him from his ghosts."

"I feel like such an idiot when I talk to her. She knows so much ... and she seems to be reading your mind when you talk to her. I wonder why Marvin is with her ... she's so much older than him."

"We all have our reasons for the things that we do, even when we're mistaken," Eulogio said, looking into the smoke that trailed from his cigarette.

That night was December 18, 1941. As the two friends talked, a group of Italian sailors from the Decima Flottiglia MAS was preparing to attack the British at the port of Alexandria. Under the command of Marquis Luigi Durand de la Penne, the men slipped in on the submarine Scirè on a mission to blow up the British boats in the harbor at Alexandria. The Italian sailors, piloting three manned torpedoes, were to plant explosives on the two docked British battleships, the *HMS Valiant* and the *HMS Queen Elizabeth*. The time planned for the explosion was six o'clock in the morning.

Alexandria's residents, blissfully ignorant, went to bed convinced that the next day would be the same as the day before.

The explosion woke the whole city. Catalina was frightened,

and Adela, even though she barely had the strength to breathe, began to wail.

Ylena woke up with a start and, throwing on a robe, left her room. She bumped into Colonel Sanders, who had also been woken up by the explosion.

A few minutes later, Monsieur Baudin, Fernando, Eulogio, and the two maids emerged. Ilora, who did most of the cooking, was trembling with fear; Dimitra, despite the early hour, offered to go out into the street to see what was going on. But Colonel Sanders asked her to bring him a pencil and paper first. He wanted to note down the sequence of the explosions, jotting down that the first had taken place at 05:45 on the morning of December 19. Monsieur Baudin kept asking what could have happened.

And what had happened? Three hours previously, the three manned torpedoes, each carrying three men, had carefully moved into position at the entrance to the port. At first, they had been unable to enter because of the metallic net installed by the British to help protect their ships. But luck had been on their side, because the barrier had been lifted unexpectedly to allow some other ships to enter. Once inside, the Italian torpedoes had put their explosive charges on the *Queen Elizabeth* and a Norwegian petrol tanker, the *Sagona*. Luck never lasts, though; the submersible carrying the mission's commander, Luigi Durand de la Penne, got stuck in the *Valiant*'s mooring cables. The marquis had to take the explosive out of the torpedo and attach it manually to the ship. When the frogmen finished and headed to the surface, they were discovered by a watchman on the *Valiant*.

The city was starting to wake up, and Admiral Andrew Cunningham listened in shock to the news that two Italians had been picked up by the *Valiant*. His crew informed him that the men refused to say anything more than their name and rank.

It wasn't until hours later, thanks to Ylena's contacts and Colonel Sanders' sources among Admiral Cunningham's officers, that they found out that the first explosion had been the *Sagona*, and that the explosion had damaged the destroyer *Jervis*, which was anchored next to it. A little later, a second explosion blew up the *Valiant*, and a few minutes later, the *Queen Elizabeth* suffered the same fate.

The British captured the Italian commandos, but the damage had been done. However, thanks to the shallowness of the harbor, the boats could be re-floated.

But these details, along with many others, would not be known to Alexandria's people until much later. That day, Admiral Cunningham's most important task was to make sure that neither the Italians nor the Germans knew for certain what had happened; they couldn't know the catastrophe that the loss of the boats implied. He also needed to make sure that the news didn't reach London, whose citizens were suffering under the constant bombardment of the Luftwaffe. Of course, it was one thing to keep the details under wraps, and quite another to pretend that nothing had happened. The city had been awoken by a huge explosion, and everyone knew someone who had an explanation.

Fernando and Eulogio hurried to the hospital. Catalina was worried. But no matter how many times she asked them, they had no news about what had happened, because neither Ylena nor Colonel Sanders had left the house yet to ask their friends about the events.

Dr. Naseef was in the room, his face showing his confusion. He couldn't answer Catalina's questions either. He had heard the explosions, but knew nothing of what might have caused them.

He looked at the baby and his expression became worried once again.

Fernando followed him out of the room. He wanted to know if Adela would live.

"It's a miracle that's she's still alive, but I don't know how much longer she'll last. She's not getting better, but she's not getting worse either. You should know that I'm concerned about Catalina too; she's very weak and must have lost a lot of blood in the birth. And she's alone in the room all the time … The nurses keep an eye on her, but all this suffering is taking its toll … If you could find the child's father … she needs that to happen."

He looked at Fernando, waiting for a reply that didn't come. He left quickly.

When Fernando went back into the room, he found Eulogio and Catalina arguing.

"What's going on?"

Catalina looked at him in fury, but her expression immediately turned to one of despair.

"You betrayed me! You brought me to Alexandria and told me that Marvin was here! And now you're refusing to help me see him. You just wanted me to help you escape! You needed the pistol to kill those two men, and my money to help you get away!"

"How can you say that? You know it's not true!" Fernando felt Catalina's words stab like a knife in his gut.

"Of course it's true! You don't care what happens to me! Look at my daughter ... born too soon. I put myself in danger, thinking that we might find her father. You cheated me! You only wanted to get revenge for your father and you, Eulogio, you wanted to run away because you were ashamed of your mother ... You're a pair of rats!" Catalina burst into tears, frightening Adela, who started to wriggle and wail.

"If that's what you think ... don't worry, we'll save up to buy you a ticket back to Spain. And as for Marvin ... why can't you accept that he doesn't want to see you?" Fernando's voice was filled with rage and pain.

Eulogio looked from one to the other without knowing what to say or do in the face of Catalina's despair and Fernando's anger at Catalina's words.

"You don't want me to find him. My mother said that you were in love with me ... the whole neighborhood said it ... I pretended not to notice, because you are like a brother to me, but they were right. You've taken advantage of me and now you're getting in the way of me finding Marvin."

Her rage and the anger in the room were so great that Fernando had to leave, slamming the door behind him. He didn't want to hold back his tears. Suddenly, he felt the full weight of all that had happened since the evening when he had killed the two men responsible for his father's death. The men who stalked his dreams every night.

He didn't want to think that he'd committed a murder. Every time the two men's faces surfaced in the blur of his thoughts, he immediately pushed them aside because he had no time to think about anything but survival ... running ... the train ... the storm at sea ... Adela's birth ... reaching an unfamiliar city with no money to pay their way ... the child's sickness ... But suddenly, all that had happened opened the floodgates of unbearable pain. Catalina had forced him to face the ghost inside him: the ghost of the murderer.

Eulogio looked Catalina up and down, and she could see that his gaze was filled with spite.

"You're right, it's thanks to your money that we're here. And thanks to your pistol that Fernando was able to kill those two bastards. We've used you? Right, because you've used us just as much. You wanted to escape from Antoñito and not have to admit that you were pregnant. What would he have said? What would your friends have said? Catalina Vilamar, knocked up! You ran away from shame and scandal. And yes, you wanted to find Marvin, but most of all, you didn't want to be pointed at in the street. And so you helped us and we helped you. You're right about one thing: Fernando loves you, but you don't deserve it. And now I'm leaving. As for Marvin, he never loved you, he doesn't love you and he will never love you. He's happy with the woman he's with, happy like he's never been before. You mean nothing to him. Let me say that if I feel sorry for anyone here, it's Adela. She doesn't deserve to have a mother as stupid as you."

He left the room without looking back, overcome by his rage. He swore to himself that he would never see her again.

Search as he might, Eulogio couldn't find Fernando in the hospital. He had obviously gone straight to work, and he had to go as well. He felt a stab of despair and asked himself what he was doing in Alexandria. He took the tram to get to work on time. Sudi Kamel seemed to be a nice man, but he was a stickler for punctuality.

Athanasius Vryzas greeted Fernando with a wave and then turned back to the manuscript he was reading. There were still traces of tears on Fernando's face, and a tremor in his upper lip showed that all was still not well.

All the employees at Wilson & Wilson murmured about the explosion that had taken place that morning. They claimed to know what it was, although what they said was really nothing more than rumor and conjecture. Sara tried to calm their fears by telling them to wait until the authorities released a statement, but it was difficult for them not to talk about the hellish boom that had roused them from their sleep and terrified them.

Fernando heard Akim, Sara's right-hand man in the bookshop, say that lots of people thought that Rommel had defeated the British and taken the city.

Sara smiled at the rumors.

"Rommel's not going to take Alexandria," she said bluntly.

"He took Cyrenaica ..." Akim said.

"This isn't Cyrenaica, which was already in the hands of the Italians. The British Army won't let itself lose Egypt, you'll see," she said.

"You know ..." Akim fell silent, afraid of what he had been about to say.

"Akim, yes, I know what you were going to say. Yes, I know that a lot of Egyptians are fed up with the British and are sympathetic towards the Germans because they think they'll help them get their own country back. If Rommel wins here, we'll be regretting it soon enough. I assure you that you would be the loser if that happened."

"All we Egyptians want is to rule ourselves," Akim said, not without a certain pride.

"I understand that, I promise you I do. But the way to do that is not to fall into the arms of the Germans."

Fernando listened to this conversation and others without really paying attention. He felt too sad. But he wasn't expecting Benjamin Wilson to turn up and ask Vryzas for a manuscript that he couldn't find.

The bookshop owner could see how upset Fernando was, sitting with his nose buried in his papers, barely managing a grunted, "hello." He was worried about the young man's mental state. So he spent a large part of the morning and the afternoon investigating the man who had arrived in Alexandria with nothing more than his acquaintance with Marvin Brian to recommend him.

The first thing he did was ask Marvin to meet him at the Hotel Cecil, a favorite spot among the city's British residents, a luxurious place that served the best dry martinis in all of Alexandria. The most exclusive parties were held in its ballroom, and select groups of the greatest men in the city met in its bar. So too did Armenian businessmen, Frenchmen, Jews, Greeks, and spies for all the foreign powers, as well as bored married women and Egyptians from good families.

Marvin arrived on time, concerned that Benjamin Wilson had insisted on seeing him so soon. Wilson was already sitting in a discreet corner of the bar, and he waved Marvin over when he arrived.

"Tell me everything you know about Fernando Garzo," he said bluntly.

Marvin told him all he knew. He replied to Wilson's brief questions for quite some time, not understanding why even the most trivial details seemed to interest him. He couldn't say much about Fernando, apart from the fact that he knew him to be an honest man, the son of a Republican who had fought in the war. But Wilson didn't think that Marvin's information was enough, so Marvin had to admit that Eulogio would be the best person to provide information about Fernando, since they had known each other all their lives. Their parents had been friends and had even worked for the same publishing house.

And so Benjamin Wilson had to wait until midafternoon, when his friend the builder Sudi Kamel no longer needed the services of the Spaniard. He asked Eulogio to meet him at his house.

Eulogio was a little surprised by the invitation, and turned up thinking that something serious must have happened. But Benjamin Wilson met him with friendly politeness and spoke with him about Spain for a long while. Without realizing it, Eulogio began to tell him not just about the present political situation, with Franco becoming a military dictator, but also the troubles of the war. He spoke about his father, his mother, his family, his neighbors and, of course, Fernando. Wilson listened quietly, interjecting a brief question from time to time to encourage him to continue. Eulogio bared his soul. He told him everything, apart from the fact that his mother had gone to bed with Don Antonio, and that Fernando had fled the country after having killed two men. But he didn't need to say everything, because Benjamin Wilson guessed that there were shadows in his tale that Eulogio didn't want to reveal. He would have to find out the rest of the truth himself.

In any case, by the time night fell in Alexandria, Wilson had gathered a rich trove of information, and had spoken to friends of friends who could make enquiries and find out more about Fernando Garzo and Eulogio Jiménez.

While all this was happening, Fernando worked until Athanasius Vryzas told him to go home.

"You've been at your desk all day: you haven't even had lunch. Did you put together the two reports I asked for?"

"Here they are." Fernando handed him a few well-organized pieces of paper.

"You're doing good work: the reports on the books of poetry yesterday, and then two more today … You need to do the reports on the essay on Neoplatonism and the book by that young woman on the early Christians …"

"I'm reading them now. I hope to have them finished tomorrow."

"And what about the books of poetry? Which one of them do you think we should publish? We'll be meeting with Mr. Wilson tomorrow, and he'll want to hear what we have to say."

"I liked Omar Basir's the best."

"Yes … you've got a good eye for these things. Basir writes in English and hopes that we'll publish his poems, but I think they lose the musicality that they have in Arabic. He's one of the most promising young men here. Well … enough for today. Go and rest."

The cold air of December hit him as he left the office. Sara had gone home a while earlier, and Akim was closing up the shop.

He didn't want to go back to Ylena's house. The only thing he wanted to do was disappear, to lose himself in the furthest corner of the world.

He walked for two hours without paying any attention to where he was going. A sudden shower of rain brought him back to himself.

He wasn't hungry, and didn't want to speak to anyone, so he went back to the room he shared with Eulogio and Catalina. Captain Pereira's loud voice stopped him in his tracks.

"About time … I thought you must have gotten lost." With a single glance, Pereira could see that Fernando was suffering.

Ylena appeared behind the captain, with Dimitra accompanying her.

"You've missed supper," she said, in a voice that was more severe than she herself felt.

"Don't worry, I'm not hungry. I'd like to go to bed."

"Just like that?" the captain asked.

Pereira looked at him so intently that Fernando was afraid that he could read his thoughts.

"Your friend Eulogio didn't look that happy either when he came in. What happened?" the captain insisted.

"Eulogio at least came back in time to eat something," Ylena said.

"I saved you a bit of stew and some pudding," Dimitra said, ignoring Ylena's icy glare.

"Thanks for your kindness, but I really would like to go to sleep now." Fernando wanted to be alone, and the attention of these well-meaning people was starting to upset him.

Eulogio opened the door, surprised by the noise of conversation.

"There you are … I was worried," he said when he saw Fernando.

"I stayed at work late, and then I went for a walk. I needed to get some air," he said apologetically.

"Eulogio told us that Catalina is all right and that the baby isn't getting worse," the captain interrupted.

"I thought about asking Dr. Naseef if the two of them could come here for Christmas. The captain will be eating with us, which is another cause for celebration. It's been a long time since he's spent Christmas here with us." Ylena seemed truly happy.

"Well, I wasn't intending to, but my ship was damaged by the explosion, and so I have to stay until the repairs are done."

"Christmas …" Fernando said.

"Yes, Christmas. There are only two ways to spend Christmas when you're alone: you can either get so drunk you don't care, or else fight back the nostalgia with good friends. This year I'm choosing the latter, and I think you'll be doing the same," Pereira declared.

Ylena and the captain didn't insist that Fernando join them

and chat for a while before going to sleep. The anger on his face was so clear that they swapped a glance and agreed silently that it would be better to leave the two friends alone.

Once the door to the room was shut, Eulogio spoke to Fernando. The two friends brought each other up to date and spoke openly for a while.

"How strange that Mr. Wilson should invite you to his house ..." Fernando said.

"Yes, but I don't really know what he wanted. He seemed interested in hearing things about Spain. As for Catalina ... I know that I was a little rude to her, but I couldn't stand to see how unfair she was being to you. She doesn't deserve you, Fernando."

"You've never liked her."

"It's not that ... I'd started to like her more. She was very brave on the journey over here. But to accuse us of taking advantage of her ... I can't sit and take that. You should forget her. You have to accept that she ..." Eulogio fell silent, trying not to cause his friend any more pain.

"That she'll never love me. Say it. It's not going to hurt me. I'm not stupid."

"No, but I think that deep down you still think she's going to forget Marvin."

"I don't know if I've got any hope that that'll happen ... but I know that I love her and that I love her so much that in spite of the pain she causes me, I can't stop loving her. I am stupid, after all."

"You heard Ylena, she wants Catalina to come back here for Christmas ... It was Captain Pereira who encouraged her to talk to Dr. Naseef."

Fernando shrugged. He hadn't stopped thinking all day about the two men he'd killed. He asked himself how it was possible for the murder to take up so much space in his head. He needed to think about it, to dig into his memories, to know if his awakening conscience would start to cause him more pain.

He got into bed and closed his eyes, constantly replaying the moment when he had shot those men and taken their lives in revenge for his father's. He didn't sleep until dawn was already breaking. Eulogio had to wake him up.

"You're going to be late. Hurry up. Dimitra has knocked several times already. She's worried because you didn't eat last night, and now you're going to go to work without having breakfast."

It was December 24, 1941. Catalina saw the clouds passing among the stars. She shuddered as she held Adela tight, asleep in her arms.

Captain Pereira had spent most of the afternoon with her, and Ylena had been there in the morning. She had been upset that Dr. Naseef had not allowed her to leave the hospital to spend Christmas Eve at home. He was a very strict doctor and didn't want the child to leave the hospital, even though she was slowly getting better.

Catalina hadn't dared ask Ylena or the captain about Fernando or Eulogio. They hadn't said anything about the two men either.

They hadn't come back since the morning when she had blamed them for her bad luck. She didn't regret her words. She was sorry for the pain she had caused them, but she was convinced that she was largely in the right, although she knew that she had come to Alexandria of her own volition. Perhaps Eulogio had been right and she had run away from the shame of having to admit to being a single mother in front of her friends and family. But even so, she said to herself that she loved Marvin, and that she wouldn't fail in her quest to find him and make him accept his responsibilities towards his daughter.

Of course, she couldn't stop thinking about what Eulogio had said, that Marvin didn't love her and that he was in love with another woman. She couldn't believe it. She was sure that she was very important to Marvin, but even if that weren't the case, then he would have no choice but to accept his responsibility for Adela. The baby had nothing to do with her feelings or Marvin's, and she had a right to both a father and a mother. Yes, they would be a family, and even if Marvin didn't love her as she wished, he would end up loving her because of Adela. He wouldn't be the first husband to become a good husband and father out of a sense of duty. Her father had been right: a good marriage is not based on feelings, but rather on reason and mutual benefit. It made sense that her mother thought that love wasn't the most important thing in the world.

She had never thought about it, but she suddenly thought that perhaps her mother had not received enough love. For her, reason and mutual benefit were not enough. But Catalina told herself that in this case, given the circumstances, they would be enough. The only thing she wanted was to take little Adela back home with Marvin on her arm as her husband.

Captain Pereira had brought her a box of sweet pastries. She wasn't hungry, but she had eaten a piece of honey-cake with almonds that seemed to her as delicious as it was sticky.

She thought about her parents. She imagined them eating back at home in Huesca, along with her uncle Andrés and his wife, her aunt Amparo, and her grandmother Agustina, her father's mother. Aunt Petra would be there as well. Ever since she had lost her husband, she had spent every Christmas with them.

Suddenly she felt nostalgic for the days when they all gathered around the fire with her two grandmothers cooking the meal.

She had barely known her grandfathers, because they died when she was a child, but her two grandmothers had been present during her childhood. This was especially true of her grandmother Adela, who had lived with them for so many years and who had died only a few months before the end of the war.

She remembered how the two grandmothers had been rivals, and how they had spoiled her to try to win her over to their side of every argument.

She had called her daughter Adela in honor of her grandmother. Suddenly she realized that the child wasn't baptized, and she crossed herself. If Adela didn't survive, she'd end up in limbo, and it would be Catalina's fault. How could she have forgotten something so urgent? She had to speak to Dr. Naseef to get him to allow her to take the child to a church to get her baptized. Or maybe a priest could bring some holy water to the hospital.

Dimitra served them turkey with plums. They had eaten stuffed eggplant to start: one of Ilora's specialties.

Captain Pereira had brought them a few bottles of wine, and was making headway into them along with Colonel Sanders and Monsieur Baudin. Eulogio ate heartily, but Fernando seemed distracted. He couldn't stop thinking about Catalina alone in the hospital, and blamed himself for doing nothing to fix the situation. Eulogio said that if he did go, then they would end up fighting, because Catalina was that stubborn.

He also thought of his mother. He thought that she would be alone, thinking about him. She would be crying. He suddenly regretted having left only a note to say goodbye, and not having been honest with her. He knew that he would have caused her a huge amount of pain if he had confessed to her how he had killed his father's killers. She would have been frightened and she would have scolded him, but even murder couldn't ruin the relationship between them. His mother had never failed him. If only he could write to her ... but he knew he should not. He didn't know if he was a suspect in the murder of the prison guard and his son the soldier, but if he were, then sending a letter home would be tantamount to turning himself in. And his mother would not be able to cope with that. She would not be able to bear seeing him in prison and then shot.

His mother might think that he had run away with Catalina. It was impossible that there wouldn't be hundreds of rumors in the neighborhood about the three of them.

"Do you like the turkey?" Ylena interrupted his thoughts.

"Yes ... of course ... it's lovely ... I'm just not very hungry," Fernando apologized.

"Something's up ... Young people are always hungry," Captain Pereira said, looking fixedly at him.

"I'm tired, that's all ... So many things have happened ..." Fernando replied.

"Everything is so new for us ... It's not easy to pitch up in a city like this, so far away. From home ... We've been lucky, but it's difficult for us to adapt," Eulogio said, trying to draw attention away from his friend.

"Are you going to stay long in Alexandria?" Mr. Sanders asked.

"I want to go to America as soon as possible, but I don't

know if it'll be possible now that America has entered the war. I'm waiting to see what Marvin Brian says, but while I'm waiting, Sudi Kamel is a more than an acceptable boss to work for. I'm surprised he has so much energy, at his age," Eulogio said.

"Do they know anything else about the explosion at the port?" Ylena said, looking at Mr. Sanders.

The Englishman shifted uncomfortably in his seat and took a sip of wine before answering his hostess.

"Nothing that you don't know already. If there's anyone who's well-informed in Alexandria, then it must be you."

Ylena smiled. The colonel was right; she had very good information about what had happened. She also knew that Sanders wouldn't say a word more than was necessary. He was very discreet.

"There are secrets that can't be kept," Pereira said. "I saw the explosion; I was in my boat at the time. And although the authorities try to stop people talking about what happened, it's an open secret that some Italian frogmen got into the harbor and that they are now under arrest. Here's a toast to their failure." The captain raised his glass.

"And what about Rommel?" Monsieur Baudin asked.

"He's still wandering around the desert, absolutely in control," Ylena said, with a little *moue* of irritation.

"They say that Churchill is worried," Monsieur Baudin said, looking at Mr. Sanders.

"Our prime minister is intelligent and knows that there's no point in underestimating one's enemy. It would be stupid not to be aware that Erwin Rommel is a good soldier," the colonel replied.

"Rommel might be a good soldier, but his boss isn't. Invading the Soviet Union might be the stupidest idea that's ever occurred to anyone. I think that the Japanese attack on Pearl Harbor, forcing the Americans to enter the war, might be decisive as well, in preventing Hitler from getting what he wants," Pereira declared.

"You're right, captain, Hitler has put his head into the lion's jaws by provoking Russia, and the Japanese have done the same by provoking the Americans," Mr. Sanders said.

The talk about the war stretched on into the night. Fernando and Eulogio listened attentively to these men who seemed to have everything that was happening right at their fingertips. The war in Spain seemed to be very distant to them, now that the world was so full of other battles.

A week later, on New Year's Eve, Leyda Zabat, Mr. Wilson's secretary, asked Fernando to go up to his boss' office.

"Is anything wrong, Leyda?" he asked in surprise.

"I don't think so ... it's just that Mr. Wilson wants to see you."

They hadn't seen Wilson for days. It was said that he had left Egypt; this surprised no one, as his absences were frequent. Sara could run the business without seeming to need her husband. The employees respected her good taste and judgment, and books held no secrets for her.

Benjamin Wilson seemed absorbed in some papers when Leyda opened the door to his office to tell him that Fernando Garzo was waiting outside.

"Thank you Leyda. Send him in."

Fernando smoothed down his shirt and came in, slightly worried. He spoke to Sara every day, but he had only met with Wilson a couple of times.

They looked at each other: Fernando realized he was measuring his words, but he didn't know why.

"Sit down," Wilson said.

As he did so, Mr. Wilson passed him a folder with some papers that he asked him to read.

Fernando opened the folder and was surprised to see the heading on the first page.

RESULTS OF THE INVESTIGATION INTO FERNANDO GARZO, EULOGIO JIMÉNEZ AND CATALINA VILAMAR

He looked up, defiantly, at Mr. Wilson.

"Read it," his boss said, without a trace of bashfulness.

The papers contained accurate information about Catalina, Eulogio and him: who they were, who their parents were, the effect that the Civil War had had on their families; Catalina was the daughter of victors, and Fernando and Eulogio's families had been on the losing side. There were also copies of Fernando's and Eulogio's fathers' respective death certificates: one of them shot in prison and the other dead at the front, as well as the suggestion that Fernando's father was a Freemason, and the work he had done before the war. Fernando was shocked to see the details of Piedad's relationship with Don Antonio García, and Catalina's engagement to Antoñito … and the disappearance of the three of them without a trace.

Fernando looked up angrily. He couldn't see why Mr. Wilson had gone into their lives in such detail.

"I can't see why you're investigating us. I don't think you have any right."

"Keep on reading. There's a newspaper cutting you might be interested in."

Fernando found cuttings from several newspapers, with different dates, all with a circle around a particular article: "Uproar in the capital at the murder of Roque Pérez, who fought with great valor at the battle of the Ebro, and his son Saturnino, member of the firing squad at …"; "Two men murdered in Madrid"; "Roque Pérez – former soldier and current jailer at Comendadoras Prison – and his son Saturnino Pérez were killed in cold blood outside the prison last night. Saturnino, as he did every night, was walking his father home when two bullets robbed them of their lives"; "The police suspect that the murder of these two martyrs was the work of a lone gunman"; "The families of the Comendadoras prisoners are being investigated"; "Authorities have promised the widow of Roque Pérez that they will leave no stone unturned in their search for his murderer."

He read every article in the folder, feeling his mouth fill with acid. When he had finished, he closed the folder and handed it back to Benjamin Wilson, who looked at him indifferently.

"Explain all this," Fernando said, with a bravery he didn't feel.

"You came upset to work a few days ago. You remember? It was all you could do not to cry. I was surprised. As you know, I hired you as a favor to Marvin Brian, who was pretty insistent that I give you a job. I have a right to know who's working for me. You and your friends came over on a merchant vessel looking for Marvin not so long ago. That in itself was surprising: three young people get on a boat in Lisbon and brave the waves on a ship that has to dodge German submarines all the way to Alexandria … Why? Are they running away from Franco, or from something else? Well, now I know that you killed those two men."

"Really? How can you accuse me of something like that? There's no name in the papers."

"My man in Madrid is a good investigator. Although you might not believe as much, if you can read the papers properly, then half your work's already done for you. You need to be able to make connections, analyze data, find clues hidden among all the apparently banal pages. Dates are key, and the dates fit with your flight. And your father was in the prison where Roque Pérez was the jailer. As for the son, he was a part of the firing squad that killed him. But don't worry, the police aren't going to draw the same conclusions. To begin with, your mother and Eulogio Jiménez's mother haven't said anything about your disappearance. And as for Catalina Vilamar's parents, they think that she ran away with you to get out of marrying the son of this …" Wilson looked at a paper as he spoke. "This Antonio Sánchez, to whom they owe money. All the adults in this case think that you ran away for other reasons: you to protect Catalina, who you were in love with, Eulogio to get back at his mother and get away from Antonio Sánchez as well."

"But you're accusing us of murder."

"I'm not accusing anyone," Benjamin Wilson said shortly.

"But just because our departure coincides with the death of those two men … it's an absurd argument," Fernando insisted.

"No, it's not, and I'm not going be coy with you about it."

"Well, you're within your rights to think what you want to think. I'll get my things and leave straight away," Fernando said emotionlessly.

"You can't leave."

"Is that so? Why not? I don't have to work here if I don't want to."

"That's right. But you're going to change your job."

"What? I don't understand."

"You're going to carry on working here as an editor, but I will also give you some tasks where you can be more useful."

"And if I don't want to?"

"I don't think it matters what you want, but rather whether or not you can do what I ask."

"Are you blackmailing me?"

Fernando's voice grew angrier, but Mr. Wilson seemed not to notice.

"Blackmail's such an ugly word, don't you think? All I'm doing is offering you a change in your job description that will help both of us, if you really are the kind of man I think you are, despite your youth."

"You think I'm a murderer and you want me to work for you … Are you asking me to commit murders?" Fernando said, ironically

"I'm going to ask you to carry out a task for me and I am sure you will perform it perfectly. But no, I'm not in the business of calling for murders. I hate unnecessary violence. I'm an editor and a bookseller, don't forget."

"And something else as well, I suppose?"

"Well, that's the basic part of my job, but let's just say that there are other sides to the business."

"Which is what you want me to do now … I don't know what you want me to do, but I'm going to say no."

"You shouldn't, Fernando. It won't be in your best interests."

"And so you're trying to blackmail me, assuming that I've got something to do with these murders."

"Enough! I've said I don't want to be coy. There'll be no games here. And now I'm going to tell you a few things, and you will decide what you're going to do. And if you're smart, you'll accept my offer, because I've already exposed myself to a degree of risk in talking to you, and I don't like to take unnecessary risks."

"Are you going to get rid of me if I say no?"

"Are you going to listen to me or not?"

"No. I don't like listening when I don't have a choice."

"All right, have it your way … I'm sorry for your friends."

Fernando got up and was about to leave. But Mr. Wilson's

words were a warning that there would be consequences not just for him, but for Catalina and Eulogio as well. He sat down again.

"I'm listening."

"I know everything about you, but they've probably told you a couple of things about me too. This is a business that I inherited from my grandfather. He brought me up, and I was with him until the day he died. He was an extraordinary man, who had in his turn inherited the business from his father, my great-grandfather. As well as being a bookseller and an editor, he traveled throughout the Middle East and made himself a name in London as a journalist. In his travels he met a lot of very ... interesting people. The Foreign Office asked him to work for them, and he did on various occasions. But it was not just the public side of British diplomacy that saw my grandfather's qualities. Other, more discreet organizations also wanted to make use of his experience and his knowledge. My grandfather knew that the value he had for others was, above all, based on the information that he could provide. Information he got from his analytical ability, that he gathered from people who trusted him, from the relationships that he built up wherever he traveled. He had a talent: he could see things, and hear things, and be quiet about things. And without looking to make it his job, he ended up being the last hope for a number of people who were looking for loved ones who had disappeared. He never wanted to work for the Secret Service, because he was too much in love with his liberty and independence, but his reputation as a well-connected man who knew the Middle East spread throughout the whole of British high society. And so bankers who wanted to know if their interests were in danger, suspicious businessmen, cautious investors, desperate parents looking for a child who had decided to disappear into the Orient ... they all came to my grandfather looking for comfort and information. And this information was worth money. I inherited his business, all of it, and carried on working for Wilson & Wilson. But Wilson & Wilson is, and always has been, a business that buys and sells books. And we have access to information that not even governments can acquire. People come to me in search of this or that, and if I don't know the answer to their questions already, I can find it out. My business is based on trust, and I don't work for just anyone. I have my own code of ethics. For example, there's no way in the world I would sell information, no matter how unimportant or vague, to a German."

Benjamin Wilson stood in silence for a moment, trying to gauge the effect of his words on Fernando. But Fernando sat still, and there was no interest or surprise in his eyes.

"As you may have guessed, I also inherited from my grandfather the friendship and support of a large number of people in the Middle East. But I have expanded the business and have a good number of collaborators in other places as well. I promise you that my Spanish contacts are to be trusted."

"And what does all of this have to do with me?" Fernando said, trying to keep his composure.

"You've only been here a few days, but I think you have certain … qualities."

"I'm not going to be a spy for anyone."

"Spy? No, my business has nothing to do with spying. I've told you. Spies … Alexandria is filled with spies from all over the world. Businessmen who aren't businessmen, seemingly frivolous or naive women … You'll find all kinds here."

"What do you want from me?"

"Something fairly simple. I want you to go to the bar at the Hotel Cecil this evening. It's a major haunt for people who are looking for information. You'll go with a young woman who works for me. All you need to do is sit at the bar and listen."

"I don't understand …"

"Two men will meet in the bar his evening. One of them is a German, and the other is a Spaniard called Pedro López. He passes himself off as a businessman who works with the Germans, but in fact he's one of Franco's agents. He didn't get here that long ago, just a little while before you and your friends. He will have good letters of introduction. He's supposedly here to buy cotton. His contact is Erick Brander, the German I mentioned. He has been here for many years and is married to a woman called Halima Altassan, who is the daughter of an important civil servant. They have two children. Before they came to Alexandria, Brander lived in South America. His mother is Argentine, and his father was in the wool trade. Brander spent his childhood in Argentina until his father decided to move back to Germany. The family settled in Hanover. Brander started to travel to Egypt to buy cotton. He decided to leave his family business and start his own one, exporting cotton and other raw materials, and his marriage to Halima came in very handy for this. It's his shield: not even the British dare touch him."

"Why are you telling me this?"

"Because you'll be wondering who Brander is."

"I don't care," Fernando said, too quickly.

"Of course. But you must care a little about the two men you're going to listen to this evening."

"You care, not me."

"You're right. Anyway, my attention was attracted by the fact that this man seemed to be a little too distant from his country's war. So uninterested, in fact, that it seemed suspicious."

"I'm not going to that bar. I don't need to know anything about your business, and I don't want to either," Fernando said as firmly as he could.

"The woman who will go with you is called Zahra Nadouri. She's a very singular individual: as well as being highly intelligent, she is very skilled at the belly dance. She performs a couple of times a week at a cabaret visited by all the most important men in the city. It's a respectable cabaret; the men who attend usually attend with their wives though of course not always."

"And this extraordinary young woman works for you?" Fernando sounded a little contemptuous.

"Yes, she has her reasons. Anyway, what I'm asking is simple."

"And I don't have any reason to do it," Fernando said.

"Of course you do … not just because I know that you killed two men, but also because your stay in Alexandria has the potential to get very tricky indeed … Marvin Brian could leave at any moment, and take your friend Eulogio with him … And as for you and Catalina … I think you'll stay because you don't have very many choices. Catalina wants to find Marvin, but he won't let that happen, and you don't want him to be found. And taking Adela on another sea voyage would be risky. She might not survive. You need to work, and I've given you a perfect job, just with a few added extras … but nothing that you can't do. And the salary is good."

Fernando felt a deep pain in the pit of his stomach. He suddenly hated this man. He felt cheated by him. He had been manipulated from the start and now he was being blackmailed. And it had all happened so easily.

"You don't have many choices," Wilson reminded him.

"I can always say no," Fernando replied.

"Of course. You decide." And then there was a silence. Wilson's gaze grew so intense that Fernando gave a start.

"Why me?"

"You speak Spanish. There are a lot of languages spoken in Alexandria, but you don't hear much Spanish. Erick Brander knows Spanish, and he will speak in Spanish to Pedro López. All you have to do is sit close to them and listen. You speak English well and know a little French, so there shouldn't be any trouble in getting along with Zahra."

"All I have to do is listen?"

"Yes, just that. Pay attention and listen, and … oh yes … Information is not only gathered from people's words, but also their gestures, expressions, whether or not they are comfortable … Little details, but so revelatory that just seeing them is as good as hearing an entire conversation. As for your friends … You'll understand the need for discretion. Find an excuse for going out tonight. Maybe you can say that I've asked you to show a friend of mine the nightlife. And now I'll call Sara. I think she has something for you. Wait here."

Sara soon came into the room with a package.

Her open, trusting smile disarmed Fernando a little.

"Benjamin asked me to find something for your date this evening. I think this ought to do the trick." She opened the package and took out an elegant jacket.

There was also a shirt, a pair of trousers, and a shiny pair of shoes.

"Yes, it's your size …" Sara said and helped him put the jacket on.

"I'll give it back tomorrow," Fernando said, just to make conversation; the situation had left him in a daze.

"Of course not. Keep it: you never know when you might need it. It's never a bad idea to be well-dressed in Alexandria, especially if you're young and want to get ahead in the world. I don't want to offend you, but I'd like you to come to my house when you have a moment … I'll give you some clothes." Sara looked Fernando in the eye.

He didn't feel offended; it would be hard for Sara to offend anyone. Her openness and her sweetness, as well as her decisiveness, made her a very special woman.

They left Mr. Wilson's office at the same time. His confusion must have been evident to Leyda, but Mr. Wilson's secretary did nothing more than smile goodbye.

Eulogio was lying on his bed with a book.

"You're back early. Sudi Kamel let me go early as well. You know what? I realized today just how ridiculous the work I'm doing is. Sudi Kamel is doing Farida a favor: he's got more than enough people to take him around. We speak in French, but I'm not that much help to him, as I don't understand a word of Arabic. And so here I am, with my books, trying to learn something. Farida gave it to me."

"Right … I think that Marvin knows you too well, and knows that you are proud, and that it would be good for you to do some kind of work while you're here."

"I … Well, I'll go with Marvin and Farida when they head off to America. You know that. This isn't my place, and I must admit that even if I did speak Arabic, I wouldn't want to live here … Everything's not quite right."

"It was your idea to come here in the first place," Fernando said.

"Well, Catalina insisted when she found out where Marvin was."

"We're in a trap, and you can escape from it, even if I can't," Fernando said.

"You know that Marvin would be happy to pay your passage to America … You can't go back to Spain …" Eulogio reminded him.

"And Catalina? Would you leave her here? You know she depends on us."

"Well, on you. I don't know how you put up with her, she's so stubborn."

"It's down to her that we were able to escape. You wanted to get away for one reason and I had another, but she helped us."

"Yes, to help herself," Eulogio reminded him.

"Yes, we all needed each other. But she's the weakest link at the moment. Her daughter is sick and she only wants to speak to Marvin. She's convinced that when they run into one another, all her problems will be solved."

"Marvin doesn't want anything to do with her. You know that. As for Farida … Well, she doesn't think Catalina's a problem. Any other woman in her position would be jealous or upset, but not Farida: she's a very special woman."

Eulogio looked curiously at the package that Fernando had put on the bed. He waited for his friend to tell him what was in it.

"I'm going out this evening. Sara gave me a jacket and a shirt … Wilson has asked me to take a young woman out and show her the town. She's the daughter of some good friends of his."

"And he asked you?" Eulogio said in surprise.

"Well, he asked me to come and have a drink with him and Sara at the Cecil, and I couldn't refuse. She'll come and pick me up to take me over there."

"I never thought that the Wilsons would set themselves up as matchmakers," Eulogio laughed.

"Well, Sara's very motherly … She keeps on asking me if I'm not too lonely, and if I'm eating enough. Yes, it looks a bit like a trap this evening, but I couldn't say no." Fernando felt bad to be lying to Eulogio.

"I hope that she's attractive and that you do Spain proud," Eulogio said, still joking.

"I'm not looking to go out with any girl …"

"Fernando, come on, you've got to start thinking about someone who isn't Catalina. She'll never be the one for you. I know that it hurts you to hear it, but I'm your friend, and I'm not going to say something that isn't true."

Fernando turned away. Eulogio's words hurt him, but he knew he was right. He let his friend get back to studying Arabic while he opened the package and unpacked the clothes.

Eulogio was helping him knot his tie when Dimitra knocked at the door to tell him, with admiration, that Zahra Nadouri was waiting for him in the salon.

Both the maid and Fernando's friend scampered after him as he walked down the hallway. Dimitra couldn't have controlled her curiosity even if she had wanted to, and Eulogio also wanted to meet the young woman who the Wilsons seemingly wanted to set up with Fernando.

Ylena Kokkalis was chatting calmly to the young woman. By the tone of the conversation, it seemed that they knew each other. Ylena introduced them.

"Fernando, this is Miss Nadouri … Zahra, this is Fernando and Eulogio, whom I have the honor of lodging in my house. Dimitra, please make sure that dinner is served at the same time as usual."

Eulogio looked at Zahra more slowly than good manners would normally permit. He didn't think she was particularly attractive. She was of middling height, with reddish-brown hair tied back in a bun, and was neither particularly fat nor particularly thin. Admittedly, her eyes were a surprising dark blue. She was not wearing makeup, and her skin was the color of cinnamon.

They made light small talk for a few minutes until Ylena reminded them that they should get a move on. Fernando thought that maybe his landlady also worked for Benjamin Wilson, because she had seemed surprised by Zahra's presence, and it was clear that they knew one another.

There was a car waiting for them at the door. Fernando got in uncomfortably. He didn't know what to say, and it was Zahra who took control of the conversation, asking him if he liked Alexandria and what he had seen of it. Their conversation was both formal and weightless, but it helped them keep talking as they headed to the Hotel Cecil.

When they entered the bar, a waiter came quickly over to them and guided them to a discreet corner table. Zahra ordered two glasses of champagne.

"Calm down. It won't be hard. All you have to do is listen," she said.

"Who to? The table next to us is empty."

"They'll be here. All you have to do is sit calmly and talk to me."

"And what if they don't come?"

"If Benjamin said that the two men will come tonight, then that's what's going to happen."

"And why are you doing this?"

"I have my reasons."

"Sure ..."

"And you don't have any reasons?"

"To come here and listen to a conversation? No, I wouldn't say that I've got any reason to be here. It's more that circumstances have forced it upon me."

"Look at me and smile, and then take my hand. Your countryman is here."

The waiter guided a man to the next table. His dark hair was flecked with gray and his face was sullen, but he looked well and he was perfectly dressed. He looked at them idly, although Fernando had the impression that beneath this apparent lack of interest, he was sizing them up. He ordered a martini and sat down in his chair. He didn't seem to have a care in the world.

Barely a minute had passed before a tall man with salt-and-pepper hair and a reddish face, already quite old, appeared. He was obviously looking for someone. It didn't take him long to find the person he sought, who was none other than the Spaniard. He shook the man's hand and sat down opposite him, glancing at the two people at the next table. He looked carefully at the girl, but his expression didn't change.

Zahra held out her hand to Fernando, and he took it in his own, feeling very uncomfortable. She leaned over and whispered something in his ear that made him smile.

"I've got good news," the German said in Spanish. "You've got an in at court. I'll go with you to Cairo."

"I didn't think you'd get it sorted out so quickly."

"You know that most Egyptians aren't on the British side: they are tired of being under their thumb. And there are a lot of people at court impatient for the war to start."

"And what about Marshal Rommel? There are a lot of rumors about his disagreement with the Italian High Command," the Spaniard said.

"You've barely arrived, and you're letting yourself listen to rumors … No, don't pay them any attention; Rommel has changed the course of the war in North Africa. Without his help, the British would have pushed the Italians into the sea," Erick Brander said, with pride.

"Yes, but it's not good for the Germans and the Italians to be at odds …" Pedro López waited to see what Brander would say.

"Don't forget that Italy is an ally of Germany and that North Africa is its zone of influence, and so, formally, Rommel has to report to Marshal Graziani. But please accept that Rommel's talent is superior to that of any Italian general," Brander said proudly.

"But it looks like the British aren't retreating," Pedro López insisted.

"And that's one of the things that is upsetting Rommel. Desert warfare has its own rules. It's all sand and rocks, but there are certain strategic points like the passes at Fuka, Halfaya and Sidi Rezegh. Rommel is astounded that just a year ago, in December 1940, the British general O'Connor was able to destroy the whole of the Italian Tenth Army with just two divisions, and capture more than one hundred thousand Italians. The surprising thing is that the British didn't press the attack and decided to draw back to Egypt. And that's why Rommel and the Afrika Korps are here, to stop the British from winning the war in this part of the world."

"So Rommel and Graziani have had their ups and downs," Pedro López insisted.

"Let's just say that the marshal makes his own decisions. He's here to win. And the proof of that is his successes at El Agheila and then at Marsa el Brega."

"They say that General Philip Neame doesn't have the same military genius as O'Connor …"

"Well, the British are surprising: O'Connor is now in charge of Suez. And don't underestimate Neame, because he's not too shabby as a general. But there are differences between the two of them. In my opinion, the commander of the British forces, General Archibald Wavell, made a mistake when he sent O'Connor to Suez."

"Right … Well, disagreements between generals are common

in all armies. If I'm not mistaken, General Von Paulus sent a very unflattering report on Rommel to Berlin, and pointed out in particular his failure to take Tobruk in spite of his later successes," the Spaniard pointed out.

Erick Brander shifted uncomfortably in his seat. Pedro López seemed to have very good information about what was happening on the African front. You never knew where you were with the Spanish …

"At the moment, Rommel is in charge of Cirenaica. I'll remind you that after Tobruk he faced up to one of Wavell's attacks and defeated the British tanks … Do you know what Rommel's great advantage is, besides his bravery and military genius? Information. Yes, information. As well as the radio intercepts. That's why they couldn't catch him sleeping at Capuzzo-Sollum."

"That caused Wavell problems, because Churchill couldn't cope with that kind of defeat and they relieved him of his command, all of which makes Rommel appear all the stronger," the Spaniard said.

"Don't be in two minds about it, my friend, we're going to win the war here as well. As for your trip to court … you'll be invited there in a week. As I said, I'll come with you to Cairo. Of course, this will not be an official visit. It will have to be discreet," Brander said, looking directly at his companion.

"Of course, that's the easiest way," López said carelessly.

"As for the cotton you came here to buy, I've already got the price negotiated with a good friend. You'll be able to see the results of that before you leave for Cairo. And now I'll let you get some rest. Oh, I forgot: my wife insists that you come to our house tomorrow to bring in the New Year. A few of my friends will come and the meeting should be … useful."

"Tell your wife that I'd be delighted to come."

"Well, you know where I live: if it's all right with you, we'll expect you at eight o'clock."

The two men got to their feet and said goodbye, shaking hands again. Erick Brander looked at Zahra again out of the corner of his eye as though he knew her. Pedro López also looked at the young couple subtly, but nothing about them seemed to awaken his interest. Fernando was holding Zahra's hands in his own, and both of them were whispering to each other in low voices. They stayed like that for a while after the German and the Spaniard had left. Zahra gave him a smile to say that they could stop acting.

"Now we'll go out arm in arm. We have to keep on pretending that we're a young couple in love. The car will be waiting for us two blocks from here. We'll go slowly, as though we're reluctant to part."

Fernando followed Zahra's suggestions without complaint. He felt exhausted. He had paid attention to the conversation between López and Brander, as well as pretending to be interested in Zahra, who insisted that he carry on looking at her and smiling.

When he got back to Ylena's house, he found Eulogio asleep, so he went and sat in the library so as not to wake him. He took a pen and paper and tried to write down everything he had heard.

Ylena found him there and sat down next to him without asking.

"Did you have a good time?"

"Yes ... of course ... a very enjoyable evening ..." He felt a little uncomfortable to be lying to her.

"You don't know this, but you've had the honor of dining with the most desired woman in the whole of Alexandria."

He didn't know what to say. He hadn't really seen anyone looking at Zahra in any way that was out of the ordinary, and even would have said that they had passed unnoticed. Zahra was no great beauty. Ylena seemed to guess what he was thinking.

"It's New Year's Eve tomorrow, we'll have dinner here. Captain Pereira will come and then we'll go to the cabaret where Zahra dances, and you'll understand what I mean."

"I ... well, I don't really want to go anywhere tomorrow ..."

"I understand. You feel alone in a strange country with even stranger people. But don't reject these offers of friendship. Life brings people together without asking their permission. You are here today, and I hope that when you leave, you'll keep good memories in your heart of me and of my house."

"I will always be grateful for what you are doing for us. You took us in without knowing who we were or whether we could pay our way," he replied sincerely.

428

"I'll never refuse Captain Pereira anything. He's a very dear friend. And I hope that you don't upset him by refusing to go and see Zahra."

"I wouldn't upset him for anything in the world, but ... well, you'll understand ... it's the first time I've been away from home for Christmas. I don't want to celebrate anything."

"But you have a great deal to celebrate, my friend. You have to celebrate that you are alive. Celebrate the fact that you came into harbor safe and sound, and that you've found a place where they will take you in without asking questions, where ... where you can heal all the wounds that I believe you have in your soul, which are always bleeding. Celebrate the fact that you're young, that there are years ahead of you. You can be who you want to be; you still have a chance to shape your own fate. Yes, I think you have a lot to celebrate, although believe me when I say that I understand the nostalgia you feel at missing people who are dear to you."

Ylena gave him a sad smile, as though she too had suddenly been assailed by the memory of absent friends.

Then she put a hand on his shoulder and left him alone in the library.

On the last morning of 1941, Captain Pereira listened carefully to Dr. Naseef. He had come early because he wanted to pay Adela and Catalina's bill, but mostly because he wanted to know how the little girl was.

The doctor tried never to give grounds for hope without reason, but he had to admit that the situation with Adela was extraordinary: never had he known two-month premature babies to be able to survive pneumonia. And Adela was surviving. Slowly, of course, but each day that went by was a day that she had won in her battle for life. He had even decided that she would soon be able to leave the hospital, but only if Catalina followed his instructions to the letter.

"Adela will live, I'm sure of it. A child who is born in the middle of a storm will always be able to make it in this world," Pereira declared.

After speaking to Dr. Naseef, he went to the mother and daughter's room. Catalina gave him a grateful hug and a smacking kiss on the cheek. The captain had become almost like a father to her, for all that he tried to play the role of the hardened sailor.

Pereira took Adela in his arms and rocked her from side to side. She opened her eyes, and he thought that she recognized him. After all, he had helped bring her into the world.

"She's better," Catalina said.

"Yes, Dr. Naseef is thinking about letting you go home."

"Home?" Catalina was overcome by nostalgia.

"To Ylena's house. She'll know how to look after the pair of you."

"Ylena treats us very well."

"Catalina, why don't you go back to Spain? It's hard, especially because the war is getting worse every day, but I could help you."

"I can't go home. I've been honest with you, and you know that I can't go home. It's not possible. I can't make my parents go through the shame of having to accept that I've had a child out of wedlock. They offered me a solution, which I rejected. And if I don't go home with a husband, then there's nothing I can do."

"There's a man who loves you and who would marry you in a heartbeat."

"Fernando? I know, but I don't love him, and I could never love him like a woman should love her husband. I can only marry Marvin. Adela is his child, and it doesn't matter if he doesn't love me; he has his obligations to the child."

"You can't force him," the captain insisted.

"If I could, then I would," she replied instantly.

"You'd be unhappy, the pair of you."

"Maybe to begin with he would be upset with me for forcing him to marry me, but I am sure that I'd be able to earn his love. And we have Adela: we owe her that much."

"A child is not enough of a reason for a husband and a wife to be together," the captain said, harshly.

"Of course it is. The important thing is mutual respect, a sense of duty, and kindness towards the other person. My father always said that this was more important than love."

"You are very young to believe that. You need other things at your age, not just your pride."

"Captain, I think it's important for me to do my duty and make sure that Adela has her father."

"Marvin Brian doesn't love you; he's in love with another woman. And Fernando would be a good father for Adela and a good husband for you," Pereira declared.

"I can't think of Fernando as anything more than a brother ... I can't ..."

"Well, I won't belabor the point, then. I'm leaving in seven days, ten at the most. The damage to the *Esperanza del Mar* wasn't as bad as it looked. We had a few problems because of those Italians. I don't know when we'll see each other again."

"But you'll come back, won't you? I ... I like you very much. I'll miss you a lot."

"I'll come back, yes ... But it'll be a few months, unless the war makes it completely impossible."

"Don't say that! I ... I don't want you to go." Tears began to pool at the corners of Catalina's eyes.

The captain embraced her, stroking her hair as though she were a child. He didn't know why, but he felt sincere affection for Catalina, and thought again of his daughters and his grand-daughters.

He didn't want to imagine that they might ever be in the same situation as this young Spanish woman.

Meanwhile, Benjamin Wilson was reading Fernando's report. It didn't contain anything that he didn't know, but the fact that the young Spanish man had been able not only to provide a precise resumé of Erick Brander and Pedro López's conversation, but also that he had been able to make accurate comments on what he had heard, only reinforced Wilson's conviction that he had been right to bring Fernando into his business.

He knew that the young man would resist, but also that, once the first step had been taken, future ones would be easier.

Sara came into the office and his heart leapt. The ties that bound them were stronger than love. They had the same tastes and were excited by the same things; they did not need to fill the silence with unnecessary words. They could spend hours sitting next to one another, reading or lost in their own thoughts, without the other feeling at all uncomfortable.

Everyone who knew them had been a little surprised that they had gotten married, given their age. But the last few years had been the happiest years of his life. For the first time, he realized what it was not to be alone.

"Looks like you're reading something interesting ..." Sara said, smiling at her husband.

"I wasn't wrong about the boy," Wilson said.

"Fernando? He's got ability, even for editing. He's a hard worker, and he's meticulous, and he has an instinct for poetry. Athanasius is very happy with him," she said.

"I didn't mean those abilities ... The report on the meeting between Erick Brander and Pedro López is full of little details that show how observant he is. I think he can do some other work for us ... He can work with Zahra."

"Wouldn't it be dangerous? He's not trained ..."

"Well, it's only a possibility. We'll see."

"So, you're happy with Fernando's work. I think that his biggest advantage is that he hasn't yet lost all his innocence, and I hope he'll never lose it. Well, I'm going home now. I want to make sure that everything is ready for this evening. Marvin and Farida will be coming. I think they're going to leave sooner than they had planned. They'll tell us, I suppose."

"Farida continuously surprises me," Wilson said.

"She's an extraordinary woman. She's intelligent, and sensitive, and brave and very beautiful. It's a beauty that comes from the soul, which makes her very special," Sara said.

"Well, I'll tell Athanasius to close up. Tell everyone else they can leave early: it's the last day of the year."

"For the Christians," Sara said.

"Yes, you're right, but the whole city will celebrate it. Alexandria's like that."

"You know I don't mind celebrating Christian New Year. And I accept Christian festivals, I've lived alongside them all my life. Us French Jews always had to celebrate at home, in secret."

"It's just an occasion like any other for meeting up with friends. Well, I won't be long."

Benjamin watched Sara leave and sighed. Then he sat still for a moment, letting his thoughts flow and bring him an answer to one thing that was nagging at him. He called his secretary. Leyda Zabat was very efficient and entirely trustworthy, and her greatest virtue was her discretion. He had never heard her criticize anyone or talk about people behind their backs. Everyone respected and liked her because she gave off a general sense of goodwill. He thought he was very lucky to have been able to find someone like her.

Before he left, he wanted to read the report that Athanasius had given him on the young poet, Omar Basir. The surprising thing about Basir was his command of English, which was almost at the same level as his native Arabic. Of course, it was not surprising at all once you took into account that his father was one of the richest merchants in the city, and that he had sent his first-born son to an exclusive London public school and then to Oxford, where he studied history. Athanasius had added a note to the effect that it had been Fernando who had read Basir's poems and recommended their publication. He decided to check whether Fernando, as Sara said, had the gift of knowing real poetry when he came across it. After reading several of Omar Basir's poems, he decided that it was true, the young Spaniard had a real eye for a good poem.

He asked Leyda to call him in. He didn't want to let his work go unappreciated.

Fernando came in looking serious. He seemed uncomfortable, not with Wilson, but with himself.

"Congratulations. You've got a good eye," Wilson said with a half-smile.

"That was the first and last time," Fernando said, in a tone of voice that was harder than common sense might have advised for one's boss.

Benjamin held back a chuckle. He was back to playing games with Fernando.

"So, you don't want to edit poetry ... That's a problem ..."

"Poetry? No, I didn't say that ... I thought you were talking about last night ..."

"Never assume anything, or you'll make mistakes. It's just that I agree with you: Omar Basir is a good poet. We'll publish his book. You'll work with him under the supervision of Athanasius Vryzas, and you'll also organize a reading where Basir can read his poems."

"Sorry ... I thought that ..."

"That I was talking about your report on the meeting between Erick Brander and Pedro López."

"Yes," Fernando said uncomfortably.

"That's why I'm advising you to think about what is being said before you speak, and if you're in any doubt, keep your mouth shut. You can have that lesson for free."

Fernando held his gaze in spite of his growing unease, and didn't reply to these last words.

Wilson seemed unfazed, and carried on talking:

"It's clear that Pedro López has come here for something more than to buy cotton. The proof is in the fact that he's got a meeting arranged with someone important at court. I suppose that General Franco is looking for friends where he can find them, and that López is one of his agents. I may have to send you to Cairo."

"I won't go, Mr. Wilson. I left Spain, and I don't want to be visible anywhere Franco's agents might be. I took enough of a risk last night."

Wilson said nothing. Fernando was right, but he still didn't abandon the idea of making something out of the situation.

"We'll talk about it. Now go and rest. I suppose Ylena must be organizing a special dinner this evening. Oh, and take this, It's for the work you did yesterday." And he handed him a sealed envelope.

31 December 1941

Captain Pereira turned up at Ylena's house in his dress uniform. He had trimmed his beard and smelled of cologne, which Dimitra noted as she led him to the library. Ylena was wearing a long midnight blue dress, and Colonel Sanders was in a dinner jacket.

Eulogio and Fernando wondered if they should join the group or if they should have dinner in their room.

"We can't turn up dressed like this," Eulogio said.

"But it wouldn't be polite to Ylena and the captain not to accept their invitation," Fernando said.

Dimitra knocked at the door, and said that Ylena was impatient, and that the roast was going to be overcooked.

They explained their problem, and she laughed at them. She asked them to wait while she tried to sort something out.

A few minutes later, Ylena appeared. She scolded them affectionately.

"You're at home here, you can come dressed however you want."

"You have to understand, we left Spain in a hurry and didn't even have time to pack a good shirt," Eulogio apologized.

"Fernando can wear the shirt and jacket that Sara Rosent gave him, and as for you, Eulogio … I think we can sort something out … I'll ask Colonel Sanders to lend you something … He's got a suitcase filled with clothes that he hasn't decided to get rid of or not."

She gave them no time to protest, and so when she came back with a suit that smelled of mothballs and which had seen better days, as well as an acceptable white shirt, Eulogio had no choice other than to accept them.

When they went into the library, Captain Pereira met them with a chuckle.

"Gentlemen, it was worth the wait."

Eulogio went over to Colonel Sanders to thank him for the loan of his clothes, but the Colonel waved away his grateful words.

"My friend, the important thing is for us all to sit down to table now and eat the roast that Ilora has prepared for us, because it won't be perfect if we hang around here much longer."

The meal warmed their stomachs and their souls. Captain Pereira and Colonel Sanders told stories, and even raised a glass for the absent Monsieur Baudin, who was eating at his son Philippe's house that evening.

Shortly before midnight, Pereira reminded them that he had

reserved a table at the City Club. It hadn't been easy to get one, because Zahra Nadouri was going to dance.

Sanders wanted to go to bed, saying that he had never liked cabarets, but the captain pretended to be offended, and eventually he agreed to come.

A row of cars stood in front of the cabaret, disgorging their important passengers. Men in dinner jackets and beautiful, sophisticated women in Parisian gowns spun on the dance floor, laughing and drinking champagne. Everything was festive, as though there wasn't a war going on a few miles away. Fernando was struck by an absurd thought: would Rommel be celebrating the New Year? Or General Auchinleck? Or maybe the pair of them and their general staff were preparing for the next battle? The war felt far away that night.

Captain Pereira was in a very good mood, and Ylena smiled and greeted everyone they met. Fernando realized that his landlady was a very well-connected woman.

The table that the captain had reserved for them was not far from the dance floor, and the sailor spoke proudly of how difficult it had been for him to get.

Eulogio whispered in Fernando's ear that Pereira must be exaggerating a little, given the familiarity he showed with some of the waiters, and the nods of greeting he offered some of the musicians. "The captain obviously comes here a lot," Eulogio commented.

Shortly after midnight, the master of ceremonies announced, to great applause and cheers, that the great Zahra was about to dance, and all the hubbub in the room died down.

The lights went out, and the stage went dark, while you could hear the careful breathing of people for whom this would surely be the highlight of their night.

The band started to play music dripping with exoticism and sensuality. Suddenly a spotlight illuminated the center of the dance floor and the rhythm of the music grew more pronounced.

It was like a haunting. A barefoot woman appeared, dressed in transparent pink bloomers and a short pink top trimmed with dangling medallions. Her stomach and belly were exposed, and she moved her arms slowly. A long braid of chestnut brown hair with red highlights hung down her back. As her slow movements gradually had their hypnotic effect, the murmur of the crowd gave way to silence.

The woman's hands and feet moved to the same rhythm, and then, slowly, her body started to move from one side to the other. Fernando couldn't take his eyes away from her stomach, which seemed to take on a life of its own.

The dance lasted for more than an hour, and when the spotlight cut off and the stage was left in darkness, there was a burst of applause and shouts of enthusiasm.

It had just passed one o'clock, and the dancer had filled the room with a sense of ecstasy. The conversation turned to her, and her elegant and sensual dancing, her ability to take one's breath away. Some gentlemen tried to go to her dressing room, but several bulky men blocked their path.

"She's amazing," Ylena said, without stopping her applause.

"Extraordinary. Any man would lose his head over her," Pereira said.

"But she doesn't have a suitor," Colonel Sanders said.

"Well, she's got dozens of suitors, but she rejects them all. She doesn't have a young man and never has," Ylena said.

"Well, if she doesn't, then it's clear that she doesn't want one," Sanders said, still dazed by Zahra's dance.

"What do you think, Fernando?" Pereira said.

Fernando couldn't find the words to describe the impact that Zahra's dance had had on him. It was hard for him to see in this dancer the young, nondescript woman who had accompanied him to the Cecil. The Zahra of that evening hadn't stood out in any way at all. This Zahra was a dream he didn't want to wake up from.

Captain Pereira ordered more champagne and they drank to the future. No one wanted to think about reality that evening, and especially not about the war.

Ylena introduced them to some of her friends, who had brought with them women who were as beautiful as they were forward. One of them had no qualms in asking Fernando to dance with her right away. Ylena encouraged him to go, and even asked another one of her friends to take Eulogio out onto the dance floor, though he resisted, ashamed of his limp.

They didn't get home until dawn. The captain insisted on walking back with them, because he said that otherwise he wouldn't feel comfortable.

That night, the champagne helped them all fall asleep immediately. Even so, Fernando woke up early. He couldn't stop thinking about Zahra, and why the most desirable woman in the whole of Alexandria should work for Benjamin Wilson.

He got up without making any noise so as not to wake up Eulogio, who had drunk a little too much. After taking a shower, with a headache caused by alcohol and tiredness throbbing in his skull, he went to the kitchen in the hopes of finding at least a cup of coffee.

He found Dimitra with huge bags under her eyes. She had been up to celebrate the New Year as well.

"Madame Kokkalis is resting. When she goes to bed late she doesn't want anyone to disturb her. Colonel Sanders had breakfast some time ago and has gone out for a walk. Would you like some tea or coffee?"

Fernando asked for coffee, hoping that it would get rid of the alcohol that was still coursing through his system, but he rejected the pudding that Dimitra tried to give him, insisting that it would fill his stomach and make him feel better.

Once he had drunk a couple of cups of coffee, he decided to go to the hospital to see Catalina. In spite of their argument, he couldn't help feeling worried and responsible for her.

He found Captain Pereira sitting next to Adela's cradle. Catalina, standing next to it, was talking to Dr. Naseef.

Fernando was surprised that Captain Pereira had come so early to the hospital, because the traces of last night's excesses were still visible on his face.

"I'm glad you're here: I'm just explaining to the captain and to Catalina that I have taken a decision, which is to let Adela go home. I told Captain Pereira as much yesterday. There's not much more we can do for her here," the doctor said, looking at Fernando.

"But do you think that Adela is in a fit state to leave the hospital?" Fernando said, a little frightened at the doctor's decision.

438

"It's like I've just told them: with the medicine we can provide and with her mother's care, she'll be better off at home rather than in the hospital. Also, I'm worried about her mother … just look at her."

The two men looked at the ruined face of the young woman. Suddenly Fernando realized that she was not only distressingly thin, but her face had transformed too. There were wrinkles around her eyes that made her gaze appear more solemn, and deep marks at the corners of her mouth made her look bitter. It was hard to see in her the romantic and carefree girl that she had been. She was exhausted.

"Doctor, can you assure me that Adela is in no danger?" Captain Pereira's voice was more serious than usual.

"Isn't it you who keeps on repeating that Adela is a survivor? Let's hope that's the case. I'll come and see her every day, and if there is any emergency, take her straight back to hospital. I really think that the two of them need peace and quiet, which they won't find here."

"I want to have Adela baptized," Catalina whispered.

"Well, that can wait," the doctor replied uncomfortably.

"No, it can't wait. I can't sleep for thinking that if anything happens to Adela, then she'll go to limbo instead of to Heaven. And it will be my fault. I should have gotten her baptized as soon as we reached Alexandria," she insisted.

"Limbo … who knows if it exists … in any case, I don't think that the Lord makes use of limbo," the doctor said.

"Of course it exists! I won't let my daughter go there if … if … if anything happens to her." Catalina's face crumpled further.

"We'll baptize her, don't worry about that. If it's urgent, I'll get a priest and bring him straight away to Ylena's house," Captain Pereira said firmly.

The doctor left the room. There were other children, and equally ruined mothers, waiting outside for him to examine.

Captain Pereira got to his feet and smiled at Catalina, who seemed confused and unclear about what she should do.

"Now, my dear, the best thing for you to do is to get your stuff together and leave here as soon as possible. My ship needs me, so I'll take you to Ylena's house and then say farewell. What are you going to do, Fernando?"

"Mr. Wilson told me I could take the day off."

"It's one of the things about this city: holidays for the Muslims, holidays for the Christians, holidays for the Jews. Well, the two of us will take Catalina home. I'll go and fetch us a car. We shouldn't take Adela on the bus."

Catalina and Fernando didn't speak.

The hubbub of the morning and the fresh sea air drove the fog out of his brain. Fernando was scared of the moment when they would get home and the captain would leave them alone together. He felt that Catalina was so far away from him that she was almost a stranger.

The captain got them home and left them at the door without even waiting for Dimitra to open it.

The maid gave Catalina a joyous welcome and insisted in taking Adela in her arms. Fernando wondered if Eulogio would be awake by now, or if he would still be sunk in an alcoholic stupor. To his relief, his friend had eaten breakfast and was now sitting with Colonel Sanders and Monsieur Baudin, who had come back mid-morning and was telling them all about his New Year's party with his son Philippe, his daughter-in-law, and his grandchildren.

The French businessman seemed the most pleased that Catalina was back with them. Mr. Sanders merely shook her hand and said he was glad that Adela was a little better; Eulogio didn't engage with her, only paying attention to the baby.

Ylena came in, having heard the noise in the dining room. She gave Catalina a friendly hug, and stroked Adela's pale little face.

"Now that you're back, I have a surprise for you. I haven't even spoken about it to Eulogio and Fernando," she said.

The surprise was none other than that she had prepared a small back room for Adela and Catalina to share. A few days ago, Dimitra had cleaned it from top to bottom and thrown out everything that could no longer be used. There was no room for much more than a little bed up against the wall next to the window. A slightly shabby wardrobe with a mirrored front completed the spartan furnishings. Ylena sent Dimitra to fetch what she said was a present for Adela.

Catalina was overcome with emotion. She was very relieved to be able to have her own room. Ever since they left Madrid, she had shared first a cabin and then a room with her companions. She had been bothered not by the supposed impropriety of this situation, but rather the lack of privacy.

"I thought about putting Fernando and Eulogio in here, but as you see, it's so small that there's barely room for a bed," Ylena apologized.

"But it's perfect! Thank you so much!" Catalina said, sincerely.

Dimitra appeared, pushing a little baby carriage. There was a package with some children's clothes in it on top.

"It's second-hand, but I think it will do. A friend gave it to me: it was for her granddaughter, as was the clothing ... I hope it's not an imposition."

Catalina cried a little, touched by the care that Ylena had shown her.

"I don't know how I can thank you for all that you're doing for us ..." she said.

"No, you don't have to thank me. The important thing is for Adela to get better."

Catalina stayed in her new room with Ylena and Dimitra while Fernando and Eulogio decided to go for a walk. They felt uncomfortable around Catalina, and relieved that they didn't have to share a room with her anymore.

"Ylena is an extraordinary woman," Eulogio said, as soon as they were out of the house.

"Yes, she is. I think that Catalina awakens the maternal instinct in her. You know, she's never been married or had children ..." Fernando said.

"Yes. It's a tragic story, Ylena and the captain's nephew. She must have loved him a great deal, to remain single after that ..." Eulogio said in wonderment.

"You see how much affection she has for the captain. Sometimes I think he must be feeling guilty for not having been able to rescue his nephew."

"It must have been very hard for him ... How old do you think the captain is?" Eulogio asked with interest.

"He must be more than sixty," Fernando said.

"And Ylena must be over fifty … She's still a very attractive woman."

"Yes, she is," Fernando said.

They walked aimlessly past the Museion, the Arab walls and the Caesareum until they reached the seafront. The breeze brought color to their cheeks, and the smell of salt filled them with pleasant sensations.

"I'm going to have lunch with Farida and Marvin. They've decided to go already. Marvin thinks that because the United States has entered the war, it will only get more difficult to cross the Atlantic. German submarines and boats will be everywhere. The captain told me last night that it was like playing Russian roulette to try to get across the ocean right now. I don't think Pereira will be here much longer. His boat is almost repaired, and there's no reason for him to stay here."

Fernando listened to Eulogio, but without paying him too much attention. He felt tired and disinclined to concentrate. And he was worried by Catalina's return.

"You're not listening to me," Eulogio reproached him.

"Of course I am."

"You're thinking about Catalina. I don't feel comfortable around her either, not after the argument we had last time, but at least we don't need to share a room anymore."

"Yes, it's the best for her and for the baby."

"And for us."

"I don't know what she'll want to do," Fernando said worriedly.

"She's got one choice: to go back to Spain," Eulogio said.

"But she'll try to see Marvin. You know her, I'm sure she'll get his address."

"I don't think she will: no one's going to tell her where he lives. Ylena's a friend of Farida's and she's the only one who could tell her, and she won't."

"You've seen what Catalina's capable of," Fernando replied.

"Yes, I know she's got guts, but you need more than guts to get through to Marvin. We have to help her get back to Spain, it'll be best for her and for her daughter," Eulogio said, insisting that Fernando accompany him to the restaurant where he was to meet Farida and Marvin.

442

Marvin was surprised to see Fernando, and it was Farida who insisted that he sit down to have lunch with them.

They spent a good part of the meal talking about the Wilsons' New Year's party. Farida told them that Zahra had gone there after her performance at the City Club, and Eulogio said that there was something very special about the dancer. But for all that he tried to get Farida to tell them something about Zahra's life, she only smiled and listened without saying anything.

When they finished the meal, Farida suggested that they drink a strong coffee, given that they were all suffering the aftereffects of staying up all night. The waiter served them coffee, and Marvin said that he was going to eat with Ylena and Captain Pereira that evening to try to convince him to accept them as passengers on board the ship.

"The *Esperanza del Mar* is headed to Brazil. We'll try to find a way to get to New York from there," Marvin said, looking at Eulogio.

"And what if Captain Pereira refuses to take you?" Eulogio wanted to know.

"There are other ships ... although we'd prefer to travel on the *Esperanza del Mar*. Captain Pereira is an experienced sailor, and it won't be easy to cross the Atlantic given the German blockade, which makes no distinction between warships and merchant vessels. Ylena has promised to try to convince him. I hope he agrees to take us," Marvin said.

"Will you come with us?" Farida asked, looking straight at Eulogio.

"Yes, of course. I'm not doing any good here ... I ... Well, thank you for the work that you found for me, but I know that it's just Mr. Kamel doing you a favor," Eulogio said, a little ashamed but still holding Farida's gaze.

"Yes, he's doing me a favor. But he appreciates all your help," she replied straightforwardly.

"He's very kind and speaks terrible French," Eulogio said, laughing.

"Enough for you to understand one another," Farida said, laughing as well.

"Fernando, what are you going to do?" Marvin asked.

"I can't go back to Spain. I'm an exile, and I have no country anymore. I'm as happy to stay here as go anywhere else, but it all depends on Catalina. If she goes back to Spain, then maybe I can join you, but if she decides to stay … No, I'm not going to leave her to her fate. Maybe if you speak to her … if you told her that you were going to acknowledge Adela …"

Marvin got to his feet and clenched his fists. He tried to control the emotion that seemed to fill him and cause him to shake.

"There's no reason to! I'm not going to participate in her delusions! Catalina means nothing to me, and she never has. She's being a child. And she has to face up to reality."

"You have a responsibility to her! You can't turn your back on her! A man has to face up to his actions," Fernando said harshly.

"You don't understand! I don't have anything to do with her! Everyone is responsible for their own actions. I don't have to explain myself to her, or to you. Why would I?" Marvin's voice was filled with rage.

Farida stood up and took him by the hand, pulling gently until he sat down.

"Fernando, I don't think you should push him on this. It's a shame that you've decided to side with Catalina, because it will cause you a lot of pain, but it's your choice and we respect it." Farida spoke firmly and sweetly, and Marvin, seated next to her, nodded.

"She'll look for you," Fernando said, unwilling to give up.

"And who's going to tell her where to find me? No one will. But I promise you, Fernando, that if I meet her and she dares approach me, I won't even say hello. She can't force me to be a part of her life or her daughter's life."

They sat in silence for a while. Farida stroked Marvin's face and the tension gradually drained from it.

"If you decide to stay in Alexandria, you can trust Benjamin and Sara. You're in good hands with Benjamin Wilson. He'll teach you things … He knows how to get the best out of everyone," Farida said to Fernando, trying to change the subject.

Fernando didn't say that Mr. Wilkson wanted him to work at something more than editing, but he guessed somehow that Farida already knew this.

"And he's fair, when it comes to paying people what he owes them," Marvin said.

Fernando nodded. He was, it was true. The money that had been in the envelope Wilson had given him for going with Zahra to the Cecil was more than he could have imagined. It gave him a bit of a breathing space as he waited for his salary to be paid.

"We'll go and see him tomorrow," Farida said. "Marvin's going to give him his collection. It's ready for him to print," she added.

"Wouldn't you prefer to have it printed in the United States?" Eulogio asked.

"I owe a debt to Monsieur Rosent, one I can never hope to pay. Up until now, he's been my one and only editor, and he believed in me and gave me ideas about how and what I should write. The Rosents will always be my editors, wherever I am and whatever happens," Marvin said.

"And Wilson & Wilson is a publishing house with a certain degree of prestige in the United Kingdom. Marvin's poems will make it to New York," Farida said.

"Benjamin has promised to publish it in three languages: English, French and Arabic. The French edition will come out with Rosent," Marvin said proudly.

The sun set. Eulogio and Fernando went back to Ylena's house. Eulogio didn't stop talking about his trip to America. Alexandria, he said, was not the place for him. One day, he said, they would both meet in America, a place where a person could really build their own future.

Dimitra told them that Madame Kokkalis had gone out, which didn't surprise the two friends, given that Marvin had told them that he was going to have dinner with Ylena and the captain.

"I took Catalina a bowl of soup and some cake to her room. She's in a bad way and needs to rest. But Colonel Sanders and Monsieur Baudin are in the dining room and are ready to eat, so don't hang about. Go get ready."

They didn't say so, but both of them were pleased not to have to eat with Catalina. They were too tired to pretend that everything was normal.

Over dinner, Monsieur Baudin told them about the latest rumors in the city.

"Some of the king's advisors are getting less than subtle about hiding their approval of the Germans. They seem to be in favor of Hitler's strongman tactics. There are more and more Egyptians who sympathize with the Germans, and who see the British as invaders."

"Monsieur Baudin, you always say the same things. I don't think you can be so sure that Egypt is keen to join the Axis powers," Mr. Sanders cut him off.

"My dear friend, you know more about this than me. The British tend to be realists, and I'm sure that General Auchinleck or Admiral Cunningham have no illusions about the sentiments of the Egyptians. The Italian attack on Alexandria has drawn some admiration for the Italians who carried it out. They talk about Luigi Duran de la Penne, the Italian in command of the mission, as though he were a hero."

Colonel Sanders closed his mouth in annoyance. He didn't want to admit that Monsieur Baudin was probably right. He was annoyed that the Frenchman continually reminded him of the fact that for many Egyptians, the British were little more than invaders.

Fernando and Eulogio finished eating and went back to their room, leaving Sanders and Baudin to enjoy their usual game of chess in the library.

Shortly after dawn, the two friends found Catalina having breakfast in the dining room. Adela was awake in the carriage next to her mother. Dimitra spoke to the child in a baby voice whenever she entered or left the room.

Catalina greeted them politely, without looking at them. Fernando asked her how Adela was, and she said that the baby had had a good night. Then the three of them occupied themselves with the coffee Dimitra had brought. Colonel Sanders and Monsieur Baudin came in later.

When they had finished eating and were about to get on with their respective days, Catalina, a little bashfully, asked Fernando and Eulogio to stay behind and talk for a moment.

"I'd be lying if I said I regretted everything I said the other day; I may have been unfair to the pair of you, but I said what I thought. I know that it's come between us, and that it's going to be difficult for us to trust each other again, and particularly for you to trust me. I … well, I don't have anyone else to turn to. Captain Pereira has said that he will still pay for me to stay at Ylena's house, but of course I can't accept that, and so I'll need to find some work, although it will be difficult because Adela needs me to be with her."

Silence fell. Catalina seemed not to know how to continue, and Fernando was trying to find the right words to tell her that, in spite of everything, she could count on him. But Eulogio cut in first.

"I don't regret saying what I said either. Maybe it wasn't a good idea to have come. But we all had our reasons for leaving Spain, and given that we're here now, the best thing for each of us to do is to find the best option and then do it. I'm leaving; I can't imagine staying longer in this city. There's no future for me here."

"I'm going to look for Marvin. He can't hide from me forever. I'll find him. He has to marry me. I'm not doing this out of love, but out of duty. Take me to him." As she spoke, Catalina didn't look at either Fernando or Eulogio.

"Not this again, Catalina, please. Marvin doesn't want to have anything to do with you. I'm not going to help you to find him. He's my friend, and he's made clear he feels nothing for you. And we've already told you that he's with a woman who he loves. He doesn't want anything more to do with you or the child. I'm going with them to America," Eulogio said.

"Are you telling me that Marvin is a scoundrel? A wretch?" Catalina tried to control the anger and shame that filled her.

"No, he's not a scoundrel. He's got his reasons and you've got yours. I respect his decision to have nothing to do with you, and I understand your desire to find him, even though … well, I think you should think a bit about what happened, given that everyone is responsible for their own actions," he said.

"Think a bit? You think I should think about why I might want to find the father of my daughter? Are you laughing at me?" Catalina's voice started to take on a slightly hysterical edge.

"You know I'm not laughing at you. I'm sorry, Catalina, but I'm not going to help you. Fernando and I brought you here, and perhaps we shouldn't have done that. But what's done is done. I advise you to go back to Spain. Your parents love you, and when they see Adela, they'll forgive you. And you won't be able to get married to Antoñito, so you're ahead there as well. He's a pig just like his father." Eulogio's words were filled with pain.

"And what about you, Fernando?" Catalina asked. "Are you not going to help me find Marvin either?"

"Eulogio's telling the truth: Marvin doesn't want to see you or hear from you," Fernando said, feeling that he was betraying her.

"I'm asking you to take me to Marvin, and what happens after that will be between the two of us," Catalina said.

"I can't."

"You don't want to! Say it! Say that you don't want to, because you can't bear him to be with me! That's right, isn't it?" Catalina wanted to hurt Fernando, because of the hurt she felt.

"You can believe me or not, but I promise you I've tried to make him speak to you. And I also swear that I don't know his address. Believe me that if I did, then I'd take you there at once. I told him that he should talk to you, and tell you whatever he has to tell you. I can't understand why he's so adamant that he won't see you," Fernando said straightforwardly.

"It's that woman! She's the one getting in the way of every-thing! She's afraid that Marvin will abandon her as soon as he sees Adela and me, you think I don't know that? That witch won't let him see me," Catalina said firmly.

"Marvin is in love with her," Eulogio said.

"He's not! She's bewitched him, God knows how … There are women who use magic to keep men at their side. I'm sure she's a witch. I know what Marvin is like: I know how sweet he is, how gentle, how much he loves me. He wouldn't hurt me, not for anything. But he's not thinking for himself: there's someone manipulating him."

Catalina spoke with such passion that it was clear that she believed what she said. Fernando said nothing, but he thought that maybe Catalina was right, and Marvin refused so bluntly to see her because Farida was stopping him. But what did he and Eulogio know about Farida? Only that Marvin relied on her.

Maybe the philosopher was not all that she seemed. But he also had to admit that any man would be fascinated by her, not just because of her beauty, but also because of her personality.

"Don't blame Farida or Fernando. Marvin has made his own decisions. I'm not going to tell Fernando where Marvin lives, because I know that he'd be incapable of refusing to tell you the address. I'm not going to betray Marvin for you." Eulogio made his position clear.

"You've never liked me, have you?" Catalina looked him straight in the eye.

"You're a little girl who has never been told no in her whole life," Eulogio replied.

"You think so? You're wrong. You don't know anything about me. I lost my grandfather in the war and my grandmother died of a broken heart. The war drove my aunt Amparo mad: she saw them shoot her son Andresito. The war took my uncles from me. My Aunt Adoración del Niño Jesús has never been the same since some soldiers broke into the convent and … well, you know what they did to nuns. The war drove my father into debt with Don Antonio, and to promise me in marriage to Antoñito because we didn't have anything to eat. You think I don't know what that meant for my father? The war took my aunt Petra's husband. And so don't tell me that life has always given me what I want. I've lost so many people who are dear to me. You think you're the only one who suffers because you lost your father? Or because that bastard Don Antonio took advantage of your mother and took your house? Or because you were wounded in a battle?" Catalina's words were filled with pain.

The three of them were silent for some time, time that seemed to them to last forever.

"Your family won the war," Eulogio said, impressed in spite of himself by Catalina's words.

"We won the war? How can you say that? Franco won the war, and everyone else lost. You're upset with me because I was on the winning side, but I'm not on any side: I never got to choose. You think that I'm stupid, and maybe that's true, but I'm not so stupid that I can't see what's going on in Spain. How much time is going to have to pass before we forgive one another?"

Eulogio was surprised by Catalina's words. He had always thought that she was stupid, and he still resisted thinking that her words might have a grain of truth in them.

"Listen, little girl, it was your side that started the war by rising up against the legitimate government of the Republic," he said.

"You're right, but the dead fell on both sides. You're upset about your father's death; I'm upset about my cousin's death, and my uncles' deaths. Your pain isn't better, or bigger, than mine. Your dead and my dead are worth the same."

Fernando was overwhelmed by the power of Catalina's speech. Suddenly he realized that behind her girlish appearance, there was a woman he hardly knew.

He felt that he needed to examine his thoughts, and even his feelings, about Catalina.

None of the three seemed able to say any more. Dimitra came in to remind them that they'd be late for work. The two men hurried away without even saying goodbye.

Leyda, Wilson's secretary, told Fernando that Athanasius Vryzas was waiting for him in Benjamin Wilson's office. When he arrived, Marvin was there as well. Judging by his expression, he seemed upset.

Wilson told him to sit down, and explained shortly that his editor-in-chief had recommended that Fernando take charge of editing Marvin's book of poems.

The book would have to be ready in a couple of months at the most. Vryzas reminded him that he had to prepare the English edition of Omar Basir's work as well.

"You have very good English, and it shouldn't be a problem for you to do that. And I'll deal with the French and Arabic editions," the old editor explained.

Marvin did not protest, but he didn't look very happy. Fernando thought that all the protesting had probably taken place before he turned up.

Benjamin Wilson ended the meeting and told Marvin and Athanasius to leave, but told Fernando to stay for a moment.

When they were alone, he looked at him for a moment before he spoke.

"There's nothing more to say about the poems. But I need you to do another job for me, one that's more urgent. I need you to go to Marsa el Brega. Well, maybe not quite as far as that …"

"Marsa el Brega? I don't even know where that is … And why should I go there?" Fernando asked uncertainly.

"It's Libya, Cirenaica … You'll find one of Rommel's camps there."

"That's crazy! What do you want me to do, send your best wishes to Rommel?" Fernando was confused.

"Look, don't play the fool … We're at war, you're against the fascists, and you have good reason to be. I am too. And so there's no reason for you not to work with me and do something to try to make sure that we win this damn war."

"I've already lost one war," Fernando said solemnly.

"Well, you may not have lost it completely if we manage to defeat Hitler. If we manage to do that, then Franco will be on the losing side, and maybe the Allies will decide they don't want a fascist governing a European country. If we win the war, maybe Franco's days are numbered."

"You know what, Mr. Wilson? Maybe that's how things should be, but I don't think the British are going to defend much more than their own interests. There's no guarantee that Hitler's going to be defeated, much less that if he is defeated, they'll decide to get rid of Franco."

"I understand your skepticism: you're very young to have seen so much. But believe me that we must defeat Hitler if we want to carry on being what we are: civilized countries with humane values. We can't just stand still in the face of the German army riding roughshod over Europe, applying their racist laws that mean that thousands of people are being sent to concentration camps because of their race or what they believe in. You have lost a war, of course, but I can assure you that losing this one would be much worse. Ask yourself if your father would have been silent in the face of Hitler, or if he would have done everything in his power to stop his madness."

Benjamin Wilson sat in silence while he gave Fernando time to think about the question that had just been put to him. He was sure what the answer would be.

"And what do I have to do in this place?"

"I've told you that, as well as publishing books, Wilson & Wilson looks for missing people."

"Yes, and that you buy and sell information," Fernando interrupted.

The two men looked at each other suspiciously. But then Wilson took control of the situation.

"I never said that: all I said was that sometimes I'm required to find information of various kinds. If I can, then I do, but nothing more. I'm sorry to disappoint you, but I don't play at spies."

Fernando shrugged. He couldn't help feeling unsettled around Benjamin Wilson, because he didn't trust him. He felt that, for Wilson, he was little more than a pawn, to be moved around as needed.

"Among the Italian troops under Rommel, there is one man who has sometimes worked with the British, and sometimes … with me. He is called Domenico Lombardi and he's assigned to logistics. A month ago, I received a message that I was to get him out of Marsa el Brega. He wanted to desert. I sent one of my usual collaborators. I know that he and Lombardi managed to get out of Marsa el Brega. They should be in Alexandria by now, but they haven't arrived … The man I sent knows the desert well, so I'm not sure what could have happened to them. I'm worried, and with good reason. I need you to go and find them."

"You're crazy! I wouldn't know how to cross a desert. I'm not prepared for this. You'd be sending me to my death."

"You're right, it's madness and it's more than likely that they'll arrest you and kill you. But I need someone to go there. It's really Hafid who will do the work. He's a Bedouin, and knows the desert like the back of his hand. He'll know how to find them if they are alive. I trust Hafid."

"I keep on hearing that the Egyptians prefer the Germans to the English," Fernando said.

"True. But not all of them. And Hafid is a Bedouin, a son of the desert: he's not on anyone's side."

"And why does he work for you?"

"He owes my father his life … many years ago he saved it. My father was an army officer stationed in Egypt. On one occasion, as he was patrolling the desert, he came across a group of bandits who had attacked a Bedouin encampment. They'd killed some men, and some women as well. One of the bandits tried to rape Hafid's mother. My father killed him with a single bullet. Hafid's father was badly wounded. So was Hafid; back then, he was little more than a boy. It was thanks to my father that his life was saved. He has a blood debt to me." Wilson spoke quietly, as though this were an unremarkable fact that he was passing on.

"And why do you need me to go?"

"Hafid doesn't speak a word of Italian."

"Neither do I."

"But you'll be able to speak to Lombardi, because both of you speak a Latin-based language, you'll be able to communicate. And I don't have anyone at the moment who speaks Italian. That's why I'm asking you to go, because I need someone who can speak to Lombardi, if he is still alive. The man who went to find him was one of Hafid's cousins, Basim, who is also a Bedouin; you know that the Bedouin never get lost in the desert. Something must have happened to them."

"Maybe this Basim decided to betray Lombardi and hand him over to the Germans," Fernando said.

"I don't think so. Like I said, he's one of Hafid's cousins. If he'd done it, he'd know that it would cost him his life. Hafid would kill him."

"That's crazy!" Fernando insisted.

"That's how things are in this part of the world. You need to speak to Lombardi, but above all, you need to get him out of there. The people who work for me know that I never abandon one of my own."

"And why should someone who works for the Italian army betray his own by working for you?"

"He has his reasons."

"I need to know them."

Benjamin Wilson looked at Fernando and knew that he wouldn't get him to do anything unless he told him the whole truth.

"Domenico Lombardi is the son of a judge. His father is a socialist. You can imagine how much he hates fascism. Well, father and son argued because of their political views and didn't talk to one another for a couple of years. A few months ago, they put his father in prison, and this made the younger Lombardi change his mind. Domenico is a soldier with a fierce sense of honor and duty, a man accustomed to obeying orders, but his chief loyalty is to his family, and to his father above all: he's the man who made him who he is today. His father's imprisonment and Rommel's attitude were what pushed him over the edge. Likewise, he's been rocked by the disdain which Rommel shows for people like him, so he hasn't had any qualms about collaborating every now and then. But his main motivation is the pain he feels knowing that his father is an honest man, and in prison."

"And if we don't find him?"

"Try to get back here."

"Right … You told me yourself that it was likely they'd kill me."

"Yes, that might happen."

"When would I have to leave?"

"In a couple of days. As long as it takes for Hafid to organize everything. He'll protect you."

Wilson gave him a folder with some journey details in it. Fernando looked it over and gave a start when he realized that it was more than six hundred miles from Alexandria to Marsa el Brega. He was going to protest, but instead realized he was beaten.

"Right … And what should I say to Ylena Kokkalis? And my friends?"

"Tell your friends that you've been sent to my branch in Cairo. And as for Ylena … you don't need to tell her anything. She'll understand."

Fernando sat in silence; he felt dazed as he tried to process what he had just been told. He felt that he was living in an alternate reality.

"Don't worry about Catalina. Ylena will look after her; she likes her very much."

"My friend Eulogio is going on the *Esperanza del Mar* with Marvin and Farida. Catalina will be left all alone."

"Yes, they're going, but not on the *Esperanza del Mar*. Captain Pereira refuses to take them, in spite of Ylena arguing their case. He'll only agree to if Marvin talks to your friend Catalina, and as you know, he refuses to do that. Well … they might have other plans, of course."

"Other plans?" Fernando didn't understand what Wilson was saying.

The editor frowned and he crossed his arms on the desk, but he didn't answer Fernando's question.

"We all have our challenges. Life surrounds us with unexpected events … Captain Pereira tries to protect Catalina's interests, and I need to protect myself from the interests of others."

Fernando left Wilson's office without understanding the man's words. He knew Wilson was manipulating him as he saw fit. He didn't want to go to Marsa el Brega, but he had agreed to go. And he cursed himself for agreeing.

Athanasius Vryzas was absorbed in reading a manuscript, but as soon as he saw Fernando, he stopped what he was doing.

They talked for a while about how to schedule their work and how to plan the publication dates for their current list.

"Mr. Wilson has told me that you need to go to our branch in Cairo for a few days, but I'm sure he'll give you time to do everything that you've set up."

"I'll try," Fernando said grumpily, without wishing to commit himself to something he didn't know if he could pull off.

"Mr. Wilson is very strict when it comes to publication dates," Vryzas warned him.

"I can't be in two places at once, and so I'll do what I can as best I can," Fernando said: his boss' demands were annoying him.

Athanasius Vryzas didn't insist. His young assistant seemed to be under a great deal of pressure.

They spent the rest of the day working, and although Vryzas tried to encourage Fernando to come out and have something to eat, he preferred to stay and work. He wasn't hungry, and he had no time to waste.

At six o'clock, Vryzas said he should go home. This time, he didn't protest.

When Dimitra opened the door, she said that Madame Kokkalis was waiting for him in her drawing room. Fernando didn't want to speak with anyone, not even Ylena, but he couldn't refuse, and he went in to see his landlady.

Ylena was sitting behind her writing desk reading a book of short stories. She smiled and nodded to him to sit down opposite her.

Her drawing room was very welcoming. Besides the writing desk, it had a couple of armchairs and a sofa upholstered in green leather, a few low tables with vases of flowers, and paintings of seascapes on the walls. The smell of leather and roses made the rooms seem particularly welcoming, especially when it was raining.

"I suppose you know by now that Captain Pereira isn't going to take Marvin or Farida to America, or your friend Eulogio either. His decision has been annoying for everyone ... But the captain has made up his mind, and he won't change it. He'll come and say goodbye this evening, because he sets sail tomorrow morning."

Fernando didn't know what to say, or what Ylena wanted him to say, so he said nothing.

"I understand his decision. I would have done the same, if it hadn't been for ... well, I'm Farida's friend, and Marvin's as well. It's difficult to be on everyone's side at the same time. But although I don't know why Marvin has acted as he has, I respect his decision, because Farida supports it. But ... well, I think if it were up to her, Marvin would talk to Catalina, but as he refuses to do so, then she's protecting him. On the other hand, I can't help but be moved to think about the tragedy that is Catalina's life. I'm fond of her. I understand her desperation. The question I want to ask is: what do you think we can do about it?"

"Do? You know there's nothing we can do. Marvin will go in any case."

"And Catalina? Will she agree to go back to Spain? It would be the best for her and her daughter ..."

"Yes, I think so too, but you'd have to ask her. I don't know."

"And what about you, Fernando? What are you going to do?"

"I feel trapped." Fernando regretted the words as soon as he said them.

She looked at him with curiosity, and he saw a trace of bitterness flash across her face.

"We can always choose what to do," Ylena said.

"No, that's not true," he said firmly.

"Maybe there are times when we cannot see the way out, but the door is always there."

"I don't think so."

"I understand that you see everything as black at the moment … You've left your country, you've been caught up in events you didn't expect … and then there's this city, Alexandria, which sometimes I feel weighing down on me as well. You have no real reason to stay here."

"Apart from Catalina."

"Yes, but once Marvin leaves, she'll have no reason to stay. Everything in Alexandria is strange to her: the language, the people, the way of life, even the war, with Rommel looking to take the city. You should leave." Ylena said, as she believed that it would be for the best.

"I'm not going to leave Catalina. Not while I can be of any use to her. If she decides to stay, I'm going to stay with her."

"Captain Pereira has asked me to take care of Catalina, and I will. I like her a great deal."

"I'll pay for her expenses," Fernando said.

"You have to decide what to do. Your friend Eulogio will leave with Marvin and Farida. Mr. Wilson has found them a berth on another ship that leaves for Marseille in a few days. Then, if all goes well, they'll travel on to America."

"To France?" But the United States is at war with Germany, and France has been occupied …"

"I think that your friend Marvin and Farida are going to go to Vichy to find Monsieur Rosent, Sara's father. It appears that Monsieur Rosent used a few friends to help him leave Paris and head to the free zone. Sara found out yesterday. You can imagine how worried she is."

"But Vichy is Hitler's vassal state…"

"Exactly, but they told me that everything is mixed together there. Sara Rosent wanted to go to Vichy, but Benjamin thinks that she'll be in danger because she's a Jew. Farida and Marvin have offered to go and look for Monsieur Rosent. Marvin feels like he owes him a great deal."

"Mr. Wilson didn't say anything to me about this," Fernando protested.

"Why should he have?"

"Marvin and Farida will be in danger, but Eulogio in much more. No, he can't go to France. Even before our war came to an end, they were locking up Spanish people in camps …"

"Benjamin is a very clever man. I'm sure he will have thought of everything so that they run no risk."

"They're crazy!" Fernando raised his voice; the discussion was making him agitated.

"We're at war, that's all. War makes everyone crazy."

"I'll talk to Eulogio."

"Yes, do that. As for you and Catalina, take whatever time you need to decide what you're going to do. Oh, and tonight the captain is going to dine with us. I have a little surprise in store."

Fernando found Eulogio smoking on his bed, with a serious expression on his face. He looked tired.

"I've just spoken to Ylena," Fernando said by way of greeting.

"And she's told you that we're going to France, to Vichy."

"Yes, she did. I suppose you're not going through with this madness."

"What can I do? Stay here working as an assistant to a man who doesn't need help, who I can only communicate with by playing charades?"

"You can go to Brazil on the *Esperanza del Mar*. The captain has refused to take Farida and Marvin, but he'll take you. I'll ask him. We can pay for a part of the journey with the money that Wilson's given me."

"Yes, we could do that …"

"Well, do it. It's the best thing to do. Once you're in Brazil, you can decide what you're going to do, but it'll be easier to travel around once you're there."

"Marvin told me what he's planning on doing, and asked me to go with them. He's offered to find Monsieur Rosent, but … I don't know, I think he's scared."

"Of course, he'd have to be crazy not to be. No one wants to go to France right now. Wilson is a manipulative man, a man without scruples, who makes everyone do what he wants."

"He also told me that he was worried about what might happen, and especially about what might happen to Farida, who insists that he shouldn't travel alone. I think that I give him a certain degree of security. He made me promise that I'd take Farida out of France if anything happens to him. Fernando, you have to see that I can't let Marvin down," Eulogio said resignedly.

"Let him down? Is refusing to commit suicide letting him down? I don't know what risks he and Farida might run, but you … You know that the French will arrest you as soon as you set foot in France and then they'll send you to one of those camps they have for Spaniards, if they don't send you straight back to Spain."

"I know he needs me. Marvin has agreed to do something he's not ready for. And he's done it out of loyalty to the Rosents."

"You're not ready either, not ready to cross half of France, go all the way to Vichy: do you think it'll be going for a camping trip? Please, Eulogio, face up to reality. Alexandria's driving us all crazy."

"I can see how we're all changing," Eulogio admitted.

"But for the worse, and we're losing what little common sense we had in the first place," Fernando said.

Fernando sat down and covered his face with his hands to fight back a sob.

He felt so old; it was as though the days that had passed since he left Spain had turned into years.

Eulogio sat down next to him and put an arm around his shoulders.

"There's no way back, Fernando: we can't go back to Spain. You even less than me. The only one who can go back is Catalina. You're right about Wilson, he does what he wants when he wants … Marvin told me some things … Well, the same that you told me. That Wilson & Wilson looks for people as well as publishing books."

"And why should we care? We don't owe him anything."

"We're exiles: we don't have anything and there's no future for us," Eulogio replied.

"You want to go to America to look for a future," Fernando reminded him.

"I wanted to run away from myself, from the shame I felt about my mother and Don Antonio. That's what I really wanted to get away from, as much as from Franco's Spain," Eulogio said openly.

The two friends hugged and tried to hold back their tears. They felt lost in the immensity of the ancient city, so alien to them. They still did not love old Alexandria.

Dimitra gave a gentle knock at the door to tell them that dinner would shortly be served.

Catalina was already seated when they came through to the dining room. She was talking to Captain Pereira. Fernando and Eulogio had no desire to make conversation themselves, so they listened to what Monsieur Baudin was saying to Mr. Sanders. They were both competing to show how much they knew about the war taking place in the desert. Ylena was the referee, trying to keep both interlocutors calm as they argued about the best strategy to follow with regards to the Afrika Korps. The colonel liked to mock Monsieur Baudin by reminding him that Marshal Pétain marched to the beat of the German drums.

Monsieur Baudin was not in favor of Pétain, but he was annoyed by the way in which Colonel Sanders boasted of the fact that England was still trying to rein in Hitler. For his part, although Pereira was sure that the war would be both long and difficult to win, the arrival of the United States could tip the balance of the conflict in their favor.

"And the Russians. Don't forget the Russians," Ylena said.

"You're right, my dear Ylena," the captain said. "Hitler may have made a mistake in underestimating them: the Russians are a brave and long-suffering people who will fight to the last man. They'll stop Hitler, you'll see."

"What's life like in the free zone?" Eulogio suddenly asked Monsieur Baudin.

"To be honest with you, the phrase free zone is little more than a euphemism. I have to agree with Colonel Sanders here; as a Frenchman, Pétain's decisions make me very ashamed … My friends in Paris tell me that the Germans are completely at home there … and as for the area controlled by Marshal Pétain, things aren't going well … especially not for foreigners, unless they're Germans or Italians."

After the meal, to the surprise of Fernando and Eulogio, Ylena announced that the next morning at seven o'clock they were to baptize Adela. Captain Pereira would be the godfather and she would be the godmother. That was what Catalina had decided.

"You're all invited to the ceremony at Saint Catherine's Cathedral. It won't be too long."

"No, it'll be a short ceremony, because as soon as it's over, I've got to set sail for Brazil," Pereira declared.

"It's a real coincidence that out of all the different faiths there are in Alexandria, the Catholic cathedral should be dedicated to Saint Catherine, our *Santa Catalina*," Baudin said with a smile.

"I'd be delighted to come," Colonel Sanders said, a little confused, because the last thing he would have thought he'd be invited to was a baptism.

Catalina thanked them all and then gave Captain Pereira an emotional hug.

"You've done so much for me! I'll never be able to repay you."

"Oh, don't say that. We weren't going to leave the little girl unbaptized, and it's an honor for me to be the godfather. The sea kept me away from the birth of my daughter and my granddaughters, and so it's only thanks to Adela that I know how people come into this world."

"You saved her life," Catalina said gratefully.

As soon as the captain had left, the Englishman and the Frenchman asked to leave the table so they could go and play their usual game of chess in the library. Fernando caught Catalina's eye. He wanted to talk to her. They couldn't keep delaying the conversation about what they were going to do.

Catalina, slightly annoyed, invited him to her room. She preferred not to speak in front of Eulogio.

After laying Adela down on the bed, Catalina sat down on a chair and invited Fernando to do the same.

"She's so peaceful," he said, watching Adela sleep.

"Yes, she's very good. She doesn't have strength for much, poor thing."

"But she's getting better. Adela is stronger than she looks," Fernando said.

"Well, what do you want to tell me?" Catalina suddenly grew tense.

"Eulogio's leaving in a couple of days," Fernando declared.

She felt the news like a punch to the gut. Although she didn't get along that well with Eulogio, his presence was a link to the Spain they had left behind.

"With Marvin, of course."

"Yes, with Marvin and Farida."

"To America?"

Fernando didn't know if he should tell her the truth, but he didn't know how to lie, and neither did he want to.

"No, they're not going to America for the time being. I think they're going to France. With Marvin, things never turn out the way they're planned," he admitted.

Catalina nodded, gazing vaguely up at the ceiling. She seemed defeated.

"Why won't he see me?" she said, looking him straight in the eye.

"I don't know, but he gets very irritated just to hear your name. The best thing would be for him to speak to you and for him to say what he thinks. But he refuses, and I can't understand why he's so insistent on it. He keeps saying that he doesn't owe you any explanation."

"He's given me Adela, and he can't ignore that fact," she replied.

Fernando sat in silence for a few seconds as he looked for the right words, the words he had held back for so long. He couldn't carry on without saying them, or the chasm that had opened up between them would become permanent.

"Catalina, I swear that I would give my right hand for you and Marvin to … Look, I'm not saying that I wouldn't suffer, that it wouldn't hurt, but I'm not so selfish as to want you and your daughter to live in shame. And I've understood for a long time now that you will never love me. I resisted that, I admit. My secret dream was that one day you would wake up and say that you had realized that you loved me ... But dreams are just that: dreams. So, there is never going to be anything more than friendship between us. But what I can do is offer you my pure friendship, forever. You can always count on me for whatever you need. I can't be happy, but I'll do whatever I can to make you happy."

Catalina was surprised by Fernando's declaration. She wasn't prepared for his words, so sincere that they disarmed her. She felt sorry that she had wounded him a few days before.

She swallowed and tried to think of a suitable reply.

"Thank you for saying that ... I ... I'm sorry, I wish I could fall in love with you, but ... I can't, Fernando, I can't. I love you, yes, I love you a great deal, as much as I love my family, and I don't want you to remember those horrible things I said to you a few days ago. You didn't deserve them ... Please understand ... I'm nervous ... the birth at sea, Adela's illness, this strange city, the hospital, being so far from Spain and my parents ... I ... I don't know what I would have done without you."

Catalina got up and stood in front of him, holding her hands out to him. Fernando got up and hugged her. They spent a few seconds wrapped in a consoling embrace. Then she leaned over Adela, trying to hold back her tears.

"Go back to Spain. It's the best thing for you. Your parents will take you in without question when they see Adela. Antoñito won't want to marry you, and everything will be sorted out. You don't have to keep running away," Fernando said.

"That's what Captain Pereira and Ylena recommend as well, but ... no, I'm not going back. I won't go back until I speak to Marvin and he acknowledges his daughter. If he says that he doesn't want anything to do with us after that, then ... No, even then I couldn't go back to Spain, because of the shame I'd bring on my parents. But I think that Marvin is an honorable man. You know him, you know how sensitive he is. I think it must be this woman who doesn't let him see me. I know that as soon as he's free of her, he'll come and find me and Adela. And that's why it's important for me to see him."

Fernando didn't know what else he could say. He felt overwhelmed by Catalina's stubbornness. He asked himself how she could be so blind. But he found the answer at once. He had been blind himself, to anyone who said that she would never love him.

"Alexandria is not the best place to live. You don't know Arabic, and you're not that good at English."

"But there are lots of people here who speak French ... Look, there's Ylena, and Mr. Sanders, and even Dimitra knows a few words. Don't forget that I was in the hospital for a good long time and that I was able to be understood by the nurses ... Gestures are universal. And ... Ylena loaned me an English texbook, and one for Arabic: I'm getting into them and maybe I'll be able to make myself understood. But the problem is that I need to find work, although ... well, if Marvin's going to France, I'll go too."

"You're crazy! It's the last place you should go. And they're not going to stay in France; it's only the first port on their voyage."

He explained what Marvin's task in Vichy was, and how he was going out of loyalty to his editor.

"What you say only confirms to me how kind Marvin is. A man who is capable of risking his life for his former editor is a good man. You're right, Fernando ... it's this woman who's making him stop doing the right thing by me and taking charge of Adela," Catalina said.

"I don't know what to think," he admitted.

Dawn had not yet broken when all the lodgers met around the breakfast table. They were due to meet Captain Pereira at six thirty on the dot at the cathedral entrance.

Monsieur Baudin was going to take them in his car. Ylena sat next to the Frenchman, with Catalina, Fernando and Eulogio squashed together in the back. Mr. Sanders had already set off to walk to the cathedral, as he had refused to even consider such a tight squeeze.

On the way to the church, the Frenchman told them a little bit about its history. Saint Catherine had been martyred here, and the angels, taking pity on her, had taken her to Mount Sinai, in the desert, where a vast monastery bearing the saint's name was built.

"Well, the cathedral was really built because of Muhammad Ali," Ylena said. "He gave the Catholics a bit of land in 1832 so they could build their church."

"And who was Muhammad Ali?" Catalina asked seriously as she tried to find a bit of space between Eulogio and Fernando.

"The founder of the current ruling dynasty. He fought against the Saudis and conquered the Upper Nile and Sudan. He fought against the Greeks and took back control of sacred Islamic sites in Arabia, and invaded Syria and Palestine ... he was a conqueror who made Alexandria his capital. But the great powers put an end to his conquests and his ambition. France and England forced him to settle for Egypt," Monsieur Baudin explained.

"Colonel Sanders likes to remind us all that it was Admiral Sir Charles Napier who made Muhammad Ali confine himself to Egypt," Ylena added.

"And what about the Turkish sultan? Didn't he oppose Muhammad Ali's conquests?" Eulogio asked with curiosity.

"He had no choice but to name him governor. Muhammad Ali liked to deal in *faits accomplis*," Ylena replied.

"He opened Egypt and Alexandria up to foreigners. He encouraged trade. You have to admit that he knew how to modernize the city. Alexandria is what it is today thanks to him," Monsieur Baudin said.

The Cathedral of Saint Catherine was in the square that bore its name, and Mr. Sanders and Captain Pereira were both there, impatiently pacing side by side.

They greeted one another and went into the church. Catalina didn't think this church – her saint's church – was particularly beautiful, but she said nothing. The smell of incense and candles enveloped her.

They walked quickly over to the font, where a priest was waiting for them. Ylena introduced them.

"Father Lucas will baptize Adela. He's going to carry out the service in French ..."

The priest bowed his head and asked the godparents to stand next to the font. Ylena took Adela, who was sleeping peacefully.

A few minutes later, Adela had received the holy water and

Catalina was smiling happily because her daughter was now a Catholic.

They went into the sacristy to complete the necessary forms, and Father Lucas, who was pleasant but not very talkative, was soon saying goodbye to them.

As they stood in the doorway, Catalina hugged Captain Pereira and started to cry. Pereira was going back to sea, and he himself didn't know when he was going to return. Catalina was sad to see him go. The man had treated her like a daughter. She felt safe by his side, and sure that if he were near, then nothing could happen to her.

"Don't cry, you need to be strong for Adela. And please, listen to me, go back to Spain: this city isn't for you," the captain recommended.

She only hugged him tighter. She wished she could follow his advice, and had said as much, but she was committed to finding Marvin and making him take responsibility for Adela.

After they had said their goodbyes, each went their own way. The captain headed for the port, where his crew and the *Esperanza del Mar* were waiting for him; Monsieur Baudin drove Ylena and Catalina back home; Eulogio said he was going to say goodbye to Sudi Kamel, and Mr. Sanders simply announced that he was going to take the tram.

Fernando stood to one side, and no one seemed to take much notice of him. Once everyone had left, he went back into the cathedral and sat in the back row of pews. He didn't know why. Maybe it was because this was a place that offered him the opportunity to be alone with himself, without any words surrounding him.

He let his mind wander and smiled when he thought about how surprised his mother would have been to see him there, sitting on a pew in a church. As for his father ... well, he would not have said anything. He knew that his father was an atheist, and that he never went into churches, but he had always been respectful of his mother's beliefs, and had walked with her to the door of the church and then smoked a cigarette while he waited for Mass to finish. He hadn't stopped Fernando from being baptized or taking his First Communion. But he, Fernando, had taken on his father's atheism as his own when he was a teenager, and had never again seriously set foot in a church until that day. His father had never allowed him to speak disrespectfully of religion, and had made him respect the beliefs of others.

The smell of incense was intense, but rather than bothering him, it made him feel good about himself. The candles on the high altar were lit and gave the space a ghostly, solemn air.

He was so caught up in his thoughts that he didn't see Father Lucas walking up the side aisle until he reached the place where Fernando sat. He sat down next to him, and suddenly Fernando felt uncomfortable. He was enjoying the silence and was worried that the priest would bring him back to the real world. But Father Lucas did no more than take out his rosary. They sat in silence until the priest turned to him and spoke:

"You can stay for as long as you want, but the eight o'clock Mass is about to start."

"I was just leaving …" Fernando didn't know what to say.

"I also like being here when there's no one around. It's the part of the day I like the most. You really feel the silence."

Fernando looked skeptical. It wasn't possible to feel silence. Father Lucas smiled and looked back at him.

"Yes, you can feel the silence, and enjoy it, but there are times when it can be overwhelming as well."

They sat in silence for a while, with Fernando trying to hear the silence and Father Lucas praying.

"I'm leaving now. Thank you, Father."

"Why thank me?"

"Well … the baptism was great," Fernando said, just to say something.

"Little Adela … I hope that the Lord looks after her. There are times when the Lord takes us beyond our own strength. Ylena Kokkalis told me about Catalina and you and your friend … Eulogio? Is that his name?"

"Yes … We've been friends forever. We were born in the same neighborhood," Fernando replied.

"And fate has brought you here."

"Eulogio is going to leave, and … Catalina and I … well, we don't yet know what we're going to do."

"What do you want to do?" the priest asked.

"Well, I don't know … my life was going to be very different, but …" Fernando fell silent, asking himself why he was being so open with this priest.

"Yes … our dreams very rarely fit into reality," Father Lucas said.

"You're a priest and I don't think you know very much about life," Fernando said, who was already beginning to regret this conversation.

"No one knows much about life. It's a great mystery that still has not been revealed to us. We look for explanations, and some of us look to the skies, and some inside themselves, and some people try to find the light via old legends and traditions … But who knows the truth?"

"I thought that priests had it all figured out," Fernando said.

"I can't speak for others, but only for myself."

"But you believe in God …" Fernando insisted.

Father Lucas shrugged and a group of women came into the cathedral, ready to sit down and hear Mass.

"Let's go out, unless you want to hear Mass …"

The sun was rising in the East, but its light had only just begun to spill over the horizon.

Alexandria was waking up, and the bells announced the eight o'clock Mass. They started to walk alongside one another.

"There was a Franciscan church here before," Father Lucas explained. "And now Saint Catherine's is the main Catholic church, and the archbishop's residence is just behind it."

"What about this?"

"This? It's the tomb of Sidi el-Metralli, an Islamic saint. In Spain, like in France, the cathedrals are beautiful. Saint Catherine's can't compete with them."

"And this other church?" Fernando asked, pointing to his left.

"The Church of the Annunciation. It's Greek Orthodox. This is where Ylena Kokkalis usually attends services. If you want to see a more beautiful place of worship, then you should go to the Attarine Mosque, which is near here. It used to be the church of Saint Athanasius, but in the seventh century, when the Arabs conquered the city, they turned it into a mosque. It's like the Ibn Tulun Mosque in Cairo. Do you know it?"

"No, I don't know Cairo at all."

"Right. This is no time to be a tourist, but if you are in Egypt, it's unforgivable for you not to go to the capital. Legends has it that Alexander the Great is buried in the mosque. There was a sarcophagus found in it that weighed several tons, and people thought that it must be his."

"And where is the sarcophagus now?"

"The British have it; they took it away. The most reputable archeologists now claim that it was not Alexander in the sarcophagus, but the Pharaoh Nekhut-Heru-Hebt, who lived in the fourth century before Christ."

"And what do you believe?"

"This isn't a matter of belief, but rather of science."

"But they buried Alexander the Great in Alexandria ..." Fernando insisted.

"He was buried in Memphis, but Ptolemy II had the body taken to Alexandria ... there was a terrible earthquake in the fourth century which probably destroyed the Soma, which was the Macedonian's mausoleum. It might be that the king's remains were removed from the sarcophagus beforehand, but when Napoleon came to Egypt, he ordered it be found, and his archeologists did find it, but it was empty ... Then the English took it."

"But how can you say that it was Alexander's sarcophagus and at the same time the tomb of a pharaoh?"

"The theory is that Ptolemy used the tomb of this pharaoh to bury Alexander ... But there are theories about everything, including that the body of Alexander was taken by Venetian merchants back to their home city and can be found in what is now considered the tomb of Saint Mark."

"But the tomb of Saint Mark is in the Basilica in Venice!"

"Yes."

"Thank you." Fernando's expression of gratitude was spontaneous.

"Thank you? Why?"

"For telling me this story. My father used to tell me stories of the olden days. He ... Well, he spent his life translating English literature. Shakespeare was an open book to him … But he also translated from ancient Greek."

"And you loved him more than anyone in the world."

"Yes, there was no one like my father."

"Congratulations. We don't all have good reason to admire our parents."

Fernando was disconcerted by what Father Lucas said. Suddenly he realized that they had reached the Attarine Mosque, and that the priest was entering it with firm footsteps.

He pointed out various items of interest and stopped to talk to the imam, who was seated on the floor reading the Koran.

When they went out into the street again, Fernando, much against his will, said goodbye to Father Lucas.

"Time flies when you're having fun. It's past nine. I need to go to work. I'll be late," he said.

"Take the tram. And come back when you can."

"Will you always be in the cathedral?"

"Yes, I will."

"I'll be back." Fernando surprised even himself with this affirmation.

Athanasius Vryzas greeted Fernando distractedly when he came into the offices of Wilson & Wilson. Sara was sitting next to him and they were going over a manuscript together. They barely paid him any attention, so Fernando sat down to work. He felt at peace, but he did not know why. Well, of course he knew why. Spending time in Father Lucas' company had left him with this feeling. He said to himself that the man did not seem like a priest. He did not speak like any priest he had ever known, although he had to admit that the only priest he'd had much contact with was Don Bernardo. But he was nothing like Father Lucas, even though they were both the same age, around sixty.

He looked at Sara Rosent and Vryzas out of the corner of his eye. They often worked together on their editions.

Sara had inherited her love of poetry from her father, and it was clear how much she enjoyed finding new poets.

Barely an hour had passed before Leyda Zabat came to find him and asked him to go up to Mr. Wilson's office.

Fernando liked Leyda. She was nice to everyone, and never boasted about her influence as the boss' right-hand woman.

When he came into the office, Fernando was surprised to see a tall, thin man standing next to Mr. Wilson. He had dark skin and part of his face and his head were covered in a Bedouin scarf. They were both looking at a map and paid Fernando very little attention; they were speaking in Arabic, and so Fernando waited impatiently for them to notice he was there. When they did, he felt that the visitor was looking him up and down with naked curiosity while Mr. Wilson introduced them.

"This is Hafid. You will leave at once for Marsa el Brega, although you won't have to get that far. Hafid has heard rumors that the Bedouin have found two injured men in the desert, and that one of them is a foreigner. We think that they might be his cousin Basim and Domenico Lombardi. Hafid has everything ready."

"When will we leave?" Fernando asked, disconcerted by Mr. Wilson's urgency and grave tone of voice.

"I told you already: right now."

"But that can't be … You told me that it would be a couple of days … I'm not ready, I don't have any proper clothing, I need to say goodbye to Eulogio, who's leaving the day after tomorrow with Marvin and Farida … I can't just disappear …"

"I already sent for clothes from Ylena's house. Your friend Catalina helped her put a bag together. And your friend Eulogio has been told that you have to do some urgent work for me. There's nothing to delay your departure."

Benjamin Wilson gave him a leather wallet which he said contained enough money for the mission. And then he told him to obey Hafid's instructions.

"Your only job is to speak to Lombardi, calm him down, and listen to anything he has to tell you. Hafid will take care of everything else."

"I told you that I don't speak Italian," Fernando reminded him.

"It doesn't matter: a Spaniard and an Italian can understand one another with no problem. That's why I'm sending you. But we've already been over this, so let's not waste our time."

"And how will I speak to Hafid?"

"In English," Benjamin Wilson said bluntly.

"I have a car parked very close," Hafid said, entering the conversation while still looking Fernando up and down. "If we go now, we will be able to get into the desert before night falls."

They went out into the street. Fernando walked behind Hafid, who had picked up his pace. The Bedouin pointed to the vehicle and indicated that he should get in.

It took them some time to leave Alexandria behind. It was noon and the traffic was slow. Hafid drove, concentrating on what was going on ahead of him. His silence started to weigh heavily on Fernando. A few times he almost told him to stop, because he didn't want to go on this journey, but he said nothing. It seemed like a betrayal for him to leave without saying goodbye to Eulogio. He didn't know if they would see one another again, and this terrified him, because Eulogio and Catalina were his last connection to the Spain he had left behind. He said to himself that he owed Wilson nothing, that the worst thing Wilson could do was fire him. If that happened, he'd look for another job: he was sure they'd need another pair of hands down at the docks.

Hafid's serious expression changed to a smile as soon as they started to drive through dry, flat terrain that seemed devoid of all life apart from the road that receded into the distance.

"We're close to Abusir," the Bedouin said suddenly.

"I don't know what there is in Abusir, but there's nothing here, it's a wasteland," Fernando said grumpily.

"There's more than meets the eye in the desert. We'll go into the Libyan desert now."

"And is it all like this?"

"If you can't see more, then yes, it is. Foreigners tend to like Abusir."

Fernando listened to him carefully. He couldn't imagine that there would be anything interesting in this inhospitable area. And he thought it would be a miracle if anything could live in this arid stretch of land.

"I hope we will reach Wadi Natrum in a few hours, where we

will find my uncle Ismail's camp. We'll leave the car there until we return," Hafid explained.

"Your uncle? And if we leave the car, how are we going to travel?"

"By camel, of course. I don't want Rommel's men to capture us."

"I thought they were in Libya."

"There are no borders in the desert. And the Germans have eyes everywhere, just like the British."

"Tell me what the plan is," Fernando asked.

"My uncle will invite us to eat, and we'll sleep in his camp. In the morning, we'll be off with a few members of my family. We're Bedouin, so we trade with everyone."

"It must be good to be friends with your enemy's friends."

Hafid laughed and slapped Fernando's thigh.

"Do you know how to ride a camel? You'll like it. It's the best way of traveling through the desert."

"So we'll travel by camel? It's crazy! We'll never get anywhere."

"We may get somewhere, but the important thing is that we'll get back. My uncle will lend us suitable clothes for the journey. Your bag will have to stay at the camp: what you're bringing with you won't be much use."

"But ..."

"Don't worry, nothing's going to happen to it. You don't know the desert, trust me. I've told you, nothing is as it seems. I was born in these dunes."

"How can people be born here?" Fernando asked naively.

"Where do you think the Bedouin are born? It's easy. Our mothers bear the wisdom of generations. It's no trouble for us to give birth here in the sands. I wouldn't want to have been born anywhere else. My mother told me that I was born at dawn, when the last stars were disappearing and the rays of the sun started to creep over the land. There is no more beautiful place to be born or to die. I ask Allah to allow me to end my days in the same way as I began them."

The sun started to warm them more than Fernando would have thought possible, given that it was the beginning of January.

"What's that?" he said, pointing to something that looked like a tower.

"I told you, Abusir. A city of the pharaohs," Hafid replied with pride. "You should visit it."

"Yes … maybe some other time," Fernando said unenthusiastically.

"Saint Menas is close as well. You should go there too. It's almost a city: the church and the holy well are still visible. Caravans used to pass through it. It was always a place for the caravans to stop. There used to be waters that cured illnesses there, but now there aren't," Hafid said.

"Curative waters? That have vanished? How can that be?" Fernando asked dismissively.

"I don't know." Hafid shrugged and looked out of the corner of his eye at his companion.

"I don't know who Saint Menas is," Fernando confessed.

They laughed cheerfully. Hafid drove quickly, without trying to avoid the potholes. He had decided that they had to reach Wadi Natrum before the light completely failed.

"It's not a problem, but I'd like to eat a good roast lamb with my uncle Ismail and my cousins. They're close to Deir Abu Bishoy."

"And what's that?" Fernando asked.

"A monastery. It's very old. It's full of monks who don't want to know anything about what's going on in the world. They spend all day praying."

"Right. They know what they're doing, I suppose," Fernando said cynically.

"It's good to pray. It brings peace to your soul."

Fernando thought that the Bedouin appeared to be a simple man, straightforward, with no secrets, but one who was also certain of his judgment. If Wilson trusted him, it must be because he had qualities that were less apparent to Fernando. Perhaps he was not as simple as he appeared to be.

The sun was starting to fade when they reached Deir Abu Bishoy. The color of its walls mingled with the sands of the desert. Fernando was struck by it: it was very different from anything that he had seen before, very different from Spanish monasteries.

Hafid parked the car near to the building and started to look around impatiently.

"What are you looking for?" Fernando asked.

"My uncle isn't here. We'll have to wait for him. He may be about to arrive, or he may not get here until tomorrow. If he doesn't come, we'll ask the monks to let us stay at the monastery."

They waited until the shadows of night had covered the desert sands, and then Hafid drove the car over to the north side, where there was a door. He got out of the car and knocked, and soon the door was opened by a monk wrapped in a black habit covered in grease spots.

The monk was so thin that Fernando thought he looked more like a corpse than a living man. Hafid spoke to him in Arabic, and the man invited them in.

"He says you can't see the tomb of the saint until tomorrow," Hafid explained.

"The saint? What saint?" Fernando was confused.

"I told him you were a Christian. The Christians who come here all come to pray at the tomb of Saint Bishoy."

"I … Well, I'm not really keen on praying to any tombs." Fernando's reply was honest and brusque.

"If you're not interested, they're not going to understand that. They let us spend the night here because you're a Christian, and I said that you needed to pray."

"You're such a liar!"

"You don't want to pray to Saint Bishoy? You'd be the first Christian who didn't."

"Hafid, let's leave saints out of this and do what we have to do. I don't know why we're here, but I didn't come to pray."

"But you will pray, or else you'll upset these good men. They promised me that you'll be able to do it as soon as dawn breaks. You should be aware that the saint's body is incorrupt."

Fernando was confused at Hafid's attitude. Where had the Bedouin got the idea from that he wanted to pray? Also, he didn't know who this Saint Bishoy even was. He didn't know anything about him.

The monk spoke with Hafid for a long while, and then took them to a corner of the garden where a few palm trees stood proudly. There, next to another building, he pointed to a door that Hafid opened.

It was a little room. On one wall there was a crucifix; another featured a portrait of a saint, who Fernando reasoned must be Saint Bishoy. There was no furniture in the room except for a simple pallet bed.

They left their bags there and followed the monk to the refectory, where they were offered a piece of dark bread with some goat's cheese. They also drank thirstily from the jugs of water they were offered. Once they had finished their meal, they went back to the room where they were to spend the night.

Hafid took a thin rug from his bag and spread it on the floor, then stretched out on top of it, lying on the stony floor.

"We could share the cot … it's small, but if we're careful the two of us will fit," Fernando said.

The Bedouin laughed in such a way that Fernando nearly got angry. But then the Bedouin explained that the rug was not for sleeping, but rather for prayer, which was what he was going to do at that moment. And then they'd talk about their sleeping arrangements.

As soon as Hafid had finished his prayers, they decided that each would sleep at one end of the cot. But in the end this wasn't necessary, because the monk reappeared with a sort of mattress, as dirty as his habit, but which would do for the night.

They argued for a while, each of them offering to take the mattress, but it was Hafid who had his way in the end.

"You're not used to the ground, but I sleep on the sands of the desert. Sleep, because we don't know what we are going to find when we come to the true desert."

And sleep they did.

Dawn had not yet broken when the monk knocked sharply at their door to wake them up. He made signs to Fernando that he was to follow him, while Hafid lay down and slept a little more.

The monk walked quickly, and Fernando, sleepy as he was, found it hard to keep up. He took him to a church lit by a few flickering candles. Fernando shivered. It was hard for his eyes to adjust to the darkness. The church, as far as he could make out,

476

was made of a long nave held up by arches, with a pillar of marble in the middle. This led through to the choir, and from there to what he assumed were chapels.

The monk walked him to the left-hand one, and once they were there he pointed out a chest.

Fernando thought he heard the monk say, "Saint Bishoy." He deduced that the saint's body must be in the chest. He didn't think this was the right moment to contradict the monk, and so he followed his lead and knelt in front of the chest. The monk closed his eyes and murmured a silent prayer. Fernando couldn't stop himself from looking at him as though he were seeing something inexplicable. They stayed this way for a long time, until the monk opened his eyes and was surprised to see Fernando looking at him. He grasped him by the sleeve to draw him close to the chest, and pushed him towards it. Fernando understood that he was being invited to touch the chest, or even to kiss it. He bent over unwillingly, kissing the vessel that contained the body of a saint who was both meaningless and unknown to him. His gesture seemed to please the monk, who pulled his sleeve again to make him walk. He took him back to the little room where Hafid was waiting for him, gathering his rug after his morning prayer.

The monk led them back to the refectory and gave them some bread and a glass of goat's milk. After speaking to Hafid for some time, he took them back to the entrance. The car was there, and he said goodbye to them before opening the door that led into the outside world.

"Has your uncle arrived?" Fernando asked.

"No, let's go and look for him. We'll find him in a couple of hours."

"How do you know that?"

"They told me."

"Right. And when did they tell you?"

"Last night."

"Last night?"

"Yes, the monk told me. They know everything that's happening in Wadi Natrum. My uncle and his family are eight or ten hours away from here. Someone's sick."

"I ... well ... I don't understand anything," Fernando said.

"It's easy. Instead of meeting my uncle at the monastery of Saint Bishoy, we'll find him in the desert."

"And how can you find someone in the desert?"

Hafid laughed again. Fernando's questions seemed to him almost childishly simple.

"Do you get lost in your house?" the Bedouin asked.

"No, of course not ..." Fernando said, getting ever more confused.

"Well, I don't get lost in mine."

When the car started, he felt a warm breeze on his face. Hafid recommended that he cover himself up with the Bedouin scarf.

They said nothing for a good long while. Fernando flinched when he felt his memories begin to attack him, like ghosts that had been lying in wait. Suddenly he saw again the faces of the two men whom he had shot, and felt a twisting feeling in his gut. Roque and Saturnino Pérez forced their way to the forefront of his mind.

He closed his eyes to try to get rid of the memory, but the two dead men stubbornly held on inside his mind, refusing to leave. He felt like gagging, and must have made some kind of noise, because Hafid looked at him and stopped the car dead.

"What's wrong?"

"I don't know ... something that doesn't agree with me ... maybe the goat's milk ... I'm not used to it."

"Right. Well, get out and try to vomit, you'll feel better. I'll smoke a cigarette."

Fernando obeyed and got out of the car, walking a few steps away from it. He felt relief once he had vomited, but the faces of the two men still haunted him.

Hafid gave him a canteen of water.

"Drink slowly and not too much, or you'll feel sick."

"Not now ..."

The Bedouin shrugged and didn't insist. He took another drag of his cigarette and breathed in the gray smoke. Then he threw the cigarette to the ground and put it out with his foot. Fernando was dizzy, and he felt a heaviness on his heart where the two murdered men refused to leave him alone.

Hafid told him to get in the car and they set off again. They drove in silence, although the Bedouin looked at him from time to time. After an hour, Fernando asked him to stop again. He was feeling nauseous again, and was dizzy.

It was hot, he felt sweat soak through his shirt.

"The best thing for you to do is to hang on for a while, and we'll get to my uncle's camp sooner. They'll give you something there to make you feel better."

"Perhaps we should go back to Alexandria …"

"Impossible. We need to do what Mr. Wilson has asked us to do. In my uncle's camp you can rest."

"I don't want to rest … I feel sick …"

However, Hafid was unmoved by Fernando's sorry state. His duty to Mr. Wilson was stronger than any illness that this young Spaniard might be suffering.

They had to stop four more times for Fernando to vomit, as he cursed the goat's milk that had turned his stomach. The desert seemed like a monotonous place to him. A few more hours had passed, and the sun was receding over the horizon, when Hafid stopped the car and smiled.

"We're nearly there," he said happily.

"Where?" Fernando said disconcertedly, because there was nothing in front of them apart from rocks and dark sand.

"My uncle's camp is very close."

He was right. They had barely gone a few miles further when they suddenly saw a group of black tents with some little children playing in front of them.

"Is this your uncle's camp?"

"Yes. We'll eat well here."

The very mention of food was enough to make Fernando want to be sick again. This made Hafid laugh.

He accelerated, and a few seconds later stopped in front of the tents. A few men appeared from nowhere and came over to them.

Hafid got out of the car and greeted them effusively. He waved a hand in Fernando's direction. It was clear that Hafid was talking about him, but Fernando's ignorance of Arabic meant he couldn't understand what they said.

Hafid left him standing by the car while he went into one of the tents. Fernando heard his voice and his laugh in conversation with other voices and other laughs. Then Hafid came back, bringing with him another man with dark skin and an imposing bearing. You could feel his strength and authority.

Hafid introduced Fernando and his uncle Ismail.

"So you're sick … let's give you something to make you better," Ismail said in very good English, much to Fernando's relief, as he hadn't known how he was going to make himself understood by the Bedouin.

They took him to one of the tents, and Hafid pointed to a cushion and told him to sit down.

"My uncle's wife will bring you some tea. It'll make you feel better."

"I don't like tea, and if I drink it, it will make me feel worse," Fernando said, his gut churning.

"It's not tea like the English drink. You'll like it, but more importantly, it will make you feel better. Listen to what I'm saying. Rest now, and this evening, if you feel up to it, we can dine."

He sat in the tent and a couple of children played next to him. It did not take long for a figure to come into the tent, dressed in a black garment that didn't show a single inch of skin. Only her weather-worn face was left bare. The woman's eyes shone intently, and her hands were as leathery as her face. He calculated that she must be around fifty years old. Then he thought that he didn't care how old she was, and also that it was impossible to tell such things just from someone's eyes and hands.

The woman put a chipped cup into his hands filled with a steaming liquid that gave off a comforting odor of mint. She stood in front of him and waited for him to drink it. Unwillingly, Fernando started to take small sips. He was surprised by the pleasant taste of this beverage, which was nothing like the tea he knew.

The woman waited for him to empty the cup, not moving until he had done so. When he had taken the last sip, she went to find something in the depths of the tent, and he was surprised when she gave him a cushion. She indicated that he should lie down. He obeyed. Then she said something to the two little children who were watching him curiously, and they left the tent with her, leaving him alone.

Fernando closed his eyes, afraid that the faces of the men he had killed would be back to visit him, but although their faces did appear, they were blurred and vague.

He couldn't tell exactly when he fell asleep, but when he woke up, it was dark and the whole camp seemed silent except for the crackling of campfires.

He felt better. The nausea had faded, but he was soaked in sweat and felt light-headed when he sat up. Even so, he decided to move.

There was a man next to him. It was Hafid, who was sleeping peacefully. Two other men slept next to them. One of them opened his eyes and looked at him, but said nothing, merely observing the Spaniard.

Fernando, trying not to step on either of the men who slept on the floor of the tent, walked out into the night. The cold made him feel better.

He tried not to make any noise, because everyone in the camp was asleep, and he started to walk without knowing where he was going, just to stretch his legs.

He gave a start and could not stop himself from giving a little shout when a hand closed over his shoulder and another one covered his mouth.

"Don't shout, or you'll wake everyone up," he heard someone say in English.

It was Ismail, who had appeared at his side. As Fernando calmed himself down, he wondered where the man had come from, seemingly out of nowhere.

"I didn't see you," he said.

"No, but I saw you. You shouldn't leave the camp, you might get lost."

"I wasn't trying to leave," Fernando apologized.

"Are you feeling better?"

"Yes, at least I'm not feeling sick anymore."

"Nafia knows how to cure people with herbs. It's one of her best qualities as a wife."

"Ah. Well, thank her for me."

"Hafid said that you drank fresh goat's milk. Nafia says that's what must have made you feel ill, and that you shouldn't have done it, because you're not used to it."

"I'm certainly not going to drink goat's milk again," Fernando said firmly.

"Go back to sleep; there are still a few hours to go before dawn breaks," Ismail recommended.

They went back to the camp, and Ismail pointed Fernando to the tent he should use, while he went back to another one nearby. Fernando was surprised to see a young woman appear at the entrance to the tent. She couldn't have been more than sixteen or seventeen years old. Her face was uncovered, and her hair was short and curly. Her skin was as black as night and her body was slender.

Ismail turned back before he went into the young woman's tent and his face grew stern, but then he seemed to relax and smiled before vanishing into the tent's shadows.

Fernando asked himself who this young woman might be, and what Ismail was doing in her tent. She wasn't his wife, that was clear. He stepped on one of the sleeping men without realizing, and the fellow sat up angrily. But it was really Fernando who was startled, as he saw a knife shining in the man's hands. He made apologetic gestures and made his way back to where Hafid was sleeping, trying not to step on anyone else. He thought he wouldn't fall asleep again, but he was mistaken. He sank back into a deep sleep.

It was hard for him to wake up. Hafid shook him carefully to rouse him. When he opened his eyes, it took him a few seconds to remember where he was.

"Nafia has brought you another cup of tea. She says it'll do you good," Hafid said, pointing to a cup at his side.

"Thank you … I slept like a log, even though I woke up in the middle of the night …"

"As soon as you're ready we'll go and speak to my uncle. He told me about my cousin Basim and the Italian yesterday."

"Good news, I hope," Fernando replied.

Hafid shrugged and left him to drink his tea.

Having drained the cup, Fernando wondered if he would look ridiculous asking for some water to wash himself, even if it was just a sponge bath. He decided it was worth the risk, because he felt sweaty and smelly, and his clothes were stuck to his body.

He left the tent and saw a group of women talking nearby. He went over to them and thought he recognized the woman from last night, and so he went to her to ask for water. The woman looked at him in astonishment while the others laughed uproariously. Nafia brought them back to reality. He couldn't understand what she was saying, but it was clear she was scolding the young woman. Then she did the same with the rest of them, before calling Hafid to ask what the foreigner wanted. Fernando explained to Hafid that he wanted a little water to wash. Hafid said as much to Nafia, and they discussed this with some agitation. Then Hafid sourly told Fernando to go back to the tent, and that Nafia would bring him the water.

She came to him with a small vessel and a scrap of grayish cloth. She gave it to him and left the tent, leaving him alone.

They hadn't been very generous with the water, he thought, so he had to make do with what they had given him. At least it would be enough for him to wash his face and rinse his body. He took clean clothes out of the bag and, feeling better about himself, left the tent to look for Hafid and Ismail. Nafia seemed to be waiting for him, and made him a sign for him to follow her. She took him to the entrance to a tent in which several men were arguing.

Ismail waved him in and indicated that he should sit down next to Hafid in the circle of men around him.

"My uncle says that we have to return to Alexandria tomorrow," Hafid said.

"To Alexandria? What about finding this Italian, and your cousin who was helping him?"

"They're dead," Ismail said coldly.

"Dead?" A shiver ran down Fernando's spine.

"They shot them. Once the garrison realized that the Italian had disappeared, they sent a patrol out to look for them. They found them and tried to stop them. They exchanged gunfire and a German shot the Italian. My son Basim was wounded as well, but they thought he was dead and left him there. My men found him a few days ago, badly wounded. That's why we couldn't come to Saint Bishoy. He died before my nephew Hafid and you came to the camp. Basim's body has already been delivered to the earth."

Ismail's face was emotionless. He didn't seem to be upset at his son's death. Even so, Fernando felt the need to offer his condolences.

"I'm sorry about your son ..."

Ismail cut him off with a gesture.

"Life doesn't belong to us: it's nothing more than a loan. Basim knew that he could die and accepted this. My family has a blood debt to Benjamin Wilson. We will honor Basim's death, but there's nothing more we can do."

"Nafia says you should rest for one more day before we go back," Hafid said.

"I'm feeling better ... I don't mind if we leave now," Fernando replied.

"If I were you, I'd follow my wife's advice," Ismail said.

"Thank you, but I don't think it's necessary," Fernando said.

"We're staying. It's the best thing to do," Hafid said, to Fernando's surprise.

He left the tent with Hafid. Ismail and his men carried on talking.

"Your uncle is a very hard man. He doesn't seem to be upset by his son's death. And your aunt Nafia ..."

"She cried for him all day and all night. She did everything she could to save his life. You can imagine her pain."

"Yes, but I don't know ... she's so ... so cold."

"Cold? I don't know what you mean by that. She cried along with the other women, and she washed and shrouded Basim's body before committing it to the earth. Pain will never leave her heart. No mother ever stops grieving for the child she has lost. You must know that. And now I will show you the camp: last night you saw nothing."

Fernando felt weak, but he didn't want to say no to Hafid. He asked himself what there might be to see here, apart from black tents standing firm on the ground and a corral with some horses and a few camels.

They walked among the tents. Hafid greeted several old men who sat in front of their tents, smoking indifferently.

"You see those rocks over there?" Hafid waved to his right, where a few rocks and some bare palm trees made a strange sight.

484

"Yes."

There's a well there. It's not the best one in the desert, but at least there's water."

"And why don't you camp over there?"

"My uncle prefers to look after the wells, and he says that if we camp too close to them, we'll end up ruining them."

They saw three young women coming towards them carrying pitchers. Fernando made out among them the black-skinned girl he had seen the night before.

"Who's that?" he asked, pointing.

"She's called Havira. That's the name my uncle gave her when he bought her. It means 'Favorite.'"

"He bought her? But ... how?" Fernando said, shocked.

"Yes, he bought her from some merchants in the south of Sudan a couple of years ago. It was a good purchase. Havira is strong, and will give him children, and will make his old age more enjoyable."

"But that's horrible! Havira's a ... a slave!"

"Yes, a slave. What's wrong with that? My uncle and my father aren't slave traders, but it's very lucrative. They have a few slaves for their own personal use."

Hafid's explanations scandalized Fernando so much that he looked in horror at the Bedouin.

"But your aunt ... I mean Nafia, the wife of Ismail ...doesn't she say anything about it?"

"What's she going to say? Women don't comment on men's business. Nothing would work if they did. That's why you have so many problems: you let your womenfolk talk too much. Nafia is a wise woman; she's been my uncle Ismail's only wife, and she treats his slaves well. Havira is not the first woman to warm my uncle's bed. There have been two others, who are now more or less the same age as Nafia. My uncle could have had other wives, but he didn't want there to be anyone who could be on equal terms with Nafia. She's happy with this, and accepts the slaves with pleasure. She looks after Havira as if she were her own daughter."

"She's young enough to be her granddaughter," Fernando said indignantly.

Hafid looked at the Spaniard and couldn't understand why he was so prejudiced. Of course, this was not the first time that a European had been scandalized because Islam allowed men to have more than one wife.

"My uncle is very fond of Havira, so it would be better for you not to look at her. He'd slit your throat if you did, and Mr. Wilson, though he might be upset, would understand."

They reached the bare rocks where the three women, laid out across the sand, were drawing water that seemed to Fernando to be much too thick and dark to be drinkable.

Neither he nor Hafid said anything to them. They went back to the camp.

Fernando felt himself overcome by the heat; the warm air and the sand scratched his throat. He didn't understand why they didn't go back to Alexandria straight away. He was keen to get back to his room in Ylena's house and have a real shower.

They walked among the tents for a while. Hafid spoke to the men, laughed with them, slapped them on the back, stopped to smoke a cigarette. He seemed to be enjoying these moments, which to Fernando seemed endless. And he was also starting to feel odd pinching feelings in his stomach, which he thought were a sign that he might be about to be sick again. Hafid saw that he wasn't feeling well, and suggested that he go back into the tent and sit down for a bit. Then he went to find Nafia once more.

She looked him up and down. Her eyes ran over his face, stopped at his chest, and then continued down over his stomach to his feet. Then she said something to Hafid and left the tent, leaving them alone.

"She says that she's going to bring more tea and that you need to rest or else we won't be able to leave tomorrow. You're not better yet."

"And how does she know?"

"Nafia has a gift, a gift that her mother had, and her mother's mother, and their mother before them ... She knows what we suffer from simply by looking at us, and she knows how to use herbs to cure us. I would listen to her if I were you. Come on, lie down for a bit and rest."

Fernando would have liked to resist and ignore the fact that his stomach was starting to twist with nausea once again, and that he was feeling dizzy. But instead he accepted Nafia's recommendations without protest, and fell down on one of the evil-smelling rugs that covered the floor of the tent. The smell was intense, and he wondered how he hadn't noticed it the night before.

The tea which Nafia brought him sank him back into a deep sleep from which he did not return until the sun started to fade on the horizon of the endless desert. He felt his body soaked in sweat, and the nausea pulling at his stomach. He didn't want to miss his mother at moments like this, but he would have felt better if she had been there to put her smooth, cool hands on his forehead, to comfort him with words and kind gestures.

He missed her so much that he felt a sharp pain near his heart.

Ever since he had left Spain, he had tried to stop thinking about his mother, so as not to be dragged into melancholy, which might lead to despair.

He knew that she would be worried, waiting every day to see if the mail would arrive with a letter from him.

His mother had no one left but him, and he had decided to choose revenge, even knowing that it would mean their separation. And although the faces of the two men he had killed still appeared in his dreams, he did not regret having taken their lives; at least that was what he thought, because he still hated those two men, the prison guard and the soldier, who had taken part in his father's murder. Maybe their faces, eternal ghosts, would leave him no peace or let him forget them, but he did not care, as he would never have been able to forgive himself for not taking revenge for his father's murder. Yes, murder: that's what the military tribunal had done when it added his father's name to the list of men to be shot.

He thought of Nafia, who had lost Basim. Her dark black eyes were filled with pain. But Ismail … did he feel the loss of his son so deeply? He had been with Havira just the night before …

He realized that his mouth was dry, with tiny grains of sand between his teeth. He needed water. He got up and tried to leave the tent without falling.

No one noticed him, but his attention was caught by a group of men and camels who he hadn't seen before, who appeared and added their numbers to the camp.

Hafid materialized out of nowhere and gave him a slap on the back.

"They're family members," he said, pointing to the new group of Bedouin.

"Yes, you have very large families," he said, just to say something.

"Yes, Allah blessed our women with many children."

"When can we go?"

"Tomorrow. You'll be better. That's what Nafia says. Maybe we'll go back via Deir el Baramus. You know him as Saint Baramus."

"Saint Baramus? What kind of a saint is that?" Fernando asked, confused by all these saints he didn't recognize.

"I'm not a Christian. You'll need to ask the monks."

"Right ... And why do we have to go there?"

"Well, maybe it will be better to go by Deir es Suriani ... We'll see."

"And what is Deir es Suriani?" Fernando asked, tired of Hafid's lack of explanations.

"Another monastery, like Saint Bishoy and Saint Baramus. The important thing is for us to be able to rest before we go back to Alexandria."

Nafia brought him a basin of water for him to wash himself again, and then he went out to be with Hafid again, who seemed happy to see the men of the new caravan.

Hafid told him that they came from a long way away, from the depths of Arabia, and that they had brought goods to trade. Later on, he invited him to sit with the men by the fire, and share their roast lamb, unleavened bread, olives and goat's cheese.

The women had prepared the lamb, roasting it with care, but they didn't sit down to share their dinner with the men. They served them quickly and stood around attentively.

The men spoke in loud voices and at times seemed to be arguing, but a single word or gesture from Ismail was enough for them to lower their voices. Fernando understood nothing of what they said, but from time to time, Hafid translated a few words.

They did not spend much time with those men. Nafia thought that he shouldn't have more than a little bread for his evening meal, along with that beverage that was not tea.

In spite of the fact that he was hungry, his stomach seemed to agree with Nafia. If he had eaten the spiced lamb, he was sure that he would have felt sick immediately.

He drank the tea and started to doze off. He got up, trying not to be noticed, and went back to the tent that he shared with Hafid and some of Ismail's sons.

He went to sleep straight away, and slept until his companion shook him awake.

"Get up, we're going to be late."

When they left the tent, the sky was still the color of night, but Hafid assured him that it would shortly be dawn and that it was better for them to be on their way. The car took a while to start, in spite of the fact that he had covered it with a large tarpaulin to stop the desert from swallowing it up. When the motor finally coughed into life, dawn was already in the sky.

Fernando was fascinated with the confidence with which Hafid drove. How was it possible that in the middle of this rocky landscape, he knew where to go? Everything looked the same to him, but Hafid didn't hesitate. After a while, he wanted to chat. The Bedouin was not given to confessions, and at first he was reluctant to reply to Fernando's questions, but he eventually gave in.

Hafid told him that he had a wife and four children, but that his wife was not a Bedouin, but rather a woman from Alexandria, and so they did not live in the desert. He missed camp life, the wandering from one place to the next, shivering in cold by night and welcoming the heat of the sun when it reached them in the mornings.

He had married his wife with the unwilling support of his family. His parents had given their grudging consent for him to marry a woman who was not a Bedouin. But he had fallen in love with the honey-colored gaze of the Alexandrian woman who had become the mother of his four children and who would soon give him a fifth.

She was intelligent, he explained, and she knew that it was impossible to prevent a son of the desert from finding his strength in the golden sands. And so every now and then Hafid went off with his people, taking his two oldest sons with him, letting them enjoy the freedom that came from living among the endless dunes.

Fernando felt better, but his stomach was still uneasy, so he rejected the bread and cheese that Hafid offered him. He wasn't thirsty either, but the Bedouin insisted that he take small sips of water, and Fernando obeyed him.

A little while before nightfall, Hafid told him that they were about to reach Deir es Suriani.

A monk let them in, and took them to meet the abbot. Hafid handed over a package which the holy man took with satisfaction. Fernando wondered what might be in the package, which he had not realized they were bringing with them; in the desert, people and objects appear and disappear as if by magic.

The monk invited them to go with him to the refectory. On a large stone table, they saw a jug with water with lemon, a bowl of olives, some goat's cheese and some dates.

Hafid sat down and poured two glasses of water, pushing one over to Fernando.

"Drink it, it'll do you good."

Fernando drank it down, barely pausing for breath. He was as thirsty as he was tired.

The monk asked Hafid something, and the pair of them spoke for a few minutes, looking every now and then at Fernando. They were talking about him, of course.

"They've told me that they're going to bring something that will make your stomach feel better."

A few minutes later the monk came back with a plate piled with a kind of yellowish mush. Fernando didn't know if he should try it or not, but the monk and Hafid waited expectantly for him to do so.

He didn't know what he was eating, but he soon recognized what he thought was the taste of wheat and chickpeas. He ate it all, thinking that this mash would only cause him more problems in his stomach.

Suddenly, to Fernando's surprise, the monk started to talk in English. A rudimentary and guttural English, but enough for them to understand one another.

Sameh Basir, as that was the monk's name, offered to show him around the monastery as soon as morning came. He said that the convent had been very important in the past for the manuscripts which it had held, authentic gems that the British had taken away with them a century ago.

The abbot explained that the monks had shown their manuscripts to a British diplomat – Curzon, the "honorable" Robert Curzon – and he had convinced them to let him take them away with him.

Even though it had lost its treasures, the monk assured him that the monastery was worth a visit.

They agreed that at dawn they would wake Fernando up and show him the monastery from top to bottom. The monk even suggested that he attend their religious services, which he said would comfort his soul.

Later, when he and Hafid were in their cell, the Bedouin explained that there were a lot of penitents at these monasteries, sinners who sought God's forgiveness in the desert and who had made these convents their place of retreat.

Fernando was roused from his slumbers by a hand that shook him energetically by the shoulder. The monk smiled at him and urged him to get to his feet. Just as had happened in Saint Bishoy, Fernando didn't feel capable of telling this monk that he was an atheist, and so he followed him unenthusiastically, cursing him in silence for having pulled him out of his deep and relaxing sleep.

The church of the Virgin made him shiver at the sheer beauty of the Fresco of the Ascension that was painted in one of the cupolas.

Some doors opened onto the choir, and the monk showed him some panels made of what looked like ivory, with the figures of Christ, the Virgin Mary and the Apostles Peter and Mark carved on them. Then he suggested that he look at some frescoes that showed the death of the Virgin.

The monk seemed very enthusiastic, showing him his surroundings, including another ivory panel depicting another figure, Dioscorus, who Fernando didn't know at all.

In another church, he showed him a black marble cross. Then he spoke to him about Saint Ephraim, yet another church figure Fernando did not know.

From the explanations the monk gave him, Fernando came to the conclusion that the monastery had been built by monks from Syria, hence its name: Deir es Suriani.

They hadn't finished looking at the monastery when a column of monks, all bearing candles in their hands, came into the church and sat down without looking at the pair of them.

For a long time, which seemed like an eternity to Fernando, the abbot led a ceremony similar to a Mass. Then, when everything was done, the monk made a sign and led them through to the refectory, where Hafid was waiting to have breakfast.

The monks were friendly and talkative, and a few of them knew some words of English. But "his" monk, Sameh Basir, was the only one he could truly understand.

This was how he found out that Wadi Natrum was a refuge for ascetics, and that there were still a large number of people who lived in caves and wells; some of them wanted to free themselves of their sins, and others didn't want to fall into the temptation to sin, and wanted to be closer to God, or at least that's what Fernando understood.

Sameh Basir insisted again that he eat the strange mush that he had eaten the night before, and as it hadn't caused him any harm, he agreed.

After breakfast, they set off back to Alexandria.

Eulogio had gone. Fernando felt his absence like a blow to the gut. And all because of Benjamin Wilson. He blamed himself for following his instructions, because having done so meant he hadn't even had the chance to say goodbye to his friend.

Dimitra told him that they had moved his room. The one that he shared with Eulogio was bigger and sunnier than the tiny room where Ylena had put Catalina, and now that Eulogio was no longer there, the landlady had decided that mother and daughter should be in the big room and Fernando could have Catalina's former space. Catalina had apparently protested, but Ylena had gotten her way by saying that in her house, it was she who decided who got which rooms.

Fernando not only did not protest, but also said that he was completely in agreement with Ylena's decision.

His few possessions were perfectly set up in the little room, and there was a sealed envelope on the desk with a letter from Eulogio in it.

Dear Fernando,

I'm sorry that we didn't get to say goodbye to one another, but from what Mr. Wilson tells me, he's sent you on a mission that can't be delayed. I hope that you've been able to complete it to the satisfaction of your very odd boss.

Marvin and Farida say that they are pleased I'm going with them, but as you know very well it's me who wants to leave Alexandria. They're my chance to get out of this city; I find it so strange, and I'm sure I don't want to live here. The only thing I regret is that you and I have to part and take different paths. I'd love you to have come with us, or else for you and me to head off to America together. But I know that you'd never abandon Catalina to her fate. I don't want to upset you, Fernando, but I think you need to accept that Catalina is not for you, once and for all, even if love is a mystery and has nothing to do with reason. She'll never love you like you love her, but she'll always want you to be her shield, her loyal friend, who she can turn to no matter what. But I'm worried, Fernando, that you're going to give up your life to help her live hers, without ever getting anything in return but the affection that she would have for a family member or a close friend.

Neither of us likes being given advice, but let me just suggest again that you should get her to go back to Spain and be with her parents. It would be the best thing for her and for the baby. With Adela in the picture, Antoñito wouldn't want to have anything to do with Catalina, so she'd be all right, although she'd have to cope with being a single mother. It wouldn't be easy, but at least she'd have gotten rid of Antoñito. It'll be hard for any man who isn't you to agree to marry her, but who knows what life may bring, eh?

As for you, my friend, go to America as soon as you can. What future could you possibly have in Alexandria? Yes, Wilson pays well, but do you really want to spend the rest of your days in this alien city?

I know that I'll have news of you via Marvin, because Sara will keep him up to date with everything that's going on.

As for our journey, Wilson has arranged everything, and our voyage, as you already know, will take us to so-called Free France, but you tell me how a country governed by Marshal Pétain under the control of Germany can be called "Free."

The last news that Sara Rosent had of her father was that he is in Vichy, where the seat of government is, but the friends who got him out of Paris want to take him to Lyon or somewhere further south.

Marvin wants to see his old editor because he says that it is thanks to him that he is a poet. And so he doesn't care about the risks he has had to run. As for me ... Well, as you know, I want to go to America, but it looks like that plan's got to be put on hold, at least for a while.

You know I'm not a nervous person, but I am worried about what might happen in France, given that Spaniards who support the Republic are normally put into camps.

Wilson has given us money, and also the addresses of certain people whom he says can help us. We'll see if he's right.

Look after yourself, my friend, and think of yourself before other people for a change.

Your friend,

EULOGIO JIMÉNEZ

Fernando made an effort to hold back the tears that had started to blur his vision. For the first time since he had left Spain, he felt truly alone. He knew that not even Catalina could fill the hole that his friend had left.

He fell back on his bed and closed his eyes. And with the eyes of his soul he saw Eulogio's face, and then his mother's. He saw her as she was, worthy and kind, earning the well-deserved respect of everyone she met.

He saw his father as well. He closed his eyes tight, afraid of seeing a reproach in his gaze for having run away and left his mother alone, and above all, for having killed those two men.

Even so, his father did not reproach him for anything. His vision was of a calm man, surrounded by papers, showing off a new edition of some English author: Shakespeare, Chesterton, or Lewis Carroll, the kind of writer he usually translated. And though he wanted to avoid it, he could not; here were the faces of the two men he had killed, father and son, Roque and Saturnino Pérez.

Fernando wanted to soothe his conscience by saying his killing them was all right because they were murderers, so there was nothing to blame himself for. But although he tried to dodge this battle with his conscience, he sometimes couldn't, because he was incapable of forgetting the simple lessons about Good and Evil that his mother had instilled in him ever since he was a child and which Don Bernardo had drilled into their brains when preparing him and the other children from the neighborhood for their First Communion.

His father had not been a believer, but he had let his mother do what she wanted, and it had been she who had brought him up in the rigid confines of a conscience that did not care for the wickedness of others, but which rather blamed itself for any possible faults, regardless of the provocations that one might possibly have suffered.

He fell asleep, seeing in his mind the surprise in the eyes of Roque and Saturnino Pérez when he shot them.

He was awoken suddenly, and saw Dimitra standing next to the bed.

"Finally! Good! I've been here for a while trying to get you to wake up. And you didn't seem to hear me. I thought you might be dead."

Fernando felt confused. He felt like he had only just closed his eyes, and the only thing he wanted to do was keep sleeping.

"It's seven o'clock; the rest of the lodgers are having breakfast. I suppose you'll be late for work. Mr. Wilson called Madame Kokkalis to ask after you. He knew you were back. She said that you must have found the journey exhausting, because you didn't even say hello to them and you've been asleep for a while. Even

Miss Catalina has come in a couple of times to see if you were all right."

"How long have I been asleep?" he managed to ask.

"Almost a whole day. Well, a little bit less," Dimitra replied. "Go on, get washed and come down to have breakfast. It'll do you good."

When Fernando came down into the dining room, there was no one there, only Mr. Sanders taking his second cup of tea. The Englishman was paler than usual, and his eyes shone with fever.

The colonel explained that he had been sick for a couple of days already, because he had gotten caught in a shower of rain as he was visiting Abukir.

Fernando coughed uncomfortably. He didn't know what Abukir was. The Englishman realized his ignorance and hastened to enlighten him.

"I'm surprised that you haven't shown any interest in getting to know the archeological jewels of Alexandria. Like so many others, you probably believe that there is nothing here in Egypt apart from the pyramids at Cairo, but the whole country is an archeological site waiting to be discovered."

As he explained it, Abukir was not far from Alexandria, and was once the site of a lake that had since dried up. It had been inhabited from distant antiquity.

"You know who Paris and Helen are, I suppose?" he asked, but not very hopefully.

"Of course, who doesn't know that?" Fernando replied, a little annoyed.

"And Herodotus? You know who Herodotus is?" the Englishman asked.

"Of course." Fernando felt like getting up and leaving, but he didn't want to abandon his coffee and cake.

"Well, if you ever go there, go to Fort Ramleh, where there was once a temple dedicated to Hercules. According to legend, Paris and Helen went there when they were fleeing Sparta, and asked for protection from the priests."

"Well, I didn't know that," Fernando admitted.

"The priests apparently didn't want to offer them protection because they were adulterers, but the real reason is probably that they didn't want to provoke the enmity of the king of Sparta."

They sat in silence, each one enjoying his drink. Fernando was the first to speak:

"And what were you doing there?"

Colonel Sanders thought that the question was a little impertinent. He thought that the Spanish didn't have very good manners.

"I'm an archeologist, didn't you know?"

"I thought that you were a colonel, a retired British colonel."

"I studied history at Oxford, and then specialized in archeology. Of course, I did my family duty and went into the army."

"Well, what exactly were you doing in this place, this ... Abukir?"

"Maybe the legends are close to truth ... There, right beside Fort Tewfikieh, is where Canopus ended up. I don't know if you know who Canopus is?"

"No, I don't ..." Fernando accepted the slight.

"Well, Canopus was the pilot of Menelaus' ship. King Menelaus of Sparta was cuckolded by his wife Helen. When the Trojan War was over and Menelaus went home, his ship docked close by and Canopus was unlucky enough to be bitten by a snake."

"Tough break," Fernando said, just to say something.

"What did you say?" Sanders was irritated by the lack of attention the Spaniard seemed to be paying to his tale.

"It's a tough break, surviving a war only to die from a snakebite," Fernando said.

"Well, thanks to that snakebite, he became a god."

"That's not a very good trade. It's the same as with the Christians, whose saints only after they had been martyred got to be saints. The same with Canopus, but he became a god."

"You say some very strange things ... I don't think you understand this at all." Colonel Sanders didn't bother to hide his annoyance.

"Of course, I understand ... please, don't be upset ... I'm tired and I've been sick ... you have to understand that this period in history, Canopus and all that, isn't really my area of interest."

Mr. Sanders gritted his teeth and took a deep breath. Then he carried on.

"I told you, it was a legend. And there is another legend that says Canopus was an Egyptian god. The pharaoh Ptolemy Soter gave the order that a temple was to be built where people from all corners of the country would come to honor Serapis and Isis. You should go there, I recommend it. I could take you if you'd like. It's a nice trip. I also recommend that you read the book about Alexandria by E. M. Forster, which describes everything I've told you and more about the city."

"Thank you."

"If you're not interested in ancient history, you might at last be interested in the fact that Napoleon's troops fought two important battles there. And nearby, Admiral Nelson destroyed the French fleet."

"Ah, English admirals ..."

"I sense a touch of irony in what you say ..."

"No, I didn't mean it. Mr. Sanders, I need to go to work now, but it's been a pleasure talking to you."

When he got to Wilson & Wilson, he found Sara wrapping a book for a customer. She greeted him with a nod and he went through the door that led to the publishing house, where his boss, Athanasius Vryzas, was sunk deep in the study of a few sheets of paper.

They greeted each other formally, and Vryzas said he should go upstairs straight away to see Mr. Wilson.

"Leyda has been down to ask for you. You are to go up to see Mr. Wilson without delay."

Leyda Zabat's smile calmed Fernando. It took the edge off the grave expression on the face of Benjamin Wilson, who received him straight away.

"Hafid came to see me as soon as he had left you at Madame Kokkalis' house."

"I wasn't well; I fell sick at Saint Bishoy. I think it was the goat's milk."

"So you haven't been able to bring me Domenico Lombardi," Wilson complained.

"Ismail, Hafid's uncle, swears that he's dead, as dead as his own son Basim."

"And now I have to give the bad news to Domenico's father ... well .... These things happen, but Wilson & Wilson doesn't normally give bad news. We are usually successful, which is why so many people trust us."

"You knew that it was unlikely that we would bring Lombardi back alive, or that we ourselves would make it back unscathed."

"You talk too bluntly, too impulsively ... I'm not blaming you for anything. There was a chance of success, and I like to tempt fate."

"Well, we failed, but we are still alive."

"I'm glad."

"I can't believe it. You don't care. Hafid and I were nothing more than a couple of pawns, and if we'd died then you wouldn't have cared too much."

Benjamin Wilson laughed freely. He appreciated Fernando's arrogance. He thought that the Spaniard was very much like himself, but his grandfather had taught him to keep his emotions in check: otherwise, he wouldn't have let him run the business.

"You have some books to work on. I promised Marvin that we'd bring his publication date forward. The book has to be in all the bookshops in New York by March, and I hope that it will be released in London as well, in spite of the war. As for Omar Basir's book, that needs to be done fast as well."

"I'll do my job. And now that you mention Marvin ... do you know if they made it to France?"

"Don't worry. Your friend Eulogio is fine."

Fernando worked all day, and despite Athanasius Vryzas' recommendation that he head out for lunch, he decided not to. Marvin's poems were full of sadness. They were very good. He couldn't deny that he was a great poet.

Vryzas and the rest of the employees went out to have lunch, and Fernando took a break to smoke a cigarette and think about Marvin. He thought that the intensity and beauty of his poems did not fit the man that he knew. Then he told himself that really, he only knew him superficially, that they had never been close friends. Catalina had prevented that. If she had not been obsessed by the American, then maybe his poetry would have called

Fernando to him. But Marvin had been his most feared rival, and he had been unable to see anything good in him. He still did not feel too kindly towards the American, but he was too honorable not to admit the truth, which was that Marvin Brian was a great poet.

When he got back to Ylena's house, Dimitra told him that Catalina had asked her to tell her as soon as he got back. He hadn't seen her at all that morning, although Dimitra had told him that she was in her room, feeding Adela.

He couldn't avoid her, although he didn't really want to talk to her. His relationship with Catalina, built as it was on absolute hopelessness, made him feel very depressed.

He found her in her room, cradling the baby in her arms.

"Dimitra told me that you were ill."

"I got sick from drinking goat's milk, but I'm better now."

"I'm glad … Well, you know that Eulogio has gone. He … he refused to let me see Marvin."

"Marvin doesn't want to see you: don't blame Eulogio," Fernando said tiredly.

"If Marvin didn't want to see me, he'd tell me himself … I don't know why, but all of you have ganged up to keep us apart … I don't understand it. We have a child together, and it's not good for us not to be able to at least explain things to one another."

He didn't answer. He felt too tired to start another one of their absurd arguments about the American. Catalina's attitude was irrational, as was Marvin's.

"I want you to know that I will follow him wherever he goes, that I won't accept it when you say he doesn't want to see me. For the love of God, Fernando, tell me where I can find him!"

"I've told you, they've gone to France, to Vichy, I think, to find Monsieur Rosent, Sara's father. The Nazis have taken over all the Jewish businesses, but Rosent was wise and managed to prevent his from being taken by selling it at a symbolic price to Marvin, and getting a man who had been a professor of literature at the Sorbonne to run the publishing house on a day-to-day basis. Marvin wanted to return Sara's property to her, but she prefers for him to own it while the war is still going on. When

Sara found out that her father might have escaped from Paris, she asked her husband to do everything he could to get him out to Alexandria. But we're at war, and it's not easy to get someone from one place to another, especially if they're a Jew. It was Marvin who decided to go and look for Monsieur Rosent and bring him here. That's all I know, there's no other news."

"So, he's going to come back."

"I don't know if Marvin's coming back, or if they'll head somewhere else once they've got Monsieur Rosent out of France. I swear that I don't know. I couldn't even say goodbye to Eulogio, so I don't know what they're going to do in France to get Monsieur Rosent out of there."

"So ... do you think I should wait for Marvin to come back?"

"I don't know if he's coming back ... I swear, I don't know."

Adela began to cry, and Catalina rocked her until she settled.

"She's better. Dr. Naseef says that we no longer need to fear for her life. Captain Pereira was right: Adela is a survivor."

"She's stronger than she looks; and she's certainly inherited your determination," Fernando said sincerely.

"Well, we'll stay here for a while, then ... But if Marvin doesn't come back, then I'll go to France to look for him."

"Are you just assuming that I'm going to stay here?" Fernando said angrily.

"Well ... I don't know ... yes ... I thought that ..."

"You thought that I wasn't going to leave you on your own, and that it doesn't matter if you run all over the world looking for Marvin, because I will always follow you to look after you."

"No ... I didn't mean that ..." Catalina was blushing.

"You think that, and you're right. No, I'm not going to leave you, or the child."

He left the room without giving Catalina a chance to reply. They didn't speak again until after supper, where Monsieur Baudin and Colonel Sanders had had an animated discussion. The Englishman and the Frenchman always argued, amicably enough, about everything.

5

In every life, even the most extraordinary ones, routines set themselves up silently. And routine would likely have descended if Fernando hadn't been in the orbit of Benjamin Wilson.

Not a week had passed since his return from the desert when he was called again with a new task.

"Do you remember Erick Brander?" Wilson asked, without preamble.

"Yes ... the man who met up with the Spaniard ... Pedro López ..."

"Yes, that's him. The pair of them are in Cairo. As you heard them say, López is going to meet some important people at King Farouk's court."

"Which has nothing to do with me."

"You shouldn't say that. Whatever happens in the war will affect Spain. You oppose the fascists. You must realize that it's better for the British to win, and now that the Americans are in the war, the chances of defeating the German monster are much increased. Hitler is a danger to the whole world."

Wilson lost no time beating around the bush, and asked Fernando to go to Cairo. There, he would meet with Zahra Nadouri in the Shepheard Hotel, which was where López was staying and where he had his meetings with Brander. All he had to do was accompany Zahra. He didn't ask anything more.

Fernando tried to resist, but not with any great conviction. His protests were lukewarm for one reason: Zahra. Although he was in love with Catalina, he couldn't deny the fact that when he had seen Zahra dance on New Year's Eve, it had produced such an effect on him that he still dreamed of her. Wilson was surprised that Fernando didn't offer more resistance.

Benjamin gave Fernando a suitcase with clothing that Sara had picked out for him.

"You'll need to look the part."

"Thank you, but it's not necessary."

"Please, don't turn this into a question of dignity. You fled Spain with the shirt on your back and you haven't even had time to buy clothes. What's in the suitcase is what you need for the work I've given you. When you come back, you can keep the clothes, or throw them away: you decide. But you need them now. Go back home and pick up whatever else you need. My driver will take you to the station. You'll be in Cairo this evening."

Leyda Zabat knocked at the door and came in without waiting for an invitation, followed by a tall man in Bedouin robes. The man looked at Wilson, who indicated that he should speak.

"Rommel is headed towards Benghazi," the man said solemnly.

Wilson turned to Fernando.

"Get going as soon as possible."

Fernando was astonished by the sumptuous Hotel Shepheard. Every corner was dripping with luxury, and the men and women who filled the lobby were dressed well, giving off the aura of carelessness that is the purview of the truly rich.

The receptionist greeted him in a friendly fashion; he told him that his room was ready, and that he could be taken up immediately, but that Miss Nadouri was waiting for him in the bar.

Zahra had chosen a table that was set to one side and she seemed engrossed in a newspaper. Fernando stopped for a few seconds to observe her. She did not look at all like the woman he had seen dance in the City Club. The dancer had been an explosion of sensuality, and there was nothing about the woman in front of him that made her stand out. She was elegantly yet simply dressed, she wore very little makeup, and her hair was tied back into a low bun. She could pass entirely unnoticed alongside the other women who, sitting beside their partners, seemed to have been plucked from the pages of a Paris fashion magazine.

Suddenly, she looked up from the newspaper and their eyes met. Fernando came over quickly, embarrassed that he had been caught staring at her.

"You're in time for dinner," Zahra said.

"Yes ... of course ... I haven't yet been up to the room. They told me you were waiting for me here."

They sat in silence as though they had nothing more to say to one another. The day they met, Fernando had discovered that she did not waste her words.

"Go up and change. People dress formally for dinner here. I know it's a little early, but then we can go for a walk before we head down to the cabaret."

"The cabaret?" he said, surprised.

"I'm dancing this evening. That's my cover story."

"Your cover story ... I don't know what mine is."

"You're my fling. The whim of a famous dancer. No one who's going to attract any attention."

"Wow."

"No one will be surprised that I've fallen for a handsome foreigner and that I've made you my official squeeze."

Fernando's face twisted: he was uncomfortable with the role assigned to him. Wilson had said that all he needed to do was travel with Zahra.

"Don't get upset ... How else could we justify your presence here?"

"I'll go and get changed. I won't be long," he replied grumpily.

"Your room is next door to mine. In fact, there's a door between them. It's the most convenient way," she said.

A couple of hours later, Zahra seemed to be distracted, and Fernando was enjoying a hearty meal. She barely touched her steak.

"Aren't you hungry?" he asked.

"I never eat before a performance. We're only in the dining room because we're waiting for Brander and your countryman Pedro López."

"He's not my countryman," Fernando protested.

"He's a Spaniard, like you."

"Yes, but he's a fascist, and I don't have anything to do with fascists, no matter where they were born."

"No one can stop being what they are. Though Farida Rahman says that any individual is who they are as a function of other people."

"I didn't know you were interested in philosophy."

"You don't know anything about what interests me. As for philosophy ... I'm interested in Farida's vision of humanity."

"Are you good friends?"

"We know each other."

At that moment, Erick Brander and Pedro López came into the dining room. The *maître d'* sat them down at a table next to Fernando and Zahra.

The two men seemed not to notice their presence and immediately started to speak in Spanish.

"You told me as much: the minister was very diplomatic, but obviously critical of the British presence here. He let me know that they'd prefer an alliance with Germany, and was certain that Rommel would win the war in the desert," López explained to Brander.

"The problem is that Farouk can't show his sympathy for Germany openly. The British would have him deposed immediately."

"My aim is to have Egypt sign some treaties with Spain, and make sure that we are good friends. The minister has assured me that this will be the case. He's ready to meet with some friends of mine ... men who are absolutely loyal to the Caudillo, who will sign these commercial treaties."

"And you won't forget about me, of course ..."

"Of course not. Diplomats may have their missions, but the rest of us are left to do the real work. You are a good friend to Spain, and we know how to thank you for that. Oh, by the way, I asked the minister for help, but I think you'll be able to do the job better: I need some information about exiled Spaniards in Egypt."

"I don't think there are that many of them," Erick Brander replied.

"Well, there must be some, and it's vitally important for us to have them under observation. Most of the enemies of Spain have fled to America, but some might have wriggled their way here. You'll be paid for every Spaniard you bring to our attention."

The two men carried on talking about their business while Zahra and Fernando listened intently. Zahra held her hand out to Fernando and indicated with a glance that he should take it. She smiled at nothing, as though he were saying something that made her happy.

It took Fernando a moment to get into the role he was to play, which he felt distinctly uncomfortable playing.

"Smile," Zahra whispered as she held his hand, "You don't look like a young man in love, but rather a bitter old married grump."

Before the German and the Spaniard had finished their meal, Zahra and Fernando left the restaurant and went up to their rooms. She told him that she needed to rest a little before they went to where she would be dancing.

The cabaret was in an imposing old building. Cars drew up in front of its wooden doors, and groups of men and women in elegant formalwear went in, ready to enjoy champagne, music, and whatever else the night might bring.

Zahra and Fernando went in through the artists' entrance, where the owner of the building was waiting for them. Zahra introduced them.

He was a tall man with dark hair. He looked good for his age. He looked suspiciously at Fernando, whom Zahra introduced as *mon petit ami*.

They shook hands, and Fernando heard him say what must be his name, Tarek Fazeli.

Then they went to the dressing room where a large screen divided the space in two. A maid was waiting for Zahra. Fernando sat in an armchair while she started to transform herself behind the screen. He heard the two women talking, but didn't catch a word of their conversation, which was in Arabic.

It was almost midnight when there was a knock on the door and the maid hurried to open it. Zahra was due on stage.

The owner of the establishment accompanied Fernando to his

table, next to the stage, where a bottle of champagne was being kept cool in an ice bucket. Another man was there, dressed in a very formal dinner jacket, impatient. The man barely paid them any attention, but Fernando looked at him closely: dark blond hair, blue eyes, elegant dress. He didn't miss the fact that Erick Brander and Pedro López were sitting nearby either. Brander greeted the owner and said to López: "Tarek Fazeli is the eyes of Egypt. He sees everything, knows everything." Pedro López looked at him curiously and the two of them shook hands. Brander also introduced the impatient blond man, who was sitting next to Fazeli: "Arthur Collins, Mr. Fazeli's business partner."

Fernando looked at him curiously. "So, an Englishman," he thought.

The lights dimmed and the musicians behind the stage stopped playing. For a minute, which seemed to last an eternity, there was whispering that gradually faded away until the room was entirely silent. Then a spotlight shone onto the stage. To begin with, it was almost impossible to make anything out, but then the shimmer of silk and the jangling of bracelets set his senses alight. Suddenly a hand appeared in the light, followed by a foot. And then the outline of a woman's body, moving slowly, the whole figure of a woman, who swayed as though she were in a trance.

The dancer, her eyes closed, slid onstage, and the audience grew tense and expectant. For an hour and a half, she danced. No one said anything, and when she finished, the shouts and applause were such that Fernando had no choice but to join in with the same enthusiasm as the rest of the audience.

The stage went dark again, and when a few dim lights lit up the rest of the room, Zahra was nowhere to be seen. Fernando made as if to get up and go and look for her, but Arthur Collins took his arm.

"No, she'll be back."

"There are a lot of very important men here who want to congratulate her," Tarek Fazeli added.

Fernando sat down again. Zahra hadn't told him what he needed to do, and he thought that as soon as her performance was over, they'd go back to the hotel, but Fazeli and Collins apparently had other plans.

When she came into the room, it was almost impossible for her to make her way through the crush. Men and women came to meet her, keen to hear her and speak to her.

Tarek Fazeli pushed his way through the crowd and led her to the table. Arthur Collins stood up and bowed, before kissing her hand. She ignored him.

"Magnificent, my darling! Incomparable! You should leave Alexandria once and for all and come and live in Cairo," Fazeli said as he poured her a glass of champagne.

Zahra came over to Fernando and kissed him on the lips. He stood still without knowing what to do or to say. She looked at him in annoyance.

"Cold, my friend, cold … the most desired woman in the whole of Egypt kisses you and you don't even smile," Tarek Fazeli said, looking at the pair of them.

"He's like that," Zahra said disdainfully.

"I wouldn't play hard to get, because there are many men here who would be happy to take your place, me among them," Fazeli said with a smile.

Fernando, who felt very uncomfortable, realized his mistake. There were a lot of eyes looking at them at the moment. He had forgotten the role he had to play, that of Zahra's devoted slave. The orchestra was playing on the stage and Fernando took Zahra by the hand and led her to the dance floor without saying another word.

They started to dance, and Zahra tried to fit her body to his.

"What kind of a lover are you?" she asked.

"I … I don't know what to say."

"We're supposed to be lovers, and yet here you are, holding me off as though I were contagious or something."

Fernando couldn't help but laugh, and she laughed back at him.

"I just didn't expect you to kiss me. I was stunned."

"And everyone who was watching us was surprised as well, including the German and the Spaniard."

"I'm sorry, you should have told me what you were going to do."

"Well, get used to the idea that in public we should behave like a couple in love. It's not so hard. I hope I'm not too disgusting."

"No ... no ... quite the opposite ... I ... well ... I ... This is all so new to me, and so unexpected ..."

"Well, get into the role. Come close to me, hold me tight, and kiss me. Everyone's looking at us."

"You want me to kiss you?" he asked in surprise.

"Please, don't make this so difficult! It's not that I want you to kiss me, but it's what's expected of us. Kissing is a part of the role we have to play."

"You're right, sorry ..."

He kissed her timidly, afraid of blushing and being the laughingstock of everyone who was watching them. But Zahra took control of the situation and wouldn't let him take his lips away from hers; they stayed like this for a few seconds, which to him seemed like years.

They carried on dancing and kissing. Fernando thought that he was going to be sick. He felt relieved when she said they should go back to the table, but she warned him that he shouldn't make any more mistakes.

"Behave like you are expected to behave."

Tarek Fazeli greeted them with a large smile. There were several couples now seated around them. The men were all keen to be close to Zahra, and the women looked at her with admiration and envy.

"Let's go. I'm tired," Zahra said, ignoring the efforts of Fazeli's guests to attract her attention.

They didn't speak until they reached the Shepheard. The doorman opened the car door and bowed to them. The dancer thanked him with a graceful gesture.

Fernando was in his room taking his bow tie off when the door that led to Zahra's room opened.

She had put on a pink silk robe and was barefoot. He looked at her in astonishment.

"Call down to reception and ask them to bring us up a bottle of champagne and some chocolates."

Fernando obeyed, while she sat down in an armchair and looked tired.

"As soon as they bring the champagne I'll go to my room. But the room service waiter has to see me here, and then he'll tell everyone in the hotel, and tomorrow *le tout Caire* will think that we're sleeping together."

"But ... they'll be scandalized."

"No, they expect it of a dancer: she has to have lovers who are young and handsome. I don't think that your reputation will suffer because people think that you are sleeping with me," she said sharply.

"But I was worried about what people would think of you!" he protested.

"You should worry about playing your role."

"Please don't get angry ... it's just that all this ... well ... I'm not ready."

"I can see that ... I think that Benjamin has too much faith in you."

"Mr. Wilson? Yes ... I don't know why he's got me caught up in all this."

The waiter knocked at the door and Zahra gestured to Fernando to open it, while she undid her robe to reveal a transparent slip.

The waiter put the champagne down and looked at Zahra out of the corner of his eye, while she looked at her nails, bored, waiting for him to leave.

When he had done so, she stood up and tied her robe.

"Well, now you can drink the champagne or else pour it down the sink, whatever you want. Tomorrow we'll need to mess up your room so that the staff think we've spent the night engaged in tumultuous acts of love."

"Why do you do this?" Fernando asked, although he regretted speaking as soon as the words were out of his mouth.

"Do what?" she muttered, turning her back on him.

"Work for Wilson ... do these strange things that can damage your reputation ..."

"And why did you flee Spain and come to Egypt? I know you've abandoned your family, your mother ... You have no friends here, no one, and yet ... here you are. I suppose you must have a good reason for it. I have a good reason for doing what I do."

"I didn't want to intrude or upset you. I'm sorry."

Zahra went back to her room and closed the communicating door. Fernando sat for a while, trying to understand everything that was going on. But he found no answer to his thoughts.

He fell down on the bed without undressing and awoke fully dressed the next morning, when he opened his eyes and found Zahra in front of him.

"Let's go down and have a coffee. It's past ten. I didn't want to wake you up, you were fast asleep ... Tell me when you're ready."

Fifteen minutes later, Fernando came out of the bathroom and found the bed thoroughly messed up.

"I told you to empty the bottle of champagne ... You didn't even have a glass. The trousers of your dinner jacket are on the sofa. The bow tie is good here, by the chocolates. I put my slip and my dressing gown on the bed. They'll think that last night was one for the ages."

They went down to the street and walked for a while. She seemed to know where she was going, but she didn't tell him anything. They found themselves in a cafe which seemed to be patronized exclusively by foreigners. The waiter took them to a central table from which they could see and be seen. Fernando was happy to drink a very strong coffee, which helped him wake up. Zahra ordered a coffee as well, but drank it very slowly. She held her hand out to him and muttered: "Remember, we're in love."

Fernando squeezed Zahra's hand between his own. He wanted nothing more than to touch the dancer's cool skin. He couldn't deny the attraction he felt. He was clumsy and small in her presence. He blamed himself for these emotions, telling himself that he was in love with Catalina and that he could never love another woman. But then, he asked himself, what was it he felt for Zahra?

"Look at me. You're too caught up in your own thoughts," she said.

"I'm sorry ... it's that ..."

"I know, this is all so new for you. But it's not that hard for us to hold hands and smile."

"Of course not."

"Well, now I'm going to tell you what we're going to do.

I have two more performances due in Cairo, and then we'll go back to Alexandria."

"Why is this Pedro López so important?" he said, although he could guess the answer.

"The Spaniard? All the powers in the war want to know everything about everyone else. Pedro López is here to open up a commercial relationship with Egypt. Spain is ruined and needs friends."

"But they've got Germany and Italy. Franco, Hitler and Mussolini are friends," Fernando said.

"Franco's Spain is on the side of the Axis, yes, but who knows what might happen in the future?"

"Nothing. Nothing's going to happen. The most likely thing is that Germany will win the war and Franco will be in charge forever. And yes, it's likely he's going to win," Fernando said.

"The last battle hasn't yet been fought. There are still a lot of battles left to fight, in fact. You can't say for certain what will happen."

"My country is lost. Franco is killing everyone who fought against him."

"Well, I don't admit that any battle is ever lost. And if I lose, I fight it again."

"It's easy to say that … You don't know what it is to lose a war, to be on the losing side. It negates you, turns you into nothing."

Zahra looked him straight in the eye, and Fernando was surprised to see her expression harden. He waited for her to say something.

"Well, carry on fighting, because things change and today's victors will be tomorrow's losers. Don't waste time on regrets. It doesn't help anyone."

"I don't think anyone cares about Spain. I don't think that the British, if they win the war, will free us from Franco. In any case, I've lost everything: they shot my father for fighting on the wrong side. You don't know what that means. My mother and I went to see him in prison every week … If you knew how he was … all the prisoners piled in together … his glasses fell off one day, and a guard stamped on them, broke them into pieces. My father couldn't see a thing without them, and was condemned to spend his whole life wandering in a fog. And then the fear, when they opened the cell door and read out a list of the people who they were going to execute that day. We asked for him to be pardoned, but the pardon was refused."

Silence fell between them again, but they kept their hands intertwined.

"No one will ever bring your father back. You have to accept it. All you can do is fight so that other men don't die." There was no emotion in Zahra's voice. Fernando freed his hand and sat back in his chair, looking to catch the eye of the waiter and order another coffee.

Zahra changed the subject and suggested they go to see the pyramids.

"I don't have to perform today. So we have a whole day to do what we want."

"And what about Erick Brander and Pedro López?" he asked.

"What about them?"

"What, we don't have anything more to do here?"

"Well, I've got two more performances. I told you so already. And you need to stay with me, my devoted slave."

"I was talking about Brander and López."

"I don't think they need to worry us all that much."

"Not even Brander?"

"He's a German agent and Wilson and the British have him under close observation. Brander passes information to Admiral Canaris' men. Canaris is the head of the Abwehr, the German secret service. He's not their best agent, but he's got access to information at the palace. His wife, Halima, gets him an in there."

"So Erick Brander is important," Fernando insisted.

"He is, to the extent that it is through him we can work out who at court is in favor of the Germans."

"And what about López?"

"I've told you, he's here to sound out the terrain, to open up trade links now that Spain is in ruins. His mission is important for his country, but not for us. And now, do you want to see the pyramids or not? You might not have another opportunity. I asked a friend to come and find us this morning and take us out there."

"You knew we were coming here?"

"Of course."

Fernando was tempted to get angry. Zahra seemed to be manipulating the situation as she saw fit. But she was right, he was nothing more than her fake boyfriend, a role he didn't like at all.

They went out into the street and Zahra waited until a gray car drew up and stopped in front of the cafe. She didn't hesitate, but opened the front door and sat next to the driver. Fernando had no choice but to get in the back.

Zahra introduced them. The man who was driving them was called Musim Sadat and he was an archeologist. Or at least that was what it said on his Oxford degree.

Fernando felt a little jealous as he looked at him. Musim Sadat was undoubtedly an attractive man. His black hair was perfectly cut, his mustache was neat, and he had big eyes and an air of distinction, as though he were someone who had never wanted for anything.

Musim spoke perfect English; it was so good, in fact, that if it had not been for his appearance and his dark skin, then he could have passed for a British gentleman. He told Fernando that he thought of England as his second homeland. He had spent the happiest years of his life there, but, he admitted, it had taken him a while to get used to it. But his parents had insisted that he have the best education Great Britain could offer. For her part, Zahra added that Musim's family were businessmen, as well as important members of the royal court.

Fernando listened to this in silence. He had no interest in becoming friends with this Egyptian.

But Musim was an outgoing man, and so he carried the lion's share of the conversation, explaining, in detail and proudly, the history of the pyramids.

"The pyramids are tombs that have made three pharaohs – Khufu, Khafra and Menkaure – into immortals. In ancient times, they were not as you will see them now: they were covered in white limestone. They were built during the Fourth Dynasty. You'll see them soon: Khufu is more than four hundred and eighty feet tall, and then Khafra is more than four hundred and sixty-nine, and the little one, Mykerinos, is just three hundred and twenty-eight feet tall." And Musim laughed as though he had just said something funny.

"The ancient Egyptians believed in life after death," Zahra said.

"Good for them. I don't think there's anything," Fernando said bluntly.

"Good for them, bad for you. It's always good to live in hope," Musim said.

"So you want to fool people with children's stories." Fernando was angry.

"My ancestors had a book about how to get to the next life. They called it the Book of the Dead." Musim had decided not to argue with Fernando.

"How organized! A guide to make it through to Eternity! Religion is a tool of domination for the powerful. It was in ancient times and it still is today. It's a bad thing to scare people by telling them that their soul will wander forever after death," Fernando insisted.

"Our beliefs aren't that different from yours. The ancient Egyptians believed that when a man died, his spirit was divided in two: Ba and Akh. Ba stayed with the dead man and Akh had to present himself in front of Osiris to be judged. Anubis, the jackal-headed god, had a set of scales, on one side of which was placed the dead man's soul, and on the other side of which was a feather, the symbol of Ma'at, goddess of Justice. If the scales did not balance, then the soul was punished, because that meant that the person had not been good in his lifetime. There's something like that in Christianity, isn't there?" Musim looked back at Fernando in the rearview mirror and waited for his answer.

"Yes, it's the best way to frighten people, scaring them with punishments in some imagined future life. Of course, people in power have always been the ones to set the rules for Eternity," Fernando said.

"You don't believe in anything, then?" Musim asked.

"No. And you?"

"Look around you, look at the desert, look at the sky, look at the sea ..."

"So the sea, the sky and the desert prove that God exists? Marvelous! Very rational!"

"I'll ask you a question that Farida asks a lot. Do you think that Everything is also Nothing?" Musim waited for an answer.

The Egyptian's words disconcerted Fernando, and also made him more irritated. Zahra, realizing the trip might end in disaster, decided to interrupt them.

"Let's leave God in peace, and enjoy the only one of the Seven Wonders of the Ancient World that has survived the passage of time."

And there they were, lifting themselves proudly up above the desiccated dunes, the three pyramids, making any human observer feel little more than a grain of sand in the face of their vast mystery.

Musim Sadat parked the car a distance away from them, and then they walked for a while until they reached the Pyramid of Khufu.

Until that moment, Fernando hadn't realized that Zahra had dressed for the occasion. She was wearing a pair of culottes and high boots that let her walk on the sand without any trouble. When Musim got out of the car, it looked as though he were wearing an explorer's outfit, but he was dressed in clothes that were comfortable and suitable for the terrain. Fernando was poorly dressed, in his light suit and his shoes that filled with sand at every step he took. If Zahra had planned the trip in advance, she would have done well to have told him.

Musim's enthusiasm was such that they spent the rest of the morning and much of the afternoon wandering from one pyramid to the next, looking at the Sphinx and commenting on the details of these extraordinary works of human ingenuity.

When they got back to Cairo, Musim invited them to have supper with him. Zahra accepted for the pair of them with alacrity.

The archeologist promised to send a car to pick them up at seven thirty, so they would have time to relax.

Zahra and Fernando didn't exchange a single word until they got to their respective rooms. This time it was he who knocked on the connecting door.

"I suppose it's not obligatory for us to eat with your friend."

"In fact, it really is. We'll go to his house, where there are always important people: ministers, well-placed people in King Farouk's court … sometimes the king himself comes to the Sadats' house."

"You said that our work was done," Fernando said sourly.

"Our work, my dear, will never be done until the war is over. And maybe not even then. You remember that Mr. Wilson's job is to find people. There are always people to be found."

"Well, we didn't come to find anyone in Cairo."

Zahra shrugged. She didn't seem to care about Fernando's bad mood.

"Mr. Wilson is helping the British authorities in this particular instance."

"I know. He told me that himself."

"We'll go to Musim's house. It'll be interesting, you'll see."

Zahra turned her back on him and Fernando went back to his room.

He collapsed on his bed and closed his eyes. Then, without warning, the faces of Roque and Saturnino Pérez came to his mind. He shut his eyes for a few seconds to try to get them out of his head, but they both looked back at him from death, and there was no expression in their frozen eyes.

He sat up, feeling himself start to sweat. The two men appeared and disappeared as they pleased. They came to him at unexpected moments to remind him that he had taken their lives.

"You bastards! You killed my father! Leave me alone!" he said out loud, anger in his voice.

But they did not go. They stayed with him and stopped him from resting.

Fernando had never been one to drink, but he looked among the bottles that were in a cupboard in the room and took a cognac. He poured himself a glass and tossed it back in a single gulp. The liquid burned its way down his throat to his stomach.

He threw himself down on his bed and kept his eyes open, as if refusing to close them would put off the dead men.

He asked himself how he could avoid the ghosts' assaults in the future.

He spent the rest of the afternoon looking at the ceiling and missing his mother, her house in Madrid, the little routines that had marked his life until he had decided to seek revenge for his father's death.

He resolved that there was no way he could let more time go by without sending some news to his mother. Benjamin Wilson boasted about having collaborators in Spain, and maybe he could get one of them to go to his house and tell his mother that they were well. Yes, he'd ask Mr. Wilson if he could help.

How was it possible that a woman could transform so much as to be unrecognizable? That morning, Zahra had been a woman who had almost faded into the background, with only her expensive clothing revealing that she was someone to be reckoned with. And now that she was standing in front of him, he could scarcely believe she was the same woman with whom he had been to see the pyramids.

Zahra was wearing a tight-fitting emerald silk dress. Her reddish chestnut hair was loose but carefully combed, and her dark blue eyes twinkled in what seemed to him to be a special way.

She was holding a shawl of a deeper green than the dress. He saw that she was not expecting him to flatter her, but Fernando didn't think that he would have been capable of telling her just how beautiful she was.

Musim Sadat's house was outside the city, on the banks of the Nile. It had its own dock, and a tender was bobbing gently in the waters of the river.

Fernando felt the curious glances of Musim's guests upon him. Most of them envied him. Zahra Nadouri was the best dancer not just in Egypt, but in the whole of the Middle East, and in spite of her youth, she was rapidly becoming a legend.

Musim Sadat received them affectionately, and some of his guests lined up behind him, keen to be introduced.

Zahra behaved like a queen, dispensing smiles and exchanging words every now and then, but without entering into long discussions with these people. They seemed to admire her absolutely.

Once more she gave her hand to Fernando to hold. She wanted

everyone to know that this young, dark-haired, thin man, with his unruly hair and direct gaze, was the only one who interested her and that it was useless for anyone to offer to replace him. Queens choose their favorites and then cast them aside. But the day of reckoning had not come yet for this Spaniard, it seemed.

Fernando suddenly gave a start. Erick Brander was there, talking to a group of men which included Pedro López. He squeezed Zahra's hand and she smiled.

"Of course they're here. Don't worry," she whispered.

"You knew they'd be here?"

"Of course. I told you that Erick Brander is a man with many friends at court."

Fernando was annoyed that she hadn't told him the German would be there.

"And don't you think I should have known this?"

Zahra didn't reply, but smiled at one of the guests who came over to her. The man kissed her hand solemnly, and she introduced him to Fernando, calling him "her dearest friend." Other guests started to come over so that they could stand near her for a while and then be able to say that they had spoken to her.

To Fernando's relief, most of these people spoke English, and seemed to have no problem using that language instead of Arabic.

A woman came through the crowd to them. She was tall, thin, dark-skinned, with hair that was so long that it almost came down to her waist in spite of the fact that she wore it tied at the back of her neck. She walked decisively, without looking at anyone, regal and elegantly dressed. It was clear that the dress she wore must have been *haute couture*.

"Zahra, what a pleasure! Musim told me that you were coming, but I didn't believe him, you come out so rarely ..."

The woman held her hands out to Zahra, and she took them in her own, and then the pair of them embraced.

"Thank you, Kytzia. The party is marvelous."

Kytzia smiled in satisfaction at the praise before she replied. As she paused, she looked at Fernando out of the corner of her eye.

"This must be the young man that Musim spoke to me about, and with whom he had a lively conversation this morning."

Fernando kissed her hand, just as he had seen the man doing to Zahra a minute or so earlier.

"Kytzia is Musim Sadat's wife," Zahra said drily.

"There's another Spaniard here this evening … I'll introduce you, you must have a lot to talk about. He came with our dear friend Herr Brander."

At that moment, Erick Brander and Pedro López came over, and Kytzia introduced them.

"Mr. López, this young gentleman who has the privilege to be accompanying the most brilliant dancer in Egypt is a Spaniard like yourself. And you, Erick, should have brought dear Halima with you. We haven't been lucky enough to see her here recently."

Erick Brander excused himself and apologized on his wife's behalf, and looked at Fernando with interest.

"So you're Spanish … I suppose you don't know Mr. López …"

"No, I haven't had the pleasure," Pedro López said, not showing all that much interest in Fernando or even Zahra.

"Well, if you don't mind, we need to go and say hello to some friends," Zahra said, so as not to get caught up in a conversation.

"Will you be in Egypt for a long time?" López said to Fernando.

Zahra replied for him, seizing Fernando by the arm as though he were her property.

"I hope he's never going to leave." Zahra spoke like a possessive woman, a woman in love.

Fernando was confused and couldn't find any words to say. He didn't know what was expected of him. And so he improvised, but felt clumsy as he did so.

"My intention is to stay in Egypt, for good I hope."

"How romantic! Well, romanticism is good for the young, don't you think, gentlemen?" Kytzia said with a hint of malice, trying to softly mock Fernando and Zahra.

"If you'll excuse us … there are some friends of ours and we really must say hello," the dancer insisted, pulling on Fernando's arm and leaving Kytzia with the German and the Spaniard.

Zahra walked over to a group of people whom she seemed to

know, and to whom she presented her companion, playing along with the idea that they were having a torrid affair.

"From what I can see, you're not a big fan of the dancer," Pedro López said to Kytzia.

"Of course not. She's just a dancer. She's out of place in this house," Kytzia replied with a flash of anger.

"She's the most desired woman in the whole of Egypt, and your countryman is lucky to be her chosen one," Erick Brander said, looking at Pedro López.

"Luck? Erick, I thought you were a gentleman! Do you think it's lucky for a man to fall into the clutches of a dancer?" Kytzia said indignantly.

"Yesterday they told me in the cabaret that he's her latest fancy," Erick Brander said, trying to minimize his evident appreciation of Zahra's charms.

"Right … And how long has he been this fancy?" López wanted to know.

"From what they told me, they've been together for some time now. She doesn't normally take her lovers out in public, but this young man is something special. Who knows, she might actually be in love."

"It's strange that a Spaniard should be here, and have conquered the heart of the most famous dancer in Egypt …" López said.

"Well, he's handsome enough," Kytzia said. "But I don't understand why a young man as attractive and put-together as him should allow himself to be duped by some woman from the clubs."

Pedro López and Erick Brander didn't reply. They could have given their hostess fifty reasons why a man would fall head over heels for a dancer. But it would have been discourteous on their part, so they opted instead for silence.

When Kytzia had to go and look after her other guests, López took the moment to ask Brander to find out what he could about the young Spaniard.

"It's strange …"

"Strange that he's with Zahra? I'd say he's just very lucky."

"Yes, but I mean that it's interesting how he got here, and why."

"I don't think it'll take me that long to find out. Don't you worry."

"From what I can see, there's no love lost between our hostess and the dancer," Pedro López said.

"It's natural. Everyone knows that her husband was in love with her, and if she hadn't rejected him, then Kytzia wouldn't be the mistress of this house today."

"Musim's a dark horse ... I thought he was only interested in mummies and antiques."

"Well, Zahra Nadouri isn't either of those."

Pedro López looked at the couple curiously. Kytzia's opinion aside, the majority of those present seemed to be eager to speak with the dancer. She received their tributes coolly, but from time to time spent more time with one person than another. On the whole, though, she showed herself to be much more distant than polite.

Fernando was bored. He felt out of place in this house, and he was sick of the sidelong stares of the men who envied him his role as Zahra's companion.

Some of Zahra's conversations took place in Arabic, which made him feel even more isolated. Fernando asked himself what she could be talking about with these men who came up to her, keen to get her blessing.

Every now and then Zahra asked Fernando to fetch her a glass of champagne and even suggested that he go out onto the terrace to smoke; annoyed, he would do as she asked. He realized that she wanted to keep him away from the conversations she was having with the guests. But even so, he couldn't help but be surprised that she had such a good head for champagne.

By the time the party was over, Erick Brander had discovered who Zahra's companion was. Musim Sadt had not been afraid to tell him everything.

"He's an editor, and he works with Benjamin Wilson," the archeologist had said.

"Yes ... but since when?"

"I don't know, but I know that Wilson is very keen on him, as is Ylena Kokkalis, if you know who she is ... a woman who is not only respectable, but who has friends who are close to the king."

"Wilson … I don't like that man," the German said.

"And why not? He edits books, and that's all. And his books are wonderful. It's good luck that there's a branch of a British bookshop in Alexandria," Musim said with a smile.

"Are you sure that Benjamin Wilson only deals in poetry?" the German said.

"You're almost an Alexandrian yourself, and you know that Wilson & Wilson is an institution in our city. They edit and sell books, and they offer a place where intellectuals can meet and debate. If I were you, I wouldn't worry," Musim insisted.

"And as for the Spaniard, isn't there anywhere else in the world that he can work as an editor?" Brander insisted.

"He's under the protection of Pereira, the captain of the *Esperanza del Mar*. You'll have heard of him."

"The Portuguese? Yes, he's not afraid of anyone. What does he have to do with Pereira?"

"I've told you, he's under his protection. I think Pereira's a distant relative or something like that. He took him with him on one of his journeys, and he met Zahra and didn't want to leave, and so he looked for work in Alexandria so as not to have to leave."

"Very romantic. Too romantic, perhaps?"

"All I know is that he's a lucky man. I wouldn't mind being in his shoes. It's more than a feat of arms to be able to make Zahra Nadouri fall in love with you. She's not a woman who looks kindly on everyone." Musim Sadat's words were infused with sweet melancholy.

"And what did she see in the Spaniard?" Erick Brander asked curiously.

Musim laughed. He would have liked to have had an answer to that question as well. He had set his sights on Zahra and had never managed to do more than win her friendship. She wasn't a woman who was susceptible to money or jewels. She was the one who chose her men, and she had chosen this young man. The people who dreamed of her, himself included, would have to wait until she dropped this young Spaniard and went back into the fray in order to have another chance with her.

Erick Brander explained to Pedro López everything he had

found out from his host, and the information seemed to be enough for the Spaniard. He came to the conclusion that the Spaniard was no one for him to worry about.

On the way back to the hotel, Zahra said nothing, and Fernando didn't break the silence. They didn't speak until they got back to their rooms.

"I hope the night was useful," he said, a little resentfully.

"Yes, it was, Fernando. Now we know exactly what Pedro López has negotiated for with King Farouk's ministers."

"Right! We know ... Well, I know nothing, of course."

"But I do, and that's the same thing."

"No, no it's not. I'll tell you, and I'll tell Mr. Wilson as well, that I don't want to take on the role of being a stupid companion anymore," he said angrily.

Zahra shrugged indifferently.

"Do what you want. Good night, Fernando, get some rest."

Four days later, Fernando and Zahra went back to Alexandria with Musim Sadat. The archeologist had offered to take them in his own car given that he was due at a meeting of a group of archeologists who were working on the site of the Lighthouse of Alexandria, another of the Seven Wonders of the Ancient World.

For Musim, this was the excuse he needed to spend more time with Zahra, and to get away from Kytzia. He would already have gotten a divorce if his wife had not been the daughter of a powerful family. But he knew that this was impossible, that he couldn't even consider it. Kytzia's family was more important than his, and the Sadat business would undoubtedly have suffered. And so he had no choice but to think that he was stuck with his wife for the rest of his life. Stuck with her, and dreaming of Zahra. Perhaps one day ...

Zahra and Musim left Fernando at Ylena's house. It was already late and the three of them were tired.

Dimira advised Fernando to go straight to the dining room, where the rest of the lodgers and Ylena were already eating.

Before he went in, Fernando heard Catalina laughing and was surprised. He hadn't heard her laugh for months.

Ylena was pleased to see him and invited him to sit down while Colonel Sanders and Monsieur Baudin asked him about the trip to Cairo. Before he could answer, Fernando noticed Dr. Naseef sitting at the table next to Catalina.

"Our dear doctor came by to see Adela and agreed to stay for supper."

Fernando greeted the doctor, and the pair of them weighed each other up. Fernando wondered why the doctor should scrutinize him so. The conversation ran about the treasures of Egypt for a while, especially the Pyramids, which Fernando had been privileged to see close up. Colonel Sanders, putting on his archeologist's hat, gave him a lecture about the Pharaonic dynasties and explained in detail how they had built those wonderful things that loomed over the desert.

Catalina said that she would like to go and see them one day, and Dr. Naseef offered to take her when the time came.

What had happened while he was away? Or had it been earlier, when Adela had been in the hospital? Fernando noticed a degree of familiarity between the doctor and Catalina which he hadn't seen before. Was Catalina finally abandoning her obsession with Marvin? As soon as he had the chance, he'd ask her. He had the right to know, of course, given that they were here because of her.

The next morning Catalina woke him up with a few gentle knocks on the door. Fernando opened up to see her smiling with Adela in her arms.

"I wanted to see you before you left, you go out so early …"

"Come in."

Fernando sat down on the edge of the bed and she took a chair facing him.

"I'm so happy! I've got a job!"

"A job? What kind?"

"I'm going to give piano lessons … You don't need to be an expert to deal with little children. Dr. Naseef suggested it … I told him that I needed to earn a living, and told him that I could play the piano. And he came by yesterday and told me that a friend of his has two little daughters and he wants them to learn the piano. He spoke to them about me, and today he's going to take me there to see them. I hope they think I'm presentable: what do you think?"

Catalina was nervous, and her words tumbled out all at once. Fernando was relieved to know that the reason for her joy and her laughter the night before was that she had the chance to do some work. He scolded himself for having been suspicious of the doctor, although he couldn't help but recall the man's gaze, the way he looked at him. There was something odd about that.

"I'm happy for you, but what are you going to do with Adela?"

"Ylena says that Dimitra can look after her if I go out for a couple of hours. You know that she's a very good baby and doesn't cry that much. Fernando, I have to do something … I can't live off charity …"

"Charity? How can you call it that?" he said angrily.

"I owe you so much … I owe Eulogio and Captain Pereira, and Ylena, and the doctor … I am so indebted to you all …"

"Indebted? You don't owe me anything, let's be clear about that."

"But you can't support me for the rest of my life. There must have been some point to my Aunt Petra's piano lessons, even if I was bored to tears …"

"Well, do you think it will be enough to live on, giving classes to a few children?" Fernando's voice was no longer surprised, but rather harsh.

"No, of course not, but I'll be able to contribute something …"

Catalina sat on the edge of the bed; although she was holding Adela against herself with one hand, she leaned over and tried to hug Fernando. He shivered and wrapped his arms around both of them in a hug.

"I only have you, Fernando. I wish I'd been able to fall in love with you," she admitted thoughtfully.

Fernando went back to work at the publishing house without Mr. Wilson showing the least interest in what had happened in Cairo.

It was clear that Zahra had told him all he needed to know. In fact, he couldn't have told Wilson much, as his job had been to play the dull companion, and he was still annoyed about it.

He was surprised at Athanasius Vryzas' discretion: he didn't make the slightest mention of his subordinate's absences. He pressured him, though, to have Marvin's poetry collection ready for March, along with the poems of Omar Basir.

When he got to work in the morning, the first person he met was Sara Rosent, who always greeted him affectionately and asked about Catalina and her daughter. He would usually ask about Marvin and Farida, in the hope of getting some news about Eulogio, but Sara's face would always sadden. Though she said that they had to be all right, she never had any actual news. The term "actual" worried Fernando a little, though he didn't dare press her any further for more information. He was worried about what might have befallen his friend. He reproached himself for not having been able to convince him that there was nothing in France for him.

Even having a routine didn't allow him to get comfortable in the situation in which he found himself. He felt trapped in this cosmopolitan city, this Tower of Babel. The only satisfaction he had was in gradually regaining his closeness with Catalina. He was surprised that she was so resigned to living in Alexandria. She even seemed happy now that she was giving piano lessons. The doctor had managed to get her another three students. She didn't earn much money, but was happy to be able to provide something towards supporting herself and her daughter.

Ylena sent for a man to tune the old piano that stood in the corner of the salon, and suggested that Catalina give her classes at it, so she wouldn't have to leave the house.

Fernando wasn't opposed to Ylena's suggestion, but it saddened him to feel that all the possible doors through which he might leave Alexandria for good were slowly closing in his face.

He sought refuge in his work and would take Omar Basir's poems back to the house with him, as they were giving him more trouble than he had imagined they would. As for Zahra, he hadn't seen her again, and this upset him as well. He couldn't deny the attraction he felt for her, for all that he told himself he was still in love with Catalina.

He also thought that Dr. Naseef was falling in love with Catalina. The doctor had started to visit Ylena's house more often on the pretext of checking up on Adela's health, although he managed to find the opportunity every time to stay for a while and talk to the little girl's mother.

Catalina seemed happy with these visits, and Fernando noticed that when the doctor came by, she would always go to her room and comb her hair.

Ylena trusted the doctor and knew that he was a good friend in times of need. When Naseef came by shortly before supper, telling her that he had left the hospital and wanted to come and see how Adela was before going home, Ylena invited him to eat and he would never refuse.

One night, after Dr. Naseef had left, Fernando went back to Catalina's room with her, as he normally did, to chat for a while. Adela was asleep in the bed, and they sat next to one another and spoke in low voices so as not to wake her.

"Do you like Dr. Naseef?" he asked.

Catalina blushed and shifted in her seat as she looked him straight in the eye.

"How could you think something like that? You know I'm in love with Marvin, and that there will never be another man in my life. Dr. Naseef has behaved very well with us, and Adela would never have made it without him. The least I can do is be friendly towards him," she said in annoyance.

"You smile at him in such a way … You're happy when he comes, and as for him … he obviously likes you, which isn't surprising, as you get more beautiful every day."

"The things you say! Fernando, don't see things that aren't there, and think about my situation. I'm a woman with a daughter and an obligation to give her a father, a real father."

"Yes, but I asked you if you liked him, not if you were going to marry him."

"If I like him? What a stupid question … He's a friendly man, a nice man, an attractive man … But I've told you already, I'm very grateful for what he's done for Adela and … well, I accept that I'm happy when he comes to see us … he's got a great sense of humor …"

"You like him, but you refuse to admit it," he said in annoyance.

"No, I didn't say that I liked him. For heaven's sake, don't leap to such absurd conclusions! Fernando, I don't want you to make jokes about these things."

"I'm just saying what I see," he insisted.

"Well, you're wrong. Don't make me feel bad. There's nothing further from my mind than to fall for some man. I tell you, there's only my child's father for me."

"But that doesn't stop you falling in love with someone else."

"That's enough! I've told you: I'm not interested in Dr. Naseef."

But this did not convince Fernando: he was sure that such an absolute denial was not the whole truth. She was still obsessed with Marvin, but that didn't stop her from feeling attracted to Naseef, just as he was in love with her but attracted to Zahra.

The human soul is very complicated.

6

The days passed by, each the same as the next. Too similar, Fernando's mother thought as she went to church.

Rain or shine, Don Bernardo insisted on praying the rosary on Saturdays at five o'clock on the dot. On her way to church, Isabel saw Doña Asunción and hurried to catch up to her.

"How good to see you! How's your husband?"

"He's still in the hospital; it's difficult for him to get over this last attack."

Isabel said nothing. She knew that no words of consolation on her part would be welcome, as Asunción knew the seriousness of the situation.

"Do you need me to help with anything?" she asked finally.

"Thank you. His brother Andrés and his sister-in-law Amparo have come to see him. You know them."

"Better, I suppose. I'm sure that Ernesto will be pleased to see his brother."

"Yes, but Andrés isn't that well either … you know what happened during the war."

"Yes, I know … We all suffered a lot, Asunción, all of us."

"But Andrés … Well, seeing his father and then his son shot right in front of his eyes, little Andresito … No, he'll never get over it."

"It's difficult to get over a death that tears someone away from us unfairly."

"Sorry, Isabel … don't think I don't realize how difficult the death of Lorenzo must be for you. Your husband was always an exemplary man. He didn't deserve to end up like that."

"No, he didn't. And so many others didn't as well. And they're still shooting them, Asunción. Apparently the people in charge haven't slaked their thirst for revenge against the people who fought for the Republic."

"Well, some people fought for the Republic and others fought for communism, Isabel ... Remember what Spain was like back then ..."

"Frustrated is what it was. Red and frustrated at so much injustice. That's why so many people became communists and anarchists, in order to protect themselves from the powerful, Asunción. Let's not argue about the past, we'll never have any control over it. But we can complain about the present, and I can't forgive those people who won the war and are still engaged in making anyone who opposes them disappear. These executions are all murders."

"What are you saying? Look, I like you very much, but I'd prefer not to hear you say such things. You protect your dead and I'll protect mine."

"We should agree, though, that there shouldn't be any more dead."

They fell silent. An uncomfortable silence. They liked one another, yes, but the unbreakable wall of the war rose up between them.

They got to the church and sat next to one another to pray the rosary. Don Bernardo seemed to be in a hurry, because the prayers were over sooner than usual. As always, after the prayers, they went to the sacristy to talk to the priest for a moment.

"I don't have much time, I'm going to eat with Don Fidel Nogués. I suppose you've heard that Antoñito is going to marry Mari Paz, Don Fidel's oldest daughter. You know the Noguéses ... they live near here, in the Calle Bailén ... Don Fidel and Don Antonio both want me to be there for the official proposal. We have to start thinking about the wedding," Don Bernardo told them proudly.

"Mari Paz? I know her, the oldest of the Nogués children. She and Catalina were friends ... they went to the same convent school together, the Sisters of Saint Teresa ... But I heard that

Antoñito was very keen on Lolita, the daughter of the tailor on the Gran Vía. Who would have thought it!" Doña Asunción said in surprise.

"Poor girl," Isabel said.

"What do you mean? She'll have a splendid wedding. Don Fidel is a very rich man, but an unlucky one, he lost his sight in the war. Don Antonio is a man of means and Don Fidel is a respected lawyer, although he doesn't practice very much anymore," Don Bernardo said angrily.

"A respected lawyer with no money," Isabel interrupted.

"Well, that's exactly why it's a good marriage for both families, just as it would have been for Catalina if she had married Antoñito. There's no space in this life for childish romanticism, but you have to act thoughtfully and correctly, respecting God's laws," the priest said, looking severely at the two women.

Doña Asunción felt uncomfortable, but Don Bernardo did not appear to notice. She, just like Doña Isabel, felt sorry for the Nogués girl, just as she had felt sorry in secret for her own daughter when she had been going to marry Antoñito. Her idea of a good wedding did not involve marrying a shopkeeper's son.

"And how long have they been going out?" Isabel wanted to know.

"Well, they've been seeing each other since shortly after Catalina disappeared. And Antoñito did like Lolita, but there's only one man in charge here, and that's Don Antonio, who decided in favor of Mari Paz. He's over the moon about the wedding, and as he is a generous man, he'll cover most of the expenses," Don Bernardo replied proudly.

"Is Nogués in such a bad way that he has to marry his daughter off to Antoñito?" Isabel insisted.

"They're having their troubles, like everyone is. Bear in mind that Don Fidel can't work as much as he wants to." Don Bernardo seemed very keen on the wedding that was being prepared.

"I'm happy for them, and only want them to be happy," Doña Asunción said, irrelevantly.

"Catalina had such an opportunity … Well … when is she coming back to Madrid? Is she still with your sister Petra?" the priest asked.

"Yes … they're in the countryside …" It was hard for Doña Asunción to lie.

"Well, she should come back, with her father so ill. Her main duty is to be with her father."

"Yes, of course … but Ernesto prefers her to be there … I know, Father, that it wasn't easy to break things off with Antoñito. Don Antonio hasn't forgiven us. Catalina wouldn't be comfortable running into Antoñito every day in the street."

"Catalina needs to be put in line. It's not going to be easy for God to forgive her," Don Bernardo said.

"You think God's going to punish her for breaking off her engagement? I don't think so. God has more important things to do than worry about a little girl who doesn't want to get married," Isabel said, glancing at Doña Asunción, who blushed a deep red.

"Oh, so now you know what God cares about," Don Bernardo said angrily.

"Well … I don't think that my daughter behaved very well, but God won't send her to Hell for it," Doña Asunción said.

"Really, do I have to hear such things? Look, I'm going now, but I'll see you at confession …"

Don Bernardo left in a bad mood. How dare those two women question God! If he knew!

Doña Asunción was nervous. She wasn't used to arguing with Don Bernardo and blamed herself for doing so, but she was sad that he had judged Catalina so harshly.

Isabel, for her part, was annoyed with the priest. She believed in God without any conditions or provisos, but from time to time, and she hoped He forgave her for it, she wondered if Don Bernardo was a good person to interpret His divine will.

"I'm pleased Antoñito is going to get married. Maybe then Don Antonio will stop causing us trouble," Doña Asunción said in a low voice.

"Don Antonio is a bad man, Asunción, and you should give thanks to God that Catalina didn't marry his son, who is as sick as his father," Isabel said.

"I never liked the idea of that wedding … But Ernesto thought that it was the best for everyone. You know we're in debt to Don Antonio …"

"Who isn't? The whole neighborhood owes him money and he takes good advantage of the fact."

"But he was going to forgive our debt once our children were married."

"Well, I should say that …" Isabel stopped speaking. She didn't want to hurt Doña Asunción.

"I know … I know you think we weren't right to commit our daughter to this, but what other choice did we have?"

"Don Antonio wants to buy himself some respectability. That's what he's aiming for now, by marrying Antoñito off to Mari Paz Nogués," Isabel said dismissively.

"Poor Don Fidel was left a widower very shortly after Mari Paz was born, but he brought her up well. They've never given any cause for gossip," Doña Asunción sad.

"Well now they will, what with this wedding and everything. I hope your daughter hears that Antoñito is getting married. I'm sure she'll be relieved," Isabel said.

"And what about Piedad? How's she doing in the workshop?" Asunción said, to change the subject.

"She works a lot, but she makes enough money to get by."

"Our children … They shouldn't have left, Isabel … there's not a day goes by that I don't pray for Catalina and hope that she comes back to me."

Isabel went with Doña Asunción for a while, then said goodbye to her at the hospital doors. She stood there for a few moments, watching her enter the hospital, her head bent low, all around her the murmur of words from the people coming and going. "How much pain there was here!" she said to herself. How much pain, in the bodies and souls that had survived the war. She couldn't help feeling her own pain as well, the terrible pain that squeezed her throat until she cried in despair. Loneliness was an unbearable weight for her. She never blamed her son, but his absence had emptied her life, and she asked herself what meaning anything had anymore.

7

The apartment was small, but large enough for them not to feel overwhelmed. There was one room with a medium-sized bed, another with two single beds, an office with a table and a sofa, and a bathroom and a combination kitchen/dining room.

Monsieur Rosent was ill. Farida feared for his life, but Marvin said that the old editor would make it through somehow. Eulogio agreed with Farida, but he didn't want to upset his friend. They had enough problems just surviving. Vichy was not safe. They needed to leave as soon as possible.

Jean Bonner had just examined Monsieur Rosent and insisted that he drink a little bit of the soup that Farida had prepared for him.

Bonner, a doctor, was already quite old. He looked well; he was slightly overweight, but his hair was still black with very few gray hairs. He had been in love with Sara, but had never dared tell her so. Bonner's wife had been a good friend of Sara's, and had known her since they were both at school. They had stayed close until the day that Claudine died. He couldn't forget that on that day, Sara had held Claudine's hand in her own until she drew her last breath.

Claudine had asked for Sara to look after her husband, and she had put all her efforts into pulling him out of the black hole into which he sunk following the death of his wife. They had no children, and the loneliness was unbearable, so unbearable that he wanted to die. But Sara, patiently and with dedication, had helped him come back, to feel what life had to offer, until one day he found himself feeling attracted to her. He had not dared say anything. She might have stopped them from ever seeing one another again. Sara's loyalty towards Claudine was firm, even beyond the grave.

And this loyalty, this sincere friendship that Sara had granted him, had led him to run the risk of taking Monsieur Rosent out of Paris and into the free zone.

When the Germans marched down the Champs-Elysées, he had been among the many people who had fled. His sister was married to a doctor who worked in a hospital in Vichy. She encouraged him to move in with them. He earned less money than he had in Paris, but at least he had the hope that what remained of France wouldn't fall into the hands of the Germans. His was a vain hope, because he couldn't deny the truth of the matter: the Government of the free zone was a puppet in Hitler's hands.

Even so, he had not returned to the capital. He rented an apartment in the rue de Nîmes and now, he said to himself, he didn't feel so alone, given the proximity of his sister and her four children.

"I'm worried. The woman on the first floor asked me if I had guests staying with me. I said yes, that an old friend had come to see me. She was curious because she had seen Farida coming and going with shopping bags. I said that I had a couple of friends from Paris with me, who were just passing through."

"And why is your neighbor so curious?" Farida asked.

"I suppose because she hasn't seen any woman coming or going at my apartment until now. I … I'm sorry, but I gave her to understand that you and I … well, I couldn't think of anything else that would stop her being so nosy."

"You did well," Farida said with a smile.

"We should go as soon as possible, but Monsieur Rosent is in no condition to travel," Marvin said.

"Of course not. It would be insane. But we have to be discreet, or else we'll end up in a labor camp. I'm mostly worried about what might happen to Monsieur Rosent: they'll send him to Germany, which is where they're deporting all the Jews. As for us, I've already spoken to you about the Organization Todt. This man, this Nazi engineer, needs people to work in the factories in

Germany. All the young Germans are at the front, and so they take anyone they find. Some of my patients have been taken to Germany by force," Jean Bonner said.

"We'll try not to be too visible," Marvin said, an anguished note in his voice.

"I hope that the medicine I've brought will help with the pneumonia, but even if it does, he'll take a while to get better: he's quite an old man," the doctor said.

It was noon by the time Bonner left. It was Sunday and he didn't have to go to the hospital. He was going to meet a friend who he trusted that afternoon. In fact, it was his friend who had asked him to visit. Armand Martin suffered from asthma and Jean Bonner was treating him. They had formed a good friendship.

They called Armand Martin "the Spaniard." He was a very discreet man who didn't speak much, but they said that he was Spanish, even though he had been brought up in Vichy. Bonner didn't know what his political views were. They had never spoken about politics: in France, this was something that people avoided in those days. People only shared confidences with people who they were sure they could trust. It was rumored that Armand Martin had helped lots of Republicans who had escaped Spain after the end of the Civil War. He had paid for people to travel to America, apparently. But rumors aside, what was certain was that Armand Martin had a large fortune, not just because he had a transport company, but because everyone knew that he collected art. Bonner didn't think about Martin's fortune; he was worried now that one of his neighbors would report him to the police for having foreigners in his house. This was something that happened a great deal. He didn't worry about himself, but about Monsieur Rosent. Sara had trusted him to look after her father. If he didn't, then he would be failing her; although he knew that she was married and that maybe they would never meet again, he still dreamed of her.

"Don't you think that Bonner is being a little extreme in his precautions?" Marvin asked, hoping that someone would reassure him.

"We can't blame him. He did enough getting Sara's father out of Paris," Eulogio replied.

"He's very brave," Farida said.

"I think it was crazy to come here. If the Organization Todt catches us, they'll send us to work in Germany," Eulogio said.

"Don't be so negative!" Marvin said.

"You know I'm right. Bonner's taking big risks and we are too. Benjamin Wilson knew he was sending us into the lion's den. He's a chess player, moving people around like pawns, and sacrificing them when he feels like he needs to," Eulogio said.

Marvin swung to face him. He knew how much Farida liked Wilson, and how hurt she would be by Eulogio's comments.

"Benjamin Wilson didn't force us to come here. I decided to come, and I'm glad you came too: I asked you to, but Farida and I would have come alone if need be. I wouldn't be a poet if it weren't for Monsieur Rosent. The least I can do is try to help him. He helped me in the past. Just as you did."

Eulogio saw the disappointment on the American's face. He didn't want to upset Marvin, but neither did he want to do him the disloyalty of not telling him what he thought.

"Marvin, I know that you want to help Monsieur Rosent, but do you think we can? We don't know the country well enough to travel across it. Maybe Mr. Wilson could have found people who were better at these things to do it. Luckily enough, Jean Bonner is a good man and he seems to know what he's doing."

"Benjamin must have let us come because he didn't have anyone who could do the job better. Don't think that he's unscrupulous, Eulogio, I promise you he's an honest man," Farida said.

"I'm not worried about his honesty, but rather about his good judgment in allowing us to come here. I don't want you to think that I'm not going to do everything I possibly can to help us get out of this situation. I'm not afraid of risking my life," Eulogio said.

"Of course you are! Who wouldn't be afraid of such a thing? You'd be foolish to think otherwise. I love my life, but sometimes there's nothing you can do apart from risk it. Marvin owes Monsieur Rosent a debt of gratitude and needs to help him in order to square things with himself," Farida said.

"I don't want you to be upset," Eulogio said, worried that his friends would see his fears as a lack of loyalty.

Jean Bonner knocked at the door of the pretty house near the Parc Napoleon where Armand Martin lived. A middle-aged woman dressed in black opened the door to him. She was the housekeeper. Madame Florit smiled at him and invited him in.

"Monsieur Martin is waiting for you in his office. He seems a little better today," she said, leading him to a little room on the ground floor whose windows opened onto a well-tended garden.

Armand Martin was working behind a huge mahogany desk whose surface was covered by all kinds of papers and folders.

The two friends shook hands and Monsieur Martin asked the housekeeper to bring some coffee. As they waited for Madame Florit to return, Armand Martin poured them both a glass of cognac.

"Napoleon himself never tasted anything like this," he said, holding out the glass.

After sipping the brandy, Arman Martin got to the heart of the matter.

"I didn't ask you to come here for my asthma. You can see that I'm not any worse. I'm not going to waste your time by beating about the bush either. I know that you've got some special guests staying at your house, and that you need to move them on as soon as possible. They're not safe in Vichy."

Armand Martin's words surprised and upset Bonner. He didn't know what to say.

"I understand your shock, Jean, but there's no time to lose."

"I don't know what you're talking about ..." Bonner said.

"Of course you do. You have a French Jew in your house, Monsieur Rosent, an American called Marvin Brian, a Spaniard named Eulogio Jiménez and an Egyptian citizen called Farida Rahman. Your wife Claudine was a friend of Sara's, Monsieur Rosent's daughter. And after your wife died, you maintained your friendship with Sara Rosent. She is now Sara Wilson, as she is married to an Englishman resident in Alexandria. Should I go on?"

Bonner felt tense. He didn't know if he should deny everything he was hearing, or if he should admit it. He was trapped.

Madame Florit came in at that moment with a tray that held a pot of coffee and two mugs.

She served the coffee carefully and then left the two men alone.

"I'm sorry to have come out and said so much so quickly, but I wanted you to see the urgency of the situation. I have friends, Jean, a lot of friends all over the world. Friends who owe me favors, friends whom I owe favors to. I found out about your guests and the need to get them out of Vichy from one of these friends. My friend is a friend of Mr. Wilson's, the husband of your friend Sara. I'll help you, Jean. I'll help you. You can't deal with the problem by yourself. How were you thinking of getting them out of Vichy?"

Jean Bonner decided that he had no choice other than to tell the truth.

"Sara Rosent was Claudine's best friend. I owe her a debt of gratitude. She looked after my wife right up to the end; when she died, she was holding Sara's hand."

"Thank you for telling the truth. I think Wilson should have been patient, and sent someone more skilled to rescue his father-in-law. You can't do it alone. Wilson came to you fairly urgently with the idea of saving his father-in-law, but even if you put your heart and soul into it, I think it's too much for you."

"I don't know where this conversation's going," Bonner said, as upset as he was worried.

"Mr. Wilson knows people whom I also know. He got in touch with them and asked them to take over the task of getting his father-in-law out of France. These contacts of Monsieur Wilson's got in touch with me; that's why I asked you to come and visit me today."

Jean Bonner didn't know what to say. He looked Armand Martin straight in the eye and suddenly saw a different man than the one he thought he knew. His asthmatic patient, the man he had made friends with, was now someone else. His jaw was set, with all the determination of a man who never retreats. His eyes shone with an icy gleam that suggested it would be dangerous to oppose him. He looked at his hands. Yes, he had never noticed those strong hands before, a fighter's hands, the hands of a man who would use force.

"I understand that you're confused, and even why you might find it difficult to trust me. No one knows who anyone is anymore, especially not in a city like Vichy. I have to be frank with you. I am going to help you. I'll look after Monsieur Rosent and your three friends. We'll get them out of Vichy on one of my trucks. We could take them straight to Nice and then over the Italian border. It's a porous border. But there's no time for that, I don't think, and so tomorrow we'll take your friends to Lyon and then to Switzerland. It's close by. It won't be comfortable, the journey to Lyon: they'll go in a furniture truck, but it's not too long, three and a half or four hours, so the inconvenience won't be that great."

"And what are they going to do there? They don't know anyone, and Monsieur Rosent is very ill. He's got pneumonia. I don't think he can cope with a journey, even a short one. As his doctor, I can't allow it."

"Well, he'll have to manage. He can either sit in a truck or be deported to Germany. Do you think that Monsieur Rosent could survive a labor camp? We are at war, my dear Jean, and there are not a lot of options open to us. In most cases, it is a question of where and how to die more than how to survive."

"I can't abandon them in Lyon."

"And you won't be abandoning them. You have to trust me. They'll stay for a few days in the home of a person I trust. Then they'll be carried across the border."

"Who are these people who'll pick them up in Lyon?" Bonner asked.

"I'm not going to tell you. The less you know, the better."

"But it's not about me, it's about Monsieur Rosent," Bonner protested.

"Monsieur Rosent's security depends on your own. He's a Jew, don't forget. And for the Germans, being a Jew is the worst thing it's possible to be these days."

"And for the French as well," Bonner said bitterly.

"Yes, for a vast majority of the French as well, why deny it?"

But Jean Bonner didn't understand why Armand Martin was going to take so many risks for people he didn't even know. He waited to ask the question, and only did so because he wanted to know that Sara's father would be in safe hands.

"Why are you doing this, Armand?"

Armand Martin filled his cognac glass once again. He didn't want to keep drinking, but the activity gave him a chance to come up with the proper reply to his friend's question.

"I'm not going to lie and claim that I am a good man. I don't think I'm worse than others, but I'm not a saint. Benjamin Wilson looks for people, and we've worked together on cases in the past that we have brought to satisfactory conclusions. He has his business and I have mine."

"You're wrong. Wilson is an editor, with two prestigious bookshops, one in London and the other in Alexandria," Bonner said with conviction.

"Of course he is, but he's not just that. I've told you, he looks for people, and he hunts for information. But he doesn't accept business from just anyone. He has his own code of ethics. And as for me … well, I'm the person you see, who you think you know, a businessman who deals with logistics. But like your friend Sara's husband, I do other things as well … I have my own code too."

"And what is your code?" Bonner asked.

"I decide by answering three questions: who for, why and for what purpose."

They sat in silence for a while. Jean Bonner was disconcerted, and Armand Martin was indifferent to his friend's unease.

"I need to speak with Sara," Bonner said.

"If I were you, I wouldn't call her. The only thing you'll do is upset her. She trusts her husband and she trusts you. She's convinced that her father is safe, and there's no need to bother her with details."

"But I need to know if …" Bonner fell silent.

"You need to know if you can trust me." Armand had said out loud what the doctor was worried about.

"No … It's not that."

"Of course it is, and I understand. But we're at war and the stakes are high. I can't force you to trust me. You decide, now, before you leave. I have everything ready to help with Monsieur Rosent and your friends. Accept the deal now or there won't be a second chance."

Jean Bonner felt a cold sweat trickle down his back. He hadn't felt so defenseless since the day that his wife died. He looked into the Spaniard's eyes and felt dizzy.

"I don't think I've got another choice," Bonner muttered.

Armand Martin shrugged. He understood the trouble the doctor had in making his mind up, but he couldn't waste any more time breaking down his resistance.

"Well, what's the plan?" Bonner asked.

"A truck will stop at the door to your house at eight o'clock in the morning. Two men will come up to your apartment. Monsieur Rosent will lie down on your living room carpet and the men will roll him up in it and carry him down to the truck."

"You're crazy!" Bonner said.

"No, I'm not. I know that you took Monsieur Rosent to your house in the evening and did all you could to prevent him from being seen so that no one would know that you have a Jew in your house. Well, I know, and if I know then other people will know as well. You've been clever to let your neighbors see Farida Rahman, so they will think you have a lover. As for the American and the Spaniard ... the best thing for them is to leave your house this evening. They can go to one of my garages and meet one of my men there. Then they can wait for the truck with the carpet to come back in the morning ..."

"And Farida?"

"Farida will leave shortly after they take Monsieur Rosent. She should walk slowly. Someone will come and pick her up to take her to the garage. And then they'll all travel to Lyon. Any questions?"

"Armand, I'm sorry, but this seems crazy to me ... taking an old man out of my house rolled up in a carpet ... He's very sick ..." Bonner protested.

"I know, he's old and sick and he's a Jew."

Armand Martin's plan was very nearly over before it started because Monsieur Rosent got worse.

The truck left them in the rue des Trois Maries in the heart of *Vieux Lyon*, near the cathedral.

No one paid Marvin and Eulogio any attention as they got out of the truck and walked, followed by two drivers carrying Monsieur Rosent wrapped in the carpet. Farida had gotten out a little earlier and was waiting for them at the door.

They went upstairs until they reached the first floor, and suddenly a door opened to reveal the figure of a man.

"Come in, come in ... Don't hang around outside," a calm voice said.

Farida went in first, followed by Armand Martin's two men, who left their burden on the sofa in the living room. The whole house was a large library. There wasn't a single wall that wasn't lined with bookshelves stuffed with books, and there were books all over the floor of what appeared to be the living room.

"I've got a room ready for Monsieur Rosent. I hope he'll be comfortable. As for you ... we'll sort something out. The lady can sleep in the guest room and ... Monsieur Brian can sleep with her? And as for you ... I hope you don't mind, but there's a sofa in the room by the kitchen ... My friends say it's not too uncomfortable ..."

"Thank you for your hospitality," Farida said, holding out her hand.

"Ah, sorry, I didn't introduce myself. I'm Anatole Lombard."

Marvin liked the man's firm handshake. Farida looked at Eulogio: he seemed uneasy.

Jean Bonner hadn't told them the identity of the man who was going to put them up, nor for how long he would be doing so. He had only told them that Benjamin Wilson had arranged for them to go to Lyon because it would be easier for them to cross the Swiss border there. In spite of Monsieur Rosent's condition, neither Marvin nor Farida argued with this. They trusted Wilson.

The house was dark. The windows were closed, and thick curtains barely let the light in.

Anatole Lombard gave them a chance to settle while he made coffee.

He must have been about forty years old. He was dressed elegantly, but informally. He was thin and pale, with straw-blond hair and very thin, almost feminine hands; his gaze was clear and his gestures were calm. Farida told Marvin and Eulogio that he was "too handsome."

Monsieur Rosent seemed to have lost consciousness because of his fever. He was shivering. Farida prepared an injection. Jean

Bonner had given them some medicine. She put a warm wash-cloth on the old man's forehead and sat down at his side.

"Is he very ill?" Anatole Lombard asked.

"Yes, he's got pneumonia, and given his age, he's very weak."

"I have a friend who works at the hospital. I'll ask him to come by as soon as possible."

They sat anxiously for a while, waiting for the old man to breathe calmly again.

They left the door to his room open and retired to the living room. Marvin and Eulogio were worried.

"I think the journey's made things worse," Farida said.

"But is he going to live? He has to," Marvin said, with an air of desperation in his voice.

"I don't know, it's hard for him to breathe ... I gave him the injection that Bonner gave me."

"I'm sorry about what's happening," Anatole Lombard inter-rupted. "I know it's cold comfort, but wars leave victims far from the front. I have to go. I imagine they'll have told you I'm a teacher, that I give classes at the *lycée*. My students are expecting me: I'll be back late in the afternoon. I can't return any sooner. There's food in the kitchen and ... well, use my house as you see fit. But we have to be careful. It would be better for you not to get too close to the windows, and to try to remain unseen. I've told my neighbors that I'm expecting some visitors, but at times like these, you can't be too careful. I think it would be good for you to get some rest. And, like I said, I'll bring a doctor by this afternoon to have a look at Monsieur Rosent. And now, if you'll excuse me ..."

Eulogio offered to look after Monsieur Rosent while Farida and Marvin rested for a while. Then Farida relieved him.

They didn't even dare eat a single apple from the heap piled in the fruit bowl. Anatole had said they should eat, but Farida thought they should wait for their host to return and to allow him to feed them. They didn't go out into the street either. It was better to wait for Anatole to explain to them what the situation in Lyon was.

Six o'clock had passed by the time Anatole retuned with a man whom he introduced as Dr. Girard.

The doctor read the report that Bonner had prepared, and then went into Monsieur Rosent's room to examine the patient. He was breathing with difficulty.

When he finished the examination, he came out into the hallway with Farida and said that he didn't think the old man would survive.

"He's running a high fever and isn't getting enough air into his lungs. You're giving him the right medication, but he has to go to a hospital. But even so, I don't think he'll last much longer."

"He has to live!" Marvin said in distress.

Dr. Girard shrugged. Farida took Marvin's hands between her own. Girard saw that Marvin was calmed by the simple touch of this beautiful woman.

"Do you think that it would be dangerous to take him to the hospital?" Anatole asked the doctor.

"Yes, of course … You know what's happening with the Jews … and Monsieur Rosent fled Paris, they told me … It's a risk, but it's a risk if he doesn't get the medical care he needs as well. I can come to see him every day, and bring medicine with me to add to the ones he is already taking, but it won't be enough," Dr. Girard said.

"Are you saying that whatever we do, Monsieur Rosent will die?" Eulogio asked.

Dr. Girard shrugged and looked curiously at the Spaniard, who had previously been relegated to the edges of his attention.

"In my opinion, there's not a lot we can do now apart from alleviate his suffering, although I think that he would get better care at the hospital, and maybe even improve … I've seen everything in my career as a doctor: people who we thought would die and survived, people who we thought would survive and nevertheless died … Life is in God's hands, and we are but men."

Dr. Girard's reply surprised Eulogio.

"God doesn't have anything to do with pneumonia," he said angrily.

"Of course not," the doctor said calmly.

"But …"

Girard cut him off. He wasn't there to argue with this young man, but rather to treat the old one.

546

"You decide if you want to take the risk of getting him to the hospital or if he stays here. In any case, I'm at your service. I will do whatever I can to help you."

"Do you think he's in any shape to travel?" Marvin asked.

"Travel? No, of course not. It was very reckless of you to bring him from Vichy. Where would he travel to?" the doctor asked.

Eulogio looked at Marvin and they wondered if they should answer the doctor. Anatole decided for them and replied in his calm voice:

"Switzerland. The plan is to take him to Switzerland. There's a pass we've used a couple of times. It's not entirely safe, but nowhere is nowadays."

"I think that he's not in any condition to be moved at the moment. We should wait a few days at least. It's clear that if you can get him to Switzerland he'll have proper treatment, but I don't think he'll survive the trip at the moment. He can't walk, and he's delirious with fever. No, it would be a death sentence to make him get out of bed," the doctor said.

"We can't keep him here very long either. We're putting Anatole in danger," Farida said.

"Oh, don't worry about me! I think of myself as fighting in the war, even though I'm not at the front. Helping Monsieur Rosent is my way of contributing. You can stay as long as you need," Anatole said.

"All right, well there's not much more to say. I'll come back tomorrow before I go to the hospital. If he gets any worse … Anatole, call me. I'll be along at once."

When Dr. Girard left, the teacher said that he would make them supper. Eulogio offered to help, although he admitted that he had never cooked anything before.

Farida and Marvin looked after Monsieur Rosent. He was sweating heavily from the fever and Farida undressed him so that they could clean him a little, wiping a warm sponge over his body. Then she changed the sheets while Marvin held him up, which was no great problem for him, as Monsieur Rosent had shrunk down as though he were turning back into a child, and he was extremely thin.

Eulogio came into the room with a mug of soup. Bonner and Dr. Girard had both insisted that Monsieur Rosent drink lots of liquids, and although he resisted, Farida insisted. And so they made him drink the soup in little sips. It had an egg yolk beaten into it.

After a little while the old man's breathing seemed to improve, and he fell into a less painful sleep.

Meanwhile, Eulogio had laid the table according to Anatole's instructions, and they ate scrambled eggs and a salad, as well as some more of the soup.

They did the meal justice. They hadn't eaten for a long time and they were tired. Anatole tried to distract them from their thoughts by telling them about Lyon and his work at the *lycée*. He gave classes in French literature, and it was clear that he liked the process of teaching as much as the subjects that he taught. Eulogio listened to him carefully, and seemed more interested in what he had to say than Marvin or Farida. But when the meal was over, the detente ended as well. Marvin went to Monsieur Rosent's room, and Eulogio and Farida helped Monsieur Rosent wash the dishes.

Marvin was relieved to see Rosent asleep. He was breathing slowly, but at least he appeared to be resting a little.

Anatole suggested that they drink a cup of coffee. They had to decide what to do.

"I think you're too tired to make any decisions now. You'd do well to get some sleep," he advised.

"Jean Bonner told us that you'd tell us about the escape route," Marvin said.

"I don't know the details. A friend of mine deals with it. He'll be the one to take you to the border. Someone will meet you there and try to get you to Switzerland. It's not far to the border. You can be there in a little more than an hour. The hard thing is crossing it."

"Will you come?" Eulogio asked.

"No, that's not my job," Anatole said.

"Are you a part of a group?" Eulogio surprised him with his question.

"Well, you might say that …" The teacher did not elaborate.

"And Dr. Girard?" the Spaniard insisted.

"Dr. Girard is a Catholic."

"That's not an answer."

"It is ... Here in Lyon, it is. In France, you come across two types of people: the ones who prefer to ignore what happens, who are the majority, and a few people like me who prefer to do something. Some of us act out of moral conviction, others out of ideology, others ... well ... everyone has his reasons. Dr. Girard's reasons are religious in nature," Anatole said.

"And what are your reasons?" Eulogio asked bluntly.

"I had a friend ... a friend who was very dear to me ... We grew up together. He's a Jew. They deported him to Germany, but I don't know which camp he's in, or if he's even still alive. That's one reason to fight against the Germans. A personal reason. I have other reasons, of course."

"What do you think we should do?" Marvin asked.

"Rest for a few days. Monsieur Rosent is in no condition to go anywhere. I'll get in touch with the person who will take you to the border. I think we'll be able to delay your journey by a few days. If he says it's not possible, then ... well, you'll have to go. It's not easy to get people from one side of the border to the other, and the people who do it risk their lives. People don't actually get to Switzerland that often. I suppose you know that."

"Of course," Farida said.

"Well, then, I suggest you rest this evening. I'll meet with my contact tomorrow and as soon as I find anything out, I'll get in touch with you. Meanwhile, the best thing would be not to leave this place. It might be a bit claustrophobic, but it's better not to attract people's attention."

Farida and Marvin went to sleep. Eulogio was about to do so, but he saw that Anatole was in the kitchen cleaning, so offered to help him. They spent some time putting the kitchen in order. They didn't need any words to feel comfortable with one another.

In the morning, Monsieur Rosent started to cough. Farida ran to his room. He had woken up and was moving from side to side in great agitation, as though he were drowning. They got another injection ready, while Marvin tried to make him drink a few sips of water.

Eulogio had woken up as well and came over worriedly. They spent a while with Monsieur Rosent until he started to fall asleep again. Marvin said that Farida and Eulogio should go back to sleep. It was still early, just five o'clock in the morning, but Farida said she would stay up.

Eulogio couldn't get to sleep, assaulted by memories of his mother. He wondered if she still thought about him. He knew the answer. His mother would always love him, in spite of what he did, and in spite of the pain that he had inflicted on her. He missed her. He missed the tiny attic they lived in, living poorly because of Don Antonio. He felt a wave of hatred just to think about that horrible man. The shopkeeper had taken advantage of his mother, and he had not been able to protect her.

He should have killed him, just as Fernando had killed the men who killed this father. But he had fled, because he had not been brave enough to take on the shame of knowing that his mother had put herself in the hands of that man to protect him, in order to lessen the implacable vengeance of the victors.

He closed his eyes tightly to try to scare away the image of his mother, but she seemed determined not to leave him. She looked at him sadly, but undefeated. That was the difference between his mother and him. Piedad had allowed herself to be harassed by Don Antonio, but she had not been defeated, because her honor was not connected to her poor flesh.

He tried to stop thinking about his mother and instead thought about Fernando and Catalina. He couldn't stop himself from feeling sad that his friend was so hopelessly in love with that young woman. She didn't deserve it. He was sad that Fernando was trapped in fruitless passion.

But he also decided that he should get rid of this troubling thought. On many occasions, Fernando had told him that he didn't understand because he himself had never been in love. His friends in the neighborhood put him into a bad mood when they asked him why he didn't have a girlfriend. Why had he never felt interested in any woman? He felt pain and anger growling in his stomach and decided to get up. Insomnia was bringing him unwanted ghosts. He got up and went to the sitting room. He took a book down from the shelf without looking. When he opened it, he smiled. His father had translated this book – Voltaire's *Cartes philiosophiques* – into Spanish, and he was an teenager when he read it for the first time. His father had never stopped him from reading any book.

He had learned French because of his father, in order to read all the treasures of French literature that his father translated. He dozed off rereading Voltaire's book. And that's how Anatole found him when he came into the salon just after he himself had woken up.

"Can't you sleep?" he asked.

"Monsieur Rosent had a bad night. None of us has slept that well. I woke up."

Anatole looked to see which book it was Eulogio was holding, and smiled.

"Do you like Voltaire? Can you read his French without any trouble?"

"Yes ... my father was a translator. He worked for a publishing house. He translated the great works of French literature. He helped me improve the French they taught me at school ... I think I'm not that bad when it comes to speaking ... you tell me ..."

"You speak my language well, and with a good accent. But speaking is one thing and reading is quite another, especially when it comes to works as dense as Voltaire's. I'm surprised that you speak French so well. Marvin has a bit of an accent, Farida less, and you could almost pass for one of us."

"Marvin is a poet, and he's lived in Paris, and Farida ... well, Farida is a polyglot, like all Alexandrians."

"Don't tell me any more. The less I know about you, the better."

"Why?"

"Because if they arrest me I won't be able to tell them anything."

"You didn't want to tell us why you do this, yesterday ..."

"I did. They arrested my best friend, a man I grew up with."

"Was he a teacher like yourself?" Eulogio asked.

"No ... He didn't like studying all that much, but he was very good with his hands ... He became a mechanic."

"Where did they take him?"

"They take Jews to labor camps in Germany … or at least that's what they say. I haven't heard any more about him. I tried to find him via the Red Cross, but they couldn't tell me anything."

"And is that what they'll do if they arrest us, send us to a labor camp?"

"In Monsieur Rosent's case, definitely. He's a Jew like Saul."

"Saul?"

"My friend …"

"Right … And what about us?"

"They'll arrest us and torture us to find out who the members of the group are."

"We don't know anything," Eulogio said.

"You know me, and Dr. Girard."

"We won't say anything."

Anatole smiled wanly. He saw a certain innocence still in Eulogio's eyes.

"Have you ever been tortured?" he asked.

"No …"

"Well, then, how can you say you'll never say anything? No one knows how they would react to torture. And you can't blame anyone who talks. But that's enough talking ourselves. It's getting late. I'll go and make some coffee. I don't usually have anything else for breakfast, there's bread and biscuits."

"I'll have a coffee."

They had breakfast in silence. When they had finished, Anatole left, saying that he wouldn't be back until late afternoon.

Marvin, Farida and Eulogio spent the rest of the day worried about Monsieur Rosent. They didn't leave his bedside, and there were times when his breathing was so shallow that they thought he had died.

Farida made some food and tried to get the old man to drink a bit of soup that was left over from the day before. But Monsieur Rosent could barely open his lips, much less swallow. They had to settle for wetting his lips with a little water.

It was past six o'clock when Anatole Lombard came back with Dr. Girard, who seemed to be even more worried than he had been the day before.

"We either take him to the hospital or he dies here, you decide."

"We know that they'll arrest him if we do," Anatole said.

"I know, but he can't carry on like this. He needs to be in a hospital."

"You'll have to do what you can to help him here. If we take him to a hospital, they'll put him on one of those trains that takes the Jews to Germany, and they'll doubtless arrest us."

"So the question is whether Monsieur Rosent dies here or on a train, that is, if he survives his trip to the hospital." Eulogio sounded very bitter and everyone gave a start.

Marvin was angry. He liked Eulogio very much, but sometimes he was so harsh that it upset him. Farida took charge of the situation.

"Doctor, will you come with us to the border? Anatole says that it won't take more than two hours to get there. I think we could take the risk if you come with us and look after Monsieur Rosent on the way. He can be looked after properly in Switzerland. We can't think about taking him to the hospital here in Lyon, and staying in Anatole's house isn't an option either."

The doctor stood in silence as he weighed up Farida's suggestion. If he went with them, he would be taking more risks than he had ever taken in his life, but he couldn't refuse. He would do it. He would go with them to the border. He couldn't do much more than he was doing already for the old man, but he knew that this woman and these two men would feel calmer with a doctor alongside them.

"I don't mind, as long as it's not in the morning or the early afternoon. It would be very difficult for me to explain my absence at the hospital."

"Anatole, when can we be ready to leave?" Farida asked.

"Tomorrow night. That's what we're prepared for. The people who deal with the crossing say that Saturday night is the best time to try. It has to be tomorrow," Anatole replied.

"Well, we'll go tomorrow, then," Farida said.

Anatole nodded and Marvin wrung his hands.

Once Dr. Girard had gone, Marvin insisted that he should stay the night with Monsieur Rosent, and told Farida to go and get some sleep. She let herself be ordered away, sure that if there were any problem then Marvin would come to her immediately.

Eulogio and Anatole stayed in the living room and drank a glass of wine. The murmuring of their conversation reached all the way to Farida's room, and did not end until the morning.

The next day, time seemed to run away from them. Or at least that's what Eulogio thought as he helped Farida wash Monsieur Rosent. Marvin looked impatiently out of the window. The last twenty-four hours he had been particularly nervous. His stomach was in knots, and for all that Farida insisted, he couldn't eat, and only swallowed a couple of cups of coffee. She was calm, as she always was. He was in awe of her inner strength, her capacity to cope with whatever life might throw at her. She didn't complain, she merely worked out how to deal with the situation. She placed reason above emotion, but this didn't make her cold or calculating. She just needed to dissect how life should be lived.

Meanwhile, Marvin was asking himself fearfully if they would get over the border. He remembered what Anatole had said to them: that it was as likely that they would be able to get across the border without problems as it was that they would be arrested. And also, he had said that no one could trust anyone those days.

Suddenly he thought about Fernando. What had happened to him? Benjamin Wilson was a good man, but he was engaged in a war against the Germans. Farida had told him as much. And he wouldn't care much for the pieces he had to sacrifice as he fought each battle. Marvin wondered if Fernando was one of those pieces, and felt sorry for him, because, although he had never been able to say that they were friends, he had always liked the Spaniard.

Monsieur Rosent's cough woke him up. He shouldn't fool himself anymore; Dr. Girard and Jean Bonner had both said that it was unlikely that the old man would survive. He was very weak. The months that he had lived in the damp basement owned by some friends of his in Paris had taken their toll on his health. Even so, he had survived until Bonner rescued him and took him to Vichy, where he had looked after him as though he were caring for his own father. But he had not been able to give him his health back. Things had gotten worse, and now it looked as though life itself were leaving him.

He felt a hand on his shoulder. He knew it was Fairda's before he turned around.

"I don't think he's going to live," she said in a low voice.

He turned to look at her and saw a deep sadness in her gaze.

"What can we do?" he asked.

"I'm going to give him another one of the injections that Dr. Girard gave us; they're stronger than the ones Dr. Bonner gave us. But he's dying. The only thing we can do is try to make sure that he goes peacefully. Nothing else."

"I can't accept that this is the end," Marvin replied.

"Death is a punishment which we don't deserve, but which we all know is inevitable, a battle we will never win. We can get out of the occasional skirmish, but the result of the battle is known in advance," Farida said in a neutral voice.

"It's cruel. You fight to live, but the result is always known in advance. What God could be capable of such cruelty?"

"We are matter, Marvin, and as matter we have to turn into dust to blend with the earth."

"And where is God in all of this?"

"We can't explain why we are, why we exist, why we die. There's no explanation, Marvin. We have to live with this, unless we become like little children and let ourselves be calmed by fairytales that lift our spirits. And it's not a bad choice. Sometimes we need dreams to be able to live with reality."

Anatole arrived at six on the dot. He told them that Dr. Girard would be there at eight.

"Farida and Marvin will leave the house at eleven and walk down the rue Saint Jean as quietly as possible. A car will pick them up. Another car will stop in front of the door at the same time. Dr. Girard, Eulogio and I will bring Monsieur Rosent down and settle him in the car as best we can. We'll meet Marvin and Farida at the border. And we'll have to walk a good long way to get to the pass that we hope will take us to Switzerland. I wasn't going to come with you, but as Dr. Girard is coming, I'll have to accompany you, and bring him back in case anything happens."

Farida had made a light supper for them all, a pasta salad. Anatole had said they should eat something before heading off to the border. Dr. Girard arrived at the agreed-upon time and examined Monsieur Rosent for a while. Then they waited for the daylight to fade and the cool night to set in.

Anatole kept on looking at the clock. He had to make sure that everything went according to plan. Eulogio made coffee and they waited, sitting down, as the hands of the clock made their slow yet inexorable journey towards eleven. It was three minutes to eleven when Farida and Marvin left the house. They went downstairs in their socks, shoes in their hands, so as to avoid making any noise. They walked down the street slowly, close to the wall, glad that the moon was behind a cloud and that there was not a single star visible in the sky to mark their passage through the night. Suddenly they heard the noise of a car, and indeed, one stopped next to them. A woman told them to get in quickly, and they did.

At that very moment, Anatole was going downstairs with Monsieur Rosent in his arms. The old man weighed little more than a baby. Eulogio and Dr. Girard cleared the way for him. A car was waiting for them by the door. The man driving it told them to hurry up. In barely two minutes they were inside. The following two hours seemed to last a lifetime.

They reached the outskirts of a village by the border. Marvin and Farida and a woman were waiting for them. She was the one who would lead them to the pass and then take Anatole and Dr. Girard back to Lyon. Marvin picked up his former editor in his arms and they started to walk among the trees until the noise of the car's engine had faded into the distance.

They walked for a while. The woman seemed to know the route very well, but from time to time she raised her hand to indicate that they should stop. They stood still in silence while she tried to analyze the sounds of the night.

She couldn't have been more than thirty years old. Her hair was chestnut brown. She was of medium height and had the robust appearance of someone who was accustomed to being outdoors.

Dr. Girard tripped a couple of times and Eulgio and Anatole had to help him get back to his feet. Farida didn't seem to have any problems walking through this strange forest in the middle of the night.

Suddenly the woman stopped dead and raised her hand to indicate that they should do the same. For a few seconds, they held their breath; then they saw her smile, and a minute later found themselves face-to-face with two men who greeted them almost wordlessly.

"We can cross without any trouble," one of them whispered. "We've been watching the zone for a few hours now. But don't make any noise or talk to each other."

"Help me!" Marvin said suddenly in a low voice as he stooped to lay Monsieur Rosent on the ground.

Dr. Girard rushed over to the old man. Everyone else surrounded him expectantly.

"Something's up … he was breathing very hard and then … he called for his daughter … and then … I think … I think he …" Marvin was in a state.

"He's dead," Dr. Girard said, closing Monsieur Rosent's eyes.

"No, it's impossible!" Marvin's voice broke out into the silence and startled the two men who had come to meet them.

"Shut up!" one of them said, in a cutting whisper.

Farida hugged Marvin. She felt him shuddering.

"What do we do now?" the woman who had brought them there asked.

"We do what we planned," Anatole said. "We help them across the frontier."

"And what will we do with the body?" one of the men asked.

"We bury it," Anatole said.

"But not here. We'll have to take it somewhere else. They patrol here very regularly," the other man said.

"We'll take him back to Lyon and give him a decent burial." That was Dr. Girard's idea.

"That's not possible, Doctor," Anatole said.

"All right, we'll take him back to my house. There's a vegetable garden there," the woman said. "We'll bury him in it. But it has to be tonight."

"We'll have to wait a couple of hours. His body's still warm," Marvin protested.

"Look, we're at war, and there's no time to waste on ceremonies. You have to cross the border and we'll take care of this old man's body, but don't ask us to risk our lives for a corpse." The woman's voice did not brook any argument.

"Let's go. Thank you, Dr. Girard. Thank you, Anatole …"

Farida held her hand out to the doctor and then to Anatole, and then she squeezed Marvin's hand.

The guides were relieved. They weren't ready to waste a minute more. They started to walk quickly, but they stopped when they heard murmuring behind their backs.

Eulogio was standing still, seemingly incapable of movement.

"I'm staying," he said.

"You can't stay here!" Marvin said, moving over to his side.

"Yes, I'm going to stay. I won't be far from Spain, and maybe I'll be able to go home one day," Eulogio insisted.

"You can't stay!" Marvin insisted.

"Of course I can!"

"I don't mind him staying in my house for as long as he needs," Anatole said.

"Thank you," Eulogio murmured.

"It will be all right," Farida said to Marvin, who didn't want to abandon his friend.

"Thank you, Farida." Eulogio's voice betrayed his nervousness.

"Will you look after him?" Farida asked Anatole.

"You know I will," he replied.

For a few seconds, Farida and Anatole looked at one another. Farida let go of Marvin's hand and walked over to Anatole to give him a hug, during which she whispered in his ear:

"Eulogio has suffered a great deal because he can't acknowledge who he is … You can help him."

Anatole gave her another hug, and whispered in return:

"I can try."

After this, no one looked back. Farida and Marvin disappeared into the darkness while Eulogio, Anatole and Dr. Girard followed the woman back to the car.

She drove them for a good distance until they reached a wooden house on the edge of a village. She said they should follow her.

Anatole carried Monsieur Rosent's body and Eulogio walked alongside him.

In silence, they dug a grave in the woman's vegetable garden and put the body into it. Then she invited them into her house to drink a cup of coffee.

"I need to get something warm into my stomach before I take you home."

And so they drank coffee.

8

When the day's work was over, and they were both about to leave the publishing house, Athanasius Vryzas came over to Fernando.

"It is unforgivable that you live in Alexandria, and that you are a translator of poetry and an editor, and you don't know the Al Togariya Cafe."

Fernando was surprised and didn't know what to say.

"Cavafy liked to write there. I don't think that talent is contagious, but a lot of writers go to Al Togariya," Vryzas said, surprising Fernando.

"Well ... the truth is I haven't had the chance to go to that cafe yet. I'll try at some point."

"You do know Cavafy, don't you?" Vryzas said, looking at him sidelong.

"If I hadn't known him before, then I would have gotten to know him here. Mrs. Rosent gave me a book and insisted that I read it," Fernando replied.

"As you set out for Ithaka, hope your road is a long one, full of adventure, full of discovery. Laistrygonians, Cyclops, angry Poseidon—don't be afraid of them: you'll never find things like that on your way as long as you keep your thoughts raised high, as long as a rare excitement stirs your spirit and your body. Laistrygonians, Cyclops, wild Poseidon—you won't encounter them unless you bring them along inside your soul ..."

Athanasius Vryzas, who had been murmuring the poem with deep emotion, suddenly fell silent.

"It's a beautiful poem," Fernando said.

"It's more than a poem … it's … Life itself is a long journey in search of Ithaca, but very few of us mange to reach our harbor." Vryzas was looking into the distance.

"Ithaca … my father made me read the *Odyssey* …" Fernando said.

"Don't get lost on the journey, Fernando. Don't get deceived by the sirens. Don't get wrapped around the smooth fingers of Circe. Try to get home to harbor. Don't stay here," the editor said in a low voice.

Fernando was so caught up by the deeply-felt words of Vryzas that he didn't quite catch their whole meaning. He only managed to blurt out something that he thought was banal:

"I'd love to go to the Al Togariya Cafe."

"I'd be delighted to be your guide and invite you to a cup of coffee."

They walked out to the Corniche. In spite of his age, Athanasius Vryzas walked quickly and decisively.

Al Togariya turned out to be a charming cafe, decorated in the art deco style, where Alexandrians played backgammon and foreigners hung around, trying to close deals.

A waiter recognized Vryzas and beckoned him through the crowd to a table that was just about to be occupied. But the waiter made it clear that this was a table reserved for his old friend and his young companion. He didn't ask what they wanted to drink, either, because a few minutes later he brought them a tray with two coffees on it, dark and thick as the night sky, and two glasses of water.

The editor-in-chief and his protégé didn't speak for a few minutes. They seemed to prefer each other's silence.

Athanasius was the first one to speak.

"You shouldn't stay in Alexandria. This isn't your place. Go and search for your destiny, your Ithaca."

"Ithaca? And where do you think my Ithaca is?"

"I don't know. I can't tell you, but I know it's not here."

"And how do you know?" Fernando insisted.

"I don't know much about you, just the things I've heard and that the Wilsons have said. But it's enough for me to be forward and tell you not to waste your life. You're like someone who has been shipwrecked in Alexandria; now that you're here, you've been trapped like a fish in a net. You didn't want to come to Alexandria, but you've found yourself here. Go before the passage of time turns your temporary stay into something permanent."

"Why are you telling me this?"

Vryzas paused for a few seconds before speaking again.

"Out of pity."

"I don't want anyone to take pity on me. There's no need," Fernando said angrily.

"Why does pity offend you? Don't answer that ... people reject pity because they think it makes them smaller. Pride prevents us from accepting the pity of those around us."

"I don't need your pity."

"You're wrong, my friend. We all need people to feel pity for us. We are nothing but men. Remember what Poseidon said to Ulysses when he was about to be shipwrecked?"

Fernando didn't remember. He felt too confused to remember any passage that he might have read a long time ago in the *Odyssey*. He looked expectantly at Vryzas, waiting for him to speak.

"So. 'Poseidon, what do you want from me!' Ulysses shouted. 'I want you to remember that men are nothing without gods,'" the old editor recited, not taking his eyes off Fernando.

"I don't understand what you're saying: it would be good if you could get to the point." Fernando was as intrigued as he was annoyed.

"My youngest son died a few years ago. Cancer. He was a late child. My wife and I couldn't have imagined that we were going to have another child, not at her age. After five children, along came Andreas. The Lord gave us this miracle. You can imagine how we spoiled him, how precious he was for us. His mother and I and his siblings only lived for him. Until the illness grew deep inside him and he died after a few short months. He wasn't even twenty years old. And I don't know why, but when I look at you, I see my son, I see Andreas. You have the same urge to live and the same confusion in the face of life. He could recite Cavafy's 'Ithaca' by heart, and he told me that his dearest wish was to go out and find Ithaca. My wife and I trembled at the idea that one day he would go off and make his own way in the world, that he would leave Alexandria in the search for his own Ithaca. He couldn't fulfill his dream."

"I'm sorry. I understand your pain." Fernando was deeply moved by what he had just heard. He could feel the depths of the pain in Vryzas' soul.

"I owe Benjamin Wilson a great deal. When he found out that Andreas was sick, he sent him to England to get the best care. He was so generous that he paid not just Andreas' expenses, but also my wife's and mine, and our children's, and he said that our son needed us in London. He behaved as only a man with a good heart could behave. Our suffering moved him to pity, and we accepted his pity."

Fernando listened to Vryzas speak, but still couldn't understand where the man was going with his tale. He felt more and more confused with every minute that passed.

"I'm sure that Mr. Wilson is a good man," he said, just to say something."

"Yes, a good man and a fair one. But you need to find your own path. If you stay here you'll be missing your chance to find your own Ithaca."

"And what does Mr. Wilson have to do with what I can or cannot do?"

"Mr. Wilson has a prosperous business. He doesn't just publish and sell books, as you know very well. But these other activities that he has involved you in are leading you away from your true path. I think you should know, by the way, that Mr. Wilson knows we're having this conversation."

"Well, well, well ..." Fernando's confusion increased with each word that he heard.

"I'll never be disloyal to him, never. I said that you reminded me of my son Andreas, and as a father, I would never have liked my son to have ended up entangled in a way of life that was not right for him. And this is what's happening to you. You can understand my agitation, and it was Mr. Wilson who told me to invite you to have a coffee here, at Al Togariya. But Mr. Wilson also asked me to say that once we had had this conversation, I was not to push you, and I should let you choose your own path."

They sat in silence, each of them absorbed in his own thoughts. Fernando, confused, tried to understand just what Athanasius Vryzas had just said to him. Vryzas sat and thought of his son, snatched away from him by death.

Neither of the two seemed to know how to start the conversation up again, and so they sat for a good long while, absorbed by their cups of coffee.

Fernando finally plucked up the courage to break the silence that had fallen between them.

"I feel like Alexandria is absorbing me so much that I don't know how I can ever escape from her," he confessed in a low voice.

"Leave. Book yourself a passage on the next boat out of here and leave."

"I don't know where to go. I'd like to go home, but that's impossible. I can't go back to Spain."

"Would you like to tell me why?" Vryzas asked, but there was no idle curiosity in his words, only sincere interest.

Fernando paused. Should he tell him that he had killed two men in order to avenge the murder of his father? He wasn't in any doubt as to Vryzas' good faith, but even so ... no, he wouldn't tell him. Only Eulogio and Catalina knew that he had committed these murders and he felt that no one else should know.

He tried to find words that would be honest, but would not betray him.

"You know there was a civil war in Spain. The people who rose up against the Republic won the war, but their victory wasn't enough for them. The losers, the ones who were loyal to the law, are being persecuted and imprisoned and murdered in the name of the new regime. Have you heard of General Franco?"

"Of course. He's the new strongman in Spain, the soldier who brought down your Republic, isn't that right?"

"Yes, that's it. His desire for revenge is nothing short of criminal. Every day, military tribunals pass down sentences against all those who fought on the losing side. They shot my father. He was an editor, like you, and a translator. His mistake was to stay loyal to the Republic and fight against those who would betray it. The families of the losing side are shunned. Franco and all his followers mistrust us. There's no future for people like me in Spain."

"Do you have any family?"

"I've got my mother."

"And is she still in Spain?"

"Yes."

"Why didn't you bring her with you?"

Fernando had asked himself this question, but he had always immediately pushed it aside. Why had he left his mother in Madrid? The only answer was the truth, which is to say that he would've had to confess that he had killed two men. His mother would have suffered to hear it. But there was another reason that made him feel even more guilty, and that was Catalina. He had believed that if he fled with her, had her under his protection, then maybe she would come to see him with other eyes and realize that she could love him, and this would have been impossible with his mother always between them. And this reason weighed down on his heart like the worst of all of them, worse than the fact that he had killed two men.

Vryzas didn't insist. It was enough for him to see the pain twisting the man's face to know that the answer hurt him.

The waiter came over to ask if they wanted another coffee. Vryzas said yes, and Fernando accepted as well. He wanted to stay there, in Al Togariya, getting further into a conversation that caused him both relief and panic.

"Do you believe in God?" Vryzas asked.

"In God? No, of course not. Why should I believe? My mother believes, she goes to Mass, she prays. She asks God every day to bring my father back. If God existed, then he would have done it. My father was a fine, upright, kind man."

"So, you're angry with God ..."

"It's not that I've stopped believing in God, just that he never interested me. My father didn't believe either, but that didn't make him any worse than men who cross themselves every day. He taught me that goodness, honesty, uprightness, doing good ... none of that has anything to do with religion."

"But you need to find some sort of consolation. Maybe speaking to a priest will help you deal with the weight of the burden you carry."

"Burden? I don't have any burden," Fernando said.

"I'd say you did … that you're not happy with yourself, that there are things that assault your conscience … It happens to us all."

"Conscience? Damn it!"

"You see?"

"Religion manipulates the conscience in order to turn us into slaves to its rules," Fernando said, raising his voice.

"Do you really think that?"

"Of course I do. Don't you?"

"Whether you like it or not, whether you are religious or not, we're all born with a conscience. Every man deals with it as best he can."

They sat in silence again, and the waiter gave them their fresh coffees. They saw through the windows that it had started to rain, a rain that was as intense as it was unexpected. It was February, and nothing had told them that there was a storm on the way.

In spite of the hour and the rain, there were still people strolling along the Corniche. The place seemed to be like a magnet for the Alexandrians.

"Are you a Catholic?" Fernando asked curiously.

"Orthodox. I'm Greek."

"Right … I'm surprised that there are so many faiths in Alexandria."

Vryzas shrugged and smiled for the first time that afternoon.

"It's a part of the essence of the city. Unlike Cairo, Alexandria was always open to whoever wanted to come and stay here. They say that all the various religions have attained a status quo, but it's a very delicate equilibrium. As you know, it wasn't always like that. So much blood has been spilled in the name of various religions. It's a crime to kill in God's name. The worst of all sins," Vryzas said, his face serious once more.

Fernando didn't feel comfortable with the way the conversation was going, so he decided to go back to square one and ask about Cavafy.

"You know what? I don't know much about Cavafy, apart from the fact that he is considered one of this city's great poets. As well as 'Ithaca,' I really like 'The God Abandons Anthony.'"

"You have the touch, so it shouldn't be hard for you to get into Cavafy's work."

For a while now, Fernando had been wondering if he should ask Vryzas about Zahra. He needed to know what she was doing, but he didn't dare ask Ylena, and although Dimitra could be a good source of information, he was not sure that the maid would know what he wanted to know.

He saw Vryzas looking at the clock and realized that he would not have another opportunity like this one, and so he swallowed and asked:

"What about Zahra? What role does she play in Mr. Wilson's organization? I can't see how she fits into Wilson's business."

Athanasius Vryzas looked straight into Fernando's eyes. He felt uncomfortable, as he sensed the old editor could read his soul.

"Zahra has a great many reasons to collaborate with Mr. Wilson. But she doesn't work for him: he doesn't pay her a penny."

"Right ... Well, it's just that I can't work out why she does what she does ..."

Vryzas thought for a few seconds. Fernando saw that the conversation was upsetting the editor.

"Are you in love with her?" he asked bluntly.

"No ... no ... it's just that ..." Fernando stammered and felt ridiculous as he did so, but he had never been good at lying.

"Right. You don't need to tell me. You are fascinated by her, just like most men she meets. There is something very special, very subtle, that emanates from Zahra, that awakens admiration and the desire for possession in all men who come close to her. You're not going to be any different. And, as you're so young, it's entirely understandable."

"I don't want you to misunderstand me." Fernando was trying to defend himself from what was absolutely self-evident to Vryzas.

"No, don't worry, I understand what's happened. I don't like to give people advice, and yet I've given you some today, telling you to head off in search of your own Ithaca. And now I'll give you another: don't fall in love with Zahra. She'll never belong to anyone. She can never belong to anyone. She's the last woman you should fall in love with. And not because she has any flaws – she is as good as she is intelligent – but she is ill, incurably ill, with a deadly sickness."

Fernando gave a start when he heard that Zahra was sick. It didn't seem possible. She looked healthy. He didn't want to seem inquisitive, but he couldn't avoid asking what it was that was wrong with her.

"Her sickness is a sickness of the soul," Vryzas said bluntly, and he looked into his empty coffee cup. As it was empty, he took his glass of water and drank it down at a gulp. He asked himself if he should be honest with the young Spaniard, and if it would be a betrayal of someone else's privacy if he decided to do so. But Fernando's gaze reminded him once again of his son. He felt that Andreas was looking at him from the past, or from Eternity.

"I'm going to do something I shouldn't …" And then he fell silent as though he regretted what he was about to do.

"Please …" Fernando was almost begging.

Athanasius Vryzas looked away from the young Spaniard and asked himself once again if he had the right to say what this young man was so eager to hear. He consoled himself by saying that maybe by telling the truth, he would be able to get Fernando to start on his quest for his own Ithaca.

"Yasmin and her daughter Heba were the best dancers in Alexandria. They danced for the court and were protected by the king. It is no secret to any Alexandrian that the late King Faud was a great admirer of Heba. They say that the king went wild when he found out that she had left for Germany …"

Vryzas paused and looked out through the windows. It looked like the rain was slackening off. Fernando didn't dare ask.

"As you will have seen, this is a very cosmopolitan city, so it was only a question of time before someone offered Heba the chance to dance outside of Egypt, and it was Jan Dinter who did so. Jan Dinter was the owner of several cabarets in Germany, especially the famous Rosy-Fingered Dawn. Dinter offered her a good contract and the chance to become an international artist. Imagine the first decade of the century in Berlin: the city was a dream for all artists. And so Heba accepted the offer this man made her without a second thought, ignoring her mother's pleas. Yasmin, the great Yasmin, knew what sort of a man Dinter was. But Heba was in love with him. He was tall, blond, with dark blue eyes, as blue and as dark as Zahra's eyes. All of us

Alexandrians felt the loss of Heba greatly, especially as we knew that her mother was opposed to it and that it might lead her to abandon the stage as well. Heba was little more than a teenager, a young girl who was so beautiful that everyone who saw her dance was just crazy for her. Yasmin couldn't keep her in Alexandria, and the pain led her to retire to her house by the sea. It was in a well-known part of Bolkly by the San Stefano Casino, near where the Wilsons live. Yasmin still lives there with Zahra."

Fernando was concentrating on the story. He tried not to miss a single detail so that all the pieces would fit together.

Vryzas waved to the waiter, who came over at once. He asked if they wanted more coffee, but they said no. Vryzas asked for a large jug of water: something to wet his mouth, which was dry after so much talk.

"Heba's youth didn't stop Jan Dinter from making Heba his lover and using her for his own capricious ends. He was a man with no scruples accustomed to having his own way without caring about the consequences. He fulfilled his promise in part, that he would make Heba into a great star. He filled the Rosy-Fingered Dawn every night, and people came to see her dance her belly dance. She was so exotic … her cinnamon skin, her bright black eyes and a body that, whenever she started to dance, left everyone breathless. I don't know exactly what Heba went through in Berlin, and what little I do know I don't think I should be the one to tell you. But know this: Heba never came back to Alexandria."

"What has all of this to do with Zahra? Can't you tell me any more?"

"I've told you enough for you to draw your own conclusions, and to ask Zahra if you dare. I've only told you what people know or believe."

"But you know the rest of the story," Fernando said.

Vryzas shrugged and pressed his lips together.

Fernando knew that he would not say anything else. He had opened the door to Zahra, but if he wanted to know anything more, he would have to ask her directly.

They said goodbye with a handshake. Vryzas smiled sadly and advised him once again to head off and find his Ithaca.

Dimitra was convinced that Adela recognized her when she picked her up.

Dr. Naseef said that she was still below the weight she ought to be at the age of four months, which worried not only Catalina but the rest of the household.

Catalina gave piano lessons in the drawing room, and Dimitra looked after Adela. Ylena had accepted this arrangement, as Adela was very quiet and made no noise in her little carriage. Sometimes Dimitra got so nervous at this passivity that she took Adela in her arms and bounced her a bit, to try to get her to smile or even cry, just to show that she was still alive.

Catalina's student tried very hard to follow her instructions and plink out something recognizable on the keyboard. But Dimitra suspected that this child, just like the others, came for piano lessons because her parents made her.

It was a sign of class to be able to play the piano, and most of the children of British families who lived in Alexandria could at least play something on the black and white keys.

Catalina was a patient and caring piano teacher who liked to talk to her students, which made them – although they were not very musical – happy to take lessons from her.

What Catalina should do, Dimitra thought, was get married to Dr. Naseef. It was clear that the doctor looked at her with a lover's eyes, and Catalina smiled at him in a way that showed she was not herself entirely indifferent.

But, as Dimitra had noticed, the Spaniard was stubborn and had made marrying the father of her child into an obsession.

Dimitra had recommended that she forget about Marvin and choose a good man, one who was capable of solving her problems. She thought that Catalina should choose between Dr. Naseef and Fernando.

When Catalina went to look for Adela, she found her in Dimitra's arms, with the maid pulling faces in order to get some sort of reaction out of the child.

"Thanks for looking after her. Has she been good?"

"So good that I've been bored," Dimitra said sincerely.

"It's better that way. My daughter seems to realize that she needs to behave well because I need to work. Well, I'm done for today. I'm going to take her out for a bit. Look at the sun … and it doesn't look like rain."

"Don't be so sure, even if it is March," Dimitra said.

Once out in the street, with Adela in her stroller, Catalina headed towards the cathedral. She wanted to see Father Lucas. She had confessed to him several times, but this afternoon she needed the advice of a friend as well as a priest.

Father Lucas was nothing at all like Don Bernardo, her neighborhood priest in Madrid.

She had never been able to talk so frankly in front of Don Bernardo, and she wouldn't have dared confess all her sins, sins that Father Lucas waved away, inviting her to think about the true nature of evil and not to waste time on nonsense.

It was not a sin to feel a little thrill, or a shiver, whenever she met Dr. Naseef, Father Lucas insisted. Rather, it was a completely normal reaction in a young woman and all it meant was that she liked the doctor.

Dreaming that Dr. Naseef was stroking her cheek wasn't a sin either, the priest insisted. And it wasn't a sin to forget to say her prayers every so often.

At their last meeting, Father Lucas had told her that she should stop going to confession in order to recount these petty little things.

"Look, if what you need to do is think about your feelings, then come and see me and we'll talk about this like good friends. But not in the confessional. You should come to the confessional to ask the Lord for help in curing your soul. And what you're telling me doesn't need any kind of forgiveness."

So she had decided to follow Father Lucas' advice and go and talk to him for a while. She imagined that he would be reading at this hour.

A young sacristan told her to follow him through to the garden, where they found the priest.

He was not reading, but he was sitting quietly, caught up in his own thoughts with an expression of suffering on his face.

Catalina had noticed this before. Father Lucas seemed tormented, even when he smiled.

"I'm sorry to bother you …" she apologized, worried about coming at an inconvenient time.

"Ah, it's you … no, don't worry, I was thinking. You weren't coming to confess again, were you? You came on Sunday and it's only Thursday," he said suspiciously.

"No … I came to talk to you, because I don't think what I want to talk about is a sin," she said.

"Of course the things you tell me about aren't sins. Would you like to walk a little? I would … let's walk a bit," he suggested.

He didn't give her a chance to reply, but set off at once, walking fast. Catalina had to make an effort to catch up with him as she followed, pushing the stroller.

They came to the rue Rosette, the station to their right.

"So what do you want us to talk about?" the priest asked.

"I don't know what I ought to do. I'm here, but I don't think it makes sense to stay in Alexandria. No one will tell me if Marvin will come back … I suppose he will one day because Farida is from Alexandria, but what if he doesn't?"

"Go back to Spain, as I have told you many times. Your parents love you and are bound to help you."

"My mother will help me, and maybe my aunt Petra as well, but she must be angry that I ran away from her home. But as for my father … No, I can't make him go through the shame of seeing me come back, single, with Adela. You can't imagine what they'd say to me if I came back home without a husband. This way at least no one is looking down their noses at my parents."

"You're afraid, Catalina. You can't live in constant fear of what people think about you. It's no shame to have a child."

"But I'm not married!"

"Well, that's a setback, but it doesn't mean that you should be ashamed of your daughter."

"It's a sin as well," she said.

"A sin that you insist on confessing every Sunday, for all that I tell you that God has already forgiven you."

"Do you think that Our Lord will hold it against me?"

"I'm sure he won't. He, just like your parents, would have preferred for you to have found a man, a good man, with whom you could form a family, but the Lord isn't going to send you to hell for having had a baby."

Catalina was not sure that Father Lucas was telling the truth: not because she didn't want to believe him, but because she was sure that Don Bernardo would have said quite the opposite, and would have sent her to do penance for the rest of her life, without making any promises about whether Our Lord would forgive her for her sin.

"So, what should I do?"

"Well, as you've decided not to listen to me and you don't want to go back to Spain, then you're making it quite difficult for me. Europe is at war, and here, quite close, in Cyrenaica, the Germans are plotting how to deal with Egypt. Maybe you could go to America."

Catalina said nothing. She had come to see Father Lucas to ask his help with something.

"Why don't you help me find Marvin? They'll tell you where he is. I only want him to see Adela and look me in the eyes and tell me if it is true that he really wants to have nothing more to do with us. I'm sure it's that woman, Farida, who's stopping us from seeing one another. Marvin has a great heart, and it would be impossible for him not to accept his responsibility towards us."

"You know that Marvin is in France," the priest reminded her.

"Yes, but no one will tell me where. I'm worried, because now that America has entered the war, France isn't a safe place for him. I want to know if he's in Paris … he had a apartment in Paris. I was thinking of heading there."

Father Lucas was moved by Catalina's tenacity, but at the same time, he was frustrated by how stubborn she was. She refused to accept reality, which was that the American wanted nothing at all to do with her. He wasn't the first man to fool around with a girl and then refuse to accept the consequences. But Catalina was denying reality, and had in her mind made Farida responsible.

He didn't know Marvin, but he did know Farida, not very well – he had spoken to her a couple of times, never for very long – but she did not seem to him to be wicked, or a frivolous temptress.

"Just assume, for once, that Marvin doesn't want you in his life, and that you are going to have to figure things out without him. It may be difficult for you to go back to your parents' house, but not so difficult that you should deny yourself the possibility of living your own life, of falling in love with and marrying another man. You are a little bit in love with Dr. Naseef, and I would be very much mistaken if he were not interested in you. He would be a good husband, and a good father for your child."

"But what are you saying? I mean, it's one thing to ... well, I sometimes dream of him and ..."

"Catalina, please, stop fooling yourself! Naseef likes you, and that is completely normal. He's handsome enough, and a good man. It's completely natural for you to like him, and for him to like you."

Catalina was about to break down in tears of rage. She had gone to try to get comfort and help, and Father Lucas was refusing to understand her.

"I will marry Marvin, or else I will marry no one. No. One. There will never be another man in my life."

"You are condemning yourself by refusing to accept that there is another man in the world who you find attractive," the priest said, looking at her directly.

"Yes, and that's another sin to put on my list."

"It's not a sin! What do you think God does with his time?"

"It's what Don Bernardo would tell me."

"Don Bernardo has filled your head with unfounded fears. I promise you that God doesn't care one bit about whether or not you like Dr. Naseef, and he's not going to punish you for giving birth to Adela. I promise you."

The priest was about to say something fairly rude about Don Bernardo. But Catalina trusted him: he had baptized her and shepherded her through her First Communion. And he had been her confessor. It wouldn't help him at all to say that in his opinion, this Bernardo knew very little about God. He said nothing at all, and then asked himself if he wasn't giving in to the sin of pride by imagining that the God he imagined was the true God compared to the false one Don Bernardo imagined.

He walked with her back to Ylena's house. It wasn't a surprise to see Dimitra giving Catalina a complicit wink as she told her that Dr. Naseef was in the drawing room waiting to see Adela.

Time flitted past without their really noticing it. They had almost reached the end of 1942, and apart from the weather, every month was like the one before.

Fernando saw Zahra from time to time. Wilson had insisted that they do so in order to maintain the fiction that they were lovers.

He would walk with her to the cabaret where she performed, or else take her for a stroll along the Corniche, or go to a party where *le tout Alexandrie* was gathered. They spoke in pleasantries; Zahra avoided any personal conversations. He had thought to himself on various occasions that he should tell Wilson that he refused to carry on playing the role of Zahra's devoted slave, as he disliked it so much, but that would have meant giving up on seeing Zahra. He had to choose between his pride and the need he had to feel her so deceptively close to him.

He didn't know why Wilson insisted on their maintaining the fiction, although he was sure that sooner or later he'd find out the answer.

Meanwhile, he carried on working as an editor. He had the satisfaction of knowing that Marvin's book had been a success in the States, and that it had even, in spite of the war, sold several hundred copies in England. There was no Manhattan bookshop that didn't put the book in pride of place in its window display. Critics praised Marvin Brian's capacity to make people's souls tremble.

The newspapers asked where the young poet was and when they'd have the chance to interview him. No one knew his location, and his family maintained a discreet silence.

When Fernando went into the bookshop on that warm morning in late November, there was nothing to make him think that day would be different from any of the other days of his life.

He had fallen into a routine that he felt was dragging him

down, but he hadn't been able to follow Athanasius Vryzas' advice and set out in search of his own Ithaca.

He realized that something had happened because Sara Rosent was waiting for him impatiently.

Wilson's wife came up to him as soon as she saw him come through the door. She explained that he should go straight up to Wilson's office.

Fernando gave a start. Had the British suffered a defeat in the desert? Were the Germans closing in? He discounted this possibility immediately, because he knew that last summer, just fifty miles from the city, the British had won a major victory under the command of General Auchinleck, stopping the Germans at El Alamein. The defeat had been a serious blow to Rommel. And a few months later, in October, Montgomery had definitively taken El Alamein.

But there was an expression of pain on Sara's face that made him feel intensely anxious.

He was even more surprised to find Zahra in Benjamin Wilson's office. They greeted each other briefly, and then Wilson explained why they were there.

"We've had news from Marvin and Farida. Monsieur Rosent, tragically, is dead."

"I'm sorry," Fernando said, looking at Sara.

She lowered her head so that he would not see her cry.

"When will they be back?" Fernando said, without bothering to hide his anxiety.

"Back? It's not that easy. Marvin and Farida have gone to America, and as for your friend Eulogio … he's decided to stay in France."

"But that's crazy! Why didn't he go with Marvin? Eulogio wanted to go to America … tell me the truth …"

"I can't say any more than that your friend decided to stay in Lyon."

"In Lyon? But they went to Vichy, no?"

"Yes, they were in Vichy and Lyon. And they had to escape via the Swiss border. Monsieur Rosent died just as they were about to cross. Marvin and Farida crossed over, but your friend Eulogio decided not to go with them. I don't know why."

"I'll go and find him," Fernando said decidedly.

"That's not possible, at least not now," Benjamin Wilson said.

"If you can get Farida and Marvin and Eulogio to France, then you can get me there," Fernando said.

"I'm sorry, I can't do that right now."

Zahra sat still and silent, waiting for Benjamin Wilson to say something more.

Wilson cleared his throat. And Fernando thought that the bad news was just around the corner.

"I didn't ask you here because of that. I need you to go to Prague with Zahra."

Benjamin Wilson tried to speak in a neutral voice, as if going to Prague were just as simple as going out to eat at the Hotel Cecil.

"To Prague?" Fernando said, as he tried to process Wilson's words.

"Have you very heard of Reinhard Heydrich?" Wilson asked.

"Yes ... of course ... he's ... I think they killed him a few months ago."

"Yes, on the twenty-seventh of May. Yes, he was killed. By a group of Czech patriots."

"Heydrich was one of the only men whom Heinrich Himmler and Hitler trusted completely. An implacable killer," Zahra said in the same neutral voice that Wilson had used.

"But he's dead now," Fernando said.

"And the brave people who killed him are as well. They were sent into exile by the Czech government and someone betrayed them. After the murder, they hid themselves in the church of Cyril and Methodius. But someone gave them away and they were all killed. You see ..."

"But Heydrich is dead," Fernando insisted, "and he at least can't carry on doing anything bad."

"Yes, but after his death, he added another two hundred people to his long list of victims in Czechoslovakia. Hitler ordered a town near Prague – Lidice – to be burned to the ground. All the men and all the boys older than fifteen were shot, and the women, 195 of them, were sent to Ravensbrück concentration camp," Zahra continued.

Fernando felt confused. He didn't understand why Zahra had to go to Prague now, nor why Wilson was once again getting him involved in his business of finding people.

"Heydrich was one of the bloodiest leaders of the Nazi movement. As you know, it was his wife, Lina Von Osten, who got him into the Nazi Party and who introduced him to Himmler," Wilson said.

"I don't know what you want," Fernando interrupted.

"Of course you do. You have to go with Zahra to Prague. She has a job. An old friend wants to get his daughter out of there … if she's still alive."

Silence fell. Wilson and Zahra waited stoically for Fernando's answer, but the expression on Sara's face showed how worried she was.

"It's crazy. We can't just go to Prague. How could we do it? As far as I know, there's a war on," Fernando said, sarcasm in his voice.

"The young woman you have to find is called Jana Brossler. A few months ago, she joined a group of students who tried to get in touch with the Resistance. The group was under surveillance by the leaders of the Prague Resistance from the start, and they still haven't been accepted by them. Now is not the time to trust anyone. This group knew nothing about the murder of Heydrich, and had nothing to do with it. Rudolf Brossler, Jana's father, is a well-regarded physics professor who lives in the United States. His wife died when his daughter was just a baby, and so Rudolf spoiled his daughter a little too much. Jana refused to travel to the States with her father. In fact, she tricked him. Just as they were about to get on a plane to Paris, as the Germans were taking over Czechoslovakia, she turned back and left him. She's very headstrong."

"So, we're going to go to Prague and convince a very headstrong girl to come with us. She'll be fine with that, and the three of us will go back to Alexandria, just like it was as field trip, and the Germans won't get in the way of anything at all. Is that it?" Fernando sneered.

"I don't need your sarcasm. You will go to Prague with Zahra: we've arranged for her to perform there. The Berlin high command tends to be fairly lenient when it comes to allowing their officers to enjoy the finer things in life. Zahra will go to dance in Prague. You will go with her. You're the man who loves her and who cannot leave her alone. All you have to do is that: accompany her. Your papers are in order so as not to arouse the suspicions of the Germans. Their spies in Alexandria have already sent back lots of information about Zahra and you. So don't worry."

"Right, nothing to worry about there …" It was hard for Fernando to hold back his irritation at Wilson's words.

"As for your cover, no, the mission is complicated, I admit. But all you have to do is find Jana because her father hasn't heard from her in three months and is worried. She was a pupil at the school of a famous dancer, Lenka Zmek. When you meet Lenka, you should say this password: "I would like to relax at the spa." Once you know where she is and that she's well, you'll try to bring her here, and your mission will be done," Wilson said.

"Piece of cake," Fernando said bitterly.

"You'll be off to Prague in three days. You'll go to Switzerland first, and then to Czechoslovakia," Benjamin Wilson said, ignoring Fernando's tone.

"I'll do it if you help me get to France afterwards to look for Eulogio."

"When you get back, we'll see what we can do," Wilson said, without promising anything.

In the days before the journey, Fernando was tempted to go to Benjamin Wilson's office and tell him that he was not going to go to Prague. That he refused to carry on being a puppet in Wilson's hands, even if that meant that he had to leave the publishing house.

He also thought about how worried Catalina would be, and how scared she had been when he had explained that Eulogio had decided to stay in France and that he had to go to Prague. He couldn't lie to her. If she could keep his darkest secret, how he had killed the men who killed his father, then how could he not tell her about his trip to Prague?

Catalina was a straightforward person, incapable of being hypocritical, so she was open about what she feared the most, both for him and for herself.

"If anything happens to you, what will Adela and I do? I wouldn't know what to do without you. I'm starting to think that his city is like a trap we've fallen into, and that we need to figure out how to escape. But I can't find a sensible answer when I ask myself where we should go. We can never go back to Madrid. When you come back from Prague, I'll go to France with you. And then … well, as soon as I can, I'll go to America with Adela to look for Marvin."

"We'll decide that when I come back. Don't worry. I'll come back. Keep on looking after yourself and Adela. Trust me."

He couldn't stop thinking about her frightened expression, so different from Zahra's gaze.

They were in a luxurious but discreet hotel in Zurich: their first stop on the way to Prague. Their rooms were connected to feed the story that they were no more than lovers, obsessed with one another.

They had reached Baur au Lac the night before, but it hadn't been until the sun rose that they had been able to enjoy the views over the lake. After breakfast, Zahra had suggested they take a walk. She wasn't put off by the cold or the rain.

The concierge gave them a couple of umbrellas, and they set off into the street with them.

"I'm going to show you two churches," Zahra said.

"Two churches? I didn't know you were interested in churches," he replied in surprise.

"And why wouldn't I be?"

"Well … the thing is … I didn't think you were religious at all, much less Catholic."

"I'm not a Catholic. I'm a Muslim. But I grew up in Germany. I'm going to show you a couple of Lutheran churches. They're worth seeing, the symbols of Zurich."

"So it's not your first time here."

"No, it's not the first time. When I was a child I came here with my mother, to the same hotel. We went out for walks and my mother liked to spend time sitting in churches. She said that she could think better, surrounded by silence and spirituality."

"But she was a Muslim as well?"

"Yes, but she could find the spiritual side to any place where people went to pray, be it a mosque, or a Lutheran church, or a Catholic one, or even a synagogue. There aren't any mosques in Zurich, so she visited the Lutheran churches like she did in Berlin."

The Grossmünster was not very far from the hotel, just a few minutes by foot. Zahra explained that it was a Romanesque church that had had an important role during the Reformation. Fernando was surprised by her detailed knowledge of the Christian schism. Then they walked to the Fraumünster, the church with a greenish spire that was a symbol of the city.

Zahra seemed struck by melancholy, although she was enjoying her stroll through the city.

He let himself be guided, in spite of the fact that the cold and the rain might have more reasonably suggested finding somewhere to shelter. But she seemed immune to the bad weather and walked with a light step, holding his arm and pointing out all the parts of the city she remembered. She seemed to miss the summer she had spent with her mother in the city.

"This city seems like a special place for you," he said as they walked a little quicker in the heavy rain.

"Yes, it is. I had a very good time here with my mother. It was one of the very few times that we were alone together. My mother was happy here. It wasn't hard for her to recover from ..."

She fell silent. Fernando looked at her out of the corner of his eye. He saw that her expression was one of profound sadness. He realized that if he wanted to find anything out about her, then she would never be more open, more available, than she was now.

"How old were you then?"

"About five or six."

"And can you remember it? You were very young."

"Yes, I remember it very well, because we were happy here."

"And your mother? Did she die?"

Zahra's jaw visibly tensed; equally obvious was the expression of rage that flashed across her face. Fernando didn't press her.

They walked in silence for a while, and it was a good few minutes before Zahra spoke again.

"Yes, my mother died. And since then, I've known what loneliness is like."

"You can never replace a mother, but maybe there were other people who loved you, maybe a grandmother, or other family members, your friends ..."

"You don't understand, Fernando ... is your mother alive?"

"Yes, she is, but they shot my father."

"Right ... I suppose your heart must be breaking because of your loss. There was nothing worse than the loss of my mother. It was as though the ground had been pulled out from underneath my feet, and there was nothing above me either ... I don't think you can understand ..."

Fernando didn't know if he should ask about what had happened to her mother. After all he had told her how his father had died. Shot by the victors in the civil war that had ruined Spain.

"Do you know why we're staying in the Baur au Lac?" she asked him.

"Is it where you were with your mother?"

"Yes, and my room is the same one that I had back then. I asked Benjamin Wilson to sort it out, and he got them to give me the same room."

"What did you do that summer?"

"We went out early in the morning to walk. We went to the Alps a couple of times ... They're very close, as you can see. We took a boat on the lake. We would go to the Cafe Schober and eat chocolate cake. I thought I'd take you ... But the best thing was having my mother to myself. And ... well ...I was upset that we came across some friends from Berlin, who insisted on inviting her to dine at the Cabaret Voltaire. Do you know anything about Dadaism?"

"No," Fernando admitted.

"It's an artistic movement that was born in this city. Who would have thought it? People are so serious here ... they only seem to care about money ... Well, Dadaism was invented by a Romanian poet, Tristan Tzara."

"So it's a literary movement," Fernando said with interest.

"Not just that. Artists of all kinds met at the Cabaret Voltaire: writers, painters, musicians, dancers ... They all argued in favor of free art, free from the straitjacket, free from schools that formed their own exclusive canons. My mother came back extremely enthusiastic. And although I was only a child, she told me that she had never felt so free, dancing, letting herself be carried away by the music, never thinking for a moment about having to please a crowd, just dancing, and dancing ... It wasn't any more than two or three nights, but I remember it very clearly, although we never spoke about it in the presence of other people, of course. She asked me not to tell anyone."

"Not even your father?" Fernando knew that he was trying to pry deeper than Zahra would probably want him to.

Zahra paused before replying, and when she did so, she didn't refer to her father.

"I know how to keep secrets. Our secrets."

He felt her shiver; the umbrella wasn't enough to stop the rain from soaking them. He too was cold, but he didn't dare suggest that they seek shelter somewhere, because that would mean breaking off the conversation. Zahra wasn't given to confidences. But she suggested that they end their walk.

"Maybe we should find somewhere to have a coffee. We're getting soaked."

They had lunch in a little restaurant on the Paradeplatz, near the Fraumünster. The rain stopped and they could continue their walk. It was barely five o'clock when darkness started to fall, and Zahra insisted that they have a hot chocolate at the Cafe Schober. Fernando was tired and wanted to go back to the hotel, but he didn't refuse.

He had never been closer to her than he was that day.

When he woke up the next day, he found a piece of paper shoved under his door. Zahra had left him a note to say that she would be out of the hotel all day and that she wouldn't be back until later.

He was annoyed that she had not said so the day before. The rain was still hanging over the city, so he decided to stay in the hotel. He found a corner in one of the hotel's drawing rooms and read Cavafy until he forgot his own loneliness.

When she came back, she offered no explanation other than the fact that she had been out with one of Wilson's friends, who had organized the rest of their trip. The next day, they would leave for Prague. They had all the necessary permits to head to the center of the Nazi empire. They would go to Austria, Vienna, and then take a train to Prague, but first, she had to dance that night at a private party. That was how she managed to justify her stay in Zurich.

Fernando was to go with her. That was his role. She relaxed for the rest of the afternoon. A car would pick them up at seven o'clock to take them to a lakeside mansion.

Zahra had already explained to Fernando that although she usually refused to perform at private parties, she had needed to make an exception that night. She was to dance at the birthday of a Lebanese merchant, a very rich man who trafficked in precious stones and who was married to a beautiful Swiss woman.

Benjamin Wilson had found no other way to justify their presence in Switzerland, which was necessary if they were then to travel to Prague.

At seven o'clock on the dot, a tall, gray-haired, rosy-cheeked man in an expensive suit was waiting for them in the hotel lobby. He came towards Zahra with a smile on his face and held out his arms.

"My dear, what a great honor to have you here! I am Kasper Maier. And you are …?" he said, looking at Fernando.

"Fernando Garzo." Fernando replied immediately.

"Right … Yes, they told me that the great Zahra would come accompanied by a Spanish gentleman."

Zahra gripped Fernando by the arm, knowing that he would be provoked by the comment.

"And I couldn't believe that I would be able to offer the Habib family the chance to have you dance at their party. But miracles exist, and when your agent Monsieur Chamoun called me to say that you were prepared to travel to Europe, I thanked the Lord."

Zahra looked at him indifferently as she turned up the collar of her overcoat. It was rainy and cold. A black car was waiting for them at the door to the hotel, and Kaspar Maier hurried to open the door.

On the way to the Habibs' house, Maier led the conversation.

"My dear, how is my good friend Zaid Chamoun? It's to him that I owe some of the finest spectacles that I have been able to put on in my cabarets. Spectacles of the first order. Chamoun knows that my clients are excellent people who shun vulgarity. Allow me to tell you that there are not very many dancers who can bring such elegance and sensuality to the belly dance. I had the great pleasure to see Yasmin dance in Cairo many years ago. She was older then, and yet … I still shiver just thinking about her."

Fernando sat in silence listening to the man. He had just found out that Zahra had an agent, apparently someone called Zaid Chamoun. She had never spoken about Chamoun, and neither had Benjamin Wilson. He felt once again like a puppet in their hands.

Kaspar Maier suddenly looked at Fernando and Fernando forced himself to smile. He didn't yet know if this man was a bastard or just a businessman.

They didn't get back to the hotel until after midnight. Kaspar Maier reminded them that they needed to travel to Vienna first thing the next morning, and that Zahra would perform two nights there.

Fernando was in his room smoking a cigarette and looking at the dark lake when Zahra pushed open the door between the two rooms.

She was wearing a robe and her face was clean and bright after taking off her makeup.

"Are you worried about something? I thought you were a little odd this afternoon."

"Worried? Why should I worry?"

"What's happening, Fernando? What's going on?"

He looked at her angrily. He was there for her and her alone, and Zahra didn't even think about him. His presence was only a part of the camouflage.

"I'll tell you what's bothering me. Your lack of trust in me. I don't care about Benjamin Wilson treating me like he does, but you … Do you really care so little about me?"

"I don't understand …"

"I didn't even know you had an agent, this Zaid Chamoun that Herr Maier was talking about. I thought that it was Wilson who had arranged this whole farce to get us to Prague."

She sat on the edge of the bed. There was a bitter smirk on her face.

"Benjamin Wilson did organize everything. Who do you think my agent Zaid Chamoun works for? Everything has to make sense, and I have to seem to be what I seem to be, an Egyptian dancer. That's why I have an agent, and when Wilson decided to send us to Prague he asked my agent Zaid Chamoun to organize everything so no one would think that we were doing anything that a dancer wouldn't do."

"You've just said that you have to seem to be an Egyptian dancer. What are you really, Zahra?"

"I'm an Egyptian dancer who helps Benjamin Wilson look for people. I help him gather information about various topics."

"A spy? Is that what you are?" Fernando asked, disdainfully.

"No, I'm not a spy. Helping people get away from this war by listening to conversations that might be useful to people who are fighting the Nazis doesn't make me a spy."

"Then why do you do all this?"

"I have my reasons. Reasons I don't have to share with you, Fernando. I'll just say that it is my duty to help save lives."

"Just that?"

"No, there's more. There is one reason that is mine alone."

"Wilson has his reasons, you have yours … You're just the same … You use people for your own benefit."

"For our own benefit! How can you say that! I don't earn a single penny for the work I do! Not a single penny! And as for Wilson … ask him. But it's not difficult to see that he's doing his part to help with this terrible war."

"It's good business for him to look for people."

"You really think so?" Zahra looked at him disdainfully.

"Yes, I do."

"His business is something more than just looking for people, now. Before the war, the people who were 'lost' tended to be young people who had set off for the Orient in search of adventure, or God knows what else. Some of them had gotten into trouble, others ended up being victims of blackmail ... But it wasn't just young people who disappeared voluntarily or involuntarily ... And the Wilsons looked for them, found them and in the majority of cases sent them back to England. But the war has changed everything, even this business. Benjamin has a network of agents who worked for him, and at the moment this network is very useful. Also, as you well know, he is British, but he is also a Jew, because his mother is a Greek-Alexandrian Jew. He studied in England under his grandfather, and feels an uncomplicated loyalty for the country. He'll help as much as he can in this war. If they ask him to do something, he'll do it without asking for anything in return. For years, the Wilsons set up a network which was very useful for them; they had ears all over the world and could find people who disappeared voluntarily or involuntarily. And this network of ears is very important nowadays. It's not a network of spies, don't be mistaken."

"But they act like spies," Fernando insisted.

"You don't get it at all ... Hitler is a monster: haven't you seen that yet? We all have a duty to fight in this war. Some people do it with guns, and put their lives at risk. But there are other ways to fight. I fight by dancing."

"You do it by listening to and spying on people who come to watch you dance!" Fernando said angrily.

"You don't understand ... I'm sorry ... I'm sorry for you, for me ... I'm sorry." Zahra's voice was heavy.

"And why do you need to feel sorry?" he said, disconcerted by her last words.

She didn't reply. She looked at him steadily and stood up.

"If you want to go back to Alexandria, then you can. You have the right. Benjamin Wilson can't make you do anything, and even if he could, then he wouldn't. I think you still don't realize what kind of a man he is. Good night."

Fernando couldn't sleep. He was trying to understand Zahra's explanations. But he couldn't. He felt betrayed.

He thought that the best thing for him to do would be to go back to Alexandria and convince Catalina to either go back to Spain or else to come with him to America and start a new life for themselves. But he didn't think he would be able to do that, because it would mean abandoning Zahra to her fate, and he couldn't help but admit to himself that she was becoming an obsession as deep and wide as Catalina for him.

The next morning, he found her having a coffee with Kaspar Meier. The Austrian filled the silence with his chatter. For a moment Fernando was pleased to see him there.

Vienna astounded him. He thought that it was the most beautiful city in the world. Of course, apart for a journey to London with his parents when he was a teenager, he hadn't left Spain until the day when he and Catalina and Eulogio fled to Lisbon and then to Alexandria.

Zahra and Fernando avoided one another as much as possible, and although Meier had reserved them adjacent rooms in the Hotel Wien, the communicating door remained closed.

Fernando found an ice bucket in his room with a bottle of champagne in it. A present from Meier, who assumed that there must be a close relationship between him and Zahra. The night of their arrival, Fernando drank the whole thing, which gave him a headache.

The two performances that Zahra was due to give were to take place in the Wien Volksoper, a beautiful theater built in 1898 where the Viennese would go to hear operettas. It was not a surprise that Zahra failed to conquer Vienna. The city was a *grande dame*, who looked at everything that was not known to her with distance and disdain.

Kaspar Meier put the evident lack of enthusiasm shown by the public down to their anxieties about the war. He didn't understand how the Viennese could be so distant when they saw Zahra's artistry. Regardless, he was an enthusiastic and expansive man, and he assured them that Prague would be different.

The newspapers picked up on Zahra's performance but without as much enthusiasm as Meier had hoped.

Zahra didn't seem to care either about the indifference of the public or Meier's concern about it. As for Fernando, he was still caught up in his own mental labyrinth.

The last night in Vienna, Meier took them to hear a concert of waltzes. Zahra listened with her eyes closed and a smile that soft-ened her generally tense features. Neither was Fernando immune to Strauss' music, which filled his senses.

When they came out into the street, snow had taken over the city. Kaspar Meier laughed merrily and made a snowball, which he threw at Fernando, who managed to dodge it. Zahra imitated Meier and threw a ball at Fernando, hitting him directly. Fernan-do didn't know what to do, but Zahra's smile was an invitation for him to throw a snowball at her. For a few minutes the three of them engaged in a icy battle that ended up with them heading, soaked, back to the hotel.

That night Zahra didn't open the door between the two rooms, but at least she said goodnight to Fernando with a smile.

"When does the train leave for Prague?" Fernando asked im-patiently, looking at the station clock.

It was the third time he had asked Meier this question. But the man seemed to be possessed of infinite patience and didn't get annoyed at Fernando's questioning.

"In an hour. We'll have a coffee while we wait, and I'll bring you up to date about what your program will be in Prague. I am sure that Zahra will be a triumphant success there. The city is still in mourning for the murder of the Protector of Bohemia and Moravia; I think that even Hitler advised him not to ride in open-topped cars. But Reinhard Heydrich was not a man who feared danger – he thought that other people should fear him – and he didn't give up his habit of driving around the city in an uncovered vehicle."

"I hope we'll have a bit of time to explore the city," Zahra said indifferently.

"Of course, my dear. Your agent, my good friend Monsieur Chamoun, has told me that I should do everything in my power to make your stay an agreeable one," Kaspar Meier replied.

"I really want to see Lenka Zmek's dance school. I think she is one of the best dancers in Europe," Zahra said, trying to catch Fernando's eye.

"Yes, she's a great dancer. You should have seen her perform

Swan Lake at the Viennese Opera. The public gave her a standing ovation of nearly an hour. But that was before the war started. Lenka Zmek studied ballet in Vienna: her father is Czech, but her mother was Austrian. We think of her as one of our own, but … well, a few years ago she fell in love with a Czech man and decided to go to Prague. It was an unfortunate decision … Vienna would have laid the world at her feet. Her marriage, unfortunately, didn't last very long; her husband died in a car accident. And now she refuses to leave Prague, and rejects all the contracts that are offered to her, without caring how much money they might bring. She lives completely for her dance school in Prague. It's the only thing that seems to matter to her. She even rejected a chance to dance in Berlin in front of Goebbels himself. Great artists like Lenka and yourself can get away with almost anything …"

Meier didn't stop talking, but Zahra seemed not to hear him. She responded to his questions with monosyllables. But Kaspar Meier didn't lose heart, and turned his attention to Fernando. For the whole journey to Prague, he boasted of his activities as an agent and proudly spoke of how he had brought great artists from all over the world to dance in the bleeding, war-torn heart of Europe.

Fernando would have liked to have spoken to the man about the war, and about Hitler more than anything, to see what Meier thought of his fellow Austrian. But he knew that he ought to avoid any question or conversation that had to do with politics. This was an instruction that Wilson had given him directly. You didn't have to be all that smart to know that Kaspar Meier felt at home with the Nazis, although he was not – or at least didn't appear to be – especially fanatical.

The first thing they saw when they disembarked from the train in Prague was German soldiers and SS patrols checking every inch of the station. They looked at the documentation of everyone who came in or went out. The tension and the fear were obvious.

Kaspar Meier didn't seem worried. He hugged a man who was even taller and more expansive than him, introducing him as his Prague contact, Petr Mezlik.

The man shook his hand vigorously, and as they left the

station, Fernando noticed that Mezlik clenched his teeth angrily as he saw two members of the SS manhandling a young man who had tried to escape.

"Ah, these rebels!" Meier said, as though the scene held no importance for him.

Petr Mezlik didn't reply, and carried on walking quickly.

The Hotel Paris was in the center of the city. Just like the Baur au Lac in Zurich or the Wien in Vienna, entering its doors brought you into an island of luxury and beauty, a whole new world.

Zahra said she was tired and went straight up to her room. Fernando, however, couldn't follow her because Kaspar Meier insisted that he share a drink with him and his business partner Petr Mezlik.

He accepted eagerly, because he felt a keen curiosity about Petr Mezlik. His gaze showed that he was permanently tense, and that there was some deep-seated unease in him.

Mezlik ordered Becherovka, a strong liqueur which the waiter brought them in very small glasses. Mezlik proposed a toast to Zahra.

Fernando nearly choked when the bitter liquid hit his throat. It was very cold, its bittersweet taste oddly medicinal. Kaspar Meier laughed when he saw Fernando's reaction.

"You don't like it? If that's the case, don't say anything. It's the national drink."

"But what on earth is it made of?" Fernando asked, barely able to stop coughing.

"Herbs. It's the national drink, the emperor is particularly fond of it ..." Meier said.

Petr Mezlik cleared his throat before he spoke.

"They say that it was invented by an English doctor, but in fact it was a pharmacist from Karlovy Vary who really perfected the recipe. Do you know where Karlovy Vary is?"

"No, I don't," Fernando admitted.

"It's a spa, one of the most important in Europe. People from the royal courts of all over Europe came to take the waters, as well as politicians and important people. It's a special place, between the rivers Epla and Ohre. It was in the nineteenth century when Jan Becher, the pharmacist from Karlovy Vary, started to make a liqueur that would help pains and stomach illnesses. It's strong, but it'll do you good."

Fernando felt his guts warming as he listened.

"You'll get used to it and end up liking it," Kaspar Meier assured him.

The three men drank another toast. Fernando was surprised that Meier and Mezlik both drank the amber-colored liquid as a shot, and was especially surprised that it seemed to have no effect on them,

Then Petr Mezlik laid out the program that he had organized for Zahra. Fernando knew it already, because Meier had explained it in Vienna to Zahra, but Mezlik obviously thought that he should explain it to this young Spaniard, who traveled with the dancer and who seemed to be more than just her companion.

"You'll rest tonight. It's getting late and it's going to keep snowing hard. Tomorrow we'll visit Lenka Zmek's dance school first thing in the morning. Then you'll have some free time to explore the city. I'll come with you. I hope that it doesn't rain too much and that we'll be able to walk. In the afternoon, Zahra will be able to rest until it's time for her to perform. It will be at the Vinoharady Theater, and it's sold out already."

"It will be a great honor for her to dance in the Vinoharady. It's a new theater, built in 1907," Meier added.

Lenka Zmek was a woman who made an impression. The force of her gaze was devastating. It was as though she could read into the deepest corners of your mind.

She was of medium height, with dark blond hair and green eyes, and seemed to float when she walked. She was made of harmony and elegance, but also strength.

She came to meet them almost unwillingly. Petr Mezlik made the introductions. Lenka took Zahra's hand, and the two of them observed one another fixedly for a second. Then the dancer pointed out where Zahra, Fernando, Kaspar Meier and Mezlik should stand, and told them they should be absolutely silent.

Lenka's class was made up of thirty women and ten men. They all stood in silence as their teacher started the class, although they couldn't help but look curiously out of the corners of their eyes at those unexpected visitors.

Lenka led the class for two hours, insisting that her students perform various steps until they were exhausted but had reached perfection. She was the mirror in which they observed themselves. She would perform a movement, and they would repeat it until she gave a nod.

Her voice was harmonious but firm, and the respect that her students showed her bordered on reverence: they were well aware that she was a legend.

Zahra was overwhelmed by the perfection of Lenka's movements. They seemed almost unreal. She had never seen anyone like her before.

Two hours later, Lenka lifted her hand to show her students that they had fifteen minutes to take a break.

The young people looked very tense, and it was clear that they needed a rest.

Lenka offered her guests a cup of coffee in her office, although she made it clear that they had very little time; the classes would shortly begin again and their visit would end.

Zahra wondered how she could speak to Lenka alone. It would be impossible to talk with Kaspar Meier and Petr Mezlik in the room.

They drank the coffee quickly, and Zahra asked Lenka if she could return on some other occasion to the dance school.

"I've learned so much today that I'm tempted to abuse your hospitality and ask if I could sit in on another one of your classes."

Lenka Zmek made a gesture of annoyance and said grumpily that she had only allowed them to come to one class because Petr Mezlik and she were old friends. Zahra insisted, and Lenka grew almost rude, saying that she didn't understand her interest, given the vast difference between ballet and Oriental dance.

But Zahra didn't give up, suggesting that maybe she could come and watch her performance at the theater that evening. Lenka refused the invitation, and admitted her lack of interest in Oriental dance, especially when it would be displayed in a show whose purpose was to entertain soldiers. The whole world knew that this evening, a large number of the Nazi officials who had occupied Czechoslovakia would come to see her.

Kaspar Meier agreed, adding that although the Nazis were in mourning for Heydrich, the High Command had issued an order that there was no more official mourning in Prague. It would be a privilege for them to see Zahra,

"When can I come back?" Zahra insisted.

"Dear, I don't think we have that much time. You're performing tonight and tomorrow as well," Kaspar Meier said, trying to put a stop to Zahra's insistence.

"I'm only dancing at night. The day has a lot of hours in it," Zahra said.

They waited for a few minutes for Lenka to say when Zahra could return.

"Well, I'm giving a class to my advanced students tomorrow. There aren't a lot of them, just ten. Maybe you could come and watch them dance. We start at nine o'clock sharp."

"Thank you. I'll be there."

When they left Lenka's studio, the cold enveloped them.

"If you don't mind walking, we could take advantage of the fact that it's not snowing to see a bit of the city," Petr Mezlik suggested.

"This is such a charming place," Zahra said.

"This is the Malá Strana district. It's right at the foot of the castle. It's a city inside a city."

They walked for a good long while. Kaspar Meier, who assumed that Fernando being a Spaniard meant he must be Catholic, insisted on going into every church they saw along the way. Fernando didn't want to contradict him or show that he had no religious beliefs.

Meier seemed to be enthusiastic when he told them that the next church they were to see was Our Lady of Victory.

"You're going to be amazed. It's got a lot to do with Spain, this church," he said to Fernando.

Although he wasn't a believer, Fernando was well aware of the artistic value of what he saw. His father had taught him not just to respect others' beliefs, but also to appreciate art, whether it was religious or of any other type. Fernando remembered that his father used to say that you couldn't understand Western civilization without thinking about the immense influence of the Church of Rome. He asked himself if his father would have enjoyed seeing the churches of Prague.

"As I said, this is where they keep the icon of the Infant Jesus of Prague." Kaspar Meier's voice brought Fernando back to the present. "But maybe it's better if Petr tells you the story."

Petr Mezlik carried on the explanation that his business partner had started.

"Look at this little figure of the Infant Jesus. It dates back to the sixteenth century, and was brought to Prague by Duchess María Manríquez de Lara. She was an aristocrat, married to Vratislav de Pernstein. Who would have thought that the image this fine lady brought with her would end up being venerated in Prague?"

They spent the rest of the morning looking around that area of the city, and Mezlik took them to a hidden jewel, the Library of the Basilica of Nanebevzetí.

"I had this prepared for you as a surprise. Kaspar told me that you like reading, and that you collect old books. You can't borrow anything from here, but we can at least look at them."

Petr Mezlik was very proud that he had managed to get them to open up the doors to such a zealously guarded collection of unique volumes.

"As you see, we've taken all your tastes into account. Your agent Monsieur Chamoun told me that you liked libraries. We didn't have very much time in Vienna, but here, Mezlik has prepared a pleasant surprise for you."

Zahra looked grateful, and Fernando saw how enthusiastic she was during the trip to the library. He was a little annoyed not to have known about this aspect of her interests. He didn't know anything about her, he admitted a little bitterly.

A little later they walked past a palace that Zahra asked about.

"It's the Petschek Palace," Petr Mezlik replied, looking gloomy.

"It belonged to an important banker," Meier added.

"You're right. It belonged to an important banker and now it's the home of the Gestapo." There was a bubbling anger in Mezlik's words.

Shortly before lunch, Petr Mezlik took them to his office, where Zahra had to sign a few papers.

Mezlik's office was on Celetna Street, near the Astronomical Tower, and only a few yards away from the Paris Hotel where Zahra and Fernando were staying.

After lunch, Zahra said that she wanted to go and rest. She had to prepare for her performance that evening. Snow had taken over the city once more, and the cold made its way through their coats.

Zahra pushed open the door that led to Fernando's room and found him looking out of the window. He seemed fascinated by the snow.

"We have to convince Lenka Zmek to take us to Jana Brossler."

Fernando had almost forgotten the true motive that had brought them to Prague. Jana Brossler had disappeared in his mind.

"Wilson told us that Jana was one of Lenka's students. It's the only clue we've got. He also said that someone would tell her that her father would send someone for her," Zahra said.

"It won't be easy to get this woman to tell you anything. I think that she was pretty upset that we were there. I don't know if you saw how unhappy she looked when you said you wanted to come back."

"Yes, and I understand it. She feels nothing but contempt for me."

"Contempt?"

"She's a great dancer."

"So are you."

"But she must think that my dance has nothing to do with art. I don't mind. Our aim is to find Jana and get her out of here if possible."

"Get her out of here? I don't think it will be possible. There are German soldiers everywhere. The Nazis are in charge of Czechoslovakia. It would be hard for us to bring this Jana along with us."

"We'll see. But the important thing now is to get Lenka to trust us. I've thought that you could go to see her and tell her who we really are."

"I imagine we'll be being watched. How can I justify going back to Lenka Zmek's studio?"

"Because I want to invite her to my performance this evening and I insisted that you go and ask her."

"It's not possible. You asked her his morning."

"It's the only credible excuse we might have."

"I think it would be better to wait until tomorrow. Meier and Mezlik will come with us, but I'll try to convince them that it would be better to leave you alone watching Lenka's class while we drink a coffee."

"You're right … I'm too impatient. The city is beautiful, but I feel it's oppressive. The soldiers and the SS men …"

"The SS men will come to see you dance his evening. And so you'd better get used to the idea of greeting the bosses and being as charming as you possibly can."

"I'll be myself. And you know that I don't speak to the people who come to see me. I don't have any reason to."

"We'll see what happens this evening. Oh, and I didn't know that you collected old books," he said, reproachfully.

"You didn't need to know. I didn't tell you." She looked him in the eye as she spoke.

"You and Wilson make me feel like nothing, you know that?"

"That's your problem, Fernando. I don't know a thing about you and I'm not bothered."

Fernando was wounded by her reply. Zahra had set out the limits of their relationship. He couldn't expect anything else from her.

"I don't think I'll come with you on any more trips. I don't feel comfortable with the role that Wilson has assigned me."

"Yes, you've told me already, and you should have told him. I don't decide where I go or who I go with. I only do what I'm told," Zahra said coldly.

She spent the rest of the afternoon in her room. Despite the fact that it was still snowing, he decided to go out for a walk. He couldn't bear being alone in the room.

That night, Zahra was a rousing success. The public applauded so much that she couldn't leave the stage. Everyone there, most of them soldiers, applauded admiringly.

Several officers came to the door of her dressing room demanding to see her and refusing to acknowledge the insistence of Kaspar Meier and Petr Mezlik that they should leave.

"Gentlemen, there will be a reception tomorrow where Miss Nadouri will be present, and you will be able to speak with her then. But she needs to rest tonight," Mezlik said, trying to make himself heard over the demands of the men.

Zahra insisted to Kaspar Meier that he didn't need to go with them to Lenka Zmek's studio, but the Austrian was not willing to let her out alone on the streets of Prague, even with Fernando to escort her. Petr Mezlik also thought that she shouldn't go out by herself, so both men decided to accompany her, although Zahra made them promise that they wouldn't stay with her and would let her enjoy the ballet class on her own.

"If you stay, she'll feel uncomfortable … She can't give a class in front of an audience she doesn't want to be there. I'll sit in a corner and they'll forget about me, but if the four of us are there, then she'll want us to go as soon as possible."

They agreed. Fernando convinced them by saying that maybe while Zahra was watching the class they could go and have a coffee somewhere.

Lenka herself opened the door to Zahra and invited her in.

"You're early. My students won't get here for a few minutes yet. Would you like a coffee?"

"I just wanted to be able to speak to you alone for a moment. That's why I'm here in Prague."

Lenka looked at her in surprise and her body tensed as she waited to hear what the Egyptian had to say.

"What do you want?"

"I want to find Jana Brossler. I am sure they told you that someone might want to get in touch with her."

Lenka's face grew icy, and worry flashed in her eyes.

"Jana Brossler? I don't know who you mean. Perhaps a former student of mine?"

"As far as I know, Jana Brossler was one of your favorite students. A brave but slightly headstrong young woman who didn't approve of the German occupation and who tried to join the Resistance." Zahra spoke in a low voice, almost a whisper.

"I don't know who you mean." Lenka's voice was cold and firm.

"We don't have much time, Mrs. Zmek. They told me I should trust you. And I am trusting you. Jana's father asked a good friend to help him find his daughter. Mr. Brossler wants to get her out of here. And I will do that if you tell me where I can find her."

"Even if this story were true, tell me: Why should I trust you? All I know is that you are an Egyptian dancer. I know that the Germans have a lot of friends in Egypt."

"Friends? Yes, I suppose that they have friends everywhere, shamefully enough. But I'm no friend of theirs. They told me that I should use a particular phrase to make you trust me, and I couldn't find a way to get it into conversation yesterday. But here you go: 'I would like to relax at the spa.'"

Lenka Zmek's lips twisted into a slight smile.

"All right. That's the password."

"You have to trust me. I don't have any choice but to trust you."

"It's difficult to trust anyone these days," Lenka sighed.

"I know, but we don't have any choice. Didn't they tell you I was coming?"

"They told me someone was, but not who."

"I don't know … I get the impression that Petr Mezlik …" Zahra didn't finish the sentence.

"Miss Nadouri, Mr. Mezlik is a Czech patriot."

"I'm sure of it … but it's difficult to believe, given that he's in business with Herr Meier."

"Ah, appearances! You were hired by Herr Meier as well. Should I distrust you because of it? Yes, it's a good reason, but not enough. There are many ways one can hide oneself."

"So, is Mr. Mezlik a part of the Resistance?"

Lenka looked at Zahra with her green eyes. She found the question impertinent.

"I don't know who is a member of the Resistance. That is, if any of them are left alive. Being opposed to the Nazis doesn't mean being a part of the Resistance. Well … how were you thinking of getting Jana out of here?"

"I have some false documentation. I hope it helps."

"We don't know if the Nazis are looking for her. She was never a part of the Resistance, although she knew people who … Well, the Nazis have gone crazy over the death of Heydrich. They killed the group who killed him. It was only the traitor Karel Čurda who was spared. I hope the Lord punishes him in hell. Then Himmler took his revenge by ordering everyone in Lidice be killed."

"I know all this."

"But what you don't know is that it won't be easy to get Jana out of here."

"Where is she?"

"In Karlovy Vary. It's a spa, a pretty spa, not very far from Prague."

"Why is she there?"

"Because she was in danger. Someone could identify her, tell the authorities that she was a part of the Resistance. One of her friends knew one of the young men who killed Heydrich. Jana is my best student. If the war ever ends, she might be the best dancer of this damn century. I managed to get her out to Karlovy Vary, to the house of my aunt Aneta, and she's been working there, pretending to be her paid companion, for a while."

"She's must be very exposed there."

"Sometimes it's easier to hide in plain sight. My aunt Aneta is a very special woman. She's my mother's sister. She's very quick to anger and everyone is a bit afraid of her. She's very well-known and respected in Karlovy Vary. Her musical soirees are famous. She has been married four times and outlived her four husbands. She hasn't got any children and I'm her only niece. We have one thing in common, which is that we both want the Germans out of our country, and hate the damn Nazis."

"Hitler is a madman. You only have to hear him to realize that," Zahra sad.

"No, he's not a madman. Don't be so soft on him."

"You're right. Tell me how to get Jana to Prague."

Lenka sat thoughtfully. She was trying to find a solution and it looked like she had one.

"You should come with me to Karlovy Vary. I'll invite you to the spa. I'll invite Meier and Mezlik as well. We'll go to my aunt's house. And we'll think of something when we get there. Maybe Jana won't want to leave the country. You must know that she didn't want to go with her father when he left," Lenka said.

"I know, but her life's in danger now," Zahra said.

"Yes ... they're looking for everyone who had any contact with what was left of the Resistance. They have arrested and tortured a lot of people to get useless confessions out of them, because most of them have nothing at all to do with the Resistance."

"I suggest you come to see me at the theater this evening. We have to give the impression that we've become friends. I know they've organized a reception for me this evening and I have to go to it. You could come with me. That way no one will be surprised when I go with you to Karlovy Vary."

"Go to a reception full of Nazis? Not in a million years!" Lenka exclaimed.

"You have to help me get Jana out of here. We need to convince everyone that we're friends."

"I'll come to see you dance, but I won't go to the reception. There's a limit to what I can stomach, Miss Nadouri,"

"Me too, Madame Zmek, except when it comes to saving a life. I'll try to save her and then I'll have time to feel nauseous. Always in that order."

"I'll see you at the theater tonight. Tell Petr Mezlik to send me a couple of tickets."

"What do you think of Mezlik?"

"I trust him. We've known each other for many years. It was he who told me a few days ago that someone was going to come and see me and what the countersign would be."

"So he knows why I'm here?"

"No, things aren't that simple. Someone told him to tell me the phrase that someone would use with me at some point. But he didn't know who, just as I didn't know who would come, or why."

"Was that why you were so annoyed at my presence?"

"What did you expect? I didn't know that the person who

was going to give me the countersign was you. Mezlik didn't either, and he shouldn't have."

"Yes, but you trusted Petr Mezlik …"

"He's a Czech patriot, even if he is in business with Kaspar Meier. And maybe that's useful for us, anyway."

"Who told him that someone was going to come and get in contact with you?"

"I don't know, and there are some questions that it's better not to ask. The less we know about one another, the better. There are a lot of ways of being a part of the Resistance, and ours is just one. We try to help the people who are risking their lives on the front line."

"Like Jana."

"Yes, like Jana."

The group of advanced students was really exceptional. True ballet virtuosos. Lenka Zmek forgot about Zahra's presence and didn't even say goodbye to her when she left. They had said everything that needed to be said.

There were murmurs in the theater that evening when the audience realized that Lenka Zmek had arrived. She wore a black floor-length velvet dress and her hair was tied back in a bun, and she arrived on the arm of an older gentleman, who walked with a stick.

Both of them looked elegant, aristocratic and aloof. They walked through the crowd, ignoring everyone around them.

The murmurs turned into comments: why had Lenka Zmek decided to come to the Vinoharady Theater to see the performance of an Oriental dancer? They all knew that Lenka was both proud and arrogant, and that there was no other dancer in the world whom she considered her equal. But here she was, splendid and proud on the arm of Pavel Ostry, another glorious figure on the national scene: the best conductor in Czechoslovakia, and a mythical figure in the rest of Europe.

The audience was even more surprised to see Lenka and Pavel applauding the Egyptian dancer.

During the intermission, a few waiters offered champagne to the audience. Petr Mezlik came over to Pavel and Lenka and insisted that they come to the reception organized in Zahra's honor. The dancer refused outright, but she was unsparing in her praise of Zahra. She said everything in the cold, firm voice that was one of her calling cards. Many of the people present heard her say that Zahra Nadouri was a great dancer.

When the performance was over, Zahra went to see Lenka. The audience noticed how deferent the Egyptian seemed to be in front of Lenka Zmek.

"Be careful, Ernst Gerke is here, and I think he'll be coming to your reception as well," Lenka whispered.

"Who is Ernst Gerke?" Zahra asked.

"The head of the Gestapo in Prague."

They both meticulously played the roles they had been given. Lenka did not come to Zahra's reception, but the next day all of Prague would know that the great Lenka Zmek had been friendly to Zahra Nadouri and had even praised her talents. It was a more cheerful piece of news to put into the papers than reports of how the war was going.

The reception was a success. Zahra had to make a great effort to accept the praises of the Nazi officials, who were anxious to pay homage to her and who didn't seem to care about Fernando's presence.

Neither Fernando nor Zahra failed to notice the enthusiasm that Kaspar Meier showed when one man in particular showed up; all the people present went to greet him.

"That is Obersturmbannführer Ernst Gerke, the head of the Gestapo in Prague, the most powerful and most feared man in the city," Petr Mezlik said.

"Is he friends with Meier?" Fernando asked.

"They know each other and seem to get along. Meier will introduce you, without a doubt. You could say that he is doing Zahra a great honor by coming to see her dance in the theater and now coming to the reception. Tonight, the most important officers in the whole of the German army, as well as the SS and the Gestapo, are here to see her."

Mezlik tried to keep a neutral tone to his voice, but Fernando thought he detected a touch of fear and disgust.

Petr Mezlik managed to book three more performances for Zahra, such was her success. The newspapers reported that Zahra had been invited to give a masterclass at Lenka Zmek's ballet school.

"So, we're going to stay here a few more days than we thought," Zahra said to Fernando.

"This whole plan to rescue Jana is pretty flimsy. Do you think the Nazis are that naive? They'll be watching us."

"Maybe yes, and maybe they don't care that two dancers have made friends with one another. In any case, it's a risk we need to take. Next weekend we'll go to Karlovy Vary. Kaspar Meier seems to like the idea. He'll come with us as well."

"It's clear that Meier is a Nazi sympathizer. Don't you hear the things he says? Hitler has made Austria and Germany great again, Europe will be a beacon to the world when he rules it from the north to the south …"

"That's why he should come with us. Of course he thinks that Lenka has invited me to see the spa town and to meet her aunt, who's a real character. Meier has told me that Lenka's aunt's last husband was a count, and so she's a countess. And for Meier to be received at a countess' house is something very special for him."

"Do you think Meier's a fool? He's no fool. He didn't get rich by being foolish. He may be ambitious and unrefined, but behind his apparent simplicity there's a self-made man who knows what he wants," Fernando replied.

"In any case, he's decided to come, and I couldn't find a reason to refuse him. We'll all go to Karlovy Vary," she said.

Snow fascinated Zahra. It was like the endless sand of the desert, or the infinite ocean. But she was shivering with cold. Petr Mezlik and Kaspar Meier had come to find them at dawn at their hotel. Mezlik was driving a black car on which flakes of snow were settling.

The Austrian had not stopped speaking since they left Prague. Fernando tried to follow his chatter, but Zahra was barely listening to him. She paid him no attention until they reached Karlovy Vary. The trees gave way to the sky and the sides of the mountains were dotted with houses from whose chimneys smoke stretched lazily upwards.

With her face pressed against the windows of the car, she listened to Kaspar Meier's explanations when he pointed out the Teplá River and how it flowed in front of the Imperial Spa, which had been built by two Viennese architects in 1895, barely fifty years earlier, in a Europe yet untouched by the Russian Revolution and the Great War.

"The most important people in Europe have visited this spa. Just think … Beethoven, Chopin, Liszt, Tolstoy, Goethe, Freud … and Tsar Peter I, who came and spent a couple of seasons here with the members of his court. But it wasn't just he who came here, Karl Marx stayed here too. Can you imagine? You should drink these healing waters. I am sure that dear Lenka will have arranged for you to be able to enjoy the experience properly."

Every now and then, Petr Mezlik caught Zahra's eye in the rearview mirror. He had been silent all through the journey, allowing Meier to do all the talking.

A butler waited for them at the entrance. The mansion was surrounded by old trees: so many that the house was invisible from the road.

Two maids came to help them with their luggage.

As soon as they entered the house, they found Lenka and her aunt Aneta.

"Welcome," Aneta said.

"Did you have a good journey?" Lenka asked.

Aunt Aneta invited them to follow her to the library, where a few logs were burning in the fireplace.

If Lenka Zmek was a woman of singular beauty, then her aunt Aneta was much more so. It was difficult to tell how old she was. She was taller than Lenka, straighter and thinner, with her silver-blond hair tied back in a bun and green eyes that were even greener than her niece's. Everything about her radiated intelligence, elegance and authority. Her mere presence filled the room.

The butler came at once, followed by a maid with a tray and a coffee service.

They exchanged pleasantries as they sized one another up,

and then Countess Aneta stood up and invited them to go to their rooms.

"You rest now, and I'll see you for lunch." And she swept out of the room, leaving them with her niece Lenka.

"All right," Lenka said. "Once you're settled in, we can take a stroll through the city if you want. Maybe Petr and Herr Meier would like to relax … You know Karlovy Vary very well, and it is cold this morning, but Miss Nadouri and Mr. Garzo might like to go for a walk."

"Of course," Zahra said, without bothering to ask Fernando.

"In that case, go up to your rooms for a moment and tell the maids what you want them to do with your luggage, and I'll wait for you here," Lenka replied.

"I'll stay here. It's not easy to drive that far in a snowstorm," Petr Mezlik said.

"Well, I'm not tired and I'll happily come with you," Kaspar Meier said.

Lenka couldn't prevent Meier from coming with them, but she frowned. She would have liked to speak to Zahra and Fernando without Meier as a witness.

"If you prefer, you can call me by my first name, instead of Miss Nadouri," Zahra said.

"Me too," Fernando added.

"If you'd rather it be that way …" Lenka didn't seem very convinced that they should address each other informally. But she accepted so as not to upset them. She had always protected herself from other people by insisting that formal manners mark the distances between them.

The house was not far from the center of the city. It was not easy to walk in a snowstorm, so Zahra took Fernando's arm. She did not forget that they were meant to be playing the role of young lovers.

Lenka showed them the Market Colonnade and the Mill Colonnade, both of which were built at the end of the nineteenth century; both contained springs from which the miraculous water flowed. She surprised them by taking a couple of little porcelain jars from her bag and filling them with the warm water which, she said, cured almost anything.

Fernando and Zahra drank from one of the springs.

Their faces of disgust made Lenka laugh.

"Don't you like it? Sulfurous waters, a little taste of metal at the back of the mouth, perhaps ..."

"And how do people know that this water is good for one's health?" Zahra asked.

"Charles IV, the Holy Roman Emperor, discovered it. He liked to hunt in these woods and found the hot springs that bubbled from the ground here. So in the fourteenth century, it became a place to come and take the waters. But it was in the eighteenth century that a doctor, David Bacher, made Karlovy Vary a true spa. It's a very special place, enjoyed by many important people. You could say that it's the best spa in Europe," Lenka said with pride, as she pointed out the baroque Belle Époque buildings that were crammed in together with their neoclassical siblings, making the whole city a real gem.

They had to go back to the countess' house because the snow was making it difficult for them to walk and their clothes were wet.

They were served lunch in a dining room whose vast windows opened onto a forest covered in snow.

Countess Aneta introduced them to a frail-looking woman.

"Jana is not only my lady's maid, but she also cares for my health. I don't know what would become of me without her."

Kaspar Meier looked at the elegantly-dressed young woman, who seemed so shy that she could barely lift her eyes from the floor.

"So this young woman is your nurse," Meier said.

Aneta didn't say anything: she merely smiled and beckoned Fernando to sit at her right side at the table. Petr Mezlik was seated to her left.

They spoke about nothing and about everything, but above all about the theater and art. Kaspar Meier kept on butting in to tell them about the many concerts, ballets, and theater companies in Vienna that fought for the public's attention. The countess asked Zahra about her dancing and listened attentively to her explanations.

"I would like to see you dance. I've never been to an Oriental dance show before. But news of your success in Prague has reached us even here."

"I am sorry to have left some of my luggage in Prague: the dances I do, just like ballet, require a special wardrobe."

The countess said that in spite of the poor weather, they would go to the theater that afternoon.

"The good thing about Karlovy Vary is that there are people who come here all year round to take the waters. The bad thing is that they aren't always the best people. But it does mean that our theater is open all year."

When they had finished their lunch, the countess suggested that they play chess or read or listen to music.

Petr Mezlik suggested to Fernando and Kaspar Meier that they have a glass of cognac and play cards, a suggestion which the Austrian accepted with alacrity; Fernando could not refuse. The ladies preferred to retire to their rooms and rest until the time came to go to the theater.

But they didn't go to their respective rooms, but rather all gathered in Aneta's. Once they were there, with the door shut, Zahra could speak to Jana and explain to her why they were there.

Jana Brossler listened to her, visibly moved. She hadn't been in touch with her father for months, and had dealt poorly with the uncertainty that this had meant.

Zahra explained that they were here to take her to Switzerland, where her father was waiting for her. Then the two of them would travel to the United States, if the course of the war permitted.

"But I can't leave. I'm sure they're looking for me. They arrested some of my friends simply for being friends with people who were in the Resistance."

"No one has given your name up, or you wouldn't still be here," Zahra said.

"We don't know if that's true. When the roundups started, they went to the houses of a lot of Jana's friends," Lenka said.

"Have they arrested all of your friends?" Zahra insisted.

"From what we know, some of them were only interrogated, but there are a few who have vanished from the face of the earth," Lenka said.

"Were you very involved with the Resistance? Do a lot of people know about you?" Zahra said.

608

"Well, I … I met a man who knew lots of the members of the Resistance, but I was never in the same room as any of them. They were afraid of being betrayed and never trusted anyone. I didn't even know their names," Jana said.

"Then I don't think they'll be looking for you," Zahra said.

"We don't know," Lenka said.

"The obvious solution is for you to go to your father, Jana. It's the best solution, at least if we can get you out of here," Aneta said.

"But I can't go … this is my country … We can't run away and let the Nazis take over everything."

"You're not doing anything here, Jana. You can't do anything. There's no Resistance anymore, they destroyed it after the Heydrich business," Zahra said.

"Well, we'll have to start from scratch," the young woman said.

"Yes, I'm sure someone will try again. But your involvement is impossible, as you will be putting anyone who tries to form a new Resistance group in danger. It's enough just to know someone who knows one of the people who were arrested," Lenka said.

"Let me ask how you're going to get Jana out of the country. I imagine you have a plan," the countess wanted to know. She obviously now thought it inevitable that Jana would leave.

"Well, you have introduced Jana to the world as your lady's maid and your nurse … I think I should get sick and then she should look after me," Zahra suggested.

"What do you mean?"

"We should stay here a couple of days, and the night before our return to Prague, I'll fall ill. You offer to let Jana come with me to Switzerland to look after me, and you make it clear that you expect her to come back. I'm sure that Kaspar Meier will know how to sort it out. It's the only thing I can think of doing," Zahra said, without a great deal of conviction.

"But he's a Nazi sympathizer," Lenka said worriedly.

"Yes, but he's also an idiot," Zahra said.

"I don't think he's that foolish; I think a lot of it is a front. Don't underestimate him," the countess warned.

"We came to Prague by train and we should leave by train. Jana will be my nurse. I have a passport for her under a false name: Jana but with a different surname. It's a Swiss passport. I've also got a nurse's document issued in Jana's name by the Swiss government."

"Jana isn't a Swiss name," Aneta replied.

"No, it isn't. Her new identity is as a Swiss citizen, although her mother is of Czech origin. We'll say that Jana is the name of her grandmother. That's the explanation."

"But I don't want to go," Jana protested.

"Dear, your presence here is entirely useless. Go back to your father, it will be the best for everyone," Countess Aneta said.

"Yes, we've tempted fate too much," Lenka said.

Jana's eyes filled with tears. They didn't give her any choice other than returning to Prague, and that might mean that she would be arrested, and God knows what else.

"You know, Zahra, I was very surprised when you told me in Prague that you had a false passport. You didn't know what you were going to find here," Lenka said, looking with curiosity at Zahra.

"I told you what my job was. The man who sent me here knew that you had given Jana shelter. That's why they sent me to get in touch with you. I don't know if he knew that Jana was with your aunt – they didn't say – but he may have known that as well. The people I am working with have a lot of eyes everywhere, so they told me that the only way to get out was for me to be sick and to get myself a nurse."

"But you didn't know that Jana was here," Lenka insisted.

"You told me yourself that it's better to know no more than the minimum, so I knew what was strictly necessary: I had to get in touch with you and bring a passport and a nursing certificate in Jana's name."

"And what does Fernando Garzo know?" Lenka's question confused Zahra.

"Know? What do you mean?"

"Does he know why you came to Prague?" Lenka's direct question left no room for any indirect answer.

"Yes, he's aware of everything. Fernando is … is … is my fiancé. I'd trust him with my life. He looks after me and he'll look after Jana."

"You know, I'm sure you can trust him with your life, but he needs to learn to act better. You're too distant and cold with one another to be lovers. I'd advise you to put a little bit more passion into it." Aneta's words made Zahra blush.

The first surprise that awaited them at the theater was the vault painted by Gustav Klimt. The second was the theater curtain, which Klimt had also painted. The third was the opera they were going to hear, which was none other than Mozart's *The Marriage of Figaro*, the work which had inaugurated the theater in 1886.

They enjoyed the evening. When they went back to the mansion, they were in a better mood than before.

The next day, Lenka told them that her aunt would come out with them to walk around the city. The weather was still cold, but the sun was shining, and some rays of sunshine filtered through the clouds to shine on the tops of the trees.

The countess took them to see the Castle Colonnade, where a statue dedicated to the Spirit of the Springs had been built. They also saw the church of Mary Magdalene. They didn't expect that when they went into the Thermal Baths, two of Aneta's maids would be waiting for them with everything they needed to bathe in the hot springs.

That's how they spent the day, but when they went home, Aneta asked her niece to take them to the Russian Orthodox church of Saint Peter and Saint Paul.

"Before the war broke out, lots of Russians came here to take the waters. They'll like it."

Kaspar Meier took the opportunity to curse the Red Army and say that sooner or later, Hitler would give them their just deserts. But no one answered him; the day was too beautiful for Meier to ruin it.

It wasn't until the next day that they put the plan to trick Meier and get Jana out of Czechoslovakia into action.

Fernando went down to breakfast with a worried expression on his face, and told the countess – with Meier and Mezlik in the room –that Zahra was ill.

Aneta asked if they would need to bring in a doctor, and Fernando answered that they would have to wait for Zahra to wake up, because she had been awake all night suffering sharp pains in her stomach.

Petr Mezlik was worried and said they should go back to Prague at once, where she could be seen by a doctor. Meier seconded the idea. But Fernando asked them to be calm until Zahra woke up.

He went back to Zahra's room and promised to keep them informed.

Halfway through the morning, he told Aneta to call a doctor, because Zahra couldn't stand up without feeling dizzy. She had chosen the illness she would suffer; she'd never had vertigo herself, but her mother had, and Zahra remembered the symptoms and all the illnesses that had accompanied it.

Kaspar Meier offered to go with Petr Mezlik to find a doctor and bring her back to Aneta's house.

This was one of the most exposed moments of the plan, because the doctor who was to come and see them was not in on the secret. Zahra therefore had to act, and her acting would determine all that might happen in the second half of the plan.

Dr. Novack examined Zahra closely, along with Jana, who was starting to play her role as a nurse.

Zahra was pale, her eyes closed, and begged them not to move her, because the room was spinning around her.

Jana also knew what was expected of her; before the doctor diagnosed vertigo, she suggested that this might be the disease Zahra was suffering from, and Dr. Novacks agreed.

Fernando held one of Zahra's hands between his own, and his expression of worry was very moving.

Aneta and Lenka waited at the door, and Meier and Meznik came in after them. The Viennese man tried not to miss a word of what was said, given that the English the old doctor spoke was a little rudimentary.

Zahra looked as though she were about to be sick and Jana brought over a basin and held her head. After several attempts Zahra's head fell back from Jana's hands and slumped onto the pillow.

"Doctor, I think there are too many people in the room. It's not good for her, and it's not good, given the state she's in, for so many people to be looking at her." Jana's voice was filled with conviction.

"You're right. There are too many people here and we're crowding her. The best thing is for you to stay with her. I'll prescribe her some pills that will be able to help with the vomiting, but as for the vertigo … I'm afraid there's not much I can do. It might last several days."

"But you have to do something! She can't stand on her own two feet. She can't walk," Fernando said with a touch of distress in his voice.

"I'm afraid that there is no real remedy for dizzy spells, although we might try something. The best thing is for her to stay in bed but with her head raised; that will help her get better."

Fernando followed Dr. Novacks out of the room and shut the door, leaving Jana inside.

They met up in the drawing room, where the doctor gave them his diagnosis and his recommendations, in particular that Zahra should rest for several days.

"But we can't stay here, Doctor. Miss Nadouri has unavoidable artistic commitments. And she insisted that she be allowed to go home," Fernando said.

"Impossible. How do you think she'll be able to travel to Egypt? There's no way. And even if she wanted to, she can't stand on her own two feet. She'll have to wait for a few days. And even if she gets better, it's not the best thing for her to travel."

When Dr. Novacks had gone, Aneta asked them what they thought about the situation. Fernando insisted that she should go back to Alexandria as soon as possible, Mezlik said that she should go to a hospital in Prague, and Kaspar Meier said that she should keep on being looked after by the nurse until they got her back to Vienna, where better doctors could have a look at her.

Dr. Novacks visited Zahra the next day and certified that her situation was still delicate. Jana and Fernando stayed by her side.

Three days later, Kaspar Meier couldn't hide his nerves. His business was calling him back to Vienna. He represented other artists and promoted other shows; he couldn't spend so long in

Karlovy Vary, so he said to his hostess that they should make a decision about what to do with Zahra.

Aneta suggested, cleverly enough, that they should take Zahra back to Vienna, just as Meier himself wanted.

"But can she travel?" he asked worriedly.

"We'll ask Dr. Novacks. He's just about to arrive. Let him make the decision," Aneta said.

When Dr. Novacks arrived, the maid told him to come with her up to the mistress of the house's private room.

The countess was seated behind her desk writing a letter. She got up to shake the doctor's hand.

"My dear doctor, we have a problem. Miss Nadouri is still in a delicate state, but on the other hand, neither she nor her companions can spend more time here. It's clear, of course, Mr. Meier needs to go back to Vienna and Mr. Mezlik has his own business in Prague. My niece Lenka can't be away from her ballet school for that long either. What do you think we should do?"

"Countess, it is difficult to make a decision, given Miss Nadouri's state."

"Yes, you're right, but yesterday you told my nurse not to leave Miss Nadouri by herself. Do you think that if she traveled with her, then it would be less dangerous for the patient?" Aneta asked in a deceptively sweet voice.

Dr. Novacks paused for a second. It was very reckless for someone sick with vertigo to go on a journey, but he understood that the countess must be sick of looking after her guests for so long, especially if she was ready to lend out her lady's maid and nurse to look after Miss Nadouri. Countess Aneta was an important woman in excellent health; he didn't understand why she needed to have a nurse in her service, but given that her four husbands had all died, maybe she was just the apprehensive type. In any event, he felt that he would do well to satisfy her demands.

He saw Zahra first of all. Jana said that she was still unable to stand up, although the vomiting seemed to be dying away. The doctor looked at her and smiled at the countess.

"I think that with the help of a nurse, Miss Nadouri will be able to travel."

When the countess and the doctor went into the library, Meier and Mezlik were arguing, and Fernando was watching them and smoking a cigarette.

"Gentlemen, Dr. Novacks has just seen Miss Nadouri and ... well, better for you to explain, doctor," Aneta said.

"Miss Nadouri is getting better, although vertigo isn't something that just goes away overnight. I understand that she wants to go back to Egypt, and she can do that, provided always that she is accompanied by someone qualified, like a nurse. The countess, with her characteristic generosity, is ready to give up the services of Miss Jana for a time."

"That's great news!" Kaspar Meier said with a smile.

"But how far will the nurse travel with Miss Nadouri?" Petr Mezlik asked, surprised by Dr. Novacks' statement.

"As far as necessary. If Miss Nadouri feels strong enough, she can go to Prague tomorrow. I understand that she's going to Vienna from Prague, and then back to Egypt by any way that she feels she can," the countess said.

"Thank you so much! I know that Jana is not just your nurse, but also your companion ... You are a very generous woman." Fernando took Aneta's hand and kissed it in gratitude.

"It's a wonderful solution. The nurse can look after Miss Nadouri, and then we can all feel a bit of peace of mind. It would have been a risk for her to travel without proper medical care. I will make sure, along with my friend Mezlik, that the paperwork is all in order for the nurse to travel without meeting any obstacles as she looks after our dear Zahra," Meier said.

They all were much more cheerful that evening over supper.

"And how will you manage without your nurse?" Meier asked.

"I'll get by. Jana isn't just a nurse: she's also been by my side in my loneliness after the death of my fourth husband. I feel so lonely here ... My dear niece Lenka doesn't come to see me as often as I would like."

"You know I can't leave the ballet school so long," Lenka apologized.

"I know ... I know ... I'm not blaming you. But now that I'm going to be alone, maybe you could tell your mother that she should come out here and keep me company ..."

Dr. Novacks had recommended that Zahra travel by train rather than in Petr Mezlik's car. Aneta had provided her with her last husband's wheelchair. They pushed Zahra onto the train and got her settled in a first-class carriage, with Fernando and Kaspar Meier doing the work under the vigilant eye of Jana, the nurse.

Once back in Prague, they went to their rooms in the Hotel Paris to rest before traveling to Vienna and then Zurich the next day.

Kaspar Meier went to get a travel permit for the nurse. Meier had good friends among the officials of the Protectorate Offices, as well as knowing Ernst Gerkle, the head of the Gestapo, so he thought that he would be able to get Jana's papers sorted out immediately. Meier insisted that Mezlik go with him, and he had no choice but to obey, although he was clearly upset to have to go into the building from which the Germans now governed Czechoslovakia.

Jana's passport was in the name of Jana Flugzentrele, a common Swiss surname. It stated that her parents were Swiss.

The passport seemed to be in order, but the officer who was dealing with them told them to wait while he showed it to his superior. He took some time in coming back, time during which Meier started to get irritated and Mezlik started to look worried. Finally, the man told them to come into a back room, his superior's office.

They were met there by two men, one Czech, who must have been the man's superior, and another man who said nothing, but who listened carefully to the conversation.

"Where is the young woman whose passport this is?" the clerk asked.

Meier gave all kinds of explanations about the owner of the passport and how she needed to travel with Zahra Nadouri, who was laid low by vertigo. Mezlik also answered the man's questions as he looked over and again at the pages of the passport. Finally, he gave it to Meier and then left without giving them any explanations.

"How odd, don't you think?" Kaspar Meier said to his business partner Petr Mezlik once they were out in the street.

"Odd? I don't think so. The Germans don't trust anyone who wants to leave the country."

"But the nurse ... she's not Czech, she's Swiss, her passport is Swiss and she's not important, so why should they care?" Meier said.

"Oh, my friend, you don't know how far German mistrust can go. We're all suspects here, for some reason or another," Mezlik replied grumpily.

"But you have nothing to worry about! Czechoslovakia is under the Führer's protection!" Meier said.

Petr Mezlik didn't answer, but his mouth twisted a little in a way that surprised his business partner who up until that moment, had simply assumed that Mezlik was a Nazi sympathizer like himself.

Fernando insisted to Meier that the journey back to Alexandria had to be made in stages, given Zahra's state. Meier would have preferred not to have had to keep shepherding them along, given that he had a lot of work waiting for him in Vienna. But he couldn't refuse to let them travel to Vienna and then to Zurich as Fernando suggested.

The train to Vienna was full, and they couldn't find a compartment where they could all travel together. Meier would go in a nearby compartment, and Jana, Fernando and Zahra would travel together, sharing with a man who had bought the last seat.

Fernando suggested that this man could swap with Meier and so the four of them could travel together, but he refused the offer, for all that Meier insisted. The man, with blond hair, broad shoulders and rough, poorly cared-for hands, seemed out of place in the elegant first-class carriage. He didn't speak to them nor they to him for the whole of the rest of the journey.

When they got to Vienna, Meier went with them to the hotel where they would stay that night. Zahra carried on pretending to be ill, unable to stand on her own two feet, and Jana said that she should rest.

The next morning, Kaspar Meier came to see them to say that they couldn't take the midday train from Zurich, but that they had to wait for the night train. He gave them their tickets and told them that he was entirely at their service if they needed anything during the day, and that he would come and find them at eight o'clock to take them to the station.

They had no choice but to spend the rest of the day in their hotel rooms. Zahra and Jana didn't go out, but Fernando took the opportunity to take a long stroll through Vienna. The city seemed to him as beautiful as it was fascinating.

At eight o'clock on the dot, Meier was waiting for them in the lobby. Jana pushed the wheelchair where Zahra lay with her head slumped to one side and her eyes closed, apparently unaware of everything that was going on around her.

They're making telling lies into a matter of course for us. Not to be ourselves. We are playing the roles we've been given, and it seems easy for us take on a new nature. What will become of us if we grow used to living in deceit? Fernando thought to himself.

Kaspar Meier helped Fernando get the wheelchair onto the train, and the conductor led them to their assigned compartment at the end of the carriage, next to the door. A man was sitting there, reading the newspaper. Fernando gave a start to see that it was the same man who had been with them on the train from Prague to Vienna. He made no sign that he recognized them or Meier. Jana looked at Fernando, and Zahra stayed stock still, although she too had recognized the ruddy-faced, broad-shouldered man, whose suit was of even worse quality than the one he had been wearing in Prague. There was a carefully folded overcoat and a hat on the chair next to him.

Meier said a curt goodbye. He seemed anxious to leave.

Jana and Zahra sat together while Fernando lowered himself into the chair next to the man. He was convinced that his presence couldn't be a coincidence. He shared a quick glance with Zahra, in which he read that she had exactly the same concern. Jana's eyes shone with fear.

The man seemed to be absorbed in his paper, but Fernando saw that he had not turned the page, and kept his eyes fixed on Jana.

Some time after the train left Vienna, the conductor came into the compartment. He looked at people's passports and tickets, and gave them back one by one, saying the names of their owners as he did so.

"So … this is Mr. Garzo's passport, and this is Miss Nadouri's, and this is Miss Flugzentrele, and this is Mr. Berger's," he said, handing the large man back his passport. "Good. We'll reach the first stop in a couple of hours. Fifteen minutes, in case anyone wants to get out and stretch their legs."

The conductor exchanged glances with Berger, who was sitting next to Fernando.

When the train made its first stop, Berger went out into the corridor and climbed down onto the platform. He seemed to be waiting for someone, but he had to get back onto the train.

He got out again at the second stop.

"I'm going out for a moment," Fernando said, deciding to follow the man.

"Be careful. It's clear that he's following us," Zahra murmured.

Jana grew tense. She had thought the same, but had decided that she must be imagining things.

"It's the man from the Prague train," Jana said.

"Yes, and I don't believe in coincidences," Fernando said, as he left the carriage and closed the door behind him.

Herr Berger had gotten off the train and was talking to a man on the platform. The man, who looked like him, was showing him a piece of paper. Fernando watched them as he lit a cigarette, pretending to be gazing at the view from the window. The two men looked threatening and he suddenly thought that they were policemen, surely from the Gestapo. He remembered that Petr Mezlik had said in passing that it had not been as easy as they had hoped to get Jana's travel permit. He went back to the compartment. He didn't want to alarm the two women, but he thought that it would be best if they could stay alert.

"That Herr Berger is talking to another man. I'm worried that the pair of them could be from the Gestapo," he said immediately.

"Yes, they must be," said Zahra. "We'll be on the alert. The train's going to stop again in an hour."

"Good Lord! What can we do?" Jana said, frightened.

"I suppose they're going to try to stop us before we leave Austria," Fernando concluded.

"Yes, I guess that's what they'll want to do," Zahra said.

"And why haven't they done it yet?"

"I suppose they haven't got proof of Jana's identity. Maybe the man that Berger was talking with on the platform gave him the proof."

Zahra asked Jana to pass her the little suitcase. To Jana and Fernando's surprise, the suitcase had a false bottom, from which Zahra drew out two pistols.

"We may need them," she said, handing one to Fernando.

"You're not suggesting that we shoot a Gestapo officer, are you?" Fernando said.

"Hide the pistol, but keep it close to hand. Maybe we won't have to use it, and maybe we will. But in any case, we're not going to let them take Jana. I suppose they'll want to interrogate us as well."

At the third stop, Berger met another man who got back onto the train with him. Fernando watched them, as he smoked another cigarette at the window. The conductor led this second man to a compartment close to theirs.

At each subsequent station, the two men got down and walked impatiently up and down as though waiting for someone to turn up.

The night wore on, and neither Fernando nor Zahra nor Jana were able to sleep. They were alert, aware of every single gesture and movement that Berger made. He carried on pretending to read the newspaper, although from time to time he closed his eyes and pretended to sleep.

Fernando went out into the corridor to get a bit of fresh air and met the conductor, who told him they were nearly there. "We'll be in Switzerland in four hours," he said.

After the penultimate stop, Berger came back into the compartment and looked Jana up and down.

"You'll have to come with me," he said, taking her by the arm.

"What are you saying? Why should this lady have to go with you?" Fernando said, standing up and getting between Jana and Berger.

"Move." Berger pushed Fernando.

Zahra got to her feet and stood in front of the man and smiled at him, causing him a degree of disconcertment.

"Get out of the way!" he said.

But Zahra came even closer until her body was pressed against the man's. Berger didn't have time to push her aside before a grimace of pain and surprise appeared on his face and he raised his hands to his chest.

Zahra's proximity and the noise of the train had muffled the sound of the shot. Yes, Zahra had shot him. He lay dying in Fernando's arms where he had fallen.

Zahra locked the compartment door and Fernando and Jana looked at one another without knowing what to say, much less what to do. But she didn't pause, and sat next to the corpse, going through his pockets until she found his documentation.

"He's with the Gestapo," she said, showing them his badge.

"Jesus!" Jana could barely stay on her feet.

"We're going to throw him out of the window," Zahra said.

"We can't do that! They'll find the body!" Fernando said.

"Of course they'll find it. But they'll take a few hours to do so. It's still night, and with a bit of luck, when they find it we'll be in Switzerland. We'll take his clothes off and hit his face a bit to make it harder to identify him."

Fernando couldn't speak. He was shocked by just how coldly Zahra had killed the Gestapo officer, and by the way in which she spoke about disfiguring the body.

"Isn't it enough that you killed him?" Fernando said, looking at Zahra with a blend of horror and stunned confusion.

"No, unfortunately it's not, not if we want to get out of this alive. It's them or us, Fernando, there's no other way," she replied calmly.

"I'm not going to do it," he said.

She shrugged. She seemed not to care that it would have to be her who beat the corpse's face.

"We don't need to do anything else. If we throw him out headfirst, he's bound to get his face crushed," Fernando said with a grimace of disgust.

"You're right," Zahra said. "Now help me strip him. You too, Jana."

The young dancer was incapable of speaking or moving. There was a sheen of terror on her face. But Zahra shook her and made her start taking Berger's clothes off.

"What will we do with the clothes?" Fernando asked.

"We'll get rid of them, of course. Body first, then clothes, both out of the window," Zahra ordered.

"Someone will see us!" Jana said.

"No, no one will. It's still pretty much night, and we'll throw him out when we hit a tunnel. The darkness will be more total then."

"And what if we get to the next stop and there are other Gestapo men waiting?" Fernando asked.

"I'll tell you what I think has happened. Berger followed us from Prague. Remember that Petr Mezlik told us that there were problems with Jana's travel permit. The Gestapo must have decided to follow us and have a man who wouldn't let us out of his sight. The Nazis are still looking into anyone who has any relation to the young people who killed Heydrich. Berger was waiting for the true identity of Jana to be confirmed, but there's only one more station before Switzerland, so he felt he had no choice but to arrest her now. I suppose he had decided to take her off the train at the next station," Zahra said.

"The train stops for eight minutes at the next station. The conductor told me," Fernando said.

"Let's do this one step at a time, Fernando. The first thing to do is to get rid of the body," Zahra said.

A knock at the door made them all fall silent. Berger's inert body was on the seat. Fernando tipped it over so it lay prone, covering it with an overcoat to give the impression that the man was sleeping. He beckoned the two women to sit down. There were more knocks at the door, and Fernando opened.

The man who had gotten onto the train shortly after they had left Vienna – the man who surely was one of Berger's colleagues – occupied the whole doorway.

"What do you want?" Fernando said, more decisively than he felt.

The man pushed him to one side and came into the compartment. He saw Berger lying with his head to one side and his glazed, dead eyes. He turned and pulled a pistol from his pocket, but he didn't even have a chance to threaten them. Fernando shot him three times.

"Thank you," Zahra said, and saw how Fernando's jaw was trembling.

She put her hand on his shoulder and squeezed it, as though this gesture could bring him back to reality. Fernando hadn't hesitated, and had shot the man, but in doing so he might have caused them problems.

Jana broke into tears, and Zahra scolded her. This was no time for crying, or for letting emotions take hold. They had two corpses in the compartment and blood on the floor. The conductor could knock on the door at any moment. Maybe the noise of the shots had been louder than the rattling of the train.

"We have to throw them overboard now. It will be dawn soon," Zahra said.

Fernando and Zahra stripped the two men. Fernando felt stunned by what he was doing. The bodies were still warm, and he was worried that they would wake up.

Jana folded their clothes, just as Zahra ordered.

Then the three of them managed to lift Berger's body and use the blackness of a tunnel to throw it out of the window. They threw it face down in the hope that the impact would make it into a bloody pulp that was difficult to recognize.

They stood for a second or so in silence, gathering their strength.

"Let's wait a little before we get rid of the next one," Fernando suggested.

"We can't. The conductor might come, or anyone else," Zahra replied.

They lifted the man's body. He was taller and even heavier than Berger, but between the three of them they managed, to wait for another tunnel and push him out onto the tracks.

Then Jana set herself to cleaning the floor and Zahra cleaned the seats. They couldn't allow even a single drop of blood to betray them. Then they threw out the men's clothes.

When the compartment was empty, Fernando and Zahra smoked a cigarette.

"What shall we do now?" Jana asked in a trembling voice. She was scared and her eyes were cloudy with tears.

"Wait. It may be that the Gestapo are waiting for you at the last stop before leaving Austria, because the confirmation of your identity has come through, or else because it is their last opportunity to get you. We won't know until the moment comes," Zahra replied.

"But the Gestapo will be looking out for Herr Berger and the other man," Jana said, in a voice that was almost a whimper.

"Yes ... perhaps. The conductor will tell them that Berger is in our carriage, and the other man is a little further along. We have to say that we haven't seen Berger since the last stop. We can say that maybe this was where he was getting off, because he didn't talk at all," Zahra continued.

"They won't believe us," Jana said, disconsolate.

"Don't think about what might happen. The important thing is that there are no contradictions in our stories, and that if they interrogate us, we hold on to our account to the end," Fernando said.

"If they arrest us they'll torture us," Jana said, crying once again.

"Come on, don't give up already. Maybe nothing will happen."

There was a hollow knock at the door that set them all on edge. Fernando opened the door, his hand on the pistol in his jacket pocket.

"The next station is the last one before Switzerland. We're only a hundred yards from the border. I'll bring you the wheelchair. I'll help you get the lady out of here," the conductor said as he looked at Zahra, who had closed her eyes and was playing the invalid once more.

The conductor couldn't help but notice that Berger wasn't there, and asked about him. It was Fernando who spoke.

"He left at the last stop and hasn't been back since," he explained indifferently.

"Right ... how odd ... I didn't see him in the dining car ..." The conductor was surprised.

Fernando shrugged, making it clear that Berger wasn't his problem and that he didn't care about him.

"Thank you so much in advance for your help when we reach Zurich. It's not easy to manage the chair," Fernando said.

"Right ... of course ... yes ... I'll go and see."

The train stopped at the border before entering Switzerland. There were two men waiting on the platform. Their sinister appearance and murderous air revealed who they were. They had to be the Gestapo. They spoke to the conductor and got on board the train. Zahra started once again to get into the role of patient, with her eyes rolled back and occasional retching. Jana put a handkerchief covered in cologne on her temples. They asked Fernando to go out, and if he bumped into the conductor, to ask for urgent medical help for Zahra. He didn't want to leave them alone, but Zahra was impatient.

"If those two men get on the train, we can't just sit here waiting for them."

"And what use is it to us for you to play the invalid? Do you think they'll care?" Fernando was still refusing to leave.

"Please, go and find a doctor. There must be one on the train." Zahra almost begged him.

He went nervously out of the compartment and started to knock on the doors along the way. It wasn't until he reached the next carriage that a shy-looking little man got up and said he was a doctor. Fernando explained that he was traveling with a sick woman who needed a doctor urgently.

Fernando walked with him back to their compartment. The man examined Zahra and Jana explained that Miss Nadouri had been suffering from acute vertigo for the last few days, and that she had woken up worse this morning.

"This compartment smells ... forgive me, but it smells of blood."

"Well, it's just that ... I'm sorry, Doctor ... but I'm going through that special time ... of the month ... it's a little early, but I suppose that must be because of the tension of the journey and my worry about Miss Nadouri's illness. She's very bad ..."

"Maybe you should air this place, or if you like, we could put her into the wheelchair and push her up and down the corridor a little to get some air. How long since she's eaten?"

"More than a day. She's refusing food. She hasn't even drunk any water."

"Ah, that isn't good. We'll take her to the restaurant car and get them to make her some kind of tea. And she'll be able to get some fresh air as well."

Zahra protested, pretending that she was in no condition to move. But the doctor insisted that she open her eyes, sit up straight, and look forwards to help get over the vertigo as fast as possible. With Fernando and Jana's help, they got her into the chair and went towards the restaurant car. Fernando stayed behind when he heard voices. The conductor and two men were running towards their compartment. He looked at his watch. There were barely two minutes to go before the train started off again. He ran towards the restaurant car and the train whistled.

The doctor had ordered an herbal tea for Zahra, and insisted that she drink a little water.

The voices of the conductor and the two men sounded nearby as they shouted and pushed people out of their way. The train started to move, and the two Gestapo men jumped down to the platform. The conductor went into the restaurant car and stopped dead to see Fernando, Jana, and Zahra. He felt cheated. They had looked for them in the first class compartments, convinced that they would have hidden themselves there, but they hadn't imagined that they would appear in full view of the rest of the passengers. He went over to the window and waved his arms to indicate to the two Gestapo officers that he had found their prey. But Fernando's hand closed tight on his arm.

"The young lady is unwell," he said, looking at him fixedly.

"But ... you ... you ... they're looking for you. You're criminals," the conductor said.

"How dare you insult us! You must have made some mistake. Looking for us? For us? Do you know who this woman is?" And Fernando pointed to Zahra.

"I don't know anything ... the police are looking for you ..." He insisted.

"The police? They're not looking for us. I'll tell you who this woman is. It's Zahra Nadouri, the great dancer."

Fernando took a newspaper clipping out of his wallet. It was a half-page portrait from a Prague newspaper. In it, Ernst Geske, the head of the Gestapo in Prague, was kissing Zahra's hand.

The conductor looked at the newspaper with a confused

expression. There must have been a mistake somewhere. It was impossible that the head of the Prague Gestapo would be paying homage to this lady if he had anything less than the utmost trust in her.

"I don't understand," he said.

"We will submit a formal complaint for your impertinence in calling us criminals," Fernando said.

"I owe you an apology, sir ... it was not my intention. They were looking for two women and a gentleman ... and two of their colleagues who were on the train as well. Herr Berger was in the same compartment as you ..."

Jana made a sign to Fernando to look out of the window. A sign showed that they had just entered Switzerland. She couldn't keep herself from crying.

Later, when they had gotten off the train and Fernando was looking for someone to help them with their luggage, Zahra took the opportunity to warn Jana.

"You can never, ever tell anyone about what happened in the train. Not even your father. You have to live with the secret."

"It was horrible ... those two men ..." Jana didn't know what to say.

"Listen, Fernando and I killed those two men to save your life. Sooner or later the Gestapo would have arrested you, so we risked our lives to get you out of Czechoslovakia. You owe us, Jana, you owe us your silence." There was a hint of harshness in Zahra's voice.

"I ... I don't know what to say ... thank you for saving me, but those two men ..." Jana couldn't keep the reproach out of her voice.

"Would you have preferred them to arrest you and torture you?" Zahra asked sharply.

"No, it's not that ..."

"If your conscience pricks you, there's still time to catch the next train to Prague. Go straight to the Petschek Palace and ask for Ernst Geske. I'm sure the head of the Gestapo will be happy to see you. And when you confess, don't forget to say that you helped us, that you're our accomplice." Zahra was speaking harshly, but was absolutely calm.

"Please … please … don't say these things …"

"You have two choices, Jana. Either you go back to Prague or you learn to control your conscience. You'll learn, don't you worry. It's just a matter of time. But if you speak, it should be in front of Geske, and if you close your mouth it should be forever." Mr. Brossler was walking impatiently up and down in the lobby of the Baur au Lac. He had been waiting impatiently for his daughter's arrival for a couple of days now, but it was not until yesterday evening that they had told him she would be coming in on the morning train. They had told him he should wait in the hotel, and he was anxious to see his daughter again.

Suddenly he saw a woman come into the hotel, with a tired face and a resolute expression. Jana was with her, and behind them walked a young man with a guarded expression.

Jana ran to her father. She hugged him tight and began to cry. Zahra and Fernando waited until both father and daughter had calmed down.

Brossler held his hand out to Zahra and then Fernando.

"Thank you … thank you so much … I'll be in debt to you for the rest of my life. My friend Benjamin Wilson told me that you'd bring my little girl back. I … I don't know what I can do or say to show you how grateful I am …"

"Nothing, Mr. Brossler. You don't need to do or say anything. It's a real satisfaction to have got one over against the Gestapo. As you can see, Jana is well. I think the best thing for you to do would be to take her to America with you as soon as possible. There's nothing going on here apart from the war," Zahra said.

"Sometimes I feel so selfish for not being at the front," Brossler said, looking down at the ground.

"There are a lot of ways to fight, Herr Brossler. Maybe you can do a lot of good without being right where the action is," Zahra said.

They only spent one night in the hotel. Zahra wanted to get back to Alexandria as much as Fernando did. They said goodbye affectionately to Jana, and the young dancer saw a warning in Zahra's gaze, or perhaps a threat. But she had already decided that she would learn to control her conscience. She had survived.

9

In January 1943, the leaders of the Allied Powers met in Casablanca. At the end of the month, the British Eighth Army took Tripoli, which was an unexpected blow for Field Marshal Rommel.

In February, the Soviets decisively won the battle of Stalingrad. Their victory cost them a million lives.

The war carried on as Adela took her first steps. She burbled words in several languages: Spanish, English, and Arabic, and also Greek, because Dimitra spoke to her in her native language.

At the end of April, the air was filled with the scents of spring, but this did not improve Fernando and Catalina's mood.

Catalina had more students than she could take on. Her life shuttled her between piano lessons, strolls with Dr. Naseef, and confessions to Father Lucas. Meanwhile, Fernando, after two months away, had resumed his routine in the publishing house, under the sad gaze of Athanasius Vryzas. They knew that he had argued with Mr. Wilson, but they hadn't found out yet about what. Leyda Zabat, Mr. Wilson's secretary, was extremely discreet, and never said a word out of place. No one had dared ask why Fernando had left the job, or what they had done to make him come back.

Athanasius Vryzas hadn't recommended that he leave Alexandria again, nor had he invited him for a cup of coffee.

Vryzas had not missed the fact that Fernando had returned from his voyage, wherever he had been, with another burden on his soul.

It had not been easy for Fernando to return to normality. He had killed again: the first time had been for revenge, and this time had been for his own survival, aware of the fact that the Gestapo agents wouldn't have been content with simply arresting Jana, but would have taken him and Zahra as well. But even so, he couldn't calm his conscience, because the men he had killed still lived in his nightmares.

He was also tormented by the fact that he had allowed Wilson to convince him to embark on an action which, from any point of view, was recklessly dangerous and which could have cost him and Zahra their lives. He was also frightened by what he had discovered about Zahra. Her hardness, her capacity to deal with everything that came towards her, and even her ability to kill without blinking an eye.

He still felt a flash of anger when he remembered how Benjamin Wilson had congratulated him for the rescue of Jana. Fernando hadn't accepted his congratulations, but had rather said that he wasn't going to work for the publishing house anymore.

"I'm not going to work here, much less get involved in your other activities."

"I understand that you've been through some complicated times. Zahra Nadouri explained that you had to get rid of two Gestapo agents. But you dealt with it well, Fernando. Take a few days off and then come back to work. Vryzas has a couple of books for you to edit," Wilson replied.

"I don't think you understand me. I don't want anything more to do with you, or your publishing house, or your other business. I am surprised that you don't care about having put Zahra's and my lives at risk."

Benjamin Wilson fixed his bland gaze on Fernando.

"You put your own life at risk the day you decided to kill the men who had taken part in your father's death. You became a pariah, which is why you are here," Wilson said coldly.

Fernando gave a start when he heard Benjamin Wilson's words. Though they were neutral, they hurt him more than if they had been said as a reproach.

"You don't know anything about me! How dare you accuse me of murder!" Fernando's voice cracked.

"I'm not accusing you of anything. All I'm saying is what I found out about you, and the fact that I don't believe in coincidence. It's odd that you left Madrid with your friends on the very day that someone killed a jailer and a soldier who had something to do with your father's death. My man in Madrid filled in the gaps by finding out about you and looking in the newspapers published just before and just after your departure."

"And now you're accusing me because your bagmen have filled in who knows what gaps!" Fernando shouted.

Benjamin Wilson looked at him with unmoving coldness. Fernando's anger and pain didn't alter the tone of voice in which he replied.

"You know what you've done and why you did it. But you work for me because you have a conscience. Don't get the wrong end of the stick, Fernando."

"It's you who's got the wrong end of the stick. And don't mention my father ever again," Fernando said, finding it hard to hold back the rage he felt.

"No, I never make mistakes when I choose who to trust."

"Trust? Trust to do what?" Fernando said, raising his voice again.

"To help me win this war and make sure that Hitler doesn't become the ruler of the world. That's what."

"I'm not a soldier, and neither are you." Fernando replied.

"There are lots of fronts in this war. Rommel is trying to wrest North Africa from the British Empire, and he is already very close to Alexandria. This is a front in the war. But the party at Musim Sadat's house was a front in the war as well. You remember how you went there with Zahra?"

"Yes, Musim the archeologist ... that ridiculous trip."

"It was a useful night. Zahra did a great job."

"How ridiculous! There you were, so worried about Pedro López, when all he did was make sure that he got a good price on some cotton. And I think you knew that."

Wilson shrugged, and made a gesture with his hands as though dismissing what Fernando said.

"I'm not going to treat you like a fool, because you're not a fool. I chose you to go with Zahra because I didn't at that moment have anyone who could do the job, but also because I thought you could be useful and I needed to know if you could carry out certain tasks. I needed someone whom nobody knew, and who might be taken for one of Zahra's flings. We all know each other here in Alexandria, and it would have been difficult for me to find someone who filled the role of her companion properly. Zahra needs support on the missions she undertakes. It's easier for a woman to move around with a man."

"A bodyguard. Well, look for another one, because I don't like the role, and I don't like people thinking that I'm the plaything of a dancer, her devoted slave."

"It's a good cover for her and for you."

"Well, I don't think it'll be hard for you to find someone else to take the role," Fernando said, getting to his feet and getting ready to leave the office.

"And now there's another reason that Zahra wants to work with you." Benjamin Wilson had lowered his voice.

"Really? What is it?" Fernando didn't sit back down, but Wilson's last words had made him stop.

"Because she says that you're intelligent, prudent and scrupulous. She and I see the same thing in you. Although I would add one more thing that I think is equally important. I'll tell you what it is."

"I don't care what you think about me."

"I'll tell you anyway. If you're not an assassin or a psychopath, then killing is difficult, and killing for the first time is the most difficult. But if you have done it once, then it will always be easier to do it again, especially for a cause or in particular circumstances. I don't hire assassins, people who enjoy pulling the trigger. I wouldn't trust them. I prefer people to whom every death is a blow to their conscience, one that stops them from sleeping. This is the greatest virtue I have seen in you, Fernando."

"Your words disgust me. Goodbye, Mr. Wilson."

He left the office feeling more downcast than he had when he entered it.

Fernando didn't return to the publishing house for two months. Catalina insisted that he tell her what it was that upset him. His pain caused her pain, and it was hard for her to see the deep bags that formed under his eyes and showed how hard he found it to sleep. But Fernando didn't say anything. He didn't want to depress her. Not even Adela was capable of pulling him out of his self-absorption. The little girl would come and find him and scramble into his arms while she smiled at him and looked for his affection.

Although she was extremely discreet, Ylena Kokkalis also looked at him worriedly. Maybe because she knew about Mr. Wilson's real business and thought that he and Fernando had argued; or even just because Alexandria was a city with layer upon layer of secrets, where every inhabitant had a handful of things they could never talk about.

Mr. Sanders and Monsieur Baudin also realized that something had caused him to sink into uncertainty and sadness.

The nights seemed to last forever. He smoked compulsively, standing at the window. The faces of Roque and Saturnino Pérez appeared whenever he closed his eyes. And now they were joined by the image of the Gestapo agent. The last face was vague, shapeless, but he could smell it, the harsh odor of the man and the scent of his blood.

Some nights, after dinner, while Mr. Sanders and Monsieur Baudin were playing their game of chess, Fernando would sit and smoke in the drawing room, with Catalina at his side. She would read out loud to him, convinced that books had a power that would soothe his tortured soul. Only once did she dare ask him when they would go to France to look for Eulogio. He didn't know what to reply. Not because he didn't think about his friend; he thought about him constantly. But he felt dead inside, as dead as the men he had killed, and this stopped him from taking any decision more complicated than breathing.

It was Zahra who managed to bring him back to reality.

One morning she came to Ylena's house. Dimitra let her in and was surprised when she said that she should fetch Fernando.

Fernando had been awake for a while now, and was looking after Adela while Catalina gave the first piano lesson of the day.

With Adela in his arms, he went to the library, where Dimitra had brought Zahra.

"What are you hiding from?" she asked him, without even saying hello.

Fernando was annoyed by her imperious tone of voice, but when he saw her, he had to accept that what he felt for Zahra was something deeper than simple physical attraction.

"I'm not hiding. Here I am, aren't I?" he said, grumpily.

"Why did you leave the publishing house?"

"Because I don't like your friend Benjamin Wilson, because I don't want to do certain jobs that have nothing to do with publishing books."

"You're suffering because you had to kill that Gestapo agent. I understand. It's never easy to kill, even if you kill someone as horrible as that man."

"You understand me? I'm not so sure, Zahra. You and I are not the same."

"You don't know me, Fernando. You don't know anything about me, so don't judge me so easily."

"You didn't pause when the moment came to kill Berger."

"What else could I do? He was a Gestapo agent and he was there, and so, just like his partner you killed, he would have arrested us if we hadn't. It was them or us. We had no choice but to save our own lives."

"Yes, we had another choice. We could have refused to be sent to Prague by Mr. Wilson. We could have chosen back then."

"You're regretting getting Jana out of there?" Zahra got to her feet and was looking at him, stunned.

"You're twisting things. I'm happy that Jana is safe with her father, but there are hundreds and thousands of Janas, men and women whose lives are complex. We're at war. I never forget that."

"A war you don't want to participate in. But know this, Fernando, you can't stand around and twiddle your thumbs when the freedom – not just of Europe, but of the whole world – is at stake. Hitler is insatiable, and he won't stop until he has made us all into Germany's puppets."

"I fought in one war and I lost." Fernando's voice was irritated.

"And now that you've lost, you've decided to wash your hands of the consequences. You care about Franco taking over your country, but you don't care that Hitler, one of Franco's allies, might take over the world."

"If you've come to read me a sermon, consider it done." Fernando didn't want to carry on talking to Zahra.

"I like you, Fernando. That's why I'm here. Yes, you were on the losing side in your Civil War, I'm not going to deny it, but stop licking your wounds. You can never forget what you've experienced or what you've done, but you can learn to live with it. You have to learn to live with your dead, Fernando, and with the people you killed. The question is why you did it."

"What did Wilson tell you?" he asked in annoyance.

"You killed a prison guard and his son, a soldier, who was part of the firing squad that killed political prisoners. You did it to get revenge for your father. I don't judge you for it. I understand. I would have done the same."

"How dare he make that accusation! And how dare you believe it!"

Zahra's statement had surprised him. He felt that she was being sincere. Yes, she would have done the same as he did.

Suddenly Adela, who had been very quiet and still in his arms, started to murmur that she wanted to play. He put her down on the ground. She ran for the door, and he let her go. Dimitra was nearby, so she would look after the child.

"Shall we go for a walk?" Zahra asked.

Fernando accepted. He would have liked to have told her to leave and that he didn't want to see her again, but he was afraid that if he said those words, they would become a reality.

They went out into the street. For a good long while, they walked alongside one another in silence, without touching. They got to the Pastroudis Cafe. They sat down by a window and ordered two coffees.

"I'm thinking about getting out of here. There's nothing for me in this city," Fernando said, as soon as the waiter had put down the tray with the two coffee mugs and the two glasses of water.

"I understand you."

"That thing that Wilson told you …"

"You know that knowledge is his business. He already told you everything he knew about you. Maybe not in as many words, but he did. At first, he wasn't sure about …"

"About what?" he said, cutting her off and getting ready to leave.

"About the reasons that made you leave Spain and come here with that girl, Catalina. Anyway, he would never have hired you if he hadn't done some research beforehand."

"I'm not interested in the kind of work he wants me to do."

"I understand. It's my fault really."

Fernando was disconcerted by this assertion. He looked at her, waiting for an explanation.

"Benjamin Wilson asked you to go with me that first evening to the Hotel Cecil to observe the Spaniard who had just arrived, the one who was due to make deals with Erick Brander. You know that Brander is German and likes Hitler. The British were keeping an eye on him, discreetly, of course, because he's married to a woman who is very close to the court. I don't do this kind of work, but someone asked Mr. Wilson to look into this Pedro López. He improvised. He didn't have anyone to send that night, and so he asked me, and I thought that it would be a good idea for me to be accompanied by someone who spoke Spanish, because Brander and López might talk in that language. I don't know Spanish, so the idea wasn't preposterous."

"López is a nobody, a vassal of the Franco regime. There's nothing in my country, the war …"

"Yes, I know. He brought letters to certain ministers here. And he was trying to make contacts that were more personal than could be made via diplomatic channels. Diplomats spy on one another here."

"I've learned this as I go along."

"Do you remember the party at Musim Sadat's house?"

"Yes, of course …"

"It was important for me to be there. Not because of López, although that's what Wilson told you, but because members of the Royal Family were to be there that night, to meet with some German agents. I could have just asked Musim to invite me, but I knew that would cause a problem with his wife. Kytzia is very jealous and doesn't trust me at all."

"Well, I'm not surprised at that, given how clear it is that her husband is in love with you."

"That's why Wilson thought that he should try to justify my presence in Cairo by organizing a show there at Fazeli's cabaret. He had insisted for some time that my agent get me a booking in the capital."

"And what need did you have of me?"

Zahra drank a sip of coffee while she tried to find the right words.

"The only way in which Musim could convince Kytzia to invite me was to say that there was a man in my life and that he would come with me to the party. Benjamin and I had previously spoken about finding someone who could pass for ... well, for my lover. It was difficult to find a man who could fit this role, or at least the names that he offered me were more worrying than helpful. But on that night at the Cecil, I realized that I felt safe with you, and that you wouldn't try to take unfair advantage of the situation. I told Benjamin, and asked him to make you my companion on the journey to Cairo."

"You made fun of me! You manipulated me!" Fernando was getting to his feet, ready to leave and abandon Zahra at the cafe. But she took him by the arm and pulled him down.

"Please, don't make a fuss. I don't know why, but I trusted you from the first moment I saw you."

"I had a right to know," he replied angrily.

"Yes ... yes ... I won't say you didn't. But we are at war, Fernando, and you have to be careful before putting all your cards on the table. That's what we did. Then, when Mr. Brossler, Jana's father, asked Benjamin to get his daughter out of Prague, he didn't hesitate in thinking that I had to go and that I would want you to come with me. And now you know the truth."

Fernando said nothing. He wanted to leave and leave her there and never see her again, but on the other hand, he was flattered that she had asked him to be there by her side.

"I'm sorry for causing you this upset," she said.

Fernando said nothing. He needed to think. But Zahra was waiting expectantly for his verdict. And so he decided that since she had manipulated him for her own benefit, he at least had the right to find out who she really was.

"You played a trick on me."

"I'm sad that you see it like that. It wasn't our intention."

"You can't manipulate other people, not even for a good cause. No, I can't trust Wilson and I can't trust you. You are capable of anything. You think that the end justifies the means."

"I won't speak for Wilson, but yes, as for me, I do. We have to defeat Hitler. You are right that Jana was just one of the many people who have had to face up to the horror of the war, but I'm happy to have snatched her from the claws of the Gestapo."

"Even if you had to kill a man to do so," Fernando looked at her resentfully.

"Yes, even if I had to kill Berger. I don't regret it."

"I suppose you sleep well at night."

Zahra hesitated for a couple of seconds. She looked into her empty glass, seeking an answer.

"I haven't always slept well at night," she murmured.

"Who else have you killed, Zahra?"

Fernando's voice was cold and imperious. She looked at him with something akin to indignation. But all she did was bite her lip.

"I killed my father." And as she spoke, her eyes clouded with her memories.

Fernando didn't know what to say. Zahra's statement had confused him.

They sat in silence. Each of them was lost in himself, looking for the right way to put this moment into words.

"I suppose you heard rumors … In Alexandria everyone murmurs about what they know and what they think they know."

"No … Well, I know that your grandmother was a dancer and your mother was as well."

"Dance is a tradition among the women in my family. My mother was very young when she met Jan Dinter. He bewitched her. Tall, handsome, blond, with intense blue eyes. Seductive. While he lived in Alexandria, Jan attracted the admiration and praise of many women. It was difficult not to be swayed by him. My mother started to have a certain reputation as a dancer. My grandmother had trained her well. Dinter came to see her dance and offered to take her to Switzerland, promising her money and fame. But it wasn't that that made my mother agree to go with him. She had fallen in love. My grandmother didn't trust him. She could see that there was nothing to Dinter but selfishness, and that my mother would never be anything to him. But my mother didn't want to hear it, and allowed herself to be seduced by him. And so without telling her own mother, she ran away with Dinter to Switzerland, convinced that once they got there, they would get married. She imagined a future alongside a man who in her mind had become a demigod. He moved her into a little hotel in Zurich. The Great War had not yet begun, but Switzerland, as we know, always remains neutral: that country never loses wars. Dinter's father was a German from Büsingen and his mother was Swiss, from Baden, near Zurich. And so he could have the best of both worlds. Dinter's mother's family was in the property business, and his father traded across the border. Büsingen is a pretty little German town in Switzerland. It was founded by a German knight called Buosingue, which is where it gets its name. It's a part of the Swiss canton of Schaffhausen, and then it became a part of the Austrian Empire. I'll tell you more about its history later, but the fact is that because of its geographical situation, the people who live in Büsingen feel as German as they do Swiss. In fact, they probably feel whatever's most convenient at any particular moment. Jan Dinter, in spite of claiming to be a patriot, didn't fight in the Great War, taking advantage of his Swiss identity at that time. He thought that it was fine for other men to fight for Germany while he got on with his life. He had gone into business with a distant relative of his, Ludger Wimmer, who had inherited a house at the foot of the Alps. He thought that he could turn it into a club, 'The House in the Woods,' where people could go to eat and drink and enjoy all manner of shows. Dinter's job was to hire the artists … musicians, magicians, but above all, dancers … I'm telling you this so you know why he took my mother to Switzerland. She waited impatiently for him to propose marriage. He had wooed her with honeyed words, suggesting that as soon as they left Alexandria, they would be together. But the days passed and the commitment she expected didn't materialize. It was a disappointment for her as well to have to dance in the house that Dinter had turned into a peculiar, discreet cabaret. Men didn't come there to see her dance, but rather to have fun with the women who were there to entertain them, women who worked for Dinter. My mother was not the only attraction. There were other dancers, and the girls ... well, Dinter encouraged them to be very friendly with the clients. To begin with, he wanted my mother just for himself, which made her happy; she managed to console herself, in spite of the disappointment she was starting to feel, with the thought that he was in love with her. But one night, one of the girls told my mother that Jan Dinter was married and that a few months before, he had become the father of a little boy. His wife was called Anke Ziegler and she was very beautiful. Anke's parents were German, from Munich, and friends of Dinter's parents. The two families had an even closer relationship once the war started, and Anke's parents decided to seek refuge in Zurich. You know how these 'patriots' are. But they were well off, in spite of the crisis that was wracking Germany. I think that Anke's father was a wealthy financier. When my mother asked him if it was true that he was married, he didn't deny it. In fact, he admitted it straight out. My mother started to cry and begged for him to send her back to Alexandria, but he laughed at her, saying that she had to earn back the cost of her passage and the cost of supporting her while she lived in Switzerland. Of course, by this time, Jan Dinter was already her lover. She never told me, but I think that this was the first time he hit her. A few days later he forced her to move to a house near the cabaret. It was a very small house, with only a single room for my mother to live in, but she felt lucky compared to the other girls who worked in The House in the Woods. At least she had a degree of privacy. Although being Jan Dinter's lover didn't bring with it any privileges, he was keen on her, and as he was a very shallow man, he enjoyed the envy he provoked among other men, who offered him large sums of money for the privilege of spending a night with her. Even his business partner Ludger Wimmer tried to get him to allow her to go with him. But Dinter liked to say that she was his exclusive property, for the time being."

Zahra looked for the waiter. Her glass of water was empty, and she felt her mouth becoming dry. Maybe she needed to pause her story. Fernando thought that she was visibly aging as she spoke. Her eyes had lost their sheen, her lips were pursed, her face was bitter, and her forehead was wrinkled.

He didn't ask her anything. He was moved by what she had said and was afraid that if he said a single word more, then she would withdraw from him, and wouldn't say any more of her secrets that it caused her so much pain to reveal.

Once the waiter had brought another couple of coffees and filled the water glasses, Zahra carried on talking without looking at him. It was as though she were talking to herself.

"When the Great War came to an end, Dinter decided to move to Berlin, convinced that the people would need fun and relaxation after so much suffering. My mother followed him. I had been born by his point, although Dinter had done all that he could to avoid making her pregnant, and thought that she had fallen pregnant just to tie him to her. He beat her so badly that she was in bed for weeks and almost lost me. My mother begged to be allowed to return to Alexandria but he refused, not because he loved her, but because he was infatuated with her. And the public was infatuated with her as well, all those men who came to the House in the Woods desired her. When I was born, I was registered under the name Mandisa Rahim."

"So ..." This story was making Fernando ever more confused. "So, your name is Mandisa ..."

"Not now. But that was the name I was given in the Zurich registry office. Do you know what Mandisa means? Sweet."

"And your surname?"

"My mother's father was called Abir Rahim, so as a single mother she registered me under her maiden name. Dinter was married, but he'd never have acknowledged me in any case. I was an annoyance, an inconvenience that he wanted to be rid of. If my mother had been a success in puritan Zurich, then it was clear that when the war ended, she would be a great success in Berlin. And so when the war ended, Dinter installed his family in a beautiful house on the Unter den Linden and opened a new business along with his business partner Ludger Wimmer. The Rosy-Fingered Dawn, it was called, a cabaret that soon became one of the favorite venues for everyone in Berlin. Jan Dinter by this time had had another child with his legitimate wife. We lived in a very bright apartment on Sophienstrasse, very close to the Bäckerei Balzer, where they sold the best pastries and the best cake … and the bread … I can still remember the smell of fresh bread …. Dinter had tried to push my mother to have an abortion, and once we were in Berlin, he insisted that I be handed over to the parish. He didn't want to assume any responsibility for me. He had his own children, and I was nothing more than a bastard who had pushed her way into his life. Dinter threatened her with handing me over to the parish if my mother missed even one day of work. My mother grew desperate. She didn't know anyone in Berlin, so she had no one to hand me over to while she danced. But if God exists, then He took pity on her, because in front of our apartment lived an elderly couple who took pity on my mother. The Levinsons were Jews. Gedeon had been a teacher and his wife Betania was a violinist, but because of their age and the war, they had lost a lot of their money, and so they lived hand to mouth. Frau Levinson reached an agreement with my mother that they would look after me in the evenings until she got back from the cabaret. Part of the money that Dinter paid my mother she used to pay Frau Betania. My mother worked constantly. She was the main attraction at the cabaret. The Berliners applauded her enthusiastically. She was very different from them, not simply because of her appearance, but because Oriental dances were the height of exoticism. When my mother came out onstage and danced her belly dance, the public went wild. Many men offered Dinter huge sums of money to be allowed to spend the night with her. But however much they begged, Dinter doubled down and said that she was for him alone. Some time went by, and then Dinter started to become interested in politics. There were people who came to the club who were upset at the conditions imposed upon Germany by the Treaty of Versailles. Dinter started to go to political meetings and to imitate the fury of these humiliated Germans. He didn't care how well the cabaret was doing: the Rosy-Fingered Dawn was packed every evening. I grew up in the face of Dinter's indifference. When he came to visit my mother, he sent me to the Levinsons' house. I couldn't leave there until my mother came to find me. I must admit that I didn't care all that much. I spent so much time with Frau Betania and Herr Gedeon that I had started to think of them as my grandparents. They were always kind and patient with me. Herr Gedeon taught me to read and write. He said that even though the war had made them poor, he still felt rich because of his books. I took some time to realize that Jan Dinter was my father. I didn't really think I needed a father, not until I went to school. I realized that all the children there had a father and a mother, and one day I plucked up the courage to ask my mother where my father was. She sat me on her lap and started to cry. She told me that Jan Dinter was my father and that he didn't like children very much, and it was better not to annoy him, and not to say anything to anyone. But I wanted to know, if Dinter was my father, why I had a different name. My mother couldn't give me a good answer and just told me to be happy with the name I had, Rahim, my grandfather's name. And so I was Mandisa Rahim, which made all the children in my class laugh at me and say I wasn't German, because my name was so odd. And no one had the same last name as their mother. Herr Gedeon comforted me by saying that I should be proud, that no one in Germany had the same name as me. But that just made me feel confused. My father ignored me, or shoved me away whenever I came near him; not only did I have a different name from him, I had to share a name with my mother. I think I was nine or ten the first time I saw my father hit my mother. She was sick, and when he came to pick her up, she begged him to be allowed to have just one night off from the cabaret. He wouldn't budge, and said that he was paying her living without getting anything in return. This was a lie, of course, because my mother filled the Rosy-Fingered Dawn every night. He pulled her out of bed and dragged her around the room, insisting that she get dressed. My mother begged him to stop and he started beating her. I got scared and started to shout, 'Leave my mother alone, leave her, she's sick, you're a bad man.' He pushed me to the floor and knocked me out. I don't know what happened next. When I woke up, Betania was holding me in her arms and Gedeon was promising to tell me all the stories he knew if I would only stop crying. But I shouted that I wanted to go to my mother. That was the first night I started to hate my father. I didn't see my mother until the next evening. Betania and Gedeon looked after me. My mother came back at dawn and fell into bed, exhausted. When I saw her, I was shocked to see the bruises on her arms and legs. Later, I found out that when Dinter beat her, she would put makeup on the bruises and also swathe herself in long strips of silk when she danced. The Levinsons spoke to Dinter. Gedeon didn't conceal his antipathy towards him; he said that he should intervene when he heard my mother's screams and Dinter beat her. But his wife advised him to be cautious, because he was too old to face up to a much younger man, and also his intervention would make things worse for everyone, given that Dinter had become an open sympathizer of the National Socialist Party. Herr Gedeon was a Social Democrat, and he was worried and disgusted at the way the Nazi Party was able to poison so many people with its rhetoric. And he was scared because he could see the way in which anti-Semitism, as promoted by Hitler, was becoming a big part of their worldview. In June 1926, the Berlin newspapers reported one of the speeches that Hitler had given in Munich, a speech that had helped him take over the party. The Austrian was obsessed with Jews and Marxists, and he knew how to inflame his followers. Jan Dinter never showed the slightest interest in me. He never kissed me, never showed me any signs of affection. When he came to our apartment, he ordered me to leave and I left at once. I asked myself why my father was so different from the fathers of other children. I didn't get many invitations to go around to people's houses, but when I went to birthday parties, I envied the warm and festive atmosphere that would always be on display in their homes. In Germany, in the mid-twenties, it started to be a problem to be 'different.' I was often asked if I was a Gypsy. My skin color proved that I was not a true German. And although I had German blood, Dinter's horrid German blood, I inherited barely anything from him."

"Your eyes are blue," Fernando said, regretting his words as soon as they interrupted her story.

Zahra looked at him in confusion and then smiled.

"Yes, depending on the light my eyes are dark blue ... but my skin is dark and so is my hair."

"Chestnut ... you have chestnut hair," he said.

"Do you think I could pass for German?"

Fernando paused. He didn't know what to say. Zahra seemed beautiful to him, but he had never thought that her beauty might be a question of race.

"You speak German perfectly."

"Yes, and that worries them. But I'm not really Aryan. Although the Nazis don't have anything against Arabs and Egyptians. Apparently we're acceptable races."

"So …?"

"So I never looked like the children in my school. It was that straightforward. But I have to admit that my friends' families sighed in relief when they found out I was neither Jewish nor Gypsy. It was acceptable for my mother to be an Egyptian. But the doors closed fast when they found out she was a dancer. An Oriental dancer who allowed people to see her half-naked in a cabaret. You can imagine the scandal. I was not a good companion for these children. And so I didn't go on many visits to these children's houses. But when I did, I envied them for having parents who loved them. My mother tried not to make me suffer and told me that my father was a busy man, with lots to do and not much time to give me. I got used to it. I got used to the fact that my father was little more than a stranger. Sometimes my father would come to the apartment with other men and some of the girls from the cabaret. He liked to organize what he called his 'little parties,' for all that my mother complained about him bringing these people over when I was there. But all he would do was laugh and say that I should go over to the Levinson's house, because that's what we paid Betania for, wasn't it? Once, when he came over, I was in my room and he came to see my mother. I kept very quiet, silent, so I wouldn't have to go to the Levinson's house. I liked to paint, and I was making a painting for my mother. I heard them arguing and was scared when I heard my mother cry. Jan was insulting her and beating her. I went into the room and found them naked, with her on the floor covering her face and him grabbing her by the hair and kicking her. 'Leave my mother alone!' I shouted when he came to beat her again. Dinter pushed me and I fell to the floor. He was going to kick me, but my mother threw herself over me, covering me with her body. This made him angry, and he beat her so much she lost consciousness. I was silent, under my mother's body, almost not breathing. He got dressed and left. I covered my mother with a sheet and went to look for Betania Levinson. My mother was sick for two weeks. Dinter didn't come to see her, but sent one of the girls from the cabaret to ask when she'd be ready to go back to work. That was the only thing that mattered to him. Not one day has passed since then that I haven't cursed him and prayed to God to keep him in hell forever."

Zahra's face was so twisted by suffering and anger that Fernando was frightened. The facade of coldness, self-certainty and wholeness hid more hatred than he had ever seen in his life. He asked himself if he hated the men who had killed his father with the same intensity. And for a moment he tried to fill his head with the fading faces of Roque and Saturnino Pérez, the men he had killed to avenge his father.

"Don't think that everything was bad all those years. My mother did what she could to make sure I was happy. She took me to the Romanisches Cafe to have high tea, down on the Kurfürstendamm, or else to the Buchwald Cafe to buy their specialty, a cake filled with apricot jam and covered in chocolate. At those times I was happy. I didn't need anyone apart from my mother. When we sat in the cafes and I told her all my worries, that all the children in my class were proud to be German but I didn't know what I was to be proud of, she would laugh and say that you only had to look at me to know that I was more Egyptian than German, and then she would tell me tales of the pharaohs, and of the desert, and of the bazaars, and of the joy that was Alexandria ... I was filled with a longing for things I had never seen, which was her own longing for a world she had lost. She told me about my grandmother Yasmin, describing her as a generous woman, the best dancer in Egypt. And she would cry a little as she recalled her father, who she had lost too young when she was just a girl. My mother was a very beautiful woman. You can't imagine how beautiful. I still remember a night when my father decided to take her to the Nelson Theater where the American singer Josephine Baker was performing. She was the star attraction in Berlin, the woman who made the Charleston all the rage. My father didn't normally take my mother out on the town, but that night, when his wife was on a trip out of the city, he

646

decided to go to see Josephine Baker with my mother. He had given her a ruby-colored silk dress with a low-cut top; it clung so close to her body that she looked like a mermaid. My mother seemed happy. Frau Levinson showed me a photo from the newspaper a couple of days later, in which my mother stood surrounded by several men. I felt very proud of her. It was this very photo that made Dinter's wife give him an ultimatum. She must have known about her husband's relationships with the girls at the cabaret, but she didn't think they were important. Her role was more important, the perfect German hausfrau, who gave him strong and healthy children. The girls at the cabaret weren't a danger: they were just pieces of meat for him and his friends to use. But when she saw the photo of my mother … it was too much for her and she asked him to sort the situation out. But Jan Dinter didn't want to give up my mother, much less give up his wife. His father-in-law had become one of the chief financiers of the Nazi Party, and rubbed shoulders with Hitler himself. And so Dinter decided that my mother should leave Berlin for a while. She was in poor health anyway. The Berlin climate affected her lungs, and she had suffered twice from pneumonia. That's why he sent us back to Zurich. We were happy there. I had my mother all to myself, and we weren't affected by the malevolent presence of Dinter. But the clients at the Rosy-Fingered Dawn kept on asking for my mother, so Dinter made her return. The very night that we came back, Dinter gave my mother such a beating that the Levinsons had to take her to the hospital. We were tired from the trip and she decided not to go to the cabaret until the next evening, but he turned up extremely excited at our house and didn't speak about anything apart from how lucky Germany was to have a man like Adolf Hitler at the helm. Then he ordered my mother to get dressed and go to the Rosy-Fingered Dawn, and she told him that we had just arrived and she was too tired to dance that evening. But Dinter didn't listen. He'd given an order and he wasn't going to take it back, so he did as he had done on other occasions and grabbed her by the hair and started to hit her. My mother began to cry, and he hit her with even greater force. I heard her cries; for a few seconds, I covered my ears, but then I left my room and went to my mother's. He pushed me to the floor as soon as he saw me. My mother had hit her head on the bedside table and had lost consciousness. Dinter didn't help her, he just left the room and gave me a kick as he did so. When I heard the door close I got up, trembling, and went to find the Levinsons. They took her to the hospital. The doctor who examined my mother wanted to know what had happened, but she refused to speak out against Dinter, and anyway, it wouldn't have done any good. I trembled every time Dinter came to our house. My mother sent me to the Levinsons, but I preferred to stay in my room, as I was afraid he'd hit her. I would pray for him to leave right away. I chewed my nails and pulled out my hair until I heard him leave. I was afraid of him, but I was also afraid of his business partner Ludger Wimmer. I've already said that at times he would come to our house with other men and girls from the cabaret. My mother would protest and say that he had no respect for her, but he should at least have a little respect for his daughter. But Dinter laughed and said, 'As soon as the little bitch grows up a little, she'll have to start working for me at the Rosy-Fingered Dawn, so start teaching her to dance.' The worst of this was not his threats, but that he allowed his business partner Ludger Wimmer to talk to me in a disgusting way and even try to fondle me, even while Dinter was in the room. My mother would immediately intervene, but Dinter would laugh and say that I was being unfriendly, and that all Wimmer was trying to do was be friendly. On one of those nights, Wimmer came into my room. I was in bed with the covers pulled over my ears so as not to hear the laughter and disgusting words. Ludger Wimmer sat down on the bed and … I suddenly felt his hands lifting my nightdress and heard his breath coming ever faster. I shouted as loud as I could. My mother burst into the room and threw herself on him, pushing him off me. But he knocked her to the floor with a single blow. Dinter came in and started to laugh. My mother shrieked that she wasn't going to let anything happen to me, and Dinter laughed, saying that someone needed to deflower the 'little bitch' and that there was no one better to do that than a real man like his business partner Ludger Wimmer. Two of the girls from the cabaret came into the room and helped me and my mother. They got me to my feet and gave me a robe and shouted abuse at the two men. In spite of the fact that it was still night, my mother sent me to the Levinsons' house. When Gedeon opened the door, he said nothing, merely let me in and called Betania."

"And did he never ... never show you any affection? You were his daughter, after all," Fernando said, astounded by what he was hearing.

"He never thought I was his daughter. I was nothing to him, just an object to use to blackmail my mother. When she threatened to go back to Egypt, he laughed at her and said she couldn't, or else he'd have me kept back in Germany. She could go, but without me. He said that although he hadn't acknowledged me as his daughter, my birth was registered in Zurich and I was Swiss, so I was only in Germany because of him and he could easily have me kept here. They'd have me sent to a boarding school until I was of age. And that's why my mother didn't run away. She was scared that he'd keep his word and separate me from her."

Zahra's story had made Fernando upset, and he had a pain in his stomach. He thought about his parents' unconditional love for him, and it was hard for him to understand Dinter's lack of affection towards his daughter.

"You can't imagine the atmosphere in Berlin in those years ... I was a girl, but I was aware of how anti-Jewish prejudice had risen, as the Nazis accused them of being the cause of all the problems in Germany. They picked them out, saying that economic power was in their hands, and that they were the people who exploited the German nation. The worst of it was that the Germans adopted this anti-Jewish prejudice enthusiastically, persecuting them, pointing them out in the street and blaming them for all their failures. Gedeon Levinson was sad that he and Betania were too old and too poor to be able to leave. Gedeon spoke about 'pogroms,' and said that they were going to be faced with a pogrom the likes of which the Jews had never seen. Betania scolded him and reminded him that they were Germans, good Germans, as German as the others, and that they'd done nothing wrong and so they had no reason to run away. But Gedeon knew the history of the persecution of the Jews and reminded her of the stories one by one until she and I were both drowning in worry and sadness. I didn't want them to leave. Apart from my mother, they were all I had. I couldn't imagine a life without them. I hugged Gedeon close, crying and begging them not to leave, or if they did leave, to take my mother and me with them. At night, before I went to sleep, I imagined what it would be like to live somewhere where we didn't have to see Jan Dinter. I thought that a life without Dinter would be more or less paradise. Dinter was convinced, along with the Zieglers, his parents-in-law, that only Adolf Hitler could make Germany once again into a power respected by the rest of the world. He had become a militant devotee of the Nazi Party, and the Rosy-Fingered Dawn was now one of the preferred cabaret venues for the higher party members and their financiers. They were always well-received at the Rosy-Fingered Dawn and Dinter was most generous to them. One day something terrible happened …"

Zahra's face twisted. She looked into the distance and her hands clenched in her lap. Fernando gave a start. She took a few seconds to regain her composure.

"One night at the cabaret, a SA officer became obsessed with my mother and asked Dinter to arrange a date immediately. Until that moment, Dinter had kept my mother for his own exclusive use, but whether because he was tired of her – or didn't dare contradict one of the SA high command – he ordered my mother to go up to one of the cabaret's private rooms with this man. She refused. And Dinter, as was now his habit, gave her a beating, although he held back a little more than normal because he didn't want to hurt her so much as not to be able to send her to the SA officer. My mother made a decision. She said that she would go with this man, but that he should let her put a bit of makeup on first to cover up the marks from where he had beaten her. He agreed. My mother ran out through the back door. She got a taxi and came home. I was studying. When I heard her return, I came down to see why she was back so early. I saw the mark of Jan Dinter's hand on my mother's face, and the bruises on her arms where she had been beaten. 'He's hit you again! He's a bastard, I hate him!' I said to my mother. She always tried to minimize the significance of the beatings that Dinter gave her, sometimes telling me that the marks were because she had fallen over. But I wasn't a child anymore. I was fourteen years old, and my mother was everything to me. I helped her with her bruises and then insisted that she rest. She asked me to bring her a jug of water, because she was very thirsty. I was getting her a glass of milk in the kitchen when I heard the door slam and Jan Dinter shouting. I stood still, trembling. I was scared of him. 'Bitch! How dare you disobey me! You're going to go to the cabaret right now and get into bed with that man! You're useless! You're lucky that someone noticed you. You're nothing, nothing! You're useless!' He shouted so much that I started to shake, and covered my ears so I didn't hear the horrible things that he said to my mother. Suddenly, I heard a shout that was like an animal's scream, as though someone were being murdered. It was my mother. I don't know how I dared … I found a sharp knife, and went to the room, where he stood with his belt in his hand. There wasn't an inch of her body that he hadn't beaten. Her face was a bloody pulp. She was on the floor, and as well as beating her with his belt he was kicking her. It looked like a hurricane had come through the room. I went in and asked him to leave my mother alone. I think I must have asked him, but I couldn't even hear my own voice. When he saw me, he turned to me and hit me so cruelly with the belt that I fell to the floor. Then he started to laugh and said that since she wasn't good for anything now, he'd have me take her place, and that the SA officer would be as happy to go to bed with the daughter as with the mother. I threw myself down on the floor next to my mother. She was barely breathing. He kicked her again, and I heard something crack. Then … then, I don't know how, but I got up and stuck the knife into him, at the level of his heart. I don't know how I did it, but I pushed it in with all my strength. He was confused. Blood started to gush out. He pushed me to one side … but the knife was sunk so deep in him that he started to stumble. He still had enough strength to insult me, but then he fell to his knees. I saw him lying on the ground, his gaze lost in space. I leaned over my mother's body. She was immobile, her gaze unfocused. I tried to pick her up and get her into bed, but I didn't have the strength. Dinter was bleeding out, and all I wanted was for him to do so as quickly as possible. He took some time to die. Don't ask me how long, I don't know. I stayed with my mother, covering her body with my own, telling her that Dinter would never treat her badly again. I stroked her hair and stared to feel scared when I saw how her eyes didn't move. I had to get help. I jumped over Dinter's body. He was dead, or at least he seemed dead, but I felt that I had to hurt him, so I kicked him in the face with all the strength I could muster, even knowing that he surely didn't feel anything. And I spat on him. I hated him so much! I went to the Levinsons'. Betania shrieked in fright when she saw me. My face, my hands, my legs, my clothing, everything was soaked in blood. Gedeon came to me and asked me to give him the knife, which I still held in my hand. He did so carefully, asking me to keep calm and telling me that I should tell them what had happened. I couldn't speak. I turned around and went back to my apartment and he came with me, as did Betania. They stood stock-still when they came into the room and saw my mother's body, and Dinter's. Betania hugged me, and Gedeon called for an ambulance. Then … I don't really remember what happened. I know that Betania made me take off my bloody clothes and helped me get washed and to dress myself. Then an ambulance came, and the police … They started to ask questions, but the words wouldn't come. I was mute. I didn't not want to speak, I just couldn't. I tried to hold on to my mother's hand and stop them from taking her away from me. I heard the doctor telling the policeman that he couldn't do anything, that the two people were dead. I smiled. Dinter was dead. And the smile turned into a wild laugh. But then I gave a start. Didn't he say that there were two bodies? Was my mother dead? I went over to my mother's body, which was still on the floor wrapped in a sheet. A female police officer stopped me from lifting the sheet, but I bit her and she backed off. I bent over and revealed my mother's body and started to stroke her face. They had closed her eyes and she looked like she was sleeping. Two policemen dragged me off her. I don't remember well what happened next … they took me to a room to interrogate me, but I couldn't speak. I saw a doctor, and then a psychiatrist. They spoke and spoke, but I didn't hear them. I saw them gesticulating, moving their lips, but it was like they were a long way away. I remember that my father's business partner Ludger Wimmer was there, and spoke about me. He said that my mother and I were two common prostitutes who were trying to extort money from an exemplary citizen like Jan Dinter, that he had had to reject my attempts to seduce him. He said that I did the same with Dinter, and that he had even heard me threatening him if he didn't give me and my mother money. I wanted to shout that he was lying, but the words stuck in my throat. He looked at me sidelong and I could see how he hated me. They kept me in a psychiatric institution until the trial. I saw hell in that place. I won't describe it to you. Why should I? They made me take medicine that gave me terrible headaches, and I walked around like I was a ghost. I ... No, I won't tell you what happened there ... They opened the door to my cell one night ... they kept me in restraints on the bed ... and it was him, I'm sure of it, it was Ludger Wimmer, my father's business partner ... he came laughing to my bedside ... The jailer asked him not to make too much noise, and then he gave me an injection and left me alone with him ... I don't know how long I was there ... I don't remember what happened ... I sometimes have nightmares and remember what happened ... But I don't know if it's true ... I see myself lying there, silently, unable to move, and Ludger Wimmer lifts my nightdress ... I feel deep pain, and fear, sharp fear. I can't speak, I can't shout, I can't move, but I see his hands coming close to me ... There was a trial a few months later. The day of the trial, they sat me next to a man who they told me later was my lawyer. That was the only time I saw him. He hadn't even come to see me in the psychiatric institution where they had me locked away. I saw Betania and Gedeon in the public gallery. Betania was crying and Gedeon tried to console her. They looked at me tenderly, suffering because I was suffering. The lawyer for Jan Dinter's family called them as witnesses. They had been threatened if they didn't testify against me. They were pressured again and again to state that I had murdered Jan Dinter, but they didn't. They repeated again and again that I had come to their house in an emotional state, trying to explain that Dinter mistreated my mother, but neither Dinter's lawyer nor mine would allow this to go on the record. They said that this was not the issue, and the important thing was to find out if I had killed him. Ludger Wimmer, my father's former business partner, was the chief witness. He went up onto the stand and repeated his lies, although I barely remember his words, given that the medicine I was on had turned me into a creature without a soul. He said in the trial the same lies that he had told the police. He said that my mother was trying to extort my father, that she was a prostitute and that I was one as well, in spite of my young age, and that I liked to provoke men, and that I had on more than one occasion thrown myself at him and offered myself shamelessly to him. He accused me of killing Jan Dinter. He described a scene that never took place: my mother and I threatening Dinter and demanding money from him. He said that Dinter had tried to defend himself and had struggled with my mother, who had managed to strike herself and kill herself in the struggle. Then I had thrown myself on him and stabbed him. It didn't matter that the Levinsons said the opposite, that they explained how my mother had been beaten brutally, and that this was not the first time something like this had happened. My lawyer didn't ask the doctors from the scene to be called to the stand, nor the people who had carried the body away. It was a farce, I was condemned before the trial had even begun. No one cared why I had killed Dinter. Over the three days of the trial, I constantly felt a woman's eyes on me. Anke Ziegler, Jan Dinter's wife, was sitting in the front row and didn't look away for a second. She looked at me with disgust and hatred. I thought that she must feel the same way about me as I felt about her husband. She was called to the witness stand, and Anke Ziegler said that Jan Dinter was an exemplary husband, who had been approached by my mother, and that he, like the good husband and family man that he was, had resisted the advances of 'that woman,' the dancer who performed at the Rosy-Fingered Dawn. They didn't ask her what he was doing in my house that evening, or why he had beaten my mother to death. The only important person was Dinter. The judge declared that I was guilty and that I should spend the rest of my life in an asylum. I saw the despair on the faces of Gedeon and Betania. But I was no longer a human being by then. I was just a husk in human form. My head no longer belonged to me, thanks to the drugs the doctors gave me. They took me back to a little cell, and every night they tied me to my bed. The jailer pushed me around, afraid that she had a murderer on her hands. Ludger

Wimmer came back once more. The jailer had tied my hands and I couldn't defend myself, so he could abuse me at his leisure. After a few months, just before dawn one night, a jailer came into my room, followed by three people. Two men and a woman dressed as a nurse. The nurse smiled at me and injected me with something. When I woke up, I didn't know where I was. I heard whispers and felt a hand stroking my forehead. I was comforted by the smell of flowers that came from the person who was touching me. Her hand was soft, and I heard her saying words that I didn't understand, but which calmed me. I think I took several hours to regain consciousness. When I did so, I still didn't realize that I was on a train. But I looked around and saw several people around me. Two women and two men, as well as Gedeon and Betania. The presence of the Levinsons relieved me. I was so scared of people I didn't know. Betania leaned over me and smiled, saying, 'You're free now, Mandisa, you're free now. No one can do anything to you now.' Gedeon was at her side and seemed happy. 'Child, a doctor's going to have a look at you, you'll be fine soon.' A tall man with a kind smile came over to me and started to take my pulse very carefully. I let him do it. The medicine had left me in a haze, so I couldn't resist anymore. I felt that the place where I was lying was moving, but it took me months to find out that I had taken the train from Koblenz to The Hague. I barely remember anything that happened over those days, although I remember Betania's voice. 'Do you remember the pretty stories your mother told you, Mandisa? You'll love Alexandria. You'll get better there,' she said, although I didn't understand her words. When the train stopped, a man took me in his arms, and I tried to fight him with what little strength I had left. Fear had come back and taken control of me again. I didn't want to leave Betania and Gedeon, who were my only anchors, and so when Betania came over to calm me, I held her tight round the neck. The tall, friendly man spoke to me and another man carried me. Then I realized that the tall man was the doctor and that he had decided that the Levinsons should come with me, that their presence was a part of the treatment I needed to get better. They put me on a boat in The Hague, a boat you know well: the *Esperanza del Mar*, Captain Pereira's ship. Yes,

'The Portuguese.' But I didn't even realize they were putting me on a boat. My mind was still foggy. I'll explain so you understand. Gedeon had written to my grandmother to tell her what had happened. A letter that spared no detail. He trusted that my grandmother would reply, and she did more than that: she decided to come to Berlin and bring me back with her to Alexandria. She managed it thanks to Benjamin Wilson; yes, my grandmother spoke to Wilson and asked him to help her get me out of Berlin. It wasn't easy. The Levinsons didn't know which institution I had been taken to after the trial, so the first thing they needed to do was to find me. Three weeks, yes, three weeks was how long it took Benjamin Wilson to find out where I was. I was condemned to die there. For those few months, the doctors had tried out various drugs on me, drugs that stripped away my free will, which dried out my soul, making me into a body with no thoughts, no words, no free will. Wilson is a great man for finding people, just like his grandfather was. He does what needs to be done. So when he found out where I was, he organized the operation to get me out of there. He told my grandmother to pick a new name for the documentation he would prepare with a new identity. My grandmother chose Zahra, which means flower, or bloom, or brilliant … and then added her own surname, Nadouri. And that's what my name is today, that's who I am. Mr. Wilson's man in Germany took a nurse and a doctor and organized my 'abduction' from the hospital. What they did was buy me. Yes, the people who worked at the hospital had no compassion for the patients: we were only flesh, flesh for them to experiment on. And if the doctors treated us like that, you can imagine how we were to the jailers and the guards: nothing, less than nothing. They bribed some of the men who worked there and were then able to come in and get me out of that hell on Earth. My grandmother and the Levinsons were waiting for me at the station, and from there we went to The Hague and then on the *Esperanza del Mar* to Alexandria. I owe my life to my grandmother, to Benjamin, and to the Levinsons. I told you that the doctor advised them to be close to me, as they were my only link to the land of the living. My grandmother agreed and invited them to live with her in Alexandria. Betania loved me very much, but to begin with, she didn't want to leave her home, although Gedeon had no such qualms. He was well aware that Germany was no place now for Jews, and so they traveled with us. You can imagine the rest. I took months to start to speak again, to get all the drugs that had broken my will out of my system, and above all to understand what had happened. My grandmother did all she could. And the Levinsons were an important part of my cure. They helped me put together the puzzle of what had happened that night with Dinter, and what had happened after that. I owe them so much … My grandmother, Betania and Gedeon, Benjamin and the doctors: they gave me my life back. That's why I'm here, Fernando, and that's why I do what I do. I owe Benjamin Wilson a great deal. But don't be mistaken, don't think that I regret taking my father's life. I won't tremble on the day when I go back to Berlin and kill Ludger Wimmer. I'll have to wait for the war to end, but I will kill him. I owe it to myself."

Fernando was overwhelmed by the long story he had just heard. He didn't know what to say, because any words would have been out of place. They sat in silence, each one recovering from the terrible tale. Then Zahra held out her hand to Fernando and they left the coffee shop. He followed her like she was a guide dog. She took him back to her house, a beautiful building by the sea. Zahra took him to her room and there it was their bodies that said all the words they had to say. The hours went by with no need for words. Skin against skin, eyes locked with eyes. And it was night when Zahra got up and told him to wait. She put a robe on and came back after a while with a tray which held dates, cheese, hummus, pita bread and fruit. They sat on the terrace and ate, letting their eyes drift over the surface of the water, afraid that if they spoke, their words might separate them.

Fernando wondered if there were anyone else in this house, although he knew that Zahra lived with her grandmother.

They sought refuge once more between the sheets. It was dawn when Fernando woke up. Zahra wasn't there. With a start, he got up and got dressed. When he came out of the room, he met a young woman who told him that there was a car ready to take him home. The house was silent. He didn't dare ask about Zahra. It wasn't necessary. Now he knew why she was how she was, and above all why she hadn't been in the bed when he woke up. She was someone who had traveled through the depths of hell and who had been able to escape. Someone who had beaten the demons who lived within her. Someone who, after so much suffering, would never belong to anyone.

And so he allowed himself to be led to the door. There was a car waiting for him and the door was open. He didn't need to say where he was going: the driver already knew.

When he got home, he found Ylena in the dining room looking over some papers and drinking a cup of coffee. She invited him to sit with her and Fernando accepted. She looked at him with interest, but didn't ask any questions.

Fernando looked at her with curiosity. He lived in the house of this generous Greek woman because of Captain Pereira. Pereira had been brought by fate into his life and Zahra's.

He went to Wilson & Wilson that very morning. When he went in, he found Sara Rosent dusting the shelves. She smiled and came over to meet him.

"Benjamin won't be in this morning, but he'll be pleased to know that you're back at work. Our dear Athanasius Vryzas is overwhelmed. We need you so much, Fernando ..."

Sara took him by both hands and didn't need to say any more. Fernando felt sincere affection for this woman. He had felt it ever since the first time he saw her. Everything about Sara was a question of equilibrium, serenity, and bibliophilia. There was nothing that pleased her more than books. And she had always been affectionate towards him. He was sure that he had been hired by Wilson not only because of Farida's recommendation, but also because Sara had put in a good word for him.

She took him through to the room where Vryzas and the other editors were looking closely at the texts they were preparing for the publishing house.

When Vryzas saw him, he was unable to hide the disappointment he felt that Fernando had returned. He had convinced himself that Fernando had followed his advice and was looking for his own Ithaca.

It was May of 1943, and the Egyptians were stunned by the surrender of the Axis forces in North Africa.

In the cafes of Alexandria, they were still arguing about the way in which the German High Command had fallen out, the arguments between Rommel and General von Arnim, who at the beginning of the year had been in charge of the west, while Rommel had stayed in the east with his Afrika Corps. The soldiers had argued about the best way to act, and Rommel had fought his last battle in March and then headed back to Berlin. Apparently he was in very poor health.

On May 12, the German forces were definitively routed, and General von Arnim surrendered to the British General Alexander.

For some people, the British triumph was a relief; for others, it was a disappointment. Every Alexandrian had placed his hopes on one outcome or the other.

Fernando asked himself when he would see Zahra again. They hadn't met since the night they spent together. He didn't dare seek her out, because he was sure he would upset her. He knew how much it had cost her to unveil her body and her soul. All he could do was wait, and in the meantime, sink into the routine of daily life.

It was odd for him to see Benjamin Wilson again. But he was the man he was. When he saw him sitting once again at the table, deep in a manuscript Vryzas had given him to study, Wilson came over to him and slapped him on the back. Nothing more. Not a word, not any sign other than that.

The months passed. Benjamin Wilson didn't ask him to do any more special work, and let him get on with editing under Vryzas' supervision.

10

Catalina was brushing Adela's hair and thinking about how to break down the wall that Fernando had built up between himself and the rest of the world. They hadn't spoken openly for months. They were engaged in their daily life, routines which allowed them to survive, but very little else. They hadn't spoken again about leaving. She wasn't unhappy – in fact, she felt a little ashamed about how happy she was – but she was aware that a decision was pending that would affect the rest of her life, and she had to make a choice, if only for her daughter.

There were only a few days left before the end of the year. The end of the Christian year, of course, because since living in Alexandria, they had also grown accustomed to celebrating significant Islamic dates. Friday, a sacred day for Muslims, was now a holiday for them. They also celebrated Eid al-Adha, the festival of sacrifice that took place on the tenth day of the twelfth month of the Islamic lunar calendar. And Mawlid al-Nabi, the birthday of the Prophet, or else Muharram, the beginning of the Islamic year.

It was impossible to live in Alexandria without doing so. But the city was not unaware of the celebrations of other religions. And now it was time to say goodbye to the Christian year.

Ylena had told her lodgers that she would invite some friends over to celebrate. She and Dimitra had spent days discussing the menu they would serve on the last day of the year. Ilora the cook didn't listen to them all that much. She knew she would have the last word.

Dr. Naseef had accepted the invitation, as had Father Lucas.

She stopped thinking about the end-of year-celebrations and went back to considering Fernando. She couldn't bear to think of the melancholy that now surrounded him. Not even Adela was able to pull him out of his self-absorption.

Their relationship was a special one. The girl treated him as though he were her father. She loved him with a spontaneous wellspring of love, and ran to see him whenever he came in through the door.

Fernando loved the girl. She was the only person he paid any attention to. He would sit next to her every evening and read her a story until she fell asleep. If Fernando was late home, then Adela wouldn't go to sleep. She would stay awake until she heard him coming.

On his days off, when it wasn't too cold, Fernando would take Adela for a walk along the seafront. Often a simple walk would turn into a full-day excursion. To begin with, Catalina had been worried when they had not come back at the arranged time, but she had become used to Fernando's habit of forgetting to look at the clock when he was with the girl.

They heard the street door open, and Adela ran off barefoot, leaving Catalina with the brush in her hand.

Fernando picked her up and scolded her for running around barefoot. Even so, she kissed him.

Catalina came out to meet him.

"I think she can sense when you're about to come. She was impatient and didn't want to go to bed," she said with a smile.

They carried out their nightly ritual. He read her a story, and Adela closed her eyes until she was asleep. Then Fernando went to the dining room to eat with the other lodgers.

He barely paid any attention to the discussion between Mr. Sanders and Monsieur Baudin. They spoke about the Allied advance into Italy. For Baudin, the fact that that Allies had now liberated Rome was a cause for great relief.

When they had finished the meal, Catalina asked Fernando if they could talk. He accepted reluctantly, and invited her to come to his room. He knew that when Catalina wanted to speak in such a manner, it was because she didn't want anyone to hear them.

Fernando left the door to his room half open, but Catalina closed it.

"Oh, I thought you might want to hear if Adela woke up."

"I don't think she will. She normally sleeps like a log. And if she does wake up, then she knows how to get out of her bed and leave the room. Also, she's got a pair of lungs on her ..."

"Well, what's up?" he asked.

"I don't know how to put it ... But I can't stop thinking about how much you've changed ... You're so sad, so ... absent ... I don't know what happened to you on your trip to Prague, but you're not the same as you were ... I thought that as time went by, you'd get better, but that hasn't happened ... I don't understand your relationship with ... with that dancer. The only thing I know is that you aren't well. Don't you trust me anymore? Don't you think I can help you?"

"What silly things you say! There's nothing special going on," Fernando said, but not with much conviction.

"Please, Fernando, don't underestimate me!" she said angrily.

Fernando looked at her and saw once again his childhood friend, the impatient and capricious girl who was also generous and always willing to stand up for him.

"I would never do that," he said sincerely.

"Well, then, tell me the truth. Trust me."

"The truth? What is truth? I feel trapped, Catalina, trapped in this city. The worst of it is not that I feel trapped, but that I don't have the strength to get out of here. I let the days go by and I feel ever more desperate."

"Fernando, let's get out of here. I'm all right, although it's hard to admit it; when I don't think about my parents or about Spain, then I feel peace. There are even days when I don't think ... don't think about Marvin ... But I keep asking myself if my real place is here. You said you wanted to go to France to meet up with Eulogio again, or at least find out where he is. Well, let's go. We'll be closer to Spain as well."

"Impossible. Have you forgotten there's a war on? France is in the hands of the Germans, Free France no longer exists; it isn't even a caricature of what it once was. They could arrest us, send us to a labor camp. And what would become of Adela? Don't think

I'm not worried about Eulogio. I keep asking Sara if she has any news, but she never does. As for Marvin … I told you that after they tried to save Monsieur Rosent, he stayed in Switzerland for a while and then went to New York with Farida, although I don't know if they're still there."

"Well, let's go to New York then. Mr. Wilson can help us."

"I don't want to go to New York. I don't know if I want to go anywhere."

"Because you're in love with Zahra?" she asked.

"Zahra … I won't deny that Zahra is important for me, but I don't know how much. I don't even know if staying here has anything to do with her … I don't know … I can't get my feelings in order. I move through the world day by day, trying not to think."

"You can't go on like this. You don't have to be unhappy. It's not fair, Fernando."

Catalina came over to him and hugged him tight, as tight as she could. He let himself be wrapped in her arms, though he was no longer sure of his true feelings for her.

They held one another for a good long time, in silence, each listening to the other's breath. When they eventually separated, they felt better. It was as though sharing the warmth of their bodies had allowed them to go back to the childhood they had left behind.

"Yes, we have to do something," Catalina insisted, as she lit a cigarette, which she then passed to Fernando as she lit another one for herself.

"We can't go to France, and I don't want to go to New York," he said.

"When will this war end?" she asked, knowing that there was no answer.

"Never. I don't know, I really don't know. You heard Colonel Sanders and Monsieur Baudin talking about the Allied advance. But who knows what might happen."

"At least the English have beaten the Germans here. Rommel and his Afrika Korps seemed invincible, and look what's happened to them."

"Why don't you go back to Spain?" he said, knowing the answer.

"I'd like to, believe me. And I would if it weren't for Adela. But you know that I can't go back to Spain where Adela would be looked down on, the daughter of a single mother, a daughter without a father … they'd be cruel to her and make her suffer. I'm not going back because of her, because of her and because of my parents. I couldn't make them go through this shame. I love my daughter more than anyone in the world, and I won't let anyone treat her badly, humiliate her. There's no place for us in Spain, at least not now. All I can do is go home as Marvin's wife."

"Or another man's. You could marry Dr. Naseef. He'd marry you any day of the week. You know he's in love with you."

"I don't know that … or I don't want to know. I'm not in love with him. I can't lie to you, so I'll admit he's an attractive man and I get along well with him. I'm flattered by his infatuation with me, but I wouldn't marry him."

"And you don't want to marry me."

Catalina sat in silence. Fernando saw her bite her lip, then get another cigarette out and light it.

"I don't want there to be anything left to say after tonight. I want to be honest with you. We've had time to look at ourselves, at how we are on the inside. I've been thinking about you for months, Fernando, about what I feel for you. I love you and you know that, but I'm not in love with you. Could I be? Maybe … you know how I was brought up … I was told so many times that love is something that grows over time, that the important thing is respect, affection, shared principles … You and I respect each other, and of course we have affection for one another, we love one another, we have shared principles, and we've been brought up together. But is it enough? I don't think it is, not for either of us. We both want more. We might be happy, and have a relationship with no problems, based on solid and sincere affection. It would be my salvation, but you deserve better."

"I've loved you ever since we were children," he reminded her.

"Yes, that's true, but do you still love me in the same way? I think you don't, Fernando, I really think you don't. Marvin came into my life, and Zahra Nadouri came into yours. You may not want to accept it, but I think that this woman has touched your heart in the same way that Marvin touched mine. There are two people between the pair of us: Marvin and Zahra. Can we be happy if we set them aside?"

"What's the answer, then?" Fernando asked.

"I won't lie to myself. I don't want to lie to myself. And so, because we love each other so much, because we have one another, we need to make a decision."

"If there wasn't a war on, then maybe we could, but where will we go? You don't want to go back to Spain, and I don't have anywhere to go."

"If the Allies win the war, they won't let a dictator like Franco run Spain."

"I'm not so sure, Catalina … I'm not so sure … the great powers have their own interests. We'll see who wins, and what's left of Europe when the war ends. Until then, maybe there's nothing we can do apart from wait."

"I don't want to wait. We'll grow old waiting!"

"Well, what are we going to do?"

"Leave, Fernando, go somewhere. If you won't go to France, then at least let's go to America. Why should you care about where we go? You know that I have to find Marvin and sort out once and for all my situation with him. I want him to acknowledge his daughter and see if he can deny the connection between us. My life depends on this conversation with Marvin. Help me."

"And what will we do in New York? How will we live?"

"If we've managed to survive here, I don't see why we shouldn't survive in New York. You speak excellent English, and could carry on working as an editor. Wilson could recommend you somewhere. As for me … I don't know what language I speak anymore, I can speak Arabic and English, a little Greek as well, because Dimitra teaches me phrases … I'll do anything. I don't care. I'll clean people's houses. They must need housemaids everywhere."

"Catalina, for God's sake! I'd never let you become a maid!"

"Why not? It's a job like any other. I don't know how to do anything else but play the piano. I didn't finish school."

"You had a good education."

Catalina laughed and hugged him again, although more lightly this time.

"Yes, I know when a table is properly laid. I know what each piece of cutlery is for. I never pick my nose, or sit with my legs apart. I can dress for every occasion. I can be a good hostess, I can keep a conversation going, and make sure that people are feeling comfortable. I can even chat pleasantly about things I don't really know about. Oh, and I know how to sew. Do you think that's a good education, Fernando? I'm not so sure."

"You've just drawn a caricature of how things really are. You know that a good education consists of other things."

"Really? Like what?"

"You're certainly worth more than what you've just said."

"Thank you for thinking that about me. You're the only person whose opinion I care about. I don't know what would have happened to me without you. I don't know if I could have survived. When I think about how we got here … What we went through on Captain Pereira's boat … and then in this city. I thought I was going to go crazy. I didn't understand anything, and it was all so strange to me … But I didn't like anything I saw. And now … you see, I can understand Alexandria. I won't say I've uncovered its soul, but at least I don't feel so alien in it."

They were still talking when dawn broke. Fernando had unburdened his conscience to Catalina's ears. He told her how he had been manipulated by Benjamin Wilson, and why he had gone with Zahra to Prague. He didn't hide from her the fact that he'd been forced to kill again, and that the dead came to him when he closed his eyes.

She wasn't shocked, and didn't judge him. She listened attentively, and when Fernando had finished telling her everything he had been through in the months that he had been so distant from her, Catalina told him that she understood, and that he had done what he had to do. There wasn't a single shadow of reproach in her eyes or in her words. He felt comforted to know that she was on his side.

"Sometimes you have to choose between your life and someone else's. You didn't have any choice but to kill that Nazi. I would have done the same," Catalina said.

Fernando knew that this was not just idle comfort, but that Catalina was speaking the truth.

That morning, when Fernando went to work, Sara and Athanasius Vryzas both noticed a change in him. They couldn't say exactly what was different, but the fixed expression on his face had softened a little, and he seemed calmer. Sara and Vryzas thought that this change was probably down to a woman, maybe Zahra. Yes, maybe he had spent the night with the dancer.

Fernando asked Leyda Zabat, Wilson's secretary, to tell him when her boss came in. Leyda said that Wilson wouldn't be in that day. He was in Cairo, and wouldn't be back until the next day, which was the last day of the year. He'd have to wait to speak to him.

Later on, Sara waved him over to talk to her. She invited him to a New Year's Eve party at her house; Zahra would be attending. But Fernando made his excuses, as he was to eat at Ylena's house with the other lodgers. He was already committed to this, although he thanked Sara for the invitation.

She did not try to get him to change his mind.

Catalina and Fernando seemed happy on the last night of 1943. Or at least that was how they appeared at the meal.

Ylena was surprised that Catalina seemed to be paying no attention to Dr. Naseef, for all that he was very attentive to her. She didn't miss the glances that Fernando and Catalina exchanged either, and wondered if maybe the two of them had decided to do what would be best for them, and what was of course the most sensible course of action: get together as a couple.

Father Lucas also looked at them and wondered what had happened between the pair of them, and felt sad to see Dr. Naseef's disappointed gaze. The doctor felt a little out of place.

Once they had raised a toast to 1944, the guests started to leave. It was after midnight, and tomorrow Alexandria would be the same as it always was.

Catalina went to see if Adela was sleeping, and then went to Fernando's room. Ylena saw her go in. What she could not imagine was that the intimacy between them was made of nothing more than words. Fernando spoke once again of Zahra, his feelings towards her, his confusion. They didn't hide anything from one another. They had found each other again and made up for lost time, aware that although they had been living underneath

667

the same roof for two years, they had grown very distant from one another.

They made a decision: they were not going to let more time go by without writing to their families in Madrid. They knew that Isabel and Asunción must both be suffering terribly.

Fernando did not see Zahra for quite some time. He didn't look for her, and she did nothing to let herself be found again.

They didn't see one another until well into March 1944, when he went to a literary evening at the bookshop. Sara kept on promoting Wilson & Wilson as a place where poetry and philosophy could be discussed. Fernando liked these evenings. He had managed to pick up enough Arabic to follow the thread of the discussions, although English and French were the chief languages spoken among the people who came to Sara's evening sessions.

He didn't know that she was going to be there on that March evening, when the bad news came through that the Wehrmacht had taken Hungary.

Sara welcomed Zahra affectionately, gently scolding her for not coming to the previous evenings. She apologized and reminded Sara that her grandmother was not well, and that she barely left her house except to go to work.

Fernando didn't know what to do. Should he wait for her to beckon him over, or go straight up to her himself? He chose for the second option, going to stand in front of her while he felt the gazes of the other people present fix themselves on them. There were many people in Alexandria who thought that they had been lovers, but that over the last few months, their relationship had cooled, so seeing them together was a cause for lively speculation.

Zahra smiled, and he immediately relaxed. Sara stood aside and left them alone.

"I'm happy to see you," she said sincerely.

"I didn't want to bother you," he said.

"You did right. I needed to think. After what we went through, I needed to put myself back together. It wasn't easy. And my grandmother has been very ill."

"I'm sorry," said Fernando.

"She's better now, but I feared for her life. I don't know what I would have done if … if she had died."

"If you had told me, I could have helped with whatever you needed … or at least come to keep you company."

"I didn't feel alone. Sara and Benjamin were with me."

"Oh, I didn't know that. They could have told me …"

"No, they couldn't. I didn't want them to tell you anything. I preferred not to see you, Fernando."

He didn't know how to interpret her words, but they stung.

Athanasius Vryzas came over to tell them to take their seats. The young poet was about to read from a book that had been published that very day.

They sat next to one another, and although they seemed to be listening to the poems, they were actually paying them no attention at all. Both Fernando and Zahra were trying to work out what the other felt or thought.

When the reading was over, Sara opened the floor to debate, and her guests, as they always did, participated enthusiastically. Fernando was usually one of the first to speak, but on this occasion, he stayed silent.

It was late evening by the time Sara said goodbye to her last guests. Zahra had offered to take Sara home in her car, as Benjamin had not come to the reading. She accepted, which was a problem for Fernando, as he wanted to be alone with Zahra again.

He didn't sleep well that night. Zahra was in his dreams, and he woke up early, covered in sweat. He opened the window to let the sweet spring air into his room.

He couldn't fool himself. Zahra was avoiding him. She had seemed happy to see him, and she had even sat next to him, very close, when they had been at the poetry reading. But then she had left and said goodbye indifferently.

No, he mustn't fool himself. He must realize that he had lost her.

The next day, he went to the bookshop before Vryzas and the rest of the editors arrived. Leyda Zabat was still the gateway to Benjamin Wilson. Fernando asked her if he could see Wilson, and she let him go through at once.

Benjamin Wilkson seemed worried, but he was his normal

amiable self with Fernando. They spoke for a while about the publishing house and the latest rumors about how the war was going. When the conversation started to falter, Fernando took out two envelopes and handed them over.

Benjamin Wilson looked at the addresses and waited for Fernando to speak.

"I want to make sure that these get to Madrid. Catalina Vilamar's family and mine have spent too long without hearing from us. We don't want them to know where we are, so I came to you."

"I'll try to get them delivered as soon as possible."

They didn't say anything else.

11

Madrid

It was hot. Too hot. Almost as hot as it was in Seville. The man took the handkerchief from his jacket pocket and wiped the sweat from his head. He had been living in Madrid for some time, but he didn't think of it as his turf. Seville was his home, because that's where his parents lived. But the war had upset his life, just as it had affected everyone in Spain, so he had adjusted himself to living in Madrid, which was where he could get work. He looked at his watch in annoyance. He had been walking around all morning, trying to avoid catching anyone's attention. La Calle de la Encarnación was empty and silent. Only the bells at the Monastery of la Encarnación broke the monotony. He walked back to the Plaza de la Encarnación and sat down in front of the monastery. He could keep an eye on the Vilamars' house from there. He opened his copy of the *ABC* newspaper and started to read without really paying attention. He saw a photograph of a painting of the Virgin Mary captioned "Our Lady of Mt. Carmel, Patron of the Glorious Spanish Fleet." He kept on turning the pages until he came to an article which, although it didn't really interest him, gave him somewhere to rest his eyes as a married couple and their two children walked past and glanced at him. "Yesterday, the General Secretary of the Movement concluded the Second National Council on Social Order with an interesting speech. Capitalism, Secretary Arrese said, is not a system based on respect for capital, but rather on the belief that the only thing that is produced is capital."

"Idiot, that Arrese," the man thought to himself, as he wiped the sweat away again. He kept on idly leafing through the pages until he got to the international news. "Heavy fighting continues in Normandy. Fierce fighting near Lessay and Saint Lo. New aerial bombardment."

He sank back into his reading. He didn't notice the priest who came out of the church and gave him a curious look.

He went on turning the pages, stopping on another article that drew his attention. "New one-peseta coins prepared for circulation." He moved on to the announcement of a film they were showing at one of the cinemas on Gran Vía. "Marguerite Gautier. Starring Greta Garbo and Robert Taylor."

He kept on reading the paper while trying to keep his attention on what was happening in the street as well. Finally, he gave up. Mrs. Vilamar hadn't come down to Mass as she usually did; he walked over to the building where Doña Isabel, the Garzo widow, lived.

He walked slowly to the door and stood in the shade of the porch. He went over to the staircase and walked up quickly. He had spent a couple of days loitering around this street and knew when the doorwoman's husband would arrive. He would come at two o'clock and then she'd close up her office for a couple of hours to eat. But because it was Sunday, she would be out all day.

Once he was on the third floor, he rang the bell and waited impatiently. He was lucky, because he had not yet bumped into any of the neighbors.

The door was opened by a woman who looked at him perplexedly.

"Doña Isabel?" he asked.

"Yes … that's me. What do you want?"

"To give you this letter. Nothing else. Good afternoon."

Isabel was so disconcerted to have the letter in her hand that she took a moment to react. She didn't know whether she should call back the man to ask him who had sent him or else just close the door. In the end, she closed the door.

She went straight to the living room, and when she saw the handwriting on the envelope, she burst into tears. It was her son's handwriting, Fernando's. She was sure of it. She opened the letter carefully and found several pages covered in clear, round handwriting.

My dear mother,

Forgive me for not writing to you earlier. If you knew everything that has happened ... But I don't want to worry you. I am well. But the body is one thing and the pain in my heart at being so far away is quite another. There isn't a day that goes by when I don't think about you and ask myself how you are; if you are well, and if you have forgiven me for leaving without saying goodbye.

We'll meet again someday, and when we do and I'll tell you what happened, you'll understand.

I can't say where I am so that I don't get you into trouble. I am a long way away, very far away, too far from Spain, and you don't know how much I want to come back. But I have to wait for the war to end in Europe and to see what happens to our country. There are people who think that if the Allies win, then things in Spain will change. I'm not too hopeful about that, but I hope that they're right.

I'm working, Mother, I have a good job and I think that Father would be proud of me, given that I earn my money honestly.

And what about you, Mother, how are you? Are you still working for Doña Hortensia and Don Luis Ramírez? I hope you've been able to find another job. It's not that it's embarrassing to work for other people, but it hurts me to think that you have to.

There isn't much news that gets to us here from Spain, so I don't know if things are any better.

Look after yourself, forgive me, and trust me. I promise that as soon as I can, I will do everything in my power to do what I can for us to be together again.

Tell Piedad that Eulogio is well. He can't write at the moment, but I'm sure that he will as soon as he can. I can't give you any more details, even though I know that Piedad will want to hear about her son. I'll add that Doña Asunción should also get a letter from Catalina. She is well, and her daughter Adela is a wonderful and very affectionate child. Marvin, unfortunately, doesn't want anything to do with Catalina or her daughter. He refuses to see them, and I can't abandon them to their fate. Don't think that I haven't tried to get Catalina to come back to Spain, but she refuses, because she doesn't want her parents to suffer the shame of seeing her as a single mother. You know how everything in Spain is: always caught up with this ridiculous moral code.

Forgive me for leaving you alone.

Your son, who loves you more than anything in the world,

Fernando

Isabel couldn't have held back her tears even had she wanted to. Fernando was well, and he remembered her. She trusted her son and was sure that he had a good reason for not coming home.

She'd go up to see Piedad and tell her that Eulogio was well. She would be hurt not to receive a letter, but Isabel knew that she wouldn't complain. Piedad had shown great dignity in the face of all the muttering in the neighborhood. Don Bernardo had told Isabel that she shouldn't be friends with Eulogio's mother, who he considered an unrepentant sinner. Piedad still didn't go to church and was not prepared to confess anything to Don Bernardo. Isabel had recommended that she go to church, even if only to stop everyone else from talking about her behind her back, but Piedad had refused.

She found her darning a dress.

"Come in, come in. I'm changing the waistband, which is so worn that it's almost transparent. I've got some malt; do you want me to make you a cup?"

"No, don't go to any trouble. I'm doing things around the house as well. I'm cleaning the windows. How are things at the workshop?" Isabel asked.

"Well … fourteen hours of sewing a day. But it's better than other things, so I'm not complaining. And what about the pharmacy?"

"I thank God for the work. Don Luis is a good man, I can't complain."

"It wasn't God who got you the job, but the people you work for."

Isabel laughed. Piedad was cross with Don Bernardo, yes, but also with God Himself. But she couldn't blame her friend. She had enough problems keeping her own faith after her husband had been shot.

"Yes, Doña Hortensia and Don Luis have been very kind to me. Doña Hortensia insisted that her husband take me on to help at the pharmacy, even though that meant I stopped helping at their house."

"Well, the one thing that there's more than enough of nowadays, it's servants for our new masters. You're a lady, Isabel, and I guess it must have upset this Hortensia to have you in her house ironing shirts for her husband."

"Don't say that, Piedad, Doña Hortensia is a good woman. She tried to help me get Lorenzo pardoned, and now she's given me this job. It would be ungrateful to criticize her."

"You're a saint … I don't know how you can say that Doña Hortensia and Don Luis are good people. They're Franco supporters to the core. They're guilty of getting your Lorenzo killed as well."

"Don't be so radical. Doña Hortensia and Don Luis are good people, even if they do support Franco."

"They can't be good if they went against the Republic and now aren't lifting a finger to stop all the injustice being meted out everywhere. They're still killing everyone who's not on their side. Don't you forget that, Isabel."

Piedad's voice was harsher now. It wasn't the first time that they'd argued about this topic. Piedad was upset that Isabel could find even a tiny speck of goodness among those who had supported Franco in the war and who had made people like her and Isabel pariahs in their own country. They had lost everything: their husbands, their sons, their hopes, their future. Piedad would never forgive them, nor would she be able to find anything good in them, these people who had turned their backs on the Republic.

Isabel understood the hatred that burned in Piedad, for it was the same hatred that she had felt when they shot her husband. She kept blaming herself for the fact that, in spite of this hatred, she could feel grateful to Doña Hortensia and Don Luis for the help they had given her. She had to live with this contradiction. She knew that her son Fernando wouldn't understand it either.

"Don Luis has taught me a lot. He sometimes leaves me alone at the pharmacy. But, Piedad, I came to tell you something …"

Piedad grew tense, and accidentally jabbed herself with the needle.

"Go ahead."

"I got a letter from Fernando. He's well … and he asks me to tell you that Eulogio is as well … he hasn't been able to write to you, but he will as soon as he can. He wrote about Catalina's daughter, Adela he says she's called, and says they're a long way away, but that they miss Spain."

"Nothing else?" Piedad said, trying to stop herself from trembling.

"Nothing else. It's a short letter, just sent to calm me down. Oh, and Catalina has written to her mother, to Asunción. But they don't say anything about where they are. The important thing is that the three of them are well."

"Right, but why can't Eulogio write to me?"

"I don't know, Piedad … I don't know … he'll have his reasons … we have to trust them."

Piedad's eyes started to cloud over. She only felt upset and defeated when she thought about Eulogio, the son for whose life she had sacrificed her dignity. The son who, for that very reason, refused to forgive her.

"Our sons love us, even though they have left us and we don't know why," Isabel said, to cheer her up.

"Yes, Fernando loves you, Isabel. I'm sure of it. And Eulogio loved me until … well, until he found out about Don Antonio. I curse the day I agreed to give in to that man. It would have been better if we'd died of hunger. You didn't sell yourself to anyone and you're managing to get by."

"I'd do anything for my son Fernando. And if I'd had to pay for Lorenzo's life with my body, then I swear I would have done it without blinking."

"I don't believe you, Isabel, I don't believe you. You're a believer; that stops you from doing things, because if you do them, you'll go straight to hell. But I'm in hell on Earth. And now tell me – where are they?"

"I don't know, Piedad. It was a man who brought the letter,

and I didn't even get a chance to look at him. He gave it to me and walked off without saying anything. And there's no stamp on the envelope."

"So maybe it's not from Fernando …"

"Of course it is. I know my son's handwriting. I don't know where he is or how he got the letter to me, but it is definitely his handwriting. I'm sure of that."

They spent the rest of the afternoon talking. Isabel tried to console Piedad, and Piedad tried to find consolation in what Isabel said.

Asunción walked quickly. She'd be late to the seven o'clock Mass. Don. Bernardo had been surprised that she hadn't been to Mass that morning. She had always gone to the noon Mass on Sundays with her husband, but as he'd fallen ill again recently, she hadn't been able to maintain their custom.

Ernesto had asked her to keep on going to Mass, and said that he could look after himself for a little while without any trouble. She was not convinced, but if she didn't go to Mass on Sunday, then she would be committing a mortal sin that weighed heavily on her soul.

There weren't many people in the street, but this wasn't strange. The pavement was burning hot in Madrid at seven o'clock in the evening, and so there weren't many people who would be keen to go to Mass at that time.

She walked along absorbed in her thoughts, not looking where she was going, which must have been why she bumped into a man who made her stumble. She dropped her bag and he bent over to pick it up. They apologized and each one went their own way.

It wasn't until later that evening that Asunción found an envelope in her bag.

She had headed home after Mass. Ernesto was asleep, his face showing just how much his illness was making him suffer. She looked at the clock and hurried to prepare his medicine, giving him the shot just as the doctor, her good friend Juan Segovia, had taught her. She had learned to give injections. She had no choice since her husband was so ill.

She didn't know if she should wake him to have supper. She'd make a French-style omelet and a bit of rice. They really couldn't afford to throw anything out. If Ernesto didn't wake up, she'd eat both portions.

She asked herself who the letter could be from. She looked at the envelope for a long while before opening it. She saw that it was addressed to her, Doña Asunción de Vilamar, and grew a little worried. How had it managed to get here, into her bag? She remembered bumping into the man … maybe it hadn't been an accident, and he'd taken the opportunity to slip the letter into her bag? She went into the kitchen to open the letter and was even more surprised to find two pages of handwritten paper and a photograph of a smiling child.

My dear mother,

I miss you so much! Not a single day goes by when I don't think of you and Papa. I suppose he must still be annoyed with me and I understand that, but I'd like you to tell him that in spite of our differences, I still love him, and I believe that everything he has done over the course of his life he has done in what he thought were my best interests.

I attach a photograph of Adela. My daughter. Your granddaughter. She's two years old now, and is very clever and very well behaved. Papa would be happy with her: Adela is very obedient and knows how to please people, very different from how I am.

I can't tell you where we are, apart from the fact that Adela and I are well. We are a long way away, too far away, and we hope to come back someday. I will return with my husband and my daughter. I will not come back without a husband. I'll never make Papa have to deal with a granddaughter born out of wedlock.

Oh, Mama, things are not going how I thought they would. Marvin seems to be running away from me. I think that he is being led astray, but I haven't been able to meet with him, much less get him to see Adela. You can imagine how sad I am. In spite of that, I can't stop thinking that one day he'll meet my little girl and that things will sort themselves out. Marvin is an honorable man.

Fernando is with me and is looking after me. I don't know what would have become of me without him. I owe him so much, Mother, so much that if I lived another thousand lives, I would never be able to repay his kindness and generosity with Adela and with me. The little girl loves him as though he was her father, because she is very young and doesn't know the truth about these things yet.

I'm working. Yes, Mama, I'm working. Tell Aunt Petra that her piano lessons are letting me earn a living, which is strange, after I complained so much about them! I don't know if Aunt Petra will have forgiven me. I hope you can convince her that I love her a great deal and that I am very sorry for everything I may have made her go through because of me.

I don't know when I'll be able to write to you again. But you must remember this, Mother, that I haven't forgotten you and I know that we will be together once again at some point in the future. But it will have to be a day with no shadows over it, a day when Papa does not have a reason to be ashamed of me.

With all my love,

CATALINA
And your granddaughter ADELA

Asunción read the letter again, and then once more. She felt her heart beating faster, and then felt suffocated, and then burst into tears. She looked at the photograph of Adela, her grandchild who she might never meet. She had to show it to her husband; maybe he'd soften up a little then and allow her to write to Catalina and tell her that he forgave her and that she should come home. Then she realized that even if Ernesto did forgive Catalina, she had no way to tell her daughter this fact. She looked at the envelope and saw that there were no stamps on it, no postmark. This puzzled her. She read the letter again and looked closely at the handwriting; there was no doubt in her mind that it was Catalina's.

Ernesto Vilamar was dozing when Asunción came into the room to ask if he wanted to eat. She walked noiselessly over to him, but she must have made some noise, because the sick man opened his eyes.

"Are you back already?"

"I've been back for a while, but I didn't want to disturb you because you were asleep."

"Did you take Communion?"

"Yes, of course. Don Bernardo asked after you. He says he'll come and see you tomorrow in case you want to confess ..."

"If only he didn't talk so much ... But he should come. It's always better to have a priest who will help you get things square with God. I'll confess. I hope he doesn't go too far with the penance this time. I can't really be doing with novenas at the moment."

"For God's sake, Ernesto!"

"Oh, come on, Asunción, you know I'm right. Of course I want to confess in case God wants to take me one of these days. I don't have much time left, and you know that."

Asunción sat at the edge of the bed, taking one of his hands and raising it to her lips.

"If you feel sick, we'll call Juan Segovia and get you taken to the hospital. But I don't want to hear you say these things. You're going to get better, Ernesto, I know you will."

"I don't want to go to the hospital, Asunción. Why should I? Do you think I don't know why they sent me home? Because they can't do anything for me. They would rather I die here, and I thank them for it. I'd prefer to die at home, in my bed, without being surrounded by strangers."

"Ernesto, I don't want to hear you say these things! Trust in God. I keep on praying that you'll get better."

"And I thank you for it, but I think that the Lord has decided that I don't have much more to do here. Go on, get me a glass of water. My mouth's all dry."

"Would you like to eat something? A bit of omelet and some rice, or maybe I could bring you a cup of malt and some biscuits ..."

"No, I don't want to eat anything. Just bring me the water."

"Ernesto ..."

"What?"

"I don't want to upset you, but ... We've got a letter from Catalina. She's sent us a photograph of her daughter, of our granddaughter. She's called Adela ..."

Ernesto Vilamar clenched his eyes as tightly shut as he could manage. He didn't want to hear his daughter's name. He didn't want to think about her, and he didn't want to know anything at all about her shameful granddaughter.

"Ernesto, please … she's our daughter and she loves us, and we love her … I know that you love her …" Asunción was pleading now.

"Bring me the water, please, and don't talk to me about that hussy. The Lord will take her into account as well, when he judges me," he said without opening his eyes.

Asunción left the room, but put the photograph and the letter on the bedside table.

He didn't open his eyes until she had left the room. He turned and saw the envelope on the bedside table. He was just about to throw it on the floor when he saw the photograph that lay on top of the envelope. A child was smiling in it, and he thought that she was smiling at him. He started to cry.

When Asunción came back with the glass of water, she found her husband with his head hidden under the sheets.

"Ernesto, Ernesto! What's wrong? I'll call the doctor right away …"

"Leave me, Asunción, leave me alone. Don't call anyone. Just leave me alone."

"But Ernesto …"

He said nothing. He knew that if he tried to speak he would only sob, and he would never have forgiven himself for crying in front of his wife.

A week went by before Isabel bumped into Asunción in the Plaza de la Encarnación. They greeted each other warmly.

"I'm pleased to see you. How's Ernesto?"

"He's got his good days and his bad days …" Asunción replied, looking tired. "What about you? How are things at the pharmacy?"

"I can't complain; Don Luis gives me more responsibility every day, and I'm grateful to him for that. Oh, by the way … I know that you got a letter from Catalina, and I got one from Fernando."

"Yes ... it looks like they're still together. My daughter says that Fernando is looking after her, which makes me feel a little calmer. I know that your Fernando is a gentleman who has always loved my daughter, and I'm sorry that there was nothing in her to return that love. We'd have saved ourselves a great deal of suffering."

"I don't think so, Asunción. Ernesto wouldn't have liked for Catalina to have Fernando as a match. Your husband was insistent that she should marry Antoñito."

"You're right ... but Ernesto has always liked you and he would have come around eventually. I just can't forgive this American seducing my daughter and then ... well, you'll know from Fernando: He doesn't want anything to do with her."

"Fernando said as much in his letter. You don't know how sorry I am. I hate that women have to pay for what men get away with. No one will judge Marvin for having a child out of wedlock, but they will judge Catalina."

"Ernesto ... Ernesto doesn't want anything to do with her. I'm afraid he'll die without forgiving her."

"Your husband is very stubborn, Asunción, but Catalina is his daughter and the fact that he won't let his arm be twisted about this issue doesn't mean that he doesn't love her."

"But he's very ill, and ... Don Juan has told me to accept that he may not last much longer."

"You have to have faith ..."

"Faith ... yes, of course ... I have faith ... but I think that Ernesto's really very weak. I've insisted that he let the doctor put him in the hospital, but he says there's nothing left for them to do and he's been sent back to die at home. If Catalina only knew how sick her father was ... do you have any way of writing to Fernando?"

"No, they didn't give me an address; they had someone bring the letter to my house."

"Where do you think they are?"

"I don't know, Asunción ... If I did, then I'd go to find my son. My life is meaningless without him."

"I have a granddaughter. Here, let me show you her photo." Asunción opened her bag and took the picture of Adela out of her wallet.

"She's beautiful, and looks happy ..."

"She's pretty, too, although she doesn't look like Catalina ..."

"It's still too soon to see what she'll look like."

"She's two years old now ... I'd give so much to have her here with me!"

Isabel was going to reply, but fell silent when she saw Mari, Don Antonio's wife, coming over. She was with her daughters Paquita and Marivi.

"Well, well, well ... I haven't seen you for a long time. You don't get out much," Mari said, looking them up and down.

"Work takes up all my time," Isabel said bluntly.

"Well, don't work so hard, it's not like you're going to inherit the Ramírez's pharmacy," Mari said, accompanying her words with a guffaw which her children copied.

Isabel bit her lip. She wasn't a naturally rude person, but it was hard for her to hold her tongue with Mari.

Asunción was also uncomfortably silent in the face of the shopkeeper's wife. And she blushed when Mari looked at her.

"We've just come from trying on the dresses for the wedding. Antoñito is going to get married in September. It's very good news that he's getting married to Mari Paz Nogués, who's a proper lady. It was a stroke of luck that your daughter has gone for good, because Antonito didn't want to marry her, he thought she was impertinent and untrustworthy ... But my husband insisted ... I don't know how he can have let himself be tricked by a bunch of people such as yourselves ... Well, I suppose he thought that if he got married into your family, then he might one day recover a tiny portion of the debt you owe him ... Just as well he doesn't trust you any more ..."

"Why are you so nasty?" Isabel couldn't hold back any longer.

"Nasty? How dare you call me nasty! You have a lot to be ashamed of, and you're lucky they pardoned you, despite being married to a red," Mari said, putting her hands on her hips and looking stubbornly at Isabel.

"Isabel ... please ... leave it ... it's not worth it."

Asunción pulled at Isabel's arm, scared by the direction this conversation was taking.

But Isabel wasn't prepared for his woman to sully her husband's name. Her scornful gaze locked on the bovine eyes of Mari.

"My husband was a good man and a gentleman, but you can't believe that a man might have such qualities. As for being a red ... you know what, I was happy to be married to him. I never had to be ashamed of anything, nothing at all."

"Look at her manners! She really thinks she's someone," Mariví interrupted.

"I'm going to tell my husband to take note and tell whoever needs to be told that you are proud of the fact that your husband was a red," Mari almost shouted.

"I am proud of the fact that I was married to a man who was good, kind and honest, and who was always opposed to injustice and who lived by his ideals. Yes, I am proud of my husband. Report me to the police if you want, I don't care."

"For God's sake, Isabel ... Let's go," Asunción begged.

"No, we're going, I don't want my daughters contaminated by people such as yourselves. I hope you both starve!"

Mari and her daughters turned their backs on the two women. A woman came over to them, a neighbor who had seen what happened.

"You shouldn't argue with her ... she's a bad person and because her husband is making so much money and she knows so many important people ... no, it's better not to have her as an enemy," the woman said.

"She's a witch," Isabel said.

The woman shrugged. No one dared criticize Mari in public in the whole neighborhood. Almost everyone had a debt with the shopkeeper, and no one wanted him to cut their credit.

"She's very puffed up over her son's wedding. It's going to make her so important, to have her son married to Mari Paz Nogués. Fidel Nogués doesn't have the money that he used to, but he's still an important man. And because they couldn't get your daughter, they've decided to settle for Mari Paz. When is Catalina coming back, by the way? It's almost two years since she left, and your husband's so sick ..." There was a trace of malice in the woman's words.

684

"Poor Mari Paz ... she's a good girl. I'm sorry for her, marrying Antonito isn't what I understand by a good marriage," Isabel said, changing the subject.

"Right, of course ... But Antoñito is rolling in it, and so for all the airs that Mari Paz or Catalina might put on, it's Don Antonio who has the money, and you know what they say, he who has the money ..."

12

Athanasius Vryzas seemed happy. Or at least Fernando thought he seemed happy. The old editor wasn't much given to speaking, and especially not to smiling, but this morning he was making an exception for both. He kept on taking about the news that he read in the paper on his desk.

It said that the war would soon be over, and that the Allies would win.

"Ever since the Normandy landings things have changed. Half of France has been liberated. Paris is Paris once again ... and Brussels and Antwerp are free too, the Soviets have taken Estonia and freed Athens ... you'll see," he said happily.

Fernando was hoping that Vryzas was right. He felt that Alexandria had become a prison from which he couldn't escape, and that this had made him old and bitter. He wanted to leave; he would go anywhere, given that Spain was an impossibility for him now. He was afraid that they would arrest him for the murders of Roque and Saturnino Pérez. Their names and their faces were fixed in his mind, and no matter how much time went by, he was unable to get them out of his head.

It was only Catalina who knew of his anguish. She insisted that Roque and Saturnino were better off dead. She didn't feel any remorse for having given him the pistol that he had used to do the deed, and she advised him to forget about it, telling him that he had freed the world of two bad people.

He tried to concentrate on the book of poems that he had to edit and to ignore Vryzas' chatter, but now Sara stood in front of his desk and told him to go up to Benjamin Wilson's office. Sara's face was worried, but Wilson's was not. He never allowed himself to show any emotion.

Benjamin Wilson spoke bluntly. "They've arrested your friend Eulogio. They've taken him to Germany."

Fernando was stunned, and did not know what to say. It was hard for him to speak the words that formed in his head.

"When? How?"

"Months ago ... I'm sorry, but they didn't get the news to me until now. If I had known about it before, I would have told you."

Sara took his hand and the pressure brought him back to reality.

"I have to go and find him," Fernando muttered.

"Where? We don't know where he is."

"But you can find out!"

"I'm trying. They gave me the news a couple of days ago and I've been trying since then to get more information. It's not easy right now."

"Help me get to Germany," Fernando asked.

"Where? Berlin? Munich? Frankfurt? I've told you, we don't know where they've taken him. And the war isn't over yet."

"How did you find out?"

"Zahra told me. She's just back from a mission."

"Zahra? Why didn't she tell me?" he said sadly.

"Her safety depends on her discretion, as you well know."

"But ... she could have told me ..." Fernando protested.

"I'm only telling you about Eulogio's situation precisely because she insisted I tell you. She told me what your reaction would be, and also that she's willing to help you if we find out where your friend is. But even if we did know, neither of you can go to Germany at the moment: the Nazis may not acknowledge it, but they're losing the war. And they are fighting, of course: Hitler will fight to the very last man."

"I'll talk to her," Fernando said with a hint of anger in his voice.

"I think she'll be here in a minute," Sara said, with a glance at the clock.

Sara was right. Only a few minutes later, Leyda Zabat, Mr. Wilson's secretary, announced that Zahra had arrived.

The dancer came into the office and gave Sara a kiss before turning to Benjamin and Fernando.

Benjamin asked her to explain to Fernando how she knew of Eulogio's fate. Zahra started to speak.

"I had to meet a few days ago with someone from the Lyon Resistance. I don't need to give you all the details, but Lyon has been one of the few places in France where, in spite of everything, there are still people resisting the Nazis. One of them was Anatole Lombard, Eulogio's friend."

"Anatole Lombard? I don't know who he is … Eulogio never spoke to me about him." Fernando was surprised.

"They met when Marvin and Farida and Eulogio tried to save Sara's father. You know that Monsieur Rosent unfortunately died when they were crossing the border and that Marvin and Farida decided to go to Switzerland, but Eulogio chose to stay."

"Yes, I know, but it was a stupid thing for him to do," Fernando said.

"Love makes risks seem normal," Zahra said, staring straight at Fernando.

Zahra's words made him even more confused. What was she talking about?

"I didn't know that Eulogio had fallen in love," Fernando said.

"Yes, he fell in love with Anatole Lombard, and Anatole loved him back, although maybe not absolutely," Zahra said, staring straight at Fernando.

He turned red with surprise and indignation.

"What are you saying?" he said, getting up and looking at Zahra angrily.

"What? I thought that it wouldn't be a surprise for you to know that Eulogio is … well, that he prefers the company of men."

"How dare you say something like that! You don't know him, you've only seen him once or twice in your whole life, and you've never spoken to him, and yet you dare accuse him of … of being …"

Sara got up and took Fernando's arm to make him sit down.

"We thought you knew ..." Sara said.

"Knew what? You're slandering my friend's name. How dare you!"

"You know what, Fernando, the problem isn't who Eulogio has fallen in love with. The problem is that you think this is a problem. Your friend had never been as happy in his life as he was in his months with Anatole. He was free, yes, free, in spite of being in occupied France and feeling the constant presence of the Nazis," Sara said with an understanding smile.

Fernando felt stricken. He was as offended by Sara's words as he had been by Zahra's. He felt a wave of anger build towards the two women. How could they speak like this about Eulogio?

They didn't know him, they didn't know anything about him. He hated them for being so cruel as to insist that Eulogio had fallen in love with a man, with this Anatole of the Resistance.

He knew that it was impossible. He knew Eulogio, they had been born in the same neighborhood, and brought up in the same building, in the same street. Their parents had been good friends. No, he wouldn't let them slander him.

"You must understand that I won't stay here another minute after what you've said about my friend. I'm going, and I won't be back, Mr. Wilson. I hope that you all have the decency to stop spreading such lies about Eulogio."

He was going to get up again, but once more he felt Sara's hand on his shoulder, as though by this she could hold him back.

"Please, Fernando ... you don't know how sorry I am that you are so upset ... we thought ... Well, we thought that you might at least suspect that Eulogio could fall in love with a man. It's true that he wasn't very obvious, but Benjamin and I were not surprised when Farida, once they got to Switzerland, explained to us why Eulogio had stayed behind. It was clear that it was out of love. And now, as Zahra can tell you, everyone in the Resistance in Lyon knew about the love that Anatole had for Saul Blanc, whom the Nazis deported to Germany, and how Eulogio took his place in Anatole's affections."

Sara spoke slowly and looked at Fernando in the eye, and held his hand. Zahra was silent.

Fernando thought that his head was going to explode. He hated them, he hated them all. He hated sweet Sara, and unreadable Benjamin, and even Zahra. He didn't only hate them, but he hated this city, which was so alien and where he felt like an exile.

Athanasius Vryzas had been right: he shouldn't have stayed here, he should have found the courage to set out to sea like Ulysses. And now he would. He wouldn't stay here any longer. He would take Catalina and Adela. He didn't care where they went, but they had to go. Having made this decision, he grew calmer. He felt air coming back into his lungs and his heart's frantic beating slow.

"Love has no sex, or age, or race, or place, or present, or future. Love is only love," Zahra murmured, looking straight at him.

He didn't reply. He wouldn't have known what to say. All he felt was an unstoppable desire to leave. But Sara's hand was still on his shoulder, and although he barely felt it, it stopped him from getting up again.

Zahra's words had found a toehold in him, but he was incapable of untangling them and accepting them for what they were.

Benjamin Wilson cleared his throat and offered Zahra and then him a cigarette. When he had taken the first few drags, Benjamin brought them back to reality.

"Right, now we need to think about what we are going to do. In my opinion, there aren't all that many options, given that the Allies are fighting day and night against the retreating Germans and Hitler still thinks that his army is invincible."

"But the war is not yet won," Sara said, puncturing her husband's excessive optimism.

"But it certainly isn't lost. And I'd say that after the Normandy landings and the liberation of Paris, every day that passes is a day that brings us closer to the end," Benjamin said.

Fernando listened to them talk for a while without saying a word. Benjamin Wilson seemed optimistic, Sara was more cautious and Zahra agreed with her. They seemed to have forgotten about him until Zahra mentioned Eulogio again.

"I'll explain why they took Eulogio to Germany. You'll know that the Vichy government passed a law that meant that all young men had to present themselves to work voluntarily in the German factories. As you can imagine, this was a law that didn't provoke a great deal of enthusiasm and the French tried to avoid it as much as possible. Germany needs workers, because all its men are at the front. And so the French government, when Berlin pressures them, rounds young men up and sends them to Germany whether they want to go or not. A member of the Resistance told me that Anatole had found a job for Eulogio. He was teaching drawing in a children's school and was a member of Anatole's Resistance group. His false documents must have been very well made, because no one suspected him. He pretended to be French Basque. In March, one of the roundups picked Eulogio up, but he managed to escape. He hid, but they found him. The worst of it is that the day they arrested him, he had a suitcase full of pamphlets that he was intending to scatter in the busiest square in Lyon. He was lucky not to be shot. It must be because there are so few men in the German factories. They sent him to Germany as a prisoner, and since then no one has had any news."

"There must be some way of finding out where he's gone," Fernando said, more to himself than to Zahra.

"It's almost impossible," Sara replied. "The Nazi factories are often hidden ... We know they exist, but we don't know where. They take the prisoners there to work ..."

"If Benjamin manages to find out where your friend Eulogio is, then I'll come with you. It won't be easy to get him out of Germany: all three of us will probably be killed," Zahra said emotionlessly.

"I don't want you to come with me. You don't have to," Fernando said.

"No, I don't have to, but I will." Zahra's tone left no room for doubt.

But Benjamin Wilson didn't promise or commit to anything. The chief demand of his line of work was to keep one's emotions under wraps. He wasn't prepared to send Zahra on a mission from which she had no chance of returning. As for Fernando, he considered that he had fulfilled his obligations by informing him of Eulogio's fate. But he wouldn't do anything else, not for the moment.

Sun and rain combined in the early hours of that Alexandrian afternoon. Fernando was keen to return to Ylena's house to talk to Catalina. All this emotion had made his stomach churn. He was scared for Eulogio, and was prepared to go to France with or without Benjamin Wilson's help.

Athanasius Vryzas looked at Fernando. He was upset by the pain in his distant gaze. He hadn't asked him what had happened in the meeting with Wilson and Zahra, but it was clear that they had spoken about something that had upset him.

"You're upset; maybe it's better for you to finish translating those poems at home. You'll be calmer there."

Fernando accepted thankfully. He not only respected Vryzas, but also felt something akin to a warm affection towards him, this man who had lost his son who was in search of his own personal Ithaca.

Dimitra told him that Catalina was not at home. She had gone to see Father Lucas and had taken Adela with her.

Catalina was now often to be found talking to the priest. He seemed to enjoy her company, and the girl's. If the weather was good, they would sit in the garden, or else stroll through the streets around Saint Catherine's Cathedral.

He decided to go find her. He needed to tell her about Eulogio.

Father Lucas laughed as he listened to Catalina. They seemed to be in harmony. Adela was sitting next to him playing with a doll and ignoring them. Fernando hurried over to where they were. He didn't say hello, but started to talk quickly about how Eulogio had disappeared. Catalina grew tense.

"What are we going to do?" she asked when Fernando had finished his story.

"Go and look for him. I'm going to look for him. I can't sit around here doing nothing."

"And how are you going to get to Germany?" Father Lucas asked.

"I don't know ... But I'll have to do it somehow. I'll speak to Mr. Wilson again, and if he won't help me, then I'll find a way to go myself."

"Think for a minute, Fernando, just think ... I understand your worry. Eulogio is your friend and you can't stand around twiddling your thumbs without knowing what he's going through. But you have to use your head. You can't go to Germany. How are you going to get there? The war has reached a critical moment. The news is good, the Allies are winning back territory from the Wehrmacht, but they still haven't won the war. Even for a man like Benjamin Wilson, it would be difficult to find out where they've taken Eulogio. The only thing they've told you is that they think he's been taken to one of the armaments factories they have there. But which one?"

"I'll find out," Fernando said.

"I'll come with you ..." Catalina said.

"What are you saying?" Father Lucas exclaimed. "How can you go to Germany? And what about Adela? Would you leave her here? What would happen to her if something happened to you? You're impulsive people. I understand ... I ... I find it hard to dominate my own impulses ... but you have to do it. You can't let yourselves be led by the heart alone. If you want to help Eulogio, you'll have to use your heads."

It took a while for Father Lucas to calm them down. Fernando and Catalina sketched out plans that grew ever more farfetched. The priest played devil's advocate and took apart everything they said. He liked these two young people, lost in a city that they would never have chosen. They were prisoners of circumstance, just as he was, but he had chosen his prison. First the desert caves of Wadi Natrum, and now this church, where he kept on paying his debts.

"I'm sure that Mr. Wilson will have thought about this, but maybe his contacts in Switzerland can speak to the Red Cross and find out if Eulogio is registered at one of these armaments factories or at a labor camp. That would be the first step to take, and once you know where he is, that would be the time to work out what to do."

Father Lucas' suggestion came as a relief to both Fernando and Catalina.

When they got back to the house, they apologized to Ylena and said they would not be down for supper. They told her what had happened to Eulogio and said that this was why they were not hungry.

Ylena grumbled and told them not to behave like children. It wouldn't help Eulogio for them to go without their supper, and the best way to help him was to keep their heads cool and their stomachs full. They agreed that she was right, but even so, that evening they preferred to go to Catalina's room and talk about what had happened. After a while, Dimitra came to the room with a tray.

"Ylena insists that you have something to eat."

They spent a few hours sunk in nostalgia, remembering their childhood in Spain and thinking about how much they had admired Eulogio because he was the oldest and always knew what to do. Fernando didn't know whether he should mention what Zahra had insinuated about the relationship between Eulogio and Anatole, but he decided that he should be completely open with her.

Catalina listened attentively and showed neither emotion nor surprise.

"I'm not going to put up with Wilson anymore, and as for Zahra … I didn't have her down as someone who would spread slander," Fernando said.

"Well, she might have been telling the truth."

"What do you mean? You can't believe that Eulogio … well, you know him as well as I do."

"Are you sure that we know him? He's your friend, of course, and you've both been there for each other, but that doesn't mean that you really know him. Eulogio is the only boy in the neighborhood who has never had a girlfriend … And he's always been so blunt and unsympathetic towards all of us girls. We make him feel uncomfortable. You say that you've been in love with me since you were a child, but you played around with quite a few other girls as well, and everyone knows what went on between you and Carolina, the carpenter's daughter … well, she was fairly easy, of course …"

"Catalina, please!" Fernando turned bright red.

"Well, I saw you being very lovey-dovey with her at Antoñito's birthday party at La Pradera."

"What are you saying? Carolina is a good girl and I …"

"Yes, yes, you're too much of a gentleman to talk about it …

But it is the case that out of all the young men in the neighborhood, the only one who has never had a girlfriend is Eulogio. He only spent time with the boys."

"But that doesn't mean anything," Fernando said.

"Well ... maybe it doesn't, but you have to admit it is strange. And ..." Catalina bit her lip. "Well, I've never said this to you before, but there were rumors about it all over the neighborhood."

"People are vicious!"

"Come on, Fernando, the two of us know that there are men out there who don't like women. And Eulogio might be one of those men. That doesn't make him good or bad. Poor boy, if it really is the case, he's probably having a terrible time of it. Anatole must have been very special for Eulogio to give up the chance of going to America with Marvin."

Catalina's words made Fernando feel even more confused. If he had not known that Catalina was neither malicious nor a gossip, then he would been very angry with her.

"I'll tell you something else, Fernando ... I think one of the reasons that Eulogio didn't like me was that he felt something for Marvin ... I'm not saying that they were in love, but he treated him as though he were his property, and ... I think he was a little upset that you loved me as well."

Fernando refused to admit that Catalina might be right.

"I'll go to France to talk to Anatole Lombard, and then I'll go to Germany. I'll ask Mr. Wilson tomorrow to get in touch with the Red Cross and find out if Eulogio is in a labor camp."

What he did not say to Catalina was that he was thinking of going to see Zahra.

He wanted to talk to the dancer alone, to hear her tell him once again what she had said about Eulogio's relationship with Anatole Lombard. But he didn't want to see her just for that. He couldn't deny to himself how much Zahra meant to him. He felt as strongly towards her as he did towards Catalina, although he couldn't say if his feelings towards Zahra were inspired more by desire than by love.

On the weekend, he went to the cabaret. The war might still be raging in Europe, but on that night in late October 1944, Alexandria was further than ever from the Old Continent. Soldiers killed and died in the fields and streets of every country in Europe while the men and women of the city of Alexandria prepared to forget the present. The neon signs seemed to be greeting everyone who came to the City Club where Zahra performed.

Fernando sat at the bar and saw a few people look curiously at him. Many people had thought that he was Zahra's devoted slave, and now they were sympathizing with him, as she had not been seen with him a lot in the past few months.

The barman greeted him curiously and asked if Miss Zahra was expecting him. He smiled and said nothing, but ordered a cocktail at random.

He had to wait a good long while for the lights to dim, as a prelude to Zahra's appearance on the stage.

He shuddered when the lights came up and picked her out on the dark stage. She danced and danced as though she were possessed. It was a different dance from the ones he had seen before. She seemed to be enjoying every movement she made. The applause she received was maybe even louder than normal. A few men got up and went to her dressing room, anxious for her to see them. Fernando didn't know if he should join this improvised procession. What if she refused to see him? And if she humiliated him? He hadn't worked out what was going to happen when a waiter came up to tell him that Miss Nadouri wanted to see him.

He forced his way through the crowds, and when he got close to the dressing room, he had to insist that he had been invited for them to let him pass. He rapped on the door with his knuckles and it opened halfway to reveal the face of Zahra's dresser. She stretched out an arm to him and ushered him quickly into the dressing room. He heard voices raised in protest, men who wanted to show off how important they were, the flowers they could offer her, the jewels they wanted to give her. But the door remained shut behind him.

Zahra was taking off the remains of her makeup. The goddess was turning back into a woman. She looked up at the mirror to where he was reflected and without saying a word waved her dresser away. The woman bowed her head and went to the end of the dressing room to fold her employer's clothes.

"I'm glad you're here," she said sincerely.

"I wanted to talk to you ... and I didn't know where to call you."

"You know where I live."

"Yes ... but I'd never just turn up at your house."

"Afraid I wouldn't let you in?" she said teasingly.

"Out of respect for you and your grandmother," he said sincerely.

"And where do you think we'll talk?" she said ironically.

"I don't know ... I hadn't thought ... maybe we could go for a walk ..."

"At this time of night? You think it's safe to walk through Alexandria at midnight? You know that's not the case, Fernando. The best thing would be for you to escort me home."

Her house was dimly lit. The silence let him hear the noise of the waves crashing against the embankment. The butler opened the door and nodded at Zahra.

She dismissed him, saying she would not need anything that night. Then she took Fernando's hand and led him to her room.

He remembered it. Spacious and elegant. The bed at the far end with a low divan and two armchairs next to the doors that opened onto a terrace with a view of the sea. A tray with fruit, dates, cheese and pita bread lay on a low table.

The room smelled of Zahra's perfume. He didn't know how it happened, but once they were alone, they looked at one another and the world stopped moving. They came to meet each other wordlessly. And dawn broke as they heard the angry waves mingling with the cries of the waking city.

She didn't go with him. She said goodbye to him at the threshold to her room. He knew that the driver was waiting for him. When he got back to Ylena's house, he found Catalina waiting for him impatiently. She had bags under her eyes and seemed nervous.

"Where have you been? I was worried about you ... I know I'm not one to talk, but please don't leave me on edge all night, disappearing and not saying anything ..."

Suddenly she stopped and looked at him and understood. He didn't need to say anything. Fernando gave off a special scent: his smell mingled with a woman's perfume. Zahra. It must be Zahra's. She couldn't stop herself from laughing. She realized that Fernando must be suffering. She knew that she shouldn't ask, especially not at that moment. She went over to him and kissed him on the cheek. Then she said that he should have a shower before going down to the dining room where Ylena presided over the table, as she did every morning. Mr. Sanders was usually the first to arrive, and then Monsieur Baudin. Fernando and Catalina were usually late, and Ylena would scold them for their tardiness.

A few days passed before Fernando was able to tell Catalina about his meeting with Zahra. It happened one night, when he came back from work, before they had dinner. They sat in front of one another in the library, and she listened to him attentively, surprised at a story which he told her in very few words.

"Oh, but you're in love!" Catalina exclaimed when Fernando finished speaking.

"No ... don't say that ... I don't know what I feel for her."

"I've told you. You're in love even though you refuse to admit it. Look, I think the best thing is for you to tell her."

"What am I going to say? No, it's better to leave things how they are. The only thing that worries me now is where they've taken Eulogio. This morning, Mr. Wilson told me that he has asked the Red Cross to do whatever they can to find out which camp he's in ... but he didn't give me much cause for hope. I asked him to help me get to France. I'll go to Paris and then to Lyon to meet with Anatole Lombard. Wilson said that it is very difficult, but he'll give me an answer soon."

"If you go, I'm coming with you."

"You can't come. I don't want anything to happen to you."

Catalina was cross. She got to her feet and stood in front of him.

"You don't want anything to happen to me? I gave you the pistol you used to kill those two men, which makes me your accomplice. We fled Spain, we nearly got shipwrecked in the

Atlantic, I gave birth in the middle of a storm ... We came here not knowing a word of Arabic, without any work, without a place to stay, with no friends ... and we survived, Fernando. We survived. And now you want to treat me as though I'm made of glass? No way! I won't let you do it! The Allies have liberated Paris, Monsieur Baudin told me that there were Spaniards among the people who liberated it ... I want to go to Paris! Maybe Marvin has gone back there. In any case, I'm not going to stay in this city."

"But Adela ... You can't put the child through a journey like that ..."

"Adela is a survivor. Don't forget that. She'll come with us. Nothing's going to happen. If Mr. Wilson helps us, we'll get to Paris. France is right next to Spain, Fernando, and I ... I miss my parents more every day, I miss my home ..."

They argued for a while, neither one convincing the other, but one thing was clear: both of them were determined to leave Alexandria.

Fernando slept very little that night. He wanted to finish translating a collection of poems by a young Egyptian author that Sara had discovered. He wasn't going to go and leave the job undone, but he didn't want to wait any longer either.

In the morning, he met with Sara and Athanasius Vryzas to give them the translation. The old editor had a quick look over it and seemed happy. Sara told him that a poet friend of hers had just handed over her new book and that Fernando should have a look at it and start translating it. Fernando clenched his jaw and apologized, saying that he was getting ready to go on a journey and he didn't know if he'd have time. He said he wanted to go and speak to Mr. Wilson. There was no surprise on Sara's face. She even offered to go with him to her husband's office.

Vryzas said nothing, but he guessed that Fernando was about to start on his own voyage to Ithaca.

Benjamin Wilson was annoyed that Fernando insisted on speaking to him again. He had told him all that he needed to the day before, and he didn't have any more information to give him. He didn't think he would find out where Eulogio was, but he didn't want to upset Fernando either.

Sara told her husband that Fernando was going to leave. He

was annoyed that the Spaniard was so set on this, because he had things to worry about besides Fernando. But Wilson was not a man who allowed himself to show his feelings, and so he listened patiently. But Sara had her own interests; unexpectedly, she became the chief supporter of Fernando's journey.

"It would be foolish for Fernando to try to make it to Germany, but maybe not so foolish for him to go to France. We should help him. I'd like him to go to my house, my father's bookshop. Marvin left it in the care of Alain Fortier, his former literature professor. I want to know what has happened. What I want more than anything in the world is for Rosent's bookshop to get back to being what it once was."

If Benjamin Wilson was surprised, he didn't show it. But Fernando did.

"I'd only be going to Paris to be able to get to Lyon more easily ... I want to find Anatole Lombard ..." he protested.

"You can do both things ... What you really want is not to be here. You haven't settled down in Alexandria ... well, that's not important. I understand that as well as finding out what happened to your friend Eulogio, you want to go to France so you can be closer to Spain, to your home ..." Sara said.

"Well ... it's not that. I only want to find out what's happened to Eulogio," he replied, slightly annoyed.

But Sara, sweet-natured Sara, was about to show a part of her personality that her husband knew well, but which Fernando had not yet seen.

"If you can't go back to Spain where you have business that hasn't yet sorted itself out, in the meantime you can stay in Paris. I'd like you to take charge of Rosent's bookshop, and make it what it once was, a place where young poets came with their manuscripts, anxious to get my father's opinion. When the war is over, I'll come to Paris myself. But until then, you'd be doing me a great favor if you dealt with the bookshop."

Fernando didn't know what to say. Benjamin Wilson said nothing either. The two of them mused about what they had just heard Sara say.

"Catalina has to come with me," Fernando said.

Sara nodded. She didn't mind. She didn't know the Spanish

girl, and she was sure that they'd face no risks in France. De Gaulle was back. He'd formed a government. The Americans were there. It was time to rebuild the lives that had been left up in the air.

"The war isn't yet over," Benjamin Wilson said severely.

"But the Allies are taking more and more ground," Sara said.

"They have made important advances, but the Wehrmacht has still not been defeated," Wilson insisted.

"I'll go in any case." Fernando wasn't going to let himself be talked out of this.

"It won't be easy." Mr. Wilson seemed immovable in the face of Fernando's and Sara's wishes.

"Well, it looks like we're all in agreement, then," Sara said impatiently.

"No, we're not all in agreement. I'm not. It will be difficult to go to France, as well as risky to organize. I don't think that this is the moment." Benjamin looked firmly at his wife.

"I'd like to go straight away, in a week at the latest," Fernando interrupted. "In the meantime, maybe you'll find something out about Eulogio."

Wilson said nothing. He wanted the conversation to be over and to speak to Sara alone. He was surprised that she had told him nothing about her plans for the Rosent bookshop.

A week later, Fernando was still in Alexandria.

Benjamin Wilson had told him that he could not find a way to get them to France without great risk.

The days passed slowly, seeming to stretch on forever. He wanted to leave the city before the end of the year, and it was nearly November.

Catalina told the parents of her pupils that she was about to leave and would have to stop giving them piano lessons. She wanted to leave Egypt, although she couldn't help worrying about the risks they would run to get to Paris. She wasn't so much worried for her life, but for Adela's. Fernando told her how cautious Wilson was being, and although she scoffed she knew he was right: it was foolish to set out on such a journey with the continent at war, but even so, she preferred to leave.

Dimitra burst into tears when she heard that Fernando, Catalina, and little Adela were to leave. Ylena's reaction was similar. She had gotten used to the presence of these two Spaniards, who had filled her quiet house with their noise. Initially, she had taken them in because of her friendship for Captain Pereira, but little by little, she had warmed to them, and now she couldn't imagine the house without them. Mr. Sanders and Monsieur Baudin also seemed a little put out when Catalina and Fernando told them they were about to leave Alexandria. The Frenchman said that they were taking too many risks, and Colonel Sanders said seriously that they should wait a little longer, until Hitler had been finally defeated. But neither Fernando nor Catalina were prepared to change their minds.

The more Fernando insisted, the more uncomfortable Mr. Wilson felt. To tell the truth, he wasn't making that much effort to get them to France. He had even argued with Sara. His wife was insistent that Fernando take charge of the Rosent bookstore. She had laid out her plan and made it clear that it was final. She would stay in Alexandria, or wherever it was that Benjamin Wilson wanted to live, but the bookshop and publishing house in Paris had to start running again. It was a homage to the memory of her father, but she also had to do it for herself, so as not to admit that Hitler had defeated them. The Germans had taken her father's life, and the only way to limit their victory was for the bookshop to go back to what it had been before.

Father Lucas also felt a sudden stab of loneliness when Catalina told him that she was leaving. She had become a part of his daily life. He had initially been irritated by her absurd confessions, but he had learned much about her and had ended up liking her a great deal. Catalina made him laugh, she was cheerful and argumentative, and always willing to fight against doing things she didn't want to do. He knew that she was deeply attracted to Dr. Naseef, but had decided to deny this attraction, for all that he told her she was denying herself the chance to be happy with a man who loved her. If Father Lucas was clear about one thing, it was the sincere and unconditional love that the doctor held for Catalina. But Marvin, even though he was far away, still loomed large in her life.

Father Lucas had found out as much as he could about the American and his love for Farida. No one was surprised that the American had lost his head for the Alexandrian philosopher.

Catalina refused to acknowledge that Farida might have any redeeming qualities. She had assigned her the role of the wicked seductress who prevented Marvin from carrying out his duty to her and to her daughter. For all that Father Lucas tried to convince her to forget about the American, Catalina stubbornly refused. She was sure that she would find Marvin and force him to marry her. She didn't even acknowledge the possibility that Marvin and Farida might get married.

Dr. Naseef thought that his pain must be as strong as that which Catalina felt at the absence of Marvin Brian. When she said that she was going to France with Fernando, he knew that they would be parting forever. He was sorry for himself, and for her. They were both condemned to be unhappy.

Sara, for her part, did not let up on her husband. Not a day went by when she didn't ask him about how the preparations for getting Fernando and Catalina to Paris were going. Faced with his wife's insistence, Benjamin finally gave in.

The day of their departure was set for December 20, but on the sixteenth they awoke to the news that the Wehrmacht had unleashed a counter-offensive in the Ardennes, to the north of France. It was such a large attack that the Allies were forced to withdraw. The Panzer forces advanced unstoppably. The Führer had made the decision to attack and isolate the American troops. Forty-five divisions stationed behind the Siegfried Line forced their way into French territory.

Adolf Hitler had entrusted the command of his forces to Marshal Gerd von Rundstedt, who had not been very enthusiastic about the surprise attack on France. But the operation was a success right from the start.

The news that came to Alexandria was garbled, but all reports agreed on one point: the Wehrmacht was superior to the Allied forces.

A messenger had come to the Wilson's house at dawn. Benjamin was drinking his first cup of coffee. He read the letter which he had been given and left at once, without speaking to Sara.

They didn't find anything else out until mid-morning, when Leyda said that Wilson had come in to the publishing house and wanted to see Sara and Fernando at once.

Fernando felt a secret admiration for Wilson's implacable face. There was nothing about it, apart perhaps from a suggestion of tiredness around the eyes, that showed this to be anything but a normal day.

"You can't go to Paris. I'm sorry. We need to wait to see what the result of the Wehrmacht's offensive is. When I am sure that you'll be able to travel safely, I'll tell you."

He gave no more details. There was no arguing with him, and Sara and Fernando both understood this.

Dr. Naseef felt annoyed at himself for the relief he felt when he learned that Catalina would stay a while longer in Alexandria. But he didn't fool himself: nothing would make Catalina change her mind. She wanted to go. There was nothing to keep her in Alexandria.

1944 passed away with fierce fighting in the Ardennes, and on the first weekend of the Christian New Year, Ylena invited Dr. Naseef to supper.

Colonel Sanders sad firmly over the course of the meal that the Allies would definitely win.

"I'm not going to deny that Gerd von Rundstedt's forces surprised our own and gave them a beating, but after the massacre at Malmedy, things have changed. The Americans won't forgive that."

Mr. Sanders paused, apparently expecting that the people present would insist that he keep talking. Catalina asked him to continue.

"It was a terrible thing that happened, dear, in a little village called Malmedy. Three American units were moving between Baugnez and Malmedy, and they were unlucky enough to run into the Peiper Division of the SS."

Again, Mr. Sanders paused to take a large sip of his wine, aware that he had the attention of everyone present. Fernando waited impatiently for the colonel to continue with his story. So did Ylena, and even Monsieur Baudin, who did not seem as animated as he usually was that evening, as he was suffering from a heavy cold.

"As you know, the Peiper Division is a very experienced unit that has fought on the Eastern Front and which is now a part of the First Panzer Division of the Waffen SS under General Sepp Dietrich," Sanders continued.

Neither Fernando, Catalina, Ylena, nor Baudin knew who this Dietrich was, and neither did they have any idea about the existence of the Peiper Group. But they all fell silent, aware that Colonel Sanders liked to surprise them with his exhaustive knowledge of what was happening on the various fronts of the war.

"Well, as I said, three American units met the Peiper Group, and you know what the SS are like. They took the Americans prisoner, and shot them, and the few who managed to escape took refuge in a cafe in Malmedy. The Nazis burned the cafe and everyone who was in it alive. General Eisenhower has promised to take his revenge, and I am sure he will. After Malmedy, the Americans are fighting much more fiercely. They want to get revenge for their fallen compatriots."

The soup was growing cold and Ylena encouraged them to keep on eating, saying they should not speak about the war any longer. Apart from Dr. Naseef, none of the people present paid their hostess any mind. And so the conversation about the war continued, and it was Monsieur Baudin who spoke to Fernando and wanted to know if he had set aside his plan of going to Paris.

"We'll go as soon as we can. If the Germans hadn't set off all this trouble in the Ardennes, we'd be there now. I'm glad to know that the Yankees are giving the Nazis something to think about," Fernando said.

With the meal over, Dr. Naseef took the opportunity to speak with Catalina. Fernando was playing chess with Colonel Sanders, and Ylena and Monsieur Baudin were chatting about mutual acquaintances.

"So, are you still sure you want to go?" the doctor asked her.

"Yes, I'm too far from my home here. Marvin will come here

from time to time, as Farida is an Alexandrian, but knowing him as well as I do, I have no doubt that he'll go back to Paris from time to time. He has his own apartment there, and Paris is the best place to write."

"Well, I don't think I agree with that … If someone has something to say, they can write anywhere."

"No, absolutely not. There are cities and moments that are more inspiring than others. And Marvin started to write poems in Paris," Catalina protested.

"You're still set on finding him …"

She looked at him very seriously and took him by the hand. The doctor blushed.

"I know … I know that there is something between you and me … well, that there could be something. But it's not possible. Even if I wanted it, it would not be possible. I have a daughter."

"And I love her as if she were my own," he replied.

"Yes, you've treated Adela with a lot of kindness and she loves you, but you're not her father. My daughter has the right to her own father, and I'm not going to give up without trying to find him. The war has stopped me from finding Marvin, but if I go to Paris, I'm getting closer to where he is. He has to acknowledge Adela; he can't deny her."

"I could acknowledge her as my own daughter," the doctor dared say.

She squeezed his hand affectionately. She was moved by Naseef's loyalty, his unconditional love.

"I know, but it would be selfish of me to decide what to do on the basis of my own desires rather than my daughter's needs. A few days ago, Fernando told me that he thought you … that you had deep feelings for me. And I can't deny it, but I will also say that I am fighting these feelings. I could love you, I could, but I'm not going to let myself do so. That's why I'm leaving here, to find Marvin and, if he'll marry me, to go home with him. Not a day goes by when I don't think of my parents."

"And if you find Marvin and he refuses to acknowledge Adela, what will you do?"

"That's not going to happen. I am sure he'll make the right decision when he sees his daughter."

"But ..."

Catalina wouldn't let him continue. He attracted her like no other man attracted her, not even Marvin, but she was convinced that her duty was to fight in order to make sure that Adela had her true father, because only then could she return to Spain with her head held high.

January 1, 1945 began with the announcement that the German troops had begun their retreat from the Ardennes. On January 17, Soviet troops entered Warsaw, and on January 26, they liberated Auschwitz and came face-to-face with hell on Earth.

This was also the date that Fernando and Catalina started out on their journey to France, which had been so carefully planned by Benjamin Wilson.

It had been harder for the two of them to say goodbye than they had imagined. They had been living in Alexandria for three years and had put down roots that were difficult to tear up. Dimitra couldn't hold back her tears. Ylena was unable to hide just how worried she was about what might happen. Father Lucas seemed downcast. Only Benjamin and Sara Wilson were calm.

The night before they left, Zahra came to Ylena's house unannounced. Fernando was putting his clothes in his suitcase when Dimitra announced that the dancer was waiting for him in a car at the door.

Zahra asked him to come with her for a walk and he accepted at once. She didn't say where they were going, and didn't speak the whole journey. He wasn't surprised to find that they were going to her house.

The night passed wordlessly. They didn't need words. As on the two previous occasions, Zahra got up early, while it was still dark. The sun had not yet risen over Alexandria when she opened wide the terrace door to the sea. He followed her and saw that her gaze was harsh.

"Will you help me when the moment comes?" she asked.

He knew what she was referring to, and so only nodded.

He went back to the room without saying goodbye. He got dressed, knowing that his dream had come to an end, struck dead by Zahra's request. He realized how little he knew her. Revenge was the fuel that kept her alive, and she would not pause until she had killed her father's business partner, the man whose testimony had condemned her to a psychiatric institution. Ludger Wimmer lived in Zahra just as Roque and Saturnino Pérez lived within him. He had already killed his father's murderers. This was why he didn't judge Zahra's decision.

BOOK III

1

They traveled to Marseille by boat, and then got to Paris by train and by car.

Catalina was excited when the man who was driving them told them that they were now in Paris. Adela was asleep in her arms and Fernando, although tired, was alert, as he had been throughout the journey.

Benjamin Wilson's preparation had been careful, and they had not run into any problems they couldn't handle, although the journey had not been risk-free. Wilson's organization had taken charge of them and they seemed certain of each step they took. Finally, they reached Paris safely.

The city was already awake at that hour of the morning, and Catalina pressed her face against the window of the car, keen to start getting to know the city. It didn't seem to have suffered the depredations of the war. People walked around in their overcoats, protecting themselves from the drizzling rain that made it difficult to see far.

The man who was driving them took them to a building on the rue de Sèvres, close to the boulevard Saint Germain. They were going to stay in an attic apartment owned by a couple that Sara knew and who, she assured them, were entirely trustworthy. Benjamin Wilson had agreed, and recommended they put themselves in the Duforts' hands.

Madame and Monsieur Dufort lived on the first floor, and were the owners of a few apartments in the building where they were to stay.

The Duforts greeted them with little enthusiasm. They were

polite but distant. They were fairly old: Fernando calculated that they must be past sixty. The little he knew about them was what Sara had told them: Phillipe Dufort had been her father's lawyer, and Doriane Dufort looked after the house, although she had been her husband's secretary in the past.

The Duforts took them to their apartment; Catalina liked it very much. It was very bright; it not only had skylights, but also windows that looked down onto the street. They had two rooms, a little rectangular kitchen that was also the living room, and a tiny bathroom. The apartment was clean and the furniture, although it was clearly not new, had been recently waxed. There were two little beds in one room, and they decided that this would be where Adela and Catalina would sleep.

Madame Dufort recommended that they unpack and rest. They found a loaf of bread in the kitchen, along with milk, eggs, butter and crackers. It was enough for them to take the edge off the hunger of the journey. The next day they'd get started on how to carry out the task that Sara had set them: to recover her family bookshop.

Sara had gone to the French Consulate in Alexandria and secured the necessary permissions for Fernando to be able to reclaim the property in her name. She had also granted Fernando permission to recover her apartment, which was on the first floor above the bookshop, accessible by an interior staircase.

Adela was tired, and while her mother and Fernando unpacked, she slept on a chair.

"It looks like you like this place," Fernando said, seeing the smile that formed on Catalina's face.

"Yes, I like it, of course, and I like the privacy as well. I don't want to seem ungrateful, because Ylena has been a friend as much as she's been a landlady, but it was always her house, and here it's ours."

"Well, it's not really our house. The Wilsons have rented this place until we get settled, and then we'll see what we do."

"I don't think I'd mind staying here. When they told us it would be an attic apartment, I imagined somewhere dark and cheerless, but this is a wonderful place. You know what, I'll go to Marvin's house tomorrow. I kept his address from the letter that he sent me. Maybe he and Farida are back in Paris."

"Don't be too hasty. Wait until Monsieur Dufort tells us how to get Sara's bookshop back."

"We can do both things ... I don't think it'll take them too long to tell us what to do and how."

He didn't want to argue with her, so he said nothing.

Dawn had not yet broken when Catalina woke up, feeling Adela's hand on her face. She had gotten up from the bed and was shivering. Catalina hugged her and brought her into the bed, asking her to sleep a little while longer. Adela didn't complain and settled herself against her mother before going back to sleep. But although Catalina was tired, she was unable to get back to sleep. She stroked her daughter's hair and said that she was very lucky that the little girl was so obedient. Adela never complained and always did what she was told. If her grandparents had met her, they would have been proud of her. For an instant, she felt happy. Paris was not that far from Spain, and maybe when the war was over, her parents could come to visit her. But she immediately abandoned that idea. She was in Paris to find Marvin and ask him to accept his responsibilities: to marry her so she could go back to Spain. No, she would not give in.

She heard Fernando go into the bathroom and turn on the shower. Madame Dufort had warned them that they should take showers for no longer than three minutes so as not to waste water. She looked at the watch to see if Fernando was obeying the rules, and laughed when the fifth minute passed by and he still hadn't come out of the shower.

She didn't want to criticize the Duforts, because they were friends of Sara Rosent's, but it seemed to her that they were a little strict.

At ten o'clock sharp, Monsieur Dufort knocked at the door.

They sat around the table that separated the kitchen from the rest of the room. Monsieur Dufort coughed, anxious to start speaking. He did not take long. He looked at the documents that Sara Rosent had provided, and assured them that he himself would come with them to the bookshop in the Marais to see what sort of condition it was in. Once they had done so, they could do what they thought best.

"I understand that Mr. Brian arranged for a friend of his,

Professor Fortier, to look after the bookshop. We'll see if he managed … Lots of shops were expropriated during the occupation, and now belong to other people. If that's the case, we'll have to litigate to get the property back."

Monsieur Dufort seemed annoyed that Monsieur Rosent, Sara's father, had symbolically sold the bookshop to Marvin Brian, even though he himself had been in charge of the transaction.

"This makes things more complicated. I told Monsieur Rosent that this wasn't necessary … but he insisted, saying that the Germans wouldn't dare expropriate the property of an American, whereas they would very easily take something that belonged to a Jew … Never mind, as far as I can see, Marvin Brian sold the shop to Sara Rosent, just as her father wanted."

"And in all this time, have you been to see what condition the shop is in?"

"Of course not, that's none of my business," he replied grumpily.

Fernando wondered how Sara could have placed her trust in such a standoffish man.

Monsieur Dufort owned a car and he drove them straight to the Marais. As they rode along, Catalina was ever more surprised at the liveliness of the city. There seemed to be no trace of the occupation.

Monsieur Dufort cleared his throat and then explained that the Germans had "respected" Paris.

Catalina was so excited by what she saw that she said that Paris was the most beautiful city in the world, a judgment which Dufort accepted with satisfaction.

After parking the car, they walked down the rue Rosier to the Rosent bookstore.

Monsieur Dufort stopped in front of a shop whose shutters were open, in spite of the fact that there appeared to be no activity taking place within. He pushed open the door decisively, without showing any surprise when a middle-aged man of unkempt appearance came out to stand in their way.

"It's closed," he said, trying to stop them from coming in.

But he couldn't. Adela had let go of her mother's hand and was looking around this strange place, which was filled with cardboard boxes and books all over the walls and on the floor. It looked as though it had seen better days.

If the man thought he could intimidate Monsieur Dufort, he was very much mistaken. Without further ado, he introduced himself as the lawyer for the Rosent family, in whose name he was acting to give this place back to its legitimate owners.

"You've made a mistake … this shop belongs to an American, Mr. Marvin Brian, a good friend of mine. He asked me to take care of the Rosent bookshop."

"Well, from what I can see, you haven't done a very good job of it, Dufort replied, looking at the dust and dirt that surrounded him.

"Monsieur, must I remind you that we are at war, and that although Paris has been liberated, the war is not yet over. As for my work here, I've done what I could, which wasn't much. Reading poetry was not a priority for the Parisians during the occupation, although we've sold a few books, I must admit. But I had to manage my own business, and haven't been able to give the bookshop the attention it requires. But I've kept it on its feet."

Dufort didn't say anything. In his opinion, Professor Fortier certainly hadn't given the bookshop the attention it required. He remembered the shop as a clean and orderly place. He decided not to waste any more time, and showed the man the proprietorial document in Sara Rosent's name that showed Marvin Brian had sold the property back to her.

The man read the documents carefully, as though he were looking for mistakes or loopholes.

"I can't give you the bookshop just like that. I'll need to get in touch with Mr. Brian … and given the circumstances, it won't be easy. I don't know where he is at the moment."

"Monsieur Fortier, as the Rosent family lawyer, I am now telling you to hand over the keys to the shop and a detailed inventory of all it contains. If you don't do so, I will have no choice but to move against you in the courts, where it will be shown that the property belongs to the Rosent family."

"I don't want to cause any problems, but I just need to be sure that my friend Marvin Brian agrees with what these papers say."

"You know that they are in order. Monsieur Rosent arranged

this sale so that the bookshop could not be expropriated because he was a Jew. But as you very well know, Mr. Brian is a man of honor, and he gave the property back to its original owners as soon as he could. I represent them."

Alain Fortier didn't know what to say. The bookshop was an inconvenience for him, but he still didn't know if he should hand it over to people he didn't know.

"You have to give me some time to get in touch with Marvin Brian," he said.

"Is he in New York?" Catalina said.

"As I said, I don't know, but I assume that he'll come back to Paris sooner or later. I have the keys to his house. I suppose he'll want to come and get them from me. But from what I hear, his poems have had great success in New York. He's finally gotten the recognition he deserves, and that may keep him out there. Of course I'll write to him at once."

"You can do what you think best, Monsieur Fortier, but we will be taking charge of the bookshop from now on. This man here, Monsieur Garzo, will take charge of the bookshop, as shown in the documents I have indicated."

"If you don't mind, I'd like to see my lawyer. If he thinks that I should give you the keys after having a look at these documents, then of course I will. But you must understand that I can't abandon the task entrusted to me without knowing that I'm doing the right thing."

Monsieur Dufort accepted Fortier's proposal. They exchanged telephone numbers so that they could arrange a meeting with no problems. Fernando asked if he could see the bookshop and the apartment above the shop, but Alain Fortier apologized, saying that he couldn't allow that until everything had been cleared up.

They spent the next few days exploring Paris. Catalina's enthusiasm only grew, and Fernando had to admit that the city was more impressive than he had imagined. She insisted that they head to Marvin's apartment, and although Fernando resisted, he ended up following her.

The rue de la Boucherie was close to the cathedral of Notre Dame. It was an elegant, silent street, and the building which contained Marvin's house had an impressive appearance. Catalina went to speak to the doorman, but he was not willing to give her any information apart from the fact that Mr. Brian was not in Paris at the moment.

Catalina did not tell Fernando, but she decided that, now that she knew where to find Marvin, she would come often and ask the doorman about him.

Fernando set about organizing his new life in Paris. He did not forget that as well as recovering the Rosent bookshop, his true intention was to go to Lyon and speak to Anatole Lombard in order to find out what had happened to Eulogio.

As Sara had recommended, he sent a letter to Anatole Lombard and explained who he was and his desire to come down to see him and find out about Eulogio.

As the days went by, Catalina made a new friend: a young woman who lived in the apartment across form theirs.

Cécile Blanchett was as cheerful as she was beautiful. She had been the one to strike up conversation with Catalina when they met on the stairs. They got along so well that after their very first conversation, Cécile invited her to come and have tea with her. Fernando resisted, saying that they didn't know anything about her, but Catalina insisted. What harm could Cécile do?

And so it became habitual for the two young women to meet every day and chat. Cécile was a source of valuable information for Catalina. She even offered to help adjust a couple of her dresses that she thought were out of fashion. And so one afternoon, Fernando found the two of them sitting together and laughing as they sewed.

Madame Dufort pulled Fernando aside one day to tell him that even though it was none of her business, maybe they should be a little more careful in their dealings with Mademoiselle Blanchett.

"She had rather too many German friends ... and, well, with some of them her friendship was ... very intimate ... and we all ask what she really lives on ... you understand me ..."

Yes, Fernando did understand her, and he said as much to Catalina.

"Oh, she's a gossip, that old woman! What's she insinuating

when she says that Cécile had German friends? As far as we've seen, the Parisians, with a few exceptions, haven't really made a great show of fighting against the Germans. Cécile told me that there were times when you really couldn't tell that they were at war, and that most people found ways to get along with the situation. What could they do? Cécile tells me that the Duforts are just a typical bourgeois couple who run away from their problems."

"I don't know anything about the Duforts apart from the fact that Sara and Benjamin Wilson told us we could trust them, and that if we had any problems, then they would sort them out. Maybe your friend Cécile doesn't know them that well. There's no reason for her to. By the way, what does Cécile do?" he asked, making Catalina feel a little unsettled.

She looked at him angrily, and replied with some force.

"She's the same as your friend Zahra. She's a dancer. She works at a cabaret in Pigalle."

Fernando was annoyed at the comparison. Zahra was a famous dancer, and she was known throughout the whole Middle East. And if Cécile worked in Pigalle … He didn't know much about Parisian life, but he had heard enough to know that Pigalle was not a place where ladies worked. But he didn't say as much. He knew Catalina and was sure that she would defend her new friend.

They had been in Paris for a week when Monsieur Dufort at last told them that they would meet that afternoon with Alain Fortier's lawyer to sort out the question of the bookshop.

It was a useful afternoon. Once he had looked at the documents, Fortier's lawyer confirmed that there were no objections and that the bookshop would be returned to its original owners. Also, Alain Fortier announced that he had been in touch with Marvin Brian and that he would soon be back in Paris. He was in New York, but his intention was to come back to Europe as soon as possible. Alain Fortier gave Fernando an inventory of everything that there was in the bookshop, as well as the keys, and offered to take them to the rue Rosier to explain to them whatever they needed to know.

Dufort and Fernando checked that the bookshop, in spite of being a little dirty, was in good shape, as was the apartment upstairs. Alain Fortier had behaved like an honorable man. And when Fernando mentioned that he was Marvin's new editor, Fortier gave him his card, in case he could be of any use. On the card, it said that Alain Fortier was a professor of literature at the Sorbonne.

That very night, Fernando wrote a letter to Sara to give her the good news that the bookshop belonged once again to the Rosent family. Monsieur Dufort assured him that he would get the letter to Sara.

With his duty to Sara done, Fernando's chief aim was to get in touch with Anatole Lombard, and so he also asked Dufort what the best way to get to Lyon was.

Dufort said that now was probably not the time to travel across the country because the war was not yet over, but he promised to help him find the best way to get there. However, first of all, he had to open the Rosent bookshop and get it up and running.

Catalina helped Fernando without question. She got up at dawn and took Adela to the Marais in her arms. They cleaned the bookshop and put all the books in order. The apartment upstairs was in a worse state, but Catalina managed to get it looking respectable.

A week later, Fernando declared that the bookshop was now up and running, and asked Dufort to help him get to Lyon.

Catalina wanted to go with him, but he convinced her that she would help him more by staying in Paris.

"You need to be at the bookshop. I don't think it will be difficult for you to deal with people who want to buy a book, if indeed that happens."

"But I don't know anything about books!" she protested.

"We've ordered them alphabetically by author. It won't be hard. We're only in Paris thanks to the Wilsons, and Sara in particular, so I can't abandon the bookshop just like that."

She accepted in the end, but felt very uncertain about it. And so, two days later, just as Monsieur Dufort had said, a man met Fernando in front of the Rosent bookshop to take him to Lyon.

The man said his name was René Marchant. He was friendly enough, but very taciturn, and spoke very little during the journey. But from the little he said, Marchant gave Fernando the impression that he had been a part of the Resistance, and therefore that Dufort must have Resistance connections as well, given that he had put Fernando and Marchant in touch.

It was cold. The rain made everything look darker, but Fernando was falling in love with France, and his first sight of Lyon didn't disappoint.

René Marchant parked the car close to Anatole Lombard's house and took him to the door.

Lombard opened the door and hugged Marchant and then shook Fernando's hand.

Anatole Lombard offered them a cup of coffee, which they both accepted, happy to be in from the cold.

"I'm sorry I can't give you news about Eulogio. I explained to Monsieur Dufort that I don't have any new information about him. And even so, you insisted on coming here to see me ... I understand. I know how close you and Eulogio were, and also that you wouldn't be satisfied with second-hand information."

"I hope you can understand how worried I am. If you only knew which camp he's been taken to ..."

"I promise you that I've done all I can to find out. The war has taken many comrades away from me, but also two people who I was very fond of ... Saul and Eulogio. I've done all I can to find out about the pair of them, but haven't gotten anything yet."

"But you must have some idea of where the Germans take the people they arrest in this region," Fernando insisted.

"The Germans needed labor, and Vichy offered it for free. He could be in any factory anywhere in Germany. It wouldn't be the worst thing that could happen to him. I'm sure that you've heard that the Soviets found a place called Auschwitz ... in Poland. There ... Well, more than a labor camp, it seems to have been a death camp. Saul is a Jew, and they may have taken him there. Eulogio is not Jewish, and maybe he was luckier."

"And couldn't you have done more than ask?" Fernando said, irritated at the Frenchman's defeatist attitude.

"Don't you know what's going on? The war isn't over. I can't take a train to Germany to go and find them. The Germans were right here just a few weeks ago."

"But the Allies are defeating the Wehrmacht," Fernando interrupted.

"Calm down, please," René Marchant said. "Do you really think we don't do all we can to find out about our own?"

"Yes, you're right, the Allies are advancing, but the war isn't over yet," Anatole said, feeling a little compassion for Fernando. "We have to wait a little while longer."

"There's a lot of confusion around at the moment. It's not easy to know what's happening. Camps are being liberated, but there aren't any official lists of survivors, and the soldiers who liberate the camps really don't know what to do with the ruined people they find in them. The Red Cross is taking charge," René Marchant cut in.

"And have you spoken to the Red Cross?" Fernando asked.

"Of course I go to them daily and try to find information. My friends in Paris do the same, but there aren't lists of survivors yet. I told you this already." Anatole's reply sank Fernando into deep despair.

"You're not the only one who doesn't know where his friends are," Marchant said.

But all Fernando cared about at that moment was Eulogio. Although he wasn't indifferent to other people's suffering, the pain he felt was for Eulogio, and him alone.

There wasn't much more to be said. René said goodbye, and that he would pick him up again first thing the next morning.

"You'll sleep here. Don't worry, it'll be fine," René Marchant said.

When they were left alone, an awkward silence fell. They were two men who didn't know one another and who had no personal connection. But Anatole Lombard tried to make an effort so that the atmosphere wasn't too unpleasant for both of them.

He took him to the guest room and said he should rest while he made them something to eat. Fernando accepted. He needed to be alone, and to think.

An hour later, Anatole knocked at the bedroom door. The meal was ready.

Fernando had ignored his stomach for a while, but he noticed how it was rumbling with hunger. The smell of vegetable soup was a comforting one.

Anatole filled his bowl to the brim and took a tiny cup for himself.

"Aren't you hungry?" Fernando asked him, just to break the silence.

"No, not really. Ever since they took Eulogio away, I barely eat and I don't sleep. I'm anxious. I'm not well. But what's happening to me is irrelevant compared to what others are going through."

"You and Eulogio … you were good friends …"

"I loved Eulogio. I still love him, because I think he is still alive. He came into my life at a moment when I thought I was dead because I had lost Saul. I loved Eulogio, but Saul … I found love with Saul. We found love together. Ours was a total love, a shameless love, unconditional. When they took him away, I thought that I couldn't just sit still and do nothing, just waiting, so I joined a group of people who fought in their own way against the Nazis. Sometimes I even thought that I wanted them to arrest me, so that I could be with Saul. You see how crazy love can be. Then Eulogio came along. I'd be lying if I said I wasn't attracted to him the first time I saw him. I felt bad: how could I love another man if Saul was a prisoner?"

Fernando was so moved by Anatole's story that he couldn't find any words to respond. He didn't know how to think about Anatole's love for Saul, or his attraction to Eulogio. It was the love of one man for other men. Anatole's feelings for Saul and Eulogio were like his feelings for Catalina and Zahra. How could it be?

"Is something bothering you?" Anatole asked, seeing how disconcerted Fernando looked.

"No … no … of course not … it's just that … well, I …I've never heard a man talk like this …"

"I suppose you knew that Eulogio …"

"No, I didn't, I really didn't … I'm surprised that …"

"That Eulogio was a homosexual like I am?"

Fernando suddenly felt strange. The conversation made him feel a little odd.

"You can't imagine how much Eulogio has suffered, trying to hide who he really is. He told me about his life in Madrid, in the neighborhood, all the jokes about homosexuals, about how he had to stay silent because he was scared to say who he was. His whole life was a lie until we met each other. He was very brave, because he took the first step, and decided to stay with me, although he knew that Saul would still have a part of my soul forever, and that if Saul came back …"

"But do you love him?" Fernando couldn't bear to hear that Anatole didn't love Eulogio with all his heart, and still kept a part of his soul aside for Saul.

Anatole sat silently and then got up and took the two plates away. He went to the kitchen and came back with a casserole dish containing a couple of sausages in a meat sauce. He gave one sausage to each of them and then sat down and thought of his reply.

"We haven't spent much time together. We had an immediate attraction. Well, that's what it was for me, but I think that it was more for Eulogio, because it forced him to accept who he really is."

Neither man felt much desire to carry on with this conversation. Anatole realized that his honesty had upset Fernando, and had put him in a state of mind that was too obviously uncomfortable for the pair of them to carry on talking. They finished eating in silence. Fernando didn't sleep at all that night. He felt uncomfortable admitting that Eulogio was a homosexual. He wanted to understand him, but he could not.

René Marchant left Fernando outside the Rosent bookshop just as Catalina was putting the shutters down. They hugged, happy to see one another again.

"You were only away for a day, but it seemed a lifetime," she said. They took the subway and went back to the apartment, where he told her in detail about his conversation with Anatole, the natural way in which he spoke about his love for other men, his confusion when he heard about it, and his reluctance to accept that Eulogio could love Anatole.

"He's your friend, Fernando, your best friend. You don't have the right to judge him," Catalina said.

"But … do you think it's all right for two men …? Well, you know …"

Catalina shrugged again. Then she put on Adela's coat and took Fernando by the arm, leading him out into the streets of Paris.

"Who are we to decide about other people's feelings?"

"I don't understand you, Catalina! You weren't raised like that …"

"What do you mean by 'like that?' Of course, my parents never told me that a man could love another man. Did your father speak about that?"

"No, of course not."

"Well, that's why we think that things have to be a particular way, and sometimes they are, but other times they are not. Look, we don't have any choice but to accept the people we love as they are, not as we would like them to be. And anyway, why should you care about who Eulogio likes?"

He didn't reply, because he didn't want to say that he did really care, that he had been disappointed and disgusted to discover that his friend was a homosexual. No, he couldn't accept that it was natural. The only thing that hadn't changed was his sincere affection for Eulogio. That hadn't changed at all.

They settled in Paris. Catalina spoke far less about Alexandria, although one day he caught her looking at a photograph showing her with Adela and Dr. Naseef.

"Do you miss him?" he asked.

"Him? Yes. I could have fallen in love with him."

"Why don't you just forget Marvin?" he said grumpily.

"Because he's Adela's father. And because he's the only man I have ever given myself to. He has to fix what we did."

"Fix?"

"Yes, fix. He has to marry me and give me back my respectability."

"Ah, so you're concerned about your respectability, but not that of others."

"I don't judge anyone, Fernando. Let everyone live how they please. I demand things of myself that I would never demand of other people. I owe it to my parents to return to Spain a married woman."

"Marvin doesn't love you, Catalina, you have to get that into your head."

"I'm not going to say that I don't care if he loves me, but the important thing is that he marry me. There's Adela to think of."

He was surprised at how much Catalina's contradictions irritated him. She let things slide with everyone else, and hadn't even been the slightest bit scandalized that Eulogio had fallen in love with this Anatole Lombard, but as far as she was concerned, she was particular to a fault.

The next day was Saturday and Fernando left the house very early. Catalina didn't go with him. She stayed with Adela, saying that she had things to do, but she didn't say what.

When Fernando came back in the middle of the afternoon, she met him with a smile and said that they had to talk. He waited impatiently, because he had to tell her that that very morning, Monsieur Dufort had given him an envelope containing a notebook filled with handwritten poems. As soon as he saw the handwriting, he knew they were written by Marvin. There was a letter from Sara telling him to publish the poems. They'd do a trilingual edition, in English, French and Arabic. Sara wanted it to be ready for the summer.

Marvin's previous book of poetry had been an unexpected success in the States. Well, Sara had said that in the States, his success had to an extent been confined to academic circles, but it was a step in the right direction. And Fernando couldn't help feeling proud that it had been he who edited the book, although he felt little personal sympathy for the American. But he had managed to separate the man from the poet.

Fernando showed her the letter and the notebook, and Catalina read Marvin's poems in silence. Fernando looked at her as she did so. When she had finished reading, she handed over the notebook.

"They're very dramatic but beautiful."

"That's what Marvin's poetry is like," Fernando agreed.

"When do you think he'll come to Paris?"

"I don't know. All I know is that she's asked me to publish

727

the book, but she doesn't say anything in her letter about where Marvin is or when he's thinking of coming, if he is thinking of coming."

"Right … But he will come. I know he'll come. There's nowhere else in the world he likes better than Paris. I know it."

Then she bit her lip, and Fernando knew she was going to say something that might upset him. And then she did so. She told him she had gotten a job.

"A job? Where? Who got it for you?" he asked worriedly.

"Cécile asked me what I knew how to do, and I told her that I could play the piano. She didn't think it would be much use in Paris, but the owner of the bar where she works said he needed a pianist. He had to fire the one he used to have. And so I start work this very night. It's perfect that our timings fit so well. I don't have to leave here before eight, and by then you're here, and maybe you can help me with Adela …"

"Are you insane? How could you even consider working at Pigalle?"

"You say that it's a cathouse … I'm not sure. We still haven't explored that neighborhood. Cécile insists that they will pay me well. I have to earn a living, at least until Marvin comes and I can sort out the situation. I don't want to rely on you. I was able to work in Alexandria and pay for my stay in Ylena's house," she said with pride.

"It's not the same! In Alexandria you gave lessons to the children of respectable families."

"And here I'll play the piano in a bar, and that's it."

"I won't let you," Fernando said angrily.

Catalina looked him straight in the eye. Fernando saw the little wrinkles in the corners of her mouth.

"I'm taking this job. I'm going to start work this evening. Cécile is waiting for me. I hope that tonight, you will at least do me the favor of looking after Adela. I'll look for someone tomorrow who can watch her."

"Cécile is not who you think," he protested.

"And who are you to judge? Cécile works to survive, as we all do. She's a dancer, Fernando, no more than that."

He knew that he wasn't going to convince her and regretted

that he couldn't protect her, although he was sure that something bad was going to happen.

"I'll look after Adela. You don't have to find anyone. But I thought you were going to help me with the bookshop. You know I can't run it by myself. Sara said that when I got it up and running, I should hire someone. I thought of you."

She bit her lip, as she normally did when she was considering something, but then she looked straight at Fernando. All doubt had disappeared from her face.

"Thank you, but like I said in Alexandria, I have to be able to earn my own living. And it wouldn't be fair for me to become a burden to you. We can always count on one another, but that doesn't stop me from wanting to get by under my own steam. And now I'm leaving. Cécile is waiting for me."

Fernando stayed with Adela and read her a story until she fell asleep. Then he sat down to read Marvin's poems slowly. Catalina was right: they were poems filled with drama and beauty.

Cécile hadn't stopped talking since they left the attic. She didn't even stop talking on the train to Pigalle. They walked a couple of blocks, and Catalina felt uncomfortable seeing women standing in the doorways of certain buildings, inviting passers-by to enter. But she was even more surprised to see Cécile greet some of these women.

"You know a lot of people ..."

"Yes ... Well, all us ladies of Pigalle know one another ... You'll see, you'll like them. Although you can't trust everyone ..."

"It's not a neighborhood like the one where we live."

"No, of course not! It's Pigalle, men come here to have fun. And that's why we're here, to give them their fun."

Catalina felt tense, wondering what exactly Cécile was talking about.

A man came over to Cécile and gave her a hug, which she accepted without resisting.

"You're late, gorgeous. You know Jean-Pierre doesn't like it when his ladies are late," the man said, looking at Catalina.

"My friend has a baby and couldn't leave it alone."

"This the new one?" the man asked.

"Yes. Catalina, this is Benoit. He's a blabbermouth."

Benoit tried to kiss Catalina but she pushed him away. Then he tried again and she pushed him away again, this time with a kick to the shins.

"What are you on? Cécile, tell your friend that she's got to play nice …"

"Oh, but you're a brute! It's her first day! Wait until she learns the ropes," Cécile replied, laughing.

Catalina wondered how Cécile could all of a sudden behave in such a vulgar way. She seemed different, very different from the girl who was her neighbor.

Benoit took them by an arm each and squeezed tight, and although she attempted to wriggle away, Catalina couldn't. The man stopped a little further down the street. A few neon lights showed that the club was called La P'tite Poupée.

They went into the bar. There were several women there, wearing clothes that left a good part of their bodies uncovered. Some men were fondling them nonchalantly, and Benoit slackened his grip. Cécile used the opportunity to take Catalina by the hand and guide her behind the little stage. An elderly woman greeted them. By the look of her, Catalina could see that Mamma Rose was not French, that she more likely came from North Africa.

"Is this the new one?"

"Yes, Mamma Rose, this is Catalina," Cécile said.

Mamma Rose looked Catalina up and down and then gave her some fishnet stockings and a red basque, as well as a black tulle skirt that barely covered her thighs.

"I'm not going to wear that. I'm going to play the piano, nothing else."

Mamma Rose stood in front of her and pinched her arm hard.

"You'll wear what I tell you to wear. Of course you'll play the piano, but you'll play a lot of other things as well. What sort of a place do you think this is?"

"Don't scare her, Mamma Rose," Cécile said, who had already changed into a dress that was so tight she could scarcely move. The neckline was so low that her breasts were practically exposed.

"I'm going," said Catalina. "I'm not going to work here."

"You're not going anywhere."

The three women turned around. There was a tall man standing at the door to the changing room. He was fat and unhealthy-looking, with black hair and even blacker eyes.

"Jean-Pierre, this is Catalina." Cécile pouted as she introduced them.

"You've got five seconds to get dressed and get onstage. You'll play the piano and accompany the singer. Élise is in a worse mood than I am. You should have been here two hours ago. This is a business and the clients want music, but they want to hear Élise sing especially. And so you'd better not hold us back any longer. Oh, and in case you hadn't realized, this is an establishment where the girls are very friendly to the customers."

Jean-Pierre slammed the door as he left.

"Better get changed fast. Jean-Pierre isn't very patient," Mamma Rose warned her.

Catalina didn't say goodbye to Cécile, but opened the door and walked out into the night. She started to walk without knowing where she was going. She didn't know the city well, much less this seedy neighborhood. Suddenly a hand grabbed her, and she turned to see that she was in the grip of Benoit.

"Oh, so the little lady didn't like La P'tite Poupée."

"Let me go," she said, trying to sound braver than she felt.

"Why? This is my home. I'm the boss here. The girls obey me. When Benoit tells you to do something, then you do it. You think you're worth more than the other girls?"

"I said, let me go! I'm not one of your girls and I'm not going to work at La P'tite Poupée. I told your boss as much, and if you don't let me go, then you'll have to talk to my lawyer, Monsieur Dufort."

"Oooh, so she's got a lawyer and everything!" Benoit laughed, but didn't look like he was going to let her go.

"Monsieur Benoit, if you let me go right now, then you'll be able to get back to your work and I'll forget I ever saw you. But if you don't let go of me, I'll make sure that my lawyer finds you and makes you pay."

"Since when have hookers had lawyers?" Benoît said mockingly.

"Don't insult me! Let me go!"

Benoit let her go carelessly, and she hurried away. She walked without knowing where she was going, feeling the gazes of women who stood in the doorways and the men who had come here to look for women. Some of them asked her what she charged. And a couple of pimps asked her who she worked for.

Finally, she came to an empty street that looked more familiar than the others. She sped up. She had been walking for more than two hours already, and was very lost, when she saw a man closing the shutters of a bar. She walked over tentatively and asked him for directions to the boulevard Saint Germain.

He looked at her in surprise. She didn't seem like the kind of girl who would normally be out at such an hour.

"It's a long way from here. What number are you going to?"

"I'm not really going to the Boulevard itself, but to a street off it, the rue de Sèvres …"

"Well, you've got a long walk ahead of you … I'll show you how to get there, but I'd be careful if I were you. This isn't really a good time to be out in the street alone …"

She nodded in shame and listened carefully to what the man told her.

When she got back to the rue de Sèvres, she ran to the door. She didn't feel safe until she had closed the door of the apartment. Fernando and Adela were sleeping peacefully. She didn't sleep a wink all night.

Fernando found her in the morning making coffee.

"You got up early … it's Sunday today," she said.

"And I didn't sleep well … I couldn't get to sleep until you got back."

"You were asleep!"

"You got back at two in the morning. And no, I wasn't asleep. How was work?"

Catalina looked down and blushed. He was worried. She didn't normally show such signs of weakness. Angry and stubborn, yes, but never humiliated. And that was the impression she gave now: humiliation.

"I'm not going to work there. It's not what I expected."

"Right."

"That place … well, I think it's one of those places where men go to … to …"

"To pay to spend a while with a woman."

"Yes, something like that. They were dancing there, drinking … They wanted me to put on a costume that left me half-naked. The owner, Jean-Pierre, is an Arab, or so it seemed to me … and Mamma Rose as well. And Benoit, who looks after the girls."

"Well, at least you made some good friends," Fernando said with a straight face.

"I had to threaten them with setting Monsieur Dufort on them if they didn't let me go. It was … You can't imagine what a time I had of it. Then I got lost, and walked up and down steep streets, and I didn't know where I was. I had a bad time of it, Fernando."

"You didn't listen to me."

"No, I didn't listen to you because I wanted to be my own woman, I didn't want to depend on you, I have to be able to run my own life. You don't depend on me, Fernando, so why should I depend on you?"

"Because you're a woman and need someone to look after you. That's why, Catalina."

"What kind of a world is this when a woman needs a man to protect her from other men? Better for you to change your attitude rather than to put us in cages so no one can hurt us."

"That's not how things are."

"Well, you have to change them," she said stubbornly.

"Yes, right away, madam," he said angrily.

"If you behaved as you should, then we wouldn't need any extra protection."

He felt how angry she was. He knew that she was right, but the fact that she was right didn't change how things were. He was sure that women should have the same rights as men. His father had insisted on this, but had also said that sometimes reason ran behind reality, and so you had to fight to change reality.

"And Cécile?" he asked.

"Cécile made a mistake about me. Or maybe I was mistaken about her."

"And still you stand up for her ... Madame Dufort explained to me that Cécile only lives here because her parents worked as porters in this building. And when they died, the neighbors agreed that she could carry on living in the attic. But they want her to leave now. In the war she had a lot of German soldier friends."

"Madame Dufort's just a gossip!"

"Maybe, but she only warned me because her husband is the Rosents' lawyer, Sara's lawyer. They are the ones who rent us this apartment and have made sure that we can start a new life. And I'm grateful that they warned us about Cécile."

"If she's working at La P'tite Poupée, it must be because she had no other choice."

"I don't know what her motives are, but she hasn't been straight with you. She shouldn't have tried to get you to work at a brothel."

"She didn't force me. I accepted ... well, I didn't know it was a brothel."

"And didn't you suspect when you saw the name of the place? La P'tite Poupée. What a name!"

Adela came into the room. She was not wearing any shoes and Fernando picked her up. He looked at Catalina, and the look was enough for them to declare a truce. It was Sunday and maybe they could still have a nice day together.

Spring had not yet come to Paris. The newspapers still gave over a lot of space in their pages to the death of President Roosevelt. Harry Truman was now back in charge of the United States, and some analysts tried to work out if the new president would change the relations between the various parties in the war, now that it looked like it was coming to an end. That morning, the headlines also spoke of how close the Soviet troops were to Berlin.

Catalina was tidying what had been Sara's apartment. Fernando was in the bookshop, hoping for the door to open and for a customer to come in. But poetry wasn't what most people were after those days, although some former customers had come back now that they saw the bookshop opening its doors again. Fernando had organized a large sign saying ROSENT: BOOKS to be hung at the door, so no one could fail to see it when they passed by.

The bell rang and the door opened. Fernando was surprised to see Alain Fortier, Marvin's literature professor friend from the Sorbonne who had run the bookshop during the Occupation.

The two men shook hands and Alain Fortier got to the point.

"I should have come earlier, but you know, it's sometimes hard to find the time to do the things you need to do. I'm happy to see the bookshop back on its feet."

"Well, we're trying," Fernando said.

"Well, as you know, Monsieur Rosent wasn't only a bookseller, but an editor as well. All of the poetry books he produced were of excellent literary quality. Rosent discovered many young poets, including Marvin. If Monsieur Rosent didn't think that a young poet was excellent, he didn't discourage him – maybe he would even send him to another publishing house – but he didn't publish him himself."

"Fernando nodded. He knew all this, but he didn't want to interrupt Alain Fortier.

"When Marvin asked me to take charge of the publishing house, I did so without imagining the problems it would cause. Imagine when the Germans started to persecute the Jews ... they took their businesses, their houses ... I didn't know what to do ... I did what I could. I took the name Rosent off the front door, and ... well, I took all of Monsieur Rosent's files."

"His files?" Fernando didn't know what Rosent meant.

"Yes, all his files, with names and addresses and telephone numbers, all the poets that Monsieur Rosent worked with, and his friends and his customers. If this had fallen into the hands of the Germans, some people would have had a bad time of it. Well, here they are. I suppose you'll need them to get in touch with these people."

Alain Fortier opened his briefcase and took out a thick envelope which he put on the counter. Fernando thanked him, and then they spent a few minutes talking about the war, which according to Fortier was practically won, even if Hitler was still holed up in the Chancellery.

"The Russians will get him out of there, you'll see. Germany is beaten, and even a fanatic like him will have no choice but to accept it."

Fernando agreed. He wanted the war to end soon so he could look for Eulogio. He had written to Anatole Lombard a couple of times, but had not received any news. All he could do was wait for the war officially to be over.

Alain Fortier waited silently, and Fernando knew he had something more to say.

"I told you already that I'm a professor of literature at the Sorbonne. Marvin was a student of mine and ... Well, there's a really brilliant student I'm currently teaching. Brigitte Durand. I think that her poems are wonderful. If Monsieur Rosent were still alive, I would have had no hesitation in asking him to read the poems. But I don't know if you ... Well, they told me you were Marvin's editor ..."

"I'd be happy to read your student's poems. Sara Rosent hired me to make sure that this place gets back to what it once was, and to carry on publishing poetry."

"Thank you, Monsieur Garzo. I brought Brigitte's poems, just in case."

The two men shook hands, no longer the strangers they had been when they first met.

Catalina had not seen Cécile again. They avoided one another, even though they knew that it was inevitable they would meet again at some point in the future. It happened one morning, when Fernando had gone to the bookshop and Catalina had stayed home because Adela was sick and had a sore throat, and she had been unable to sleep all night.

The girl still had a temperature at noon, and Catalina decided to ask Madame Dufort if there was a clinic nearby where she could take her. She opened the door and ran straight into Cécile, who had obviously not been home all night. Her hair was messed up, her makeup was smeared, and she had bags under her eyes and her clothes were out of shape.

"What a surprise, I haven't seen you for ages," Cécile said grumpily.

"Sorry, I'm in a hurry," Catalina said.

"You and I need to talk. You got me into a lot of trouble. Jean-Pierre was very angry with me. You caused a stir ... Look, I didn't think you were such a prude. You've got a child, you're not married, and yet you put on fancy airs and graces ..."

Catalina swallowed. She regretted having been so open with Cécile and explaining her situation. How could she have been so stupid?

"I'm not going to argue with you. I don't care what you think of me, but you're clearly wrong. And now, if you don't mind, I need to go."

"But I want to talk to you," Cécile said.

She had drunk too much, and the alcohol was still in her system.

"Some other time."

Catalina went down quickly to the first floor. She was lucky to find Madame Dufort at home, and she recommended her a doctor who had a surgery not that far from where she was. She offered to go with her. Catalina accepted gratefully.

When she went upstairs to fetch Adela, Cecilia was still waiting on the landing. She was waiting for her.

"Hey, I said that you and I need to talk," she said, trying to grab hold of Catalina.

Cécile didn't expect that Catalina would give her a shove. She let go of her and stood in surprise for a second, then went into her house and slammed the door, saying loud enough to be heard by everyone, "Who does that little Spanish bitch think she is?"

Luckily enough, Adela wasn't very sick. The doctor said she had a throat infection and that was what was causing the fever. He gave her a prescription and said that Adela shouldn't go outside for a couple of days at least.

The next morning was when they came for Cécile.

Fernando was just getting dressed when he heard her shouting. Catalina heard her as well.

Male voices ordered Cécile to come with them.

"What's going on?" Catalina asked, rubbing her eyes, barefoot, in a robe.

"I don't know, I think it's got something to do with Cécile," Fernando said.

Catalina didn't think twice and opened the door.

"Go back inside, madame!" one of the men ordered.

"What's going on? Why are you taking her?" Catalina asked in alarm.

"She's a collaborator," the man said.

"Help me!" Cécile said, trying to break free.

"Get back inside if you don't want to get into trouble," another man said.

"Come on, Catalina, let's go inside," Fernando said.

"But we can't just let them take her away!"

In the end, they didn't do anything because there was nothing they could do. One of the men said that they shouldn't stick their noses in unless they wanted to get in the same trouble as this "slut."

Fernando took Catalina's arm and dragged her inside. She protested, but he stopped her from going out onto the landing again. The voices faded away.

Even though Catalina was angry with Cécile, she couldn't stop worrying about her. As soon as she was dressed, she went to the Duforts' apartment.

She told Madame Dufort what had happened.

"It's odd that they didn't come sooner. She's not the first collaborator to be taken by the FFI."

"The FFI? Who are they?" Catalina asked.

"The Forces Françaises de l'Intérieur, men who were in the Resistance," Madame Dufort said, but she didn't know where they had taken Cecilia nor what might happen to her. She didn't seem to care that much. It was obvious how much she disliked Cécile.

Even though Catalina tried to convince Fernando that they should try to find Cécile, he held firm.

"A few days ago, you were complaining about her taking you to Pigalle, and now you want to save her? I told you that our landlady doesn't think very highly of her. She went out with German soldiers and had no qualms about bringing them back here. Your friend Cécile isn't really popular around here."

"Yes, she tricked me, but I don't want anything to happen to her ... poor girl," Catalina said.

"She's a whore," Madame Dufort interjected.

Doriane Dufort's unequivocal statement surprised the two Spaniards so much that they didn't know what to say.

"Well, it's not that she's a whore per se – people find the work they can – but rather her relationship with the Germans. She's a collaborator," Madame Dufort said.

"And what? Did all the Parisians work with the Resistance?" Catalina said angrily.

"Of course not, my dear, but some people had the good taste to be discreet. They didn't fight against a powerful enemy who had taken control of our city, but they didn't fraternize with them either."

"That's impossible, Madame. The city as a whole collaborated, and only a very few people stood up against the Germans. They ... they felt right at home here," Catalina said.

"You're very young, and you don't know what happened here," Madame Dufort scolded.

Two days later, Cécile knocked at Fernando and Catalina's door. Fernando opened and was struck dumb.

Cécile's beautiful red hair was gone. Instead, only her cracked bald scalp was visible.

Cécile burst into tears, and Fernando let her in. Catalina gave her a hug. Then they listened to her in astonishment.

Cécile had paid for her relationship with the Germans. She thought that she had saved herself, but the balance of power had swung the other way, and she was to be punished.

Catalina couldn't be Cécile's friend again, but neither could she abandon her to her fate. Cécile didn't even dare go out and buy bread, so Catalina took it upon herself to do all the shopping she needed. What she did not do was stay to listen to Cécile's complaints. She was very upset because her hair would take months to grow back, and if she didn't start working soon, then she'd lose her apartment.

After that day, everything happened so quickly that they were barely capable of taking it in. The news that appeared on the front pages of the papers was an open invitation to hope.

The Soviets had taken Berlin. The partisans had killed Mussolini. Adolf Hitler had killed himself in his bunker in Berlin. The

German army was surrendering in places where they had until recently been fighting: Italy, Holland, Denmark…

On the seventh of May, Monsieur Dufort came to find Fernando and Catalina and told them in a choked voice that he had just heard on the radio that Germany had surrendered.

Catalina burst into tears and scared Adela, who didn't understand why her mother was crying.

"We've won," Catalina said, as she tried to wipe the tears away with the back of her hand.

Monsieur Dufort invited them to come and celebrate the end of the war at his house with some friends.

"We've got a couple of bottles of Bordeaux saved from an excellent year that my father laid down. There hasn't really been a reason to celebrate anything these last few years. We'll drink them tomorrow," Dufort said, his voice thick with emotion.

The days started to pass ever more quickly; or at least that's how it seemed to Catalina and to Fernando, who had finished editing Marvin's new poetry collection and felt particularly satisfied with the result. He had asked Alain Fortier to promote the book, given that the professor wrote reviews for various literary publications.

At the beginning of July, Fernando received a message from Sara. She and her husband were in Paris and were staying at the Ritz, but they were keen to see the bookshop – and above all, her apartment – as soon as possible. They'd come to the bookshop early that very afternoon.

Catalina said that she would buy the flowers for Sara herself. She was nervous, and so was Fernando, both of them waiting impatiently for Sara to bestow her approval on what they had done.

The taxi drew up outside the bookshop at three on the dot. Sara Rosent came out impatiently without waiting for her husband. She went into what had once been her father's bookshop, now her own, and burst into tears. Everything was as it had been the last time she had been here, if maybe the smell of polish was a little stronger.

Fernando came over to her with Catalina behind him, both trying to hide their nervousness. Adela, very quiet, was sitting on a chair behind the counter. Catalina had told her not to move, and she was obeying to the letter, seeming to understand the solemnity of the moment.

Sara briefly greeted Fernando and Catalina, and then went over to the shelves to look at the books; there wasn't a speck of dust on them. She took a few down, turned the pages, smelled them. She stroked them with the tenderness reserved for something one has not seen in a long time. She couldn't speak, she was so overwhelmed.

Benjamin Wilson stood in silence, as did Fernando and Catalina. They were aware that they had to let Sara find herself once again. They saw her wipe away a tear that ran down her cheeks, and it was not until Adela spoke that she seemed to realize that there were other people around.

"Mama, can I move now?" the little girl asked.

Then words started to burst out of all of them, questions, because Sara wanted to know everything that had happened. Then they went up to the apartment, where she was either unwilling or unable to contain herself, and she cried freely. She closed her eyes, and for a moment she imagined her father, thinking that when she opened the door, he would be there.

She smiled to see the vase of flowers on the dining table, and passed her hand over the surface of the furniture, as though just by touching these items she could travel back into the past, back to the years she spent with her parents.

Benjamin Wilson came over to his wife and took her by the hand. She smiled gratefully and then invited them all to sit down around the table.

"Is everything all right?" Catalina asked worriedly.

Fernando explained in detail what they had done, and gave them all the documents that Monsieur Dufort had drawn up, as well as an inventory of what there was in the shop and the house. He showed them the French edition of Marvin's poems and asked their permission to publish the poems by Brigitte Durand, the poet he had been recommended by Marvin's friend Alain Fortier.

They spent the rest of the afternoon talking and catching up on what had happened in Paris, but also what was happening in Alexandria. Ylena missed them, and Dr. Naseef had given them a present for Adela. The biggest news was that Captain Pereira had come home on the *Esperanza del Mar*.

When Ylena scolded him for being away so long, the captain had explained that they had been caught in a gale and nearly shipwrecked. They had sought refuge in Africa and remained there for several months while the old *Esperanza del Mar* was prepared once again to face the mysteries of the open sea. But that had not been his only adventure. Once they reached Brazil, the ship suffered an accident that almost sent it down to Davy Jones' locker.

Catalina was very moved to hear that Pereira had asked after her and her daughter, and that he was sad not to find them in Alexandria.

It was already dark when Benjamin Wilson suggested that they accompany him to have dinner at the Ritz. He said that Monsieur Dufort and his wife would be there as well. Catalina said that she couldn't come because she wasn't dressed for it, and that she had to look after Adela, but Sara said that the child wouldn't be any trouble at all, and that they had to all eat together. Adela spent a very happy afternoon with her coloring book.

They made a strange group in the Ritz's elegant dining room. Sara was wearing a wine-dark silk dress. Benjamin Wilson was in a dark blue suit, so dark it seemed almost black.

Doriane Dufort was in a simple black dress. Her husband, Phillipe Dufort, had a dark suit and a sober tie. Catalina knew that she and Fernando didn't fit in with this group, as they were wearing their work clothes: she was in a tweed skirt and a white shirt with a cardigan, and he was wearing a jersey and corduroy trousers. Adela wasn't dressed up either. But no one seemed to pay them any attention.

Benjamin Wilson and Phillipe Dufort spent a good part of the evening talking about the Potsdam Conference that was currently taking place, especially the absence of Churchill, who had lost the elections.

"No man is indispensable," Monsieur Dufort said, but Benjamin Wilson said that without Churchill, they wouldn't have won the war. "He was the only man who never wavered in his belief that we had to stand up to Hitler. It was hard for our North

American friends to decide to join the war, but victory would have been much more difficult without them." Dufort acknowledged this, and added that they shouldn't forget the millions of dead that the Russians had added to the reckoning.

Catalina listened to them in silence and Fernando hardly spoke. Sara seemed distracted, and as for Adela, she was barely there. Her mother had told her that she should be good and not get in anyone's way.

Dufort didn't know if Truman, Stalin and Attlee could agree at Potsdam. Benjamin Wilson had no doubt that the decisions which the three presidents would make would mark the future of Europe. He said that Sara would be staying in Paris, but that he would be going to Berlin at some point in the next few days.

After dinner, when they were saying goodbye at the hotel door, Sara opened her bag and took out two envelopes.

"I saved it as a last surprise for you," she said, giving one envelope to Fernando and the other to Catalina.

Catalina nearly shrieked when she recognized the rounded handwriting of her mother. Fernando said nothing.

They wanted to be alone to read the letters. They barely spoke on the journey back from the Ritz. The Duforts said nothing to spark conversation either.

My dear daughter,

I am as nervous as I am excited to think that this letter will find its way into your hands. I am writing and I can't stop looking at the photograph of your daughter, my granddaughter, little Adela. The same name as my mother.

I can't understand why you didn't just send us a letter, why we can't know where you are, and why your news has always come to us through mysterious channels. A man came up to Isabel, Fernando's mother, in the street, and said that if we wanted to write to you, he'd pick it up in a couple of days. Isabel told me at once. I can't understand why it has to be this way, but I do understand that it can't be any other way.

I'm sorry, I don't want my first words to you to be a reproach. That's the last thing I want. If there's one thing that

I desire with all my heart, it is to have you close to me and to look after you and Adela.

And now the bad news. You know how sick your father has been. Ever since you left, he has gotten worse and worse, and it seemed that he had lost the will to live and to fight. I suppose you won't have forgotten about Juan Segovia, our doctor and friend, who has been very helpful these years while your father's health has been worsening. Thanks to him, your father has been well cared for after the four times he has been sent to the hospital, the last time only a month ago. Your father had a stroke, so he can no longer speak, and half of his body is paralyzed.

Catalina, my daughter, please, if you can, come back to Spain. Your father loves you and he has suffered and suffers, just as I do, from your absence, for all that he was strict with you before. He has always wanted the best for this family and thought that the way to protect you in this new Spain was to get you married to someone with influence and a good relationship with the regime. He was wrong, yes, and he has never forgiven himself. I want you to know that he punched Don Antonio when he spoke ill of you.

All I want to say is don't judge your father, because although he is wrong, he has always acted in what he thought were your best interests.

Before the stroke, there was one other time when we thought we would lose him, he seemed to be dying, and my heart broke to hear how he called for you. But the Lord wanted him to live, although the effects of the stroke are severe: he can't leave his bed and he is difficult to understand when he speaks.

Your father and I were brought up to live in peace, but we went through a war and suffer the hatred of people we don't even know.

My daughter, I will say it again. Come back, come back to us, come back home. I know that it will be good for your father to have you around, and getting to know our granddaughter will make him as happy as it will make me.

As for the gossip: what can we do? Of course they'll criticize us, but we can't live our lives worrying what other people will say. We'll hold our heads up high and we won't let anyone insult Adela because her father won't acknowledge her. That's what has happened; am I wrong? If the American had behaved like a gentleman, then he would have married you and you would be here, so if you are not here, then it must be the fault of the dishonorable behavior of Mr. Marvin Brian.

Your aunt Petra has forgiven you, and insists that I tell you as much. You made her very upset when you ran away, because she was in charge of you, and she couldn't stop blaming herself for not having been able to stop you. The poor woman cried for months, and every time she came to our house, she kept on asking forgiveness, and accepted your father's reproaches without complaint. She suffered so much that she fell ill, and couldn't eat anything for a long time. She lost a lot of weight. Now she's calmed down a bit and wants to meet Adela just as much as I do. She says that when she comes to Madrid, she'll get her a place at the convent school where she still gives piano lessons. It's a good school and it's close, in the Corredera Baja de San Pablo.

Antoñito is happily married, apparently. Maria Paz Nogués, the daughter of Fidel the notary. He seems to have calmed down a bit too.

Maria Paz was always a good girl, sweet and religious. They've had two children already and she is pregnant with the third. You can't imagine how much of a fuss Don Antonio and his wife make of their grandchildren, and Antoñito behaves as though they were the only children in the world. I won't tell you that they're a more refined family now, because that would be impossible, but at least they're a little more relaxed.

Prudencio, Don Antonio's brother, has been promoted and has an important job to do in logistics. As for Paquita and Mariví, Antoñito's sisters, they're still single, which is unsurprising.

Don Bernardo keeps on asking me about you. He is annoyed that I don't tell him where you are and why you left, and has even threatened to refuse me absolution in the confessional until I tell him the truth. But I held firm and said that if he didn't want to hear my confession, then I would go to another church and confess to another priest. I'm not so simple as to think that I can upset God just by not telling Don Bernardo where you are. On the other hand, I don't know where you are, so there's that as well.

I run into Piedad, Eulogio's mother, quite often in the neighborhood and we say hello in a friendly enough way. She's even come to have tea with me and Isabel a couple of times. I am very proud of her for still holding her head up high even with everything people have said about her friendship with Don Antonio. She is still a beautiful woman, but all the suffering has left its mark on her. The worst of it is that she doesn't know where her son is, but in his last letter, Fernando said that Eulogio was well.

Who are we to judge other people? We all have our weaknesses and our little sins.

Don Bernardo scolds me for being so sympathetic towards Piedad, but I have to say – and may the Lord pardon me for doing so – that I quite enjoy annoying Don Bernardo, and so I commit little sins that I'm sure God won't care about, like being nice to Piedad, or inviting her to our house for a coffee. I don't think the Lord will punish me for that. And I don't think that Our Lord of all Mercy and Kindness, who sacrificed himself on the Cross for all of us, is going to send me straight to Hell, or even to Purgatory, for getting along with Piedad. If I go to Hell, and I pray that I don't, then it will be for something else.

As for Isabel, she is as worthy a woman as always. She has a natural authority that makes everyone respect her. She's a good woman, and she's suffering from Fernando's absence, just as I suffer from yours and Piedad suffers from Eulogio's.

The man who will pick up our letters has told Isabel that he is sure they will get to you soon. I hope so, and more than anything else, I hope that you come home to see us.

Your loving mother,

ASUNCIÓN

Catalina had been so eager to read her mother's letter that she hadn't noticed that Adela was asleep fully dressed on the bed. She went over to her daughter and hugged her as she cried. She felt such strong nostalgia that the only thing she wanted to do was to pack her bags and go straight back to Madrid. But she knew that she couldn't let herself be carried away by nostalgia; in spite of her mother's goodwill and her father's forgiveness, life would not be easy for them if she turned up with no husband and with a child. She knew her neighbors too well, and her old friends from school, and they wouldn't hesitate to criticize her harshly for being a single mother.

No, she couldn't go home because of the hurt it would inflict on her and on her daughter. It would mean making her daughter suffer the stigma of being the daughter of a single mother.

She cried for a while as she held her daughter tight. Adela slept and didn't notice her tears. She slept the sweet sleep of innocence.

Catalina heard Fernando's nervous footsteps. He had gone to be alone in his room and read his mother's letter. Isabel would ask him to come home, just as her mother had asked her to. But neither of them could do it. She needed to protect Adela and she was also implicated in what Fernando had done. She had given him the weapon with which he killed those two men, Roque and Saturnino Pérez. Sometimes she asked herself if maybe Fernando regretted killing them. She had to admit that she did not regret giving him the pistol that her Aunt Petra kept carefully because it had belonged to her husband in the war. Yes, she was complicit in the deaths of those men, and one day she would have to confess what she had done; she had not yet done so, for all that she had been tempted to do so on several occasions with Father Lucas. She hadn't confessed because the secret was not hers to share, and she would not betray Fernando, even if that meant eternal damnation. The thought frightened her, and she decided that she would confess on her deathbed when she was very old and no one could do anything about it to either of them.

My Dear Fernando,

What a joy to know that his letter will soon be in your hands!

A few days ago, the usual stranger came to Luis Rodríguez's pharmacy, which is where I work now. He said that if I wanted to, I could write to you and he could make sure that the letter got to you. He also said that if Catalina's mother wanted to do the same, then he could get a letter to her as well. He made me jump when I first saw him, but now when I see him coming, I know that I'll have news from you, so I smile whenever I see him.

My son, I never stop praying for you, and asking God to protect you and guide you. I know that you are a good man and that you always remember what your father taught you.

I dream that one day, instead of that stranger, it will be you who walks through the door so I can give you a hug. Until that day comes, I'll make do with the knowledge that you are well, or at least this is what this strange messenger tells me when I try to get more information out of him. He's a taciturn man, but he says he knows that you are well and that things are going well for you, although he refuses to tell me where you are.

My son, I still can't understand why you can't tell me where you are, but I respect your decision because you must have a very good reason for not doing so.

The only thing this man tells me is that Catalina is with you, and that calms me down. I'm thinking of her as well as you. I know that you'll look after one another.

Have you and Catalina perhaps decided to bind your lives, to get married and start a family, or maybe you are still friends as you were when you were children? And I worry about Eulogio, and why he doesn't write to his mother. Piedad suffers in silence. She always asks me if I have any news of you. Is Eulogio still with you and Catalina? Tell me so that I can calm her. She asks me about the American, Marvin Brian, and is certain that he can give you a hand. As for Spain … I suppose you know what's going on here, because wherever you are, you will know what's happened; you must read the papers.

There is fear everywhere, Fernando, fear because the executions are still going on, death sentences are still being signed. There are lots of men and women in prison whose families get no news from them at all.

No one dares say out loud what they really think, except the people who are supporters of the new regime, of course. They can speak freely, and it's a freedom they have that we don't. We're always losing; we not only lost the war, we continue to lose it every day. The losers have become survivors, nothing more. And that's why I also feel a great pain not to have you by my side, although I also want you to be somewhere where you are a free man, and where you don't have to bite your tongue so that people don't know what you think, and where you can walk freely through the streets without someone reporting you to the police as an enemy of the regime.

I only hope that one day you ask me to come to visit you. Don't doubt for a second that I will come at once, no matter how far away you might be.

I can only imagine what your life must be like; mine goes by with very little new happening in it. I work at Don Luis' pharmacy, and I'm very grateful to him, and to his wife Hortensia, for trusting me. I know that you'd frown if you were here, and that you'd ask me how I could possibly be grateful to these people, the victors in the unfair war we fought. But ideas are one thing and people are another, and Don Luis and Doña Hortensia are good people. They think that it's best for Spain that their side won the war, and we think that it was a tragedy, because it put to an end once and for all our dream of building a fair and democratic country. But that doesn't make us better people or them worse ones, and it is how we treat others that should be the only thing by which we are judged. And I swear to you, Fernando, that I have nothing but good things to say about them; they have treated me well and I have never felt undignified or belittled. They know that your father was a Republican and that he fought in the war, but they never say anything that could upset me. And they never boast about being on the winning side. Doña Hortensia likes to say that we should think about the future instead of going over the past again and again. One of her brothers was shot, and every death causes the same kind of pain, Fernando.

Everything is more or less the same in the neighborhood except for the fact that Don Ernesto is very ill: he had a stroke and half of his body is paralyzed. Asunción looks after him night and day. As you know, they're very much in debt. Don Ernesto's brother still has control of their lands, but they don't bring in very much, and so they live very modestly, although Asunción doesn't complain. She's a good woman, who tries to do as best she can with the little they have. As you can see, Fernando, Asunción is another example of someone who is good, even though their ideas are not the same as ours. I don't want you to think that all ideas are equally good; no, not at all. There are monstrous ideas that only cause death and destruction, and which don't respect other people, but that's not the case with Asunción and Ernesto, who may be right-wing and very monarchist, but who are not bad people.

All I can say about Don Antonio is that he's as proud as a peacock of his son's new father-in-law. I told you that Antoñito was going to marry Mari Paz, the daughter of Don Fidel Nogués. You don't know how happy Don Antonio and his wife are. Even Antoñito seems happy. As for Mari Paz, she's always been a good and obedient girl, and she accepts her husband and his family without complaint. They've had two children now, and she's pregnant again too.

I want to ask you, Fernando, to try to get Eulogio to write to his mother. Piedad doesn't deserve to suffer so much. Children shouldn't judge their parents, and Eulogio certainly shouldn't judge his mother for making such a great sacrifice to save her son. When you speak to him, try to make him understand. We normally go out for walks together on Sundays. She comes to meet me when I get out of the noon Mass, and if the weather's nice, then we walk down Gran Vía and maybe have a coffee at the Viena Capellanes Cafe. Some Sundays, Asunción asks us to tea. Ernesto sits in his chair, motionless, staring into space, but I think he's thankful to us for keeping his wife company.

Fernando, my dear son, when can I see you? You have to know that I only want to hold you tight, and that alone gives me the strength to keep on living.

All my love, forever,

YOUR MOTHER.

Benjamin Wilson went to Berlin next. He seemed impatient to be in Potsdam, close to the place where he said that Stalin, Truman and Attlee would decide the fate of the world. Sara did not go with him. She was eager to turn what had been the house of her childhood and youth into the home of her adulthood. Although she knew all too well that Benjamin Wilson would never move fully back to Paris, it was no problem for them to have a house where they could spend long periods if need be. She needed Paris, just as much as her husband needed Alexandria and London. "Although he is half English, the same old poison – fascination with the Orient – runs through his veins," she said.

It was clear that the Wilsons had a lot of money: if that hadn't been the case, then it would not have been possible for them to buy the apartment next to theirs on the first floor of the old building on the rue Rosier where the bookshop was. Benjamin was always prepared to support his wife in these matters, as he didn't want to make her live in cramped quarters. The windows and the terrace of their house in Alexandria opened onto the sea and she needed not to feel trapped by the walls of the apartment she had inherited from her parents.

And so she poured all her enthusiasm into the building work that made her apartment not just her home in Paris, but also a large independent office space from which her husband could manage his affairs.

Fernando asked Wilson to do all he could while he was in Berlin to find out where Eulogio had ended up. He still hadn't heard anything from him.

As for everything else, Catalina and he sank into a new routine. Everything was pretty much as before apart from the fact that they had to listen to Sara's opinion on everything. She was not only overseeing the work on her house, but also needed to know about the catalogue of publications that Fernando was preparing. Rosent's bookshop would once again become a hub, not just the place where the best books of poetry were sold, but also where they were published. They waited impatiently to hear what Sara had to say about Brigitte Durand, the poet that Alain Fortier had recommended. Sara had liked the poems a lot, and had also liked the poet, a mousy-looking girl who nonetheless had wonderful sensitivity and talent.

Sara liked that fact that Fernando had listened to Alain Fortier. Not just because he was a well-respected professor of literature, but because without his guidance he would have been lost, try that he might to call all the poets whose names appeared in Monsieur

Rosent's files. Some of them had been deported to German extermination camps from which they would never return; others had been robbed of their inspiration by the face of the war, and their only aim was to see their loved ones once again and survive. In the middle of all this confusion, Fortier was capable of recommending some of his students who he was sure had great poetic talent.

Adela started to go to school on the day that Japan surrendered. The war in the East had carried on until the Americans decided to put a stop to it all by dropping nuclear bombs on Hiroshima and then Nagasaki. Europe was a great plain filled with corpses, and so her citizens were not all that interested in the terrible effects of those destructive bombs.

Catalina and Fernando had decided to carry on living in the attic apartment that the Duforts rented to them, and had even told Sara that they would start paying their own rent.

Sara had raised no objection to having Catalina work in the bookshop behind the counter, while Fernando grew ever more focused on his work as an editor with the help of Alain Fortier. Neither Catalina nor Fernando thought of asking for a salary, but Benjamin Wilson decided how much money he should pay them, and was very generous when he did so. And so Fernando and Catalina made the decision to stop living off the charity of others and work for their daily bread.

They had found a place for Adela in a lycée near the rue Rosier. The three of them would go there every morning on the subway.

Catalina was worried about how her daughter would adapt to the lycée, given that she only had a few words of French, but Adela made herself understood. She had developed her own language: a mixture of Spanish, Arabic and English, with a little Greek and now some French.

Life might almost have been pleasant for them had it not been for the hollow feeling born of their exile, stopping them from being close to their loved ones and wrapping them in an embrace.

In December, Benjamin Wilson came back to Paris with Marvin and Farida. As for Eulogio, to Fernando's despair, Wilson told him that his men were looking for him all over Europe, but it was as though he had vanished. Fernando said that they had to keep on looking for him, and Benjamin Wilson, maybe so as not to upset him, said that they would.

As for Marvin, he was to spend a few days in Paris. Sara and Benjamin asked Fernando to organize a poetry reading to which the most famous poets of the city would be invited. His last collection, *German Notebook*, had been praised by the most demanding critics in America and Europe, as had his previous works, *Spanish Civil War Notebook* and *Alexandria Notebook*. Marvin was now one of the elite, an Olympian.

Sara asked Alain Fortier to take charge of the invitations, as he would know better than anyone who to invite.

Fernando didn't hide the fact that he was worried about how Catalina would react when she found out that Marvin was in Paris.

Benjamin Wilson cleared his throat and looked at him.

"You'll have to find a way of talking to Catalina. We don't want to get involved in Catalina's private life, or in Marvin's, for that matter. However, he said he would only come to Paris on one condition: he must be sure not to see Catalina. He's afraid that she'll insist on seeing him. I like Farida a great deal, and she has been a friend of mine since we were both very young. She's worried that Marvin might be upset by any scene that Catalina might cause," Benjamin Wilson explained.

"I can't stop Catalina wanting to see Marvin. He's within his rights not to want to see her, but she's totally within her rights to try to see him," Fernando said.

Benjamin Wilkson was not a man accustomed to being refused, and so he pursed his lips and looked away for a few seconds before continuing.

"I am sorry, Fernando, but my priority is Marvin Brian. It's not just because we are his editors and we owe it to him, but also because it was Sara who led him on his first few steps as a poet, and convinced his father to pay attention to his gift. Sara can't forget Marvin and Farida's bravery in going to France in the middle of the war and trying to save her father, even if, very unfortunately, Monsieur Rosent died when he was about to cross the Swiss border."

"Well, Eulogio helped them too," Fernando replied.

"Yes, that's true." Benjamin Wilson's tone grew stern.

The two men looked at each other, aware of how difficult the situation was. But neither of them could back down. They both had made unbreakable vows and had things they were required to do, although Fernando was aware that if he broke things off with the Wilsons, then Paris would cease to be the safe refuge that it had become for him and for Catalina. It wasn't easy for people to live in the city as refugees.

He spent the rest of the day in a state of unease and was surprised that Sara said nothing to him about Marvin, although they didn't have any time to be alone because they were with Alain Fortier going over the books that they were about to publish. Then came lunch, and she left the office at lunchtime, saying that she wouldn't be back in until the next day. Fernando was sure that she was going to see Marvin and Farida.

He waited for night to fall before talking to Catalina. Adela was asleep and they sat down to discuss the events of the day together, as they always did after eating.

"Marvin is in Paris," he said without looking at her.

Catalina gave a start. She felt very uncomfortable. Of course, it was clear in her head that she had to get Marvin to acknowledge Adela and marry her to give the pair of them back a little bit of respectability. But she wasn't fooling herself: her dreams of love with him had been worn down over time. Sometimes she asked herself if she had ever really been in love with him.

Silence fell between the pair of them. Fernando was waiting for Catalina to speak, but she needed to get her emotions in check before she did so.

"I'll go and see him tomorrow. I suppose he'll be staying at his apartment on the rue de la Boucherie."

"I don't know. All Benjamin Wilson told me was that Marvin and Farida were in Paris. He wants me to organize a poetry reading. Alain Fortier will choose the place and the guest list."

"What else did Wilson ask you?" Catalina looked straight at Fernando. She knew him well enough to see when he was hiding something.

"The Wilsons don't want you to see Marvin. He made it a

condition of his coming to Paris that they stop you from approaching him. Farida thinks it will affect him."

Catalina's face twisted with rage.

"How dare they! No one can stop me trying to speak with Marvin! No one! I left Spain to find him. I've been through … you know what we've been through, and now they want me to sit around and twiddle my thumbs. I won't!"

"Don't shout, you're going to wake Adela."

"I'll speak with Marvin. He has to listen to me. Let's see if he's brave enough to look me in the eyes and say that he won't care for his daughter. If he does, then he's … he's … a bastard."

"Calm down. We need to think about what we're going to do."

"We? Who's we?" she said suspiciously, already knowing the answer.

"We need to think about what is best for you and for Adela."

"And for you as well?" she said, angrily, as though Fernando were a stranger.

"We've come a long way together, Catalina, we've pulled together and we've gotten here together. Everything that has to do with you affects me and has an effect on my life."

"If you're going to ask me not to see Marvin …"

"No, I'm not going to ask you that. I've told Benjamin Wilson that it's your decision. Of course, whatever you decide will have consequences."

"Will they throw us out of the apartment?" she asked, her voice both hostile and somewhat fearful.

"He made it clear to me that the Wilsons are his editors, and that they owe Marvin a great deal, as well as the fact that they are friends with both him and Farida. I think they'll prefer to avoid any conflict. I don't know what decision they'll make if Marvin … well, if Marvin feels that you're putting him under pressure."

"I'm going to see him, Fernando. I'll do it. I owe it to my daughter and my parents."

"I can try to talk with him …"

"You know what happened in Alexandria."

"A lot of time's gone by, and maybe he'll listen to me now."

"But what kind of man is Marvin if he's scared to talk to me?"

"I don't know him all that well. And we were never friends, you know that."

"You're his editor."

"Yes, I'm his editor, and as his editor, I am aware that he's one of the best poets I've ever read. I love and honor the poet, but not the man himself. You can be a genius and a bastard."

"I'm going to see him, Fernando."

"Let me try, please."

"No! There are things that a person has to do for themselves. I know that you've always gone out of your way to protect me, but I'm rejecting your protection now. And that's final."

They stopped speaking. Fernando knew that he had no choice but to let her do what she wanted.

It was raining and the wind held her back. She had gotten up very early. She had left a note for Fernando telling him that she'd be late to the bookshop.

Adela walked holding her hand. They had taken the subway to Nôtre Dame and she would have liked to say an Our Father, but the cathedral was shut. The rain soaked her overcoat. She turned up her collar and Adela took her hand.

The doorman was sweeping the entrance and he stood in front of her mistrustfully, blocking her way in.

"Good morning, Miss."

"Good morning."

"What do you want?" the doorman said, looking her up and down, then looking at the quiet little girl holding her hand.

"I'm going to Mr. Brian's house," she said with a false tone of confidence.

"Mr. Brian ... Well, you'll have to wait and let me ask if they're seeing people at the moment. I have orders to prevent anyone from bothering them," he said, proud of the responsibilities that he had been given.

"I'm a friend of Mr. Brian's. Tell them that it's Catalina Vilamar."

The doorman hesitated. He thought that this young woman

wouldn't agree to wait peacefully in the doorway and would try to follow him up to Mr. Brian's apartment. He thought that he'd take the elevator, but then he saw that she'd see which floor he was headed to, and so he walked up the two flights of stairs, his arthritis complaining all the while.

He rang the doorbell several times. It was as though there was no one there, but he knew this could not be the case, given that he hadn't seen Mr. Brian leave, neither him nor the elegant woman whom he treated as his wife.

The door opened a crack. The lady was wearing a silk robe. The doorman apologized and said that there was a woman with a young girl waiting downstairs. Farida couldn't hide her surprise when she heard the name Catalina Vilamar come from his lips.

"Tell this young lady that Mr. Brian will not see her. And please, tell her not to keep trying to see him. He won't see her today or any other time."

The doorman was surprised at how blunt the reply was, and had no time to answer, because Farida had softly shut the door.

Catalina was waiting impatiently by the doorway.

"Can I go up?" she asked anxiously.

"I'm sorry, miss, but the lady says that Mr. Brian can't see you."

"Did she say when ..."

The man was uncomfortable and hesitated, before replying in a whisper.

"The lady says that Mr. Brian won't see you on any other occasion either. I'm sorry."

She stood still, as though her feet were nailed to the ground. She had feared this reply. She had almost expected it.

She took an envelope out of her bag and handed it to the doorman.

"I'd be very grateful if you could get this to Mr. Brian. Personally."

The doorman took the envelope and assured her that he would. He had no choice but to accept, because Catalina waited until he had gotten into the elevator. She wouldn't go until she knew that the letter was in Marvin's hands. She had written it the night before, thinking that Marvin might refuse to see her.

She felt sick and tearful, but she held herself together until the doorman returned.

"I gave the letter to the lady. She promised me she'd give it to him."

Farida shut the door and turned around to see Marvin waiting impatiently in the doorway to the living room.

She held the letter out, and he looked as though he would refuse to take it.

"She won't leave us alone," he said, a little upset.

"No, she won't," Farida said.

"Well, let's go. We'll fly to New York," he said.

"You shouldn't do that. It's important that the French critics support you, because Sara has said that they want to see you, and interview you, and come to your reading. You're a poet, Marvin, and you have obligations to your readers, because they are the people who make you what you are."

"She's crazy. How can she think of coming here with the girl?"

Farida said nothing, but walked over to him and took him by the hand.

"I'm going to make some coffee. Go back to bed. I'll bring you your breakfast."

"No, I can't sleep any more. Catalina gets to me."

"You have three choices. You can speak to her, or you can run away, or you can avoid her, as you have until now."

"But she doesn't give up!" he said.

"And neither do you," she advised.

"But how are we going to avoid her? She's quite capable of turning up at the reading and making a scene."

"No, I don't think so. A scandal's not what she wants. She wouldn't gain anything, and she'd make herself look ridiculous."

"So, what are we going to do?"

"We stick to the plan. Make France surrender to your new book of poems. We'll ask Benjamin to deal with Miss Vilamar."

"The ridiculous thing is that Fernando Garzo is my editor, and he's the one standing up for her."

"You've told me several times that Fernando is in love with her."

"The truth is that we don't really get along with one another ... I don't know why Sara got him to edit my poems ... Athanasius Vryzas could have done a much better job ..."

"Sara's a mother figure ... she saw something in the boy that moved her and she decided to help him. Monsieur Rosent was an editor, and you know that Fernando Garzo's father was an editor as well until they shot him ... I suppose she thought she had to help him. In any case, you have to admit that Garzo is a good editor and has looked after every last detail of your collection."

"Even so, I think I'll ask Sara if I can work with a different editor. I'm upset by the very idea of seeing Fernando again, especially now that Eulogio's no longer in the picture."

Farida sat in silence. He knew that she was not there, but rather drifting along the gray waters of her thoughts. She was trying to make sense of a fate that had tied the four of them – Fernando, Catalina, him, and her – into an impossible tangle.

"Read the letter while I make the coffee," she said, opening the door and closing it softly after her.

Marvin opened the letter, and the first thing he saw was the photograph of a girl who seemed to be smiling at him. He put it back in the envelope without paying it any further attention and settled down to read the letter.

Dear Marvin,

If you are reading these lines then it is because you have refused to speak with me.

I really don't understand why you insist on this: how can I hurt you if we just speak? If we're honest with one another?

After all the time that has gone by since we met each other in Madrid, and after what happened, I can understand, for all that it hurts me deeply, that you are not in love with me and you never were. On that night, I was no more than a girl who lost her head and let herself be seduced. Maybe I was lying to myself when I said that you were as infatuated with me as I was with you. And so I accept that you do not love me. But we have a daughter together: I attach her photograph. You and I both have obligations towards her.

She is not guilty of our mistakes, and she deserves to have both of us make sacrifices for her so that she can go through life with her head held high and doesn't have to suffer the indignity of having "father unknown" on her documentation.

I don't ask you to marry me; no, although that is what in all good conscience you should have done. But at least recognize Adela as your daughter, give her your name and behave towards her as a father, let her grow up knowing that you're her father.

Our daughter is now going to school, and a few days ago she told me that all her friends have a Papa, and she was wondering if she could say that Fernando was her Papa; she thinks he's her father. I had to tell her the truth, that Fernando is not her father, and that her father travels a great deal but she'll meet him soon. I won't hide from you that she was disappointed that Fernando was not her father, but I don't want to tell her lies, and sooner or later she'll have to know the truth.

I don't even ask you to support her. I can do that myself. All I'm asking is that you don't make Adela pay for our mistake.

And please, don't make our problems fall on Fernando's shoulders. If you complain to Wilson he might fire us both, which might be fair in my case, but would be entirely unjust when it came to Fernando. As far as you are concerned, he's the best editor you could have, but not only that: he's an honorable man, a gentleman who has helped me and Adela more than I can say. We would be dead without him.

I hope that your conscience makes you rethink the situation, and at least accept that you have a daughter and have obligations towards her.

I look forward to your reply.

Yours, with all my love,

CATALINA VILAMAR

He started to crumple the letter and would have torn it up if Farida had not come in at that moment with a breakfast tray.

"What are you doing? Come on, don't behave like a child," she said as she put the tray on the table and picked up the pages from the floor.

She poured him a cup of coffee and read Catalina's letter. When she had finished, she drained her cup.

"What do you think?" Marvin asked.

"I still think you've got three choices …" Farida said straight-forwardly.

"I don't care about the girl. She's not my problem," he said angrily.

"I'm afraid that like it or not, she is your problem, at least until she convinces herself that you will never, ever take on this responsibility."

"I'll call Benjamin and Sara at once. They promised me that Catalina wouldn't bother me," Marvin said.

"It was an impossible promise. You know that."

"Yes … We shouldn't have come," he complained.

"Don't say such silly things. You have to assume that this girl will follow you wherever you go, and will insist that you recognize the child as yours. The important thing is to make sure that this doesn't affect you."

"I can't deal with her stubbornness, trying to make me take on a responsibility that is hers alone."

"She's right about one thing … if you complain to Benjamin, he'll fire Fernando, which wouldn't be fair. He's a good man, and if Benjamin fires him, his life will get very complicated … and he's a good editor. The best book you've produced has been the *German Notebook*, in the English and the French versions especially."

"We never liked one another, but you were in his corner right away."

"Yes, I tend to sympathize with people who have to fight with their ghosts. And we know from what Eulogio told us that he definitely has his ghosts. Well … I recommend you don't change your editor."

"I don't know. And now that you mention Eulogio, I'm upset that Benjamin hasn't been able to find any trace of him. I don't want to think that he died in one of those camps."

When Catalina arrived at the Rosent bookshop, she found the door to the back room open and Fernando standing with Sara and Alain Fortier. She went over to say hello to them, and saw that Sara's face was very stiff.

She set herself to organizing some shelves, trying to calm down. She worked at the bookshop only thanks to the generosity of the Wilsons. If they fired her, she would have to rely fully on Fernando again, and it was impossible for her to be a permanent burden on him, for all that she was accustomed to his support and his presence.

They had lived together for more than four years and she felt nothing but gratitude towards him. He had never tried to take advantage of the defenseless situation in which she found herself, and he had shown her generous and unconditional affection.

She knew that if Marvin complained to the Wilsons about her insistence that he recognize Adela, then they might fire her and get rid of Fernando. Benjamin Wilson and Farida were old friends, and he would do what it took to please her.

She was worrying away at these thoughts when Alain Fortier's voice brought her back to reality. Fortier was saying goodbye. He smiled at her, and as soon as he closed the door behind him, she went to the back room where Sara was seated and Fernando was standing.

"I'm sorry to interrupt you, but I'd like to speak to you, please, Mrs. Wilson."

Sara looked at her seriously but invited her to sit down.

"As you know, and well, if you don't know you'll find out soon, I went with my daughter to Marvin Brian's house this morning. He didn't want to see me, but I gave the doorman a letter for him. I know that this will be unwelcome news for you and for Mr. Wilson. You don't want Farida or Marvin to be upset in any way. I understand this: they're your friends. If my presence here makes things difficult, I'd understand it if you decided to get rid of me, but I only ask that my personal issues – which are mine alone and my decisions – have no effect on Fernando. He is not responsible for my decisions, nor does he participate in them. I'll tell you one more thing, Mrs. Wilson: I will try to speak to Marvin again, and if I don't manage to do so in Paris, now that the war is over, then I will follow him wherever he goes. I accept the consequences of my actions, and if you and Mr. Wilson decide that my unbreakable vow to speak to Marvin Brian is annoying and will cause you problems with Marvin himself, I understand if you fire me at once. But I beg you, one more time, don't make Fernando pay the price for my actions, which have nothing to do with him."

Catalina had spoken in a rush, without giving Sara a chance to interrupt her. Fernando looked at her worriedly and she could see that Sara was weighing up the words she was about to say.

"Yes, you've put us in a tricky situation. Marvin called me and my husband just now to say that you were at his apartment and that you had written him a letter. You yourself acknowledge that this is very vexing for him. He's only in Paris because I insisted in no uncertain terms that he come. Now that he is starting to make a name for himself as the excellent poet that he is, it seemed to me essential that he return to Paris. The *Poet of Pain* ... that's what they called him in the United States and in England ... and it is important for him to get the support of the French critics, because that will guarantee him success in the rest of Europe. Now that the war is over, we need poetry so that we can feel human again," Sara said sadly.

Fernando looked at both women without knowing what to say. Catalina had really made things difficult for the pair of them. And although he needed the job, he wouldn't carry on with it if that meant his humiliation. Sara spoke again.

"We owe a debt of loyalty to our authors, but Marvin is also important because I discovered him. I can still remember the day he came into the bookshop, nervous, asking for my father. I told him that he wasn't there, and he gave me a folder and asked me to give it to my father. I promised I would, and then as he was leaving, he turned back and looked at me with a smile: 'Maybe you could read my poems, and if you like them give them to Monsieur Rosent.' And that's what I did, because as soon as I started reading them, I was swept away by the symphony of his words. My father was the only one who decided that they were worth publishing. Until then, I never had anything to do with deciding which authors we would publish. That was my father's job. The poets, and above all the critics, trusted him. If my father published something, it was because its literary value was undeniable.

I was sure that the poems that the young American had given me were extraordinary, but I was also interested to see what my father would say. If I close my eyes I can see him even now, saying: 'Now I know that the Rosent bookshop will outlive me. This young man that you recommended to me has an extraordinary talent. He's your author. You take charge of him.' Until that moment, I had just helped out at the bookshop, but now I started to help my father editing books. Marvin is 'my' author and I am very proud of him and of me. I've edited lots of other poets, very talented poets, but none of them means what Marvin means to me."

Sara fell silent. Fernando wrung his hands, and Catalina listened to every one of her words very carefully.

"As for Farida," Sara continued, "she's a very dear friend of Benjamin's, and not just because she's a great philosopher, a cultivated and sensitive woman, but because the two of them grew up together and know each other well. Benjamin can't deny Farida anything, and she can't deny him anything."

"In that case, there's no more to be said. I see that you have to dispense with my services. I'm sorry, because I felt very useful here. I never thought that books would be so ... important for me. I'll get my things. All I can do is say thank you for everything you've done for me."

Catalina turned and Fernando followed her. Sara didn't try to stop either of them from leaving.

"Catalina ... wait ..." he begged.

"I'm sorry, Fernando. I'm sorry to have put you in this situation. I should be making every sacrifice for you, but my chief obligation is to my daughter. Please stay. I hope the Wilsons don't make you pay for my problems with Marvin."

Fernando felt stunned by the situation, although he knew that his primary loyalty was to Catalina. And so he turned back and went into the back room.

"I am sorry about what has happened, and I want to thank you for all you've done for me, for us. I'll never be able to repay you for your generosity. I hope that you understand that I ..."

"Calm down. Has anyone said that you need to go? I don't think you should. You're a good editor and I trust you. You've shown how good you are at running the business and that you also have an eye for finding new talent. No, I don't want to lose you. I know that Catalina is a good girl and has done her fair share of the work over these last few months. You've managed to get this house back on its feet. I appreciate the work she has done, and I don't want to get rid of her either, but with her attitude, it's very hard for her to stay here. I owe Marvin a lot, Fernando. You have to understand this. You've edited a few poets and you know that you owe them a lot, that you can't ignore their circumstances."

"I don't know what to do," Fernando admitted.

"Tell Catalina not to be so hasty. Let her finish her day's work, at any rate. I'm going to have lunch with Benjamin and Farida and Marvin, and I'll be back later this afternoon. I'll have a definitive decision as regards Catalina by then. As for you, Fernando, nothing has changed, and your position here isn't in question."

Catalina was putting on her overcoat when Fernando caught up with her. They whispered to one another. Fernando couldn't convince her to stay. The two of them knew that she would never give up her pursuit of Marvin until she had managed to make him acknowledge Adela, and that the Wilsons couldn't allow her to work for them as long as she remained a threat to their dear Marvin.

"But let's not ruin it all. You should stay. What do we win if they fire us both?" Catalina said.

Fernando agreed, but he felt uncomfortable with himself. He didn't want to leave the bookshop, but his conscience said he should show solidarity with Catalina. And he told her as much. She insisted, even saying that they should be practical. If he left the Wilsons' shop, what would they eat? It wouldn't be easy for him to get a good job in Paris, much less to find a place where they could live that was as nice as the apartment that the Duforts rented to them at such a reasonable price.

Fernando spent the rest of the day upset and agitated, asking himself what he should do. He deeply hated Marvin Brian, who he blamed for all their current problems. He did not for one minute think about blaming Catalina for her stubbornness. He thought that Marvin was a bastard, a coward who hid from a woman he had taken advantage of. He had been a witness to the event when he saw them together; she had been drunk on the wine that Antoñito had brought for his birthday, and Marvin had taken advantage of the situation. She was little more than a girl back then, someone who had fallen in love with the American because he was very different from all the other boys around her. Catalina had built up a romantic dream about Marvin. It wasn't unreasonable, given the black years of the war in which there had been no room for hope.

He was about to lock up when the Wilsons' car stopped in front of the bookshop, which was not unusual, given that the first-floor apartment was now their home.

Benjamin Wilson seemed annoyed, and Sara frowned, which showed that she was worried. Fernando closed the bookshop and walked back to the back room of the publishing house.

"Well, let's get things straight," Benjamin Wilson said without preamble.

"Of course," Fernando replied, feeling the tension in all the muscles of his body.

"We've been with Farida and Marvin and spoken about the situation," Sara said.

"Marvin doesn't want to meet Catalina or the child. He's made it very clear that he doesn't want anything to do with them. We're his editors and we respect his decision. And you should respect it as well." Benjamin Wilson fixed his blue eyes on Fernando.

"You have to understand it," Sara said, crossing her hands on her lap.

Fernando felt disappointed, knowing that either he would have to accept Marvin's conditions or else he would have to resign. He couldn't help feeling grateful towards Sara, because it had been thanks to her that he had become an editor. She had trusted him without knowing him all that well, and had helped him make his dream come true: to be an editor like his father. He was happy and felt indebted to her. He did not feel the same towards Benjamin Wilson, for whom he felt no sympathy and who he viewed as a manipulative person.

"Could I stop being Marvin's editor?" he asked, hoping that they would allow this.

"For the time being, Marvin Brian is our most beloved author.

Not just because he is a great poet, but because he is a friend. His collection had a great deal of success in the United States. Critics have praised him and say he will be one of the most important poets of his generation. And in London and Paris, they've been favorable as well," Sara said.

"Let's be honest here: ours is a little publishing house dedicated to publishing poetry. We don't publish just anyone: it's not enough to be a good poet, you have to be excellent in order to be published by Rosent or Wilson & Wilson. You already saw that we only have two other people working as editors in Alexandria. There are four in London; in Paris, until the business starts working like it did before the war, there are only two, you and Alain Fortier. But Fortier isn't really an editor and doesn't want to take on this job, for all that he's one of Marvin's friends. And we're publishing Marvin's book in English as well, and Alain Fortier doesn't know English. So ... you have to decide what to do."

"Whether I should stay or go," Fernando said.

"Exactly," Wilson replied.

"Don't delude yourself ... there is no solution for the situation between Marvin and Catalina. Marvin won't give in to Catalina. He hates her. Do you have to sacrifice your present and maybe your future for something that has no solution?" Sara asked.

"I don't understand why Marvin doesn't want to speak with her ... Let him say what he's got to say to her face. If he does that, then I'm sure Catalina won't insist ... But she can't stop trying to speak with him, she's got a daughter whose future is at stake," Fernando protested.

"I don't judge my authors' decisions and I don't judge my friends' decisions. I accept them and that is it," Benjamin Wilson said impatiently.

"I can't accept this decision of Marvin's, so I'm not the right person to be his editor," Fernando said.

Benjamin Wilson shrugged. He couldn't decide for Fernando.

"Your job is to be an editor, Fernando, and being Marvin's editor is a part of that job. Catalina will carry on trying to speak to Marvin, and he will keep on avoiding her, and their wills will clash, and those of us around them will be unable to influence them one way or the other. And so we should let them get on with it and do our own things," Sara said.

"I can't be loyal to both of them," Fernando said.

"Marvin needs a good editor, and Catalina needs unconditional friendship. You can do both," Sara said.

"I don't think so," Benjamin interrupted.

"I agree with Mr. Wilson," Fernando admitted.

They sat in silence. Three wills facing one another. Fernando got up, ready to leave, already missing the job he was abandoning. Sara had given him the chance to make his dream of being an editor a reality, to be like his father, and when he left the bookshop, he would put a final end to that dream. He wasn't fooling himself. No one was going to employ a Spanish refugee as an editor.

"You have to try ..." There was a degree of obstinacy in Sara's voice, the sound of someone who doesn't want to give in to fate.

Benjamin looked at his wife. From the day that Marvin had told him that Fernando's father had been an editor and that he had been shot, Benjamin had decided to help him, and meeting him in person only reaffirmed his decision. He saw in Fernando values on another level. He had almost adopted him, giving him clues about how to edit books, solving his problems, teaching him and giving him responsibilities beyond what might have been entirely reasonable. He hadn't stopped asking himself about why Sara behaved this way towards Fernando, but he thought that on one level, he was probably the son she had never had. He loved her more than anything, and although he knew that it was ridiculous that Fernando should be Marvin's editor, he decided to give in to his wife.

"Think about it. Talk to Catalina," Benjamin said, a little frustrated.

"I'll come down to open the bookshop tomorrow. If you're not there, it'll mean you've decided to leave us," Sara said.

Fernando reported verbatim to Catalina what he had said to the Wilsons and what the Wilsons had said to him. She listened in silence. She knew that Fernando wouldn't do anything that could hurt her, much less betray her. He needed her to absolve him so that he could carry on doing the job he loved so much. And she had already absolved him. She didn't have the right to ask him to be so loyal as to destroy himself. He had been more than generous towards her. She wouldn't have survived without him. If Fernando had not been at her side, then she could have been lost forever. She needed him, but it was not out of selfishness that she was going to ask him to carry on at the Rosent bookshop. Rather, she would never forgive herself if he left.

When he had finished talking, she stood up and gave him a hug. Fernando was disconcerted – almost uncomfortable – to receive such an unexpected embrace that he almost didn't return it.

Then she asked him, almost begged him, not to leave the bookshop and not to stop working as an editor. If he did, she would never forgive him or herself.

"I'm not offended that you're Marvin's editor. Why should it offend me? What there is between us is too strong for it to be changed by the fact that you edit his poems. You'll never be friends. I know that. You can't be friends, but that doesn't mean that you can't edit his poems. It's just a job, no more, for all that you tell me that the editor and the author have to communicate. I don't believe it. It can't always be like that. There must be occasions when you feel connected to the author, but that can't mean that you only edit the poetry that you like or the work of poets who share your sensibilities … No, don't give up your job. I'm not asking you to, and Marvin doesn't deserve you to give all this up on his behalf. The Wilsons have helped us, and it would have been a lot more difficult without them. I've only resigned because I know their loyalty to the friendship they bear to Marvin and Farida. It doesn't matter that I've stopped working at the bookshop. You have to carry on. We're doing well, Fernando. You like what you're doing; you're a good editor like your father was before you. And as for me … I like this apartment, Adela seems happy although she's finding it hard to speak French … she still mixes up her languages … and we're closer to home. Neither you nor I can return for the time being … but who knows, maybe our mothers could come out to see us. I'll try to find a job, Fernando, and I promise that I won't make a mess of it like I did with Cécile."

Fernando closed his arms around Catalina's shoulders and they stood for a long while, holding one another tight.

The room was small but it was packed. Professor Alain Fortier had called all the most respected critics from the Paris newspapers. Sara Rosent had decided that it was best to celebrate this reading as an intimate occasion, with a few well-chosen guests. She didn't tell Fernando, but her husband had hired a couple of men to stop anyone bothering Marvin.

The reading had been announced in the papers, so Catalina knew where and when it was to take place.

"Promise me you won't cause any fuss," Fernando begged, when he told her the reading was the next day.

"I'm not going. You think I'm going to put your job in danger? No, I won't go to the reading, but I will go to Marvin's house. I'll stand by the door until I manage to speak to him."

The doorman had been given instructions by Farida to tell them if the young Spanish woman turned up again. And so, for three days straight, when he had seen her turning up with the child's hand in her own, he had gotten into the elevator and gone to tell Farida.

She heard him out impassively and told him to stop this young woman from coming up to their apartment. For this, she gave him a good tip. The man relied on the help of his wife, who stood in the doorway and wouldn't let anyone who didn't live in the building come up.

Marvin started to suffer anxiety attacks from the constant presence of Catalina, and Farida decided that when he had given the poetry reading for the Wilsons, they would leave Paris.

Benjamin Wilson hired a car and a driver for them, as well as a couple of men to make sure that Catalina didn't get close to Marvin. The first day she tried to get into the building, one of these men held her back and threatened to call the police. From that day on, she had stood with Adela's hand in hers by the door and had waited for Farida and Marvin to come down, when she would try to get close to them, although another man held her back, as they got quickly into the car. Her struggling and shouting was all in vain. Marvin didn't even look at her, although Catalina and Farida exchanged glances on occasion.

One day, she saw the driver coming out of the door carrying a couple of suitcases and shouted even louder.

"Marvin! For God's sake! Listen to me! Marvin, this is Adela! Your daughter, look at her!"

He got into the car right away, embarrassed at the scene. Some of his neighbors had commented on how disagreeable it was to have this young woman shouting under their windows every morning.

Catalina found out where Marvin was going. The *Herald Tribune* announced his return to London, and she decided she would follow him there.

Fernando did not try to talk her out of it. On the contrary; he collected all the money he had been saving and gave it to her.

"I don't think it will be better for you there than here, but if you need to go, then you need to go."

Adela vomited on the crossing. The waves on the English Channel seemed to be about to swallow the boat. Catalina felt sick as well, but knew that she couldn't show any weakness because Adela needed her.

The journey to London was a little better, although Adela, tired, asked "why can't we stay with Papa Fernando?" She called Fernando that, for all that Catalina constantly reminded her that her father's name was Marvin. But Adela didn't care. She wanted to have a father, like all her friends at school, and Fernando was there for her.

At the station, they were given a recommendation for a little hotel off Oxford Street. They were told that it wasn't too expensive and that the sheets were always clean.

Catalina wouldn't have known where to start looking for Marvin, but Fernando had said she should start in Wilson & Wilson. She should be careful, he said, because it was the main bookshop and publishing house in Wilson's business empire.

The hotel was fairly modest, but they could not afford to spend a pound more than necessary, so they moved in right away. The doorman told them that Wilson & Wilson – one of the best bookshops in London as well as a famous poetry publishing house – was in Bloomsbury near the British Museum. Catalina listened patiently to these explanations; then, with Adela holding her hand, she went off to look for clues to Marvin's whereabouts.

Wilson & Wilson was an attractive four-story building. The ground floor and the first floor were the bookshop, and the top two floors were where the publishing house and the Wilsons' apartment were to be found. This explanation was given to her by a tall, thin woman, who must have been about her age, who came over to her as soon as she went into the shop.

Catalina said she was looking for a book by Marvin Brian, and the woman smiled.

"You must be aware that we don't only sell Marvin Brian's books, but we are his publishers as well," she explained with pride.

"Yes, I know ... I know Mr. Brian."

"Oh, so you know him!"

"We met in Madrid. You'll know from his poems: he spent a part of the Civil War in Madrid."

"Of course ... And which book in particular are you looking for?"

"It's for a present ... I don't know ... give me some help."

"Well, you are Spanish, so the *Spanish Civil War Notebook* is maybe the obvious choice ... the *German Notebook* is also very interesting ... he wrote it after the European war, he went all over Europe going to those camps where the Germans did horrible things to their prisoners. I don't know if you know, but people say that he lost a friend in one of those German camps ... I think it's better than his Spanish book ... but have a look for yourself."

Catalina had read the *German Notebook* and had realized that he had traveled to Germany after the war. Suddenly, she realized that he must have gone looking for Eulogio. She was sure of it. The friendship between the two of them had always surprised her with its solidity and intensity. It was not a surprise to her that Marvin had tried to find Eulogio, even though he had failed.

Sara had told Fernando that her husband wouldn't stop looking for Eulogio, but she hadn't said that Marvin was involved in it as well.

The woman took her to a bookshelf where Marvin's books were laid out. Then she left Catalina to take as much time as she needed to browse.

Catalina opened the *German Notebook* and had a look over

his other works. Adela stood still and quiet next to her mother.

After a while, she took the *German Notebook* over to the saleswoman.

"You're right, it's extraordinary. I'll take it. Can you wrap it up for me, please?"

"Of course. You've made an excellent choice."

The young woman carefully wrapped the book of poems, and Catalina put on her best smile.

"I'd so like to be able to say hello to Marvin ... I'd give him such a surprise!"

"Well, he's got a house only two blocks away from here, and I know that he's there at the moment. The *Times* wrote an article about him yesterday. Maybe I've got a copy here ... I'll give it to you."

Two blocks. Catalina tried to keep her hands from trembling. Marvin was only two blocks away.

"Maybe I'll stop by and leave my card, and see if we can meet up," she said casually.

"Well, he's got a very efficient housekeeper. I'm sure she'll pass the card along at once."

"And where is the house? On the left or the right?" she said innocently.

"Well, go out of the shop and turn left, then walk two blocks. It's a two-story house, imposing-looking."

When they got out into the street, Catalina wanted to burst into tears. The friendly young woman had helped her more than she could have imagined.

"Do you like London?" she asked Adela.

Her daughter shrugged and let out a soft and uncomplaining "yes."

Following the young woman's instructions, Catalina took little time in getting to a building which she thought must be Marvin's London home, a Victorian red-brick house with some stairs leading up to it.

Nervously, she rang the bell. A large, well-dressed woman in a black dress buttoned up to the neck opened the door. Catalina said she was a friend of Mr. Brian's and hoped she might see him. The woman looked her and Adela up and down.

"I'm afraid that Mr. Brian is not at home, but if you would care to leave your card …"

At that moment a door opened. Through it, a vast library and Farida were visible. Catalina was not intimidated when she saw the Egyptian coming towards her. She recognized that Farida walked like a queen, and her beauty was so great that it would leave no one unmoved.

"Mary, I'll speak to the young woman."

Mary curtseyed, and with a "yes, ma'am," walked quickly out of the hall.

"You're Farida Rahman," Catalina said, holding Adela's hand tight.

Farida nodded, but her face was stern.

"I want to see Marvin. I've come to London to speak with him."

"I'm sorry, but he's not at home. Also, as you well know, Marvin doesn't want to talk to you."

"This is his daughter," she said, putting her daughter in front of her. "The only thing I want is for him to acknowledge this fact. Just that. I don't ask for anything for myself. What we did together is over now, but I can't let Adela keep paying the price."

Farida looked at her and her face gave nothing away. Then she patted the little girl's head.

"Marvin will not speak with you. Please don't insist, and don't make us do things that might be unpleasant … think of your daughter."

"If I didn't think of her, I wouldn't be here. I don't want anything for myself, I just want Adela to have a name."

"Miss Vilamar, I'm going to have to ask you to leave, and not come back. You are not welcome here. It would be very unpleasant for you if you were reported to the police. I don't think that it would be good for you or your daughter if there were a scandal. Marvin has been very patient with you, but your scandalous behavior in Paris has exhausted his patience and … well, now you dare come over the sea and follow him here … please accept his decision."

"All I want is for him to listen to me," Catalina said stubbornly.

"Please, go away. Don't make me use force. And don't come back, Miss Vilamar, please. There's no point."

"I won't go, Madame Rahman."

"Then we'll have no choice but to report you to the police."

Catalina took a step back, trying to gauge the import of these words, and Farida took the opportunity to push the door closed.

"Mama ... Mama, why are you crying?" Adela was scared to see her mother's tears.

"I'm not crying ... don't you worry."

"You are crying, I can see you," the girl said.

They walked for a good distance without talking. By the time they got back to the hotel, Catalina had decided not to give up.

"I will go back to that house in Bloomsbury tomorrow, and the day after, for as long as it takes."

The next morning, she went with Adela to stand in front of Marvin's door. And she stood there until mid-morning, when he came out with Farida. A car was waiting for them. When they were just getting into it, Catalina started to shout: "Marvin, Marvin! For God's sake, speak to me, listen to me!"

A few passers-by looked at her in surprise and Marvin, nervous, got into the car. Farida closed the door with a bang and the car pulled off.

But Catalina did not give in, and stayed there with Adela the rest of the day. Her daughter was very tired.

It was late when the car came back. Another car pulled up at the same time, and two men got out of it, flanking Marvin. Catalina tried to force her way through to stand by his side, but the men stopped her. One of them stood in front of her.

"Miss Vilamar?"

"Yes ..."

"I'm Detective Morris. I have to ask you to stop bothering Mr. Brian, or else we will have to arrest you."

"Arrest me? I haven't done anything wrong."

"Of course you have, ma'am. You're harassing a citizen and that's a crime."

"But he ... he knows me ... this girl is my daughter, and also his."

"Miss Vilamar, I'm not interested in your personal problems.

If you have a legitimate complaint against Mr. Brian, you can go to the police or the courts, but you can't follow him to the door of his own house and provoke a public scandal. There are neighbors who have complained. You've spent the whole day in front of his house and that worries them. If you carry on like this, I'm going to have to enforce the law. That means that you will be arrested until you can be taken to trial, and your daughter will be put in the hands of the social services."

"You're threatening me, Mr. Morris."

"Of course I'm not. I am telling you that here has been an official complaint made against you, and that Mr. Brian fears for himself. He can't tell if you will be dangerous or violent, given your very strange attitude. You can decide for yourself, ma'am, but I tell you again that if you have any legitimate complaint against Mr. Brian, you can make it in front of a judge."

"But how dare Marvin behave like this to his daughter!" Catalina said indignantly.

Detective Morris didn't reply. He didn't care at all about the romantic affairs of a poet and a young woman. His boss had told him to accompany the Brians back to their house because they had made a formal complaint against a young Spanish woman who was following them, motives unknown. He had to tell the Spaniard that she should stop following the poet or else she would be hauled up in front of a judge. And that's what he had done. He hoped that the young woman wouldn't force him to arrest her.

Angrily, Catalina said she was going. She was afraid that her insistence might lead to Adela being taken from her. And she hated Marvin so deeply that she started to retch harshly and uncontrollably.

She cried all night, and the next day at dawn, she decided to return to Paris. But one thing was sure: she would not give up.

In Paris, she fell back into a routine based on the protection that Fernando offered her. She would force Marvin to acknowledge that he had a daughter. She could not go back to London, because he had made an official complaint against her, but Marvin wouldn't stay in London forever, and she would follow him wherever he went.

2

Her wait lasted three long years. Meanwhile, thanks to Madame Dufort, she got a job teaching music at a music school. The owner, Monsieur Girardot, hired her to look after the smallest children. The pay wasn't very good, because, as he said, "you have no qualifications."

It wasn't until June 1949 that they had news from Eulogio.

Fernando would never forget that moment. It was about eight o'clock in the evening, and he had just come home to find Catalina packing a suitcase. She was going to go to Boston the next day. Marvin and Farida lived there. At least, this was what she had read in the *Herald Tribune*, which had reported that Marvin was going to give a course on poetry at Harvard, and that the university was overwhelmed by the number of students who wished to study with him. Catalina had seen an opportunity in this, and Fernando had not been strong enough to resist.

Adela was helping her mother fold her clothes and put them carefully in the suitcase. She kept on asking what America was like, and why her father lived there.

Catalina answered her in monosyllables, thinking about what would happen if Marvin avoided her once again and she had to come back to Paris. Maybe they wouldn't let her carry on teaching at the music school. But she knew that whatever happened, Fernando would help her. He had paid for her trip to Boston, in spite of their arguments about it, because he didn't want her to take Adela. He thought that if things went badly, then the child would suffer. Adela was nearly ten years old. She was aware enough to know what was going on, and the trip to Boston would interrupt her schoolwork. But Catalina ignored these arguments. If the *Herald Tribune* said that Marvin was in Boston, then she would go to Boston.

She was just about to close the suitcase when the telephone rang. Fernando hurried to answer.

As he listened to the person on the other end of the line, his face showed first joy, and then concern, and finally anguish. When he hung up, he sat down and tried to pull himself together.

"What is it? Who was it? What did they say?" Catalina asked worriedly.

"It was Benjamin Wilson ... they've found Eulogio."

"Wonderful!" she said happily.

"No ... no ... he's not well ..."

"Is he sick?" she said, worried at what the answer might be.

"He's lost his mind. That's what they told Wilson, and that's why it's taken so long to find him."

Catalina said nothing. She didn't know what to think or what to say.

Adela was quiet as well, aware that something serious was happening.

"I didn't know that the Wilsons were in Paris again; I thought they were in Alexandria," she said.

"Neither did I. I think they must just have arrived. They've arranged to see me tomorrow at seven. I won't be able to take you to the airport."

"No, of course not ... maybe I shouldn't go ... maybe it's better for me to stay and come with you to find Eulogio."

"No ... you should go to Boston. I'll look after Eulogio."

"Eulogio is more important. Marvin can wait," she said sincerely.

"I'll call you, and tell you what happens. But you have to go to Boston. You'll never forgive yourself if you don't. It's a real opportunity."

"Yes, we've spent all our savings on the tickets, even though it might all be useless," Catalina said.

"No, it won't. it was hard for me to accept, but I understand that you want Marvin at least to acknowledge Adela."

At six-thirty in the morning on June 10, 1949, Fernando said goodbye to Catalina and Adela. He had asked Monsieur Dufort to be kind enough to take them to the airport, or at least to find someone he trusted to do so.

When he arrived at the rue Rosiers it was already seven o'clock, and the doorwoman was cleaning the doorway. She was not surprised to see him, given that Fernando often came early to the bookshop before opening it up to the public. He liked to work in the quiet of the back room where the publishing house was. But that day he didn't go into the bookshop, but rather went up to the Wilsons' apartment.

Sara opened the door. She was already dressed and had her makeup on. She invited him to come through into the living room. Benjamin, who was sitting down reading the paper, got up to shake him by the hand.

A maid appeared with a tray with coffee on it. Fernando was nervous and wanted to know the news.

"Zahra has found your friend Eulogio. It wasn't easy. He was working in a German factory and … well, he made friends with a man who was …" Benjamin seemed unable to find the right word.

"Homosexual, like him," Sara said easily.

"They weren't the only ones. There were other men like him in the factory. Of course, they hid who they were. It was almost as dangerous to be a homosexual in Germany as it was to be a Jew. The man that Eulogio befriended was a Frenchman, René Roche. An engineer and a communist. They worked in a factory near Weimar. They had been deported in the same group of forced laborers that France had sent to Germany. The conditions at the factory were essentially slavery. Eulogio didn't know anything about René Roche, but René saw that he was a homosexual and tried to help him as much as he could. Once, when Eulogio fainted, René took over his shift. We don't know exactly what happened … but apparently someone reported them for being homosexuals in the factory where they worked, and they were given a harsher punishment. They were sent to Buchenwald. They worked for Gustoff, a munitions company, there. Lots of German factories relied on forced labor. And the factories that were supplied by laborers from Buchenwald were the most important.

And conditions in Buchenwald were essentially slavery. In this place, near to Weimar, the place where Goethe lived, the SS became the lords and masters of thousands of human beings. Buchenwald was not just a camp."

Benjamin paused for a moment and drank a sip of coffee to allow what he was saying to sink in.

"In Buchenwald, when they decided that a worker was no longer useful, they killed him in the gas chambers, just as they did with the Jews. Thousands of people died in the Bernber and Sonnestein chambers. Your friend Eulogio got a lung infection, but René Roche advised him to hide it, because if they found out about it, they might get rid of him. But the worst of it was not having to work while sick, without enough to eat and being unable to rest. The doctors at Buchenwald were keen experimenters. They infected the prisoners with all kinds of viruses. Many of them were given typhus deliberately. But this wasn't the worst either. Don't forget this name: Carl Værnet."

The door to the drawing room opened and a woman came in. Fernando felt something like a sudden blow in the pit of his stomach. He got up and walked over to her.

"Zahra ..." he said.

She looked at him without any particular emotion. Sara stared at her expectantly, and Benjamin waved that she should take up the story.

"No, Fernando, don't forget that name, Carl Værnet. Although his real name is Carl Peder Jensen. He's Danish. He was the son of a horse trader; he studied medicine, then specialized in endocrinology and became friends with Knud Sand, an endocrinologist who supported the idea of castrating homosexuals. Carl Værnet dedicated himself keenly to experiments that might 'cure' homosexuality. He was one of Hitler's favorite scientists, and as such, enjoyed all the privileges one might imagine. For a time, he lived in Prague, dealing with homosexual prisoners who were brought to him to experiment on. Then he went to Buchenwald. He had been appointed a major in the SS, and he carried out his experiments under the auspices of the camp commander. Don't forget this name either: Karl Otto Koch. A monster. A demon in human form. In the infirmary in Buchenwald, they carried out experiments that ended the lives of hundreds of people. The doctors experimented, and the camp commander, Karl Otto Koch, benefited from these experiments. He loved objects made from human skin. He had a lampshade of the stuff. His wife, Ilse, an equally evil person, had a bag that he had given her, made from human skin as well. Erich Wagner – don't forget this name either – was the doctor whose specialty was removing the skin from prisoners. The camp commander was keen on tattoos, so he would find out which prisoners had tattoos that he liked. Dr. Wagner would inject them with phenol and flay their skin to get an extra tattoo for Koch's collection. But I'm digressing. Why should you care about any of this?"

Zahra got out a cigarette and lit it. Fernando was feeling nauseous and it was hard for him to carry on listening to this story. He couldn't believe that what Zahra was telling him was the truth. No human would be capable of such monstrous behavior. He felt his hands trembling and accepted the cigarette that Sara put between his lips.

"Carl Værnet experimented on the homosexuals he had under his control in Buchenwald, and submitted them to terrible tortures. He castrated some of them, and sterilized others, and in the worst cases, he injected hormones into the groin or else transplanted monkey testicles into them. Most of the men who were subjected to these practices didn't survive, and those who did … Well, Eulogio was one of Carl Værnet's victims … he survived, but his mind was broken."

Fernando clenched his fists. He felt a wave of repulsion and anger.

"Where is he?" he asked, and there was incredulity, pain and anger in his voice.

"He's in the hospital. We arrived late last night. It wasn't easy to find him … I've been on his trail for months … But it's almost impossible to find a man with no identity, a man who doesn't know who he is …"

"So you found him," Fernando muttered.

"Yes, I've been living in Germany for months now, going from one side to the other, visiting camps, going through the files that each camp commander put together, visiting the survivors …"

Zahra pushed a strand of hair back from her forehead, as though she needed to wipe away the image of what she had seen. Fernando could see how she had changed, how life had made itself known in the little wrinkles on her forehead and the bitter expression in which her face rested. And he thought that she would never recover from what she had seen in her journey through the remains of Germany.

"We'll go and see him. But you need to be aware that he might not recognize you, that he might not speak … Who knows where his mind is …" Sara said, holding Fernando's hand.

"And Anatole? Does he know that …?"

"I've called him and told him what has happened. He'll come from Lyon this afternoon. But we must be realistic. It wouldn't be fair to ask Anatole Lombard to take care of Eulogio. He's a young man, and although they did have a relationship, who knows if it was important enough for him now to decide that he should look after Eulogio indefinitely." Benjamin spoke coldly, and it was this coldness that so irritated Fernando.

"Eulogio has me … I'd never ask anyone else to take care of him. But …. Well, maybe it would do him good to see Anatole … he was very important for him …"

"I think that the best thing would be for his mother to take care of him. No one can look after a child better than his mother," Sara said, speaking calmly to make sure that Fernando took in what she was saying.

"Piedad? How's she going to do that?" he asked in confusion.

"We wanted to ask you before we did anything. We think that the easiest thing would be for her to come to Paris and take him back to Spain with her. Of course we'll help her … she can't travel alone with Eulogio in his state … we'll find a nurse, someone who can take the train with them to Madrid …" Sara looked directly at Fernando.

"Piedad … the poor woman! She doesn't deserve to suffer so much!" he said, talking to himself.

Benjamin's car was waiting for them at the door. The Rosent bookshop would be closed that day.

When they arrived at the Hôpital Pitié Salpêtrière, the Wilsons and Zahra walked firmly to the stairs. They seemed to know where they were going.

They came to a room where a nurse came out to talk to them. Benjamin didn't give her a chance to turn them away: they were here to see a Spanish patient, Eulogio Jiménez. He had been brought there the night before, and he had a permission slip from Dr. Courtois that allowed him to go and see him whenever necessary. He provided the slip.

The nurse spoke to another nurse, an older woman who appeared to be in charge of the room. Then she let them in.

Eulogio was in bed, and Fernando protested angrily when he saw that he was tied up. Leather straps kept him in place.

"What's this! Take them off at once!" He didn't wait for anyone to help, but immediately went to undo the straps himself.

"Stop it!" the nurse tried to make him stop.

"My friend isn't an animal … I'm not going to let him be treated like this … I'll take him with me at once … This is terrible!"

The nurse couldn't manage to stop Fernando, but another nurse had gone to fetch Dr. Courtois, who came in and spoke angrily to Fernando.

"How dare you! Leave at once, and I'll give them orders not to let you back in."

Benjamin Wilson put his hand on the doctor's arm and spoke to him in a firm voice.

"I'm sorry, Doctor, but you have to understand that we were surprised to see our friend tied up. You said yourself last night when you examined him that he wasn't any danger to himself or to others … And Miss Nadouri here traveled with him and a nurse from Germany without him causing any problems. And so we'll be taking him now. You must have a diagnostic chart for him, and you can tell us what we need to do."

Benjamin Wilson had not spoken in order to convince Dr. Courtois, but rather to make it clear to him that they would do what they wanted to do.

Dr. Courtois looked at Benjamin Wilson with what might have been a shrug, ordering the nurse to get Eulogio ready to leave. Then he asked them to come with him to his office and handed the medical report over to Benjamin Wilson. Wilson looked at it and then looked up at the doctor.

"Yes, what you're seeing here is final. He'll never be well again. His mind has sunk into itself in order to allow him to survive. We don't know if he recognizes anyone, or if he even hears them … He can't speak at the moment."

"And in the future?" Fernando asked, feeling an unbearable pain in his chest.

"We know very little about the human brain. But in my opinion … well, you can read it in the report, but I don't think that Monsieur Eulogio Jiménez will ever be the man we knew again. Could he improve? I couldn't say one way or the other. Maybe a calm environment, surrounded by people who love him … but it's a long shot," the doctor said.

"Well, he recognized me," Fernando said.

The Wilsons and Dr. Courtois looked at him with sympathy and disbelief, but they didn't answer.

"I know that he recognized me," Fernando insisted.

One hour later, accompanied by Paulette Bisset, the nurse who was pushing Eulogio's wheelchair, they left the hospital. Fernando put his hand on Eulogio's shoulder and walked alongside the chair. Zahra and the Wilsons followed them in silence. It wasn't easy to get Eulogio into the car, and it was even harder to fit them all into the car after him, so Benjamin Wilson took control of the situation and offered to take a taxi with Sara.

"We haven't even said where we're going to take him …"

"We'll take him to my apartment. Catalina isn't there … she's gone off on a trip and won't be back for a few days."

"If I'm not mistaken, the apartment has two bedrooms …" Sara said questioningly.

"Yes, that's right," said Fernando.

"Well, Nurse Bisset can stay with you until Eulogio's mother gets to Paris," Zahra said.

"Let's talk about this when we get home," Fernando said shortly.

Catalina had left the house tidy. A bouquet of woodland flowers waited in a vase on the living room table with a note for

Fernando. He put it in his pocket to read when he was alone.

Eulogio allowed himself to be moved around. He didn't say anything, but he seemed calm. His eyes were vague and lost.

"Shall we put him in bed, or can he sit upright?" Fernando asked the nurse.

"Well, I think that he can stay up, except when he makes signs that he wants to lie down. Maybe we can sit him next to the indow."

And that's what they did. Fernando told the nurse that she could sleep in Catalina's room. They would put Adela's bed in his room, and he would sleep there with Eulogio.

Sara and Benjamin arrived shortly afterwards. They had to decide what to do with Eulogio. Sara spoke first.

"The easiest thing is for his mother to take care of him. It's what she would want. You can't look after him, and as for this friend from Lyon, Anatole Lombard ... we can't ask him to take on the responsibility of looking after Eulogio, even if he asks for it. It has to be his mother who decides what's best for him."

"As soon as I get to my office, I'll call Madrid and get them to find his mother. They can tell her what's happened and offer her a train ticket to Paris," Benjamin said.

"No, you can't tell her what Eulogio's situation is. Tell her that he's sick and needs her help, but no more details. Imagine how upset she'll be until she has a chance to see him. I ... I'd prefer it if I could talk to her before she saw him," Fernando knew that it would be a hard blow for Piedad to see her son in his condition.

"Well, if we're all agreed, then I'll get things moving straight away to bring Doña Piedad across as soon as possible," Benjamin Wilson said.

"And don't worry about the bookshop. Stay with Eulogio until his mother arrives. I'll look after it. It'll be like going back to my youth," Sara said with a little smile.

Zahra remained silent. She listened carefully to what was said, but she knew that it was not her business even to opine about what should happen to Eulogio. But when the Wilsons had left, she stayed in the apartment.

"I'll give you a hand," she said, as an explanation for why she stayed.

"Thank you, but I think that I can sort everything out with Miss Bisset."

"Of course ..." Zahra seemed to hesitate before speaking again.

The nurse interrupted them, saying that it was lunchtime and the patient needed to eat. Zahra offered to cook and Fernando did not object. There was a pot of vegetable soup in the fridge, as well as some meat.

To begin with, Eulogio did not want to eat. He refused to open his mouth, but Fernando sat at his side and patiently managed to make him swallow a couple of spoonfuls of the soup. It wasn't much, but at least he got something in his stomach.

Eulogio's eyes were fixed on the wall and he moved his head from side to side without making any noise. The nurse spoke calmly to him, and the sound of her voice seemed to tranquilize him.

Zahra helped Fernando get the rooms ready, and took advantage of the couple of minutes they had alone together.

"I know this isn't the right time, but do you remember that I told you that one day I would ask you to help me finish off Ludger Wimmer?"

Fernando had to search his memory ... Ludger Wimmer. And then he remembered that he had been Zahra's father's business partner, the man who had accused her of murder and who had gotten her locked up in the psychiatric institution where he had raped her.

He had blocked this memory from his mind because of the harsh feelings it provoked in him. It was enough to see the faces of Roque and Saturnino Pérez, the murderers of his father, without being haunted by even more unfortunates.

But here Zahra was, reminding him of his promise to kill this man.

She had searched Germany from top to bottom looking for Eulogio, and she had found him, his body alive and his mind dead. Now it was his turn to hold up his end of the bargain.

"Yes, I remember," he admitted.

"I didn't find him while I was in Germany. I only found out that he disappeared as soon as the war was over. Maybe he left even before Berlin fell. He was clever enough to know that he had left too many witnesses to his fraternization with the Nazi high command, and that the Rosy-Fingered Dawn was a hive of depravity for the SA and the SS. He had too many friends among the murderers. He owed them favors, and they owed him. Anyone might have pointed the finger at him. And so he disappeared. But I will find him."

"He might have died," Fernando said.

"No. He's alive."

"How do you know?" Fernando said, annoyed that her absolute affirmation left no space to be questioned.

"I know he's alive, Fernando."

"And where do you think he is?"

"I've got a lead … When I leave Paris, I'll follow it. I need to find someone else as well. A job for our friend Benjamin Wilson. Lots of people have disappeared."

"Yes, I suppose business must be booming for Benjamin Wilson," Fernando said bitterly.

"I know that you don't like Benjamin … you can't forgive him for getting you involved in his affairs … but you mustn't judge him. He's a good man and he helps other people."

"And gets paid for it."

"Yes, of course, but not always. There are people who have come to see him, desperate people who had no money, and he has never turned them away: he's taken on the case and done what he could."

"Well, if you say so …"

"I do say so. Who do you think paid for the hunt for Eulogio? Haven't you asked? Well, it was him. And he did it for you, without expecting anything in return. Why should he care about Eulogio? He barely knows him. Sara told him how worried you were, and … well, he's spent a year looking for your friend. I won't lie, he's looked for other people at the same time, but every time that he thought there was a clue to where Eulogio might be, however unlikely or expensive it was, I followed it up because Benjamin Wilson supported me. Yes, Fernando, we look for people, but it's not just a business, as you still haven't managed to understand."

Fernando felt uncomfortable. He didn't want to say anything to Zahra, but he still didn't trust Benjamin Wilson. He had been manipulated by this man and had not forgiven him. He had carried a gun and fired it because of him. No, he could never forget the journey to Prague, when they risked their lives trying to rescue that girl … what was her name? Jana? Yes, Jana Brossler. They risked their lives to save hers.

"I don't want to argue with you," Fernando added.

"Why would we argue? Of course the truth is sometimes uncomfortable. All I'm doing is saying that you should be grateful to Benjamin Wilson."

Fernando grew tense and looked at Zahra; she held his gaze defiantly.

"What do I have to thank him for? That he took advantage of me? That he sent me on an absurd mission into the desert where I risked my life? That he made your friends believe I was your devoted slave? Should I thank him for sending us to Prague to look for that girl? Tell me, please, there's a lot I need to thank him for …"

Zahra looked disappointed, and that hurt him.

"Marvin Brian told Sara and Benjamin Wilson the story of your father and asked them to hire you. Well, Farida asked them. Sara was moved to find out that you were the son of an editor, a man of letters shot by Franco's forces, and she didn't hesitate to help you, because her husband wanted to help you as well. The Wilsons looked after you during your time in Alexandria. Do you think that the only person who could give piano lessons in the whole city was Catalina? The Wilsons have made you into who you are, an editor, which is what you and your father both dreamed you would become. Even when you stood up to Benjamin and told him you wouldn't go to hunt for more people for him, he didn't abandon you. When you wanted to leave Alexandria and come to Paris, they helped you, recommending you to the Duforts, your current landlords, and they helped you take your first few steps. The Wilsons put the Rosent bookshop into your hands, trusting you with it, trusting that you would edit books of poetry for them. You owe them a lot, Fernando. You owe them everything you are today."

He didn't argue with her. He didn't care what she said. He was too upset about Eulogio to feel anything else. And although he couldn't help trembling with emotion whenever she was close to him, he would have preferred Catalina to be with him at that moment. Catalina would have understood.

The sun had not yet risen that morning, but June was nearly at an end. The leaden sky promised rain, and the breeze did not smell of springtime, but rather brought shivers of cold.

Fernando had arrived early to the station, and was nervously walking from one side of the platform to the other.

The train came in slowly, grayish smoke spiraling up from its smokestack. He stood very still, watching the doors open. Tired-looking travelers with sleep-reddened eyes started to drag their suitcases over the platform, scanning the crowd for the friends and relatives who might be waiting for them. He waited, eyes skimming over him, and started to get worried. Suddenly, he saw her. She was standing by the train, nervous and impatient, looking around until finally she saw him and relief flooded her face. He walked quickly over to her.

"Piedad!" he called, raising his hand.

He gave her a fierce hug and she let herself sink into the embrace as though it was a preview of the one she would get from her son.

"How are you? How was the trip?" he asked.

"How wonderful to see you … And my son?" she said.

"I'll take you to see him straight away," Fernando said, avoiding the question.

"I don't understand anything … A man came to the house and …"

Fernando wouldn't let her continue. He picked up her suitcase in one hand and took her by the arm with the other, guiding her through the station.

"Come on … Come on … we need to talk. I know you are very tired and want to see Eulogio, but we need to talk first."

She nodded, but couldn't help feeling an oppressive weight on her heart.

They left the station and went to a nearby cafe. Fernando ordered two coffees and a couple of croissants.

"You must be hungry."

"I'm tired, but I'm worried more than anything else. Why don't you take me to Eulogio? What's happened to him?"

"What did they tell you in Madrid?" he asked.

"I told you already: a man came to my house. He said that he was calling on behalf of some friends, and that he would help me to get a passport to go to Paris to see my son. You can imagine how shocked I was. I didn't know who this man was. If he hadn't given me your letter, I think I would have thrown him out of the house. But you told me to trust him and to follow his instructions. And so I did. He gave me a train ticket and ... well, he must have been important, because it only took them five days to issue me a passport. You told me in the letter that Eulogio needed me and that I had to come to Paris. I told your mother and ... well, she wanted to come with me. She insisted, thinking that she'd find you here as well. She told Asunción too. She couldn't think about coming, because she has to look after Ernesto, but she gave me a letter for Catalina. Is she with you?"

"No, no she isn't ... but that's not important at the moment. Look, I want to tell you about how Eulogio is before you see him."

He didn't spare her any details about Eulogio's state, although he didn't talk about fleeing to Alexandria and their life there. He spoke about Eulogio's work in France, his business with the Resistance, how he had been sent to Germany and how he had suffered in the camps.

Piedad listened to him in silence, without holding her tears back. She felt in her own flesh the pain her son had experienced.

"We were able to find him thanks to some friends. In the camps, the Nazi doctors experimented on certain prisoners. They were able to do what they wanted with them. Their lives were worthless."

"Experiment?" Piedad gave a start. "You told me they took him to a labor camp, a munitions factory ..."

"Yes, and there ... there were other prisoners, who were ..."

"Who were ...?"

"I don't know how to tell you ... Eulogio ... Eulogio ..."

"For God's sake, Fernando, tell me now!"

"While he was in Lyon, Eulogio fell in love. It was an intense love, generous, complete. He … well … he felt free to unleash all his emotions, his tastes, his personal truth."

"Why won't you tell me clearly what's going on?"

"He fell in love with a man. I'm sorry." Fernando looked down to the table in embarrassment.

Piedad passed her hand over her face and sighed before she spoke.

"So, he finally accepted it," she said in a whisper.

"What do you mean?" Fernando said in confusion.

"You think I don't know what was upsetting my son? You think you can really trick a mother? Eulogio was fighting against himself and …. He never forgave me for telling him when he was a teenager to always be open about what he felt, never to live in shame. But he … well, he denied to me what I had seen about him, and from that moment on, he never felt comfortable around me because I knew his secret … It was his most intimate secret and he didn't want to share it with anyone, not even me, and that tormented him. My husband refused to accept it, and told me that this was just my imagination, and he got angry when I told him that our son was suffering. As you know, Eulogio loved his father above all things, and knew that his homosexuality would have been a disappointment to him. And so it was impossible for me to help him. You know why he never got on with Catalina, why he was so angry at her all the time?"

"Well, I guess they were different kinds of people," he said, just to say something.

"No, it wasn't a question of character. It was because Eulogio was in love with you. Catalina was his rival. He knew that you weren't inclined the same way as he was and that if you found out what he felt, then you would surely break off your friendship. But even though he knew it was impossible, he couldn't help himself and he disliked Catalina a great deal. And you ran off with her, and he ran off with you, in spite of her."

Fernando felt that he was blushing. He couldn't cope with what he was hearing. His sentiments were a mixture of pity and revulsion. Suddenly his friendship with Eulogio had taken on an unknown dimension. Piedad realized how uncomfortable he was and was scared that this revelation might lead him to turn his back on Eulogio.

"Who is this man he fell in love with? Was he loved back in return?"

Fernando couldn't find the words to speak to Piedad. She had always known and the only thing that seemed to worry her was how her son had suffered.

But he didn't blame her, he didn't judge her.

"He's French … he's called Anatole Lombard, and as I told you, he lives in Lyon, but when I told him that Eulogio had been found, he didn't hesitate and said he'd come at once. You'll meet him now. That's why I wanted to talk to you …"

"Tell me how Eulogio is," she demanded.

"There was a doctor called Carl Værnet in Buchenwald, who was trying to cure homosexuality. The homosexual prisoners in the camp were subject to his experiments. Some of them had monkey testicles implanted into them, others were given hormones; people were castrated and sterilized …"

"Shut up!" she said, trying to hold back her tears.

"I'm sorry … I … Eulogio was a victim of these experiments. He survived where others did not … His body is here, but his mind is lost … he doesn't speak, and the doctor says he doesn't recognize anyone, he looks into space … and … he cries, he cries in silence every now and then. He purses his lips and clenches his fists and shudders and cries."

"Take me to him now, please," she begged.

The nurse opened the door to the apartment. Anatole was sitting next to Eulogio and reading to him out loud in French. Piedad stopped still and watched her son, and recognized Verlaine's "Chanson d'automne":

> *Les sanglots longs*
> *Des violons*
> *De l'automne*
>
> *Blessent mon cœur*
> *D'une langueur*
> *Monotone.*

Tout suffocant
Et blême, quand
Sonne l'heure,

Je me souviens
Des jours anciens
Et je pleure;

Et je m'en vais
Au vent mauvais
Qui m'emporte

Deçà, delà,
Pareil à la
Feuille morte.

Anatole Lombard raised his eyes to see Piedad. It seemed to Fernando that they were speaking to each other across the silence.

"Piedad, this is Anatole ..."

He closed the book and got up, extending his hand to Piedad. She shook it quickly. Then she stepped aside and walked around to her son.

Piedad hugged Eulogio's inert body. She stroked his hair and kissed him gently and whispered words that neither Fernando nor Anatole heard. Eulogio made no motion of protest, but his face showed no emotion. His mind was elsewhere.

The nurse came over and introduced herself.

"Madame, I'm Paulette Bisset, your son's nurse."

Piedad nodded, but didn't stop stroking her son's face. Tears ran down her cheeks and she made no effort to stop them. Suddenly Eulogio's wandering gaze fixed on her. He made no gesture, no movement to show that he had recognized her. He still looked vague.

Fernando left the drawing room because he was unable to hold back his tears. Piedad's painful silence was unbearable for him. He took a few seconds to pull himself together, then returned to the room.

"You should rest for a bit, or at least freshen up after your journey," he said to Piedad.

"The only thing I want to do is hold my son, but you're right, I've been traveling all day and need to tidy myself up a bit. But there's no time to rest."

She allowed Anatole to take her place and let Fernando guide her to the room where he slept with Eulogio.

"You can sleep here with Eulogio, and I'll sleep on the sofa."

She didn't argue. All she wanted was to be close to her son. Fernando had put her suitcase on the bed and she opened it, taking out a few garments.

She came back to the salon after about half an hour. The nurse was seated next to Eulogio, and Fernando and Anatole were talking in low voices.

"You look like a different woman, but you need to dry your hair," Fernando said, just to say something.

Piedad's hair was still wet, and she smiled briefly. She didn't care whether she had dried herself properly. She felt light after the shower.

"Can we talk?" Anatole asked.

She nodded and sat down next to Fernando. She crossed her hands in her lap and waited.

"As you've heard already, I'm a good friend of Eulogio's. I won't say that my suffering is anything like yours, but believe me that I am very sad to see him in this state. I … I have loved him, I love him, and I am sorry that I don't have in my hands the power to make him be as he once was. I suppose you'll take him back to Spain, and if you'll let me, I would love to come and visit him now and then … I am a teacher, so it would have to be in the school vacations … I'll write to you in advance."

Piedad listened to him carefully. She would have liked to feel some degree of sympathy for this attractive man with whom her son had fallen in love. But she blamed him for Eulogio's bad luck. Why had they taken Eulogio instead of him? It was irrational, she knew, but she couldn't help herself.

"Yes, write to me … I don't suppose there'll be any problem in your coming to visit," she said noncommittally.

"I was waiting for you to come so I could meet you. I'm going back to Lyon today. I have been in Paris for a few days already. When they called me to say that they had found Eulogio I came at once, and here I've been, by his side. Although he doesn't even know I'm here."

"The doctors say that faced with all this unlimited suffering, his mind tried to leave his body and got lost somewhere," Fernando tried to explain.

"Yes … you already told me that," Piedad said.

"Maybe he will come back to us someday," Anatole said.

She looked right at him, and her gaze was that of a wolf about to attack. How dare this man try to console her with a vain hope?

"Miracles do happen," Anatole insisted.

"You're lucky to be able to believe in them," Piedad said disdainfully.

"Well … my train leaves early in the afternoon and I need to visit a friend first … I'll be off …"

Anatole was on his feet, and Fernando got up quickly as well. Piedad got slowly to her feet. Without offering her hand to Anatole, she merely said, "I hope you have a good journey, Monsieur Lombard," before turning back to look at her son. She took Eulogio's hands in her own, and this seemed to comfort her. Anatole gave Eulogio a kiss on the forehead, and then left without saying another word.

Piedad insisted on meeting Zahra. She wanted to see the face of the woman who had rescued her son. Fernando had spoken about her without giving too many details about who she was or what she did. But Piedad didn't care about the details. All she wanted to do was meet this woman.

Zahra came to see them two days after Piedad had arrived. On that June afternoon, Paris was drenched with rain.

The two women got along well from the start. Piedad gave Zahra a spontaneous hug, and Zahra let herself be caught up in her thankful embrace. Then they spoke openly, and Zahra told her various unknown details of the crimes the Nazis had committed, and the shame and guilt that they had inspired in the victors of the war, who seemed eager to cover up as soon as possible all that had happened. The Nuremberg trials were taking place, but Zahra was upset that not all the murderers of Hitler's regime were on trial. "It's been a kind of catharsis, but millions of people will go about their business without justice touching them in any way," she said angrily. "The very man who tortured Eulogio, Carl Værnet, has disappeared, and really they just let him disappear. They took him to a camp in Denmark, but he escaped, or rather, they helped him escape." And then, speaking in a lower voice, as though to herself, she added: "One of the biggest sources of shame is the fact that many of the experiments that the scientists and doctors who were working for Hitler carried out have aroused the interest of ... well, of the victors. Many of them are being protected and granted a new identify. Maybe Værnet is one of them."

Fernando heard Zahra speak in astonishment. He thought that she must be wrong: how could the people who had defeated Hitler "save" the monsters who had worked for him? No, that couldn't be right. Zahra must be speculating because she was so filled with hatred towards these people.

Zahra carried on speaking, explaining to Piedad just how difficult it had been to find Eulogio, and how she had come across him in a mental asylum.

Fernando followed the conversation without daring to interrupt. There was a direct communication between them that he couldn't touch.

Night had already fallen when Zahra said goodbye to Piedad. He insisted on walking her home, and she accepted.

They walked for a while without speaking. She let him put his arm around her shoulders, and each felt the heat of the other's body.

"She's a brave woman," Zahra said.

"Piedad? Yes, yes she is. She's suffered a lot."

"When are they leaving?"

"The day after tomorrow. The nurse will go with them to Madrid and will stay with them for a few days. Piedad doesn't want the nurse to go with them, but she insisted. It's better for her not to be alone on the train. It's a long journey, and who knows how Eulogio might react."

"Well, I wish he would react ... I brought him all the way

from Germany, and he didn't cause any problems at all. He's not there, Fernando, he's not there. He's a body that you can pose as required."

"The doctor said that you never know when it comes to illnesses of the mind. I won't be happy if Piedad doesn't have at least a little help on the journey."

"And your mother?"

"Piedad brought me a letter. She wants to see me. She's asking if she can come to Paris …"

"Will she come?"

"Although there's nothing I want more in the world than to see my mother, I'd prefer it if she didn't come."

"You're scared."

"Scared? What do you mean? How can I be scared of my own mother?"

"You're scared of explaining to her the real reason why you left."

Zahra was right, and Fernando didn't argue. No, he wouldn't be able to look her in the eyes and tell her that he had killed those men. The ghosts of Roque and Saturnino Pérez still visited him. The passage of time had not erased their presence: father and son were ever more focused on tormenting him.

He loved his mother above all things and knew that if she were standing in front of him then he would not be able to lie to her, even though he knew the immense pain and disappointment it would cause her to know that her son was a murderer. How could she live with this knowledge? His mother believed in God, and if she had ceased to believe in earthly justice, she still had faith in divine justice; she was convinced that Roque and Saturnino Pérez would be judged for their crimes. But knowing that her son was responsible for their murders … no, that would ruin her. And so he preferred not to see her, because if he did, then he would be unable to lie to her.

"Your mother will understand," Zahra insisted.

Fernando pursed his lips and said nothing.

They walked for a good long while, apparently wandering, until Zahra suddenly stopped in front of a little hotel in Montparnasse. She didn't let go of his arm and he followed her. The room was large and comfortable. A suitcase was open on her bed with her clothes folded inside it. She closed it and put it on the floor.

"I'm leaving as well," Zahra whispered.

"When?"

"Tomorrow."

"Will you come back?"

"I'll call you when I find Ludger Wimmer."

Fernando woke up with a start. The light was starting to filter through the windows. He slid his hand across the bed and found no one there. He sprung out of bed, aware of Zahra's absence. The suitcase was gone, as were the clothes that she had worn the day before, formerly discarded, item by item, on the floor of the room. He was annoyed with himself for not having realized that she had gone. How could it have happened? He felt a knot in his stomach, and he got dressed as quickly as possible.

The receptionist told him that the young lady had left little more than an hour ago, and that the room was paid for.

When he got back to his apartment, Piedad was combing Eulogio's hair. He sat still and indifferent, and the nurse made coffee.

They sat down to breakfast and made small talk. Then Piedad said that she was going to pack her bags, because they were leaving the next day.

"What do you want me to say to your mother?" she asked him.

"That I'm well, and that not a minute goes by when I don't think about her."

"She'll ask me if you're going to come back ..."

He sat in silence. It was difficult for him to lie to Piedad, but he had no other choice.

"I'm going to the United States. Catalina's waiting for me there. I'm only in Paris because they told me that Eulogio had turned up," he apologized.

"Right ... but this apartment ..."

"It belongs to some friends."

"Is that Catalina's daughter?" she asked, pointing to a frame with a photo in it, showing the three of them: Fernando, Adela, and Catalina.

He said nothing. Did Piedad know that Catalina had a daughter? She realized what he was thinking and smiled.

"Yes, I know that Catalina was pregnant and that's why she left, and you and my son with her."

"Eulogio told you …"

"He didn't need to tell me … he left without saying goodbye, just as you and Catalina did. But I had heard Eulogio and Marvin talking about her … and you and Eulogio were always so full of secrets … and then when Asunción told us that they were sending her to stay with some relatives … Lots of things have happened over these years, Fernando. The three of us, the three mothers, have joined forces. Isabel, Asunción and I have our three vanished children in common. We couldn't talk to anyone, so we spoke among ourselves. And so we've spent a lot of time wondering where you might be. Your mother is very discreet and said nothing about Catalina's pregnancy, but one afternoon Asunción couldn't cope anymore and broke down and told me everything. When she got the first photograph of her granddaughter, she was so proud … Catalina has to come back to Spain. Her mother doesn't care what the others might say. We've changed, Fernando, we're no longer the same women you knew. The suffering and uncertainty caused by your disappearance, have made us strong. You'll be surprised when you hear Asunción speak. She's not the weak lady she was before, but a strong woman who will stand up to anyone who says anything out of place about her daughter."

"Catalina won't come back to Spain until Marvin marries her, or at least acknowledges his daughter," Fernando explained.

"Ah, Marvin! He's not the man for Catalina. She's too lively for him, and …" Piedad stopped herself.

"Whatever the case may be, he's Adela's father."

"And all these years you've been trying to get Marvin to acknowledge the child?"

"Yes, but he won't even speak to her."

"And what do you think?"

"Me? Well, I've tried to speak to Marvin, but as soon as I mention Catalina, he flies off the handle. And so I can't do anything other than protect her."

"Are you still in love with her?"

He was silent. He didn't have an answer to this. He sometimes thought that the only woman he could truly love was Catalina, but then he saw Zahra and all his certainties began to tremble.

"I'll never leave her," was the most honest answer he could say.

"Right ... And Zahra? I don't want to stick my nose in, but ... it's clear that there's something ... I mean, I don't think you're indifferent to her."

Fernando lit a cigarette. The conversation was making him nervous. He would have liked to have asked her to stop asking these questions, but he didn't dare. Piedad had known him since he was a little boy, and her husband and his father had been friends, and now she and his mother were particularly close.

"Zahra is ... a very important person for me. But Catalina is much more important."

"I know that this conversation is upsetting for you, but I feel like I have to ask you, as your mother will ask me when I return and she'll want to know what you're really like, what your lives are like."

"Tell her the truth, that I'm well and I miss her. I hope that she's been getting the letters that I've sent over all these years ..."

"Yes, the letters that appear mysteriously in our mailboxes. No postmark, no stamps ... as though they fell from the sky. And they make your mother and Asunción even more worried, particularly Asunción, because she never stops asking herself where Catalina and her granddaughter might be."

"And now you can tell them that we are well."

"And you're not coming back?"

"No ..."

"Just because of Catalina?"

"Lots of things have happened in these years ... I don't want to come back to Spain, I couldn't live under the suffocating Franco regime. I will always be the son of a red, a man who was shot by the regime. I have no future in Spain."

"And your mother?"

"I hope we can see each other at some point in the future, but not in Spain." He knew he was lying.

"Paris isn't that far away ..."

"We don't live in Paris. I told you, Catalina is in the United States, and I'll go to meet her when you and Eulogio are back in Madrid."

"Do you at least have a letter for your mother?"

"Yes, it's written, but it only says that I love her, that there's not one minute that I don't think about her."

Piedad knew that he was lying. That this was not an apartment that a friend had let him use. The photos, the clothes in the wardrobes, the papers on the desk ... no, this was not just somewhere they were passing through, but the place where Fernando and Catalina shared their lives.

The next day he took her to the station. He was nervous, and didn't stop giving the nurse instructions. Piedad didn't know this – she didn't even know they existed – but the Wilsons had once again shown their generosity. They hadn't only spent money looking for Eulogio, not stopping until they found him, but now they were paying Nurse Bisset's wages and also the price of three first-class train tickets.

Piedad had said that she didn't need the nurse to come with her, but Fernando had convinced her that she did.

The nurse led Eulogio by the arm. He walked slowly, looking into space, allowing himself to be led.

The passengers got into their carriages, and Fernando helped Piedad and Eulogio find their place and sit down. The nurse stayed with Eulogio, and Piedad came to say goodbye to Fernando.

"How are you going to manage when you get to Madrid? They've told me that you're in a workshop, but you can't leave Eulogio by himself."

"I'll sew things at home, it's the only solution. I know enough about sewing to make a living at it. Maybe they'll give me work at the workshop to take home with me. I won't leave him alone for a moment. I have my son back, and my life means nothing more than caring for him now."

"But what will happen to Eulogio in the future? You ... Well, we're all getting older, and he ... he can't be alone."

"I know what you're saying ... you're worrying what will become of him when I die."

"No ... I didn't mean that ..."

"Yes, you did mean that. You're a good friend of my son, and although you haven't told me much about it, I know you've gone through a lot together. I'll tell you the truth, Fernando. The day I know I'm going to die, I'll take him with me."

Piedad looked at him defiantly, but Fernando held her gaze. There was nothing else to say, and he didn't judge her for what she had just confessed to him.

They heard the whistle of the train and the voice of the conductor asking the passengers to take their seats. She got onto the train and didn't look back. Fernando came to the train window to say goodbye to Eulogio. His friend was leaning against the window and Fernando wanted to believe that he was trying to say goodbye, but his gaze was still blank.

3

It wasn't easy for him to return to normality. The days he had spent with Eulogio had filled him with a sadness he couldn't shake off. He had looked desperately for some sign of life in his friend's eyes, but the emptiness behind that gaze seemed boundless.

He hoped that the routine at the bookshop and in the publishing house would save him. But they didn't. If it had been hard for him to accept that Eulogio was a homosexual, it was harder still for him to accept Piedad's assertion that he had been in love with him.

He asked himself how it had been possible that he had not noticed, but then told himself that it must have been because he loved him that Eulogio had never allowed himself to inconvenience Fernando. He was his best friend, and he'd never have another man like him.

Sara surprised him by giving him a new book of poems by Marvin.

"It's very short, only fifteen poems, but we'll publish it anyway. *Poet of Pain*. Marvin identified very strongly with that description."

He didn't argue. Marvin was the most important author of the Rosent publishing house. And Sara would publish him, even if it was only a single poem. And so he asked her when she would like the book ready by, and she said that September would be a good month to aim for. Sara also surprised him by asking after Catalina.

"She's well," he said bluntly.

"Yes, I can see that. Well enough to go and see Marvin give a lecture at Harvard. Admission was free," she said severely.

So, she knew she was in Boston. Fernando hadn't told the Wilsons, but he didn't think that he was being disloyal to them. He thought that Catalina had the right to do what she felt she needed to do, even if that meant upsetting Marvin. He felt no empathy for the American, and he was upset with him in private, given that he was his editor. He lived in an impossible state of tension between the promise he had made to protect Catalina and his duties as an editor. But he hadn't lied to Sara or Benjamin: if the delicate balancing act broke down, then he would side with Catalina.

"They had to throw her out of the hall. When Marvin finished his talk and the professor who had introduced him asked if there were any questions, she stood up and said, 'Hello, Marvin, this is Adela. We've come to see you. When will you talk to me?' Luckily the organizer of the day's events thought that she was a friend of Marvin's and that she was just there to give him a surprise. He interrupted her and said, 'Lady, I'm sure that Mr. Brian will be happy to talk to you, but we're only here to talk about poetry this evening. It's a great honor of us to have the *Poet of Pain* with us here at our university. You can talk to him later.' Catalina tried to speak again, but the professor wouldn't let her talk. The event didn't last long. Marvin started to feel unwell, so after only five or six questions he left the room. Catalina tried to follow him, but when she tried to find him he had already disappeared."

"You know what I think, Sara, we've talked about this already. Catalina has a daughter and she needs to stand up for her. The least he can do is listen to her. She won't give in, she'll follow him wherever he goes. It's very easy for him to deal with this situation, which is for him to speak to her and hear what she has to say, but this ridiculous insistence on avoiding her won't help anyone."

"I'd say that it's Catalina who's ridiculous, constantly making a spectacle of herself."

"I'll always support her, you know that," he said tiredly.

"Yes, I suppose it was you who paid for her flight to Boston. Will you make her come back?"

"I can't make decisions for her. She needs to know that she can always count on me."

Sara pursed her lips. She was also upset by the conversation, but Benjamin had insisted she speak with Fernando.

"We have to find a solution to this ..."

"The only solution is for me to stop being Marvin's editor ... there's no point my staying on with him, really. We only speak to each other by letter or via you. I don't understand why we're publishing the English version here. It would make more money if we did it in New York."

"Rosent is a French publishing house and Marvin is our author. His poems will leave this place published in all the languages we decide. There's no point arguing about that. I thought you liked your job ..."

"There is nothing I want more than to be an editor. It's been my dream since I was a child, to be like my father and do what he did. I know that I owe you everything, Sara, and that I would have fallen off the map without you, but never ask me to give up on Catalina, because I won't, even if that means I have to leave. I have never lied to you; my primary loyalty has always been to Catalina."

She subtly changed the conversation. She'd sort things out with her husband. Benjamin had told her that she seemed to have adopted Fernando, and treated him like an unruly son whom she spoiled. Maybe he was right. She remembered something by Pascal: the heart has its reasons of which reason knows nothing.

4

They were walking together by the sea. It looked calm. She had bought the *Boston Herald* and wanted to sit down to read it. But she had to wait until she got back to the hotel.

She had just enough money left to pay for one more week at the hotel. Adela had said that she wanted to go home to Fernando. She missed him. For all that Catalina had tried to explain that they were here because they had to see her real father, but Adela didn't care. She had asked for a father because she had hoped that it would turn out to be Fernando, and did not understand why her father had to be this man that her mother kept on pointing out to her.

Catalina decided to get a job. She could do something. Maybe she could give piano lessons like she had done in Alexandria and Paris. She didn't know how to do anything else, although she was prepared to work at whatever might be necessary. Because she wasn't going to go back to Paris. She had promised Fernando that if Marvin refused to speak to her she would come back, but she wasn't going to.

Adela was now eight years old, and she would soon know what it was to be the daughter of a single mother.

She rationed out the money she had and so she bought food for Adela but made do with a sandwich herself, although it wasn't a real meal. She told herself she didn't have any appetite.

When she opened the paper, she found a photograph of Farida and Marvin. She was smiling; he looked scared. The caption was brief: "His time at the University of Harvard finished, Marvin

Brian, the *Poet of Pain*, will stay on in Massachusetts at his family home in Cape Cod as he works on a new collection."

Where was Cape Cod? Catalina asked herself, feeling a wave of irritation swell inside her. Now she had to find where this place was, although it couldn't be that far, as it was still in Massachusetts. But this was America, and distances were measured in days.

When she got to the hotel, she asked the receptionist how to get to Cape Cod. The receptionist explained pleasantly enough that she should go from Boston to Provincetown by boat, or else the whole distance by road. She gave her some details as well: "You should know that it was to Provincetown that the *Mayflower* arrived in 1620. You'd like it. It's a very important historic site for Americans." She seemed proud of her country.

Catalina asked her if she could recommend any cheap places where she could live in Cape Cod. The receptionist hesitated, then said in a low voice that she had a cousin who lived there and who might be able to rent her a room, although maybe not, because her cousin's husband didn't like them having lodgers, although they didn't have that much money. She said that she'd write a letter and Catalina could deliver it personally.

When Catalina asked her if it would be easy to get a job there, the woman laughed. "Of course not. There are only beaches and forests there. People go to Cape Cod to enjoy the solitude. There are lots of writers, painters, university professors. Eccentrics who flee civilized spaces."

That night, as soon as Adela was asleep, she wrote a letter to Fernando. She wanted to know how his meeting with Eulogio had been, and she had to tell him that she had changed her plans and would stay in the United States.

She knew Fernando would be upset, and even might regret having helped her get to Boston in the first place, but he knew her and he knew that she wouldn't rest until Marvin officially recognized Adela as his daughter. She couldn't finish the letter and decided to write it as soon as she was in Cape Cod, that strange and foreign place.

The boat docked in Provincetown. Adela had been sick on the journey. Catalina hadn't been that well herself, but at least she'd been able to avoid throwing up.

She asked a man where she might find Snow Street, and they walked along the beach until they came to it. The house was a simple one and Catalina prayed that Mrs. Jones would rent her a room.

The door was opened by a fat woman with a pleasant face. Catalina introduced herself and held out the letter from her cousin in Boston. Mrs. Jones hesitated a moment before inviting her in.

"Come in ... my husband doesn't like strangers coming in while he's not here ... but I don't think you and the girl are likely to be dangerous."

Mrs. Jones opened the envelope and read the letter, written in the spiky handwriting she knew so well. She read it carefully and slowly, lifting her eyes up from time to time and keeping them on Catalina.

"My cousin Stephanie recommends you. She says that you're a gentlewoman who has come to America with your daughter looking for work."

"Yes, that's right," Catalina said.

"But my dear, this isn't the right place at all. Why didn't you stay in Boston? You might have found something there, but here on Cape Cod, the only people are the ones who were born here or who have come here to find solitude. There's no work here. You should go back to Boston, or even try New York."

Catalina insisted, saying she was looking for somewhere quiet to raise her daughter. Mrs. Jones looked at her suspiciously. She didn't believe her. No one came to Cape Cod to make their fortune.

"I can't decide anything until my husband gets back. He works at the post office. He'll be back later. Of course you can leave your suitcase here ..."

Adela was tired, but didn't complain when her mother said they should play at the beach for a while. The wind was cold, and the horizon seemed to threaten rain. Even so they ran on the beach, sat on the sand, hugged one another and let time go by.

It was late afternoon when they decided to go back to Mrs. Jones' house. They were hungry, but more than that they were exhausted.

Mr. Jones was back and he was addressing himself to a plate of roast lamb. It was clear from his questions that he mistrusted her. Was she a writer? A painter, perhaps? There was no other way in his mind to think that someone would go to Cape Cod. If she was really looking for a job, better for her to try Martha's Vineyard, with the rich people and their vast houses, but there were only bohemians here.

Catalina patiently explained to him that she wanted to stay for a while, even if only a few days. Maybe she had made a mistake in choosing the place, but she liked small towns where everyone knew one another and where her daughter could grow up in safety. As for how to earn her living … she didn't know.

The most that she managed to get was for Mr. Jones to agree to rent her a room for a week. After that they'd see. He asked her for the rent in advance and they agreed that she would have breakfast and supper with them every day as well.

When they were finally able to get into their room and shut the door behind them, both mother and daughter fell fully clothed onto their bed and went straight to sleep. They didn't even hear the wind blowing the sand around.

Mrs. Jones knocked insistently on the door. Catalina gave a start. She opened her eyes and for a moment didn't know where she was. The light filled the room and there was a noise that was like a roar. She stood up and shook her dress out before opening the door.

"It's almost nine o'clock," Mrs. Jones complained.

"I'm sorry … we were tired … we fell asleep and I don't think we'd have woken up if it hadn't been for you."

"Mama, Mama." Adela's voice softened the patrician visage of Mrs. Jones.

"You'll have to have breakfast."

"Yes, give me a couple of minutes and I'll be right with you."

The water in the shower was none too warm, and that woke her up very thoroughly. Once she was dressed, it was Adela's turn. She shivered but did not complain. Adela never complained.

Mrs. Jones had put two bowls of milk and a box of cereal on the table, as well as scrambled eggs and bacon.

Adela turned up her nose, but Catalina cast a warning eye on her and that made her eat the eggs. She didn't like cereal either, but she made an effort so as not to upset her mother, much less this strict-looking woman who seemed to be watching her to see that she ate all her breakfast.

"Can I help you, Mrs. Jones? Maybe there are some errands I can run ... or clean a room ... or iron," Catalina said.

"Of course not, my dear. It'll be enough if you keep your bedroom and your bathroom clean."

"Of course ... Well, I've remembered that I have a friend who has a house in Cape Cod ... We haven't seen each other in some time ... I don't think he can even imagine that I'd ever come here ... But he spoke to me so much about this place. Maybe you can tell me where his house is."

Mrs. Jones' face showed frank curiosity. It was almost unimaginable for her that this foreigner might have friends in Cape Cod.

"Tell me what your friend's called ... if I don't know him, then maybe my husband will, you know I told you he works in the post office."

"Marvin Brian. I suppose you might have heard of him ... he's a great poet ..."

"Of course! The *Poet of Pain*! And you know him?" Mrs. Jones was incredulous.

"Yes, we know one another. I know he's here. He's been teaching in Harvard this semester, but I think he came to Cape Cod to relax and write in peace and quiet ... They told me that his family had a house here."

"Well, as you probably know, Marvin Brian is a member of a wealthy Massachusetts family. The Brians bought a house here several years ago, but I've not seen them use it much. Rose Brian is a woman of the world and prefers her house in Martha's Vineyard. As for her husband Paul, well, he doesn't have all that much time to spend on holidays. They've always said that the Cape Cod house was bought for Marvin because he likes solitude, and although you can find solitude in Martha's Vineyard, there's too much social life up there. Marvin came here several times while he was teaching at Harvard. I heard that he got here a few days ago with that woman ... they say she's his wife ... I don't know ... she looks a lot older than him ... but you know what poets are like. They don't like to have visitors, although Marvin's brother comes to see them every so often."

"Right ... and can you tell me where the house is?"

"Of course. We're very proud of having the *Poet of Pain* as one of our neighbors here in Cape Cod. I haven't read any of his books, but I'm sure they're marvelous."

Mrs. Jones explained in detail how to find the house. She had to walk for three miles and then she'd find it, not far from the beach, half-hidden among the trees.

The wind was blowing the sand that morning, but Catalina didn't care, and she walked out holding Adela's hand, telling Mrs. Jones that she would take a little trip to the Brians' house.

Adela ran along barefoot by the sea and seemed happy, although Catalina had to admit that her daughter never complained about anything. She didn't ask questions and she accepted with good humor every situation, no matter how strange it might seem.

They had walked a long way and they had seen no one apart from a couple, walking along at a good pace. Mrs. Jones said that most of the properties here concealed themselves from prying eyes. If they weren't here to see Marvin, then she would have enjoyed the landscape and the loneliness. They had walked for more than an hour and Adela had decided to stop running. Suddenly she seemed to see in the distance a man walking a dog that jumped around him as he went. She decided to catch up with him and ask him how to find the Brians' house. They were close to the man when he looked up and saw them. He seemed to give a start and then began to walk off fast. Catalina ran towards him. "Sir ... Sir ... please, sir ..." But suddenly she recognized him. She stopped dead. Adela looked up at her expectantly.

"It's your father! It's him! Run on, run to him ..."

Adela didn't know what to do, but her mother gave her a push and she started to run towards the man who was walking even faster now with the dog leaping at his heels.

Catalina began to run as well.

"Marvin! Marvin! For God's sake stop! Marvin!"

He started to run with them in pursuit. He shouted. The wind stopped Catalina from hearing what he said. Suddenly a man and a woman appeared from among the trees and ran to him. The woman held out her hand and he ran to her as though he were saving himself from shipwreck. The man stood his ground and waited for Catalina and the girl to come. When they got there, Marvin was lost among the trees.

The man blocked Catalina's way.

"What do you want?" he said angrily.

"I'm looking for him," Catalina said, pointing to the trees.

"For who?" he insisted.

"For Marvin Brian. We're friends … I have to speak to him. This is my daughter … and his," she said defiantly.

He looked at her scornfully. He was young, tall and athletic. He seemed very sure of himself, and certain that he could stop her from running after Marvin.

"Listen, lady, why don't you stop persecuting my brother? You're making a fool of yourself. He doesn't want anything to do with you. He's made that clear enough."

She stood still and silent. So, this young man was Marvin's brother. Yes, Marvin had spoken about him. The perfect brother, the one who looked after the company business, the one who had decided that Marvin should not waste his talent and that he should dedicate himself to poetry.

"You're Tommy, Marvin's brother?" she said, although she knew the answer already.

"Yes, I'm his brother," he said defiantly.

"Adela, darling, this is your uncle."

The man looked at the girl and held her curious gaze. She said nothing, but she didn't seem scared either.

"You shouldn't use the girl …"

"Use her? Of course I'm not using her. I just want her to know her father and for him to acknowledge her. I used to want Marvin to marry me, but now all I want him to do is admit he has a daughter. She's not the guilty party here."

They stood in silence for a while. Catalina tried to dodge past him, to walk into the trees, but he grabbed her by the arm and stopped her.

"I'm sorry. I've already said that my brother doesn't want anything to do with you. Accept it and leave."

"I will not leave until I speak to him. I followed him to Alexandria, to Paris, and now here … Let him at least have the guts to speak to me!"

"Lady, it's not a question of guts … You … you have to accept that things are how they are. My brother will not speak to you. He never will. Do you understand? So stop humiliating yourself."

"You think I feel humiliated? Not at all. Everything I'm doing, I'm doing for my daughter."

"You shouldn't get her involved in this situation …"

"You can't stop me from talking to Marvin."

"I think I can. I think that he's already in a car, driving away from Cape Cod."

"He's left?" she exclaimed.

"That's what he said he'd do. He can't stay here, not with you roaming around the place. And that's annoying, because he likes this place a lot and he and Farida were happy here."

"Farida, of course … she was the woman who was running alongside you."

"Of course. And when she saw you, she was certain that they had to leave at once."

Catalina sat down on the sand. Adela put her hands around her neck, as though she could take her mother's pain away with this simple action.

Tommy Brian didn't seem moved, but rather upset at her stubbornness.

"So …"

"I've told you. They've left. And it's your fault that Marvin will probably never come back here again."

"Mama … Mama…" Adela seemed scared and grabbed onto her mother with even more strength.

"Your daughter doesn't deserve what you're doing to her. Accept it, accept once and for all that you will never, ever get anything from my brother."

"Tell your brother that I, Catalina Vilamar, will never, ever surrender. Tell him, because even if he goes and hides himself in Hell I will find him."

She stood up, gripping Adela's hand hard in her own, then turned around and walked back towards the Jones' house.

She spent the next few days lost in her own thoughts. She got up early and spent the whole day without any real aim, letting Adela run free on the beach. They came back late in the evening, exhausted from so much time in the fresh air by the sea. They tried to eat before Mr. Jones got home, and then went to their room.

After a week, Mrs. Jones reminded them that if they wanted to stay, then they would have to pay again in advance.

"I think that if you want to stay then you'll have to find a job, but a day on the beach, apart from giving you sunburn, won't help you at all. It's a shame that you weren't able to speak to your friend Mr. Brian. I don't think you'll be able to speak for a good long time, and all. It was in the newspaper today that Mr. Brian's headed off to Asia now."

"We're leaving tomorrow, Mrs. Jones. Your husband was right ... it's difficult to get a job here. I'll try my chances in Boston."

If Mrs. Jones was surprised at Catalina's decision, he said nothing. All she did was tell her the ferry schedule.

She had very little money left, although she had spent her few remaining dollars modestly. She had enough for two more days in a hotel in Boston, and then she would either have to find a job or go back to Paris. The wisest choice was to go back to Fernando. He would know where to find Marvin and she was sure that he would help her find him again. She'd send him a telegram to say that she was coming back. And as she made this decision, she felt the relief of someone who is going home.

5

Fernando didn't blame Catalina for her failure, even though he had warned her of the slim chance of success when she had first decided to go to Boston. Catalina had come home almost defeated. Almost. Because she would never give in.

The Wilsons had left Paris after making it clear that they were very upset by Catalina's presence in Cape Cod. They didn't blame Fernando for Catalina's mistakes, but they were hoping that he would find a way to make it clear to her that it was a big mistake for her to follow Marvin around. And they avoided speaking directly about Marvin with Fernando. In fact, Sara spoke about nothing at all that had to do with Marvin or Farida, except for the most important part: his poems. The French edition of his fifteen poems was ready, and Fernando had to prepare the English edition. As for the Arabic version, Athanasius Vryzas, his old editor in Alexandria, would deal with the translation and the editing.

Before Sara and Benjamin left, Fernando had tried to get Sara to give Catalina her old job in the bookshop back. He had a point, which was that he would have to deal with the editing work and there would be no one to man the shop. But Sara did not accept this. Catalina had put them in an impossible position when she had gone to Marvin's house in the rue de la Boucherie, and then done the same in London and Boston and Cape Cod. Catalina's obsession was starting to wear away at Marvin, and he wouldn't understand it if the Wilsons gave shelter and space to Catalina. Fernando was upset by the reply, but he couldn't blame Sara for anything. Marvin was her author and she would protect him.

Two years went by before Catalina asked Fernando to help her again. The *Herald Tribune* published an article from their Tokyo correspondent in which it was made clear that Marvin Brian, after two years living in Japan, was finishing his stay in Hiroshima. The *Poet of Pain* honored his nickname and had gotten deeply involved in the events of Hiroshima.

Apparently his poems could only blossom in places where the traces of suffering were visible.

"I want to go to Hiroshima," Catalina said, showing him the newspaper.

"No," he said bluntly.

She was surprised. He never usually replied so severely as he had with this "no."

"Marvin will be there."

"I know, I read the papers as well. I'm saying no because you can't go there. First of all, we don't have the money to go on another journey, and secondly, you can't carry on like this. You're wasting your life and you're going to cause your daughter problems."

"Adela needs a father," she said in a tired voice.

"She has a father. I'm her father. I have been her father since the day she was born. I look after her, I look after her when she's sick, I help her do her homework, I take her to school, I taught her to ride a bicycle … she has a father, and I have a daughter."

Catalina didn't know what to say. She didn't want to upset him, but she didn't accept his reasoning either. Yes, Fernando had behaved like a father to Adela, but he wasn't her father. And she needed to put her situation in order so that she could go back to Spain to live with her parents. She couldn't do that if she weren't married, with her head held high.

"Thank you for everything you do for us. It's true that you're behaving like a father to Adela, but … Fernando, you are not her father. You just aren't. She has the right to know who her father is and to have him take responsibility for her. Marvin is not the best of men, I've realized that, but he is Adela's father, and although he doesn't love me, he has to acknowledge that fact."

"That's enough, Catalina! Stop kidding yourself. Marvin will never acknowledge Adela and he will never marry you. You have to face up to reality. And don't you see what you're doing to your daughter? She's not so little anymore."

She felt Fernando's barely repressed rage. Maybe it was just weariness. They had been living together for more than ten years, sharing their troubles and their occasional joys. They had learned to survive alongside one another, abandoning their own lives. Fernando was still haunted by the ghosts of Roque and Saturnino Pérez, the two men he had killed. She knew this because she sometimes heard him call out at night, and then heard his pacing on the floor as insomnia devoured the rest of his night. He couldn't go back to Spain because they would arrest him and kill him. He would live in exile aware that this had been his only choice, and he would not complain. If she had not been dependent on him, then maybe he would have decided to fall in love with Zahra. She was sure that Zahra was more important for Fernando than he would ever admit.

"I am sorry, Fernando, but you're mistaken if you think this has anything to do with stubbornness. I am only looking for justice."

"Justice? When has there ever been justice in the world? We have to accept things as they are. Marvin doesn't love you, he hates you, and he will never recognize Adela as his own. He won't do it because he has no other wife than Farida; she is his past, his present and his future, and he has no life outside of her. And you have to face up to your life without fooling yourself with the idea that he'll change his mind."

"I won't change mine either. I'll go wherever he is and try to make him listen to me until he finally hears me out."

"Well, not in this case you won't. You don't have any money to go to Japan." His voice hardened.

"Maybe I can ask Monsieur Girardot to advance me a year's salary …"

"Oh, just like that. Your boss has a little business, and I don't think he'll give you a year's salary in advance. And do you think he'll let you leave right in the middle of the academic year? He'll have to find someone else to give the music theory classes."

"You don't lose anything by asking."

Monsieur Girardot refused to give Catalina a year's salary in advance. And he reminded her of the time she had gone to Boston, promising she'd be away for only a week, and then had lengthened her "vacation" far beyond what had been agreed.

Catalina wept with rage. Ever since she had come back from Boston, her chief aim had been to find out where Marvin might be. Not even Fernando could help her, because Sara Rosent avoided giving him any information about where Marvin was. She had spent almost two years trying to find out where he had gone, and now that she knew, she didn't have the means to get to him. She tried once again to get Fernando to help her. He listened to her carefully, and when she had finished speaking, he made her an offer.

"Marry me. It's the best choice for you and for Adela, who will have a father who acknowledges her and a proper name for herself. It will let you go back to Spain. Everyone there knows that we ran away together, and so no one will be surprised if you go back with a daughter who bears my name. You can stay with your parents and you don't need to feel ashamed of anything. As for me ... well, you can say that our marriage didn't work out and that you decided to go back to Spain. Your parents will accept what you say, and as for the rest ... Well, it's a plausible story at least."

She bit her lip until she felt blood mix with her saliva. She didn't want to offend him by saying no. Fernando had always been generous and patient with her, and he loved her, yes, he loved her so deeply, in ways that he had never loved anyone else. But she had no right to tie him to her for the rest of his life, because Zahra existed, because Marvin existed as well.

She hugged him, and he returned her embrace, and for a few seconds the two of them asked themselves silently what they were doing with their lives.

"I'm not going to marry you, because you don't deserve to have me take advantage of you."

"You're not going to marry me because you don't love me," he corrected her.

"I love you more than anyone in the world, I love you as much as I love my daughter and my parents. I have never lied to you, and you know that I have never been and am not in love with you, it would be wrong for me to fix my situation by ruining yours. You know, Fernando, that it's my fault you have no life of your own. Everyone who knows us thinks that we're a couple, no one criticizes us for it, France is like that. But you and I know the truth. I think that you should abandon me and go and try to find Zahra. You can have the life you deserve with her."

Fernando laughed, a nervous laugh. She had hit the bullseye when she referred to his love for Zahra.

"You're not a burden on me. You say that you love me … I love you too. I've been in love with you since we were children."

"You say that I'm obsessed with Marvin, and you may be right, but you're obsessed with me, Fernando. At least let one of us be happy."

"I am happy if you're by my side. I don't ask for anything more from life, although if a miracle did take place and Marvin came back for you one day, I would stand aside."

They hugged once again, and their tears mingled.

"Mama … Papa Fernando … Why are you crying?" Adela asked fearfully.

Catalina tried to be content with the very little information that Fernando brought her about Marvin every now and then. And that only happened when Benjamin and Sara were back in Paris. Time seemed to pass unbearably slowly. She would go to the newsstand every morning and buy the newspapers, and would pray that she would see some news about Marvin. She tried not to make her agony visible to Fernando, as it seemed that he was less unhappy in Paris than he had been in Alexandria.

6

Alexandria

It was the mid-1950s, and the Wilsons lived the greater part of the year in London, but they went back to Paris often enough. For Sara, keeping the Rosent bookshop and publishing house going had become her life's mission.

Sara very rarely visited Alexandria, but she was worried about what was happening to Egypt since the military coup. King Farouk's reign had drawn its last breath on July 18, 1953, when the monarch had gone into exile. To begin with, the new head of the government, General Mohamed Naguib, had seemed prepared to come to some arrangement with the West, but the real strongman in the situation was another soldier who knew what he wanted and who wouldn't rest until he got it. Benjamin Wilson distrusted Gamal Abdel Nasser.

Foreigners started to notice changes, even in cosmopolitan Alexandria. At this time, nationalism flowed through Egypt's veins. And so Benjamin Wilson put his business in order, placing Athanasius Vryzas in charge of the Egyptian branch of his affairs, and moved to London. He carried on running his most profitable business from there: looking for people.

The Second World War had left a vast number of people missing, and the survivors wanted to know if they were even still alive.

Benjamin wanted Zahra to come to live in London. But she refused. Her grandmother had died and there was nothing left for her in Alexandria, but she was grateful to the city, which had been there for her when she had been lost. She still lived in her grandmother's handsome old house, woken every morning by the noise of the waves beating against the shore. Although she did not abandon Alexandria, she spent more and more time out of the city.

She carried a photograph of Ludger Wimmer in her wallet, and not a day went by that she didn't look at the face of this man, the object of her hate, who she had spent ten years searching for.

She received a telegram that very morning from Benjamin Wilson to say that she should come to London. She suspected that this time, it wouldn't be for a job.

She finished putting on her makeup. She felt the loneliness in the shell of the house where her grandmother had patiently helped her cure the wounds inflicted upon her soul. She missed her. She had no one now, no one apart from herself. Even the public was starting to forget her: she performed less and less often. She could no longer sink into the music and feel it start to move her body.

She was due to dine with Farida and Marvin that evening. They had come back to Egypt, because Marvin wanted to see how the country was being reconfigured by military nationalists. He could sense that beneath the excitement of the days there was loss and suffering. He wanted to see how the Egypt he had known was transforming itself. But in particular, he wanted to be there because his poems grew from his own pain and that of other people.

There were rumors circulating in the city that Nasser was the country's new strongman. Apparently he was the one the soldiers preferred.

Farida met her with a warm hug. The rain beat against the windows, and stopped them from seeing the Corniche.

Marvin seemed calm and put all his efforts into his duties as host.

Zahra didn't judge Farida. She wouldn't have dared to do so, but she couldn't help but admit that of the two of them, Farida was both the more committed and the more distinguished. She was a famous philosopher when she had met him, and Zahra asked why she had fallen in love with him. He was an attractive man, but no more so than other men: the difference between him and them was the anguish visible in his eyes. That night, though, they seemed serene.

Zahra congratulated Marvin on his *Hiroshima Notebook* and asked about his new work. He explained that he had also published what he thought of as a minor work. He wasn't writing at the moment, he said, but was rather allowing himself to fill his senses so that he could feel what was going on around him.

"A new Egypt is being born. And I want to see the results. A monster, maybe, or maybe the dawn of a new era," Marvin said. "Whatever it is, I want to see it, feel it, write it."

Farida was worried about what might happen.

"I don't think it's a step forwards. Nasser's hatred for foreigners will end up having consequences for the country."

"They can't close Egypt off from the world," Marvin said.

"They're doing it already," Zahra said.

They spoke about the future. Zahra said that she would be going to London in a couple of days. Farida and Marvin would stay a few days in Alexandria. They praised the Wilsons, who they all loved for different reasons.

"I owe it to Sara, everything that I am. Her support pushed open the doors of the temple of poetry for me," Marvin admitted.

"And she was right to pick Fernando as your editor," Farida said.

"Yes, in spite of the fact that we don't get on all that well because of Catalina. She's a nightmare, that girl. As soon as she finds out where I am, she turns up and causes a scandal without the slightest hesitation. I'm sorry for the girl, but she … she makes me feel quite, quite sick."

Zahra said nothing, but glanced at Farida.

"Will you be in London for a long time?" her friend asked her.

"I don't know."

"Benjamin's doing a good job over there, and I think it must be a business that makes a lot of money. It's something to be pleased with, finding people whose families think they are lost. You were able to find Eulogio. You know that Marvin went all over Europe looking for him. We weren't successful, but you were."

"It was hard to find him. He had lost his identity. He didn't speak, he didn't know who he was. He had been taken from one place to another. I was lucky."

"Lucky? No, it wasn't luck. You're the best when it comes to finding people."

"You know, Farida, it's not enough to do things well. You have to be lucky too."

7

Eulogio was sitting in the living room by the window. Piedad wondered if there were any thoughts in his mind, or if he was just thinking of nothing.

She spoke to him as she sewed, knowing that she wouldn't get an answer, but maybe her words would have some impact on his brain.

It was starting to get dark and she looked at the clock. Isabel must be about to get back from work, and she would come up to see them as she did every day.

They found comfort in one another's company, and this comfort was only increased when Asunción joined them.

Recently, Ernesto had gotten worse, and he had needed to go to the hospital again. She hadn't been able to go and see him, because she didn't have anyone she could leave Eulogio with apart from Isabel, but they spoke to one another every day on the phone and she was up to date with what was happening to Ernesto.

The doorbell rang and Piedad got to her feet.

"It's Isabel, here to see you," she said to Eulogio, and went to open the door.

Isabel came in, walking briskly, her face tired.

"How is Eulogio?" she said by way of a greeting.

"You know, the same as always ... but calm."

"I asked Don Luis to let me leave a little earlier in case you need to make a delivery. I can stay with Eulogio for a while," Isabel offered.

"That would be wonderful. If it weren't for you, I wouldn't be able to leave the house. I have to deliver an overcoat and a couple of skirts. They're for the Prado woman, the one who lives in Arenal with her two unmarried daughters."

"Yes, I know who she is. Go and take it over to her and I'll look after Eulogio."

"Do you want me to make you a cup of malt?"

"No ... no need. Go on, take the sewing over to them."

Piedad didn't take long to get there and back, happy because Mrs. de Prado had paid her in full and had also given her one of her daughter's overcoats to switch out the lining.

She earned just enough to keep her and Eulogio, but she felt happier than she had in years. Having her son with her was the only thing she needed.

When she got back, she found Isabel reading the newspaper to Eulogio.

"Are you back already? You didn't take any time at all. Well, I'll go home now."

"You don't know how grateful I am for your help with Eulogio. I'd take him everywhere with me, but I'm worried when we go out into the street; he gets so nervous."

"Don't thank me. If we didn't help one another ... And ... well, I'm worried about Asunción ... I don't think Ernesto's got much longer ... he's weaker every day."

"The poor woman! I'd love to go and see her."

"If you'd like I can sit with Eulogio on Sunday for a bit, and you can go to the hospital."

"Well, thank you, I'd like that."

"Piedad, there has to be some way of getting the news to Catalina. The house you were at in Paris ... do you have the address? Couldn't we send a letter there? Since you came back from Paris I've had a couple of letters from Fernando, and Asunción and Ernesto have gotten letters from Catalina, but ... you know, they turn up mysteriously in the mail, no stamp, no postmark ... Why don't they want to tell us where they are? I don't understand it. And I think they're in Paris, anyway."

Maybe ... I told you that I had the impression that the apartment wasn't just a stopping point for them ... but he was so sure about it ... he said that he was going to the United States with Catalina ..."

"But there has to be a way for us to get in touch with them! Look, I've been patient and I don't want to judge my son, but I can't understand why they don't want to tell us where they are or make it easy for us to get in touch with them."

"They'll have their reasons, Isabel, reasons which we don't know. I've told you that Fernando has made it clear to me that he'll never leave Catalina."

"Yes, but you also said that she was still hoping that Marvin would marry her. My son's throwing his life away for no reason."

"Look, don't worry, if you want we'll send a letter to that address and see what happens. If they took Eulogio there, it must be because they know someone who lives there ... I don't know, there's no harm in trying."

"Oh, by the way, Mari Paz, Antoñito's wife, is pregnant again, Don Bernardo told me. But then I heard someone say in the pharmacy that the pregnancy's going badly ..."

"The poor thing, she lost the last one. They've got two kids, a boy and a girl, but even so ..." Piedad said.

"I met Don Antonio and his wife in the street the other day and they asked me about Fernando. I didn't know what to say ..."

"The whole neighborhood knows he ran away with Catalina. Your son has always been so in love with her that it was no surprise that they ran off together."

"Yes, I know. But I get nervous when they ask about him. Don Antonio said something like Fernando was a bad son because he didn't come back to visit me. I had to bite my tongue not to give him a piece of my mind."

"They're bad people, he and Mari. Two sinners finding one another, and that's why the marriage works."

"And poor Mari Paz ... I don't know how she can cope with that family. She's always very nice when she comes to the pharmacy, but Antoñito ... he comes with her sometimes, and you don't know how arrogantly he treats me."

"Write to your son and we'll send the letter to the Paris address tomorrow, and ... well, it's so long since I was there ..."

8

Fog seemed to envelop the city. Zahra got out of the taxi in front of Wilson & Wilson and felt the damp passing through her coat into her bones.

Benjamin met her with a serious expression on his face. Scarcely had he greeted her before he gave her a folder. She had come directly from the airport to Wilson's office. She hadn't even had a little bit of fun as she usually did, walking through the lower floors of the bookshop.

The building, situated in the heart of Bloomsbury, had always been one that she loved. It was like an endless symphony of words, hidden in the volumes that covered the walls of the two lower floors. But up here, in the apartment and Benjamin's office, the atmosphere was different. There were books all over the walls as well, but there were spaces for large paintings, and you could tell that Sara had a hand in the decoration from the presence of flowers in vases on little tables here and there.

Benjamin poured himself a glass of port. Zahra opened the folder, looking carefully at the photographs it contained and reading the papers that accompanied them.

When she had finished, she looked up at Benjamin.

"Are you sure?"

"As sure as one can be in such cases. My man was looking for an SS officer who had disappeared in the days after the war ended. Someone wanted to settle a score with him. Someone who lost his mother and his father at Auschwitz. His only goal was to bring this man to justice. I have spent five years looking for him, and I think I have found him, but as you can see from the folder, one of the men who is next to him in the photos I've taken looks astonishingly like Ludger Wimmer, your father's former business partner."

"Yes, it could be him. Who is your man?"

"A good investigator. A Jew. His father was a judge, a man who had given his life over to the law. He decided that his wife and son should leave Germany as soon as Hitler was made chancellor. My client was ten years old back then and didn't want to go. He thought that he was a German and didn't understand why suddenly they treated him as though he were no longer one. But leaving saved his life, because his father and his grandparents and his uncles and cousins all died at Auschwitz."

"What's his name?"

"Johan Silverstein. He's a journalist, so he was able to go hunting without arousing too much suspicion."

"And why did the Silverstein family decide to flee to Chile?"

"You'll have to ask him. All I can tell you is that one of his mother's sisters was married to a Chilean diplomat, which made it the most convenient choice. Johan grew up in Santiago, where he finished school and where he now works as a journalist. There's a large German colony in Chile, which makes it a good place to look for former Nazis. Johan found me another man I was looking for there as well."

"And what happened to this man?" Zahra asked.

"I don't know. I gave the information to the people who were looking for him. All I had to do was find him."

"All right, I'll go to Chile."

"And you'll kill him," said Benjamin.

"Yes."

"Do you want one of my men to go with you?"

"I'll ask Fernando to come with me."

"Fernando? You know that he doesn't want to have anything to do with this business, much less with killing anyone. He was able to kill for personal reasons, and would only do it again if it were for the same cause."

"He'll come with me. He doesn't have to kill anyone. I'll do the killing. This will be the only time that I pull the trigger for pleasure."

Benjamin knew that Zahra didn't need Fernando to help her on the mission, but in order to save her from herself afterwards, so he nodded.

"I'll tell Sara that she needs to do without Fernando for a few days."

"Yes, I suppose it will be a bit of an inconvenience."

"Well, the Duforts are always good at sorting this kind of thing out. I'm sure they'll find someone."

"What about Catalina?"

"She could look after the bookshop while Fernando's not there, but Marvin would never understand it. She's obsessed and follows him everywhere. We owe it to him not to get her involved."

"Well, it would be the best solution while Fernando is with me."

Benjamin shrugged resignedly.

"Are you coming to eat with us this evening?"

"Thank you, but I'd rather get started on the trip to Paris to find Fernando. I'll need someone in Santiago to get me a gun."

"Yes, I know. I'll give you a man's address. Don't get Johan involved: he only looks for people."

"I won't."

"Good luck."

Zahra smiled and left the office, and was not surprised to bump into Sara a few hours later on the train to Paris. Sara had decided that it would be she who took charge of keeping the bookshop's doors open while Fernando was away.

9

Paris

Fernando was in the back room talking to Alain Fortier about a book of poems by another young hopeful that the literature professor taught. The door from the back room to the shop was open in case any customers came in, but it had been a quiet morning and looked to be a quiet afternoon as well. But the door to the bookshop did open; there, to his surprise, was Zahra. He stood up and apologized to Professor Fortier, and went out to say hello to the dancer.

When he saw her he knew what she wanted.

"Ludger Wimmer is in Chile," she whispered.

"Are you sure?"

"Yes, it's good info." And she opened her bag and took out a photograph that showed a group of men chatting unconcernedly. One of them, had his face circled in red pen.

"So ..."

"You agreed to come with me," she reminded him.

"When?"

"Tomorrow. I'll come and pick you up this evening when you close the bookshop. We can have dinner together and I'll tell you all, the details."

"All right," he said, trying not to show the resignation in his voice.

Zahra came back two hours later. Professor Fortier was saying goodbye to Fernando, and he couldn't help looking out of the corner of his eye at this woman. He had seen her a few times in the bookshop along with the Wilsons. He shook hands with Fernando and left.

Fernando knew that Sara was coming. She had come to the bookshop and told him to take all the time he needed to help Zahra. Neither of them referred to the kind of help that Zahra required.

Fernando thought about Sara's surprising nature while Zahra took him to a little restaurant in the Quartier Latin, in the rue de l'Ancienne-Comédie.

He felt a bit confused when they went in, because he immediately thought that he wouldn't have enough money to pay to eat there. The opulent decoration had the air of former times.

"Don't you know this place?" Zahra said, realizing that Fernando was a little uncomfortable.

"No, we never go out to restaurants. We sometimes splurge and go out for a coffee …"

"They say that Le Procope is the oldest cafe in Paris … Rousseau ate here, as did Diderot and Voltaire … Danton, Marat and Robespierre all conspired here … and I like the onion soup," she said with a smile.

Fernando barely ate a thing, but Zahra had a healthy appetite, so the dinner went on late into the night. She gave him the details of the trip they were due to take the next day. Benjamin had arranged for her to perform at a cabaret that, according to the information he had available to him, was one that Ludger Wimmer regularly visited. The German had a good relationship with the owner of the club, and some people even thought that he was a silent partner.

"Are you worried about Catalina?" Zahra asked suddenly.

"No … well, I don't know what explanation I can give her."

"Tell her the truth: that I'm looking for someone and have asked you to come with me. She knows that I work for Benjamin and that he looks for people. It won't be the first time that you come with me on trips of this kind. She doesn't need to know more than that."

"Right …"

"Don't worry so much about Catalina. She's not a child. Although it's hard for you to admit it, she doesn't need you as much as you think."

"What do you know?" he protested.

"Well, I know that you're all tangled up like a ball of wool, but you could live perfectly well without one another. I even think that it might help, because you won't have real lives until the ball of wool is properly unwound."

He was annoyed at how honest Zahra was. He refused to tell anyone, not even her, about the strength of his relationship with Catalina. Catalina was the person who made him remember who he was, where he came from, and why his life had worked out as it had.

Zahra saw the tension in Fernando's mouth. He was obviously fighting with himself.

"You know why I'm going out there ... and although you did promise to come, I'd understand if you backed out now."

"It's you that should back out."

"No, you know that's impossible."

"I'm surprised about your attitude towards death. It's like taking a life hardly matters to you."

"It doesn't weigh me down, Fernando, it doesn't weigh me down at all to have killed people who deserved it. Are you still tormented by having killed the men who murdered your father, or the Gestapo agent who followed us from Prague?"

"Drop it. I'm coming with you."

"You don't have to kill anyone, Fernando, all you have to do is come with me."

"Yes, that's what you said when we set off to Prague, and I ended up killing a man."

"A murderer, a Gestapo murderer."

"A man, for all that."

When the waiter brought them the bill, Zahra wouldn't let him pay, and Fernando was offended. He didn't want to rely on her, and he didn't want to let her treat him to a meal.

"Look, let's be practical. We're about to set out on a journey which will cost us a great deal of money. And it wouldn't be fair for you to have to make sacrifices. I'm going to pay for everything, so let's say that the journey starts tonight and I'll pay the bill."

But he refused. He couldn't pay for the flights, but he could at least pay for a meal at the oldest restaurant in Paris.

Later, when he told Catalina that the following day he would be going to Chile with Zahra, he realized that she was deliberately refraining from asking questions. She had always been cautious when it came to Zahra, and was afraid of saying a single word too much.

She offered to pack his suitcase and he accepted because it would give them more time to talk.

Adela couldn't hide how upset she was that Fernando was going on a trip.

Adela seemed to be afraid of anything that might disrupt her daily routine, which was based on Fernando and Catalina, whom she considered her parents. This was enough to keep her happy. So first she begged Fernando not to go, and then she asked if she and Catalina could go with him, and then she made him promise not to stay away too long.

10

Santiago

Johan Silverstein was waiting for them at the airport terminal. He was a young man, not too tall, with chestnut-brown hair, bright eyes, and a ruddy face. There was nothing about him that attracted too much attention apart from the goodwill that shone from his contained smile.

"I've reserved a room for you at the Carrera Hotel. You'll like it; it's the best hotel in the city and it's not that far from the cabaret where you are going to perform," he said, smiling at Zahra.

Silverstein was right. The Carrera was a modern hotel, built in the 1940s in the Art Deco style, with marble columns and leather chairs that created a cosmopolitan atmosphere.

They sat in a corner of the bar so that Johan could bring them all up to date.

"The owner of the cabaret is called Jorge Prat, and he's a fascist. His friends include the worst people in the country, everyone who is trying to hold back democracy, who think that workers only have one right: the right to work. He'd rather have an army officer in charge of the government than a politician, and he supported hard crackdowns on students and anyone who dares question the rotten government of this rotten country. At the end of the 1930s, he was in Berlin for a while and married a German woman, Matilde Schmidt. And from what I've been able to find out he was in business with a famous Berlin cabaret, the Rosy-Fingered Dawn. It was one of the favorite cabarets of the high officials of the SA and the SS."

Zahra shuddered, although neither Fernando nor Johan realized how upset she felt.

"When he got back from Berlin," Johan continued, "he opened a cabaret near the Avenida de la Alameda. It was called 'La Nuit' and all the most influential people of Santiago came there. Businessmen who funded unhappy military men, politicians keen to get rich at the country's expense … and over the last few years, it's been the haunt of foreigners, Germans among them. I know that Benjamin Wilson has explained to you that my father and a part of my family died in the gas chambers at Auschwitz. And I, just like very many others, am not going to put up with the idea that just because a few of the Nazi higher-ups have been sentenced at Nuremberg then we need to accept that thousands of other people who were also responsible for it all get to walk free. Some of them have changed their names, some have fled, lots of them are safe at home, back in their villages, as though they'd done nothing at all. But as far as I'm concerned, I'll do whatever I can to unmask them and make sure they are brought to justice."

"It's an almost impossible task," Fernando said.

Johan nodded, and offered cigarettes. He waited for Fernando and Zahra to light theirs and then lit his.

"There are other people who think as I do. Have you heard of Fritz Bauer? Or Simon Wiesenthal? Or Jan Sehn, or Tuviah Friedman?" Johan asked.

"No," Fernando said.

Zahra started to speak:

"Fritz Bauer, a Jew, a man of the law, wasn't killed by the Nazis because he spent the war in Denmark and Sweden. He's trying to make sure that the people who were responsible for the crimes committed at Auschwitz and other places don't remain at liberty. Simon Wiesenthal was at Mauthausen and then, when the camp was liberated, he went to Linz where he founded a center for historical documentation … I think that his book *KZ Mauthausen* was published in 1946, a year after the war ended. And then a year later, he published a book about the Mufti Amin Al-Husseini. The book has never been translated out of German; not even Benjamin Wilson has considered translating it into

English. And as for Tuviah Friedman … he's like Wiesenthal, and has tried to bring Nazi collaborators to justice. He's living in Israel now, frustrated with constantly seeing how Austria tries to forget its Nazi past. His archives are in Jerusalem, at Yad Vashem, the center built to memorialize the Holocaust."

Fernando listened to Zahra in surprise, asking himself why she hadn't shared this information with him before. He could answer the question himself. Zahra was like these men, whose aim was to unmask criminals, but she would be content to ensure justice came for one man: her father's business partner, Ludger Wimmer.

"You've done your homework," Johan Silverstein said, looking at Zahra.

"As for Jan Sehn … it's thanks to him that we know the worst details of what happened in Auschwitz, especially insofar as the medical experiments carried out on the prisoners," Zahra continued.

"What does this Jan Sehn do?" Fernando asked

"He was the chief prosecutor in the case of Rudolf Höss," Johan said.

"And the High Commissioner for investigating the crimes committed by the Nazis in Poland. He was a part of the Polish Military Commission for Investigating War Crimes," Zahra added.

"I think you should rest. I'll come and find you later," Johan said, looking at his watch.

Zahra's room led through to Fernando's through a small vestibule containing a low table with a bouquet of flowers on it, as well as a card that Zahra glanced at indifferently.

"An admirer?" Fernando asked.

"It's from Jorge Prat, the owner of the cabaret."

"Look, I don't think it's a good idea to dance here. Ludger Wimmer might see you. He knew your mother and he knows you."

"Jorge Prat must have known my mother as well. That's why he hired me, because he remembered how successful my mother had been dancing at the Rosy-Fingered Dawn. He wants to offer his customers the same that Wimmer and my father offered them back in Berlin. But don't worry. Prat doesn't know who I am. For him, I am nothing more than an Egyptian dancer."

"But Ludger Wimmer will recognize you. And your name ..."

"I'm the bait so that Wimmer will let himself be seen. He'll be curious to see the show, an Egyptian dancer whose name doesn't mean anything to him. I'm Zahra Nadouri now, but when ... when what happened happened, I was a girl and my name was Mandisa Rahim: I told you that I had my mother's name then. Wimmer won't connect me with Mandisa."

"I'm not so sure about that," Fernando said.

The telephone brought them back to the real world. They had fallen asleep and he saw that the world outside was dark.

Fernando sat up and listened to Zahra replying monosyllabically to the person on the other end of the receiver.

"Jorge Prat will come and meet us in an hour to take us to dinner."

"But Johan said that he'd come ... we have to warn him."

"Call him while I get myself ready," she said, getting to her feet.

Jorge Prat was a tall man, plump running to fat, with gray hair. His smile worried Zahra.

"My dear Miss Nadouri! What a great honor to have you here! I hope you were able to get a little rest." Prat ignored Fernando; he had eyes only for Zahra.

She extended an indifferent hand to Prat, then looked at Fernando and drew him close.

"Mr. Prat, this is Mr. Garzo. He's a good friend whom I have been very close to for a long time."

Prat and Fernando sized each other up as they shook hands.

"Yes ... they told me that you would be coming with the gentleman ... Well, I hope you enjoy your stay in Santiago, and I am sorry for insisting on coming to see you this evening, but I was very keen to meet you. I know that you're a legend in Alexandria."

Zahra didn't bother to reply. Fernando did instead.

"Miss Nadouri is by far the most famous dancer in the whole Middle East."

"Well ... if you think it's all right, I suggest we eat at the hotel. And if you'll allow me, I'll tell you a little about La Nuit, where we've had all the tables reserved for weeks for people to come and see you."

Zahra was very *distraite* during the meal, whatever Jorge Prat told her. Fernando shouldered the bulk of the conversation and asked the businessman lots of questions. And so they found out that years ago he had been in Berlin and did business with a number of businessmen. On one occasion, he had the chance to see an Egyptian dancer himself.

"Heba, I think her name was … yes, Heba Rahim. Did you ever hear of her?" he asked, looking fixedly at Zahra.

She shrugged and drained her glass of champagne.

"Egypt has a long tradition of Raqs Sharqi dancers."

"Yes, and this was a good while back. When Heba was dancing in Berlin, you must have been little more than a girl. It was a wonderful time … Berlin was the capital of Europe and … well, it could have been the capital of the world … It was a shame that Germany lost the war, don't you think?"

Fernando was about to answer, but Zahra got in first.

"I really don't care, Mr. Prat. Egypt has enough problems of its own for us to bother with those of others. I'm not interested in politics: it's men's business, and men never think of women when it's a question of war or of peace."

"Interesting," Prat said, looking scornfully at Zahra. He now dismissed her as a woman with no interests, and he was even starting to fear that she wouldn't be as good a dancer as he had been promised.

"And what about you, Mr. Garzo? What do you think?" Prat insisted, trying to draw out Fernando.

"What do I think about what?"

"About the result of the war."

"It's all history now, what does it matter? The important thing is the future. Don't you agree?"

"Of course, of course …"

Jorge Prat looked at his watch, bored by this tedious conversation with the dancer and the Spaniard. He looked at Zahra out of the corner of his eye and couldn't help comparing her with the wonderful dancer who had lit up the Rosy-Fingered Dawn club so many years ago in Berlin. He not only remembered her name, but also her sensuality and her beauty. Jan Dinter, Wimmer's business partner, the owner of the Rosy-Fingered Dawn, had enjoyed her favors, although from time to time he had shared her with some of the Nazi top brass.

When he had mentioned to Ludger Wimmer that an artist's agent had offered him a belly dancer for his club, Wimmer had told him not to hesitate and to book her, because she would be a guaranteed success. And he trusted Wimmer's business sense. He had admired the man ever since he had met him in Berlin, when he had been the co-owner of one of the most exclusive cabarets in the city.

That's why he hadn't hesitated when the chance had come up to offer him a role as co-owner of La Nuit, when Ludger Wimmer had turned up in Santiago just before the end of the war. He was open and told him that he didn't want to tempt fate. He had managed to get out of Berlin before the Russians arrived, and as a forward-thinking man, he had had the good sense to separate his business dealings from his sympathies. He was a dyed-in-the-wool Nazi, but his faith in Adolf Hitler didn't get in the way of his reason, and so he had taken his money out of Germany and put it in a Swiss bank. When he came to Santiago, it was not as a refugee seeking shelter, but as a capitalist, with money to invest. Wimmer's interests now went beyond cabarets, although he still seemed to enjoy being an investor in La Nuit, which he visited occasionally.

"You're very thoughtful." Zahra's voice shook Jorge Prat out of his musings.

"I'm sorry, how impolite … I thought that you might be tired after such a long journey and that maybe I was rude to insist that you dine with me."

"Of course not. We're very grateful," Zahra said, her face bored.

"Well, let's meet up tomorrow. I told you already, I am expecting you to dance at eleven o'clock. I'll send a car to pick you up at nine o'clock, if that seems a good idea. You'll have a maid in the cabaret to help you dress."

"Thank you very much, Mr. Prat, you're right, we are tired." Zahra got to her feet.

They had said goodbye to Mr. Prat barely half an hour previously when the doorbell made them jump. Fernando opened up.

"How did the dinner go?" Johan Silverstein asked in the doorway.

"Well … we weren't expecting it," Fernando said.

"You told me not to come because you were dining with Mr. Prat, but I couldn't help myself coming to see you," Johan said.

Zahra appeared in the salon, barefoot and wearing a silk robe.

"You were right. He's dangerous," she said to Johan.

"Yes, there's a scorpion hiding behind his good manners. You have to be careful with him," Silverstein replied.

Fernando put three glasses of whisky on a tray and offered one to Johan.

"Do you think that Ludger Wimmer will come to La Nuit tomorrow?" Zahra asked worriedly.

"I can't say for sure, but I would say that yes, he would. I told you, the rumor is that Wimmer has a stake in the business. He doesn't normally come out to cabarets, because in Santiago he's better known as a businessman in the textiles market. He's a partner in a textiles factory, and he has a couple of menswear shops. But he's discreet. He doesn't take part in the city's nightlife, although he has been seen on occasion at La Nuit."

"And what if he doesn't come?" Zahra asked worriedly.

"We'll look for him … he's discreet, but he's not invisible."

"Johan, I don't want you to get caught up in what I've come here to do," Zahra said.

"I don't know what you mean …"

"I will dance at La Nuit tomorrow, but what I need most of all are details of Ludger Wimmer's life in Santiago. His address, his habits. Just that. As soon as you get me this information, get as far away from me as you can."

The young journalist looked at her, trying to work out what lay behind the woman's eyes. Her tone betrayed no emotion, but her words and her attitude were worrying.

"My aim is to bring the largest possible number of Nazis to justice. Ludger Wimmer isn't on any list of fugitives from justice. He came to Chile legally, and the authorities haven't got anything on him. But you're looking for him because you know he's a dangerous Nazi. At least we can unmask him and make sure that his name and his photos appear in the newspapers, stop his life here from being so easy. Maybe you can get a German court to extradite him … Isn't that enough?" Johan asked, trying to see into Zahra's inscrutable face.

"No," she said sincerely.

"So …"

"Help me by getting me the information I have asked for, and then stay away from me," she insisted.

"Benjamin Wilson asked me to help you. I have been working with him and others for some time now, looking for Nazi criminals, but my only task is to bring them to justice. What do you want to do?"

"What would you do if you found the people who killed your grandparents and your family members at Auschwitz?" Zahra interrupted.

"Do? I've told you, try to bring them to justice."

"And if you found yourself face-to-face with them, wouldn't you try to perform justice yourself?" Zahra asked.

"No! Of course not! There is no justice outside of the law," Johan replied, alarmed at the turn the conversation was taking.

"What law? The laws of Hitler's Germany? There were courts and tribunals there as well," Zahra said.

"You know what I mean. I am a German, and I feel sick to think about what happened in Germany. I know that it wasn't just the fault of the Nazis, but that it was normal people, our neighbors, some of our friends, people we thought we knew but who preferred to look the other way. They too are responsible for what happened. And that's why I'm not going back to Germany, because I'm afraid that I won't be able to see anything but the faces of killers, people who ended lives through what they did, and because of what they left undone. But one thing is clear. I will never, ever do anything that will put me on the level of these people."

"You're sure of your moral superiority," Fernando said reproachfully.

"I am sure that I don't want to be like these people, and even if I know that justice isn't always just – and I know that lots of these monsters will never be brought before a court, or even if they are, then they will be given sentences that are trivial in comparison to their crimes – even with all this in my mind, I will never do anything that might bring me down."

They fell silent and lit cigarettes.

"You're a good man," Zahra murmured.

"I remember the day my mother and I left Berlin. My father said that as soon as he could, he'd follow us. He couldn't make it. They took him to Auschwitz along with my grandparents, my uncles and my cousins. My mother and I were the only survivors from my entire family. And know that not a day goes by when I don't remember the last words my father said to me as the train was about to leave: 'Johan, whatever happens, don't let anything or anyone turn you into someone who can't look in the mirror without feeling ashamed.'"

"So you decided to resign yourself to the situation," Fernando said, feeling a sharp pain at the words he had just heard.

"Resign myself? No, of course not, but I've never forgotten the words my father said. And believe me, there is a great relief in being able to look at yourself in the mirror without feeling ashamed."

Fernando felt Johan's words like a knife to the gut. Time hadn't stopped Roque and Saturnino Pérez from appearing before him. They turned up in his dreams, reminding him that he had taken their lives, and even though he shouted at them, blaming him for having taken his father away from him, they still pointed at him and called out "Murderer!" And the face of that other man, the Gestapo agent, was there as well. But it wasn't the voices or faces of Roque or Saturnino or the Gestapo man that made him suffer, but his father's face, and his voice: "You shall not kill, Fernando, you shall not kill." He knew that his father would not accept that his son had become a killer. He had disobeyed his father's warning and the man who stood in front of him had followed his father's instructions to the letter.

Zahra and Johan looked at him in silence. What they saw in Fernando's eyes was loss beginning to bite.

"Everyone sorts things out as best they can," Johan said. "And I don't judge anyone."

"Sometimes, we must take the law into our own hands," Zahra whispered.

Johan looked worriedly at her. He was starting to work out what this woman's intentions might be.

"You've done everything you can and we're grateful to you," Zahra added.

"I will go to La Nuit tomorrow. I'll help you do whatever you think you need to do," Johan insisted.

"Find out where Ludger Wimmer lives. I need that information," Zahra replied.

It was Saturday, and the streets of Santiago were getting ready to party.

Zahra was getting dressed with the help of a maid who wouldn't stop talking. But she didn't listen to her.

Jorge Prat had insisted to Fernando that he sit at the table he had reserved for himself and his most special guests. He had barely taken a sip of the whisky that they had given him, and although Prat had introduced him to the couple seated at the table, he was finding it difficult to pay attention.

The woman had dye-blond hair and was dressed in red. She seemed bored. Her companion, an older gentleman with a sharp gaze, was telling Jorge Prat about how the Government needed to be given a little "push."

A few tables further along, Johan Silverstein seemed to be having fun, chatting to a couple of young men like him. Fernando asked himself who they might be.

A man marched directly over to the table. Jorge Prat got up and gave him an affectionate hug.

"My dear friend, how wonderful to see you here this evening! I hope that the dancer is good enough to meet our expectations. I know that she can't possibly compare with the pretty little thing from the Berlin cabaret, but I'm also sure we won't be disappointed. Am I right?" Jorge Prat said, turning to Fernando.

"Miss Nadouri is one of the best dancers of Raqs Sharqi around," Fernando said.

"Raqs Sharqi? What's that?" the blond asked.

"Oriental dance, in this case belly dance, a specialty of Egyptian dancers," explained the man who had just arrived.

"Allow me to introduce you. Mr. Garzo is the companion of tonight's dancer. And this is my dear friend Ludger Wimmer. And you, my dear general," he said, looking at the white-haired man, "I think you know him already."

Ludger Wimmer nodded to the general, kissed the blond's hand, and held out a hand for Fernando to shake while he looked him carefully up and down.

"And so, your friend is Egyptian, and you are ... Spanish? Am I right?"

"Yes," Fernando said.

The lights in the room started to dim and Jorge Prat nervously asked them to be quiet. "The dance is about to begin," he whispered.

The musicians started to tune their instruments and the lights faded completely. A single spotlight lit up the center of the room. The murmurs of the public died away, and only the clink of glasses suggested that there were even people in the room. Suddenly the music grew louder and louder, and when it reached a climax, Zahra appeared in the spotlight.

She started to move slowly, as though time did not exist for her, and everyone in the room became aware of the movements of her body.

Fernando didn't stop looking out of the corner of his eye at Ludger Wimmer. He was surprised by the sensation of disgust that overpowered him, running from his stomach up to his mouth. This was the man who had raped Zahra, who had locked her away in a psychiatric institution, who had made every possible effort to destroy her.

Ludger Wimmer looked at Zahra. He kept his eyes fixed on her, and Fernando was afraid that he had recognized her. It only took a second for their eyes to meet. A second, barely enough time for the recognition to happen. But in a flash it had: Zahra's eyes filled with overwhelming hatred, and Wimmer's with the memories that were coming back to his mind.

The applause filled the room and Zahra and Jorge Prat both

enjoyed their moment of success, seeing so many men on their feet and applauding.

"I've never seen such a reaction. My dancer is as good as your Berliner," Prat joked, slapping Wimmer on the back.

Ludger Wimmer didn't say anything. His lips were pressed together and there was something like hatred and stupefaction in his eyes.

"Will she come and have a drink with us?" he asked his friend Prat.

"Well ... I don't think so ... there's a clause in her contract that states she won't meet any customers," Jorge Prat said reluctantly.

"But here is her companion. Sir, will you refuse us a chance to speak with the lady?" Ludger Wimmer said to Fernando.

"It's like Mr. Prat said. Miss Nadouri never speaks to customers in the places where she dances. It's a custom she has never broken, and which I support."

"But this is a cabaret ... the dancers know what that means. It's impossible that she should insist on such conditions when she comes to dance in a place like this." Ludger Wimmer's voice showed barely contained rage.

"Miss Nadouri's contract is extremely clear, and Mr. Prat signed off on it, and if he hadn't accepted her conditions then we wouldn't be here." Fernando also sounded tense.

"Come, come ... let's not get angry," the general said. "You have to understand, young man, that men like us need to show our admiration for such an extraordinary woman ... you shouldn't be jealous."

"I have no cause to be jealous, general. And now if you'll excuse me, I'm going to go see Miss Nadouri. She'll be tired and want to go back to the hotel."

It wasn't until much later, when there was no longer a single customer at La Nuit, that Ludger Wimmer asked his friend and business partner Jorge Prat about Zahra.

"Doesn't she remind you of our dancer from Berlin?"

"No, not at all, my dear friend. I mean, yours was undoubtedly a beautiful woman and a good dancer, but this one ... she has something special."

"I don't know …"

"You don't think it was the same woman, surely?" Jorge Prat said ironically.

"Of course not. That's not possible, but … I don't know … there's something about her that is familiar …"

"Oh, Ludger, what's familiar is that she's an exotic dancer. They all look the same."

"Possibly …"

Ludger Wimmer didn't sleep well that night. The eyes of that dancer … they reminded him of other eyes … the eyes of a girl that he had personally tried to destroy. He knew that she was dead. That's what they'd told him at the sanatorium when he'd gone back determined to rape her again.

"They've taken her away," the nurse had said. And then in a low voice she'd added that it wasn't the first time that the authorities had decided to get rid of someone like her, a "social parasite." And then she had also said, "Who cares if someone like that lives or dies?" But he had insisted, and the nurse had shown him the register. They'd taken her to a halfway house … yes, a halfway house between life and death. A hospital for the incurably demented.

Right, so Mandisa Rahim was dead. There was no doubt about it. As dead as her mother, Heba Rahim. But those eyes … they had only locked eyes for a second, but he was sure that she had looked at him with hate.

He didn't go to sleep until dawn was nearly breaking, and he woke up because he heard a shout. It was his own shout at Mandisa Rahim coming back to take his life.

Zahra didn't sleep that night either. Johan Silverstein had given her a piece of paper that evening with Ludger Wimmer's address. She thanked him.

"Will you be able to live with yourself?" Johan asked her, looking her straight in the eye.

He didn't need to ask anything else for him to know what she intended to do.

She nodded. They shook hands. Johan paused for a few seconds before leaving.

"I'm not going to say anything, but … whatever happened, whatever you do, it's going to be tough on me."

"You don't know anything about this, Johan, nothing at all. Don't let your imagination get the better of you."

But he felt guilty, and as he left the hotel, he asked himself if he could look at himself in the mirror without feeling shame.

Zahra and Fernando left the hotel late in the morning. They walked for a good distance before they found a taxi. Fernando told him the address; it was in Chuchunco, near the station.

It wasn't hard for them to find the modest house of the man who Benjamin had recommended to them. The man who might sell them a gun.

They knocked on the door. When it opened, all they could see was a face covered in scars, one eye almost closed.

"Alfredo Zúñiga?" Fernando asked.

"What do you want?" the man said shortly.

"We were sent here by a friend. I think he told you we would be coming to buy something from you …" Fernando said, asking himself if this man really was as trustworthy as Benjamin had said.

"Who sent you?"

"We were told to ask for Alfredo Zúñiga on behalf of his good friend Tomás."

The door opened and the man waved them in. The house was in shadow and smelled of rotten food.

He didn't ask them to sit down. He stood and waited for them to tell him what it was they wanted.

"You sell weapons, don't you?" Fernando said.

"What kind of weapon?"

"Small, but powerful," Zahra said.

The man looked her up and down, but she ignored him. Fernando felt uncomfortable to see the man's eyes running up and down Zahra's body.

"Is it for you?"

"I need a small but powerful weapon that I can easily use. I want a gun that doesn't jam, and that has a silencer," she replied.

"I'll see what I've got."

The man opened a door and disappeared, closing it after him. Fernando was about to speak, but Zahra put a finger to her lips.

Better not to say anything. A few minutes later the man came back to the room.

"Here you go … this'll do you," he said, handing a gun to Zahra.

Fernando held out his hand and took it. He looked at it for a few seconds, trying to work out how it worked. It seemed like it might do, although he knew very little about guns.

"How much?" Fernando said.

"A bargain, because I'm not going to charge you for the silencer."

And then he named a price which was higher than they had imagined, but Zahra didn't protest, and her eyes told Fernando to pay. They had agreed that it would be he who dealt with this man, because he wouldn't have understood it any other way.

"I don't know you and you don't know me," the man warned.

"Of course we don't know each other," Fernando said.

They left the house quickly. Fernando felt the weight of the gun in his jacket pocket. He wanted to go back to the hotel as soon as possible, but Zahra was intent on walking past the place where they had been told Ludger Wimmer lived.

They walked in silence, alone with their thoughts. They didn't stop another taxi until they had gone a good long way. They gave him the address they had been given for Ludger Wimmer.

"We don't know if he's at home," Fernando murmured.

"The important thing is that we know where he lives. We'll deal with the rest later."

"We have to be careful to make sure he doesn't see us," Fernando said.

"I was half naked last night, and covered in makeup."

"But I was wearing clothes, so he might recognize me," Fernando said with a touch of irony.

The discreet two-story house had the look of a place where someone who was rich but who didn't like to attract attention might live. They saw a woman coming out, but they were too far away to see the details of her face.

Fernando didn't calm down until they were back at the hotel. Zahra was above such nervousness.

"You shouldn't do it," he insisted.

She didn't say anything. She was immune to all attempts to dissuade her. She took the gun and looked at it without hiding a grimace of dissatisfaction.

"You don't like it?"

"No, it's not the kind of weapon I like. It's not very accurate. But it'll do."

They wanted to be alone, so they went to their separate rooms. Zahra needed to plan how and when she was to kill Ludger Wimmer, while Fernando wanted to forget all about what she was going to do.

At nine o'clock, they were told that Mr. Prat's car was waiting for them downstairs. Zahra had heavily made up her face, and transformed herself into a strikingly different woman.

She danced again at La Nuit, and as she did so she felt a gaze on her. She knew whose it was without looking up. Ludger Wimmer was there.

Jorge Prat insisted once again that Fernando sit with him at his table, and Ludger Wimmer had not taken long to join them.

The German looked at Zahra as though he were dissecting her, and Fernando was afraid that he had recognized her.

Wimmer pursed his lips and furrowed his brow as he followed Zahra's movements as though hypnotized, but he didn't join in the enthusiastic applause at the end of her performance.

"She's incredible! Congratulations, Mr. Garzo, you're a lucky man," Jorge Prat said, holding the flame of his gold lighter to Fernando's cigarette.

"She's a great artist," Fernando said.

"More than that ... look ... look around you ... even the women have fallen for her charms ... No one can resist her dancing. Don't you think the same, Ludger, my dear friend?"

Wimmer nodded. He seemed uncomfortable, upset.

"Of course," he said, but not with any great enthusiasm.

"Do you think that we might be able to get Miss Nadouri to stay a couple of days longer with us? I'd like to see her dance in Viña del Mar. I opened up a bar there not so long ago ... It would be a great success!" Jorge Prat was completely taken with Zahra.

"I don't think it will be possible. Miss Nadouri is already committed to other performances, back in Europe."

"I'm ready to compensate you for the cancellation of those performances … A few days more … Just stay here a few days more … If I had known how extraordinary she was, then I wouldn't have accepted a contract for just a week. I have the place booked solid for the days she's going to be here, and there's a waiting list. You can't imagine how many people call me personally to ask me to get them a table because the *maître d'* has said that there wasn't one available. I'll talk to her, try to get her to stay another week at least."

"Miss Nadouri never breaks her agreements, and so we can't help you. We can't stay for another week. But I am sure that she will be happy to return on another occasion," Fernando was speaking firmly, trying to sound absolutely convincing.

"How long have you known her?" Ludger Wimmer asked suddenly.

"We've been good friends for several years now."

"Where did you meet her?" Wimmer insisted.

"In Cairo. It's a very special city. Do you know it?"

"And has she always lived there?" Wimmer was not going to allow Fernando to sidetrack the conversation.

"Miss Nadouri travels all over the world. She's a well-known artist. Her official residence is Egypt, although as I said, we travel from one place to the next."

"Where did she learn to dance?" Ludger Wimmer was speaking in an ever-more threatening voice.

"My dear friend, you must really have been taken by Miss Nadouri!" Jorge Prat exclaimed.

"You know that the belly dance is an Egyptian specialty. Lots of women learn to dance it, although few of them do so professionally."

"But someone must have taught her," the German insisted stubbornly.

"No one is born knowing how to dance, but again, Mr. Wimmer, it's difficult for a woman not to learn how to belly dance in Egypt. And, if you'll allow me … I'm surprised at your curiosity," Fernando's voice was cold.

"I'm sorry, I didn't want to seem impertinent. It's just that … well, she reminds me very much of someone I knew a long time ago."

850

"My friend Ludger was the co-owner of one of the best cabarets in the whole of Berlin. There was a belly dancer who was one of his most important artists. She was extraordinary! But not quite as extraordinary as Miss Nadouri. I don't understand why he thinks that Miss Nadouri reminds him of his dancer ... they don't look like one another. His dancer was curvier, more sensual, and drove men mad, but she wasn't as elegant as Miss Nadouri. I'd say that his dancer was more earthly, and Miss Nadouri seems to have stepped out of the air."

"Has Miss Nadouri ever danced in Germany?" Wimmer asked.

"No. Let me remind you that Germany is still suffering the effects of the war. The Berlin which you all seem to miss so much no longer exists, and I don't think that there are cabarets where they offer belly dancers anymore ... Maybe I'm wrong. But no, we've never been to Germany."

Suddenly Jorge Prat got to his feet. The room was filled with applause and shouts. Zahra walked along with her head held high and came over to them. Fernando felt himself break out into a cold sweat.

"I was waiting for you. I'm tired," Zahra said, ignoring Prat and Wimmer.

"I'm sorry ... I got talking to these men. If you'll excuse us ..."

Ludger Wimmer started to speak to Zahra in German. She looked at him and said nothing.

"Ludger, what are you doing? I'm sorry. Ludger, how could you think of talking to the lady in German?"

"Excuse me. It's just that one can't help speaking in one's native language when one has something important to say," Wimmer said, looking Zahra up and down.

"I understand. It happens to me as well, on important occasions, I find it hard not to speak in Arabic, which is my mother tongue. I'm sorry I didn't understand you. Maybe you'd like to say what you said in English?" Zahra said coldly.

"No, don't worry ... I was just expressing my admiration for your talent."

"Are you German?"

"Yes. Do you know my country?"

"No, I've never danced there, but the chance may come up one of these days ... Although I'm finding it ever harder to leave Egypt."

Wimmer spoke to her in German again and she, with a tired expression, cut him off.

"Mr. ... I'm sorry, I don't know what you're called ... we haven't been introduced ... I'm sorry, but I don't understand what you're saying to me. I don't speak your language," she said.

"Of course ... I don't know why I insisted ..." Ludger Wimmer said by way of apology.

She shrugged and held out her hand to Fernando.

They didn't talk until they reached the hotel. When Fernando closed the door she came in and hugged him. He held her close and she calmed down in his arms.

"He recognized you," Fernando said. "We have to get out of here."

"No, he didn't recognize me. He can't recognize me. I was a girl when he ... No, he doesn't know who I am ..."

"Whether or not he knows he senses something. Why else would he speak to you in German? He wanted to see if you understood him."

"But I didn't make any sign that I did or didn't."

"He gave me the third degree. He wanted to know if you knew Germany, if you'd danced there ... where you had learned to dance ..."

"And you told him what we agreed you would, right?"

"Yes, but he's not an idiot, Zahra, and although he can't be sure that it is you, you remind him of the girl that you once were."

"And according to the documents that Benjamin Wilson prepared, she was taken to a sanatorium where they get rid of people with mental problems. Mandisa Rahim doesn't exist, Fernando."

"But it won't be hard for him to pick up your trace. Everyone in Alexandria knows who your grandmother was, and who your mother was as well ..."

"Calm down, Fernando. In a few days, Ludger Wimmer will no longer exist."

"No, I can't calm down. You know that this man has his suspicions about your identity."

"You think he'll be able to find anything out in four days? No, he won't."

"Come on, Zahra. Let's forget about him."

"Oh, so now you're telling me to forget about him? You, who killed your father's murderers? You, the man who became a pariah for having killed those men!"

"Shut up! Don't talk to me about ... don't talk about my father."

They sat in silence looking at one another sadly. Fernando felt the blood pounding in his head. She held out her hand to him and pulled him down to sit on the sofa.

"We can't lose our cool. It's what Wimmer's trying to do, to make us nervous, open a gap between us. But we can't let that happen. I'm going to kill him. There's not a single day that goes by when I don't think of this moment. I understand why you're worried. I was selfish to bring you here. You shouldn't have made me the promise you did. You accepted because you thought we'd never find Wimmer."

"You're wrong. I knew that if he was alive, then Benjamin Wilson would find him for you."

"Go on, Fernando, go home tomorrow. Go back to Paris."

"I want to, but with you."

"You know I'm going to kill him," she said in a tired voice.

"Then let's pray he doesn't find out who you are. You have four days to do it."

"Pray?" Zahra smiled. "Yes, I can imagine you praying. You told me that your mother taught you to pray when you were a child, although your father never prayed because he didn't believe in God."

"And I don't believe in him either," he said angrily.

"You? Maybe you believe without knowing it ... It's difficult for us to abandon the things we were taught when we were children. It's there ... hidden ... without us knowing about it ... but the seeds they sowed will always be there, Fernando."

That night, each slept in their own room. There was nothing more to be said. The day had barely dawned when Zahra woke

Fernando. She told him that she was going to Wimmer's house. She wanted to see when he left and where he went.

"We did that yesterday," he said, still foggy with sleep.

"I'll go today and tomorrow as well. I'll kill him in two days."

"It's crazy, your plan," he said, knowing that she wouldn't listen to him.

He wanted to go with her, but she wouldn't let him.

"I don't want to waste any more time, and you still need to get up. I won't be long."

She wasn't back for four hours. Fernando sat impatiently in the hotel bar, holding his third cup of coffee in his hands.

Zahra explained that Ludger had left the house at the same time as the day before, and had gotten into a dark-colored car.

"I know how I'm going to kill him."

He didn't say anything. He had given in.

"You told me that when I finished my act, Wimmer stayed with Jorge Prat."

"Yes, that's what's happened the two times he's been there."

"Well, the last night, when I finish dancing, you'll be waiting for me in the dressing room and we'll leave at once. We can walk. Wimmer's house isn't that far from La Nuit."

"It's a good trek," Fernando said.

"But we'll definitely get there before he does. We may have to wait all night. We'll be ready, and when we see him come in his car, I'll go over to him before he has a chance to get out. I'll shoot him then."

They argued for a while, but then called a truce, both of them tired by their discussion.

That night, Ludger Wimmer came back to La Nuit and sat at Jorge Prat's table, where there were other men keen to see Zahra dance.

Zahra's success was even greater than on previous occasions. Prat was very excited.

The dance had barely finished when Fernando said goodbye to the two men.

"But you must stay and have a glass of champagne! Everyone wants to meet Miss Nadouri. Please do me the favor of bringing her," Jorge Prat said to Fernando.

"I'm sorry, but I've said no already, as well as the fact that it's written in her contract. Miss Nadouri leaves when she has finished dancing. She never stays to drink with her admirers."

"But you have to convince her! Look, the men with us today are some of the most important businessmen in the whole of Chile, and they want to be near her," Prat said.

"You'll have to excuse her. And if you'll allow me, gentlemen …"

Fernando nodded goodbye to the two men and could hear, even through the hubbub of the cabaret, Ludger Wimmer's voice saying, "I don't like that Spaniard."

The next nights followed the same pattern. When Fernando went over to Prat's table, Ludger Wimmer was already there with his glass of champagne.

Tonight was going to be different. It was Zahra's last dance.

While she finished putting on her makeup, Fernando walked up and down the room. He felt tension and fear in every muscle of his body. He had spoken continuously, trying to dissuade Zahra from her course of action, but she only listened to him and packed her bags, and then she asked him to leave her so she could put on her makeup.

The next day, their plane was due to leave early in the morning. They would stop in Buenos Aires on the way. Jorge Prat had said he would send a car to take them to the airport, and she had accepted.

When they reached La Nuit, Zahra went straight to her dressing room where the maid was waiting for her. She had put the pistol she'd gotten from Zúñiga in the bottom of her bag.

Fernando sat in his usual spot at Prat's table. The impresario unleashed a cloud of praise for Zahra, trying to persuade him one more time to speak with her and get her to come back to Santiago as soon as possible.

Wimmer came by at that moment and sat down at the table. Jorge Prat continued.

"My dear friend. I'm not selfish, and so I've spoken to several of my friends who have bars and cabarets in the city, and after all I've told them of Zahra, they are very keen to hire her. Could we bring her back in three or four months' time?"

"I am not Miss Nadouri's agent, and I don't know exactly what is on her schedule," Fernando said drily.

"Then who are you, exactly?"

Ludger Wimmer's question disconcerted Fernando for a few moments. He looked so angrily at the German that Jorge Prat felt obliged to intervene.

"What an absurd question, Ludger! Come, now … let's drink a toast to the success of Miss Nadouri and hope that this is not the last time she dances at La Nuit." Jorge Prat didn't want his business to be spoiled by Ludger Wimmer's obvious animosity towards Zahra and Fernando.

They had argued about it. Wimmer had not been able to give a rational explanation for his mistrust of the dancer. His German business partner seemed both to hate her and to fear her. From Zahra's age, it was clear that Wimmer could not have known her in the past, so he had to discount the idea that it might be something personal between them. Maybe, Prat thought, he had had some mishap involving an Oriental dancer in the past.

The lights had barely gone up at the end of Zahra's performance when Fernando got up to say goodbye. All Jorge Prat's guests looked at him enviously because he was Zahra's companion.

Fernando didn't shake Ludger Wimmer's hand, but merely nodded at him.

Jorge Prat reminded him that he would come to find them at the hotel and take them to the airport the next day. "It's the least I can do for such a great artist," he said solemnly, looking at his guests.

Zahra was already dressed to leave when Fernando came into the dressing room. The maid was putting her dancing clothes away in a bag.

They said goodbye to the young woman, and Zahra put a banknote into her hands as she did so.

"Oh, ma'am, that's not necessary!" the maid said, putting the note in the pocket of her apron.

"I know, but buy yourself something nice and remember me."

Neither Zahra nor Fernando had any desire to speak, and so they walked along thinking their own thoughts until she guided them to Ludger Wimmer's house. It took them about an hour to get there, and they met no one on the way. It was cold, and that late at night, there were few people who would venture out onto the streets of Santiago.

"Let's wait here," Zahra said, and put her hand on Fernando's arm to stop him.

She had decided to hide behind some trees that were themselves behind a group of parked cars.

"He normally leaves his car here, along the sidewalk, in the first spot he finds. His house is here. You don't have to do anything. I'll go over to him, shoot him, and then we'll go. I hope the silencer works properly."

He didn't feel like saying anything, and so he just stood still where she indicated. He was going to light a cigarette, but Zahra stopped him.

"No one can see us here, but if someone looked out of the window for whatever reason, they might see the light of a cigarette. I want to smoke as much as you do, but we need to control ourselves."

They were lucky. The street remained empty. No cars, no pedestrians. They were there, tense and impatient, and it wasn't until nearly three o'clock in the morning that they heard a car motor grumbling up the street.

"It's him," Zahra said. She took the pistol out of her bag, thumbed back the safety and cocked it.

"You don't know if it's him." Fernando wanted to hold her back.

"I do know. Please, do as I say."

The man driving the car had parked it now. He didn't see a figure coming out of the darkness and opening the passenger door.

"Good evening, Mr. Wimmer."

"You! But what are you doing here? Who are you?" Wimmer was disconcerted.

"My name is Mandisa Rahim and I'm here to kill you. Look at me."

He threw himself at her, and she took advantage of his movement to shoot him in the stomach and the heart. He looked at her incredulously and put his hand to his wounds. With the other hand, he tried to grab her. He failed. He was going to shout but she put a hand over his mouth.

Fernando had come over, and when he saw them struggling, he opened the door of Wimmer's car and put his hands around his neck with all his strength.

Zahra took the opportunity to shoot him again. She did so twice more, angry to see that he was still alive.

Fernando felt Wimmer lose all his strength, in spite of the fury that still glowed in his eyes.

"Go to hell, you and your friend Jan Dinter," Zahra whispered.

"You are … you are … your father … Jan was your father …" Wimmer breathed his last words.

"Let's go," Fernando said.

"No, not until he's really dead." She shot him again. Wimmer's face became a mass of blood.

"He's dead," Fernando said, trying to take the gun from her.

Zahra shot him again, where he had once had eyes, a mouth, a nose. Fernando grabbed her wrist and forced her to drop the gun.

"It's over! Let's go!"

Fernando pushed the body onto the floor of the car. They'd find it, of course, but this would slow them down a bit. Then he took Zahra by the arm and made her follow him.

They threw the pistol down a storm drain. They had wiped it down and Zahra had been wearing gloves so there would be no fingerprints. Fernando felt relieved to realize that he was wearing gloves as well, because of the cold. They wouldn't find his fingerprints on Wimmer's neck. He looked at his watch. It was four-thirty in the morning. Day would be breaking soon. They walked quickly. When they got to the hotel, Johan Silverstein came out to meet them.

"I've been waiting for you all night. You shouldn't go in through the main door. There's a back door with a watchman on it, but from what I see he's dozing off. I can distract him …"

Zahra nodded and kissed him on the cheek.

"Why are you helping me? You don't know what we've just done ..."

"And I don't want to know. Don't say anything. I'm only here to help you get to your room."

They went into the hotel via the service door. No one saw them. When they got to their room, they realized that their clothes were stained with Wimmer's blood.

"Take off your clothes and I'll wash them," she said.

"We'll wash everything, both of us, but Prat is coming to get us at seven."

They worked hard to get the bloodstains out of their clothes and packed the clothes in their suitcases. Fernando wondered what would happen if they made him open them at customs.

Once they had taken a shower and put on clean clothes, they sat down to relax for a moment. It was only a few minutes before they were due to get the call that Jorge Prat was there to pick them up. If they didn't, then that might mean he'd already found Wimmer's body.

But Prat turned up at seven on the dot and smiled with satisfaction in spite of the tiredness on his face.

"It's a shame that you're leaving so soon; my customers were so happy with your performance that they drank more champagne than ever. I almost had to throw them out to get here on time to pick you up."

They got to the airport. There were photographs of Zahra dancing in La Nuit on the front pages of the newspapers. They said that she was a great artist who had revolutionized the cultural life of Santiago de Chile.

They didn't feel at ease until the wheels of the Douglas DC-4 had lifted off the ground and the plane had hidden itself among the clouds.

Zahra fell asleep. Fernando was exhausted, but he could not rest. She had killed Ludger Wimmer, but he had squeezed his neck to hasten the process, and he was sure that one more ghost would now join the Gestapo agent and Roque and Saturnino Pérez. And he remembered his father, on the day that he left for the front, telling him, "Fernando, I don't want you to go to the front, I don't want you to live tormented by the memories of the men you had to kill."

And he saw himself, replying to his father's words: "Killing fascists is justified. They started this war. You're going to the front and you'll have to kill, let me go with you, Father, don't keep me from fighting."

"Son, you can help by doing things that aren't fighting. The Republic is also being defended by the people in the rear-guard. No, Fernando, you shall not kill. I'll have to live with this burden, but you shall not kill."

The memory was unbearable, and he covered his hands with his ears, but his father's voice kept on pursuing him: "You shall not kill … You shall not kill."

When the plane landed in Paris many hours later, they were both very tense. They hadn't spoken during the journey, much less referred to the night's events. Somebody would have found Ludger Wimmer's body by now, and maybe someone had seen them or suspected them.

When they were waiting for their luggage, they saw Benjamin Wilson coming towards them. Zahra wanted to run to him and hug him, but she held herself back.

"I've got a car by the door. You're coming to our house. Sara has insisted that you don't stay alone at a hotel."

"Thank you, Benjamin."

"Do you have any news about …" Fernando started to ask.

"Over. Over and done with," Benjamin replied as they left the airport.

"Are you sure?" Zahra asked.

"Yes. Done and dusted. All you need to do now is start living."

Zahra didn't even look at Fernando when he got out of the car. She knew that they had lost one another forever.

11

Adela had changed, or at least that's what Fernando thought. He hadn't been gone for all that long, but suddenly it seemed that the teenage girl was becoming a woman. As for Catalina, she hugged him tight and said how much she had missed him. "I'm not used to being without you," she admitted.

"Neither am I," said Adela, "and now that you're here, I need to say that I've decided to leave. Mama agrees with me."

"Leave? Where to?" Fernando felt incapable of processing more emotions.

"To the United States. As soon as the school year ends, I'll be off to Boston. I've applied for a scholarship to study there, and I think they'll give it to me," Adela said.

"But ... when did you make this decision? You didn't say anything to me."

"We couldn't because you were in Chile," Catalina said.

"But I was only gone for ten days ..."

"And in those ten days, Mama and I went on yet another trip to try to find that man, my father ..."

If he had not been so exhausted, maybe Fernando would have been angry, but given his state, he simply listened to the two of them provide a disjoined explanation of what had happened.

"Mama read in the papers that Marvin Brian was in Italy, in Sorrento, where he was going to spend some time relaxing. You can imagine what she decided to do ..."

And Adela spared no detail of the story while Catalina looked at her in silence.

They had traveled by airplane as far as Naples and then they had taken a train down to Sorrento where they looked for a place to stay. Marvin was staying at the Hotel Excelsior.

"An earthly paradise," Adela said. "The gardens are the stuff of dreams, it's where Augustus Caesar had his palace … there are still some ruins there … and you can imagine what the people in the hotel are like … it was like another universe."

For a couple of days, they had stood waiting outside the doors of the hotel, but hadn't seen Marvin or Farida enter or leave. On the third day, Catalina decided that she would go in and ask for him. She took advantage of one of the guards looking the other way to climb over the fence and go through the garden into the hotel.

They walked through the garden ringed with orange and lemon trees and breathed in the smell of the flowers. The hotel was a little palace, and the receptionist had told them that the Great Caruso himself had stayed there. It was a place where aristocrats and people with money went to avoid being disturbed.

A very friendly doorman came out to meet them before they got to the door of the hotel building, and when Catalina said, very sure of herself, that Mr. Brian was waiting for them, he told them where to find him on the terrace. Marvin and Farida seemed happy, looking out at the Bay of Naples. The hotel was built on some rocks and had incredible views.

They were talking peacefully, laughing, holding one another's hands. There were other guests, all of them dressed very elegantly, and they seemed to be enjoying the spot, and the calm that came from such beauty.

Adela felt that she was in the way here, an intruder, and begged Catalina to turn around and head back to Paris. She didn't feel like she could face another scene. But Catalina walked forward with determined steps and stood in front of Marvin and Farida.

"Good morning, I'm sorry to bother you, but I hope you won't run away again. I'm here with Adela."

Marvin got to his feet and ran into the hotel followed by Farida. Catalina ran after them, but the concierge came out and stood in her way, grabbing her by the arm.

Adela felt incredibly embarrassed to hear Marvin shouting "Throw that madwoman out of here!" And that's what they did:

throw them out. Two men made them leave, stopping Catalina from chasing Marvin, who had disappeared as though the ground had swallowed him up.

Catalina protested, and said she wouldn't go without speaking to Marvin, but the two men practically dragged them out, and told them that they would call the carabineers if they saw them again.

They had a fight when they got back to where they were staying. "Never again, do you hear me? Never again am I going to let you embarrass me like that! This man doesn't want anything to do with you, or me. Let's not humiliate ourselves any more. At least, I won't humiliate myself. I don't need him. I don't need him to be my father!"

Catalina assured her that she would never give up, that she would follow him forever until he acknowledged her as his daughter. But Adela had made the first important decision of her life. "You can do whatever you want. But I'm not having anything to do with it. I won't go with you again, anywhere that you go looking for him. And I forbid you from demanding that I acknowledge him. I don't want him as my father," she said furiously.

And that's why she had decided to leave. She didn't want her life to hang on the hope that her father might acknowledge her; that would stop her from being herself, just as it had stopped her mother from having a normal life.

"I refuse to allow this poet to control how I live my life," Adela said.

And Fernando knew that they had lost her.

It was not easy for him to get back into his routine, and he barely had time to talk to Sara because two days after they got back from Chile, she and Benjamin went to Alexandria. They didn't want Zahra to travel alone, and knew that she needed them.

Sara had time to mention the last incident that had occurred between Marvin and Catalina.

"I know that you can't do anything, but ..."

"No, I can't do anything. And I don't know if I want to," Fernando said, sincerely.

"Sometimes I ask myself if I wasn't a little selfish to make you Marvin's editor."

"It's not just your decision. I could refuse to do it as well."

"Yes. In spite of everything, I think you're very lucky to be his editor ... think about what he's become ... the whole world applauds him. There's not a single critic who's against him."

"I'm an editor who deals with his writer via someone else, via you. I am sure that he'd be happy with the change, but you've insisted that I carry on with the job, and I don't know why."

"Because the day I met you there was something about you that moved me and ..."

"And you decided to take me under your wing, just as you have done with Marvin, and Zahra, and everyone who you think needs you."

"It's not a question of need so much as who deserves a hand from me. Marvin is the *Poet of Pain* and his ailing soul makes his work sublime. Zahra ... well, I don't need to tell you how she built herself back together piece by piece. And you ... I still think you're trying to escape from yourself. Your conscience pricks you, what you did ... even though you had a good reason to do it. You and Marvin are held together by pain. A permanent, un-bearable, intense pain that stops you from being happy. He has found something akin to peace at Farida's side, but you ..."

Fernando didn't want to let her carry on with her voyage through his soul.

"We deal with our own pain as best we can. When will we get a new book from Marvin?"

"It's still soon ... but he is writing. He went to Sorrento to do just that."

Two days later, when he got home from work, he found Madame Dufort waiting for him, holding a letter.

"It came this afternoon. It's from Spain," she said, pointing to the postmark.

Catalina wasn't back yet, and Adela was in her room study-ing, so he sat down to read the letter alone. His mother's name was on the back of the envelope.

My dear son,

I write this letter in the hope that it will come into your hands. Although you told Piedad that you were going to America and that the address in Paris wasn't a fixed one, she thinks that it's not a house like that, but rather the place where you and Catalina live in Paris. I hope she's not wrong, because that would mean having you close to me. Even so, we sent the letter to Monsieur Dufort, whom Piedad says is the owner of the building. I hope it gets into your hands.

The first thing I have to tell you is that there has been a tragedy in Catalina's family: her father has died. He was very frail and couldn't get over his last heart attack.

Ernesto died with the sorrow of not seeing Catalina again, and never knowing his granddaughter.

I don't want you to see any reproach in these lines, but why don't you come back? What's stopping you? I promise you that Ernesto and Asunción care very little about what the neighbors might say about Catalina's daughter. Ernesto did care, but in spite of everything, he did love his daughter. He stood up to Don Antonio and Antoñito himself to defend Catalina.

No one in the neighborhood knows that Catalina had a daughter, but I promise you that the child would have been a joy for Ernesto and Asunción.

Asunción asked me to tell you about Ernesto's death so that you can tell Catalina. She didn't feel strong enough to write to her. She is distraught and does nothing more than pray that her daughter will come home. If there is anything you could do to convince her ...

You can imagine how she is. She has looked after Ernesto for years, has never left his side, has suffered in silence watching her husband slip away. Asunción says that it was only the hope of seeing his daughter again that kept him alive.

And now Asunción doesn't know what to do, because if there's one thing she needs, it's her granddaughter and her daughter. Please, Fernando, do whatever you can to have them at least go and see her, or have her come to see them.

As for Eulogio, you can rest assured that he's well. You can imagine how Piedad looks after him. She never leaves him alone. She gives herself, body and soul, to her son. She left her job at the workshop and now makes a living doing piecework for ladies. I won't say that she's happy, but having her son back has made her a lot more serene.

I told you that Antoñito was married to Mari Paz Nogués. They have two children, a girl and a boy, both of them now teenagers. Mari Paz has been pregnant on other occasions, but has never managed to have another child. It seems like she can't have more children.

Sometimes I ask myself, the Lord forgive me, how they could have had two such good children. Mari Paz has brought them up well. Don Antonio has plans for his grandchildren: he hopes to have them inherit his property, because as you know well, Antoñito isn't the sharpest knife in the drawer and can't really do more than follow his father.

As for our neighbors, the Gómezes are as stuck-up as ever. Their son Pablo has got married and had a baby girl. He comes by a lot to see his parents. As for your friends, they are all married and have children, but most of them don't live in the neighborhood any more.

And so, that's the news, and now I need to ask about you.

Why don't you come home? I know how unbearable it would be for you to live here … it is. … well, you know … but even if you don't want to stay, why don't you come and see me?

There's nothing stopping you from coming to Madrid. If it's a question of money, then I save pretty much everything I earn, which isn't a lot, but I am keeping it saved for you, for the future or for any need that you might eventually have.

If you are in Paris, maybe I could come to see you. You're not that far away, and the journey wouldn't be too hard.

I'm old now, Fernando, and I pray to God that what happened to Ernesto doesn't happen to me. I don't want to leave this world without seeing you again, and knowing that everything is going well for you, and that you're happy.

All my love, forever,

YOUR MOTHER.

Fernando let the tears flow down his face. He felt like a terrible person for allowing his mother to suffer, but he couldn't tell her the truth: he couldn't confess that he was not coming back because he had killed two of his father's killers. He couldn't tell her that sometimes people make decisions that there's no coming back from. And he didn't know if they had decided to close the investigation into the deaths of Roque and Saturnino Pérez, or whether the case was still open.

And it would be hard for him to return to Franco's Spain after so many years of living in freedom.

No, he couldn't get used to silence, and lying, and keeping his head bowed low.

He heard Catalina's voice calling out a greeting. Adela called back, and said that Fernando was at home as well. She knocked on his door.

"Fernando? I'm here ... I ended up talking for too long to the mother of one of my students ... are you all right?"

He opened the door and she saw his tears. Without saying anything, she held him tight. They stayed like that for a few seconds, then he gently pushed her away.

"Let's go into the salon, and tell Adela to come too."

Catalina and Adela sat and waited for him to speak. It was a few seconds before he could calm down.

"I got a letter from my mother," he said.

"What? Where did she send it?" Catalina asked.

"Here. When Piedad came to see Eulogio he was here, and when she got back, she told my mother that she was sure we lived here."

"Well, it's obvious that it isn't just a boarding house," Adela interrupted. "Anyone would have realized that."

"What did your mother say, Fernando? What's going on?" Catalina was nervous, guessing that something must be happening.

"I'm sorry ... I'm sorry ... It's your father, Catalina ..."

"What's happened to him?" she asked, feeling the words catch in her throat.

"He's dead. Your father is dead."

Catalina covered her face with her hands. She was devastated.

She knew about her father's poor health, but she thought he would live forever. How could he possibly die? Death had never been a part of her thoughts about him.

Adela went over to her mother and held her. It was the first time she had seen her mother cry. Catalina had always been so sure of herself in front of her daughter, and had never shown the least sign of weakness.

Fernando and Adela let her cry. Neither of the two found the words to console her. For Adela, this dead grandfather was someone who had neither face nor voice. Catalina had never spoken at length about her parents, or about her life in Spain. It was as though she had abandoned her past and never looked back.

But Fernando was a part of this past and he knew why she was devastated. She had turned Marvin into an obsession for herself, and she had done this because of her parents, so they wouldn't have to feel ashamed because of her, so that no one would murmur about her behind their backs or point her out to people. Maybe she had even stopped loving him, although she didn't admit that to herself.

He didn't interrupt her tears. He cried along with her.

They both agreed that they would carry on pretending that they didn't live in Paris.

Fernando wrote back to his mother, and included the following passage.

Although I got this letter, I beg you, please don't make me tell you where I am. You can carry on writing to me at Monsieur Dufort's address. He'll know how to get the letters to me.

I am sorry, Mother, I know that you won't understand my attitude, but at least believe me when I say that not a day goes by when I don't think about you and miss your hugs. All I hope is that one day you'll forgive me for the suffering I'm causing you. Catalina is distraught and incapable of dealing with the news of her father's death. Adela has moved on. She's decided to embark on her own life now. Yesterday she was barely more than a child, and she's become a woman without us realizing. Her absence makes us even more aware of how devastated we are. I keep trying to make Catalina go back to her mother.

I think that her place is not with me, and certainly is not so far from Spain. But she is still stuck on the idea that she will only come back when Marvin acknowledges Adela, which I think may never happen.

Mother, I keep on asking myself what we have done, what Catalina and I are doing with our lives, and the only answer I can come up with is that we are wasting them. But we have reasons that stop us from coming back, and I am afraid that these reasons will never disappear.

In Catalina's letter to her mother, she couldn't hide her despair. She felt lost. The death of her father and the absence of Adela were two wounds that were difficult to heal.

Monsieur Dufort agreed to be their intermediary and put the two envelopes with their letters into a larger envelope which he sent to Fernando's mother's address in Madrid. Isabel took Catalina's letter to Asunción. For all that they spoke about the decisions that their children had made, neither of them could understand why they didn't come back to Madrid, and why they refused to allow them to come and visit. Piedad couldn't help them find any answers. Isabel asked her to tell her one more time how Fernando was, and she said, holding Eulogio's hand, that "he's changed, he's not a child anymore and I don't think he's happy."

But who could be happy, after a war that had taken the lives they dreamed about away from them?

Piedad didn't dare confess to Isabel and Asunción that she almost felt happy. She had Eulogio back by her side and that was more than she had expected from her life.

12

The years went on, but life did not. Their lives stopped. To begin with, Adela's absence was unbearable for them. They didn't admit this to one another. They had learned not to complain, to content themselves with whatever they were given.

Adela had begged her mother to stop pursuing Marvin, and told her about the shame she had felt for all those years when they had followed him around the world and he hadn't even looked at them. But Catalina refused to promise anything, and that opened a rift between them which, in spite of the pain that it caused them, they were unable to heal. And so, what was initially going to be a few years studying journalism in Boston turned into a whole new life. When she finished her studies, Adela decided not to come back to Paris, but rather to look for work in New York. She couldn't face going back to being part of her mother's obsessions to make her father acknowledge her.

When she was a girl, she didn't really care that this man might be her father. She didn't even really want to meet him. But when she became a woman, she couldn't stop asking herself why Marvin Brian had rejected her. The man the critics called the "Poet of Pain" had repudiated his daughter hundreds of times. Wasn't he aware of the pain that his contempt might cause her?

On one of her rare and brief trips to Paris, she asked Fernando why Marvin ran from her mother and from her. He didn't know what to say, so she only had one choice left to her: to try not to think about this father who refused to be one.

Fernando carried on working at two jobs: running the bookshop and editing poetry. Catalina carried on teaching at the Academy, giving lessons to children whose mothers wanted them to be great artists.

They didn't have any friends, but sometimes accepted an invitation to supper from their landlords, Philippe and Doriane Dufort. The Duforts were convinced that Fernando and Catalina were a modern couple, like so many others, who preferred to live together without going through the business of marriage. Madame Dufort suspected that Catalina had been married before, and that because there was no divorce law in Spain, she had decided to run away with her lover, Fernando, and her child from the previous marriage.

Alain Fortier, Marvin's professor friend from the Sorbonne who helped edit the books, also believed that Catalina and Fernando were a couple.

But they didn't really speak to anyone outside their work. They avoided the Spaniards who lived in Paris, even though lots of them were Republicans, socialists or exiled communists.

Fernando preferred not to have to invent a story to explain why he lived in Paris, and Catalina didn't want to run the risk of meeting someone who knew a member of her family and having the news get back to them.

And so they lived on the margins of the Spanish exile community. They didn't take much interest in the events of May 1968 either, with the young people keen to stop the world so they could change it.

Fernando and Catalina both thought that the student revolution had nothing to do with them, or with their interests, or with their hopes. They weren't indifferent, but they looked at the world around them as an object of curiosity rather than as something relevant to them. Catalina told Fernando that some of the students were worked up by the events of that May, thinking that the world would change, but neither she nor Fernando thought that at all.

And so they waited as the years went by, without hoping for anything, because who could be happy, after a war that had taken the lives they dreamed about away from them?

Catalina was surprised one morning to find several white hairs on her head, and couldn't stop herself from calling to Fernando, who was just about to head off to the bookshop.

"Come and look!" she called.

He came into the bathroom worried: she had cried with such urgency.

"What is it?"

"You'll think I'm silly, but I hadn't realized I had so many white hairs. Do you know what this means?"

"Well, I've got some myself, I don't know if you've seen. And you ... well, I thought you'd seen them, but you've got more than one ... it's normal."

"So ... We're growing old!"

"Hadn't you noticed yet? We're not children anymore. We left Spain at the end of 1941 and now it's December 1973. Just count the years."

"But ... it's not possible ..."

"It is. It might seem like yesterday that we fled, but you can see that our lives are slipping away from us."

"And what are we going to do about it?" she said, looking lost.

"Do? I don't know what you mean ... We can't do anything ... Well, I can't do anything. I have to stay here, but you ... you can go home, I've told you that many times. You've gone into an exile that isn't really necessary. You know that Marvin is a lost cause and that you won't get Adela back until you admit it," Fernando said, looking severely at Catalina.

"Adela doesn't understand that everything I've done and do is for her, because I don't want her to lack a father she has a right to."

"She's told you in no uncertain terms that she doesn't want Marvin as her father. Leave her alone. I've asked you to marry me and give her my name, and I've even said I'll acknowledge her as a daughter if you don't marry me," he replied.

"Adela always wanted you to be her father," Catalina admitted.

"And you denied her that possibility," he said reproachfully.

"Let's not argue, Fernando, I'm not going to give up, I'm going to carry on trying to get Marvin to acknowledge Adela."

"Your mother is very old and needs you," he reminded her.

"And your mother's old too, and needs you," she said angrily.

"There's a difference between us! I can't go back!"

"You could let her come and visit you!"

"Why won't you let your mother come? Look, let's not argue. I'm going to work and … well, as for your white hairs, just think for a second … you're more than fifty years old."

"Oh Lord, my life's slipped through my fingers!"

Fernando heard these last words and thought that Catalina was right: they had lived without realizing that they were alive. He walked more quickly. He had to open the bookshop and he wanted to meet with Sara and Benjamin, who had arrived from Paris the day before.

The Wilsons didn't normally say when they were coming, and on more than one occasion he had arrived at the bookshop to find the doors open and Sara looking at the shelves.

That December day it seemed that the couple were in a bad mood.

Sara was nervous. Fernando started to tell her about the sales figures for Marvin's latest book.

Vietnam Notebook had consolidated his position even more as the *Poet of Pain*. Several thousand copies of the book had been sold in North America, but in Europe it had become an instant classic, a cry sent out against the war that was being unleashed in the jungles of the former Indochina. Ever since *Vietnam Notebook* had been published, Marvin had not written anything else; although Fernando didn't particularly care about this, he was aware that Marvin was the one truly successful poet they published.

Benjamin Wilson listened distractedly. He seemed worried by other things. Five years had passed since the youth of Paris had taken to the streets, and Benjamin was sure that the world had changed, and all the certainties that had ruled his past were no longer present. You didn't have to be too aware of how things were to see that. The fuse had been lit in Paris, and a change was going to come.

Marvin and Farida spent most of their time traveling, even though they had made New York their home. He found his inspiration in pain and grew as a poet in every one of his books.

Fernando and Marvin hadn't seen each other again. His manuscripts would arrive via Sara and the two of them planned their editions together. Sara had given up on trying to bring Marvin and Fernando back together and they had agreed to allow their lives to be handled by this strange woman with short salt-and-pepper hair.

It was she who told Fernando that she and Benjamin would go with Marvin to Israel.

"Farida asked us to go with them. It won't be easy for her to make this journey," she explained.

"Can Farida go to Israel? I thought that as she was an Egyptian she couldn't … Nasser's regime is an enemy of the Jews," Fernando said.

"She has a British passport. The British used to be in charge in Egypt," Benjamin said.

"Right …" Fernando said.

"It's not going to be a pleasant trip for Farida or for me. I'm a Jew, but I'm an Egyptian Jew who has had to take all his business to London. But that doesn't mean that I don't care if the Israelis and the Egyptians kill one another," Benjamin admitted.

"It shouldn't be like that … but who's to blame? I can't understand how stubborn the Arab leaders are in refusing to accept the resolution of the United Nations that recognizes the right of the Jews to their own country. It's what's causing all these wars," Sara said.

Fernando realized that Sara and Benjamin had their own differences of opinion on this matter, and he didn't care much about it wither way.

"I'm an Alexandrian, Sara, and I hate the fact that a lot of my friends have lost their lives fighting against Israel. I can't help it, I think I'm an Egyptian," Benjamin replied.

"Well, I was French. I didn't think I was anything apart from Parisian, but one day many of the people who were our friends turned into enemies. Here, yes, right here in this marvelous and civilized city, lots of people had no qualms in turning their backs on the Jews, in pointing us out to the authorities, in remaining silent when they took our houses and businesses, in looking the other way when they deported us to the extermination camps. If anyone had told me that this might happen in Paris, I wouldn't have believed them."

"And Egypt took you in like one of their own," Benjamin interrupted.

"Egypt? No, it wasn't Egypt, it was you who welcomed me as your wife. And I won't deny that I was happy in Alexandria and that I feel the suffering of our friends, but no more than that of the Jews who are fighting against being pushed into the sea. You remember that a few months ago the Syrians and the Egyptians attacked Israel again, taking advantage of it being Yom Kippur." Sara looked straight at Benjamin.

"You've become a Zionist," he said.

"Zionist? Of course. What else can one be as a Jew? Have we been left any other choice? Israel is a necessity for the Jews. Don't kid yourself, Benjamin, the Jews are a nuisance for the rest of the world. We're tolerated but little more. And so it's time for us to stop being guests, guests who are only sometimes accepted in the countries we end up settling in. Israel is a piece of land that gives us the right to exist. That guarantees that right. I'm sorry, Benjamin, and I understand how you are suffering because your friends are losing their lives in this war, but this is a war they unleashed against Israel. The Arab leaders keep repeating that they won't stop until they've driven the Jews into the sea. Well, we're not going to stand by and let them treat us like animals. If they wage war against us, we'll defend ourselves. Our very existence is at stake," Sara said bitterly.

"Let's not bore Fernando with our differences of opinion," Benjamin said. "Anyway, we're going to Israel with Farida and Marvin."

"Marvin wants to write two books, one of them dedicated to the pain of the Jews, and the other to the pain of the Palestinians," Sara said.

"Whose side is he on?" Fernando asked.

"Whose side? Well, Marvin is on no one's side apart from his own, and Farida's. Suffering is the match that lights his sensibility, that feeds his talent. The *Poet of Pain* ... Yes, Marvin has made pain the fuel of his life." Sara's words sounded to Fernando like ice cracking.

"Is it safe to travel there? The Yom Kippur War was very recent, it's only been three months, hasn't it?"

"The Day of Atonement ..." Sara said.

"Well, the situation seems under control, and if it weren't then we wouldn't go," Benjamin said.

"Do you want to come with us?" Sara asked Fernando.

"No ... of course not ... My presence wouldn't be any use," Fernando said uncomfortably.

"What are you thinking, Sara? And who'll run the store?"

"You're right, it was just a passing thought. Oh, and please, do what you can to stop Catalina going to Israel. She'll find out because Marvin has given a few interviews where he talks about his next trip," Sara said, looking straight at Fernando.

"I'm sorry, Sara, but I'll never deny Catalina her right to go wherever she wants, and much less will I stand between her and Marvin," Fernando said in annoyance.

"It's a pity that she ... well, everyone does what he wants with his own life, but Sara is right that it would be very uncomfortable to find her there," Benjamin said.

"If she finds out, she'll do what she thinks fit," Fernando said, bringing the conversation to an end.

13

Israel – Palestine

Afine rain fell on the city. She had gone out to walk along the seafront. She needed to think, and walking helped with that, even if she was unable to get over the cough that had bothered her for the last few days. She had a temperature, and didn't need a thermometer to tell her so. She was covered in a sticky sweat and her head hurt.

She had arrived the day before and was afraid that the journey had been in vain.

Ever since she had read in the *Herald Tribune* that Marvin was to travel to Israel, Catalina had been sure that she would have to go there too. Fernando hadn't even tried to stop her.

Adela had come to Paris to spend Christmas with them, but when she realized that her mother was going to go to Israel, she left. She didn't even stay to have dinner on Christmas Eve. She argued with her mother and Fernando was unable to calm them down.

"Accept it. He hates you. Don't humiliate yourself any further, and don't humiliate me by insisting that he acknowledge me!" Adela had shouted.

Catalina stood in front of her and said that if she didn't make the effort, it would be tantamount to admitting that she had wasted her life. Adela looked at her angrily and said, "Well, admit it, then. It's clear that your life has been useless. That's not the worst of it. The worst part is that you don't have any dignity. And I don't want to be a part of your madness."

She had risen to her feet and gone to her room. A few minutes later, she had come out with her suitcase in her hand. Fernando tried to make her stop but all she did was give him a kiss and say, "I'm so sorry for what my mother has done to you."

After that night, they hadn't spoken to her again. She didn't return Catalina's calls or Fernando's. Even though Catalina was very hurt, she wasn't ready to give up. And that's why she was in Tel Aviv at the end of February of 1974.

Marvin and Farida were still in Israel, while Sara and Benjamin had gone back to London. She knew this from Fernando. As for Marvin, she didn't know where to find him, but she hoped it was in Tel Aviv.

She had found a room in a little hotel by the beach. It wasn't very expensive, and the rooms were simple but clean. When the owner of the hotel saw her passport she smiled and said, "I'm a Spaniard too." She was a Sephardic Jew who said her name was Veronica Baraen.

It wasn't hard for them to understand one another, for all that some of the words she used were strange to Catalina.

Adela loomed large in her thoughts and she said to herself that the only way to get her daughter back was to show that it had been worthwhile, all this effort to make her father acknowledge her.

The world had changed, apparently, that's what Adela said: it didn't matter if one didn't have one's father's name on the birth certificate. But she didn't believe her, and anyway, she wasn't going to throw away all the sacrifices that she had made, abandoning her parents and turning herself into a pariah, even though she had to admit that she had left Spain to avoid marrying Antoñito just as much as she had left it to marry Marvin. Just thinking about Antoñito made her feel sick.

She had to stop and cough for a while. Her headache was now coupled with sharp pains in her chest and she decided to go back to the hotel.

The next morning she made a great effort to get up. Veronica Baraen was looking after some guests, and Catalina waited for her to finish.

"Tell me, how can I find out if Marvin Brian, the *Poet of Pain*, is still in the city?" she asked.

Veronica not only didn't know if he was in Israel, she had never even heard of him. But she said that she would call the Sephardic Center to see if anyone knew anything about the poet.

Catalina waited patiently while Veronica made the call, trying to work out the upshot of the conversation from her gestures.

"Well, it looks like you're right, and he's a very important poet. They gave him several interviews when he first came here a month ago, but they don't know where he is now. According to the interviews he was going to travel across the country and talk to everyone, Palestinians as well ..."

This information didn't tell her anything she didn't know already. Marvin's talent fed on the pain of others, and so he would look for inspiration by moving between the two communities, the Israeli and the Palestinian. The question was where to find him. Veronica was still giving her the summary of what she had discussed with the Sephardic Center.

"The man who picked up the phone is a good friend of mine and he said he'd call me in a while, that he's going to call a friend of his who's a journalist, who might know what this poet's up to. But why are you looking for him?"

"Oh, I'm not really looking for him ... he's an old friend and they told me he was here ... I'd like to see him if possible ... give him a surprise."

She went out for a stroll to pass the time. She was sick and the fever clouded her vision, but she preferred to be outside, moving about, rather than waiting inside for Veronica's friend to call back.

She looked at her watch every now and then, regretting that the minutes seemed to pass so slowly.

When she got back, Veronica greeted her with a huge smile. "Good news!"

Marvin Brian had been in Jerusalem for a month. He was staying at the American Colony Hotel, which was proof to Veronica that he had to be very rich, especially as he had previously been in the King David Hotel with a couple of friends, but had moved out when they left.

Catalina thanked her and asked how she could get to Jerusalem and where she could stay if she decided to be there for a few days.

Veronica explained that there was a bus that could take her to Jerusalem and that she could stay in one of the Christian hostels there, or maybe stay as a lodger … "Well, I've got a friend who might be able to rent you a room for a few days, it's something she does every now and then, although it couldn't be for more than five or six days, she doesn't want to have permanent lodgers … she's a widow and she has two children and from time to time she needs a bit of help … it's hard to raise two children by yourself."

Catalina spent the rest of the day in her room. She was exhausted. Her cough seemed to be chronic now, and her chest hurt every time she breathed. Veronica had given her a pill and told her that it would help, and even brought her up some soup to the room and insisted she drink it.

At eight o'clock the next morning, she was on a bus to Jerusalem. Maybe it was because of the way the vehicle rattled and jolted, or maybe it was just because of the fever, but she was exhausted when she reached the city.

Lea, Veronica's friend, couldn't have been more than thirty years old, and was the mother of ten-year-old twins.

She greeted Catalina without too much enthusiasm, and made it clear that she would have to be gone in a week.

"My house is not a hotel or a guesthouse. Sometimes I take in people that Veronica sends me. Breakfast is in the kitchen at seven, but you'll have to have lunch and supper out. As for your timetable … well, I have two children, so try to come in at a reasonable hour. I won't give you a key, so if you're back any later than nine, then the door will be shut until tomorrow."

In spite of how severe and dry Lea was, Catalina couldn't help feeling a little dash of sympathy for her. She knew what it was for a single mother to have to face life by herself and bring up children alone. In Lea's case, her responsibility was double.

Lea's house was in the Old Town, by the Zion Gate. It had three bedrooms and a little inner courtyard. Catalina had to share the bathroom with Lea and her daughters. But it was all very clean and her room was large, so she felt comfortable and at home.

Lea explained where the American Colony was.

"It's a very special place," she said. "It used to be the palace of a Pasha, and then it was bought by a Christian community and they used it for charitable works until the beginning of the century, I think in 1902, when they turned it into a hotel. It's very luxurious, and people come there from all over the world. The person you are here to find must be important, but be careful, it's in the Palestinian zone ... well ... don't get into trouble."

Catalina nodded. Veronica had told her that Lea's husband had been wounded in 1967 when the Israelis had taken the city. The wounds had left their mark, and he had died two years later.

In spite of Lea's directions, it was hard for her to get to the hotel. It was a long way away, or that's what she felt. It was hard for her to walk because the air didn't get into her lungs, and her fever made her sweat.

When she got to the hotel, she couldn't help but admire it. The stone walls opened onto an elegant building with well-tended gardens. She asked the receptionist about Marvin.

"No, Mr. Brian isn't here at the moment. He went out first thing in the morning along with Mrs. Brian. I don't know when they'll be back. I don't mind if you wait, but bear in mind that I don't know when they'll return ... maybe it would be better for you to leave a card and for them to get in touch with you."

Catalina decided to stay at least for a little while, but two hours later the pain that shot through her chest was so intense that she found it hard to breathe. Also it was getting late and she was scared to walk home alone through the dark labyrinth of streets.

She got back to Lea's house, and when Lea saw her she was alarmed.

"What's up with you?"

"Nothing ... I've just got a bit of a cold. My head hurts, but I'll be fine tomorrow."

Lea seemed to soften up a bit and told her to go to bed, and then brought her a glass of milk with honey.

The next morning, she woke up with a raging temperature and all her senses overwhelmed and stifled. It was hard for her to move, or to think, or open her eyes. With a huge effort, she got to her feet. The shower would have helped her to wake up, but it wasn't very hot and so she just shivered all the more. Lea and the children had left, but she found a bottle of milk, some biscuits and a jar of honey on the table. She didn't feel that she could drink or eat anything.

She walked slowly to the American Colony. It was cold, but she felt the sweat running down her back. When she got to the hotel, the receptionist looked at her sadly.

"Mr. Brian left first thing this morning," he said.

Catalina put her hand to her forehead.

"He's gone? But that's not possible … I know he's going to be in Jerusalem for a while," she said with all the conviction she could muster.

"I didn't say that he'd left, just that he was gone and he'll be out of the hotel for the rest of the day."

Catalina left the hotel lobby and tried to find somewhere to sit down. She needed to have a coffee to wake herself up and gather her strength to go to Lea's house once more.

The waiter was more talkative than the receptionist, and when he asked her if she was staying in the hotel and she said she had only come to see her friend Marvin Brian, the man smiled.

"Ah, Mr. Brian! He and Mrs. Brian are very nice people. We were talking about Jericho this morning. My mother is from there, although I was born in Jerusalem."

"Jericho?"

"Yes, the oldest city in the world. More than ten thousand years old," the waiter said with pride.

"Right … how interesting. Is it very far from Jerusalem?"

"That's just what Mr. Brian asked. They were planning to go there this morning. And no, it's not far, just an hour or so away. Mr. Brian seemed very interested in seeing the old ruins of the city, but I told him that there were other things which were worth seeing. Mrs. Brian is keen on going up to the Monastery of the Temptations."

"The Monastery of the Temptations?"

"Are you a Christian?" the waiter asked.

"Of course I am, I'm a Catholic."

"Then you'll know that Jesus spent forty days in a cave in the desert and was tempted by the Devil."

"Yes …" Catalina remembered that story from Bible classes at school.

"I'm a Catholic as well," the man said with a smile.

She couldn't stop her face from showing a little surprise.

"Mr. Brian was surprised when I told him, too. Not all Palestinians are Muslim, although most of us are, but there are Christians like me among us as well."

"So, Mr. Brian's gone to Jericho," Catalina said.

"Yes, and I'm sure that he's gone up to the Monastery of the Temptations, which is also known as Saint George's Monastery. It's an orthodox monastery, but it's where the cave of Jesus' Temptation is to be found. Oh, and I also recommended that he go to visit the ruins of the Summer Palace that Herod built, and the Palace of Hisham ... if you decide to go, you should see these places too."

"And how can I get to Jericho?"

"Well, I'd go by car ... if you want, my brother-in-law can take you. He's a taxi driver and he normally parks by the door to the hotel in case there are any tourists who want to travel out there."

At that moment, one of the receptionists appeared, showing some curious tourists round the hotel. When he saw the waiter talking to Catalina he started to scold him in Arabic. The waiter was apologizing when Catalina interrupted.

"I'm sorry, it was my fault ... I was just asking about some excursions ..."

The receptionist and the waiter looked at her in astonishment. The last thing they expected was for this woman to be able to speak their language.

"Of course, madame, don't worry," the receptionist said.

"Do you think your brother-in-law could take me to Jericho now?" Catalina asked, once the receptionist and the tourists had left.

"If he's there, there shouldn't be any problem. Let me go and have a look for him while you finish your coffee. And ... well, you speak very good Arabic."

"I lived in Egypt for a long time," she explained.

The thick black liquid had woken her up. The coffee had performed a miracle on her mood, or maybe it was just the chance of seeing Marvin once again.

The taxi driver, the waiter's brother-in-law, had no problem with taking this tired-looking and fragile woman to Jericho. He said that he would wait for her until she had finished looking around, and even that he would be her guide, if she so desired. They agreed on a price.

In Jericho the weather was more spring-like, and they encountered several Israeli checkpoints. They were stopped on more than one occasion by soldiers. They were friendly enough, but wary, although they seemed to accept Catalina's explanation that she was a good Catholic eager to see the Monastery of the Temptations.

The taxi driver told her that the first port of call should be the ruins of old Jericho. He pointed her in the direction of the little hill and explained that the city had only been destroyed through divine intervention.

"Are you a Christian as well?" she asked.

"Of course. We're an old Christian family. You know what my name is? Boulos. Paul. And, as I was telling you, Jericho was taken by Joshua who followed the instructions of God. He surrounded the city, and on the eighth day he sounded his trumpets, and the walls came tumbling down," he said with pride.

The fact that Catalina spoke Arabic with a degree of fluency made it easier for them to get along with one another. But in spite of the taxi driver's enthusiasm, she was unable to summon up any emotion in the face of these ruins.

As they were looking around, a little group of French people came along, also trying to force their imaginations to see what ten thousand years before had been a great city.

Catalina thought to herself that the trumpets of Joshua must have been cannons, because they hadn't left one brick on top of another.

After seeing the ruins of Jericho, Boulos wanted to take her to the ruins of the Palace of Herod.

"He ordered them to build his palace here because of the weather. I suppose you can guess what it meant to have a moderate climate here. It was far too cold in Jerusalem in the winter, and far too hot in the summer, but here ... you see how it is."

But Catalina didn't think that she had the strength or the

desire to carry on looking at ruins, and suggested that they go to the Monastery of the Temptations.

"We could go by horse. I have a cousin who can take us," Boulos offered.

"Can't we go by car?" she asked worriedly.

"No, madame, my taxi wouldn't make it: it's a stone path that leads up there."

She accepted, although she felt very dizzy, and Boulos got her to his cousin's house, where his cousin's wife, seeing how sick she looked, made her an herbal tea.

Catalina tried to resist. The smell of the infusion made her feel nauseous, but the woman insisted that she drink it all, right down to the last drop.

Then they sat her on a mule and let her be guided by Boulos' cousin, who said he too was a Christian and that his name was Boutros.

"You know what Boutros means?" he asked proudly.

"No ..." she admitted.

"Peter! I'm called Peter."

The road up to the monastery was a torment to her, not because of the mule, which was a well-behaved beast, but because of the uneven road. Boulos and Boutros seemed to be accustomed to climbing up the steep paths which led up the holy mountain, and spoke ceaselessly, catching up on the doings of their respective families.

Catalina was sure that she would find Marvin and Farida up there. Her intuition led her to believe that Marvin was likely to seek inspiration for his poems at the Monastery of the Temptations.

To her surprise, the herbs that Boutros' wife had made her drink were gradually making her feel better. She didn't feel well, but she was breathing more freely and her head hurt less.

The view over the monastery was impressive. Boulos explained with pride that it was a building from the fifth century AD and that it was more than one thousand one hundred and fifty feet above Jericho. Lots of hermits had climbed up there to live in the caves that filled the area. For his part, Boutros recommended she look across to the horizon where she could see the river Jordan. What she found most impressive was the construction of the monastery itself, which seemed to have been hewn out of the very rocks.

"There was an initial structure built in the fourth century AD, and then it was destroyed by the Persians in the sixth century, and then it was rebuilt in the twelfth century but was later abandoned," Boutros told her as he pulled along the reins of the two mules. Catalina was not able to walk up the hundreds of steps that led up to the Monastery of Saint George.

The door to the monastery was half open, and when Boulos gave it a push, a monk came out to meet them. She asked if he hadn't by chance seen a couple of Americans.

"There was a group that came this morning, but they're gone now."

Catalina insisted, describing Marvin and Farida.

"She speaks Arabic, she's Egyptian ..."

The monk scratched his chin and then smiled.

"Oh, I know them! A man and a woman, very friendly ... they came up by themselves ... I don't know if they've gone already ... They were in the Cave of the Temptations ... head over there ... or they might be in one of the other caves ..."

"How many caves are there?" she asked in exhaustion.

"About forty ... one of them is the cave that Jesus stayed in for forty days and forty nights while he was in the wilderness. There's a little chapel there. I recommend that you pray there."

"And the other caves?" Catalina insisted.

"They're scattered all over the mountain. They were used by monks and hermits."

Catalina thought about Father Lucas. He had lived like a hermit in the caves at Wadi Natrum.

The cave where Jesus had sought refuge was small, and held a little chapel. Catalina fell to her knees and prayed for a long time, hoping that Jesus Christ would help her in her quest to have Marvin acknowledge Adela.

She prayed devoutly, trying to overcome the nausea and the dizziness she felt. Then, with the monk as her guide, she explored the rest of the monastery, caught up in the unique spirit of the place.

The monk explained that the prophet Elijah had also spent some time on the mountain as well as Jesus Christ.

Catalina listened to him with interest. She could not fail to note the spirituality that flowed from this sacred place, for all that she regretted not having found Marvin. She had come too late.

As they went back to Jericho, she had to hold tight to the reins because the mule seemed more nervous than before. When she was back in the taxi, she closed her eyes in exhaustion.

Night was falling when Boulos left her back at the Jaffa Gate in Jerusalem.

She found Lea making supper. She asked her how she had spent her day, and Catalina told her about the trip to Jericho.

"Well … so much stuff to see in Jerusalem and you decide to go to Jericho." Lea's comment seemed like a reproach.

"I wanted to pray in the Monastery of the Temptations," she said.

"Maybe you should start off by praying in the Holy Sepulchre, like all the Christians do when they come here. Or the Cenacle, which is only a few yards from here."

"The Cenacle?"

"Where your people celebrated the Last Supper. You should know all this!"

"Yes … you're right … But I didn't know the place still existed …"

"Well, it's only a few yards from here. I'll tell you how to get there."

"You're right … I'll get up early tomorrow and go there first thing."

In spite of her stern appearance, Lea was an empathetic person, and she was moved to see this frail sickly-looking woman, so she invited her to eat with her and her daughters.

"No … really, no … I don't want to get in your way … if you don't mind I'll have a shower and go to bed."

"You have to eat something. You've got a cold, you're all stuffed up, you look awful … Have a bit of soup, it'll do you good."

Although she wasn't hungry, she didn't want to refuse Lea, given that she was being so nice to her. When they had finished eating, she didn't have strength to have a shower, and so she got straight into the warm bed and fell asleep. But her sleep was in no way calm. When she woke up, she felt like she'd been through a battle.

Lea and the children were just about to leave when Catalina came into the kitchen.

"The coffee's still hot, and I've left you out a little bit of bread and honey."

Catalina thanked her. She took a couple of sips of coffee and got ready to go out and look for Marvin again, but first she decided that she would do what she had promised Lea the day before. She would go to the Cenacle and then the Holy Sepulchre.

It wasn't hard to find. Just as Lea had told her, it was only a few steps from her house. The two-story stone building was almost empty, which surprised her. This didn't look like the place where Jesus had celebrated the Last Supper with the Apostles, or at least it didn't look like the place depicted in any art that she had ever seen. She sat there, thoughtful, trying to make the iconography that was so dear to her fit with this space. A few voices brought her out of her self-absorption. A Franciscan was explaining the history of the place to a group of pilgrims. They were speaking Spanish. She realized at once that they were Mexican. She walked over surreptitiously to try to hear what the Franciscan said.

"And then Jesus told his disciples to come to the city, and that they would find a man carrying a pitcher of water and they should follow him, and they should ask the owner of the house where the Master and his disciples could eat … And this was the place. It was a synagogue, and then a mosque … and in 1347 the Franciscans took over the Cenacle. I haven't told you, but the tomb of King David is on the ground floor …"

Catalina listened fascinated and frankly incredulous. It was almost impossible for her to believe that this was one of the spots where so many of the events that she had read about in the Scriptures might have taken place. She crossed herself.

When the group left the building, she followed them openly. She had heard them say that they were going to the Holy Sepulchre.

There were several men kneeling on what seemed to her to be an enormous stone. She immediately found out what it was, because the Franciscan spoke to the Mexicans in a low voice: "This is the stone of Unction." Catalina lowered her head and listened carefully. Then she followed them down some stairs to a chapel that the Franciscan said was Golgotha, the place of the skull. They knelt down and prayed for a few minutes, and she did the same. She was overwhelmed by the spirituality that flowed from the stones of the chapel. She prayed for a good long while, absorbed in the words that she spoke, repetitively, without thinking, just as she had done when she was a little girl. She didn't realize that the Mexicans had left the chapel. She went down the stairs and found the same group waiting to get into what looked like another chapel.

There weren't that many people in it. Once Christmas was over, before Holy Week began, the flow of pilgrims dwindled. And so she followed the Mexicans down to where she could kneel at the tomb of Jesus and pray for a few minutes for him not to abandon her.

Then she found a corner to carry on praying. She hadn't felt so at peace with herself or with God for many long years. In fact, she felt so peaceful that she almost forgot how much she was suffering from her fever.

She had lost all sense of time, and when she left the building, it was already noon. She didn't feel strong enough to walk to the American Colony, so she convinced herself that she was unlikely to see Marvin and that it was better to wait for the evening.

She decided to walk around the city and got lost. The narrow streets, heady with the scent of spices, made her dizzy. She felt very weak and thought that this must be because she hadn't eaten anything. She stopped and bought a pastry filled with nuts. She didn't feel at all scared because the voices she heard were not foreign to her. They were the same sounds, the same words that she had heard years before in Alexandria.

She asked an old man how to get to the American Colony. The man said that she should follow the street straight along until she got to the Damascus Gate, and then he told her which streets to take to get to the hotel.

She felt very tired and couldn't stop coughing. And so she walked slowly to the hotel.

The receptionist seemed fed up to see her.

"No, Mr. Brian isn't here, he left very early this morning and hasn't reserved a table at the hotel for this evening ... Madame, leave your card and we'll give it to him. We've already told him that you were asking for him. But you didn't say who you are, and of course he won't see you if he doesn't know who you are."

She smiled and said that she would be back later, but that she wouldn't leave a card because she wanted to give Mr. Brian a surprise. Her statement was received with a degree of suspicion from the receptionist.

The pain in her chest barely allowed her to breathe, and her head hurt so much that any sound, no matter how soft, hurt her.

At the entrance to the hotel she met Boulos, the taxi driver who had driven her to Jericho the day before. He was smoking a cigarette with the other drivers, and came over when he saw her.

"Madame, madame ... Do you want me to drive you somewhere? You don't look very well."

Catalina tried to smile, but she had no strength to stand. The taxi driver took her by the hand to try to stop her from falling.

"I'll take you where you need to go ... you don't look well ..."

When they got to Lea's house, they found her helping her daughters with their homework.

"We've already eaten, but there's a bit of soup."

"Thank you ... you're very kind ..."

"Are you sick? You seemed a little under the weather yesterday, and today ... Well, you don't look well, and you didn't look well when you came either. Look, if you're sick, it's better if I call the doctor."

"No, there's no need. It's just a cold that I can't get over. Oh, I went to the Cenacle and the Holy Sepulchre today."

Lea looked at her worriedly and insisted on calling a doctor, but Catalina refused. She ate the soup quickly and went to bed. She wanted to get up early to get to the hotel before Marvin left.

The next morning, she found it very difficult to breathe. She was confused. She didn't know where she was, and it was hard for her to feel what was happening. Her vision was blurry and her legs found it hard to hold her up. She had to stop from time to time to lean on walls so as not to fall over.

When she reached the American Colony, a young footman came out to meet her. She muttered that she was looking for Marvin Brian and the young man must have taken pity on her, because he told her that the gentleman and the lady had left a while back in a taxi, to go to the Old Town. Catalina thanked him and had to grab hold of his arm. She felt so dizzy that she was barely able to stand on her own two feet. He told her to sit down and wait in the garden until he could bring her a glass of water.

She could barely swallow the water, but she did so because she didn't want to seem impolite to this young man. The footman ordered her a taxi because she didn't look well, and she accepted this offer with gratitude.

The taxi left her at the Jaffa Gate, the best place for her to then find her way into the heart of the city. She decided to walk to the Wailing Wall, leaning against the walls the whole time so as not to fall over.

Lea had told her that the wall had been built on the ruins of the Temple of Solomon. And that was where she saw him. Marvin was standing by the wall with Farida and another man with whom they were talking in a lively fashion.

She couldn't help but admire the elegant figure of the Egyptian, dressed in a leather overcoat and a hat to cover her hair.

She walked over to him, and when she was close enough, she put her hand on his shoulder. He turned towards her and his eyes showed first shock and then astonishment.

"Marvin … you have to listen to me! Please!"

"You're insane! How dare you come here? Go away, leave me alone!" he shouted.

"No, I won't go … you have to acknowledge Adela. I don't want anything for me. She is your daughter, you have an obligation to her. Please!"

She felt her legs trembling, her vision clouding over, and she grasped his arm because she felt her strength leaving her, but he pushed her away and she fell to the ground.

"Let's go! She's crazy!" he shouted, grabbing Farida by the arm to the astonishment of the man who was with them.

"The lady … she seems ill," the stranger said.

"She's insane! She's following me around the world. Let's go, please, hurry up," Marvin said nervously.

Catalina no longer saw or heard anything. When she opened her eyes, she was scared. She didn't know where she was. A room, bare white walls, and her arm … her arm with a needle stuck in it …

She tried to shout but no sound came out of her mouth. She couldn't move either. She could hear some murmuring noises. She closed her eyes and drifted back into nothingness.

When she returned to consciousness, she looked up to see a woman in white who seemed to be talking to her.

"How are you? Calm down. I'll call the doctor."

The nurse left the room and came back with a man who said he was Dr. Haddas, although Catalina wasn't sure that this was exactly what he'd said.

"You're very ill. You've got pneumonia. You have to let us get in contact with your family. They'll be worried not to have heard from you. You've been here a week …"

It was hard for her to remember the number of the Paris apartment, but Dr. Haddas didn't seem to be in any hurry, and told her not to worry. Then she fell back into sleep and dreams which numbed her pain.

Fernando listened carefully to Dr. Haddas. He had only arrived in Tel Aviv a few hours ago, and he hadn't wasted any time in looking for a taxi to take him to Jerusalem. When he got to the hospital, the doctor had come to see him right away. He said that all he knew was that she had been picked up by the police at the Wailing Wall, where she had apparently tried to attack a man who had pushed her away in self-defense and made her fall over. But the cause of her state was not the fall, but rather the pneumonia. She was very sick, and must have spent several days with a high temperature and infected lungs. He thought that she was out of danger, but that she shouldn't be moved. She was very weak, and although it had been controlled, the pneumonia was still not beaten.

When they took him to the room where Catalina lay, Fernando thought at first that there had been some mistake. The woman who was in the bed looked nothing like Catalina. She had many more white hairs than before and her face was wrinkled and wracked with pain. The shrunken body was that of a little girl or an old woman.

He went over to the bed and took her by the hand. She opened her eyes and tried to smile.

"You came ..." she murmured.

"I'm with you, don't worry, nothing's going to happen. Don't speak, don't tire yourself out, I'll take care of everything."

"Marvin ..."

"Forget about him!"

And he ran the back of his hand across her face to wipe away the tears.

Fernando stayed at her side for a whole month. Although Dr. Haddas told him that the worst was now past, he still wouldn't let her leave.

For the entire time, he tried to get Adela to come and see her mother, but she refused. When Fernando called her to tell her that Catalina was in a hospital in Jerusalem, Adela started shouting.

"I'm not surprised! You know it was in the papers? Yes, even *The New York Times* noted that the *Poet of Pain* had been assaulted by a woman in Jerusalem, a woman who follows him wherever he goes. Can you believe it?"

"She is your mother and she is very ill," Fernando said.

"Yes, she's very ill, but the worst of it is not the pneumonia, but the fact that she's sick in the head."

"Don't say that. Don't judge her. You don't understand anything."

"No, you're right, I don't understand anything. You are a mystery, the pair of you. I'll never understand why you live together without ... well, without having any kind of romance. I don't know why you support her in her madness. I don't know why you have given up your life. I don't know how she can have lost her senses so much as to follow a man who despises her. No, Fernando, I'm not coming. I'm not going to participate in her madness. I left Paris because of this, and I warned her that if she carried on following Marvin Brian around, then she would lose me forever. She's made her decision."

"Adela, you have no idea what it meant to your mother to bring you into the world. You don't know Spain. You would have been shunned, pointed out in the street … You would have been the daughter of a single mother and you would have felt the effects of that your whole life."

"No, I don't know Spain, I don't have anything to do with your country, even though I still have a grandmother, an aunt, and who knows what other family still living there. My mother wanted to come back triumphant with a husband on one arm and me on the other, and now, look, she's lost the both of us. I've made my choice, Fernando, I've built up my own identity. I'm an American now. I thought I'd tell you the last time I saw you, but … well, you know what happened."

"An American? But why?"

"Because I have to be from somewhere. Where is someone from, if they were born in the Atlantic, grew up in Alexandria, became a woman in Paris?"

"That doesn't matter now … you have to come. Your mother needs you."

"No, she doesn't need me. She doesn't need anyone, apart perhaps from you."

Fernando thought back over this conversation as he watched over Catalina's sleep. This conversation had been a month ago. A month during which he had barely moved from Catalina's side, holding her hand in his, cleaning the sweat from her brow, trying to make her, little by little, eat some food. A month during which everything else had stopped mattering to him.

When he had called Sara to say that he was going to Jerusalem, she was already aware that Catalina had gone there in search of Marvin, although she didn't know that she was ill.

Fernando didn't lie to her: he told her that he would stay with Catalina until she got better, and that he didn't know how long that would be until he got to Jerusalem. He could almost hear Sara pursing her lips as she did when something upset her, but she said nothing more than that she would look after the bookshop and the publishing house until he got back, and he thanked her.

He had slept by Catalina's bed that night, like every night, in a chair. He had lost weight and the bags under his eyes seemed there to stay. Every night the dead came to visit him. Roque and Saturnino Pérez came like clockwork. The last man whom he and Zahra had killed, Ludger Wimmer, came to see him as well.

At seven on the dot, the nurse came in.

"The doctor has said that he'll be here in half an hour. He might let her leave the hospital today."

The doctor came later than he had said he would. Catalina was impatient to be allowed to go. She wanted to go back to Paris. She knew that Fernando and she would have to talk about what had happened, because for that whole month he had asked her no questions and had not blamed her for anything. But he deserved an explanation. Once again he had shown how much he loved her.

When Dr. Haddas said that she could go, she could no longer contain herself, and instead of shaking his hand she gave him a hug.

"Thank you, Doctor. I was so ready to leave this place," she said.

To which he replied that he hoped she would come back someday, but not as a patient.

14

They arrived back in Paris in May. Madame and Monsieur Dufort met them at the airport and Catalina's face grew full of emotion.

Doriane Dufort, who was usually so reserved, seemed pleased to see her, and said that she had looked after the apartment in their absence, and that when Fernando had called to say that they were coming home she had gone out and bought a couple of things, to make sure they didn't come home to an empty fridge. And that she hoped this didn't bother her.

Madame Dufort had also put a vase of flowers on the salon table, and a brown envelope, one of the ones that came every now and then with two letters inside: one from Asunción for Catalina, and one from Isabel for Fernando.

As soon as they were alone, they hugged one another.

"I owe you so much …" she said.

Fernando wouldn't let her speak. They were home, together, and needed nothing else. Or that's what they wanted to believe, at least.

Then, alone in their rooms, they opened the letters they had been sent.

My dear Fernando,

I'm worried that I haven't heard from you for a long time. I am sorry to have to write to you with bad news. A few days ago Piedad and Eulogio died. I'd like to be by your side now, to hold you tight and comfort you. I know how close you were to Eulogio, a friendship that grew up between you when you were still children. And you know how friendly your father and I were with Piedad and her husband, that good man, Jesús.

Asunción and I are both very upset. We couldn't have imagined it would actually happen.

Piedad was worried about what might happen to Eulogio if she died, and she had said to us on several occasions that if she were ever to fall seriously ill, then she would end her own life and that of her son as well. We said that if she died then Eulogio would be looked after by an institution, but she didn't accept that as a choice at all. She didn't want to think of her son being abandoned in an asylum.

A few months ago, we saw that she looked worried. She said that it was because of her work, but she looked bad, she had bags under her eyes, and was getting thinner all the time. I was worried to see her still taking in new sewing.

She didn't want to confide in Asunción or in me, knowing that we would try to dissuade her from what she was going to do.

On Sundays, Asunción and I go to Mass together, and then we usually join Eulogio and Piedad and go out for a walk. A few days ago, just before I was about to go out to church, Piedad came and knocked at the door. She was very pale and I asked her if she was well. She said she was fine, but she just wanted to tell us that she wouldn't be coming out for a walk with us on Sunday. I asked if she needed anything, and she said no, but that she just wanted to spend a peaceful day with Eulogio. She even said I shouldn't come up to see her, because she wanted to rest.

Although I was worried, of course I obeyed her request. And then on Monday, I went out to work early, and when I got back in the afternoon to see them, I knocked on the door and no one answered. A neighbor came out onto the landing and said that there was a very odd smell coming from Piedad's house. I rang the bell again and again. I thought that maybe she was out delivering some clothes, but I couldn't help thinking that the neighbor was right, and that it did smell odd. A little later, the doorman came by to the house. She said that it smelled of gas, that the smell was coming from Piedad's house, and that she was going to call the firemen to open the door.

897

The firemen came and ordered us not to stand close while they broke open the door. In fact, they knocked it off its hinges. They came and opened the windows and looked for the cause of the accident. The gas tap was on.

They found Piedad and Eulogio sitting on the sofa. They looked like they were asleep. Eulogio's head was resting on his mother's shoulder and she had her arms around his shoulders. I know because as soon as the fresh air started to clear the gas I went into Piedad's house. The firemen shouted at me to get out and I didn't pay them any attention, but I did feel dizzy and they had to help me.

There was a letter addressed to Asunción on the table, and another one addressed to me. We couldn't open them until the police came. We couldn't read them until the next day, when they called us to the police station.

It was an open and shut case. Piedad had killed herself and had taken her son with her, just as she had promised to do on other occasions.

She had found out that she had cancer of the pancreas. The doctor had told her the truth, that there was no chance of a cure, and that she only had a few months left to live.

She decided that before the sickness stopped her from moving about, before they took her son away from her, she would end the lives of the pair of them. And that's what she did.

I don't judge her, Fernando, you know that I'm a Catholic born and bred and that suicide is a mortal sin, but I don't judge her or condemn her, because I know that the Lord has taken her into his bosom. Piedad's only sin was to love her son, to want to protect him, to hope that he would always be looked after. I am sure that the Lord has forgiven him and that Piedad and Eulogio are by his side.

I know that this letter will make you sad, cause you pain, and I would do anything I could to make you feel better, even though I must admit that since that day I have not slept very much at all.

Although Eulogio and Catalina never got along very well, she is a good person and she will feel sad for him.

You have one another. Help each other.

I don't want to blame you at all, my son, but wouldn't it be possible to put an end to this farce? Piedad was sure that you and Catalina lived together in that apartment in Paris where we send the letters. Please, Fernando, it would help me calm down a little, to know where you are, even if you don't want me to come and visit you.

With all my love, my son,

YOUR MOTHER, who only
dreams of being able to hold you again.

Fernando was crying bitterly when he saw through his tears Catalina standing in the shade of the doorway.

He hadn't heard her knock or come in. She sat at his side and hugged him tight. He couldn't hear the words she said, but he no longer felt so alone. They stayed holding one another.

It wasn't Roque and Saturnino Pérez who came to him that night, but Eulogio.

He saw Eulogio, lost and vague, suddenly coming to himself and looking over at him and smiling. He shouted. He shouted as loud as he could, and Catalina tried to wake him up.

"Did you see him?" she asked.

"Yes, I saw him ... he was here ... he seemed dead but then ... then he smiled at me."

"He's your friend, Fernando, you mustn't be afraid of him."

"I'm not afraid of him ..."

"We're all afraid of the dead. Eulogio won't hurt you ... I even think he's in Heaven, protecting you, just like your father."

Fernando couldn't help but be surprised at Catalina's straightforward way of viewing the world. She might have grown white hair, but she hadn't lost her childish innocence. She had never stopped believing.

Routine once more became a part of their lives. They understood one another with no need for words. Fernando was tormented by the fact that Marvin had pushed Catalina away and left her lying on the ground. In his eyes, he was no more than a bastard. And it was hard from him to get over Eulogio's death. He couldn't help blaming Piedad for having killed her son, but Catalina calmed him down, asking what choice she had. He turned on her, and said that her Catholic convictions left a lot to be desired. She didn't get offended.

He felt that they were closer than ever, especially because since Eulogio's death, they had realized just how fragile life was.

Sara carried on trusting in Fernando, so much so that now she no longer accepted books of poems for the publishing house without asking his opinion. While he had been away, Professor Fortier had tried to interest her in the work of another one of his students who he considered highly talented. But Sara had said that they should wait until Fernando came back. And she had also held off on replying to a journalist who had sent his book of poems along via a mutual acquaintance.

But it still surprised Fernando when, a few months after he returned, Sara called him to her office to tell him that Benjamin's health had worsened.

"Benjamin is very ill. He hid the fact that he has liver cancer. The doctor is not very confident, so ..."

"I'm sorry," he managed to say.

"Well, I know that you never got along well with my husband," Sara said, looking him straight in the eye.

Fernando didn't say anything because he didn't want to lie to her. It was useless even to try. He still didn't know why she had always protected him and trusted him, so he owed her a debt of gratitude, but as for Benjamin ... the years hadn't made him change his mind. He still thought Benjamin was manipulative, unscrupulous, heedless of the fates of others except where they fitted with his plans.

"No, you never understood him. You never understood what he did, and the many lives he saved," she said.

"To save some lives you need to sacrifice others," Fernando dared to mutter.

"Lives that are worth losing," Sara's voice had grown harder.

"And who decides that?" Fernando felt so agitated that his heart was beating far too fast.

"You must admit that if someone had killed Hitler, then the lives of many innocent people would have been saved, and so

I think that his life, Hitler's life, was one that deserved to be cut off at the root. My husband never sent a just man to his death, but he tried always to make sure that worthwhile lives were saved. And anyway ... you yourself decided to take the lives of two men when you were very young, men who had taken what was most important to you: your father's life. You decided that these men didn't deserve to live. Do you think you're better than Benjamin?"

Roque and Saturnino's faces swam before his eyes and he rubbed his eyes to make them go away. Sara waited in silence for him to reply.

"I'm not going to argue with you. I understand how much pain you must feel at Benjamin's illness, and believe me when I say I don't wish him any harm."

"No, you can't wish him harm: all he's done is protect you and treat you well. Do you think that if he'd been against it, you would have been put in charge of the Rosent publishing house? Of course not. He always approved of you. He trusted my decision, but also your qualities. Well ... I'm leaving tomorrow to go to London. I don't know how much more time Benjamin will live, but I don't want to miss a second of it."

"I understand."

"Oh, by the way, Zahra is in London."

He didn't reply. He felt his soul twist within him, if that was possible.

"You're two stupid people. You've given each other up for nothing," she said in annoyance.

Fernando had fallen silent. He wouldn't talk about Zahra, not even with Sara.

Silence had become his life's chief companion. He and Catalina never spoke about Adela. They didn't let the worry they felt come out in words whenever Monsieur Dufort gave them brown envelopes containing letters from their mothers. Catalina had stopped talking to him about Marvin, and he had stopped mentioning Zahra.

Their life was nothing more than getting up in the morning and chatting about the news on the radio as they drank a cup of coffee.

Their life was nothing more than the music lessons that Catalina carried on giving at the neighborhood music school, and the poetry collections that Fernando edited without feeling any emotional inspiration.

Their life was nothing more than forced conversations with the scholarly customers at the Rosent bookshop, the people who came in not to buy books but to chat with the shopkeeper for a while.

Their life was nothing more than getting up later on Sundays, and walking through the city and going to the cinema in the afternoon.

They seemed to have given up on life, except when every now and then something made them look it in the eyes.

Benjamin's death was one of these events. He died on September 1, 1974. Sara called to tell them. Catalina told him he should go to London for the funeral, but he didn't think he needed to. He knew that Zahra would be there, and if he was sure of one thing, it was that he didn't want to see her.

Sara didn't blame him. She didn't expect him to go. Benjamin's death led Sara to decide that her true home was really Paris. They had no children, and she kept on running Wilson & Wilson in London, but she found someone else to handle the shop's daily operations, flying in once a month to look at the accounts and see how the business was going.

Fernando was used to not having a boss to tell him what to do, and he was worried that Sara's presence would put in danger what had until that moment been a satisfactory working relationship for the pair of them.

But Sara very rarely pulled rank on him. They did agree that Fernando would stop editing Marvin's books. He didn't ask her if it had been Marvin's decision, and she didn't tell him. This change was a relief to Fernando and a source of pride for Sara.

In March 1975, Marvin gave Sara a new manuscript. *Notebook of the Holy Land*.

"It'll be another success," she predicted.

"His books generally are," Fernando said.

"I want to get it edited as soon as possible, maybe for the end of the summer. We'll need the French version and the English one ready. We'll do a book launch in New York, one in Harvard, and one in Paris. I hope you won't be upset by what I'm going to say, but please, I want you to do everything in your power to make sure that Catalina doesn't do anything. I asked you in the past, and you always said that you didn't want to get involved, but this time ... Farida isn't well, and I wouldn't like her to have to put up with another one of Catalina's scenes."

"I didn't know that Farida was sick ..."

"There wasn't any need for you to know. She's a little older than I am. Do you know how old I am?"

He looked at her and it was as though he were seeing her for the first time. When he had met her in Alexandria, Sara must have been around forty years old, and as for Farida, she had always seemed to him to be ageless.

"I'm seventy years old, Fernando, and Farida is five years older than me. We don't have very much more time."

"You don't look like you're seventy years old ..."

"Of course I look it! You'd have to be blind not to see my wrinkles, or the fact that I'm moving much more slowly than before. And so just think: Farida's five years older than I am. Seventy-five. And like Benjamin, she's got cancer. Breast cancer. They've operated and the doctors are optimistic, but with cancer you never can tell. It's not just Farida who worries me. Marvin's worse than she is."

"Marvin?"

"Yes, he's got Parkinson's disease. His hands shake and he had a heart attack a month ago. It wasn't the first one: he had another a few years ago ... do you remember when Catalina went to find him in Sorrento? He wasn't there writing his *Mafia Notebook* ... he needed to recover from a heart attack."

"I didn't know anything about this ..."

"No, of course, it's something that he and Farida have been very private about: they only told Benjamin, Zahra and me. And as for Zahra ... well, she's not in the best health either."

It got to him. Yes, it got to him to know that Marvin and Farida were both ailing. Suddenly all the people around him were sickening and dying. During the Civil War, he had accepted that the people around him would die, but when they killed his father, he rebelled. Then Benjamin Wilson and Zahra had put him in situations where he had to kill. The dead carried on coming to him at night, but he felt that there was a difference between the ones who died of sickness and the ones who died through violence.

Don Ernesto, Catalina's father, he had been the first. Then Piedad and Eulogio, then Benjamin Wilson, and now Sara was telling him that Marvin and Farida were fighting for their lives as well. And Zahra. Sara had just told him that Zahra was ill.

"Aren't you going to ask me what's wrong with Zahra?"

"Yes ... of course ... I was."

"It's her heart. She's suffered two heart attacks."

"Where is she?" he asked, lowering his voice.

"In Alexandria."

"But there ... she's alone there, her grandmother died."

"Yes, she's alone. I tried to convince her to come to Paris, but she refused. She'll never leave her city. It's the only place that makes her feel she has an identity of her own."

"I'm not going to hide from Catalina the fact that Marvin's coming to Paris, and even if I wanted to she'd find out. The newspapers would be talking about it ..."

"I'm not asking you to hide it, but please ... for her good as well, she has to understand that she has lost her battle with Marvin."

"Catalina will never give up," he said, "but I'll try to stop her from causing herself any more harm. What happened in Israel was terrible for her."

Sara seemed to accept the reply, and they were in this way able to carry on working together as though nothing could happen to alter the apparent harmony between them.

"Franco is dead." Catalina dropped her coffee cup. Fernando was in the shower, but came out wrapped in a towel when he heard her shriek.

"What's going on? You scared me."

"He's dead ... he's dead. My God ..."

"Francisco Franco died in the early hours of the morning. The streets of Madrid are peaceful now ..."

The newsreader kept on telling them what had happened. Fernando stood still and tried to work out what he was being told. Catalina twisted her hands nervously and started to feel the sound of her own heart beating. For a few seconds, she thought that what she was hearing on the radio was impossible. They had reported that Franco was unwell on the radio, but she'd never imagined that he might be dead.

"What are we going to do?" Catalina asked nervously.

"Nothing. What can we do?"

"Franco's dead! You can go back to Spain ..."

"The fact that he's dead doesn't mean that the regime's just going to vanish. And ... Catalina, I don't have a life in Spain anymore. I gave it up on the day when I ..."

"On the day when you shot Roque and Saturnino Pérez ... but that was more than thirty-five years ago ... and no one has come to find you, no one has accused you of these murders ... and now ... Fernando, Franco is dead! Everything will change, you'll see. It will all be like it was before the war."

The sound of the telephone made them both jump. Fernando still had a towel wrapped around his waist, but he hurried to pick up the receiver. Adela's voice was nervous.

He listened to her for a while, then passed the receiver to Catalina.

"It's Adela."

Catalina felt her soul tremble. She hadn't spoken to her daughter for more than a year. And their last conversation had been formulaic, routine.

"What are you saying? Why didn't you tell me? No, I don't want to argue with you either ... I thought you only wrote about culture ... My mother? It's just ... No, it's not that I don't want to tell you, it's that ... All right, take a note of this: Calle de la Encarnación 6, third floor on the left. Careful ... she's very old ... yes ... yes, of course ... please call us and tell us if you see her ..."

She hung up. She seemed dazed. Fernando went over to her and took her by the hand.

"You know what she's going to do ..." Catalina murmured.

"She just told me. She's been in Madrid for two days. Her newspaper sent her to Madrid to help with its coverage of Franco's illness. It's the first time she's been to Spain, so it's only logical that she should feel a bit out of place."

"She wants to go to my mother's house, and she wants to go to your mother's house as well. She says that they're her grandmothers, and she needs to meet them."

"She's right. She needs to get answers. What we've told her over the years hasn't been enough."

"My mother … I don't know how she's going to react when she sees her …"

"I do, Catalina."

15

Madrid

The street looked quiet enough. It was a shortish street, and above all a well-proportioned one. One side of the street was occupied by houses, while the walls of an enclosed convent took up the other.

Adela shuddered. Her mother and Fernando had been born here. They had played here as children. They had grown up here. Their mothers still lived here. This had been the world they had escaped from. She knew why her mother had left, and in Fernando's case, she guessed that it was something more than the unconditional love he had always felt for Catalina.

Adela found number six and went in. It was a grand building. The doorman came out to meet her.

"What do you want?"

"I'm going to the Vilamars' apartment," she said, with a voice that was less certain than it might have been.

"Third floor left. Are you expected?"

"They've been waiting for me for a long time."

She went up in the elevator and paused for a few seconds in front of the door without daring to ring the bell. She didn't know if she should turn around; she took one little step backwards. She heard the bell ring inside the house, and then some slow footsteps walking towards the door. It opened and she saw an elderly woman with a kind face and white hair tied back in a bun, dressed in a gray skirt and a gray jersey.

"Good morning. What can I do for you?" the old woman said, looking at her in surprise.

"Asunción Vilamar?"

"Yes, that's me."

"Grandmother ..."

"Good Lord!"

They spontaneously hugged one another, and Adela felt how fragile the old woman was.

"It can't be ... it can't be ..." Asunción said.

"Yes, Grandmother, it is me ... I've wanted to see you so much!"

They cried and hugged one another. Neither of the two tried to hold back their tears. Adela felt her grandmother's body shaking and was afraid that the surprise might hurt her. They stood for a while holding one another. Asunción Vilamar was afraid that if she let go of her granddaughter, then Adela would disappear like a dream.

Then, when the two of them had hugged enough, Asunción invited her granddaughter in.

The living room looked out over the street. Two balconies looked onto the convent wall. It was very clean, but the armchairs showed the passing of the years.

Asunción insisted on getting Adela something to eat, but she resisted.

"Please, all I want to do is see you, be with you, get to know you ..."

"It's early. At least have a coffee ..."

And they spoke. They listened to one another. They had to catch up on thirty-four years of news; Adela's entire age.

And she told her grandmother everything. That she had been born in a merchant ship on the Atlantic while a German submarine was trying to send them to the bottom of the sea. Her happy childhood in Alexandria. Her teenage years in Paris. Her youth in Boston. She asked the questions which Catalina had never answered to her satisfaction. Had Spain really been so bad in those years, to make her mother feel that being pregnant meant that she had to leave? She had been in Madrid for two days and didn't think that the people were like Fernando and her mother had described them. She hadn't seen Spain as a sad and oppressive place, but rather one where the people had a burning desire for freedom.

Asunción explained to her in detail what the Spain that had

sprung up after the Civil War had been like. She acknowledged the fact that she and her husband, as they were Catholic and supporters of the monarchy, had initially been relieved at Franco's triumph because the country was being overrun with anarchists, but then, as the years had gone by, they had asked themselves if Franco had really been the best solution.

"When so many people have had to learn to live in silence, to lie, you realize that this isn't normal. If people are scared, then it's because things aren't how they should be. We'll see what will happen now, with Franco dead … I'm sure that it will all turn out for the best. Young people don't have to inherit our mistakes. They have the right to look for their own path through the world, for themselves and for Spain. It's their time, and we should let them decide. The Spain of today is not the Spain of my youth, where a woman was marked for life if she ended up pregnant outside of marriage. You know, although she's suffered a great deal, I think Catalina did right not marrying Antoñito, and she did right as well by refusing to let them condemn you here. She only made one mistake."

"What was that, grandmother?"

"In her choice of father for you. The *Poet of Pain* … I've read a few of Marvin's books and I can see that he's a great poet, but he's a bad person. He should have acknowledged you. But men are like that, they take advantage of a moment of weakness and then abandon the woman forever. I wish that Catalina had had that moment of weakness with Fernando."

"He has always been my father. I can't imagine another father that isn't him."

"But haven't they gotten married? All those years living together …"

"Together but apart. They're not a couple, and it's been hard for me to accept, but it is the case. I'm sure that Fernando would marry my mother even now, but she doesn't want him to. She is obsessed with Marvin, and she also says that it's not fair for Fernando to give up his life for her. But she's allowed him to do that anyway. There was a woman … Zahra …"

"Yes, Piedad told us about her; she saw her when she went to Paris to fetch Eulogio."

"A special woman. She's not so much beautiful as possessed of an extraordinary force. I think that Fernando was in love with her, but he's as stubborn as my mother. She's decided to marry Marvin, and he's decided to marry her. If they don't succeed, then they'll think that their lives have failed, but they are aims that run in parallel, and will never flow together."

Asunción spoke of her husband Ernesto, of his shame at Catalina's departure, of how he had plucked up the courage to face up to Don Antonio, of his sickness, of how he had died with Catalina's name on his lips.

And she told her about Isabel and Piedad. About their diminished lives, their widow's lives, their renunciation of everything that wasn't the return of their sons.

It was afternoon when Adela said goodbye to her grandmother, promising to come back when it was time for supper. Asunción said she would invite Isabel, who, just like her, thought that she would die without being able to hold her son one last time.

She also tried to get Adela to stay the night in her house, but Adela rejected the idea. She had been sent to Madrid by her newspaper, and she was in Madrid to work, but she promised that she'd come and see her every day. She didn't want to say that there was a reporter from CBS here as well to cover the death of Franco and that they'd been living together for some time now. Maybe that would be too many surprises for one day.

That night, when Adela came back to her grandmother's house, she met Isabel. Fernando's mother held back a shout when she saw her and looked across at Asunción as though she wanted to tell her something without using words. But Asunción avoided her gaze.

Just as she had done that morning, Adela spoke and spoke, trying to give suitable answers to Asunción's questions. She didn't lie to them. She told them that the house where they sent their letters was the same one where Fernando and Catalina had lived since they left Alexandria, as well as the fact that although she had insisted again and again that Fernando and Catalina should go to Madrid, they had refused. In her mother's case, it was because she was determined to return to Madrid as Marvin's wife, and in Fernando's case … well, she had to admit that she suspected that there was more to it than a simple desire to be with Catalina, and that it was something that only he and Catalina knew. Isabel assured her that she couldn't guess what this reason might be, but that she too was sure that it existed.

Catalina and Fernando waited expectantly for Adela's phone calls. Ever since going to Madrid, she had called them assiduously. She seemed happy, although she never stopped blaming her mother for all those years that she had kept her from her grandparents. They had lost a lot of time. Adela couldn't stop thinking about how it would have been to grow up with a grandmother like Asunción. She even missed her grandfather Ernesto; she had talked about him with her grandmother so much that she could almost imagine they had met. And Asunción's house in the Calle de la Encarnación was full to bursting with photos of the family.

When she spoke to Fernando, he insisted that she tell him what was happening in Spain. It wasn't that he didn't already know, given that he watched the news and read the papers, but it was as though the information that came directly from Adela was more valuable.

She was clear that the Spaniards were preparing to take the reins of their own future. She had always thought of Spain as a sinister kind of country, but here she was, right in the middle of a dynamic new society that wanted to join the rest of the world.

"I'm telling you, the regime will never survive. Don't worry," she assured Fernando.

"But Arias Navarro is president! You have no idea who that man is!" Fernando said.

"He won't last long; he doesn't get along with the king."

"But the king was installed by Franco!" Fernando shouted, convinced that Adela didn't know anything and didn't understand anything.

"Look, I'm actually here, and I'm speaking to people, and I promise you that Juan Carlos has no intention of perpetuating Franco's regime. He's going to dismantle it bit by bit, but he has to be careful."

"We don't want a king! ¡Viva la República!"

"Well, you're going to have a king, whether you want one or

not, so you'd better get used to the idea. And it's not a good or a bad thing in itself to have a king. What matters is whether or not Spain becomes a democratic country, and if anyone can help with that transition, it's him. Unless you all want to go back to shooting at one another."

"You don't know what you're saying!"

"I'm telling you that Juan Carlos is the head of state and the head of the military and that the army obeys him through gritted teeth, and so that it's only carefully and patiently that he can take apart a regime that has lasted forty years. I know that you Spaniards are very black or white about such things, that you don't have a good head for shades of gray."

"You're Spanish yourself, at least in part. Even if Marvin is an American."

"No, I'm a citizen of Atlantis," she joked.

"It's going to be a catastrophe," Fernando said.

"No, it won't be. Not unless old pig-headed men like you insist that it will be."

"Whatever you say, there's going to need to be a reckoning, and the Franco supporters are going to have to be put on trial and then shot. There's no forgiving what they did."

"If you, the people who lost the war, decide to do to the former winners what they did to you, then there's no hope. You want the next forty years to be more reprisals, more tit-for-tat, more exiles and more suffering? I think that people don't think like you, or at least the majority don't. People here want to turn over a new leaf and start again."

"I'm not talking about reprisals, I'm talking about justice … What do you know about what they did? They shot my father, and he was a good man whose only crime was to fight in favor of the Constitution."

If they couldn't agree about politics, they agreed even less about Asunción and Isabel, or, as Adela referred to them, her grandmothers.

"You should stop being stupid and come and see your mother. Do you know how old she is?"

"Of course I do. She's my mother!"

"She's eighty. And so is Asunción."

But for all that Adela tried to get Fernando to come home, kept on avoiding the question.

Adela had equally bad luck with her mother. When she said that she should come back, Catalina said nothing, for all that Adela assured her that Spain was not what it had been when she was a child, and that now no one cared if people were single or married, that they wanted to be free, and that was it. But Catalina just pursed her lips and said nothing.

She didn't want to tell her daughter that she didn't come home not just for her own sake, but also because of Fernando. She couldn't leave him. She was tired and wanted to see her mother, but the price she would have to pay would be abandoning her most loyal companion, the man who had loved her and provided her with ample protection without asking for anything in return.

Fernando would never go back to Spain, she was sure of that. She knew that he was afraid of what would happen. He had killed two men, and they could punish him for their deaths. She couldn't tell Adela this, though. Only she and Eulogio had known what Fernando did that afternoon next to the Comendadoras prison. She could be considered an accomplice, because she had given Fernando the weapon he had used to kill Roque and Saturnino Pérez.

Adela didn't understand her mother, and she didn't understand Fernando. They were stuck in the past and pictured a Spain that no longer existed. It was a Spain that must have been as terrible as they remembered it. No one can live thorough a civil war without scars. But a country is not a photograph, a snapshot frozen in time.

And she was enjoying her time in Madrid. Not just because she had met her grandmother and found that part of her that had never been allowed to grow, but also because she was in a relationship that made her happy. Peter Brown was a colleague of hers from CBS and she had started a relationship with him before they had been sent to Spain. Neither of them imagined that they were going to be sent to Madrid, and so they felt a double passion in these days. Passion for one another, and passionate excitement at living through a historic moment.

They saw one another very little during the day, but the nights

...la invited Peter to her grandmother's house and
...e.

...d Isabel to come by the evening that Peter and
... Peter was impressed at how dignified the
... were. There was suffering etched in every one of
...nkles, but they didn't mention it, although he couldn't
...p himself from asking their opinion about everything that was
going to happen in Spain.

Asunción summarized their feelings: "I won the war and Isabel lost it. But actually, we both lost. Do you think it was easy to live in a country where the ground is sown with dead men? No, we all have our dead, we all have unsettled scores."

Isabel nodded and then decided to add something herself: "It wasn't easy to live, supressing your hate, knowing that the person you met in the street could be the very man who shot your husband in the head, or your brother, or your son, or else had betrayed them to the authorities, or who had been in the firing squad ... Not all the victors were like Asunción, and not all of them behaved like she has behaved. Some of them were arrogant and gave free rein to their bitterness, and we who had lost everything had to suffer the blows and keep our mouths closed. We learned to live in silence, fearing that one word in the wrong place could get us sent to hell. Then ... then you get used to it, and you think that the way you're living is almost normal. But that's a lie: there's no normality in any life unless you're free. You'd be fooling yourself if you said that you'd never give in, because one day you give up on hope."

"And now?" Peter said, looking respectfully at the two old women.

"Now it's the young who have to make a future for themselves. They can do it. This isn't going to last much longer. Arias Navarro can't last. Our country is an anomaly within Europe," Isabel said.

"So you don't think the regime will fight for its survival?" Peter asked.

"It might try, but it can't. You can't go against history, and today's society has nothing to do with the society that existed during the war," Isabel said.

"Will there be a settling of accounts?" Adela asked.

"A settling of accounts?" Isabel seemed not to understand what Adela said.

"Yes, if Arias Navarro falls, and there's a democratic government, do you think that they'll try to call Franco's supporters to account?"

"We should, but I don't think people will want to. Or at least I don't think that the majority will want to. Another confrontation … no, we've had enough already. All these years we've lived alongside our enemies and they have lived with us, their former enemies, even though they beat us. Young people today have the chance to make a different country, and they can't do that if they insist on settling the scores of the past."

"Do you like the king?" Peter asked.

"I'm not a monarchist, I don't like the monarchy. And this king … well, let's see what he can do. I think that apart from Asunción and a few other people in Spain, there aren't many monarchists left anymore. Not even Franco's supporters are monarchists."

Adela and Peter listened with interest to the two old women, surprised that in spite of their profound political and biographical differences, they were firm friends. There was something that united them: suffering, and neither of the two of them wanted to take a step back.

Peter helped Adela run some interviews with some of the opposition figures. They were all waiting to see what the future might hold.

Catalina and Fernando had to accept that Adela would reveal to her grandmothers that they were living in Paris. They didn't even protest when she told them that she had done so. They had lost any influence they held over Adela a long time ago, and it wouldn't have made any sense to blame her. She did what she wanted, and she had decided to tell these two old women the truth, or at least the part of the truth that she knew.

Isabel and Asunción insisted that Catalina and Fernando allow them to come to Paris with Adela and Peter, but they refused. They couldn't see their mothers again, because if they did, they would fall apart and be unable to carry on living the fiction that their lives had become.

Adela wasn't pleased with them. She even threatened not to see them again, but Catalina and Fernando were unmoved by her threats and asked her to respect their decision. She couldn't accept it, though, because she had met these two old women, and saw that if one thing were keeping them alive, it was their desire to see and hold their children once again.

Time sometimes runs faster than one would wish. Without any of them realizing, 1976 had arrived, and Adela was called back to New York. Arias Navarro had resigned as president on the instructions of the king, who preferred to have a younger man by his side. Adolfo Suárez was the man who would deal the final blow to a regime that had to be swept away.

Peter was going to stay in Madrid, which made Adela even less happy. But she had no choice. If she was clear about one thing, it was that she only wanted to live in New York. She certainly wouldn't go back to Paris, for all that her mother and Fernando were there. And she wouldn't have stayed in Madrid. She didn't dislike the city, but it had been hard for her to establish her own life there. She was no longer tied to her mother. The price she had to pay for her independence was moving a long way away and feeling slightly lonely, a loneliness that she had started to feel her way out of with Peter.

But she still felt at peace after having met her grandmother, that woman who had helped her put some of the pieces of her identity back together.

16

Paris

Sara gave Fernando a copy of *Notebook of the Holy Land*.

"It's the best thing Marvin's ever written," she said proudly.

"And the one he spent the most time correcting."

"Well, it was worth it. We'll release it in New York first of all, and then in London, and in Paris in the autumn …"

"Will you go to New York?"

"Yes, and … Zahra will go as well."

Zahra. Sara had stopped mentioning her, and she had gradually become one of the ghosts that stopped him from getting to sleep.

He didn't even speak about Zahra with Catalina. It hurt him to think of her. He asked himself if he had ever loved her, and told himself that he had only ever really loved Catalina. He had felt passion for Zahra, a passion that had made him tremble. He had killed for her, but he never thought that he would give up Catalina to be with her.

He hadn't realized that he had fallen silent until Sara cleared her throat.

"Would you like to come with me to New York?" she asked.

"No, of course not."

They looked at one another. She gave a small smile and took him by the hand.

"Well … I wanted to say something to you … I don't need to tell you that I'm very old … too old. I've decided to sell Wilson & Wilson. I've got a good offer from a chain of bookshops in London."

"But … Benjamin wouldn't have liked that …"

"Of course not. But we spoke about it. We didn't have any children, and he hasn't got any direct family, no brothers, no nieces and nephews …"

"I understand," he said without understanding anything.

"As far as the Rosent bookshop is concerned, I'd like to talk to you about it."

Fernando grew tense. He was afraid that she was going to tell him that she was going to close the bookshop.

"I inherited it from my father, and he got it from his father, and my grandfather got it from his father … I don't want it to disappear, but, like Wilson & Wilson I don't have anyone to leave it to. I thought that … well, I thought you might like to buy it."

"Buy it? I … I don't think I could pay you what it's worth … There's nothing I'd like more, but … " He was so surprised by Sara's proposal that he didn't know what he thought or what he should say.

"I know you don't have the money to buy the bookshop, but I don't want to do business with you. I really thought that I would just leave it to you, but I spoke to a lawyer and he said that it would be much too complicated for you if I did that: you'd have to pay so much in taxes that it would be impossible for you to come out ahead. No, it's best that you buy it: I'll sell it to you for a symbolic sum, with the proviso that the sale only comes into effect on the day of my death. I'll still own it until that happens. I won't be able to get used to walking in front of the bookshop and feeling that it's not mine."

Sara named her price and he waved a finger at her to say no. It was such a small amount that it made him feel ashamed.

"I told you that it would be symbolic. The Rosent bookshop is important to you, an important part of your life. So important that you don't know what you'd do if you weren't here. You are older now, and even if you did go back to Spain, I don't think you'd be able to adapt very well to life there."

"I don't have children either. What would happen to the bookshop when I die?"

"Oh, that would be your problem! I'd be dead, I wouldn't care. You could leave it to Adela, you could sell it, or maybe you'll decide to have your own life after all, and marry a younger woman and have a child. Whatever happens, you deserve to have the Rosent bookshop belong to you. If you accept my offer, we'll tell Monsieur Dufort. I asked him to get the papers ready, and all you have to do is sign them."

Fernando didn't know how to thank her for her generosity. She had chosen him to be the son she had never had.

"Thank you. I know I don't deserve your generosity. You've looked after me from the first day we met."

"Yes, the very first day you came to Wilson & Wilson in Alexandria, I don't know why, but I adopted you. Maybe it was your melancholic eyes. Or your determination, your sensibility. Benjamin laughed at me for it. When he spoke about you, he called you my adoptive son. He liked you, Fernando, although he never showed it. He always knew that the Rosent bookshop would become yours, and he never tried to talk me out of it."

Fernando gave her a hug, and she felt how warmly he meant it. She had always seen him as a little lost boy.

"You're right, Sara, I'll never go back to Spain."

"Of course you will, but you'll never stay there. It's too late. But you'll have to go, so you can look the past in the face. You can't change it, but you can make your peace with it, become reconciled to what you left behind. They're saying that there might be an amnesty. If that's the case, then you can go back without any trouble, although no one will connect you to the deaths of those two men anyway. Benjamin knew it, but he was always very good at putting the pieces together. And anyway, you confirmed it, because you were naive. When he told you about the two men who had been found dead near the prison where your father had been held, he had no way of knowing that you had anything to do with their deaths."

"He tricked me!"

"No, he didn't trick you, he was just smarter than you, than all of us. I'll tell you something else, which is that he was always ready to protect you. If anyone had tried to lay the blame for this on you in Spain, then he ... well, he'd have fixed it."

"You asked him to do that," Fernando said with a smile.

"I didn't need to. He was always ready to do anything for my 'adoptive son.' You know, I think I would have liked to have met your mother, but it's too late now."

"And she would have liked to have known I had a guardian angel."

They laughed as they shook hands. They had never felt closer than they did at that moment.

What Catalina and Fernando did not expect was for Adela to turn up on a visit to Paris. They hadn't seen her for years, and she had not agreed to have them visit her in New York.

She was only there for one day, which was time enough for her to argue with her mother and recriminate Fernando for his stubbornness.

She spoke to them about Isabel and Asunción, about their loneliness, about the pain they felt because they couldn't understand why their children refused to see them.

"I don't understand it either, and I think that the three of us deserve an explanation," she challenged Fernando and Catalina.

They were eating in La Coupole. It was Adela's favorite restaurant, where she had celebrated her birthday every year when she was a teenager. She liked the dining room, always filled with people. The noise of the conversations, the way the waiters treated her like an adult although she had only just stopped being a child.

La Coupole was a part of her best memories of Paris, and she wanted to have the discussion she was due to have with Fernando and Catalina there, as though the place itself would be enough to bring back harmony to the situation. But it was not to be.

"We don't have to explain anything to you. It's our decision. It's the best for everyone, for our mothers as well," Catalina said annoyedly.

Adela looked angry and put down the glass of champagne that she had just been about to bring to her lips.

"So, you don't think we deserve to know because … you don't … you're heartless. Your mothers are very old, and they have lived on in the hope of seeing you again. I'm not even asking you to come to Spain, because I'm not even going to try to understand why you won't do that, now that Franco's dead, but to refuse to allow them to come to see you in Paris … I could bring them …"

"No," said Fernando dully.

"Have your mothers done something unforgivable for you to punish them like this?" Adela's voice shook with anger.

"They're the best mothers anyone could hope for," Catalina said, without changing her tone.

"Then why are you punishing them?" Adela shouted.

"That's enough! It's nothing to do with you. Please, don't insist," Fernando begged.

Adela got up and left without saying goodbye. Catalina thought that maybe she had lost her daughter forever.

They didn't hear anything from Adela after that. She didn't answer their calls and didn't call them. This was how she punished them. But they kept on getting letters from Isabel and Asunción.

My dear son,

Adela has come back very sad from her trip to Paris. She told us that she tried to get you to come to see us. We said thank you, because it's the only thing that's keeping us alive. If it weren't for the hope of one day seeing you again, I think I wouldn't mind dying.

Asunción at least has had the joy of seeing her granddaughter. Adela has made her years younger. She's even getting ready to go to New York. She might go to the wedding. I know that Adela hasn't told you, but she's going to get married. Peter is a man who seems to care for her a great deal. He's a journalist like she is; he works for CBS. They get along well and he's very supportive of Adela.

I'd like to see her get married as well, but I don't feel strong enough to go to New York, and I don't think it's really my place, although Asunción insists that I go with her to keep her company. I don't have much money, but with what I've saved and my pension, maybe I could go along.

I was speaking to Asunción downstairs a few days ago, and Pablo Gómez came along to see his parents. He's always very rude, and he said: "I wonder how the happy couple's doing. They've had time to have plenty of children by now." He was obviously talking about Catalina and you. Asunción turned pale. We didn't answer him.

Fernando, I don't want to blame you for anything, but I am old, and maybe I don't have that much longer to live. I don't know if it's useless for me to tell you that my only desire is to see you one more time, but that's how it is. I'd go to the ends of the earth to see you again.

I'm not going to ask that you come to Madrid. I don't understand why you refuse to come, but it's even harder for me to understand why you refuse to let me come to Paris.

What have I done, my son, for you to refuse to see me? I keep on asking myself why.

Fernando, you'd be surprised about how things are changing here in Spain. There might be elections. Yes, free elections. You know that I'm not a monarchist, but maybe this king is going to make things happen, and maybe it wasn't a mistake for him to pick Adolfo Suárez.

I'm not going to say that everything is sorted out now, but I think there won't be any more steps back. We are all scared, scared that it will turn out to have been a dream, that something will go wrong. But I think you'd like to see what's happening here.

I respect your decision not to see me anymore, even though I don't understand it, but I want to ask you not to let me die without telling me why.

Please write when you can.

All my love, forever,

YOUR MOTHER.

Fernando was afraid of what Catalina's reaction would be when she found out that Adela was going to get married, but she accepted it with resignation.

"There's no reason for you not to go back to Spain," Fernando insisted.

She looked him straight in the eye and said, without raising her voice:

"Yes, there is a reason. You."

"For God's sake, Catalina! I don't want to hear you say things like that. If you're staying because of me, then you can pack your suitcase right away. I'll be able to survive without you," he laughed.

"Of course you'd be able to, but even so, I'm staying. Fernando, we left together, and we'll go back together or not at all. Only if ..."

"Only if what?"

"Only if there'd been a woman ... if you'd decided to have a life with Zahra or some other woman, I'd leave."

"I'm not going to let you sacrifice yourself for me," he said angrily.

"I'm not sacrificing myself, Fernando, it's just that I can't imagine my life without you. I've found it impossible to love you as a husband, but I love you more than anyone else in the world. I don't know if you can understand what I'm saying, but it's the truth."

"I'm not going to go to Spain, Catalina. My life is here. You know how generous Sara's being: the bookshop will be mine. If I go back to Spain, how would I live?"

"Adela's right that there's no reason for us not to see our mothers. They could come here."

"No, not mine. I'd have to explain to her why I've been gone so many years, and I'd have to confess that I killed two men, and she wouldn't be able to bear it. I know that I've hurt her deeply, but the damage would be far greater if she knew that her son was a killer. I've told you that my father stopped me from going to the front, that he didn't want me to have to kill anybody. He kept on saying the same thing to me, again and again: 'You shall not kill. A man who takes somebody's life, however just the cause, will never be the same again. You shall not kill. You shall not kill.' He made my mother promise to stop me from enlisting, after he himself left for the front, so that I'd never have to kill anybody. And my mother kept her promise. She wouldn't let me fight."

"Stop torturing yourself for what you did. Those men ... Roque and Saturnino were two bad men. You don't deserve to suffer for what you've done."

"I haven't stopped thinking about them since the day that I killed them. Every day. Every single day ... And at night ..."

"I know ... I've spent years listening to your screams."

"They come to me every night. The other two are there as well, the Gestapo agent and Zahra's father's business partner ... but they don't make me feel so bad. Roque and Saturnino ... it's as though my father would blame me for my actions."

"He wouldn't, Fernando, he wouldn't. You have to stop tormenting yourself, because I promise you that the world has lost nothing through the deaths of those four men you killed."

"You know, I never understood why this didn't matter to you."

"Well, Fernando, it doesn't matter to me. I don't lose any sleep over the fact that you killed those wretches."

"In any case, you should go back to Madrid."

"No, Fernando, I can't. I can't bear the thought of your mother's eyes if she asks me the truth. I could only keep quiet if you were with me. That's why you should think about this. Nothing will happen if they come to see us. Think about it."

Catalina got a letter from Asunción at the end of the year. The letter made her very upset, but she didn't let herself cry. She hadn't allowed herself to cry since she left Spain, thirty-five years before.

My dear daughter,

As I told you I was going to in my previous letter, I went to Adela's wedding. It wasn't what I expected, but at least I saw her get married.

The ceremony was quick, in the town hall. There weren't all that many people there, just their closest friends, and Peter's mother. His father didn't come because he lives in California. Well, I didn't think it was a good reason, but apparently when children leave home in the United States, they stop being their parents' responsibility.

Then they threw a dinner at a restaurant in SoHo. It was a warehouse, with the walls made out of unmasked brick, and all the pipes painted in different colors, and low tables with candles on them. Apparently it was very "in," whatever that means. It was an experience, anyway, and very good for me to see my granddaughter get married.

I liked New York a lot. I couldn't have imagined that a city like that could even exist, and I loved discovering it with Adela. She made me stay in her apartment, which has lovely views over the Hudson. It's small, much too small, and so they're going to live in Peter's apartment, which is a little bigger. But not much bigger. If they have children, they'll have to move out.

Isabel didn't come with me, but I went by myself very happily. You can imagine that everyone in the neighborhood wanted to hear what had happened. Going to New York is for young people, they said, but now that I don't have you anymore, I need to enjoy my granddaughter for as long as I can. Well, the doctor said that I've become years younger since meeting Adela.

I haven't told you about this yet, but when Adela turned up, everyone in the neighborhood wanted to know who her father was and when you would come back. I didn't answer these questions. They asked Isabel as well, because everyone thinks that Adela is Fernando's daughter.

One day we bumped into Don Antonio and his wife. Oh, and they were shameless and stepped out of the way to stop us.

"Oh, Doña Asunción, introduce us to your granddaughter," Mari said, looking me straight in the eye. And I did introduce her, with pride, as there's no other way to introduce a granddaughter like Adela. She was charming, gave Mari a kiss on the cheek, smiled at Don Antonio and behaved like she'd known them all her life.

You know how coarse Don Antonio and Mari are, and so they didn't hesitate, but came right out with it: "Well, it's a real surprise to see you here. We haven't heard any news from your mother for years, but what about your father? Your father's a bit of a mystery."

And I turned pale, but Adela laughed in their faces and replied to them just what they deserved to hear.

"A mystery? Well, maybe it's a mystery for you. I know who my father is. Maybe it's an issue in your family, not knowing who your parents are, but I promise you we all know who our parents are in my family."

Adela's like that. I felt so proud of her. But you can imagine how much they've criticized her now, comparing her to Fernando.

We met Pablo and his wife and children as well. They were coming to see his parents, who still live on our street. He looked like he was going to stop, but I pretended we were in a hurry. That boy always drove you up the wall. Well, he's not a boy anymore: he's bald and he's put on a lot of weight.

Adela has promised to come and see me when she can, but she can't very often because of her work, and I've said I could go to New York. I won't deny it, the journey is a tough one and the time change gets to you, but it's worth going through any trouble to be with my daughter. I'll never be able to thank you enough for having Adela, but I'm just sorry I didn't meet her sooner.

I know I always ask you the same thing, but couldn't you come to see me? I don't think anyone would dare ask you who Adela's father is, but if they did, then you could copy your daughter's answer and keep your head held high.

I also want to tell you that I'm worried about Isabel's health. She looks more and more drawn every day. And I have Adela now, but she doesn't have anyone. You have to convince Fernando to come and see his mother. He'll regret it if he doesn't, because Isabel is very old, as old as I am, and we've got lots of aches and pains. Well, I don't really get you, but that's nothing new, I stopped trying years ago.

All my love,

YOUR MOTHER.

Sara had been right. The critics thought that *Notebook of the Holy Land* was Marvin's best book of poems. From New York to London, from Paris to Jerusalem, from Amsterdam to Berlin to Stockholm to Rome ... the book acquired an instant cult following wherever it appeared. Marvin had reached his apotheosis.

1976 was his year. He was awarded the Nobel Prize.

Catalina took the news with indifference.

"Is he as good as you say he is?" she asked Fernando.

"You know he is. He's behaved like a complete bastard to you, but he's an extraordinary poet."

"Is he going to come to Paris?"

"Yes, Sara's organizing a grand reception."

"And Farida?"

"She'll come with him. She never leaves him. Marvin doesn't go anywhere without her. They delayed coming to Paris because she had to have an operation. You know she's very ill."

"Cancer …"

"And he's sick too … Sara says he's got heart trouble, and his Parkinson's disease is getting worse."

"It must make it difficult for him to write."

"I don't know. I try not to speak to Sara about him, and she tries not to tell me anything more than is absolutely necessary. What are you going to do?"

"What do you mean?"

"I was wondering if you're going to try to see him again."

"I don't know … I'll have to think about it. You'd be very upset if I … well, if I stood up to him again."

"Yes, of course I'd be very upset, but not because it would upset Marvin or even Sara, but because you don't deserve to humiliate yourself in front of him. Adela was right about that."

"So tell me, Fernando, what other point has there been to my life, other than being with you? I've given it all up, Fernando, I've given up the chance of falling in love again, of having a family. I couldn't be with my father when he died, because I didn't want him to be ashamed of me. You know that I didn't go to Madrid back then because I didn't want them to pick on Adela as the daughter of a single mother. And you're asking me to forget about all of that. If I do that, then my life will have had no meaning."

"He won't want to see you, and he's nothing but a sick old man."

"Yes, I know, he won't want to see me, and I don't really want to see him either, but I can't turn back, Fernando, I can't, because then I'd think that all my life had been in vain."

"It'll be difficult for you to get close to him anyway. He's won the Nobel Prize. He's bound to have security around him."

"Yes, I suppose. Don't worry. I'll try to do things as discreetly as possible."

Marvin came to Paris on June 15, 1977, the same day that the first democratic elections were held in Spain. Sara was nervous and worried that things wouldn't run smoothly. He wasn't "her" poet any longer: he'd won the Nobel Prize, and that made him the poet of the entire world.

Catalina and Fernando were nervous as well. They had been listening to the radio and the television all morning.

The elections were taking place peacefully, which was the most important thing to them. Then they heard that the UCD had won, which upset them. Fernando had thought that the Communist Party would win: who else could it be? Catalina didn't agree; she had been following the reports published in the French newspapers and she also didn't really want the communists to win. Fernando had asked her on many occasions to define herself politically for him, and she had tended to say that the only thing she was clear about was that she was not a Franco supporter, but she remembered how scared people had been at the activities of the Popular Front, and so she preferred any choice that had absolutely nothing to do with what she had already been through.

Days later, when they were sitting in front of the television, they saw images of La Pasionaria, Santiago Carrillo, and other communist leaders. Fernando was very moved.

"There would be no democracy without the generosity of the left. Who would have thought that the leaders of the Communist Party, people who have just gotten out of prison or returned from exile, were going to take up seats in Congress ...? But it still seems unfair that they didn't win. You know, it's hard for me to see them talking to people who were part of the regime ... look ... look at these pictures ..." Fernando said, pointing at the television screen.

"I think it's a good idea. It's the only way to get rid of the idea of Two Spains. If they can't speak to one another, what then?" she asked.

"Yes, but it must be hard for them," Fernando said.

"Well, it's the two extremes who need to talk. Come on, don't make that face. What were you expecting?"

"Justice."

"Justice? You know that God writes the future with a crooked pen."

"God's got nothing to do with the elections, Catalina."

"Look, Fernando, either you wipe everything clean, or it will all be how it was before the war started. I don't know about you, but I wouldn't want that to happen in Spain again. We've had enough with forty years of Franco. It's better to try to find spaces where people can understand one another ... There's no way to fix the past."

"But it's not fair that the left didn't win the elections. People are so forgetful."

"We don't know anything about how Spain is, Fernando. We only know how it was. We should respect people who've voted in this way. And I don't really mind Adolfo Suárez. Maybe I'd have voted for him, if I'd been in Spain."

"But you know what he's done ..."

"Clean slate and start again, Fernando. All that I know is that he called for democratic elections and that's why the PSOE and the PCE took part. Look at how young the socialists are. Well, I might have voted for Felipe González, I like him as well."

"You don't have very clear ideas, Catalina."

"That's what you think."

"As if there were no difference between Adolfo Suárez and Felipe González!"

"Yes, but, although I don't know why, I'd have very little problem trusting either of them."

"You can't say one thing and then its opposite, but that's what González and Suárez are," he said.

"Hey, I don't tell you what to think, so maybe you should let me think whatever I want to."

"But you're contradictory, and in politics, you need to have everything clear."

"I am entirely clear. I don't want the Spanish to carry on fighting. I think we have to support each other. I like the fact that Carrillo and Fraga are both in Congress, because that means it's representative of the true Spain."

A few minutes later, Catalina's face changed. Marvin's face filled the screen. "The *Poet of Pain*, accompanied by his faithful companion, the philosopher Farida Rahman, arrived in Paris this afternoon. Marvin Brian will be received by the President of France, and will then go to the Académie, where he will read poems from his new book, *Notebook of the Holy Land*. In other news ..."

"So he's here ..." she said, more to herself than to Fernando.

"He's only going to be here for three days. Sara said that he was almost going to cancel the tour because his heart can't take it. As well as the Parkinson's, he's had two heart attacks. He's traveling with a doctor just in case, but his cardiologist wants to swap out two of the heart valves they put in him several years ago, and he thinks that he should go back to New York as soon as possible."

"I hope he doesn't get too worked up when he sees me," she said emotionlessly.

"You should think about what you're going to do. You're not a child anymore. Marvin has won the Nobel Prize, and if you get close to him, there'll be a great scandal."

"Do you think I'd lose my job? They pay me a pittance and I'm about to retire. If they fire me I'll find another job: they always need people to clean houses."

"Don't be stupid! And I think that if you make that much of a fuss, then they won't even hire you to clean houses."

"I'm sure I'll find a way to earn my living. Let's stop thinking about Marvin for a minute. Go on, change the channel, maybe there'll be more information about the elections in Spain."

17

The *New York Times*, the *New Yorker*, *The Washington Post*, the *Boston Globe* ... All these papers, and many others, reported the "attack" that the Nobel Laurate Marvin Brian had suffered.

Adela read the press release, feeling as angry as she did ashamed.

> Marvin Brian, this year's Nobel Laureate, was the object of an attempted attack in Paris. Brian was leaving the Académie Française after giving a reading when a woman came up to him and tried to force him to speak with her. The woman, who broke through the security surrounding Mr. Brian, took him by the arm and shook him so that he would pay attention to her. They were separated immediately.
>
> The assailant allegedly suffers from a personality disorder.
>
> The police held her for several hours, but released her without charge. She does not seem to suffer from any condition apart from an obsession with the Nobel Laureate.
>
> Sources indicate that this is the same woman who has tried to approach Brian on various previous occasions.

She's done it again, Adela thought. Yes. Her mother had stood in front of Marvin and tried to get him to acknowledge her as his daughter. She didn't want her to do this. Even if Marvin were willing to acknowledge her, she would still reject him. She didn't need him as her father, and felt nothing for him, absolutely nothing.

She was tempted to call her mother, but she held back. If she did, then it would be to break things off with her forever. She couldn't cope with her mother exposing herself to any more ridicule, especially not in her daughter's name.

She didn't understand how her mother failed to grasp that the best thing she could do for her would be to stop insisting that she forge a connection with a father she didn't want.

She also wondered why Fernando didn't stop her mother from making a fool of herself. He had never done so.

The telephone made her start. Peter's voice brought her back to reality.

"Did you read it?" he asked.

"Yes," she said bluntly.

"I'm sorry, I know that these things affect you. At least no one puts you and her together."

She was annoyed at the comment, although she knew that Peter meant well.

"I don't care," she said.

"Are you going to call her?" he asked.

"No, because then we'd argue, and that would only make things worse. And my mother is deaf to anything I might say on the issue."

"Talk to your grandmother. Maybe she can get her to see sense."

"No, my grandmother's too old to get upset over something like this. And it won't be any use, I told you already. Well, I'll let you go. I've got work to do."

She drained her coffee and tried to calm down. She had to write up an interview she'd done the other day with a famous dramatist. She thought he was boring, but he was fashionable, and her boss had told her to do it. She knew that he might turn up at any moment to get the interview.

It was later that she got the call from Fernando. She was about to hang up on him, but she loved him too much to do this to him, even though she blamed him to some degree for not being able to control Catalina.

"You'll have heard already," Fernando said by way of greeting.

"Yes, it's been in all the major newspapers in the States, and I guess it's the same in Europe as well," Adela admitted.

"Yes, that's how it's been."

"Couldn't you have stopped her?"

"No, and I didn't even think about trying to. Your mother has the right to do whatever she wants," Fernando said bluntly.

"And what about me? Doesn't she care how this might affect me?"

"Everything she's done, she's done for you."

"I'm going to be thirty-six, and I should be able to decide if I want my mother to do what she's doing for me."

"She thinks it's only fair for Marvin to acknowledge you."

"I don't want him to be my father. I never wanted him to be."

"But he is, Adela. You can't choose your parents."

"My grandmother is proud of me, and she doesn't care that my mother brought me into the world when she wasn't married. I don't know what things were like when you left Spain, but now no one cares what their neighbors do, and if they do care, then it doesn't matter."

"I know that's what you say, but it doesn't stop your mother from wanting to get Marvin to make amends for what he did."

"And what did he do?"

"She was a girl who fell in love and he took advantage of her. Although it might be hard for you to believe, we grew up in a society where young women were very innocent and your mother was one of the most innocent of them all."

"If you say so ..."

"Of course I say so. I called you because I thought that the news would have upset you, and also ... Well, maybe it's time for you to step in."

"Me? You know that my mother won't listen to me."

"No, but maybe Marvin will."

"Marvin? Are you crazy? Every time he saw me and my mother together, he ran off screaming. As the years have gone by, it's clear that he doesn't want anything to do with me, and I don't want anything to do with him either."

"It was just an idea ... maybe it's not a good idea, but I couldn't think of anything else that might put an end to this situation."

"Well, I can think of something else: my mother could stop making a fool of herself. It's the best choice. Tell her from me."

Scarcely had she hung up when she saw her boss coming to her desk.

"Have you got the interview?"

"I'm on it."

"Well, in the morning meeting, we thought that we needed to interview Marvin Brian, and find out more about this woman who's spent years following him around. You're on it."

"You know that Marvin Brian doesn't give interviews, and as for this incident in Paris, I don't think it means anything."

Her stomach was hurting. She tried to keep looking at her boss; he seemed to be studying her carefully. She felt herself blushing.

"What's up?" he asked, looking at her suspiciously.

"Nothing. Why?"

"It's like you're upset to be given this interview. Look, it doesn't have to be tomorrow. Marvin Brian is coming to New York tomorrow, and then they're taking him straight to the Mount Sinai Hospital. His heart's very weak. Maybe they'll operate on him as soon as he gets here, who knows. I want you to stick to him like glue, find out what he's doing, where he's going, what he's going to do, and find the best moment to interview him. As for the madwoman who's running around after him, find out what you can. I've asked our Paris correspondent to send us everything he can about her. It'll be a great story."

She felt herself growing dizzy. She felt like a fly trapped in honey. Maybe she ought to explain to her boss that she knew all too well who this woman was and why she was following the *Poet of Pain* around. But if she did so, then he would force her to write the story, and even make her appear in a photo or two. She could see the headline: "Daughter of Paris Madwoman tells all. Mother says that she is Marvin Brian's daughter." She'd become a laughingstock, and even Peter would feel ashamed of her. She started to shudder and ran to the bathroom. The coffee she had just drunk was fighting to escape her stomach.

When she called Peter later to tell him what had happened, she could tell that he was annoyed.

"Look, you've got to sort this out, or you'll end up in all the papers, starting with your own, and I don't want to imagine what my bosses will ask me to do ... They'll think it's great that my own wife is the daughter of a Nobel Prizewinner, according to a madwoman."

"Don't you dare call my mother mad!"

"Of course she is!"

"You know very well that Marvin Brian lived in Madrid, and that my mother had a fling with him, and that I was what came of it, and that he's never wanted to have anything to do with me."

"That's what your mother says, of course."

"How dare you!"

"Look, the only thing I know is that your mother's crazy behavior is going to end up hurting us: you and me both. She's my mother-in-law. I've got a mad mother-in-law! Marvin Brian, as well as winning the Nobel Prize, is one of the best poets in English, known all over the world, living a perfect life with his faithful companion Farida Rahman, a respected philosopher ... That's all I know. And, well, I'll say something that I've never said before, but maybe I should put it out there: you don't look anything like him."

She felt Peter's words like blows. He didn't know it, but he had just ended their marriage. She didn't trust him anymore, could never trust him again. He looked down on her just as he looked down on her mother.

To say those things ... that she didn't look like her father ... that her mother was crazy ... that they were going to be affected. She suddenly felt more alone than she had ever felt before.

She left the office. She hadn't finished the interview with the dramatist, but she didn't care if her boss got angry, or if he fired her. She needed to put her thoughts in order. She needed to process what Peter had said.

She went to Central Park. It was sticky and hot, as it was in New York every summer. She sat on a bench and let herself cry.

When she got back to the office, she had already made some decisions, all of them difficult and some possibly mistaken, but at least she knew what she had to do.

Her boss came over to her desk shouting.

"Where do you think you work? This is a newspaper! You left without handing in the interview!"

"You'll have it in five minutes. Don't expect it to be great literature, because this dramatist is a real idiot. Oh, and as for what you asked me to do with regards to Marvin Brian, I'll do it. It won't be easy, but I'll do it, but you need to give me time and let me do it my way. And above all, don't ask me questions. You'll get your story, I promise."

Marvin's operation was a success, or at least that's what the hospital spokesman said. They had changed two of the valves in his heart, and his cardiologist recommended that he take a good long time to rest.

His editor, Sara Rosent, released a statement saying that Marvin Brian was going to suspend all his engagements until such time as he was fully recovered.

The statement was a short one, and Sara Rosent refused to answer any more questions.

Adela had gone to the press conference. They caught sight of one another. She knew that Sara had recognized her. As the rest of her colleagues left, she walked over to Sara.

"I'm ..."

Sara raised her hand to stop her talking.

"I know who you are. I know you're a journalist as well. Fernando has kept me up to date with everything he hears about you. He loves you like a daughter. I remember you from when you were a girl. You used to come with your mother to the bookshop."

"I need to speak to you. Please."

Adela's tone of despair made Sara pause. But Adela insisted.

"Please. I promise you I won't keep you very long."

"All right ... come and see me at five o'clock at the Hotel Pierre. Look for me in the bar. I'll be waiting for you."

"Thank you."

They parted without saying anything else.

At five o'clock sharp, Adela walked into the bar of the Hotel Pierre. She cast a quick glance around to get a feel for the place and the people who were there. There were some elderly couples drinking cocktails, businessmen, a group of middle-aged ladies and there, in a corner, Sara Rosent.

Adela had always admired Sara, for her elegance, her calm gestures, the way her face showed her love for her fellow man.

"Thank you for agreeing to talk to me."

"Sit down. What would you like to drink?"

"Nothing ... Maybe some mineral water ..."

"I'm drinking water as well. I'll ask the waiter."

While the waiter poured her glass of water with the same care as though it had been champagne, Adela turned over in her mind what she wanted to say to Sara.

"I am sorry that my mother constantly harasses Marvin Brian. Not because I feel much sympathy for him, but because of the harm it does my mother."

"I see you've decided to be direct, without caring all that much about the fact that I am very fond of Marvin," Sara said, annoyed.

"Mrs. Rosent ... Sorry, I mean Mrs. Wilson ..."

"You can call me Sara. Rosent is my surname, Wilson was my husband's surname, but we'll understand one another better if we stick to first names."

"I'm desperate. I've tried to get my mother to give up her obsession with Marvin for years. I don't care whether or not he's my father, or that he doesn't want anything to do with me. I haven't got any father apart from Fernando, who I love; he has made himself my father. And so I have to make it clear that I don't want anything from Marvin Brian, and even if he did decide to acknowledge me, then I would reject him."

Sara looked at her curiously, weighing up how emotion and truth were balanced in what Adela was saying.

"So, what is it you want?"

"I think that if Marvin met just once with my mother and said what he thinks he has to say to her, then she would accept it and stop trying to get him to acknowledge me. But all these years he has run away from her, he has ... well, in my opinion, he has mistreated and humiliated her when it would have been much easier for them to resolve their differences over the course of a single conversation. He's not the first man, and he won't be the last, to refuse to acknowledge paternity of one of his children."

"You know that Marvin Brian's not in very good health," Sara said, looking directly in Adela's eyes.

"I know, and I also know that this isn't the best moment for it, but maybe you could convince him that when he is better, he could speak to my mother and they could sort out this problem once and for all. Look, they don't know at my newspaper that I'm ... who I am ... I've always used my mother's second surname, Blanco, and changed it into White occasionally, and now I use Brown, my husband's name. My boss has told me that I have to interview Marvin. But not only that, he's told me to find out why a Spanish woman has spent years following him around. You can imagine how I feel."

Adela wrung her hands nervously, and there was tension in every line of her face.

"And what are you going to do?"

"As far as my mother's story is concerned, I'm going to tell lies, and as far as the interview with Marvin is concerned, I'm going to ask you to help me fix it up. I even thought that I could tell my boss that Marvin had only given me the interview on the condition that I didn't ask about the Spanish woman who's been following him around, because that would only give her the oxygen of publicity. But if I get at least a part of what my boss ordered, then it should be enough."

"So, you're asking me to get Marvin to agree to an interview with you and also sit down and speak with your mother? Well, you know what you want, I guess!"

"I know that I'm asking a lot of you, but I don't have any other choice. I don't want to become a story in the newspaper, and I don't want my colleagues to hound my mother, trying to get her to admit that she had a one-night stand with an American thirty-five years ago, and I don't want Marvin to mark my life and ruin it like he has ruined hers. She's got very nineteenth-century ideas about certain things, though she can be surprisingly modern as far as others are concerned. You can't imagine what Spain was like in the 1940s. A single woman, a single mother, would be pointed out and scorned. No one would marry her, they'd think she was easy, and her family would suffer the consequences as well. My mother ran away to avoid the consequences for her parents and for herself. She also thought she was in love with Marvin, but now … well, I don't think she feels anything for him. I think she doesn't know as much yet, but the person she really loves is Fernando. It's a love that's built up without their being aware of it. He … well, I think he's still in love with my mother, although Zahra was very important for him. My mother and Fernando have something strong between them, something that can never be broken."

"Yes, they have an absolute love, although your mother is obsessed with Marvin."

"Will you help me?"

Sara said nothing. She took a sip of water and looked aside for a few seconds, avoiding Adela's eyes. She was trying to reach a decision.

"If Marvin gives you the interview, will you ask him about your mother?"

"No, I won't. I swear. I will only ask him about his poems, about his literary career, about how pain is the source of his inspiration. I won't upset him by talking about my mother."

"I can't promise anything. I'll think about it, and if I decide to help you that doesn't mean that it will happen: it's still a decision that Marvin and Farida have to make. He doesn't agree to anything without Farida agreeing as well. Maybe I should speak to her first of all."

"When can you tell me something?"

"I'll call you. Give me your number. I don't know when."

"Please!"

"I understand your concern. I'll call you, and now, if you'll excuse me, I need to go upstairs and change. I'm going to eat with Marvin and Farida this evening. When I call you, who should I ask for: Adela Blanco, Adela White, or Adela Brown?"

"Ask for Adela, that should be enough. If they ask for a surname, use Brown."

Adela was unable to sleep that night. Her hand slid over to the empty side of the bed. Peter and she had decided to take a break. She felt that he didn't understand her, and he admitted as much.

Peter had blamed her for feeling upset when he questioned Catalina's behavior, given that he was sick of hearing her say much the same things about her mother. "You let yourself criticize your mother, but you get upset when other people do it. It's irrational, and a part of your Spanish blood. If there's one thing that I can be sure about with Spaniards, it's that they are very good at being irrational."

She had decided to leave the apartment they shared and rent a small one in SoHo. It was tiny, but she didn't care.

She didn't hear anything back from Sara until the end of September. She had told Fernando that she had spoken to Sara and he had said that sooner or later Sara would call her back. Meanwhile, the summer had served as an excuse for her boss to put less pressure on her. Well, the summer and his divorce, because his wife had left him and taken their three children away with her, which had led him to suffer attacks of anxiety that ended in a heart attack. Adela wasn't enjoying the man's personal tragedy, but it was very convenient for her.

She got back to her studio and made herself a sandwich while she sat down to write an article on Constructivist Art due the next morning. She picked up the telephone on its first ring.

"It's Sara Rosent. You can go to Marvin Brian's house tomorrow at two o'clock. Farida will see you. Talk to her first. Good luck."

"Mrs. Wilson … Sara … thank you. Thank you very much."

"Now it all depends on you."

Sara hung up without giving her a chance to say anything else. Adela called Fernando.

"Sara just called me."

"I know. She said she'd call you. You have to know that it was very difficult for her to get them to meet with you, and her friendship with Marvin and Farida has been at the breaking point on several occasions. Play your cards right, Adela, you owe it to Sara."

"I will. What about my mother?"

"She's sad. No one has wanted to hire her since she got fired from the music academy. She doesn't know it yet, but I spoke to Monsieur Dufort this morning."

"Our dear landlord."

"Yes, Phillipe Dufort is a good man, and Doriane, his wife, is a good woman. I've asked them to look out for a job for your mother, which is hard because she's nearly at retirement age. And we might be about to go back to Madrid."

"Madrid!"

"Yes, it's not certain yet. But the Government looks like it's taking things seriously."

"That would be wonderful. How happy the grandmothers will be! You know what, Fernando, I've never understood why you hurt your mothers so much; they don't deserve it."

"No, you don't understand, because you can't understand."

"Because you never wanted to explain it to me."

"You're right. I never wanted to, and I still don't want to. But if certain things change, then we might go back to Spain."

"I'd like to come with you."

"Concentrate on the interview with Marvin."

"Yes, I'll do that. Can you keep this a secret for me and don't tell my mother anything about the interview? She's perfectly capable of turning up in New York."

"You're not going to speak with her?"

"No, I'm still not ready to ... We'd argue. I need some time."

Marvin Brian lived in a luxurious apartment facing Central Park. Adela was trembling when a maid opened the door and invited her in.

"Madame is waiting for you."

Farida had the majestic bearing of a woman who had once been a real beauty, but more than her features, it was her personality that was truly striking.

She was sitting behind a rosewood writing desk. She looked up at Adela, then stood and came over to her.

"Welcome."

"Thank you ... I ... I'm very grateful that you've agreed to meet me."

"It's difficult to deny anything to Sara. You must have been very convincing, because she stood up to Marvin until he finally agreed to meet you."

"I ... well ... I'm sorry that you've argued because of me. I hope that you understand that the situation isn't easy for me either."

"No, it isn't. I remember you as a child, holding your mother's hand, your eyes very wide and filled with fear and shame. I always felt sorry for your situation. Well, our lawyer will be here in a few minutes. You have to sign a document that guarantees that everything you talk about this afternoon will be confidential. You will never be able to publish it, never, and if you do, then you'll need to rob a bank to pay the legal fees. Our lawyer is very thorough and has put together a document that leaves no loophole whatsoever for you to interpret your agreement here."

"I promise you I have no intention of causing anyone any pain."

"But for our peace of mind, it's better if you confirm that in writing."

The maid knocked gently at the door before coming in. A tall, pleasant-looking man with a briefcase in one hand came into the room.

"My dear ..."

"Jim, this is Mrs. Brown. I hope you've put all her aliases down in the document."

"Don't worry, it's just like we discussed. Mrs. Brown, please read this document carefully and if you agree to it all, then sign it."

Adela didn't dare argue with them. She hadn't expected something like this to happen, but she was ready to sign anything if it would help her untie the knot that was strangling her life and her mother's.

Once she had read it, she took a pen out of her bag and signed it.

"All right, so you accept all the terms. You've accepted a lot, Mrs. Brown," the lawyer said.

She nodded, and smiled. Then the lawyer gave Farida a kiss on the cheek and left the room.

"You want to know about the piece of his life that doesn't fit. Sit down and listen, and when I've finished speaking, then you'll learn who Marvin really is. You won't be with him for more than a few minutes. He's not really in any state to answer questions. But I'm sure that you'll be able to compose a few and he'll provide written answers to them. I'll get them to you."

"All right," Adela said.

"Do you smoke?"

"No ... I've never smoked ... well, when I was younger in Paris, I smoked in secret."

"You should never hide something that is pleasurable. If you don't mind, I'll smoke. It's one of the pleasures that I'm not going to give up, in spite of the fact that the doctor has forbidden it. Breast cancer. I've been operated on twice and it's come back again. If I'm speaking freely, it's because you can't use a single word of what I say here."

"Yes, I know what I just signed."

"You'll also know that neither Marvin nor I have much time left. I'm older than him; I'm past seventy-five. I'll tell you everything you want to know. First of all, Marvin is not your father."

Adela couldn't help but frown, surprised at how clear and firm Farida's assertion was.

"I'll tell you why. Marvin was a young poet who came to Spain shortly before the start of the Civil War. This wasn't because he cared about what was happening in the country, but rather because he loved the literature of the place: Cervantes, Quevedo, Lope de Vega, Góngora ... But the war broke out and he decided to stay. A friend asked him to work as an interpreter for some American journalists. He accepted. He was keen on new experiences, and a war was an experience that he knew would leave its mark on him, make him a better poet. I'm not going to bore you with details. One day, when he had to take a journalist to the front, he was wounded. This happened in spite of the efforts to protect him made by a young soldier, Eulogio Jiménez, who saved his life and was left crippled in return. Marvin was wounded in the genitals. He had to undergo an emergency operation, and lost a part of his genitalia, which stopped him from having any sexual relations for the rest of his life."

"You can give me a cigarette now," Adela almost begged.

"Of course." And Farida held out the packet.

"I'm sorry, but I don't understand ..."

"Yes, you've completely understood. Marvin cannot have sexual relations."

"And Eulogio ... Did he know this?"

"Of course. He saved his life, dragged him back from the front line. Eulogio was infatuated with Marvin, but his real love was Fernando. Marvin was exotic, American, blond, with blue eyes, handsome, a poet. He had all that was needed for a sensitive man like Eulogio to fall in love with him."

"But ... he ... he never told Fernando, about Marvin, I mean ... and he didn't tell my mother." Adela tried to hide her despair.

"No, he didn't. Marvin made him swear never to tell anyone. Eulogio kept his word."

"Who else knew that Marvin ...?"

"The doctor who operated on him at the front, and no one else. And the doctor can't tell anyone because the next day, he was hit by a mortar shell while sewing someone up."

"But I can't believe what you just said ... Fernando found my mother lying on the floor in Marvin's arms. Fernando doesn't lie."

"You're right. Fernando found your mother in Marvin's arms. She was semi-conscious. She had been assaulted. She had just been raped."

"My God!"

"But it wasn't Marvin. He couldn't have done anything, even if he had wanted to."

"So ..."

"Marvin heard her shouting. He had drunk too much, which was what he did back then. It wasn't easy for him to be among young men and know that he was mutilated forever, that he would never be able to have a woman. He was throwing up when he heard shouts. He stumbled over to where they lay. A young man was on top of your mother. He had ripped her stockings and her skirt ... her underwear was pulled down ... you can imagine the scene. The young man who was raping your mother didn't realize that Marvin was there, but when he heard him say 'What the hell are you doing?' he got up and ran. Marvin went over to your mother and was trying to help her when Fernando arrived."

"It can't be!"

"That's what happened."

944

"And the other man ... the one ... the one who raped my mother?"

"You'll have to find the answer to that in Madrid."

"In Madrid? But why?"

"Marvin thinks he knows who it was, but it was dark, night was falling, and he never said anything for fear of accusing an innocent man. There are two hypotheses. The first is that your mother was flirting with this man and then let him have his way to a certain extent, but got scared and told him to stop it when he was going too far. The other hypothesis is that this young man decided to take advantage of your mother and didn't give her a chance to say no because he jumped on her and assaulted her right from the start. That's what we think happened."

"But my mother is sure that ..."

"For a long time, Marvin was sure that your mother was falsely accusing him. You don't know how many times we've sat down to talk about what happened that night. And with time, we came to the conclusion that your mother hadn't gotten over what happened. We even asked a good friend of ours who is a psychiatrist; he explained that if something traumatic happens, then many people refuse to acknowledge it."

"My mother isn't a liar," Adela said, trying to hold back her anger.

"I haven't said that she is, I'm saying that she was in a state of shock. She lost her bearings. Her brain refused to acknowledge the rapist. Any psychiatrist will tell you that when someone suffers a traumatic shock, the way for them to survive is to erase what happened. She only remembered that she was in Marvin's arms, and that calmed her down. When later on she found out that she was pregnant, she thought that what had happened – the thing she kept hidden in the secret part of her brain – could only have happened with Marvin."

"But why didn't Marvin say anything? Why didn't he tell my mother what happened that night ..."

"Because he would have had to explain that he was incapable of having sexual relations. That his genitals were mutilated. And he wasn't prepared to share that information with anyone. After he was wounded at the front, his parents did all they could to bring him across to the United States. They operated on him again. But they couldn't give him back the manhood he had lost. As a result of his wounds, he has had to live with pain and a certain degree of ... difficulty. It's his secret, and he doesn't want to share it with anyone. And that's his right."

"Eulogio, did he know what happened that night?"

"Yes, Marvin told him what had happened and who he thought had raped Catalina."

"But Eulogio said nothing, not to Fernando, not to my mother."

"Eulogio was absolutely loyal to Marvin, and you know that."

"But he could have said something to Fernando ... they'd have found the rapist and forced him to confess."

"Yes, that's what they should have done, but they didn't."

"And why did he let my mother chase him around all those years? Why didn't he tell her what he knew?" Adela insisted.

"I've told you already, because he would have had to admit that he had been injured in that way, and no one has the duty to confess something so intimate, something that has caused him immense suffering. It was not easy for Marvin to live, knowing that he was mutilated."

"I'm confused ... I don't know what to think ... I can't believe it."

"It's the truth," Farida said calmly.

"My mother ..."

"Your mother knows who raped her."

"You just said that my mother was traumatized, in a state of shock!"

"She knows it without knowing, she has the truth hidden in the deepest part of her brain. She needs to speak to a good psychiatrist."

"Could you give me another cigarette?"

Farida passed one over. Adela lit up, and drew the smoke down into her lungs.

"The rapist is one of the young men in the group who went to the Pradera de San Isidro. You know who it is; Marvin told you," Adela said, looking firmly at Farida.

"Marvin has told me who he thinks it was. He's pretty certain."

"Tell me, please."

"If you want to know the truth, you'll have to go to Madrid."

"Please tell me … please …"

And Farida spoke a name, which made tears start to flow down Adela's face.

"You have no choice but to go to Madrid and find proof. You can never use Marvin's name, and you can never tell Fernando or your mother what you have heard this evening."

"I know." There was a hint of despair in her voice.

"And now I'll take you through to see Marvin. A few minutes, and nothing that might upset him. Write me down the questions you're going to ask. I'll make sure you get the answers tomorrow."

Marvin Brian was sitting on a dark green leather chair with his head on the headrest and his eyes half closed. He opened them and looked first at Farida and then at Adela. Farida nodded to him and he nodded back.

"Adela Vilamar," he said, looking fixedly at her.

"Yes."

"Do you have the answer you were looking for?"

"Yes."

"I hope you know how to be discreet."

"Yes, I do, there's no need for you to worry. I'll be discreet not just because of the paper I've had to sign, but also because I want my mother to suffer as little as possible."

"You can't stop her from suffering. Catalina has no choice but to face up to reality."

She was about to say that he was guilty of at least a part of her mother's suffering, and that it was his fault that she had spent her life chasing after him, and that it was down to him that she was getting divorced from Peter, and that Fernando's life was still unused, untasted. His silence had saved himself, but wounded many others. But she didn't say so.

"Is there anything else I can do for you?" he said indifferently.

"No thank you, Mr. Brian. Thank you for the interview."

"I am not your enemy, Adela. But I am not your father, either."

"I'm not your enemy either, Mr. Brian, and let me assure you that I never wanted you for a father."

"Good afternoon, Adela."

"Good afternoon, Mr. Brian."

Farida led her to the door.

"Your last trip before finding the whole truth," Farida said.

"Thank you for allowing this interview."

"Thank Sara Rosent. Marvin owes everything to the Rosents, and this is the only thing that Sara has asked in return her whole life. It was a real wrench for Marvin to accept that you would know what had happened, and especially the consequences of the wounds he received at the front during the Spanish war."

"I understand. I'm a stranger to you all."

"Good luck, Adela."

They shook hands. In spite of all that separated them, they couldn't help feeling sympathy for one another.

The next day, when she got into the office, she found a letter-sized envelope on her desk. She knew that it contained Marvin's answers to her questions. They were typed, and very long.

Her boss had to admit that all her effort had been worthwhile. He also said that he had received a phone call the previous day from the owners of the newspaper saying that Mr. Brian would be most upset if they published anything about the woman who had appeared at his public events on several occasions. And, given that he had been kind enough to grant an exclusive interview to one of the paper's journalists, he hoped that the newspaper wouldn't go into any potentially scandalous detail about this woman and himself.

"And so, for the time being, we're not going to write anything else about that Spaniard ... I tried to convince the high-ups that there has to be a juicy story here somewhere. But they're the bosses ... So, forget about her, at least for the time being."

She called Sara to say thank you, but Sara barely gave her a chance to speak. "I hope it was worth it," was all she said.

The interview was a great success. It was years since Marvin Brian had given an interview: he hadn't even given one when he was awarded the Nobel Prize. This was not just because of how sick he was, but because the passing of the years seemed to have solidified his misanthropy.

Peter called her to congratulate her and to try to get them to celebrate together, but Adela could think of nothing but the task ahead of her, and that task did not involve Peter.

A friend at the office gave her the phone number of a psychiatrist, telling her that he was the best psychiatrist in Manhattan. "You'll love him."

The psychiatrist was very much in demand, and his waiting room was filled with stressed businessmen. In spite of the personal recommendation, there was no way for him to offer her an appointment until ten days later. Those ten days seemed like an eternity to Adela. But she didn't want to go to Madrid until she had spoken to an expert in the human soul: in the end, she thought, that's what a psychiatrist is.

Dr. Ward was a young man, about forty years old and quite attractive, which explained her friend's enthusiasm. The question was whether he was competent as well as handsome.

Adela told him that she wanted to present him with a hypothetical case for him to pass clinical judgment on. He didn't seem very enthusiastic, but in the end accepted.

She asked him what reactions one might expect in a woman who had been raped. Dr. Ward looked at her worriedly.

"Traumas are difficult to handle. When a person suffers from a traumatic experience, it can set a defense mechanism in action which blocks out the trauma. Any type of traumatic event can cause an alteration in one's thought and behavior, as well as cause harm to the unconscious. It is completely possible that someone who has been raped might suffer gaps in his or her memory, and might block out reality. In these cases, therapy would be used to help the individual go back to the moment of the trauma and then confront it in order to be able to overcome it."

"Can it be the case that someone who is traumatized doesn't acknowledge reality?"

"It's as I've just said: there can be a disconnection between the subject and the traumatic event. Sometimes they experience delayed reactions."

Dr. Ward tried to get Adela to say if she had been the victim of a rape. "In that case, you would need help. You shouldn't have to deal with this yourself. Many women blame themselves for what happened. Sometimes they never become intimate with men ever again."

Adela nodded. Dr. Ward was right. Her mother had never slept with a man since that night. She lived with Fernando as though they were brother and sister. She had found it difficult to accept because when she was a little girl, she had thought that Fernando was her father, but now she understood. There were no men in her mother's life.

Dr. Ward also explained to her that science had not yet found a way to confirm paternity. The proofs that could be gathered were not conclusive.

"You need to take a blood sample. It's called the RH test, but it can only be used to show that someone is not the parent of an individual, rather than confirm that he is."

18

"We can go to Madrid," said Catalina, looking intently at Fernando, checking his reaction.

It was a Sunday, and they had gone for breakfast to a place close to the Louvre, in order to go into the Museum afterwards and see an exhibition. Fernando had been behaving oddly during the past few days.

She knew him well enough to know that there was something in his mind that he was not sharing with her. She imagined it was probably connected with Sara, perhaps she was ill. She decided to insist on traveling to Madrid.

"Why aren't you saying anything?"

He looked in her direction with renewed interest. They had been discussing the same thing for days.

"Not yet, we need to wait and see if it is true that they're going to pass the Amnesty Law. I'm sure you've heard on the radio that they're still negotiating it."

"They'll pass it."

"We'll see."

"We should let our mothers know that we are considering coming back. We can't just turn up without letting them know."

"Why don't you go first? If they pass the Law, I'll come afterwards."

"We've already talked about this, and you know that I won't leave Paris without you. You're still afraid."

"Of course I am. I wouldn't like to be arrested at the border. Imagine the irony, to end up in jail while all those who took up arms against our country and choked it for all these years are now becoming respectable people."

"No one will put you in jail, Fernando. In all these years, no one has come looking for you, or has demanded that you be arrested and sent back to Spain. In Alexandria, we went to the consulate to renew our passports, and no one asked us anything. We've renewed them in Paris too. If there was some kind of warrant out for you, they would've tried to keep you there, and me as well. After all, I am your accomplice. I gave you my uncle's weapon. You need to let go of what you did."

"Let go? You know that's impossible, that I have never forgotten those two men."

"Do you regret what you did?" asked Catalina, lowering her eyes to give him a chance to form his answer.

"No, I don't. And that is even worse than what I did."

"If you don't regret it, don't think any more about it. I don't regret having given you the gun, either."

"But you didn't pull the trigger."

"Who cares? It doesn't matter either way. I gave you a gun to kill because I agreed with your actions. That makes me your accomplice," insisted Catalina.

"I would prefer not to be worried, but I am."

"We ought to risk it, Fernando, we need to go back. Our mothers are too old now, and if they die without us having given them one last kiss, we will regret it for the rest of our lives."

"Adela is in Madrid."

"Is she now? And when did she tell you?"

"A few days ago. She and Peter were having problems."

"And she has found refuge with her grandmother."

"Your mother and Adela are good friends now."

"Tell me, Fernando, what's the matter? And please don't say it's nothing. You are sad, I know. I know that something is the matter."

Fernando simply kissed the back of her hand.

"Finish the croissant and let's go into the Louvre," was all he said.

19

Madrid

Adela had gotten up early. After making breakfast, she placed it on a tray – along with a single flower – and took it to her grandmother's bedroom.

Asunción had a cold, and Catalina had insisted that she stay in bed a little longer, but nonetheless she found her grandmother up and about, sticking the last hairpins into her bun.

"I wanted to surprise you!" Adela protested.

She had been in Madrid for a few days. And it hadn't been easy for her to talk to her grandmother. She had been as honest as possible. She had to find her mother's rapist, but without telling her grandmother everything she knew, and definitely without telling her that Marvin Brian was not her father.

But Asunción was too sensitive not to realize that her granddaughter needed some help, so she had answered all her questions without asking any in return.

"Today we'll have the day to ourselves. I made a reservation at La Taberna del Alabardero, that restaurant that you and Isabel are so keen to visit. But let's go for a walk first. Is that a good idea?"

"You've forgotten the main event … Mass. It's Sunday. Isabel and I always go to noon Mass."

"I know… Let's see, I'll come with you to San Ginés, and then I'll meet you at the end of the service. We can go for lunch, and afterwards come back here. It's getting cold in the early evening these days."

"I only have a tiny little cold, and it's not chilly at all, it's only

October. But I am very thankful for all the care you take of me."

Asunción extended her hand towards her granddaughter, who bent down to hug her grandmother. She was surprised by how much she loved this woman, given that they had only recently met. She wondered why her own mother was so little like her. Her grandmother had told her that Catalina had the same personality as her father. "Ernesto was a good man, but very stubborn. It was impossible to make him change his mind," she was fond of saying when talking about her husband.

Isabel arrived at half past eleven. They walked slowly to San Ginés, and maybe because it was starting to rain, or perhaps because her grandmother was grasping her arm firmly, she ended up going into the church and staying for Mass. To tell the truth, she didn't pay attention to anything the priest said, but she found comfort in the litany of the prayers muttered by the believers.

Once Mass ended, they saw that it wasn't raining anymore, which allowed them to take a short walk around the Plaza de Oriente before going into La Taberna del Alabardero.

"This restaurant belongs to a rather peculiar priest. He is called Luis Lezama, and, if the rumors are true, he helped a lot of youngsters get clean and abandon a life of petty crime; he became the protector of the illegal bullfighters looking for a second chance, and opened this restaurant to help his 'boys,'" explained Isabel.

"But I've also heard rumors that he's a socialist, a 'red,' even if he was the assistant of Cardinal Tarancón, who was also peculiar in his own way… But what I think Father Lezama does is take the New Testament seriously," added Asunción.

Adela was listening carefully. They sounded thrilled to eat at that particular restaurant, so close to their homes, owned by a priest. She herself had to admit that having a priest as a restaurant owner wasn't usual. They ate while talking of everything and nothing, and then they had the chance to meet the priest.

He had a medium build, quick step, and vivid eyes, and he entered the place with some gentlemen that Asunción recognized.

"Goodness! All those men with him are writers, and very famous ones as well."

The priest heard her words and came to their table to greet the ladies.

His hello only lasted a few seconds, but Isabel and Asunción were very taken with the priest's manners and worldliness.

Asunción said she did not want anything for dessert, and Isabel said the same, but a waiter left a tray with a selection of sweets on the table, and they couldn't resist.

Once the meal was over and Adela asked for the bill, they were surprised to see that they had not been charged for dessert.

The priest would never know it, but from that moment on, Asunción became one of his most fervent admirers, capable of showing her claws if someone attacked the "red priest."

They spent the rest of the afternoon talking to each other and watching television. Isabel spent some time with them, but eventually she decided to go back to her house.

"She's very lonely," said Asunción.

"I know, and I feel sorry for her. I've grown fond of her."

"She is a very good person, and... I'm sorry, but I cannot understand Fernando. Although to tell you the truth, I don't understand Catalina either..."

"Grandmother, I cannot understand them either."

On Monday, Adela got up early, and she needed a while to get ready. She was worried. What she was about to do could go catastrophically wrong. But she owed it to her mother, and to herself. It was time to break the wheel. She insisted in staying in and tidying the apartment while her grandmother went out to make the most of the autumn sun, trying to buy bread and coffee, though the shop didn't have any coffee. Afterwards, when the old lady returned, Adela got ready to leave.

Her grandmother didn't ask her where she was going. She didn't want to force her to answer.

Adela walked along, mentally organizing the torrent of words that she knew she would have to say. She hesitated for a second, but eventually she stopped a taxi, giving him the address of the place where she hoped to find the answer to what had happened to her mother thirty-five years ago.

The hospital was near the city center. She entered the lobby and looked for someone she could ask for directions. She found an energetic-looking nurse.

"Turn right and follow the hallway to the elevator. Go up to the third floor; you'll find her there."

Adela didn't doubt it. When she came out of the elevator, she looked for another nurse to help her find Sister Dolores.

"I think she's in charge of the infirmary, at the end of the floor."

She walked briskly to the information desk where she stood for a few seconds, looking at a team of nurses who were taking instructions from a nun.

The nun was more or less her own age. Ample forehead, prominent nose, brown eyes, slim. The only thing remarkable in her appearance was her smile. Every time she talked to any of the women, she smiled. She also looked in control.

Perhaps it was due to Adela's insistent stare, but Sister Dolores turned to look at her.

"May I help you?" she asked.

"I..." stuttered Adela.

"Are you looking for someone?" insisted Sister Dolores.

"Well, I was actually hoping to talk with you. But I can see that you are very busy."

Sister Dolores looked Adela curiously, and she asked her to walk with her. She took her to a sitting room with an oil painting and a statue of one of the saints. A sofa and a few chairs were placed around a coffee table. Everything looked worn, but clean.

"What do you want?" she asked in surprise.

"I know that what I'm about to say will surprise you... Maybe you won't want to listen to me."

"Well, even if I am surprised, I'll listen to what you have to say."

"It won't be easy."

"You look anxious and scared... What's the matter? I know! You have a sick relative!" Sister Dolores could not hide her curiosity.

"You might not want to hear what I have to say, and you might throw me out of here."

"Whatever you say, I won't throw you out. Is that enough?

I am here to help whoever needs me, and it seems to me that you need help, although I don't know what."

"You are a nun, and, well... What I'm about to say is tough."

"I'm not exactly a nun, my daughter, the Sisters of Charity have vows that we renew from time to time. But nun or not, I'm sure that whatever it is that you are going to say won't frighten me too badly."

Adela sighed, and then, looking into Sister Dolores' eyes, she started to talk.

"Thirty-five years ago a young man raped my mother. I was born as a result of that rape."

"My Lord! Poor little lamb!"

"Your father was the rapist."

"What on Earth are you saying?"

"My mother suffered a shock and blocked the events from her mind. Another young man found her, and he saw the rapist leaving the scene."

"What on Earth are you saying? Why are you accusing my father?"

"Because the young man who saw the rapist leaving swears it was your father."

"Perhaps he is saying this to exonerate himself... He wouldn't be the first person to blame someone else for what he has done... It couldn't be my father, my father is a respectable man, a good man. I can assure you of that."

"I understand that it's difficult for you to believe. I won't hold it against you."

"The man who accuses my father... Why?"

"For thirty-five years, my mother believed that it was he who had raped her, and that he was incapable of admitting it."

"He could be lying!"

"No, he couldn't."

"In that case, it must be some other man... He could have made a mistake..."

"There's only one way to find out the truth. That's why I'm here."

Sister Dolores looked more serious now, surprise and fear plainly showing on her face.

"I can't allow my father's memory to be insulted, to have him made the scapegoat for such a horrendous act. You don't know him. He is the best father in the world."

"No, I don't know him. And I don't want to either."

"What do you want, then?"

"To know the truth, so my mother can face it. There's only one way of finding it out, if you agree to help me. We would need to do a blood test. If your father is innocent, the analysis will rule him out. Unfortunately, there is no technique precise enough to positively determine paternity, but it is sophisticated enough to rule people out. If your father is not the man who raped my mother, the analysis will tell us."

"But if the analysis doesn't rule him out, then…"

"Then your father could be guilty of raping my mother. I need you to bring your father here, and take that blood from him, and then we will send it to a laboratory."

"But how could you think I would do such a thing? You show up here, saying that my father raped your mother, and that you are the fruit of that rape. All of this is according to another man, who is the one your own mother thinks is the one who raped her, who blames my father instead. And on top of that, you're asking me to bring my father here so we can test his blood? This is the Devil's work! No, there's no way… I don't even know your name…"

"You're right, I haven't told you who I am. My name is Adela Vilamar. My mother is Catalina Vilamar. I am sure you've heard about my mother, and that you've met my grandmother, Asunción."

Sister Dolores raised her hand to her brow. She felt dizzy, incapable of accepting what she was hearing from this unknown woman.

"Yes… I've heard about Catalina Vilamar… I wasn't born when she left, but for many years, people talked about her in the neighborhood."

"She left because she got pregnant as a result of the rape. I don't know Spain very well, but you know that in the 1940s, a single woman who got pregnant was considered a disaster. My mother wanted to spare her parents the shame, and she also wanted the man who she thought was my father to meet me."

"Catalina Vilamar… You must forgive me, but it could be that your mother invented the story about the rape, that she gave herself to a man, and afterwards…"

"My mother did not invent anything, Sister Dolores. My mother was raped, and she got pregnant, but being raped is traumatic and her mind defended itself. Of course her memory blocked out what happened, so when she opened her eyes she saw that the boy she liked was trying to help her out, she decided that whatever had happened had been with him: it was her way of dealing with what had happened. But that boy could not have done it."

"You must forgive me, but I'm finding it difficult to believe all this…"

"I'm not surprised. I'm also finding it hard to believe that you and I could have the same father. I assure you that my mother and I are not looking for any financial compensation. I'm quite willing to sign a document stating that I will not make any kind of claim, not now, and not in the future. I don't even want to meet him. I don't want anything, except the truth."

"I need to talk to my father… He'll know what to do."

"I beg you, don't do it. At least not until we have the results."

"Do you think you can come here and sit in front of me, telling me that my father is a rapist? That's a terrible accusation! You're saying that he's a criminal. He could be sent to prison. And what about my mother? Have you given her any thought? Would she have to accept that her husband is a rapist? And what about my brother? Do I call him to tell him that his father is a rapist?"

"I'm sorry. I apologize for putting you through all this. I came to you instead of your brother because I was told he works for a charity in Rwanda."

"Yes. You see, it turns out that my father, who you describe as a monster, taught us such solid values that both me and my brother work at the service of others."

"I'm not here to judge your father. I assure you that the only thing that I want is to know who raped my mother. If things happened like I think they did, I know that my mother will suffer another shock, but I also know that she will be able to come to terms with it for the future. I can assure you that the last thing that my mother would want is to see your father, ask him for anything, know about him. I can assure you that."

"I don't believe you... I don't know you... I can't know what your intentions are... My father is a good person, a good man."

"I'm not here to question how your father has been with his family. That's for you to know. You may be a nun, but you are also a woman. I'm sure you can put yourself in the shoes of a young girl who was raped and got pregnant. If you turn me away, if you don't help me find out the truth, which kind of nun are you? Do you prefer injustice to flourish rather than allow yourself to be shaken from your comfortable life?"

"Comfortable life? You have no idea what the Sisters of Charity do."

"You're right, I have no idea. I know nothing about nuns. But I do know that God won't forgive you if you deny me your help. And if you do deny it ... I'll be forced to sue him for paternity. He will have to face the scandal."

"Oh my God! You can't do that."

"Of course I can, Sister Dolores. I have spoken with a lawyer, and I can assure you that your father will be forced to do the test, and if he refuses, then a jury could validate the paternity claim even without a test. Besides, he would have to face the scandal."

"My mother is unwell... You can't do this! You're blackmailing me!"

"I'm asking you to resolve this situation quietly. You get some blood from your father for a test, and I'll get a sample of mine, and when the lab gives us the results, if they're negative, you can forget about me. You will never see me again. I swear."

Sister Dolores looked at her, scared, while she wrung her hands. Adela Vilamar was right. It would destroy all her certainties in the world if she found out that her father was a rapist.

"And if it isn't negative?"

"Then I'll talk to him. Your mother won't need to hear anything."

"Let me think about it. Come back tomorrow. I need to pray."

"Pray, Sister, pray as much as you need to. I'll come back tomorrow."

When she got back to her grandmother's house, she didn't feel like talking, so she sat next to her in front of the television and pretended that she cared about the people on the screen, although she was really neither watching nor listening. She said that she had a headache and went to bed early.

Asunción looked at her worriedly, but didn't ask her any questions. She decided to wait for Adela to confide in her. The next day, Adela went to the hospital early in the morning.

When she got there, they told her to go and wait in the room where she had spoken to Sister Dolores the day before. She waited there impatiently for a few minutes.

Sister Dolores came into the room looking tired. Her red eyes and the bags underneath them showed that she had spent a night of suffering and insomnia.

"Good morning," Adela said.

"All right, I'll get my father to do the test. But I'll need to find an excuse, because there's no reason for him to have his blood drawn."

"How will you convince him?"

"He's got bad kidneys. I'll tell him that he looks bad and that it would make me feel better if he came to the hospital and had a blood test. Just promise me that whatever the result is, my mother won't find out about it. I won't make you sign anything, but I'll trust you to keep your word."

"I have no intention of hurting your mother. I just want to know the truth."

"If it turns out that we are sisters ..."

"Well, we can never feel that we are truly sisters. There's nothing that ties us together. And I don't need a sister and neither do you. Why should we pretend to be something that we're not?"

Sister Dolores promised to bring her father to the hospital in a couple of days. For her part, Adela had now found a laboratory to perform the analysis with guaranteed results and absolute confidentiality.

Two days later, they met at the door of the laboratory.

Sister Dolores was nervous.

"I went to my parents' house yesterday. I told my father that he didn't look well and that he should come into the hospital for a blood test. He said he was well and that he saw no reason to come in. But my mother told him to listen to me: 'If Dolores says you look bad, then listen to her. She is a nurse, after all,' she said. And so he came in this morning. Here's a sample."

Adela took the tube and walked away. They were waiting for her in the laboratory, where the only thing they could tell her for sure would be if this man was not her father.

The train arrived on time. Eight o'clock in the morning. They had traveled all night. The Amnesty Law had been passed a week before, and Fernando had decided that he could risk coming back. Catalina thanked him for it. She was tired of having lived through such a long exile. Above all, she was afraid that she might lose Adela forever.

The two of them were nervous, full of nerves for the moment they would see their mothers. They imagined that they would be the same as they were the day they left, but they knew they would be meeting with two old ladies.

Fernando was scared when the conductor took their passports. But he only glanced at them idly.

Adela was waiting for them on the platform. She hadn't wanted Asunción or Isabel to come to the station, but suddenly, as the train drew in, she saw them walking over to where she stood. She frowned, but then smiled. She understood them: how could they bring themselves to spend the day waiting at home? They had been waiting for this moment for thirty-six years.

Fernando stepped down first, helping Catalina after him. They saw Adela and the two old women coming towards them.

"It's them," Catalina whispered.

And then they broke into a run. Catalina cried as she held her mother tight, stretching out her arm to her daughter as well. Fernando paused for a few seconds before approaching, and looked at Isabel, wiping the tears from his face.

They held each other and cried for a while, unable to find the words that they had both spent so long rehearsing for this moment.

When Fernando walked into his mother's house, he felt that he had gone back in time. Everything was as he remembered it. His father's old overcoat was still hanging by the door.

His clothes were still in his wardrobe, as were his pencils and notebooks, and the book he was reading when he left, *Macbeth*. And there was his soccer ball, in the corner under the table, a present his father had given him as a child.

He hugged his mother again, and they spent most of the morning repeating the hug, trying to get back all the hugs that they had lost.

Catalina cried when she went into her house. Like Isabel, Asunción had made time stop within the walls of that house.

Catalina's room was extremely tidy, her bed covered with a crocheted bedspread that Asunción had made. Her dolls were piled on a shelf. Her clothes were all clean and ironed.

She sighed, thinking that she had felt homeless for thirty-six years, and that suddenly her life was here, everything she understood and loved, between these four walls.

Over the next few days, Fernando jumped whenever the doorbell rang, whether it was the doorman bringing up a letter or the grocer delivering an order from the shop. He couldn't stop himself from thinking that one of these days, the police would come to accuse him of having killed those two men thirty-five years ago. He tried to calm himself down, saying that the Amnesty Law would wipe the slate clean for supporters of Franco and of the Republic alike.

His mother hadn't asked him to explain why he had been gone for so long. She waited for him to choose the moment. And Fernando knew that although he was afraid of doing so, he would have to face up to his actions. But now he was playing for time. He needed to get to know his mother again, and his friends from those bygone days, and his city.

Madrid had changed. It had become a major capital city, but also one that had to accept the passage of time. He was surprised to hear people talking so much about the future and so little about the past. They seemed keen to turn over a new leaf, to forget the forty years of Franco's dictatorship.

He eagerly read the newspapers and sat down with his mother

to watch the news on television every evening. He thought that if he had been able to vote, then he would have voted for Santiago Carrillo, but he had to acknowledge that his mother was right, and that what the country needed was a renewed left wing in its politics, and that this newness was represented by the young socialists, led by Felipe González.

"I voted for Felipe," his mother said. "And I think your father would have voted for him as well. You know that he was more on the side of Indalecio Prieto."

They had lunch most days with Asunción and Catalina and Adela, as well as with Petra. Asunción showed her enthusiasm for Adolfo Suárez whereas her sister Petra regretted the poor results obtained by Fraga Iribarne.

Catalina had asked her aunt's forgiveness for having run away. Petra was nearly ninety years old and seemed to be afraid of the changes that were taking place in Spain. More than the political discussions they had as they ate, however, Fernando and Catalina were worried that Petra would ask about her husband's pistol.

One afternoon, after tea, Petra asked Fernando and Catalina to come to her house, with the excuse that her knee was hurting and she was worried that she might fall over. Neither Isabel nor Asunción looked surprised.

When they left the house, Fernando told them to wait while he hailed a taxi, but Petra didn't let him leave.

"We'll walk, it's not raining and it's not that cold."

"But, Aunt Petra, if your knee is hurting, then it's better for us to take a cab."

"Well, my knee isn't really hurting, or at least it's no worse than it was yesterday. I wanted to speak to the two of you alone. I don't want your mothers to be scared, or little Adela."

"Scared? Scared of what?" Catalina asked worriedly.

"Of what you did with your uncle's pistol. You disappeared, and it disappeared as well. Why?"

Catalina looked at Fernando, and she spoke before he had the chance to.

"We didn't know what might happen to us. We didn't have any money, we had to sleep in the street, we were exposed to all kinds of hardships and problems. I was absolutely certain that

I was going to leave, but I was scared, so I said nothing to Fernando and took the pistol just in case. Look, he's only just found out about it now."

"Didn't you tell him?"

"No, of course not, he'd have left me if he'd found out about it, we were arguing a lot in those days. I hid the pistol and didn't decide to get rid of it until we were on a train to Lisbon. I told you, we got on as stowaways. I threw the pistol out of the window because I realized that we weren't going to need it."

Petra looked suspiciously at her niece. Fernando said nothing and didn't know what to do.

"So you just found out that Catalina took my husband's pistol?"

"Fernando knew nothing about it, Auntie, he'd have been very upset."

Fernando nodded and felt the sweat spring out on his neck.

"You're a caution, Catalina! Look, Fernando's gone all pale."

"I'm just shocked by what I've heard," he managed to say.

"Well, now all that's cleared up, I think you should go and hail me a cab."

They had agreed to meet at nine on the dot at the door of the laboratory. Sister Dolores had arrived half an hour early and was walking nervously up and down the street. Adela turned up five minutes early as well.

They said hello, and they went in together. A few minutes later, they got the results from one of the laboratory technicians who had carried out the tests.

"Sit down, please … here's the report. I have to tell you that the test result was not a negative, so you are likely to be the children of the same father. I hope that this is good news for you."

"Of course," Adela said, seeing that Sister Dolores was trying to hold back her tears.

"Sister, I understand that you're emotional, and I'm pleased that this is the news you were expecting. You can't imagine the problems that there are in families when they find out that the head of the family has been spreading himself around a little …

as might be the situation in this case. Anyway, the results say that you could have the same father."

Adela paid for the test results and they went out into the street. She had to hold on to Sister Dolores' arm to stop her from falling over.

"It can't be ... it can't be ..." she murmured.

"Now all that remains is to find out the truth, and that's something only your father knows."

"My father is the best person I know, and he ... he would never be capable of raping a woman ... He's never had eyes for anyone but my mother ..."

"Your father married your mother after raping my mother, so it might very well be the case that once he was married, he never looked at another woman. But I don't care. The only thing I want to do is confirm that my mother was traumatized, and that as a consequence of the trauma, she entered a fugue state that led her to believe that another man raped her that evening."

They had to go and sit in a cafe so that Sister Dolores could drink a glass of water and pull herself together. Adela ordered two coffees.

"I prayed all night to our Lord for truth to prevail," the nun said, wiping away a tear.

"Well, He listened to you, because truth has indeed prevailed."

"And what are we going to do now?" Sister Dolores said, looking at Adela with fear in her eyes.

"Nothing. As far as you're concerned, you should just forget that any of this happened. I'll never be in touch with you again."

"But ... But we might very well be sisters ... half-sisters ... my father is your father ..."

"Look, Sister Dolores, the fact that your father raped my mother thirty-six years ago doesn't make us anything more than strangers. I don't want to hear from you again. Learn to live with this secret. It's the best you can do, for yourself and for your parents."

"But he ... you ... you hate him ..."

"Hate him? I don't even know what I feel. I'm not worried about him, I'm worried about my mother, and I'm doing all this for her."

"He … he doesn't know what happened … he made a mistake … maybe he didn't rape her … maybe she let him …"

"Don't even say that! If you dare insult my mother, I'll report your father to the police for rape, and I'll do everything in my power to destroy him."

"Don't threaten me!"

"Of course I'm threatening you! Don't think for a moment that I'm not threatening you!"

Sister Dolores promised that she would keep this burdensome secret.

"Offer your suffering up to God," Adela said angrily.

"You and I … Well, we're sisters, maybe we could see each other again …" the nun suggested.

"Never! We'll never see each other again! I don't want to have anything to do with you or your family."

"I'm not to blame for what went on between my father and your mother … we should try to understand one another."

"No."

Adela turned and stopped a taxi, leaving the nun alone in the middle of the street. She didn't even feel like looking back in the rear-view mirror.

She told the taxi to take her to the practice run by a psychiatrist Dr. Ward had recommended to her. The American had told her that he had met Dr. Fuentes at a conference and that he had made a very good impression on him. He had given her the address of his practice in Madrid, which was where she went now, as she had arranged a meeting for that very morning.

Dr. Fuentes looked very like Dr. Ward, only a little older. He was very tidy. He listened to her without asking any questions until she had finished her story.

Adela had told him the essentials of the story, but had been very careful not to reveal that for three decades her mother had thought that Marvin Brian, the *Poet of Pain*, was her father.

"The most surprising thing about this story is that my mother never said, nor suggested, that she might have been raped. She seemed to think that she gave herself voluntarily to this … this man who was a friend of hers; she was in love him and he found her stretched out on the ground …"

"It's normal for a person who's suffered a shock to activate a dissociative defense mechanism to try to avoid further suffering. There are people who have a great degree of inner strength or who possess psychological defense mechanisms that allow them to face up to trauma, but there are other people who don't, and what they do is to disconnect the rational part of their brains. When the trauma is a serious one, the disconnection is serious as well, and can even wipe out the actual memory of the traumatic event. But I can't give a proper diagnosis until I speak to your mother."

They agreed that he would speak to Catalina, because if there was one thing that Adela was sure of, it was that Catalina would suffer an even greater shock once she found out the truth.

She walked over to the Plaza de la Encarnación and sat in front of the railings. From there, she could see the first few houses along Arrieta Street. She had to put the second part of her plan into action.

She had spent days watching the man who might be her father. She was sure that he was, that Marvin had identified him correctly.

The man came out for a walk in the middle of the afternoon, leaning on a stick.

When she saw him, she followed him for a while before stopping him.

"Good afternoon," she said, standing by his side.

He looked at her in surprise, and something like worry appeared on his face.

"I'd like to speak to you."

"Right. What about?"

"About what happened thirty-six years ago at the Pradera de San Isidro."

He stepped back and looked her up and down scornfully.

"Thirty-six years ago, you raped Catalina Vilamar."

"Don't be so stupid. Where did you come up with such a story?"

"There was a witness."

"A witness? A witness to what?"

"Are you going to deny what you did that night?"

"I don't have anything to deny, and I don't have anything to say to you. Go away."

"I want to hear you say the truth. If you do, then I'll leave you alone forever. If you don't, then I will make an official report and cause such a scandal that you'll never be able to stick your nose outdoors again. You decide which you prefer."

"An official report? What about?" The man laughed and looked at her scornfully.

"I will make a paternity claim. You are my father. A father that makes me feel sick just to look at: I wouldn't take your name for anything. But I need to hear the truth."

"You're insane!"

"No, I'm not insane. I'm prepared to destroy whatever is left of your life, even if it doesn't look like there's all that much. You choose. If you tell me the truth, I'll never bother you again. Or else you can see me in court."

They looked at one another. There was nothing but anger and hatred in their gazes.

"You had a blood test a few days ago. A friend got me a sample of your blood, and I took it to a laboratory for a paternity test. You are my father."

Adela looked this man in the eyes. She had lied to him, but she was sure that he was too old to know that blood tests weren't yet able to establish paternity.

"A blood test? What are you saying?"

The man was now unable to hide his worry. He asked himself if perhaps his daughter had betrayed him, but he pushed the thought aside. She was a nun, and she was his daughter. How did this woman know that he'd had a blood test, then?

"Have you made up your mind? Either truth or a trial. I have the proof that you're my father, but I want to hear you say what happened that night."

"Your mother was … she liked to flirt. She knew that all the boys were crazy for her. She liked an American who paid her no attention. She drank more than she should have. She flirted with everyone, and a friend and I bet that we might be able to get further with her. I was the one who did the deed. She didn't hesitate, and came with me into the trees. Catalina was trying to make the

American jealous. I don't care why she followed me into the dark. She was so drunk that she didn't realize I was taking her clothes off. I'm a man, I've always been a man, and so we got to a point where she shouted and tried to fight me off, but I didn't stop. Why should I have stopped? No decent girl would have drunk what she did, or flirted with everyone. She deserved what happened to her. She cried, but I was sure that she had her fun as well."

"What you did was rape her," Adela said, trying to keep her voice level.

"What I did was what all men do when a girl isn't decent and doesn't know how to defend her virtue. A woman who gets drunk knows what she's asking for."

"So you admit that you raped her."

"The only thing I'll admit is that I took her behind the trees and did what had to be done."

"You said that she shouted and tried to fight you off," Adela said.

"Every girl knows what's likely to happen if they go with a man to a dark place. So why should I have stopped?"

"Your rape had consequences. Me."

"That's what you say. She left, disappeared. She left with Fernando Garzo, a kid from the neighborhood. I don't care what he did with her. I'm not going to acknowledge you as my daughter. If you and your mother are after money, you can crawl back under the rock you came from. I'm not going to give you a penny."

"Money? Do you really think we're looking for your money? You haven't understood this at all. Look, let's make things clear. You've confirmed to me that you raped my mother, which is all I wanted to hear."

"I didn't rape her ... she came with me voluntarily ... then she changed her mind and started to shout and struggle ... Fucking hypocritical little slut!"

The man stood still, frozen for a second. The woman had just slapped him in the face with the back of her hand. He was surprised.

"If you insult my mother again, you'll pay for it dearly."

Adela opened her jacket and he could see that she had a tape recorder strapped to her body.

He looked at her in confusion.

"You recorded me?" he asked in alarm.

"Of course. And I don't think your wife would like to hear this recording. And even a judge might think that it was interesting."

"What do you want? Tell me how much you want ..."

"I never want to see you again. Never. You hear me. Never."

She turned and walked away, leaving the man trembling and lifting his hand to his heart. She heard a noise. But she didn't turn around. Someone shouted that a man had fallen over.

Adela called Dr. Fuentes and asked him to be prepared to come to her grandmother's house at any moment.

Then she called her aunt Petra and asked her to come so that she would be there with Isabel and Fernando as well. They had all accepted, thinking that Adela only wanted to organize an afternoon of drinking tea and chatting.

Asunción was serving coffee when Adela thought that the right moment had arrived.

"I've invited you all here today because I have something very important and painful to tell you. Mother ... I'm sorry ... I'm so, so sorry ..."

Catalina shuddered. Adela's voice scared her.

"What is it? Is something wrong?" Her lower lip started to tremble.

"A month ago, I went to see Marvin Brian."

"Marvin! I don't understand ..." Catalina looked confused.

"Sara Wilson managed to get me an interview. I went to see him in New York. After you went to the Académie Française, Marvin Brian went back to New York. He had to have an operation on his heart. Sara went with Farida and I managed to talk to her."

"You were with Sara? That's impossible ..."

"We spoke, and I don't know why, but in the end she decided to help me. She said that she couldn't promise anything, but she would try to get me an interview with Marvin. My newspaper had asked me to interview him, but not just that, they wanted me to write about the unknown woman who followed him all over the world. About you. You can imagine how bad I felt. I made a decision: we needed to put an end to this situation once and for all, for your sake, for my sake, for all our sakes. You've never accepted that I don't care about Marvin and that I had no interest in acknowledging him as my father. After a few days, Sara called me and said that Farida and Marvin would meet me. I went to their apartment in New York. I spoke to Farida and we had a conversation that ... well, that was very illuminating. But I signed a non-disclosure agreement. If I passed on or used anything of what I am telling you now, I would owe them ten million dollars. And their lawyers will try to get me sent to jail. I signed this document. So, if any one of you breathes a word of this, then you'll be sending me to prison. And I don't have ten million dollars lying around."

"What are you saying? I don't understand ..." Catalina's hands were trembling now.

"Marvin Brian was wounded at the front when he was working there as a translator for an American journalist."

"We know," Fernando interrupted.

"What you don't know is that he was castrated."

"What?"

"He was shot in the genital area and the operation to save his life led to part of his genitals being amputated. He couldn't have children; he didn't have much to have children with. Marvin Brian is not my father, because he couldn't be my father. He couldn't be anyone's father."

Catalina got to her feet and looked like she was about to hit her daughter.

"You're accusing me of lying! You're saying that I've made all this up! How dare you insult me like this!"

"No, you haven't made anything up, at least not consciously. I've spoken to two psychiatrists, one in New York and the other in Madrid, and they say that if someone suffers a sexual assault, then they can dissociate what they experience from themselves as a kind of self-protection, a defense mechanism. This is how people deal with trauma, how they keep on living. They set their memories aside."

"Oh, and you were told all this by a pair of psychiatrists!" Catalina was getting increasingly angry.

"Yes, Mama, I was told this by two reputable and fairly famous psychiatrists. This is exactly what happened to you. You were raped and your reaction was to deny the existence of the rape, causing a disconnect in your mind."

"Marvin's lying! He lied to you!" Catalina shouted.

"No, he didn't. I swear. I'm sorry, I'm so, so sorry."

"You said that your mother was raped," Fernando said, looking very serious.

"Yes. Marvin thought he knew who did it. You were at the Pradera de San Isidro, and he went into the trees because he needed to throw up. He saw a couple on the ground. The woman was shouting. He went over and saw a man on top of my mother, and she asked him for help … the man who was raping her fled when he heard someone coming, just did up his trousers and ran away. Marvin found my mother with her skirt undone, her stockings ripped, her underwear pulled down. She was crying and in a state of shock. He tried to get her to stand up, but she couldn't move. He didn't feel that well himself, and stayed there for a few minutes trying to get her to calm down. Then you came along, Fernando, and you saw them. You thought that my mother had been seduced by Marvin, that they were doing what they both wanted to do. You saw them sitting on the ground, her in a daze with her clothes all disheveled, and him with her in his arms."

Fernando took Catalina's trembling hand. Asunción, Isabel, and Petra sat in silence, not daring to move or speak in the face of Adela's narrative.

"Who was it, who did it?" Fernando asked, afraid of what the answer might be.

Adela took out the tape recorder and turned it on. For a few seconds, they listened in silence to the voice of the man confessing his crime. Catalina started to tremble even more.

"Antoñito Sánchez, Don Antonio's son. He raped my mother."

"No … No … No!" Catalina was screaming now.

She stood, but suddenly fainted. Fernando was the first to help her. Catalina took a few seconds to open her eyes, and then curled into the fetal position, giving little shouts of pain.

Adela went over to the telephone. She called Dr. Fuentes, asking him to come at once, just as they had agreed.

Fernando managed to pick Catalina up, although she refused to move. He put her on the sofa and Petra made her drink some water. Asunción was very upset and held tight to her daughter's hand as she cried. As for Isabel, she looked worriedly at both Fernando and Catalina, afraid that her son was suffering a shock as well.

The only one who seemed to be calm – although in truth she was very far from calm – was Adela. She knew she had no other choice. Dr. Fuentes had warned her of what her mother's reaction might be.

When Dr. Fuentes arrived, Catalina was convulsing, crying, and murmuring words he did not understand.

The doctor gave her an injection; she relaxed and became drowsy.

"We have to take her to the hospital," he said.

"Why?" Asunción asked in distress.

"Are you her mother?" Dr. Fuentes said, looking sympathetically at this elderly woman.

"Yes ..."

"Your daughter needs treatment to help her face up to what Adela told her. She has kept herself free from trauma for years by using dissociation techniques. She's suffered from what we call Dissociative Amnesia, which has stopped her from remembering what happened to her on the night she was raped. She has to get better, and to do that, she needs to accept the truth; she has to travel from grief to pain in order to overcome it. It won't be easy, but we'll help her manage."

"Where are you going to take her?" Doña Asunción said, scared for her daughter.

"To a hospital, at least for a few days. Then she can come home and continue with the treatment that might help her face up to reality. But now we need to take her to the hospital. I'll call an ambulance."

"No ... please ... let me take her ... Do you have a car?" Fernando asked.

"Yes ..." the doctor replied.

974

"Please, take her in your car. I'll come down with you and travel with her. An ambulance would be worse ... I'm sure of that."

Several days passed since Catalina had gone to the hospital. Days during which Fernando felt the void caused by her absence. Days which held more silence than words.

That Sunday afternoon, Fernando was reading while Isabel pretended to read but was in fact looking at her son. It was easy for her to see the child that he had once been in this gentleman with salt-and-pepper hair and wrinkles at the corner of his mouth. She knew that her son was suffering. The day before he had called Sara, the owner of the bookshop. She was in Alexandria, apparently. He didn't know what she had said, but Isabel had seen Fernando's face form a hard mask.

When she asked if Sara had given him some bad news, he said nothing, but put on his overcoat and left. He came back a couple of hours later. He didn't say where he had been, and she knew that she shouldn't ask, because the suffering in her son's face left her no need for questions. He had barely spoken since then, and had no appetite.

She was worried that he would go back to Paris, but above all, that he would do so without explaining why he had left all those years before.

She had spent days trying to pluck up the courage to ask him, but the words caught in her throat. She decided that she could no longer avoid the conversation, for all her worry about the effect it would have on her son.

"Tell me the truth, Fernando. Did you leave here just to help Catalina, so that her parents didn't have to be ashamed at her pregnancy? If you're going to lie, don't say anything. I won't say that you owe me the truth, but I'd like there to be nothing left between us, and I'd like to be able to understand you. Your absence has been so harsh, I couldn't understand it ... The fact that you wouldn't let me know where you were, where you were living ..."

He looked her straight in the eyes, holding out his hand to pull her down next to him.

"I'll tell you the truth. It will be hard for me, Mother, because I don't want to cause you any pain, and I'm afraid you won't understand me. But I will do it, and I ask you to forgive me for what I did, and for my disappearance."

Isabel smiled slightly and squeezed his hand.

"I left because I killed two men, two of the men who killed my father. Do you remember Roque, the ugly-faced prison guard? The one who stepped on Father's glasses when they fell to the ground, the one who didn't give him our letters, who laughed at the prisoners? His son was a soldier, Saturnino Pérez, and he was in the firing squad. I … I felt a hatred for them that I couldn't control. They killed my father, they killed him for his loyalty to the Republic. Every day that passed, I hated them more and more. They weren't happy with having defeated the Republic; once they'd won the war, they seized their chance to exact their revenge on the losers with unusual cruelty. They'd won, so why shed more blood? I was raging, and I needed to take revenge for my father's death."

His mother's gaze twisted his soul within him. He put his fingers to her lips to stop her speaking, not until he had finished.

"If I'd told you I was going to take my revenge, you would never have let me do it. You would have tried to convince me not to, and I would have obeyed you. That's why I didn't tell you, Mother. Catalina and Eulogio knew what I was going to do, and Catalina gave me her uncle's pistol; she made me promise to take her with me in exchange. I resisted, but she held firm and I finally gave in. I've told you how we got to Lisbon, and then to Alexandria, the years we spent in Paris … And now you know why I left, and why I didn't write to you, and why I didn't want you to know where I was … I was scared that the authorities would connect me to the two murders, that they'd arrest me … that you would lose more and more, first your husband and then your son. But I didn't only kill those two men … I killed two others. A Gestapo agent and a Nazi war criminal. The circumstances I was in forced my hand. Forgive me, Mother, forgive me."

Isabel was sitting stock still, as if all the movements and sounds of her body had frozen solid. She took a few seconds to react.

"Oh. 'You shall not kill, Fernando, you shall not kill.' You remember? Your father told you that no one is ever the same after having killed, even if it is for a just cause. Your father wouldn't have wanted you to live with this … with the weight of having taken other people's lives. 'You shall not kill' was what he said when he came back from the front. Oh, Lord, how much he would have suffered if he'd known what you did!"

They both broke into tears, without embracing one another, without knowing how to console one another. Then Isabel wiped her tears away with a handkerchief and stroked her son's face.

"Mother, not a single night has gone by when I haven't seen the faces of Roque and Saturnino Pérez. I've had no peace since that day."

"I understand. You feel guilty."

"No … no … I don't …."

She shook her head. She knew that conscience does exist, even if we wish we could ignore it.

"I forgive you, my son. I forgive you. But you will have to ask God for forgiveness one day."

"I'm not a believer, Mother, and Father wasn't either."

She nodded.

"Even so … One day, Fernando, do it."

She got up and left him alone in the room. They both needed some time to themselves.

Fernando wanted to rid his head of his father's words, the ones his mother had brought back into his mind: "You shall not kill, Fernando, you shall not kill."

Roque and Saturnino came to visit him in the night, breaking his sleep. When dawn came, he woke suddenly, feeling a pressure in his chest. All was still.

After a while, he got up to get a drink of water and heard a murmur coming from his mother's room.

"Mother? Are you all right?"

He opened the door and saw her lying on the floor with her eyes open. He cried out, then bent down, picked her up, and put her on her bed. She calmed down when she heard him speak.

"I'm not feeling well … my stomach hurts, and I want to be sick … I wanted to go to the kitchen, but I fell over and couldn't get back up."

"Don't worry, I'll make you a chamomile tea, that'll settle your stomach. Just lie there, and I'll be along in a moment."

He went to the kitchen to boil some water. Then he got down the box where his mother kept the herbal teas. He made chamomile tea with a little sugar.

When he came back to the room, his mother was still lying in the same spot, immobile, her eyes looking into nothingness. Fernando dropped the teacup and went over to the bed. He sat next to her and closed her eyes, then put her head back on the pillow and sat still, waiting as the heat left his mother's body.

He cried as he spoke to her and asked her forgiveness.

He didn't need the doctor to tell him that his mother's heart had broken. He had broken her heart. He had killed his mother by confessing his own past crimes. Now he had a new victim to add to his list.

For an instant he wished he could believe in God, because then he would think that his mother and father were together again. But rationality stopped him from finding a way past his pain.

They buried her the next day. They didn't tell Catalina, because she wouldn't have been able to bear it, and wouldn't have been able to stand seeing Fernando cry.

He locked himself away, unable to speak, unable to allow himself to be consoled.

He didn't dare close his eyes, because if he did so, then he saw his mother's face, and heard his father's words: "You shall not kill, no, you shall not kill."

Adela forced him to come back to reality, coming to his house every day and sitting with him in silence until, little by little, she was able to get a few words out of him. And one morning, when she came to find him and take him for a walk, he said: "I'm going back to Paris."

Adela asked him to wait until Catalina left the hospital, and that if her mother wanted to come with him to Paris, she would convince her that she should stay in Madrid.

"She needs someone to look after her, my grandmother and my great-aunt will do it, and I will too. I've decided to stay in Madrid. I'm going to write about Spain for the newspaper. We've come to an agreement already."

Fernando accepted the idea and waited until the day that Dr. Fuentes said that Catalina could leave the hospital.

Fernando went to pick her up. Catalina had asked him to come alone. She wanted to speak with him with no one around.

He found her dressed and talking to Dr. Fuentes.

"We've agreed that we'll see each other two days a week at my office. But she's much better. I've said she can go home."

She smiled scornfully but nodded. She had lost weight, and the medication seemed to make her particularly vague.

She held Fernando's arm. They walked to the elevator, and she didn't smile until she had left the hospital behind her.

"Together again ..." she said.

"That's how it has to be," he replied.

"I want to say something ... I don't know if you'll be angry..."

"Of course not! You can say what you want."

"I've thought about it ... a lot ... Not just about what happened, but about my whole life, with the doctor, and ... well, I've come to a decision ..."

"You want to stay in Madrid. You're not coming back to Paris with me. Is that it?"

"How did you know?"

"Because I know you as well as you know me. And I understand you. It's the right thing to do. You have your mother here, your aunt ... they'll look after you. You need them to look after you, you need a family. Adela is happy because she has a family at last, she loves her grandmother and her great-aunt. She's very good friends with Petra."

"And you? I don't want you to go, Fernando."

"I have to go, Catalina, there's nothing left for me here. I'm very old, and I wouldn't find any work. How would I live?"

"Stay here, Fernando ... I ... I don't know how to live without you."

"We have to learn to live without one another. It'll take a few months, but you'll hardly miss me after a while. You have your mother, your aunt, your daughter ..."

Asunción opened the door and gave Catalina a hug. The two of them made an effort to hold back their emotions. Adela hugged her as well, and Petra struggled to get into the hug too.

Adela said she would cook "something French."

They laughed and enjoyed the meal, but more than anything, they felt that Catalina had returned from the shadows of the trauma that had affected her for so many years now.

After the meal, Fernando got ready to leave.

"I need to finish packing. My train leaves at seven o'clock. A good thing that the station's close," he said.

Catalina walked over to Fernando and hugged him, almost despairingly.

"Don't go ... please stay here ... I can't bear it ..."

Asunción let out a little sob, and Petra tried to contain herself.

"I can't ... you know that I can't ... I've got the bookshop ... one day it'll be mine ... I came to an agreement with Sara ..."

"Please, I'm begging you!" Catalina's grip was so firm that Fernando couldn't break away.

"I'll come and see you, and you'll come to see me in Paris ... you can all come ... that's it ... all of you, come to see me ..."

"Fernando, don't go!"

"Mother, please, don't make this difficult," Adela said to Catalina.

"I have to say something ... I ... I didn't say it this morning, but I'll say it now ... we can get married. Stay here. We'll get married and stay together. You always wanted that, and I didn't know it, but I only ever loved you ..." Catalina waited, smiling slightly.

Fernando stood still. He couldn't think, he couldn't speak, he couldn't even feel. He had waited all his life for Catalina to say that she loved him. But her words meant nothing to him now. He would have given anything to have heard them half a lifetime ago, but when he looked at her now, all he felt was tenderness, nothing more. He loved her with all his soul, but it was a love that had no room for anything but pure affection.

"We'll see each other soon, I promise," was all he felt able to say.

"So … it's over between us …" Catalina murmured.

"No, never, I could never leave you, because it would be like leaving myself. And now I must go back to Paris, and I promise we'll see each other soon. I'll call you every day."

He left the dining room, hearing Catalina's desperate shouts behind him.

"Oh, God! What have I done all these years! How could I have done what I did! How could I have treated Fernando like that!"

"Mama, calm down … let him go to Paris … Fernando loves you, he's never loved anyone else. He needs to put himself together, like you have put yourself together, like I have put myself together. It's difficult for all of us to deal with: how do you think I feel? I thought that Marvin was my father, and I wanted Fernando to be my father, and my real father turned out to be someone I can only hate. I've lost the father I always wanted to have."

Adela tuned away so her mother wouldn't see her cry. She knew that they had both lost Fernando forever.

Fernando was almost done packing when Adela rang the doorbell.

"I'll take you to the station," she said, without giving him the chance to protest.

"And your mother?"

"Asunción and Petra are trying to calm her down."

"You should have stayed with her."

"I needed to be with you, to say goodbye … I'm afraid, Fernando, afraid that you'll be gone forever. Tell me the truth: why are you going to Paris?"

"Because there's nothing left for me here, and there are still poets to discover in Paris. I wouldn't be able to make a living in Madrid, but in Paris there's the bookshop. It'll be mine one day, but even if that weren't the case, I could still carry on editing poetry there regardless. Sara needs me; she's very old."

"You love her a great deal."

"Yes, she's looked after me like a mother, but without imposing herself, without my realizing. She's always protected me. Ever since Benjamin died, she's been alone. I'm the only one left."

"You know … maybe you'll be annoyed to hear this, but I thought that maybe you were leaving because of Zahra … I know she means a lot to you."

Fernando stroked Adela's face before replying.

"Zahra's dead. She died a couple of days ago. Sara called me from Alexandria to tell me. A heart attack."

"I … I didn't know she was sick."

"Her heart was weak. She forbade Sara from telling me anything. And so now you know, I'm not leaving your mother for another woman, if that's what was bothering you."

"I'm sorry." Adela looked down at the ground.

"Don't apologize, there's no need."

"My mother loves you, Fernando, and she has always loved you, but she was ill, and she's been sick all these years without knowing it, without us realizing. I'll never forgive Marvin and Farida for allowing my mother to destroy her own life, and your life, and almost my life as well."

He said nothing. All he did was close his suitcase.

The train was waiting on the platform. The passengers were getting on and heading to their respective compartments. Adela helped him find a place for his suitcase, and then grasped him by the arm.

When they heard the first whistle, they hugged and Adela burst into tears.

He helped her down onto the platform, then got back on the train and leaned out of the window to say goodbye. They held hands. The train started moving and Adela tried to hold Fernando's hand for a few seconds longer.

"Tell me the truth, and don't lie to me. Are you coming back?"

"No, I won't come back … I'll die in Paris."

Glossary of historical facts and events

Abraham Lincoln Brigade: Organization of American volunteers that fought for the Second Spanish Republic during the Spanish Civil War.

Abwehr: German military intelligence organization in operation from 1921 to 1944.

Afrika Korps: German military forces in Africa during World War II; commanded by Erwin Rommel until February 1943, when he was replaced by Hans-Jürgen von Arnim.

Amnesty Law: Law that came into force in Spain in October 1977 granting amnesty to political prisoners imprisoned by Franco's forces.

Atomic bombings of Hiroshima and Nagasaki: Nuclear attacks on the Japanese cities of Hiroshima and Nagasaki carried out on August 6 and 9, 1945. The attacks, ordered by President Truman, led to the surrender of Japan in World War II.

Attack on Pearl Harbor: Military strike by the Imperial Japanese Navy Air Service on the American naval base at Pearl Harbor (Hawaii) carried out on December 7, 1941. The attack led to the United States' entry into World War II.

Battle of El Alamein: Military conflict that took place between October 23 and November 4, 1942; led to the retreat of German troops from North Africa.

Battle of Stalingrad: Military confrontation between the Red Army of the Soviet Union and the armed forces of Nazi Germany for control of the city of Stalingrad (now Volgograd).

The battle took place between August 1942 and February 1943 and ended in the defeat of the German army.

Battle of the Bulge: German offensive campaign that took place from December 1944 to January 1945 in the Belgian region of Ardennes; it ended in victory for the Allies.

British protectorate of Egypt: British occupation of Egypt from 1882 to 1953.

Buchenwald: Concentration camp located near the German city of Weimar that was in operation from July 1937 until April 1945.

Checas: Unofficial jails located in Republican-controlled areas during the Spanish Civil War; used to interrogate, torture and execute those suspected of collaborating with Franco's forces.

Cyrenaica: African region comprising a plateau around 80 miles wide that runs along the north-eastern coast of Libya.

Establishment of the Republic of Egypt: Coup d'état that forced King Farouk I to abdicate in 1952 and established the presidency of Lieutenant Colonel Gamal Abdel Nasser.

FFI (French Forces of the Interior): Secret military organizations formed by members of the French Resistance to support the Allied forces in France.

First democratic elections in Spain: First free elections held in Spain since the Second Republic and after the dictatorship of Francisco Franco. They were called by Prime Minister Adolfo Suárez and held on June 15, 1977.

Gestapo: The official secret police of Nazi Germany.

Invasion of Tripoli: The liberation of the city of Tripoli (Libya) from Italian control by the British army in January 1943.

"Kyrie Eleison": One of the oldest prayers in Christian liturgy; also called "Lord, have mercy."

Liberation of Paris: Entry of Allied forces into Paris in August 1944, followed by the liberation of the city from Nazi control.

Lidice Massacre: Assassination of 340 inhabitants of the village of Lidice in the Czech Republic in retaliation for the attack on Nazi leader Reinhard Heydrich.

May 68: Period of civil unrest carried out by left-wing student unions; supported by most of the French working class.

Occupation of France: Occupation of part of France by the German army after the defeat of the Allied forces in France, which continued from June 1940 to December 1944 and divided the country into two zones. The north and west, which became known as the occupied zone, were taken by Hitler's forces; meanwhile, the southern part of France, known as the free zone, remained under the rule of a puppet regime with its capital in Vichy.

Organization Todt: Third Reich civil and military engineering organization founded by Fritz Todt, a senior Nazi; based on the use of forced labor.

Panzer: German tank used during World War II.

Pogrom: Extermination of an ethnic or religious group, or any other minority, accompanied by the seizure of their possessions. This term is used in particular to refer to acts of violence against Jewish communities.

Potsdam Conference: Meeting held in the German city of Potsdam in 1945 at which the leaders of the Soviet Union (Joseph Stalin), UK (Winston Churchill and Clement Attlee) and USA (Harry S. Truman) decided how to govern Germany after its surrender.

Raid on Alexandria: Attack carried out on December 19, 1941 by the Italian Navy with two manned torpedoes on two British Naval battleships moored in the port of Alexandria.

Raqs Sharqi: Style of belly dancing developed in Egypt during the first half of the 20th century.

SA (Sturmabteilung): German Nazi Party organization that played an important role in Adolf Hitler's rise to power.

Service du Travail Obligatoire (STO): The forcible recruitment of workers in occupied France to be deported to Germany, where they were exploited and sent to work camps.

Siegfried Line: German defensive line stretching approximately 390 miles between the German city of Kleve on the Dutch border to Weil am Rhein on the Swiss border.

(SS) (Schutzstaffel): Main intelligence and security agency in Nazi Germany; also operated throughout occupied Europe until the end of World War II. The masterminds behind the Holocaust emerged from this organization.

Treaty of Paris: International agreement signed in 1947 by representatives of the victorious Allied powers in World War II and the governments formerly aligned with the Axis (not including Germany), with the aim of resolving territorial conflicts in Europe following the war.

Treaty of Versailles: Peace treaty ratified in 1919 that marked the end of the First World War.

Wehrmacht: Name of the unified armed forces of Nazi Germany.

Yom Kippur: Jewish holiday celebrated over 10 days to commemorate the Day of Atonement.

Glossary of historical figures

Alexander, Harold: General named Commander-in-Chief of the Allied Forces in North Africa and the Middle East during World War II.

Ali, Muhammad: Governor of Egypt between 1805 and 1848.

Auchinleck, Claude: Commander of the British Army in North Africa during World War II from July 1941 to August 1942.

Bauer, Fritz: State prosecutor in the Federal Republic of Germany who launched the Frankfurt Auschwitz trials.

Dannecker, Theodor: SS captain in charge of the "Dannecker Report" identifying all Jews living in occupied France.

Ernst, Gerke: Head of the Gestapo in Prague and a lieutenant colonel in the SS during World War II.

Farouk I: King of Egypt from 1939 to 1952; forced to abdicate following a coup d'état by the Free Officers Movement led by Gamal Abdel Nassar.

Forster, Edward Morgan: English writer born in 1879 who lived in Alexandria during the First World War, volunteering for the Red Cross. In 1922, he published Alexandria, a fascinating work about the history of the city and the best possible guide to discover it.

Friedman, Tuviah: Director of the Institute for the Documentation of Nazi War Crimes in Haifa, Israel following World War II. He played a key role in the capture of the Nazi leader Adolf Eichmann.

Goebbels, Joseph: Third Reich minister between 1933 and 1945, and one of Hitler's closest associates.

Graziani, Rodolfo: Named Marshal of Italy during Mussolini's Fascist regime; acted as Viceroy of Italian East Africa and Governor-General of Italian Libya. Graziani is remembered for the massacres that he ordered in these territories.

Heydrich, Reinhard: High-ranking Nazi official and one of the main architects of the Holocaust; assassinated by a Czechoslovakian soldier in Prague in 1942.

Himmler, Heinrich: leading member of the Nazi Party who was responsible for the construction and supervision of the death camps.

Koch, Karl Otto: SS officer who was in charge of four of the main concentration camps in Nazi Germany.

Montgomery, Bernard Law: Marshal in the British army, also known as the "Spartan General," who fought during World War II in France until 1942. He was then transferred to North Africa, where he led the Allied forced at the Battle of Al Alamein. There, he was victorious over the German army commanded by General Erwin Rommel.

O'Connor, Richard: General who commanded the British army during the campaign in North Africa, stopping the advance of the Axis troops.

Paulus, Friedrich: General in the German army who commanded the failed invasion of Stalingrad.

Pétain, Philippe: General and Marshal of France who acted as Chief of State in Vichy France in Occupied France.

Rommel, Erwin: Marshal in the German army during World War II, who was nicknamed the "Desert Fox" for his ability to command the Afrika Korps forces during the North Africa Campaign.

Sehn, Jan: Polish lawyer who was a member of the Commission for the Investigation of Nazi War Crimes and who led investigations in the Auschwitz-Birkenau concentration camp.

Vaernet, Carl: Doctor who tried to eradicate homosexuality by using cruel methods on prisoners at Buchenwald concentration camp.

Von Arnim, Hans-Jürgen: General in the Nazi Army who lead the Afrika Korps from December 1942 until May 1943, when he was captured by the British army.

Von Rundstedt, Gerd: Nazi field marshal during World War II.

Wavell, Archibald: Senior officer in the British Army during the North Africa campaign, in which he was defeated by Nazi Army commander Erwin Rommel.

Wiesenthal, Simon: Mauthausen concentration camp survivor who dedicated most of his life to identifying and tracking down Nazi war criminals to bring them to justice.